James Bruce Ross was professor of medieval and Renaissance history at Vassar College for many years. She is the author of studies of medieval Flanders and Renaissance Venice, including a translation of *The Murder of Charles the Good* by Galbert of Bruges.

Mary Martin McLaughlin is a medievalist and independent scholar, with special interests in the history of medieval women. She has written on various other subjects, including the medieval University of Paris, the history of childhood, and Heloise and Abelard.

James Bruce Ross and Mary Martin McLaughlin also co-edited *The Portable Renaissance Reader*.

Each volume in The Viking Portable Library either presents a representative selection from the works of a single outstanding writer or offers a comprehensive anthology on a special subject. Averaging 700 pages in length and designed for compactness and readability, these books fill a need not met by other compilations. All are edited by distinguished authorities, who have written introductory essays and included much other helpful material.

The Portable

Medieval
Reader

Edited and with an introduction by
JAMES BRUCE ROSS
and
MARY MARTIN McLAUGHLIN

PENGUIN BOOKS

PENGUIN BOOKS
Published by the Penguin Group
Penguin Group (USA) Inc., 375 Hudson Street, New York, New York 10014, U.S.A.
Penguin Group (Canada), 90 Eglinton Avenue East, Suite 700, Toronto,
Ontario, Canada M4P 2Y3 (a division of Pearson Penguin Canada Inc.)
Penguin Books Ltd, 80 Strand, London WC2R 0RL, England
Penguin Ireland, 25 St Stephen's Green, Dublin 2, Ireland (a division of Penguin Books Ltd)
Penguin Group (Australia), 250 Camberwell Road, Camberwell,
Victoria 3124, Australia (a division of Pearson Australia Group Pty Ltd)
Penguin Books India Pvt Ltd, 11 Community Centre, Panchsheel Park, New Delhi – 110 017, India
Penguin Group (NZ), cnr Airborne and Rosedale Roads,
Albany, Auckland 1310, New Zealand (a division of Pearson New Zealand Ltd)
Penguin Books (South Africa) (Pty) Ltd, 24 Sturdee Avenue,
Rosebank, Johannesburg 2196, South Africa

Penguin Books Ltd, Registered Offices: 80 Strand, London WC2R 0RL, England

First published in the United States of America
by Viking Penguin Inc.
Paperbound edition published 1955
Reprinted 1956 (twice), 1957, 1958, 1959, 1960 (twice),
1961 (twice), 1962 (twice), 1963, 1964, 1965 (twice), 1966 (twice),
1968 (twice), 1969 (twice), 1970, 1971, 1972, 1973, 1974, 1975
Published in Penguin Books 1977

40 39 38 37 36 35 34 33

LIBRARY OF CONGRESS CATALOGING IN PUBLICATION DATA
Ross, James Bruce, 1902–   ed,
The portable medieval reader.
Reprint of the 1949 ed., which was issued as 46
of the Viking portable library.
Bibliography: p. 38.
1. Literature, Medieval. I. McLaughlin, Mary
Martin, 1919–   joint ed. II. Title.
PN667.R6   1977   808.8   77-1658
ISBN 0 14 015.046 3

Printed in the United States of America
Set in Linotype Caledonia

Contents

PART TWO: THE CHRISTIAN COMMONWEALTH

THE SPIRITUAL AUTHORITY

PART FOUR: THE WORLD PICTURE

PART FIVE: THE NOBLE CASTLE

The Makers

POETS AND STORY-TELLERS

Introduction

I

ENTERING the lists in the enduring controversy between past and present, between "ancients" and "moderns," Walter Map, a twelfth-century writer, complained that "the illustrious deeds of modern men of might are little valued, and the castaway odds and ends of antiquity are exalted." In similar vein, a scientist of the same century, Adelard of Bath, deplored the domination of the present by the past, accusing his own generation of thinking "nothing discovered by moderns worthy of acceptance."

But Adelard's contemporary, Bernard of Chartres, called "the most copious fount of letters in Gaul in modern times," said of the relationship of his age with its ancient past, "We are like dwarfs seated on the shoulders of giants; we see more things than the ancients and things more distant, but this is due neither to the sharpness of our own sight nor the greatness of our own stature, but because we are raised and borne aloft on that giant mass."

Yet, whatever their differences of perspective on the past, whether they resisted the authority of the "ancients," or paid admiring tribute to their greatness, these men of the twelfth century were profoundly aware of living ties with the past. In fact, they, and their predecessors and successors as well, were confronted with the problem of the past in a particularly acute form. For

1

theirs was the task of recovering and assimilating a vast cultural legacy from pagan antiquity and of reconciling it with the Christian revelation and way of life. Although they were by no means deficient in pride in their own achievement, the weight of their debt to the past often lay heavily on them.

In our "modern times," we seldom have occasion to lament the hold of the past on the present, and we rarely feel dwarfed by its greatness. We are not often inclined to take a humble view of our own stature or to acknowledge a close kinship with the past, especially with the age represented by these men of the twelfth century. As Americans, we are separated by geography from the physical environment and many of the tangible evidences of this phase of the past, and by our truncated national history from the long "middle age" of Western culture which is as truly ours as it is that of European peoples. We are often still further divorced from our remoter history by a grandiose conception of progress in which our own role looms large and that of the future larger still. This orientation is a common one, although the optimistic theory on which it rests has grown somewhat threadbare in an age when human advancement appears more and more as "a slow crablike movement sideways."

Yet there is much evidence today of a haunting awareness of failure, of dissatisfaction with modern perspectives, of an anxious pursuit of enlightenment in the sources of our culture. We are increasingly conscious of the fact that while in a sense history, as Voltaire cynically put it, is a pack of tricks the living play upon the dead, it is also a pack of tricks that the dead have played on us. We are pathetically eager to consult the past, as we might a psychiatrist, to discover when and where things went wrong, to probe for the roots of modern neuroses. Seeking to comprehend the meaning of our own experience, and to restore a sense of continuity with the past, we read the "great books," we take courses in contemporary civilization and its background, we pore over complex works of historical interpretation. All this is surely a healthy sign that, whether we regard the past as a burden or as a legacy, we recognize that our ties with it are inseverable, and that we may possibly profit from its experience.

But perhaps, even in these efforts, we view the past too much through the distorting lenses of the present. Great books and lesser ones, too, have great value, but really to be understood they must be read in the context of their own times. Probably no age can fully escape bondage to present-mindedness; when it looks into the mirror of the past, it sees, like Narcissus, its own image. Yet, in order to see ourselves at all clearly in the mirror of a different age, we must try to understand that age in its own terms, we must attempt to relive its experience and to rethink its thoughts. By transcending the limitations of the present, we may extend our experience in time and space, and perhaps come to know ourselves better.

The middle ages of Europe were the spawning ground of the modern Western world. In the teeming life of the medieval centuries many aspects of modern society—its nation-states, its institutions, its class structure, its urban way of life—existed in embryo or in more advanced stages of development. But medieval culture was complete and distinctive in itself. Although this culture and its modern descendant have much in common, they also differ profoundly and often in the most striking ways. Emphasis on the differences, rather than on the similarities, between medieval thought and experience and our own has often encouraged the feeling that this is a dead past, with no significance for the present. Yet no area of the past is dead if we are alive to it. The variety, the complexity, the sheer humanity of the middle ages live most meaningfully in their own authentic voices, for as Walter Map said of the ancients, "their diligent achievement is in our possession; they make their own past present to our times." Not only in their "great books," in the works of their extraordinary men, is the medieval achievement still vital, but also in the records of the lives and work, the pleasures, sufferings, and strivings of their ordinary people.

The aim of the *Portable Medieval Reader* is to provide, by means of selections from these sources, a little mirror of the middle ages in which medieval men and women may appear as they saw themselves and in which we may see the evidences of our kinship with them. Perhaps it may also fulfill the expectations of the medieval writer who said, "I believe that in future times there will be men, like myself, who will eagerly search the pages of historians for the acts of this generation, that they may be able to disclose occurrences which have taken place in past ages for the instruction and amusement of their contemporaries."

II

If it is true that the middle ages are significant for us both as a distinct culture and as the ancestral form of our own, why does this period often seem dim and alien and in some way sharply cut off from our own? How did the concept of a "middle age" develop, and how has the term medieval acquired its rather vague and derogatory connotations of dark and barbarous? "Medieval" men like Walter Map and Adelard of Bath clearly thought of themselves as "modern" in relation to the "ancients." Perhaps the arbitrary divisions and conventional characterizations of history do not represent eternal verity, but rather the special interests or the blind spots or the arrogance of different ages. The kind of thinking which tries to confine the unwieldy and intractable past in neat pigeonholes is one of those tricks which the living of one age play on the dead of another. It tends to exalt those periods with which a particular age may identify itself more closely and to pass over those which for one reason or another are less agreeable.

When the later humanists, feeling that they had discovered man and the world anew in the light of pagan antiquity, used the word *renascita* or renascence to describe their own time, they also characterized as the "middle ages" the period which in their view separated them from their antique models. By stressing the idea of a breach between their own time and that which preceded it, they asserted their independence of their immediate predecessors, and the novelty and originality of their own particular awareness and revival of the ancient heritage. This concept of a breach between the "middle ages" and the succeeding age, and its corollary, an opprobrious view of the earlier period as Gothic, dark, and barbarous, were adopted and developed from their own special viewpoints by the contemporaries and successors of the sixteenth-century humanists.

In breaking with the medieval Church, the Protestant reformers also emphasized the gap which separated them from a period dominated by that Church, rather than the continuity with medieval Christianity which much of their doctrine and practice represented. From another point of view, which made both Catholicism and conservative Protestantism the objects of its mocking assault, the rationalists of the eighteenth century liked to consider themselves infinitely remote, in their enlightenment, from "the thousand years of barbarism and religion," a phrase with which one of their most eminent representatives, Edward Gibbon, dismissed this long period. It is possible to ask, with Carl Becker, whether the "heavenly city" of these eighteenth-century philosophers was, in the faith on which its basic premises of the perfectibility of man, illimitable human progress, and their corollaries, rested, as unmedieval as its exponents chose to believe. Does the eighteenth-century outlook reflect, as Becker suggests, an age of faith based on reason as contrasted with a medieval age of reason based on faith? At any rate, to the men of the Enlightenment, and in the nineteenth century to many men of science, the middle ages were a period, generally speaking, of religious obscurantism and intellectual darkness, in which the light of progress shone but dimly, if at all.

The more violent phases of the French Revolution, and its aftermath, altered the outlook of many thinkers. In reaction, there was an increasing emphasis on the continuity rather than the breaches of historical development. In the conservative view, such as that expressed by an opponent of revolution like Edmund Burke, the state as it had developed historically appeared as a tree, and society as a contract between the dead, the living, and those yet unborn. In the light of this interest in the continuous thread of historical growth, and reacting against the rationalism and classicism of the eighteenth century, the exponents of romanticism, such as Victor Hugo, Sir Walter Scott, and others, tended to glorify and idealize the middle ages. They saw in this period an age more spirited and glamorous, more romantic, than their own nineteenth century, and sought to restore to life its people and its atmosphere.

From still another source, the nineteenth-century preoccupation with science and the application of scientific method to the study of man, a truer evaluation of the middle ages was fostered. Not only the long perspective of the evolutionary theory, but the scientific urge to see things as they really are, or were, which motivated many historians, has contributed largely in the last hundred years to the fuller and more objective study of the middle ages. As R. H. Tawney has said, "The past reveals to the present what the present is capable of seeing and the face which to one age is a blank to another is pregnant with meaning." The great surge of enthusiasm for St. Francis, the "little poor man" of Assisi, is a striking instance of the modern rediscovery and revaluation of the middle ages, so often inspired by romanticism and then developed by the more critical zeal of scientific history. The Christlike humanity of this saint, his tender love for man and for all the works of nature, made a profound appeal to the romantic idealism of the earlier nineteenth century, which responded ardently also to the poetry, paintings, and architecture of the land and century of St. Francis. His cult, always active among Catholics, spread widely beyond the circles of the Church and led to that scholarly probing into the sources of his life and work which has created a large school of Franciscan studies.

III

Whether the conventional divisions of history are viewed as reflections of the special concerns of successive periods, as conveniences of thought, or as substitutes for it, or perhaps as a legacy from the medieval conception of a series of well-defined ages, the use of these categories can hardly be avoided. Although the term middle ages is quite widely accepted for the period from the "fall of the Roman Empire" to the fifteenth century, few historians will venture to say precisely when the period began or when it ended. In order to define its limits it is necessary to decide what is specifically "medieval," and ten centuries is a very long time to characterize as a whole. Some historians have preferred to consider as separable phases of development the earlier period, from the fifth to the eleventh century, and the high and later middle ages which are the focus of the *Medieval Reader*. This conception is supported by the fact that the eleventh century was in many respects a definite turning point in European history.

By this time, the process of fusion of the varied elements, classical, Christian, and barbarian, which went into the making of Europe was well under way. In the breakdown of the ancient order, the Christian Church had emerged as the most direct heir of the organization and functions of the Roman Empire, to assume the task, in the earlier middle ages, of converting the barbarian peoples. After the collapse of the short-lived empire of Charlemagne and the renewed barbarian invasions of the ninth and tenth centuries, the civilizing influence of the Church and the emergence of feudal bonds had restored some measure of order in society. The energies hitherto absorbed in meeting assaults from without and disorder within were now freed; by the eleventh century, Latin Christendom was moving from the defensive to the offensive.

Feudal society was approaching the fullness of its growth, and the medieval Church was advancing toward the height of its power. The revival of religious enthusiasm found expression in new monastic orders, in the Crusades, in efforts to reform the Church, and in the increasingly articulate assertion of its independence and supremacy in medieval society. That massive achievement, the recovery and assimilation in the twelfth and thirteenth centuries of a great body of Greek and Arabic philosophy and science, marks the real beginning of European intellectual leadership. In the integration of society in Church and empire, and in lesser forms of corporate organization, these centuries saw the attainment of a unity which, though imperfect, was far more complete than any which the modern world has achieved. Yet an intensified diversity of thought and action was manifested in every sphere. "There have been few periods in the history of the world when the movement of thought and of life was more rapid than in the twelfth and thirteenth centuries." This accelerated vitality was expressed in the rise of feudal states and the extension of royal power; in the growth of towns and of the new middle class; in the expansion of economic activity, of geographical and intellectual horizons; in the spirit of revolt expressed in heresy and in communal uprisings. The creative genius of the age produced not only great corporate expressions of its constructive powers, institutions like the universities and works of art like the cathedrals, but smaller and homelier objects of revolutionary significance, such as clocks and spectacles, buttons and forks.

In the fourteenth and fifteenth centuries, the vigor of medieval civilization, though still great, was more widely diffused. As earlier efforts to coordinate the parts of society within a larger unity weakened, the parts themselves waxed stronger and more independent. The empire, always greater in shadow than in substance, became the victim and the prize of dynastic rivalries, and the authority of the Church, especially of the papal monarchy, was challenged by temporal claims, by schism and heresy, and by movements for reform. The successes of feudal monarchies like France and England strikingly demonstrated the effectiveness of the smaller unit. Political thought, increasingly independent of theological speculation and more acutely aware of political realities, made fresh attempts at the perennial goals of medieval Christendom, unity and peace. While a political theorist like Pierre du Bois in the fourteenth century still sought these ends through the time-honored means of a crusade for the recovery of the Holy Land, he looked for their achievement not to the universal institutions of Church and empire, but to the newer national monarchies. The corporate and hierarchical structure of society was increasingly strained and shaken by the conflicts between the various "orders of men," by peasants' revolts and urban struggles. In the spheres of artistic, intellectual, and religious activity, the earlier attempts at coordination and synthesis gave way to a more vigorous individualism, a more independent and secular spirit. The gradual triumph of the parts over the whole may be seen in the growing separation of science and philosophy from theology, of art from the Church, in the increase of mysticism and in the appeal of lay religious movements.

Yet these later centuries saw the continuance and sometimes the perfection, as well as the transformation and decline, of many earlier ideals and institutions. In most respects the old feudal order was decaying, its basis and its functions undermined by the encroachments of kings and burghers and peasants, by new ways of warfare and of government. But not until late did the courtly ideal and the outward trappings of feudal chivalry attain a formal perfection in the extravagant refinement and splendor of the Burgundian court. And even if the enduring visions of universality and peace as embodied in the weakened Church and empire were dimmed, they had not yet faded. Dante in the fourteenth century, crying in the night for his lost Caesar, and

Nicholas of Cusa in the fifteenth, seeking the *Concordantia Catholica*, still strove to realize their ideals through the purifying and strengthening of the old institutions. But when in the middle of the fifteenth century, Pope Pius II called for a crusade against that latest threat to Christendom, the Ottoman Turks, the response to the papal plea revealed that Latin Christendom could not revivify by common action the ideals which it still acknowledged.

In this time of profound change, which has been described both as the "waning of the middle ages" and the "dawn of a new era," the old foundations had become dilapidated but they had not yet been replaced. Alfred North Whitehead has said that sometimes the period of transition is an age of hope, sometimes it is an age of despair. The later middle ages were both. If this period suffered from upheavals and catastrophes on a larger scale than did the preceding centuries, and from the weakening of the older forms of security, social and spiritual, it also experienced the opening up and broadening of new freedoms and opportunities. At its end, it beheld the discovery of the new world.

To fix the geographical limits of medieval civilization is as difficult as to determine precisely its temporal span. Yet, as Roger Bacon said in recommending the study of geography to his contemporaries, "The things of the world cannot be known except through a knowledge of the places in which they are contained." The focus of the *Medieval Reader* is the culture of Latin Christendom, which was an entity both larger and smaller than the Roman Empire it replaced in the West, just as it was both more and less in theory and in fact than the Europe of modern times. Latin Christendom, "the whole commonwealth of Christians obedient to the Roman Church," was never a geographical unit, but a spiritual body, always reaching out to embrace new lands and new peoples. From its core in western and central Europe, medieval Christendom, through missionary labors and the work of conversion, through crusades, conquests, and commerce, extended its frontiers to the north, east, and south, and even reached out to farther Asia.

The Mediterranean unity which was the great achievement of Roman civilization had been profoundly shaken in the last centuries of the empire by the incursion of barbarian peoples in the north, and by the concentration of imperial authority in the east, which both reflected and enhanced the divisions between Greek East and Latin West. This unity was finally shattered in the seventh and eighth centuries by the rise and expansion of Islam. What was formerly one cultural sphere had now become three. To emphasize the medieval culture of the Latin West is not to minimize the roles of Byzantium and of Islam, which were pre-eminent in the early middle ages, or the enrichment of Western culture from these sources. But by the twelfth and thirteenth centuries Latin Christendom was clearly in the ascendancy in the Mediterranean world. The Greek and Muslim East are seen in these selections chiefly in terms of the interaction of peoples which was the result of Western expansion. Until the late fourteenth century, Latin Christendom was actively engaged in the early stages of that process by which Western European civilization has extended its influence throughout the world. Its eastward expansion was checked, and its frontiers pushed back, by the westward advance of the Ottoman Turks. Henceforth its expansive energies were directed toward the south and west, and concentrated on the maritime enterprise and exploration which heralded the great age of discovery.

IV

In a small book of essays called *Velvet Studies*, C. V. Wedgwood tells of her electrifying discovery of the direct route to that world of the past with which she was already enchanted. She had found out, at the age of twelve, that men and women long dead had left behind them all manner of records. So dazzling was the revelation that "immediate contact could be made with these dead" that, she says, she breathed for hours on the showcases in the British Museum copying off all the documents on view. For most people to whom the reality of the past is revealed, it is first in some such way as this, in the shock of recognition, a sudden sense of personal contact, a flash of sympathy and comprehension. The act of imagination by which the barriers of time and space are dissolved and the past is endowed with very present reality is the true beginning of understanding.

The medieval materials for this process exist in bewildering quantity and variety. Men and women of these centuries have left their account of themselves in many forms, in paintings and buildings, monuments and artifacts of all sorts, as well as in the written records to which the *Medieval Reader* is restricted. They wrote, as Hugh of St. Victor said of the "ancients," more books than we are able to read. Their public activities and aspirations and their more intimate thoughts and emotions are recorded in biographies, chronicles, histories, in laws, letters, and journals, in little songs and in great prose and poetry. The articulate members of medieval society, though few in number as they are in any age, were men, and sometimes women, of the most varied ranks and conditions; they were churchmen and laymen,

famous and obscure, naïve and sophisticated. Among
them were monks and friars like William of Malmesbury
and Salimbene, secular clerics like John of Salisbury,
scholars and theologians like Adelard of Bath and
Thomas Aquinas, great prelates like Archbishop Becket
and Pope Pius II. There were laymen of different classes,
such as that "gentlemanly journalist," Jean Froissart,
the Italian bourgeois, Villani, the English surgeon, John
Arderne, and women like Christine de Pisan, who took
up writing to support her children.

The motives which inspired their work were as varied
as the individuals; some wrote from a desire for private
and personal communication, or more formally to amuse
or to instruct a contemporary public, or, to use a good
medieval phrase, "for the perpetual memory of the matter," and incidentally, of themselves. The products of
this educative ardor are quantities of learned and popular treatises which provide, besides edification, insight
into the life of different classes, and into medieval theories about that life. And the range is very great, from
the "mirrors of princes" and the handbooks of statesmen,
such as John of Salisbury's *Policraticus*, to advice for the
good wife in the care of house and husband and to the
rules of love carefully enumerated by Andrew the Chaplain. Fortunately, many medieval writers, although they
may have worked for their own gratification and that
of their contemporaries, were not unmindful of posterity.
Giraldus Cambrensis was moved, as he said, to draw the
portrait of King Henry II, "so that those who in future
ages shall hear and read of his great achievements, may
be able to picture him to themselves as he was." Whatever the nature or the intention of these records, whether
they are casual or formal, inventories of household furnishings or the finished products of intellect and imagination, through them we may make contact not only

with the inner life of "nature's microcosm or little world, which is man," but thereby with the larger world in which these individuals moved.

Letters of the past have a special appeal, because though reading the correspondence of one's contemporaries is frowned on, reading that of the dead is permissible and rewarding. A charming and playful letter like that of Thomas Betson to his young betrothed, urging her to eat her meat like a woman so that she may soon grow up and marry him, makes the writer no longer simply an obscure fifteenth-century merchant, but the friend and contemporary of the reader. In letters like those of Heloise to Abelard, and that of Peter the Venerable telling Heloise of Abelard's last days and death, there is a direct revelation of the personalities and relationships of three individuals. "Who," Heloise herself says, "could read or hear these things and not be moved to tears?" And in reading them we are introduced to the tumultuous, creative twelfth century, for the writers and recipients of these letters moved with other great figures at the center of their world, Abelard as the renowned teacher and philosopher, Heloise as a most learned abbess, and Peter the Venerable as abbot of the widespread order of Cluny.

The abounding vigor of mind and spirit which charged the life of this age, which revitalized the monasteries and filled the schools, was manifest in them, as it was in their contemporaries. It found outlets in every sphere of activity, in the passionate study of the classics and of logic and law, in theological speculation and lyric poetry, in crusades and the building of churches and the government of men, in reforming ardor and even in revolt. The abbot of St. Denis whose "machinations" Heloise deplored was that same Suger who was the counselor of two kings of France and who ordered for his abbey church the construction of a revolutionary new choir which was the beginning of the Gothic style. Heloise's judgment of Norbert and Bernard as "false apostles" was extreme, as was her provocation. They were moving spirits in the reform of monasticism, and the austere personality of St. Bernard, abbot of Clairvaux, was a most powerful force in his age. He was the formidable adversary of both Abelard and his friend the eloquent and unfortunate Arnold of Brescia, whose zeal for reform, turned against the worldly power of the Church and finally to revolt, hastened him to the "sad noose."

John of Salisbury, who wrote a brief account of Arnold's career, had sat at the feet of Abelard, the Peripatetic of Palais, in the course of long years of study in France. His life span made him a link between the first and second halves of his century, and because of the breadth of his interests as scholar, humanist, and churchman, he was active in both the sphere of the schools and the larger orbit of church and court. For John, who died as bishop of Chartres, was the friend and adviser of popes, the secretary and loyal supporter of Thomas Becket in the long struggle with King Henry II which ended in the archbishop's murder. His younger contemporary, that lively archdeacon Giraldus Cambrensis, of flourishing ego and busy pen, was another of those men of the twelfth century who went everywhere and knew everyone of importance. His acute observations and wide experience are recorded in many books, one an account of his own deeds in which his vivid personality is but imperfectly concealed by the use of the third person. He wrote with a naïve vanity and self-concern which moved him to report that an old abbot, on beholding his physical perfection, had cried, "Can such beauty die?"

When Giraldus died, the thirteenth century was already well begun, a century, like the twelfth, of vigorous activity but of a different spirit. Its special qualities and interests, its great movements and their centers, like those of the preceding age, are reflected in the lives and relationships of its individuals. The court of Sicily under the last of the Hohenstaufen emperors, Frederick II, whose "misfortunes, follies, and death" are described by the ubiquitous friar Salimbene, was a center of political experiment and sophisticated culture, just as were those Italian cities of the north of which Salimbene himself was a child. Out of this flourishing urban life, enriched by commerce and often torn by strife, came that renewal of the Christian spirit, inspired and personified by St. Francis, and spread by his Friars Minor, of whom Salimbene was one. Among the Italian cities, the Rome of Boniface VIII, whose career marks a turning point in the history of the Western Church, was still the heart and core of medieval Christendom. And in Florence, of which Villani was the chronicler, was born the "sweet new style" in Italian literature and art embodied in the works of Dante and Giotto. Another sphere of the thirteenth-century world was the France of Louis IX, in whom the ideal of feudal and Christian kingship was fulfilled, and of his faithful vassal and biographer, Joinville; its focus was Paris where the schools of the twelfth century had crystallized in that great university where Robert de Sorbonne and Roger Bacon and St. Thomas Aquinas worked and taught.

Among the men and women of these and other medieval centuries, there are many whose lives and works illuminate not only their age and its experience, but the timeless greatness of the human spirit. In the goodly company of such as these, boredom, which was to the middle ages one of the deadliest sins, is impossible.

v

If the Gothic cathedral has become, especially
through the influence of Henry Adams' *Mont Saint Michel and Chartres,* a familiar and still valid symbol of the
medieval spirit, the school, comprising all the forms
of education, is an equally valid one. For the culture of
the middle ages was essentially architectonic in its ideals
and achievements. Its "peculiar genius" for embodying
its ideals in institutions constructed not only monasteries, churches, and castles, but schools and universities, encyclopedic works and systems of thought. Out
of diverse traditions and intractable materials men of
the middle ages were building a civilization, and in
both the cathedral and the school are reflected the
premises on which this task was based, and many of its
problems.

The corporate activity by which the cathedrals were
built is but one aspect of the vast effort to order the
diverse and conflicting elements of society in a harmonious whole. The work of individual and recognized
artists reflects the role of the more articulate and self-
conscious individuals in society. The balance of high
tensions in the Gothic cathedral has been called the
classic expression of the Western spirit, as final as the
temple of the fifth century B.C. was of the Greek spirit.
A cathedral like Amiens or Chartres is as dynamic and
active an organism as the society which produced it.
And its purpose was as functional, in theory, as that
of other parts of society. The cathedral was a monument
of the arts coordinated in the service of religion, and
it was a school of religion, for, as Durandus said, "pictures and ornaments in churches are the lessons and
scriptures of the laity." In these pictures and images the

great popular devotion to the saints, and above all to the Queen of Heaven, is mirrored. The cult of the Virgin, the "welle of mercy," found expression in the innumerable portals, chapels, and cathedrals built in her honor, as it did in the names of flowers, the Lady's slippers and Mary-buds, and in the little stories of her miracles, and in great poetry.

In the cathedral, the whole Christian revelation, the drama of medieval religion, is made manifest in tangible forms with those symbolical meanings which Durandus explained at length. Very little that medieval men built or painted or wrote can be fully comprehended without some understanding of that mode of observation and thought which expressed itself by means of symbolism and allegory. In this way of looking at things and thinking about them, the visible object is clothed with supernatural significance, and the abstract conception given concrete form in an image. The ox is not only a beast of burden, it is the symbol of Luke the Evangelist, because the ox is an animal fitted for sacrifice; it has two horns, moreover, representing the two testaments; it figures Christ, the sacrifice for man.

The "Unam Sanctam" of Pope Boniface VIII is a small compendium of the more familiar symbols. The Church is the dove of the Canticle, the spouse of Christ, the body of Christ, the seamless garment. Here also are the two swords, symbols of the spiritual and temporal authorities, although "the priesthood of the sun and the imperium of the moon" were often preferred as symbols in the great conflicts between these powers. To the medieval mind symbolism explained the observed facts of nature in terms of the Christian and eternal facts of life. It exalted and justified both image and concept, supporting them with the weight of tradition and of divine authority.

But if the cathedrals and tapestries and illuminations are filled with symbolical meaning, the leaves, flowers, and animal forms which decorate them reveal also a loving and accurate observation of nature. This kind of detailed scrutiny of nature is an aspect of that empiricism which was so significant in the development of medieval science and technology. In the long history of man's peering into the mirror of nature, of his efforts to extract her secrets, to understand and apply them, the contribution of the middle ages was by no means negligible. Adelard of Bath's "natural questions," in which he instructed his bumptious nephew, provide an insight into the scientific interests of a twelfth-century scholar, in whose ideas are mingled a naïve curiosity and a real comprehension of some scientific principles and problems. Roger Bacon's concern with the observation of nature and with the development of an experimental science and method are better known than much of the equally important work of his contemporaries and successors, that of Albertus Magnus, for example, in botany and biology, or that of the fourteenth-century physicists.

An intensely practical and experimental attitude toward everyday life and work, as characteristic of the middle ages as the more theoretical approach, was responsible for those notable advances in technology by which now nameless artisans and inventors helped to revolutionize human habits. Just as the making of forks and of buttons wrought great changes in domestic life, so the invention of spectacles in the late thirteenth century meant that men could now read more and later in life. The form and distribution of reading matter, and every phase of late medieval and modern life, were deeply affected by another kind of domestic revolution. For the process of making paper, which spread from Spain to Italy in the thirteenth century, pulp was required, and the increased use of linen in clothing during the fourteenth century supplied the needed rags. "The *siècle de chemise* introduced the century of printing." Although some of its advantages may be debatable, probably no medieval invention has been more important for modern science than that of the mechanical clock, which made possible the precise measurement of time so essential to scientific method.

In the middle ages, someone has said, almost everyone was always trying to educate or to advise everyone else. The schools, the whole effort of education, like the cathedrals, were expressions of this didactic spirit, at once practical and theoretical. Yet there were no colleges or departments of education, and a large part of the work of instruction was not even carried on in formal schools, but in feudal courts and the workshops of artisans and in the manorial fields; it was an organic part of the social structure. And in keeping with the functional character of society, the training was vocational. Each order and group assumed the responsibility of educating its members, and as in Dotheboys Hall, men learned by doing. The young nobleman, like Jörg von Ehingen, the craftsman, the merchant, the artist, the novice-monk, the student in the university, all served an apprenticeship in their calling, and were ultimately subjected to a test of their ability. The monastery was, *par excellence*, a "school of the Lord's service," but in a sense all education was a school of service, both that of the Lord and of man in society. For in the medieval view, education was moral training, a preparation for the "good life," and, since the real business of life was salvation, for eternity.

Like religion, with which it was so closely allied, the educational process pervaded medieval life. The passion for learning and teaching, in its more intellectual as-

pects, had its formal embodiment first in the monastic
and cathedral schools, and then more completely in the
universities, which from the thirteenth century on were
the workshops of thought and the molds of public opinion. In centers like Paris, Bologna, and Oxford, students
from every corner of Christendom were trained as teachers, doctors, lawyers, and theologians, absorbing a cur-
riculum which was a legacy from antiquity, expanded
gradually in the earlier middle ages, and more spectacu-
larly in the twelfth and thirteenth centuries. Here men
confronted, in its intellectual forms, the great task of
harmonizing a Christian view of things with the ordinary life of man. The advent of "Our Prince," Aristotle,
and his Arabic companions acted as a catalyst, sharpen-
ing and intensifying the persistent efforts of medieval
thinkers to reconcile complex classical traditions with
Christian revelation, to satisfy the demands of both
reason and faith. In philosophy and theology, a most
comprehensive solution was the massive synthesis of St.
Thomas Aquinas. His system was, however, but one of
many responses to a challenge which stimulated bold
speculation and the most varied currents of thought. The
"learned ignorance" of Nicholas of Cusa, emphasizing
the primacy of religious experience, reflects the increasing tendency of later medieval thinkers to separate,
rather than to harmonize, the domains of reason and
faith.

VI

According to a fifteenth-century description of the
symbolism of arts and sciences, the art of writing should
be represented by a "little old man with a strainer in one
hand and a written book in the other." The strainer is
an equally appropriate symbol for anthologists, espe-

cially for those who boldly attempt to make from the multitudinous records of several centuries a selection that is both discriminating and representative. Our effort has been to seek out some of the best, the most authoritative, vivid, and direct expressions of medieval experience and thought, whether in poetry or prose, familiar or little known, previously translated or not.

From those sources already available in translation we have drawn gratefully and, we hope, well. But a vast amount of significant material is still accessible only in its original language, either in Latin or in the vernaculars. In some cases where, in our opinion, an important or revealing record was not yet translated, we have tried to remedy the lack. For example, Froissart has written the best-known description of the Battle of Poitiers, but that of Geoffrey le Baker, which we have translated, is the most vivid and accurate. Some works of unique value, hitherto familiar only to scholars, are also represented in our own translations: Hugh of St. Victor's little guide to study and teaching, so influential throughout the middle ages; the inquisitor's manual of Bernard Gui, containing perhaps the fullest account of the beliefs and habits of medieval heretics; the history of surgery by an eminent fourteenth-century surgeon, Gui de Chauliac; the treatise on "learned ignorance" of Nicholas of Cusa, the great and too little known churchman and philosopher of the fifteenth century.

Many of our selections are narrative and descriptive, some are didactic, others are lyric; some are of considerable length and others brief. All have been chosen to speak for themselves, without special comment or explanation. The straining process has often been difficult and sometimes painful, and the limitations of space, of available materials, and of our own knowledge and tastes are responsible for many of those sins of exclusion which often seem more unforgivable than those of inclusion. In general, documentary sources have been avoided; we have used only a few, of great intrinsic interest and general value, such as the bull "Unam Sanctam" of Pope Boniface VIII and selections from the visitation records of the reforming archbishop Odo and from university and municipal records.

Of the rich imaginative literature of the middle ages, we have sought to include as much as possible and to illustrate both its unique qualities and its varied forms. Because the large body of courtly romance is familiar to most readers, and, in addition, had much the same relation to real life as does modern "soap opera," we have omitted all but a small sample in order to have more room for selections from less-known works, such as *Piers Plowman*, that "first authentic cry of the poor in history." The great works of medieval literature should be read as a whole and, if possible, in their own language; we have deliberately refrained from making selections from *The Divine Comedy* and *The Canterbury Tales*, available in many translations. It is our hope that an acquaintance with the culture of the middle ages from other sources may make these supreme expressions of its spirit more meaningful, and also that the reader who mourns the absence of old favorites may take comfort in finding new ones.

When, in their own accounts of themselves, the men and women of the middle ages are encountered familiarly and directly, the sense of instant comprehension is often so strong that any barriers between us and them appear insignificant—mere accidents of time and environment, the differences perhaps between the complicated plumbing fixtures of a modern house and the simpler, cruder furnishings of a fifteenth-century manor house. But suddenly we are brought up short by the realization that, although we may meet medieval people on the common ground of humanity, and of much else besides, some of the differences are not accidental and superficial, but really profound. Medieval culture was, as has been said, a distinct one; many of the aspirations and ways of thinking which shaped its life are not those of the modern world. The attempt to understand calls for more than sympathy and imagination; it requires a penetrating insight into the factors which molded this society and held it together, the ideals which dominated it, and the forces which challenged and changed it. The personal records must be set in a larger framework, as the individuals who produced them were parts of a larger whole. An interpretation of medieval culture is both implicit and explicit in the selections and organization of the *Medieval Reader;* it is, we hope, a valid reflection of what men of those centuries thought about themselves, in harmony with their theories as well as with the actual structure of their society.

When they discussed the nature, activities, and problems of society, most medieval writers, certainly from the twelfth century on, based their ideas on a simple analogy. They thought of society as a living organism, and compared the functions of its parts with those of the human body. According to the classic statement by John of Salisbury, "a commonwealth is a certain body endowed with life." The commonwealth, "the whole body of Christians," is one expression of the unity and universality for which medieval men sought, just as "The Body Social" is another. "Christian Commonwealth" and "Body Social" are really two aspects of the same entity, which was coextensive with the Christian Church in its broadest sense. The place of the Church in medieval society or of society in the Church, depending on the point of view, is one important reason why it is impossible to separate the strands of medieval life along conventional modern lines in political, social, economic, and religious categories. Medieval men, whatever their failures and backslidings, would not have conceived of religion as a separate compartment of human activity. The Church aimed to be, as Tawney says, "not a sect, but a civilization," and it was in practice a vast institution with universal claims, a system of government and social organization, pervading and deeply involved in every sphere of medieval life.

To a lesser extent, though in very important ways, the growth of feudal organization, based on loyalty and land, was a unifying force in society. It provided a principle of order in a world of conflicts and struggles, an answer to the needs of men for protection and security, just as the Church, the vessel and means of salvation, cared for the security and salvation of men's souls, as well as often for their bodies. Both were based on co-operation among men and on the coordination of activity. Both Church and feudal organization were expressions of that striving for order, social, intellectual and spiritual, which is so striking a quality of medieval life.

According to Boniface VIII, "the law of divinity is to lead the lowest through the intermediate to the highest things. Not, therefore, according to the law of the universe, are all things reduced to order equally and immediately; but the lowest through the intermediate, the intermediate through the higher." Society with its hierarchy of orders and ranks of men, the Church and the feudal state with their hierarchies of officials, the structure of lesser corporate bodies such as universities and guilds, and the hierarchy of arts and sciences culminating in theology, reflected, though imperfectly, this eternal order. When men worked, as they frequently did, for the reform of society, they thought of it as "the proper ordering of the spiritual and temporal estates."

But though society was in theory and practice closely woven, it was by no means a seamless fabric. It was, as it conceived itself to be, a living organism; it was always changing, challenged and ultimately rent by conflicts and tensions which it sought constantly but with varying success, to harmonize and resolve. The ideal and the actuality, the unity and diversity, the struggle and violence of this society are all illustrated in the sections of this book called "The Body Social" and "The Christian Commonwealth," which are concerned with social and institutional life. They are also manifest in the other parts of our framework, which represent more special aspects of the same whole. In "The House of Fame," which contains portraits of a few great men and women, this larger whole may be viewed in the microcosm of the individual. The expansion of this society, its mobile and adventurous spirit, its relations with other peoples and cultures, are shown in "The World Picture." Dante's conception of "The Noble Castle," inhabited by the great poets and sages of antiquity, suggested the title of the last section, illustrating "Melodious Musyk, Profound Poetry, and Drawyng of Picture," the liberal arts and higher sciences, and culminating in the medieval *summum bonum*, the vision of God.

VII

To medieval men, whether consciously or unconsciously, their past was ever present, in the Christian tradition of the Bible and the Fathers, in the ghost of the Roman Empire, in all those "flowering, perfumed, fruitful works of the pagan world" which shaped the humanist tradition. And as H. O. Taylor pointed out, "through the labor of making their inheritance their own, the middle ages produced whatever of lasting value it was their fortune to hand on. No period of human history shows more clearly how little of what goes before is lost in the most signal creations of the human spirit."

The magnitude of our own debt to medieval labors and the directness of our ties with this past are evident not only in living institutions, in the products and traditions of art and thought, but less tangibly in common ideals and problems. For we share with medieval men many of the noblest human aspirations, for the brotherhood of man, freedom, the security of human life, unity, and peace. Although their reach often far exceeded their grasp, they made no distinction between ideal and reality. To them the ideal, even if they failed to achieve it, was real.

Even in the homelier aspects of modern life, we still carry about a great deal of the unconscious baggage of medieval custom and convention, as well as of medieval invention and discovery. In the strangeness of our familiar things, such as the basic form of our letters and numbers, the nursery rhymes of children, in our manners and habits of courtesy, in our trivial sayings, and in many of our common assumptions may be seen permanent marks of the middle ages. When we say firmly that we will do something "by hook or by crook," do we think of the serf who was allowed to gather only as many sticks in the manorial woodland as he could secure without cutting? When we appeal to a friend for "aid and counsel," does the origin of the saying in the obligation of feudal lord and vassal flash through the mind? Although most of us are familiar, even though vaguely, with the heliocentric theory, for us, as for men and women of the middle ages, the sun still rises and sets. It is good to remember, too, that the middle ages preserved and illuminated, in both its earthly and its eternal significance, the classic definition of man as a "mortal, rational animal, capable of laughter."

The theme of indebtedness, on which this introduction opens, is an appropriate one on which to close. In compiling this reader we have been conscious above all of what we owe to the intellectual stimulation and training of our teachers in the field of medieval studies, at the Universities of Nebraska and Chicago and at Columbia University. To a number of friends and colleagues at Vassar and Wellesley Colleges we wish to express our gratitude, and especially to Professor Henry F. Schwarz of Wellesley College for his generous contributions of original translations of materials on German history. His translation of a large part of the *Reformation of the Emperor Sigismund* is the only English version of that remarkable document. Special thanks are also due to Smith College, and particularly to Professors Leona C. Gabel and Florence A. Gragg, for permission to use freely excerpts from the translation of *The Commentaries of Pius II*, which is being published in several installments in the *Smith College Studies in History*. The extensive search for materials represented in this book was made easier and more pleasant by the interest and cooperation of the staff of the Vassar College Library and by the courtesy of the staff of the Widener Library of Harvard University; to both we express our appreciation. Finally to the patience and industry of Marie Kelley and Elizabeth Salmon, who typed the voluminous manuscript of the book, our warm thanks are due.

M.M.M. and J.B.R.

Chronological Table

1050-1500

LATER ELEVENTH CENTURY AND TWELFTH CENTURY

	POLITICAL AND INSTITUTIONAL	SOCIAL AND ECONOMIC	RELIGIOUS AND CULTURAL
1050	*Height of Holy Roman Empire* Henry III, 1039-56 *Papal reform movement and investiture conflict* Pope Gregory VII, 1073-85 vs. Henry IV, 1056-1106 *Expansion of Normans* Conquest of England, William I, 1066-87; conquest of Sicily, Roger, d. 1101	← *Feudalism* → ← *First Crusade, 1095* →	*Reform movement in Church* Peter Damiani, d. 1072 Cistercian Order founded, 1097 *Revival of culture in Western Europe* Study of logic and theology Romanesque art and architecture: Abbey of Cluny; St. Albans Abbey, 1078; Durham Cathedral, 1093; Abbey of Vezelay, 1096
1100	*Rise of feudal monarchy* Anglo-Norman: Henry I, 1100-1135 French: Louis VI, 1108-37, and Abbot Suger, d. 1151 Spanish: expansion of Leon, Castile, Aragon	← *Rise of communes* → *Reclamation and colonization within Western Europe*	Recovery of Greek and Arabic science, philosophy begins: Adelard of Bath, fl. c. 1130 Rise of cathedral schools: Chartres, Laon, Paris Philosophy and theology: Peter Abelard, 1079-1142; Hugh of St. Victor, d. 1160; Pet r Lombard, d. 1160

Papacy and empire
Concordat of Worms, 1122

1150 *Papacy and empire*
Continuation of conflict: Frederick I, Barbarossa, 1152-90, vs. papacy and Lombard communes
Height of Hohenstaufen empire

Feudal monarchy, expansion and conflict
Anglo-Norman gain of Anjou and Aquitaine, Henry II, 1154-89, vs. Louis VII, 1137-80; Angevin-Capetian conflict: Richard I, 1189-99, vs. Philip II, 1180-1223; John, 1199-1216, vs. Philip II
Angevin loss of Normandy, Anjou, etc., Battle of Bouvines, 1215

← *Second Crusade, 1147* →

Importation of sericulture to Sicily

Eastward expansion of German people

← *Heretical movements* →
Albigensian and Waldensian

← *Third Crusade, 1189* →
First windmills in Europe

Humanistic studies: Bernard of Chartres; John of Salisbury, d. 1180

Study of Roman and canon law
Beginning of Gothic style—art and architecture: Abbey of St. Denis, 1140
Latin literature: Goliardic poetry
Vernacular literature: French—chansons de geste; Chrétien de Troyes; Marie de France, *Lais;* Provençal — troubadour lyrics; Spanish—The *Cid*
Historical writing: Otto of Freising, d. 1158; William of Tyre, c.1130-1190; Giraldus Cambrensis, c. 1146-1220
Rise of universities: Bologna, Paris, Salerno
Gothic cathedrals: Sens, Laon, Notre Dame de Paris, c.1160

Agricultural economy predominant. Serfdom and manorial organization. Revival of trade; rise of towns and middle class.

31

THIRTEENTH CENTURY

POLITICAL AND INSTITUTIONAL	SOCIAL AND ECONOMIC	RELIGIOUS AND CULTURAL
1200 *Feudal monarchy: constitutional and territorial growth*	← *Fourth Crusade, 1202* → Sack of Constantinople, *1204*	*Height and synthesis of medieval culture* 1200
English: Henry II, centralization; John, feudal reaction, Magna Carta, 1215; Henry III, 1216-72, growth of constitutional principle		Rise of mendicant orders: Order of Friars Minor, St. Francis, d. 1226; Order of Preachers, St. Dominic, d. 1221
French: Philip II, centralization in expanded royal domain	*Fairs of Champagne*	Full development of universities: Paris, 1215; College of Sorbonne, 1250; Oxford; Padua, 1228; Rome, 1245; Salamanca, 1250
Spanish: Union of Leon and Castile, 1230	Pioneer engineering work in Northern Italy	
Height of medieval church and papacy		Philosophy and theology: Recovery of complete Aristotle; attempts at synthesis—Albertus Magnus, d. 1280; Bonaventura, d. 1274; Thomas Aquinas, d. 1274
Centralization and extension of authority: Innocent III, d. 1216; Fourth Lateran Council, 1215; Papal Inquisition	← *Expansion of Teutonic Knights in Prussia from c.1230*	
Papal conflict with empire for control of Italy	← *Development of Italian and Flemish cities* →	Scientific interests: Robert Grosseteste, d. 1253; Albertus Magnus; Roger Bacon, d. c.1292
Fall of Hohenstaufen Empire Death of Frederick II, 1250	Spread of use of Hindu (Arabic) numerals	

1250 *Feudal monarchy at height*

English: Edward I, 1272-1307, conquest of Wales and Scotland; statutes and Model Parliament, 1295

French: Louis IX, 1226-70, expansion and centralization; Philip IV, 1285-1314, growth of bureaucracy, Estates General, 1302

Spanish: strong monarchy and estates in separate kingdoms

Holy Roman Empire
Interregnum, 1254-73
Rise of Habsburgs: Rudolf I, 1273-91

Papacy: assertion and decline of authority
Boniface VIII, d. 1305; *Unam Sanctam*, 1302; conflict with national monarchies—France and England

---

Maritime rivalry of Venice and Genoa

Use of compass by Italian sailors

Invention of gunpowder in Europe or Syria

Travels to Far East Merchants → Marco Polo

Spectacles made in Northern Italy

Height of Gothic architecture: cathedrals of Rheims, Amiens, Chartres

Growth of vernacular literature: French—fabliaux, *Roman de la Rose*; Italian—lyric poetry; German—minnesang

Missionary efforts of Friars: John of Pian de Carpini; William of Rubruck

---

Continuation of manorial economy. Expansion of trade; merchant and craft guilds; increase of urban centers and population; wealth and influence of middle class.

FOURTEENTH CENTURY

POLITICAL AND INSTITUTIONAL	SOCIAL AND ECONOMIC	RELIGIOUS AND CULTURAL	
1300 "Babylonian Captivity"—popes at Avignon, 1305-76 Pope John XXII, conflict with Louis of Bavaria and Spiritual Franciscans *Beginning of Hundred Years' War between France and England, 1337* *Rise of tyrannies in Italian city-states* *Holy Roman Empire: dynastic rivalries, Habsburg, Luxemburg, Wittelsbach* Henry VII, 1308-13; Louis of Bavaria, 1314-47 Independence of princes and free cities→ Rise of Hanseatic League→ Growth of Swiss Confederation, 1315-1386 Charles IV, 1346-78; King of Bohemia; Golden Bull, 1356, Seven Electors	Perfection of mechanical clock Use of firearms—small cannon	*Increasing independence and secularization in life, art, and thought* Political theory: Pierre Dubois; Marsiglio of Padua, c.1270-1342; William of Ockham, d. c.1349 Philosophy and theology: Duns Scotus, d. 1308; William of Ockham, nominalism Science and medicine: Arnald of Villanova, d. 1313?; Peter of Abano, d. 1320; John Buridan, fl. 1335 Universities: new foundations—Perugia, Valladolid, Prague, etc. Vernacular literature: Italian—Dante, d. 1321, *Divine Comedy*; Petrarch, d. 1374, *Sonnets*; Boccaccio, d. 1375, *Decameron*	1300

1350 *Advance of Ottoman Turks; cross to Europe, 1356*
National monarchies: France and England
Continuation of Hundred Years' War: Poitiers, 1356
Political and constitutional development: France—Estates-General at Paris, 1356-62; the Great Ordinance, 1357; victory of Charles V, 1364-80; foundation of absolute monarchy; beginning of Burgundian power
England—Edward III, 1327-77; parliamentary control of taxation and anti-papal statutes; Richard II, 1377-99, attempt at absolute monarchy, Lancastrian revolution, Henry IV, 1399-1413
Schism in the Church, 1378-1417
Popes at Avignon and at Rome

← *The Black Death, 1348-50* →

← *The Jacquerie, 1358*

Lollard heresy in England →

← *The Peasants' Revolt, 1381*

Art and architecture: Giotto, d. 1336; flamboyant Gothic style in northern Europe
Increase of mysticism and of lay element in religious life: Ruysbroek, 1293-1381; Gerard Groot and the Brethren of the Common Life
Further growth of vernacular languages and literature: French — Guillaume Machaut, Jean Froissart; English — William Langland, *Piers Plowman*; Geoffrey Chaucer, John Wyclif, English Bible
Humanistic interests: Richard de Bury, 1281-1345; Petrarch; Coluccio Salutati, 1331-1406; Leonardo Bruni, 1369-1444

Decline of manorial economy. Social and economic conflict in towns. Beginning of shift in trade routes and expansion of maritime trade.

FIFTEENTH CENTURY

POLITICAL AND INSTITUTIONAL	SOCIAL AND ECONOMIC	RELIGIOUS AND CULTURAL
1400 *The Church, efforts toward reform, the triumph of papal monarchy*		*Continued dominance and development of scholastic philosophies and theology—especially in northern Europe* **1400**
Continuation of schism		*Movements and theories of Church reform*
Conciliar movement: Council of Pisa, 1409		Pierre D'Ailly, 1350-c.1420; Jean Gerson, 1363-1429; Nicholas of Cusa, 1401-1464
End of schism: Council of Constance, 1414-18; burning of John Hus, 1415; election of Martin V, 1417		*Humanist studies predominant in Italy*
Restoration of papal monarchy: Council of Basel, 1431-39; Pope Eugenius IV, 1431-47; Pope Nicholas V, 1447-55		Poggio Bracciolini, 1380-1459; Lorenzo Valla, 1406-57; Aeneas Silvius (Pope Pius II), 1405-64
The national monarchies: continued conflict		*Pre-eminence of Italian and Flemish artists*
English victory and domination: Agincourt, 1415, King Henry V; civil war—Anglo-Burgundian Alliance; career of Jeanne d'Arc, 1429-31		Masaccio, 1401-29; the Van Eycks; Roger van der Weyden, c.1400-64; Donatello, d. 1466; Brunelleschi, 1377-1446; Alberti, 1404-72
Restoration of French monarchy: Charles VII, 1422-61 Hundred Years' War ends, 1453	*Economic leadership of cities of South Germany and Low Countries*	

1450	The greater Italian states—consolidation and centralization	Decline of overland trade with Far East, search for new routes	First printing with movable type, Mainz, c.1450
	Venice, Milan, Florence, Papal States, Sicily		Vernacular literature
	The fall of Constantinople, 1453		Christine de Pisan, c.1363-1431; development of French and English religious drama; Charles of Orleans, 1391-1465; François Villon, 1431-1489; Philipp de Commines, 1447?-1,11?
	The height and fall of the House of Burgundy		
	Philip the Good, 1419-1467; Charles the Bold, 1467-77	Prince Henry the Navigator, 1394-1460	
	The Holy Roman Empire: beginning of Habsburg domination		
	Frederick III, 1440-93		
	Maximilian I, m. Mary of Burgundy, 1477		
	The "new" monarchies; territorial expansion and consolidation		
	France: Louis XI, 1461-1483		
	England: Wars of the Roses—York vs. Lancaster; Henry VII, Tudor, 1485-1509		
	Spain: Ferdinand of Aragon m. Isabella of Castile, 1469		

Disintegration of manorial economy. Consolidation of tenures; emergence of free labor. Growth of capitalistic enterprise in trade, industry, banking.

SUGGESTIONS FOR FURTHER READING
(REVISED, 1997)

SINCE 1949, when the *Medieval Reader* first appeared, and especially since 1967, when these suggestions were last revised, the literature on the middle ages has grown enormously, and many works of both general and specialized interest have become more accessible than ever in paperback editions. During recent decades, the expansion of scholarship and interpretation in diverse directions, concerning more varied topics, has fostered both wider perspectives on medieval societies and intensive investigation of large and hitherto neglected aspects of the medieval world. Whatever the lasting outcome of this encompassing activity, the impact of theory and empirical research has enlivened current study and understanding of the middle ages. A glance at this revised list may suggest something of the scope of an enterprise that now embraces women, children, and private life; the poor, prostitutes, criminals, and others on the margins of society; fixes attention on such basic aspects of human life as the body, gender, and sexuality; and poses new questions to medieval sources, including those represented in this collection.

Like our earlier lists, this revised selection has been drawn from works written in or translated into English; wherever possible, the best paperback edition of both older and newer editions has been indicated. In general, individual sources or books devoted to individuals, as well as textbooks and studies of strictly national scope have rarely been included. For reasons of space, bibliographical references have been restricted, in general, to the publisher, commercial or academic, and the date of publication or reprint. Paperback editions are indicated by the letter p.

Among works of reference, the *New Cambridge Medieval History* will replace its predecessor, now out of print. Of the seven projected volumes (Volume IV is to be divided into two parts) only Volume II, (c. 700–900), edited by Rosamond McKitterick, has been published (1996). The first three volumes of the *Cambridge Economic History*, all now candidates for revision, deal with the middle ages. Especially active in the production of works devoted to large aspects of medieval society, the Cambridge University Press publishes such collaborative series as the Cambridge Studies in Medieval and Renaissance Music. Another important collaborative series is *A History of the Crusades*, edited by Kenneth M. Setton of which all six volumes have now been published (University of Wisconsin Press, 1955–1990). A more encompassing series, the Medieval Academy Reprints for Teaching (MART), published by the University of Toronto Press, features books specially selected and is designed to keep in print the very best medieval scholarship, modestly priced for students. Placing the medieval world in its geographical contexts are several atlases, among them the *New Penguin Atlas of Medieval History* edited by Colin McEvedy (1992) and *The Cambridge Atlas of Warfare: The Middle Ages, 768–1487* (1996).

Also available are several continuing series of medieval sources in translation, some accompanied by the original text such as the new series the Cambridge Medieval Classics, edited by Peter Dronke. Among the several published volumes are: *Nine Medieval Latin Plays*, edited and translated by Peter Dronke (1994) and Dante's *Monarchia*, edited and translated by Prue Shaw (1995). Nelson's Medieval Texts also includes original texts. The Penguin Classics series offers an extensive selection of medieval classics in new, complete translations, while the Paulist Press offers translations of medieval classics in its Classics of Western Spirituality.

I. WORKS OF BROAD SCOPE AND INTEREST.

Anderson, Bonnie S. and Judith P. Zinsser. *A History of Their Own: Women in Europe from Prehistory to the Present.* (Vol. I, HarperCollins, 1988, p).

Barber, Malcolm C. *The Two Cities: Medieval Europe, 1050–1320.* (Routledge, 1992; 1993, p).

Bartlett, Robert. *The Making of Europe: Conquest, Colonization, and Cultural Change, 950–1350.* (Princeton University Press, 1993).

Bell, Rudolph M. and Donald Weinstein. *Saints and Society: The Two Worlds of Western Christendom, 1000–1700.* (University of Chicago Press, 1982).

Benson, Robert L. and Giles Constable with Carol D. Lanham, eds. *Renaissance and Renewal in the Twelfth Century.* (University of Toronto Press, MART, 1991, p).

Binski, Paul. *Medieval Death: Ritual and Representation.* (Cornell University Press, 1996).

Bitel, Lisa M. *Land of Women: Tales of Sex and Gender from Early Ireland.* (Cornell University Press, 1996).

Bloch, R. Howard. *Medieval Misogyny and the Invention of Western Romantic Love.* (University of Chicago Press, 1991, p).

Boswell, John. *Christianity, Social Tolerance, and Homosexuality: Gay People in Western Europe from the Beginning of the Christian Era to the Fourteenth Century.* (University of Chicago Press, 1981, p).

Brown, Peter. *The Rise of Western Christendom: Triumph and Diversity, A.D. 200–1000.* (Blackwell Publishers, 1995).

Cohn, Norman. *The Pursuit of the Millennium.* (Oxford University Press, 1975, p).

Contamine, Philippe. *War in the Middle Ages,* translated by Michael Jones. (Blackwell Publishing, 1992, p).

Geary, Patrick J. *Before France and Germany: The Creation and Transformation of the Merovingian World.* (Oxford University Press, 1988, p).

Grant, Edward. *The Foundations of Modern Science in the Middle Ages.* (Cambridge University Press, Cambridge History of Science, 1996, p).

Herrin, Judith. *The Formation of Christendom.* (Princeton University Press, 1987; 1989, p).

Holmes, George, ed. *The Oxford Illustrated History of Medieval Europe.* (Oxford University Press, 1988; 1990, p).

Kieckhefer, Richard. *Magic in the Middle Ages.* (Cambridge University Press, 1990).

Klapisch-Zuber, Christiane and Arthur Goldhammer, eds. *A History of Women in the West, Vol. II: The Silences of the Middle Ages.* (Harvard University Press, 1992; 1994, p).

Krautheimer, Richard. *Rome: Profile of a City, 312–1308.* (Princeton University Press, 1980, p).

Lindberg, David C. *The Beginnings of Western Science: The European Scientific Tradition in Philosophical, Religious, and Intellectual Context, 600 B.C.–A.D. 1450.* (University of Chicago Press, 1992).

————. *Science in the Middle Ages.* (University of Chicago Press, 1978).

Moore, R. I. *The Formation of a Persecuting Society: Power and Deviance in Western Europe, 950–1250.* (Blackwell Publishing, 1987, p).

Morris, Colin. *The Discovery of the Individual, 1050–1200.* (University of Toronto Press, MART, 1987, p).

Mundy, John H. *Europe in the High Middle Ages. 1150–1309.* (Basic Books, 1973; 2nd edition, Longman Publishing, 1991, p).

Murray, Alexander. *Reason and Society in the Middle Ages.* (Oxford University Press, 1978, p).

Rosenthal, Joel T., ed. *Medieval Women and the Sources of Medieval History.* (University of Georgia Press, 1990, p).

Solterer, Helen. *The Master and Minerva: Disputing Women in French Medieval Culture.* (University of California Press, 1995).

Southern, Richard W. *The Making of the Middle Ages.* (Yale University Press, 1961, p).

II. SOCIETY AND POLITICS.

Atkinson, Clarissa. *The Oldest Vocation: Christian Mother-hood in the Middle Ages.* (Cornell University Press, 1991).

Bloch, Marc. *Feudal Society,* translated by L. A. Magon. (2 vols., University of Chicago Press, 1961, p).

Brooke, Christopher. *The Medieval Idea of Marriage.* (Oxford University Press, 1989).

Brundage, James A. *Law, Sex, and Christian Society in Medieval Europe.* (University of Chicago Press, 1990, p).

Cadden, Joan. *Meanings of Sex Difference in the Middle Ages: Medicine, Science, and Culture.* (Cambridge University Press, 1995, p).

Dillard, Heath. *Daughters of the Reconquest: Women in Castilian Town Society, 1100–1300* (Cambridge University Press, 1990, p).

Duby, Georges. *The Early Growth of the European Economy: Warriors and Peasants from the Seventh to the Twelfth Century,* translated by Howard B. Clarke. (Cornell University Press, 1978).

———. *Love and Marriage in the Middle Ages.* (University of Chicago Press, 1996, p).

———. *The Three Orders: Feudal Society Imagined,* translated by Arthur Goldhammer. (University of Chicago Press, 1980).

Ennen, Edith. *The Medieval Town.* (Oxford University Press, 1979).

Fossier, Robert. *Peasants of the Medieval West,* translated by J. Vale. (Blackwell Publishing, 1984).

Gold, Penny Schine. *The Lady and the Virgin: Image, Attitude, and Experience in Twelfth-Century France.* (University of Chicago Press, 1987, p).

Goody, Jack. *The Development of the Family and Marriage in Europe.* (Cambridge University Press, 1983).

Guenée, B. *States and Rulers in Later Medieval Europe,* translated by J. Vale. (Oxford University Press, 1985).

Hanawalt, Barbara A. *Growing Up in Medieval London: The Experience of Childhood in History.* (Oxford University Press, 1993).

———. *The Ties That Bound: Peasant Families in Medieval England.* (Oxford University Press, 1989, p).

Herlihy, David. *Medieval Households.* (Harvard University Press, 1985, p).

Holmes, Urban T., Jr. *Daily Living in the Twelfth Century: Based on the Observations of Alexander Neckham in London and Paris.* (University of Wisconsin Press, 1962, p).

Howell, Martha C. *Women, Production, and Patriarchy*

in Late Medieval Cities. (University of Chicago Press, 1988, p).

Labarge, Margaret Wade. *A Small Sound of the Trumpet: Women in Medieval Life* (Beacon Press, 1986, p).

Le Goff, Jacques. *Time, Work, and Culture in the Middle Ages,* translated by Arthur Goldhammer. (University of Chicago Press, 1982, p).

Leyser, K. J. *Medieval Germany and Its Neighbors, 900–1250.* (Hambledon Press, 1982).

Mollat, Michel. *The Poor in the Middle Ages: An Essay in Social History,* translated by Arthur Goldhammer. (Yale University Press, 1990, p).

Otis, Leah L. *Prostitution in Medieval Society: The History of an Urban Institution in Languedoc.* (University of Chicago Press, 1985).

Platt, Colin. *King Death: The Black Death and Its Aftermath in Late Medieval England.* (University of Toronto Press, 1996).

Pounds, Norman J. *An Economic History of Medieval Europe.* (Longman Publishing, 1974).

Reynolds, Susan. *Fiefs and Vassals: The Medieval Evidence Reinterpreted.* (Oxford University Press, 1994; 1996, p).

———. *Kingdoms and Communities in Western Europe, 900–1300.* (Oxford University Press, 1984).

III. RELIGION AND THE CHURCH.

Bornstein, Daniel and Roberto Rusconi, eds. *Women and Religion in Medieval and Renaissance Italy,* translated by Margery J. Schneider. (University of Chicago Press, 1995).

Brentano, Robert. *Two Churches: England and Italy in the Thirteenth Century.* (Princeton University Press, 1968; University of California Press, 1988, p).

Brooke, Rosalind B. and N. L. Christopher. *Popular Religion in the Middle Ages: Western Europe, 1000–1300.* (Cambridge University Press, 1984).

Brundage, James A. *Medieval Canon Law.* (Longman Publishing, 1996).

Bynum, Caroline Walker. *Holy Feast and Holy Fast: The Religious Significance of Food to Medieval Women.* (University of California Press, 1987, p).

———. *Jesus as Mother: Studies in the Spirituality of the High Middle Ages.* (University of California Press, 1982, p).

———. *The Resurrection of the Body in Western Christianity, 200–1336.* (Columbia University Press, 1995).

Constable, Giles. *The Reformation of the Twelfth Century.* (Cambridge University Press, 1997).

Elliott, Dyan. *Spiritual Marriage: Sexual Abstinence in Medieval Wedlock.* (Princeton University Press, 1993).

Henderson, John. *Piety and Charity in Late Medieval Florence.* (Oxford University Press, 1994).

Johnson, Penelope. *Equal in Monastic Profession: Religious Women in Medieval France.* (University of Chicago Press, 1991).

Lambert, Malcolm. *Medieval Heresy: Popular Movements from the Gregorian Reform to the Reformation.* (2nd edition, Blackwell Publishing, 1992).

Ladurie, Emmaneul LeRoy. *Montaillou: The Promised Land of Error,* translated by Barbara Bray. (Random House, 1979, p).

Lawrence, C. H. *The Friars: The Impact of the Early Mendicant Movement on Western Europe.* (Longman Publishing, 1994).

————. *Medieval Monasticism: Forms of Religious Life in Western Europe in the Middle Ages.* (2nd edition, Longman Publishing, 1989).

Leclercq, Jean. *The Love of Learning and the Desire for God: A Study of Monastic Culture.* (New American Library, 1961).

Le Goff, Jacques. *The Birth of Purgatory,* translated by Arthur Goldhammer. (University of Chicago Press, 1986, p).

Little, Lester K. *Religious Poverty and the Profit Economy in Medieval Europe.* (Cornell University Press, 1978).

Moore, R. I. *The Origins of European Dissent.* (University of Toronto Press, MART, 1994, p).

Morris, Colin. *The Papal Monarchy: The Western Church from 1050 to 1250.* (Oxford University Press, 1989).

Morrison, Karl F. *Tradition and Authority in the Western Church.* (Princeton University Press, 1969).

Newman, Barbara. *From Virile Woman to Woman Christ: Studies in Medieval Religion and Literature.* (University of Pennsylvania Press, 1995, p).

Peters, Edward M. *Inquisition.* (University of California Press, 1989, p).

Rubin, Miri. *Corpus Christi: The Eucharist in Late Medieval Culture.* (Cambridge University Press, 1992, p).

Russell, Jeffrey Burton. *A History of Heaven: The Singing Silence.* (Princeton University Press, 1997).

Southern, Richard W. *Western Society and the Church in the Middle Ages.* (The History of the Church, Penguin, 1970, p).

Swanson, R. N. *Religion and Devotion in Europe, c. 1215–c. 1515.* (Cambridge University Press, 1995, p).

Tellenbach, Gerd. *The Western Church from the Tenth to the*

Early Twelfth Century, translated by Timothy Reuter. (Cambridge University Press, 1993, p).

Venarde, Bruce L. *Women's Monasticism and Medieval Society: Nunneries in France and England, 890–1215.* (Cornell University Press, 1997).

IV. THOUGHT, LEARNING, AND EDUCATION.

Carruthers, Mary J. *The Book of Memory: A Study of Memory in Medieval Culture.* (Cambridge University Press, 1992, p).

Clanchy, M. T. *From Memory to Written Record: England, 1066–1307.* (Oxford University Press, 1979; expanded edition, Blackwell Publishers, 1993, p).

Cobban, A. B. *The Medieval Universities: Their Development and Organization.* (Methuen, 1975).

De Ridder-Symoens, Hilde, ed. *A History of the University in Europe, Vol.1: Universities in the Middle Ages.* (Cambridge University Press, 1991).

Holmes, George. *Florence, Rome, and the Origins of the Renaissance.* (Oxford University Press, 1986; 1988, p).

Jacquart, Danielle and Claude Thomasset. *Sexuality and Medicine in the Middle Ages,* translated by Matthew Adamson. (Princeton University Press, 1989).

Jaeger, C. Stephen. *The Envy of Angels: Cathedral Schools and Social Ideals in Medieval Europe, 950–1200* (University of Pennsylvania Press, 1994).

Le Goff, Jacques. *The Intellectuals in the Middle Ages,* translated by Teresa L. Fagan. (Blackwell Publishing, 1992, p).

McKitterick, Rosamond. *The Carolingians and the Written Word.* (Cambridge University Press, 1969, p).

———. *The Uses of Literacy in Early Medieval Europe.* (Cambridge University Press, 1992, p).

Labalme, Patricia H., ed. *Beyond Their Sex: Learned Women of the European Past.* (New York University Press, 1984).

Petrucci, Armando. *Writers and Readers in Medieval Italy: Studies in the History of Written Culture,* translated by Charles M. Radding. (Yale University Press, 1995).

Smalley, Beryl. *Historians of the Middle Ages.* (Thames & Hudson, 1974).

Southern, Richard W. *Medieval Humanism and Other Studies.* (Blackwell Publishing, 1970).

———. *Scientific Humanism and the Unification of Europe.* (3 vols. Blackwell Publishing: Vol. I: *Foundations: Aims, Methods, and Places.* [1995; 1997, p]. Vol. II: *The Heroic Age.* [1998]. Vol. III: *Disunity, Decline, and Renewal.* [1998]).

Stock, Brian. *The Implications of Literacy: Written Language and Models of Interpretation in the Eleventh and Twelfth Centuries.* (Princeton University Press, 1983).

V. LITERATURE, MUSIC, AND THE VISUAL ARTS.

Alexander, Jonathan J. *Medieval Illuminators and Their Methods of Work.* (Yale University Press, 1994, p).

Auerbach, Erich. *Literary Language and Its Public in Late Latin Antiquity and in the Middle Ages,* translated by Ralph Manheim. (Princeton University Press, 1993, p).

Belting, Hans. *Likeness and Presence: A History of the Image Before the Era of Art,* translated by Edmund Jephcott. (University of Chicago Press, 1994).

Borsook, Eve. *The Mural Painters of Tuscany.* (revised edition Oxford University Press, 1980).

Branner, Robert. *Gothic Architecture.* (George Braziller, 1961, p).

Camille, Michael. *The Gothic Idol: Ideology and Image-Making in Medieval Art.* (Cambridge University Press, 1991, p).

Coleman, Joyce. *Public Reading and the Reading Public in Late Medieval England and France.* (Cambridge University Press, 1996).

De Hamel, Christopher. *A History of Illuminated Manuscripts.* (David R. Godine, 1986).

Dronke, Peter. *Medieval Latin and the Rise of Latin Love Lyric.* (2 vols., 2nd edition, Oxford University Press, 1968).

————. *Women Writers of the Middle Ages: A Critical Study of Texts from Perpetua, (d. 203) to Margaret Porete, (d. 1310).* (Cambridge University Press, 1984, p).

Duby, Georges. *The Age of the Cathedrals: Art and Society, 980–1420,* translated by Eleanor Levieux and Barbara Thompson. (University of Chicago Press, 1983, p).

Hearn, M. F. *Romanesque Sculpture: The Revival of Monumental Stone Sculpture in the Eleventh and Twelfth Centuries.* (Cornell University Press, 1985, p).

Hughes, Andrew. *Medieval Music: The Sixth Liberal Art.* (2nd edition, University of Toronto Press, 1980).

Larrington, Carolyne. *Women and Writing in Early and Medieval Europe: A Sourcebook.* (Routledge, 1995, p).

McGee, Timothy J. *Medieval and Renaissance Music: A Performer's Guide.* (University of Toronto Press, 1988, p).

Meale, Carol M., ed. *Women and Literature in Britain, 1150–1500.* (revised edition, Cambridge University Press, 1996, p).

Paterson, Linda. *The World of the Troubadours: Medieval Occitan Society, c. 1100–c. 1300.* (Cambridge University Press, 1995, p).

Petzold, Andreas. *Romanesque Art.* (Harry N. Abrams, Perspectives, 1995, p).

Radding, Charles M. and William W. Clark. *Medieval Architecture, Medieval Learning: Builders and Masters in the Age of Romanesque and Gothic.* (Yale University Press, 1992, p).

Schapiro, Meyer. *Late Antique, Early Christian, and Medieval Art.* (George Braziller, 1979).

———. *Romanesque Art.* (George Braziller, 1977).

Simon, Eckehard, ed. *The Theatre of Medieval Europe: New Research in Early Drama.* (Cambridge University Press, 1991).

Wieck, Roger S. *Time Sanctified: The Book of Hours in Medieval Art and Life.* (George Braziller, 1988).

VI. LATIN CHRISTENDOM AND ITS NEIGHBORS.

Angold, M. *The Byzantine Empire, 1025–1204: A Political History.* (Longman Publishing, 1984).

Cohen, Mark R. *Under Crescent and Cross: The Jews in the Middle Ages.* (Princeton University Press, 1994).

Holt, P. M. *The Age of the Crusades: The Near East from the Eleventh Century to 1517.* (Longman Publishing, 1986).

Hussey, Joan M. *The Byzantine World.* (Greenwood Publishing, 1982).

———. *The Orthodox Church in the Byzantine Empire.* (Oxford University Press, 1986).

Lombard, M. *The Golden Age of Islam.* (Oxford University Press, 1975).

Nicol, Donald M. *The Byzantine Lady: Ten Portraits, 1250–1500.* (Cambridge University Press, 1996, p).

Riley-Smith, Jonathan, ed. *The Atlas of the Crusades.* (Facts on File, 1990).

———. *The Crusades: A Short History.* (Athlone Press, 1987).

———, ed. *The Oxford Illustrated History of the Crusades.* (Oxford University Press, 1995).

Rodley, Lyn. *Byzantine Art and Architecture: An Introduction.* (Cambridge University Press, 1994).

Setton, Kenneth, M., ed. *A History of the Crusades.* (6 vols., University of Wisconsin Press, 1955–1990).

Whittow, Mark. *The Making of Byzantium, 600–1025.* (University of California Press, 1996, p).

I. THE BODY SOCIAL

The Body Social

JOHN OF SALISBURY

Twelfth century

A COMMONWEALTH, according to Plutarch, is a certain body which is endowed with life by the benefit of divine favour, which acts at the prompting of the highest equity, and is ruled by what may be called the moderating power of reason. Those things which establish and implant in us the practice of religion, and transmit to us the worship of God . . . fill the place of the soul in the body of the commonwealth. And therefore those who preside over the practice of religion should be looked up to and venerated as the soul of the body. For who doubts that the ministers of God's holiness are His representatives? Furthermore, since the soul is, as it were, the prince of the body, and has rulership over the whole thereof, so those whom our author calls the prefects of religion preside over the entire body. . . . The place of the head in the body of the commonwealth is filled by the prince, who is subject only to God and to those who exercise His office and represent Him on earth, even as in the human body the head is quickened and governed by the soul. The place of the heart is filled by the senate, from which proceeds the initiation of good works and ill. The duties of eyes, ears, and tongue are claimed by the judges and the governors of provinces. Officials and soldiers correspond to the hands. Those who always attend upon the prince are likened to the sides. Financial officers and keepers . . . may be compared with the stomach and intestines. . . . The husbandmen correspond to the feet, which always cleave to the soil, and need the more especially the care and foresight of the head, since while they walk upon the earth doing service with their bodies, they meet the more often with stones of stumbling, and therefore deserve aid and protection all the more justly since it is they who raise, sustain, and move forward the weight of the entire body. . . .

Then and then only will the health of the commonwealth be sound and flourishing, when the higher members shield the lower, and the lower respond faithfully and fully in like measure to the just demands of their superiors, so that each and all are as it were members one of another by a sort of reciprocity, and each regards his own interest as best served by that which he knows to be most advantageous for the others.

From *Policraticus*, trans. J. Dickinson (New York: Appleton: 1927).

The Orders of Men

THE CLERGY: THE PRAYERS AND THINKERS

The Monastic Ideal

PETER DAMIANI

Eleventh century

ON CONTEMPT OF THE WORLD

FOR when we have renounced the world, we have constituted God as our property and consequently we have become His property in such a way that He has become our portion and we are His peculiar heritage. . . . If then the omnipotent God Himself deigns to be our portion, what kind of riches, I ask, will it avail anyone to acquire which could exceed in merit this matchless treasure? For that treasure is such that even if it be alone, all riches can truly be possessed in it. "In the heart of Jesus are hidden all the treasures of wisdom and knowledge." . . .

How, O monk, do you mean to lay Christ up in your

cell? First, cast out money, for Christ and money do not go well together in one place; if you shut them both up at the same time, you will find yourself the possessor of one without the other. The richer you may be in the poor lucre of this world, the more miserably lacking you are in true riches. Therefore if money is there, let it retire forthwith into other halls so that Christ may find vacant the cell of your heart. That great Guest seeks indeed to descend into the recesses of your lodging-place, and He wishes to dwell alone there, without any companions. For how can you try, in the poor corner of your cell, to put strange companions with that One whom the vastness of heaven and earth cannot contain? Let terrestrial wealth give way where celestial treasure is admitted! . . .

This treasure, then, namely Christ, our God and Lord, who was made for us as both redeemer and reward, He Himself both the promiser and the prize, who is both the life of man and the eternity of the angels—this, I say, store away with diligent care in the recesses of your heart. On Him cast the anxiety of any care whatsoever. In Him delight through the discourse of zealous prayer. In Him refresh yourself by the nightly feasts of holy meditation. Let Him be your food, and your clothing no less. If it should happen that you lack anything of external convenience, do not be uncertain, do not despair of His true promise in which He said, "Seek ye first the kingdom of God, and all things shall be added unto you." . . .

Nor do I deem it possible, dearest brother, to exclude this from your memory, that we have often grieved among ourselves in familiar intercourse about that baneful habit of the monks; we have suffered in fraternal love over the brothers who are restless and sinking to their ruin through the vice of roaming about. For there are some who, when they bore the burden of service in the world, were weary under this yoke of human servitude with running hither and thither, and therefore they resolved to go over to monastic peace through love of liberty. Now, however, they burn with such a great flame of pernicious restlessness that when no occasion of going to a distance presents itself, they seem to be shut in by the dark horror of prison confinement, which without doubt the astuteness of the old enemy is not ignorant of. For those whom that most evil rider drives to this, he urges on to the dangerous incitements of wandering so that they, returning to the vanity of the world, may perish and turn others away from seizing the path of true salvation. . . .

From this poisoned root of restlessness so many shoots of vices spring that whatever plant it is perceived in is stripped of all the fruit of monastic perfection like a withered tree. . . . For, to name only a few out of many, a monk while travelling is not able to fast because the hospitable kindness shown him does not permit it. He does not recite the psalms as he should because the loquacity of the moving company prevents him. He does not persist in nightly vigils because the privacy of isolation is lacking; he does not sweat on bended knees in prayer because the toil of travel does not agree with the zeal of holy devotion. He is in no way constrained by the rule of silence because frequently when occasions arise, though unwillingly, he gives way to much speaking. . . .

Whoever, therefore, as a monk hastens to attain the height of perfection, let him confine himself within the walls of his cloister, let him love spiritual quiet, let him have a horror of running about in the world, as he would of immersing himself in a pool of blood. For the world is more and more every day polluted by the contamination of so many crimes that any holy mind is corrupted by the mere consideration of it. . . .

ON THE MORTIFICATION OF THE FLESH

And so there is nothing but the love of God and the mortification of yourselves. For if the apostolic maxim lives in us, which says, "Always bearing the dying of Jesus in our body," because carnal love does not have wherewith to diffuse itself within us, by necessity all our joy transfers itself, raised on high, to God; and our fire, leaping up, lives there because within us it does not have room to spread. The man who is wise and earnestly intent on guarding his salvation watches always with such great solicitude to repress his vices that with the belt of perfect mortification he girds his loins and his reins, his belly as well as his flanks, on all sides. This indeed is then done, when the itching palate is repressed, when the bold tongue is restrained in silence, when the ear is closed to evil speaking, when the eye is forbidden to look at illicit things, when the hand is restrained lest it strike cruelly, the foot lest it go off wandering idly; when the heart is resisted lest it envy the good fortune of another's happiness, lest it desire through avarice that which is not its own, lest it cut itself off by wrath from fraternal love, lest it arrogantly praise itself above others, lest it yield to seductive luxury through pleasure, lest it sink immoderately into grief, or in joy open the way to the tempter.

Therefore, dearest brothers, seize the arms of all the virtues—sobriety, humility, patience, obedience, chastity, charity—and fight not on behalf of fields or cities, not for children or wives, but for your souls which rise above every emotion of relationship. Especially should you fast, so that your youth may acquire strength, and pray, for the reason that fasting subdues the vigour of the flesh and prayer raises the soul to God. It should be known, however, that some, while they indiscriminately carry out the fast, do not receive the benefits of fasting; for whatever they deny themselves one day, the next they gorge on at will. And so it is that one day of fasting serves for the following day. . . .

That one fasts well who on the day of refreshment [after fasting] is content with the common fare, if, that is, while he does not reject any kind of food, he does not also exceed the daily portion of those eating. Nevertheless, do not, ascribing too much importance to fasting, lose sight of obedience which is the golden road to heaven. . . .

Be content with garments mean and few. Accustom yourself to wearing light and scant clothing. This indeed is done at first not without travail but as habit grows, when it becomes natural, the discomfort of cold is easily assuaged. Moreover, the poverty of clothing and the scarcity of food forthwith drive out all avarice from the heart of a monk. For what should I long for that does not add either to food or clothing? Therefore, as beginners we shudder not without a certain dread at the bareness of feet, and scarcity of clothes, the hardness of bed, the harshness of food, the drink of water, imagining sauces and other such things; persevering and persisting for a long time, however, we find these things easy henceforth and bearable. Frequency indeed mitigates severity, and custom makes rigour agreeable. . . .

Come now, brother, what is this body which you clothe with such diligent care and nourish gently as if it were royal offspring? Is it not a mass of putrefaction, is it not worms, dust, and ashes? It is fit that the wise man consider not this which now is, but rather what it will be afterwards in the future, pus, slime, decay, and the filth of obscene corruption. What thanks will the

worms render to you, who are about to devour the flesh
you nourished so gently and tenderly? Come, I say, why
did Christ suffer? That He should wash away His own
sins and blot out the faults of His own trangression?
But hear Peter on this, saying, "Who did no sin, neither
was guile found in His mouth." For whom then did He
suffer? Peter himself answers, "Christ suffered for us,
leaving us an example that ye should follow in His
steps." . . . Why then do we read that Christ suffered,
unless we follow His example from His footsteps? . . .
Let the holy mind not fear therefore to share the cross
of Christ in scourging, let him not blush with shame at
the nakedness of the body, since He says, "For whosoever shall be ashamed of Me and of My words, of him
shall the Son of man be ashamed, when He shall come
in His majesty." . . .

ON THE MORTIFICATION OF THE SPIRIT

Now let me speak with chagrin about those who follow after the rabble of the grammarians and who, abandoning spiritual studies, lust to learn the trifles of earthly
art. Counting as little the Rule of Benedict they rejoice
to apply themselves to the rules of Donatus. These,
scorning the experience of ecclesiastical discipline, and
panting after secular studies, what else do they seem to
do but abandon the chaste spouse in the marriage bed
of faith and descend to actresses and harlots? . . .

Moreover, the one who endeavoured to lead the
troops of all the vices placed the desire for learning as
head of the army, and so in her train brought all the
crowds of iniquities into the unhappy world. What marvel, therefore, if in the daughter of Eve still vibrates that
same spear which formerly the old enemy thrust into the
same Eve? . . .

Moreover, tears which are from God approach the

tribunal of divine grace confidently, and obtaining what they seek, are assured of certain remission of our sins. Tears are mediators in the peace to be negotiated between man and God, and truthful and learned masters in any uncertainty whatsoever of human ignorance. For when we doubt whether something is pleasing to God or not, never do we receive greater certainty than when we pray, truly weeping. . . .

O tears, spiritual delights, even above honey and the honeycomb, and sweeter than all nectar! how you refresh minds raised to God with the pleasant sweetness of secret savour, and water arid and wasting hearts in the inmost part with the draught of supernal grace. . . .

From *Opuscula varia* (Migne, *Patrologia Latina*, vol. 145), trans. J.B.R.

The Cistercian Order

WILLIAM OF MALMESBURY

Early twelfth century

IN HIS time [Pope Urban II] began the Cistercian order, which is now both believed and asserted to be the surest road to heaven. To speak of this does not seem irrelevant to the work I have undertaken, since it redounds to the glory of England to have produced the distinguished man who was the author and promoter of that rule. To us he belonged, and in our schools passed the earlier part of his life. . . . He was named Harding, and born in England of no very illustrious parents. From his early years, he was a monk at Sherborne; but when secular desires had captivated his youth, he grew disgusted with the monastic garb, and went first to Scotland, and afterwards to France. Here, after some years' exercise in the liberal arts, he became awakened to the love of God. For, when manlier years had put away childish things, he went to Rome with a clerk who partook of his studies; neither the length and difficulty of the journey, nor the scantiness of their means of subsistence by the way, preventing them, both as they went and returned, from singing daily the whole psalter. Indeed the mind of this celebrated man was already meditating the design which soon after, by the grace of God, he attempted to put in execution. For returning into Burgundy, he was shorn at Molesmes, a new and magnificent monastery. Here he readily admitted the first elements of the order, as he had formerly seen them; but when additional matters were proposed for his observance, such as he had neither read in the rule nor seen elsewhere, he began, modestly and as became a monk, to ask the reason of them, saying, "By reason the supreme Creator has made all things; by reason He governs all things; by reason the fabric of the world revolves; by reason even the planets move; by reason the elements are directed; and by reason, and by due regulation, our nature ought to conduct itself. . . . See then that you bring reason, or at least authority, for what you devise; although no great credit should be given to what is merely supported by human reasons, because it may be combated with arguments equally forcible. Therefore from that rule [of St. Benedict], which, equally supported by reason and authority, appears as if dictated by the spirit of all just persons, produce precedents, which if you fail to do in vain shall you profess his rule, whose regulations you disdain to comply with." . . .

Two of the fraternity, therefore, of equal faith and learning, were elected, who, by vicarious examination, were to discover the intention of the founder's rule; and when they had discovered it, to propound it to the rest. The abbat diligently endeavoured to induce the whole convent to give their concurrence, but . . . almost the whole of them refused to accept the new regulations, because they were attached to the old. Eighteen only, among whom was Harding, otherwise called Stephen, persevering in their holy determination, together with their abbat, left the monastery, declaring that the purity of the institution could not be preserved in a place where riches and gluttony warred against even the heart that was well inclined. They came therefore to Cîteaux; a situation formerly covered with woods, but now so conspicuous from the abundant piety of its monks, that it is not undeservedly esteemed conscious of the Divinity Himself. Here, by the countenance of the archbishop of Vienne, who is now pope, they entered on a labour worthy to be remembered and venerated to the end of time.

Certainly many of their regulations seem severe, and more particularly these: they wear nothing made with furs or linen, nor even that finely spun linen garment, which we call Staminium; neither breeches, unless when sent on a journey, which at their return they wash and restore. They have two tunics with cowls, but no additional garment in winter, though, if they think fit, in summer they may lighten their garb. They sleep clad and girded, and never after matins return to their beds: but they so order the time of matins that it shall be light ere the lauds begin; so intent are they on their rule, that they think no jot or tittle of it should be disregarded. Directly after these hymns they sing the prime, after which they go out to work for stated hours. They complete whatever labour or service they have to perform by day without any other light. No one is ever absent from the daily services, or from complines, except the sick. The cellarer and hospitaller, after complines, wait upon the guests, yet observing the strictest silence. The abbat allows himself no indulgence beyond the others—everywhere present, everywhere attending to his flock; except that he does not eat with the rest, because his table is with the strangers and the poor. Nevertheless, be he where he may, he is equally sparing of food and of speech; for never more than two dishes are served either to him or to his company; lard and meat never but to the sick. From the Ides of September till Easter, through regard for whatever festival, they do not take more than one meal a day, except on Sunday. They never leave the cloister but for the purpose of labour, nor do they ever speak, either there or elsewhere, save only to the abbat or prior. They pay unwearied attention to the canonical services, making no addition to them except the vigil for the defunct. They use in their divine service the Ambrosian chants and hymns, as far as they were able to learn them at Milan. While they bestow care on the stranger and the sick, they inflict intolerable mortifications on their own bodies, for the health of their souls. . . .

But to comprise briefly all things which are or can be said of them—the Cistercian monks at the present day are a model for all monks, a mirror for the diligent, a spur to the indolent.

From *Chronicle*, trans. J. A. Giles (London: Bohn, 1847).

How the Friars Came to Germany

JORDAN OF GIANO

Thirteenth century

IN THE year of our Lord 1219, and the thirteenth year
of his conversion, Brother Francis held a general
chapter at Santa Maria della Porziuncola, and sent
brethren to France, Germany, Hungary, Spain, and
those provinces of Italy which the brethren had not yet
reached. . . . The German mission was led by Brother
John of Parma with some sixty or more brethren. When
they were come into Germany, not knowing the language, and when men asked whether they desired lodging or meat or any such thing, they answered *Ja*, and
thus received kindly welcome from some· folk. Seeing
therefore that this word procured them humane treatment, they resolved to answer *Ja* to all questions whatsoever. Wherefore, being once asked whether they were
heretics, come now to infect Germany after the same
fashion wherewith they had already perverted Lombardy, they answered *Ja;* so that some were cast into
prison, and others were stripped of their raiment and led
to the common dancing-place where they were held up
for a laughing-stock to the inhabitants. The brethren
therefore, seeing that they could make no fruit in Germany, came home again; and this deed gave the brethren so cruel a report of Germany, that none dared return
thither but such as aspired to martyrdom. . . .

So in the year 1221 . . . St. Francis celebrated a
General Chapter at Santa Maria della Porziuncola . . .
and the brethren there assembled were reckoned at

three thousand. . . . What tongue could tell the charity, patience, humility, obedience, and brotherly cheerfulness which reigned at that time among the brethren? And, albeit the multitude of brethren was so great, yet the people ministered unto us so cheerfully that, after seven days, the brethren were constrained to close their gates against further gifts, and to tarry yet two days in order to consume these offerings. Now, at the end of this Chapter, St. Francis bethought him that the order had not yet been built up in Germany; and, because he was then infirm, Brother Elias spake for him whensoever he would have spoken to the people. So St. Francis, sitting at the feet of Brother Elias, twitched him by the frock; and he, bending down to learn the saint's will, rose again and said: "Brethren, thus saith the Brother" (that is to say, St. Francis, whom the brethren called "the Brother" by excellence). "There is (he said) a certain land called Germany, wherein dwell Christian and devout folk who, as ye know, often traverse our land with long staves and wide boots, singing praises to God and His saints, visiting the holy places in the heat of the sun and the sweat of their brow. And, seeing that the brethren once sent thither were evil intreated and came home again, therefore the Brother would constrain no man to go thither; but if any man, inspired with zeal for God and men's souls, will now go thither, the Brother will give him the same commission—nay, an ampler commission still—than to those who go beyond the sea. Wherefore, if there be any willing to go, let them now arise and stand apart." Then some ninety brethren, inflamed with love, offered themselves for death; and, departing from the rest according to the saint's bidding, they waited until it should be ordered who and how many and how and when they were to go.

Now there was a certain brother present at that Chapter who was accustomed in his prayers to beseech the Lord that his faith might not be corrupted by the Lombard heretics or shaken by the ferocity of the Germans; but rather that God of His mercy would deign to deliver him from both. He, seeing many brethren arise and show their readiness for the German mission, and thinking that they would soon be martyred there, and grieving that he knew not the names of those brethren who had been martyred on the Spanish mission, was resolved to order things better in this case. Arising, therefore, from the throng, he went to these ninety, and asked of them one by one, "Who and whence art thou?" for he thought it would redound much to his glory if they chanced to be martyred, and he could say: "I knew that man, and I knew that other."

But among this company was a certain brother named Palmerio, a deacon, who was afterwards warden of the friary at Magdeburg; a jocund and sportive man, from Monte Gargano in Apulia. So when that curious brother had come to Palmerio asking, "Who art thou, and what is thy name?" then he answered "My name is Palmerio"; and, laying hands on him, he added, "Thou too art of us and shalt go in our company," wishing to take this brother with him among those very Germans of whom he had oftentimes besought the Lord that He might send him whithersoever He would, so that it were not to Germany. Now therefore, shuddering at that name *Germans*, he made answer, "I am not of your company; but I came hither desiring to know your names, not to go with you." But the other, overmastering him in his jocund way, clave fast unto him and drew him to the ground, for all his resistance in word and in deed, and constrained him to sit down among the rest; and meanwhile, while this curious brother was thus held captive there, he was assigned to another province and proclamation was made: "Let such a brother go to such and such a province."

But while these ninety were awaiting their answer, Brother Caesarius the German, of Speyer, was chosen minister provincial of Germany, with power to choose whom he would from that company. He, finding this curious brother among the rest, was counselled by them to take him. And, seeing that he desired not to go thither, and ceased not to protest, saying, "I am not of your company, for I arose not with the purpose of going with you," he was led to Brother Elias. And the brethren of the province whereunto he had been assigned, seeing that he was a weakly man and that the land of Germany is cold, strove to retain him; whereas Brother Caesarius sought by all means to take him. At last Brother Elias cut short this strife, saying: "I command thee, brother, by holy obedience, to resolve once for all whether thou wilt go or leave it."

He therefore, thus constrained by obedience, and still doubting what to do, feared to choose for conscience' sake, lest in so choosing he should seem self-willed; for he feared the journey on account of the cruelty of the Germans, lest his patience should fail him for suffering and his soul be in mortal peril. Halting thus between two opinions, and finding no counsel in his own heart, he went to that sorely tried brother who (as we have said) had suffered fifteen times in Hungary, and besought his advice, saying, "Dearest brother, thus and thus hath it been commanded to me, and I fear to choose and know not what to do." To whom the other made answer: "Go then to Brother Elias and say: 'Brother, I am unwilling either to go or to stay; but I will do whatsoever thou shalt bid me': truly thus shalt thou be freed from thy perplexity." Thus then he did, and Brother Elias commanded him by holy obedience to go with

Brother Caesarius to Germany. And he is that Brother Jordan of Giano who writeth these present words; thus it was that he went to Germany; but he escaped from that fury of the Germans which he had feared, and was among the first to plant the order of Friars Minor in that land, with Brother Caesarius and other brethren. . . .

On their way, they entered into a certain village to find food, wherein they begged by two and two from house to house; but men answered them in the German tongue, "*God berad!*" which is, being interpreted, "May God provide for you!" One of the brethren, seeing that with these words nothing was given to them, thought within himself, "This *God berad* will slay us today!" Wherefore he ran before the brother who was wont to beg daily, and began to beg in the Latin tongue. Then answered the Germans, "We understand no Latin; speak to us in German." So that brother, speaking corruptly, said, "*Nich tiudisch*" (which is to say, "No German," the words "I know" being understood). And he added in German, "Bread, for God!" Then said they, "Ha! thou sayest in German that thou knowest no German," and they added, "*God berad!*" So that brother, exulting in spirit and smiling and making as though he knew not what they said, sate him down upon the bench; whereupon the man and his wife, looking at each other and smiling at his importunity, gave him bread, eggs, and milk. He, therefore, seeing that by such profitable dissimulation he might relieve not only his own necessities but those of the brethren also, went to twelve houses and begged in like fashion; whereby he gained enough to feed his seven brethren.

From *Chronicle*, trans. G. G. Coulton, *Social Life in Britain* (Cambridge, Eng.: Cambridge University Press, 1918).

A Preacher and His Miracles

SALIMBENE

Thirteenth century

WE COME now to Brother Berthold of Swabia [Berthold of Regensburg]. He belonged to the order of Friars Minor, and was a priest and a preacher, and a man of honourable and holy life, as becomes a monk. He composed an exposition of the Apocalypse, from which I copied only the parts on the seven bishops of Asia, who are brought forward as angels in the beginning of the Apocalypse. I did this to know who those angels were, and because I had Abbot Joachim's commentary on the Apocalypse, which I esteemed above all others. Moreover, Berthold made a large volume of sermons for the whole course of the year, both for feast days and for the Sundays of the entire year. Of those sermons I copied only two, because they treated most excellently of Antichrist. . . .

And mark you, Brother Berthold was favored by God with a special gift of preaching, and all who have heard him say that from the apostles even to our own day there has not been his equal in the German tongue. He was followed by a great multitude of men and women, sometimes sixty or a hundred thousand. Many times an unnumbered crowd gathered together from many cities, that they might hear the honey-sweet words of salvation which poured from his mouth, by His grace who "gives His voice a voice of might," and "gives word to them who preach with much virtue."

He was accustomed to ascend a belfry or a wooden

tower built almost in the form of a campanile, which he used as a pulpit in the fields; on its summit was also placed a banner by those who set up the tower, so that the people might see which way the wind blew, and know where they ought to sit to hear best. And, wonderful to say! he was as clearly heard and understood by those far from him as by those close by; and no one stood up during his preaching and withdrew, until he had finished. When he preached on the Last Judgment, everyone trembled, as a rush trembles in water. And they begged him, for the love of God, not to preach any more on this theme, because they were fearfully and terribly troubled when they heard him.

One day it happened that, when Brother Berthold was to preach in a certain place, a peasant begged his lord for God's sake to let him go to hear Brother Berthold's sermon. But his lord answered, "I shall go to the sermon; thou shalt go to the field to plough with the oxen, as it is written in Ecclesiasticus, 'Send him to work, lest he be idle.'" When the peasant had begun one day in the early morning to plough the field, he heard, wondrous to relate, the first word of Brother Berthold's sermon, although he was on that day thirty miles away. Immediately he freed the oxen from the plough, so that they might eat, and he himself, sitting down, might listen to the sermon. There came to pass here three most memorable miracles. First, that he heard and understood him, though he was so far away, thirty miles. Second, that he learned the whole sermon and kept it in his memory. Third, that after the sermon was finished he ploughed as much as he was accustomed to plough on other days of uninterrupted work. So when later this peasant inquired of his lord concerning Brother Berthold's sermon, and he could not repeat it, the peasant did so, from beginning to end, and explained how he had heard it in the field and had learned it. So the lord, knowing that this was a miracle, gave the peasant complete freedom to go and hear Brother Berthold's preaching as often as he wanted, whatever work he might have to do.

Now it was Brother Berthold's custom to arrange the sermons which he intended to preach, now in one city and now in another, at different times and in different places, so that the people who flocked to hear him might not lack food. Once a certain noble lady, inflamed with a great and fervent desire to hear his preaching, had followed him for six whole years from city to city and town to town, with a few companions and her riches, yet she could never have private and intimate conversation with him. But at the end of the six years, and after the spending of all her wealth, on the Feast of the Assumption that lady and her faithful companions had no more food to eat, so she went to Brother Berthold and told him her story, which I have related. When Brother Berthold had heard all this, he sent her to a certain banker, who was considered the richest of all in that city, and commanded her to tell him in his name to give her as much money for her food and other expenses as the value of one single day of that indulgence which she had gained by following Brother Berthold for six years. When he heard this, the banker smiled, and said, "How shall I know the worth of the indulgence for one day on which you have followed Brother Berthold?" And she said, "He told me to tell you to place your money on one scale of the balance, and I will breathe on the other scale, and by this sign you will know the worth of my indulgence." Then he poured in his money abundantly and filled the scale of the balance. But she breathed into the other scale, and immediately it was weighed down, and the money flew up as if it had suddenly become as light as a feather. When the banker saw this, he was greatly astonished, and heaped more and more gold pieces on his side of the scales, yet he could not outweigh the lady's breath, for the Holy Ghost lent such weight to it, that no amount of money could counterbalance the scale on which she breathed. Then the banker, seeing this, went with the lady and her women to Brother Berthold, and told him all that had happened. And the banker said to him, "I am ready to restore all my ill-gotten gains and, for God's sake, to distribute my own goods among the poor, and I want to become a good man, for truly I have seen marvellous things this day." So Brother Berthold commanded him to supply abundantly with the necessities of life that lady with whom he had had this experience, and her companions also. This he fulfilled eagerly and generously to the praise of our Lord Jesus Christ, to whom is glory and honour forever and ever. Amen.

From *Chronicle*, F. Bernini, ed. (Bari, Italy: G. Laterza, 1942); trans. M.M.M.

Monastic Reform in the Fifteenth Century

JOHN BUSCH

Fifteenth century

THE monastery of St. Martin, in Ludinkerka, of our order, in Friesland, in the diocese of Utrecht, which was previously an abbey of our order, began to be reformed in the year 1428. Before its reformation there were but few priests there, and a great many converts—

more than thirty or fifty—who had entered into an agreement with the converts of a neighbouring monastery of the Cistercian order, a mile off, that they would mutually help each other with a hundred armed men. The consequence was that they had subdued all that part of Friesland. A certain vassal, however, who lived in the town about the monastery, by advice of the lawyers, of whom there are plenty among the priests in Friesland, reported their ill life and conversation to the archbishop of Utrecht. None of them was chaste, all were proprietors [that is, possessed something which they called their own in money or goods], and they had nuns with them in the monastery who sometimes brought forth children. I knew the abbot there, a learned man, whose father had been called a convert, and his mother a nun. He afterwards resigned his abbacy and entered into a monastery of our chapter near Haarlem, and having there become a monk, he ended his days well.

The bishop, however, Frederic de Blankenheym, a wise and learned man, sent his ambassadors, men learned and skilful in the law, who, visiting the inmates of that monastery, found that almost all the converts had entered without rule or profession, and that they had remained up to that time, a period of many years, in that predicament. Being asked how they came to take upon them the habit of converts, they answered, "When first we came here, we saw many persons clothed with white tunics and scapulars, and at the same time wearing arms, so we bought ourselves white cloth, and had it made into white tunics, white hoods, and scapulars, and put them on ourselves." It was asked whether they had heard anything about a rule. They answered, "Never; but each one took to himself a nun, a female convert, or other woman, with whom he cohabited without being married." The bishop of Utrecht, therefore, hearing this, by the advice of men learned in the law, in which he too was learned himself, adjudged and decreed that all the persons of this description were not monks, but might lawfully go out and marry wives, and be secular persons; and that they should put off that habit, and resume their secular dress; and this they immediately did, and also made protestation that they had no right or claim to the monastery, or any property belonging to it. A few, however, two or three, obtained leave to remain there, because they were old; and for a time retained also the women who had belonged to them, that they might wait on them in their infirmity, until all the women being expelled, they were collected together and formed into a monastery of our order hard by. After this the agents of the bishop sent to Windesheim to request that they would bring the monastery into a proper state of reformation; and upon that the prior of Windesheim sent thither some monks of Windesheim and of Mount St. Agnes—viz., Jacobus Oem, afterwards prior of Tabor and rector of the nuns in Bronopia, Gerard Wesep, John Lap, priest of Berg, and Engelbert Tentinel, with one convert who was very expert in temporal matters; and these first began the reformation in that place, with John Gerard of Zwoll, professed in Berg, whom they appointed rector there. But as they had not monks enough for its reformation and refoundation, the prior of Windesheim sent Godfrey de Tyela, and one John Busch, to the aforesaid monastery, in order to make up the number for its complete reformation; and he said to me, "Brother John, you did not do much out beyond Cologne, at Bodingen; you may see whether you can convert the Frisians."

In the year 1429, therefore, on the festival of the Conversion of St. Paul, I was sent to Ludinkerka, where we carried forward the reformation already begun, repairing the choir, refectory, dormitory, and other buildings of the monastery, and taking in clerks for its new reformation, and instructing them according to rule and discipline; and in like manner lay brethren and servants.

When, therefore, in obedience to the apostolic see (for the pope had laid the diocese of Utrecht under his ban; and the Lord Rudolph of Defolt, whom the towns of Deventer, Zwoll, and Campen, with their adherents set up, and the Lord Zweder of Culenborch, to whom the pope had given it, were striving for the bishopric), all the monks of the Overyssel district were compelled to leave it, the prior of Mount St. Agnes, of our order, by the advice of the prior of Windesheim, with all his convent, came to Ludinkerka with the lay brethren and servants, and completely reformed the monastery there, according to the rule of our order, in every particular. And there are now more than fifty persons, as well brethren as laity, faithfully serving the Lord God in the simplicity of their hearts day and night, and maintaining themselves on the fields and pastures, which are very rich, and well suited for cattle; the name of abbot being exchanged for that of prior, owing to its incorporation into our chapter of Windesheim. Therefore, "my song shall be alway of the loving-kindness of the Lord," who hath made me a partaker of all the good that shall be done there for evermore. For at first we suffered a great deal for the want of furniture and other necessary things; and, there being very few trees in that part of the country, the wind, in the winter time, blew round us on every side, and the cold became intense, so that, after the service of the canonical hours, I sat in bed to warm myself. And the water, even in the canals and running streams, having a salt taste from being so near the sea, which is apt to run into them, disagreed with me very much. For in all reformations or new foundations of monasteries it is necessary that the first set of monks who go there should take a great stock of patience with them, otherwise they will never be able to live there without words of disgust and murmuring; and thus, murmuring and seeking their own, instead of the things that are Jesus Christ's, they will go away without credit and without fruit.

From "Autobiography of John Busch," *British Magazine*, vol. XIX, 1841.

Archbishop Baldwin of Canterbury

GIRALDUS CAMBRENSIS

Twelfth century

HE WAS a man of a dark complexion, of an open and venerable countenance, of a moderate stature, a good person, and rather inclined to be thin than corpulent. He was a modest and grave man, of so great abstinence and continence, that ill report scarcely ever presumed to say anything against him; a man of few words; slow to anger, temperate and moderate in all his passions and affections; swift to hear, slow to speak; he was from an early age well instructed in literature, and bearing the yoke of the Lord from his youth, by the purity of his morals became a distinguished luminary to the people; wherefore voluntarily resigning the honour of the archlevite [arch deacon], which he had canonically obtained, and despising the pomps and vanities of the world, he assumed with holy devotion the habit of the Cistercian order; and as he had been formerly more than a monk in his manners, within the space of a year he was

appointed abbot, and in a few years afterwards preferred first to a bishopric, and then to an archbishopric;
and having been found faithful in a little, had authority
given him over much. But, as Cicero says, "Nature has
made nothing entirely perfect"; when he came into
power, not laying aside that sweet innate benignity
which he had always shewn when a private man, sustaining his people with his staff rather than chastising
them with rods, feeding them as it were with the milk
of a mother, and not making use of the scourges of the
father, he incurred public scandal for his remissness. So
great was his lenity that he put an end to all pastoral
rigour; and was a better monk than abbot, a better
bishop than archbishop. Hence Pope Urban addressed
him, "Urban, servant of the servants of God, to the most
fervent monk, to the warm abbot, to the lukewarm
bishop, to the remiss archbishop, health, etc."

This second successor to the martyr Thomas, having
heard of the insults offered to our Saviour and His holy
cross, was amongst the first who signed themselves with
the cross, and manfully assumed the office of preaching
its service both at home and in the most remote parts of
the kingdom. Pursuing his journey to the Holy Land, he
embarked on board a vessel at Marseilles, and landed
safely in a port at Tyre, from whence he proceeded to
Acre, where he found our army both attacking and attacked, our forces dispirited by the defection of the
princes, and thrown into a state of desolation and despair; fatigued by long expectation of supplies, greatly
afflicted by hunger and want, and distempered by the
inclemency of the air: finding his end approaching, he
embraced his fellow subjects, relieving their wants by
liberal acts of charity and pious exhortations, and by the
tenor of his life and actions strengthened them in the
faith; whose ways, life, and deeds, may He who is alone

the "way, the truth, and the life," the way without offence, the truth without doubt, and the life without end,
direct in truth, together with the whole body of the
faithful, and for the glory of His name and the palm of
faith which He hath planted, teach their hands to war,
and their fingers to fight.

From *Itinerary through Wales*, trans. Sir R. C. Hoare (Everyman's
Library [1908]).

A Model Parish Priest:
St. Gilbert of Sempringham

JOHN CAPGRAVE

Early twelfth century

THIS man Gilbert was born in that same place called
Sempringham. His father was born in Normandy,
his mother was a lady of this place aforesaid. His father,
they say, was a knight of Normandy who came to this
land with King William at the conquest and wedded the
lady of this place. . . . Then was this man born of two
bloods, Norman on the father's side, English on the
mother's side. . . . So it seems that this man was not
born of a wretched nation, nor in serfdom, but of people
gentle, freemanly, and generous, both on the father's
side and the mother's. He was in his youth and in his
simplicity full gracious, like to Jacob, whom for his
cleanness and innocence the mother Rebecca, through
the inspiration of God, preferred to be lord of all his
brethren, as this man is preferred to be master of all this
religion. . . . He was at that age set to school and
grounded in those sciences which they call liberal, as

grammar, rhetoric, logic, and such others. But his heart
at that time was more inclined to learn good manners
than subtle conclusions. . . . Because afterward he was
ordained to be a teacher of virtuous living, it was fitting
that he should first be a disciple in the school of honesty.
In all his youth he was clean from such vices as children
have, like lying, wanton raging, and other stinking conditions. Even then he began to be like a religious man,
to which life he was applied by God.

In that same secular life and at that tender age, he
followed, as he could and might, the rules of religious
life, and to those over whom he had any power he full
benignly gave example to follow the same rules. For
first he was a master of learning to the little ones, such
as learn to read, spell, and sing. The children who were
under his discipline he taught not only their lessons in
the book, but besides this he taught them to play in due
time, and he taught that their play should be honest and
merry without clamour or great noise. For though he
had not at that time experience of the good customs
which are used among religious men in monasteries, yet
our Lord God had at that age put in his breast these
holy exercises, for he taught the disciples whom he had
to keep silence in the church; all at one hour to go to
bed, and also to rise to their lessons; they all went together to their play or any other thing. His greatest labour and desire was to win souls to God with word and
also example, for the best sacrifice unto God is the jealous love of souls. . . .

When he was promoted to the order of priesthood,
and had souls in governance, and also had received
power to make ministration of the spiritual gifts which
by virtue of our Lord's blood are left in the church, then
as a true steward of his Lord's treasure . . . the word

of good exhortation was not hid in him, but he dealt it out freely to those who would learn. For his auditors were so endowed with learning that it seemed in all their governance they had been nourished in the monastery among the servants of God. They engaged in no insolent drinkings, no long sitting there, nor used to run to wrestlings, bear-baitings, and such other unthrifty occupations, which some men nowadays prefer before divine service; this they did not, but they used to pray devoutly in the church, to pay their tithes truly, to walk about and visit poor men, to spend their goods in such a way as is pleasant to God and a comfort to the poor. Whoever had seen them within the church might soon discern whether they were Gilbert's parishioners or not, he had taught them so well to bow their backs and their knees to God, and so devoutly to say their beads.

From *Life of St. Gilbert*, J. J. Munro, ed. (London: Early English Text Society, Orig. Ser., no. 140, 1910); trans. M.M.M.

An Attempt to Enforce Clerical Celibacy

ORDERICUS VITALIS

1119

GEOFFREY, the archbishop, having returned to Rouen from attending the council at Reims, held a synod in the third week of November, and stirred up by the late papal decrees, dealt sharply and rigorously with the priests of his diocese. Among other canons of the council which he promulgated was that which interdicted them from commerce with females of any description, and against such transgressors he launched the terrible sentence of excommunication. As the priests shrunk from submitting to this grievous burden, and in loud mutterings among themselves vented their complaints of the struggle between the flesh and the spirit to which they were subjected, the archbishop ordered one Albert, a man free of speech, who had used some offensive words, I know not what, to be arrested on the spot, and he was presently thrust into the common prison.

This prelate was a Breton and guilty of many indiscretions, warm and obstinate in temper, and severe in his aspect and manner, harsh in his censures, and, withal, indiscreet and a great talker. The other priests, witnessing this extraordinary proceeding, were utterly confounded; and when they saw that, without being charged with any crime or undergoing any legal examination, a priest was dragged, like a thief, from a church to a dungeon, they became so exceedingly terrified that they knew not how to act, doubting whether they had best defend themselves or take to flight. Meanwhile, the archbishop rose from his seat in a violent rage, and hastily leaving the synod, summoned his guards, whom he had already posted outside, with instructions what they were to do. The archbishop's retainers then rushed into the church with arms and staves, and began to lay about them, without respect of persons, on the assembled clergy, who were conversing together. Some of these ecclesiastics ran to their lodgings through the muddy streets of the city, though they were robed in their albs; others snatched up some rails and stones which they chanced to find, and stood on their defence; whereupon their cowardly assailants betook themselves to flight and sought refuge in the sacristy, followed closely by the indignant clergy. The archbishop's people, ashamed of having been discomfited by an unarmed,

tonsured band, summoned to their aid, in the extremity
of their fury, all the cooks, bakers, and scullions they
could muster in the neighbourhood, and had the effron-
tery to renew the conflict within the sacred precincts.
All whom they found in the church or cemetery, whether
engaged in the broil or innocently looking on, they beat
and cuffed, or inflicted on them some other bodily injury.

Then Hugh of Longueville and Ansquetil of Cropus,
and some other ecclesiastics of advanced age and great
piety, happened to be in the church, conversing together
on confession and other profitable subjects, or reciting,
as was their duty, the service of the hours to the praise
of God. The archbishop's domestics were mad enough
to fall on these priests, treated them shamefully, and
so outrageously, that they hardly restrained themselves
from taking their lives, though they asked for mercy on
their bended knees. These old priests, being at length dismissed, made their escape from the city as soon as they
could, together with their friends who had before fled,
without stopping to receive the bishop's licence and
benediction. They carried the sorrowful tidings to their
parishioners and concubines, and, to prove the truth of
their reports, exhibited the wounds and livid bruises on
their persons. The archdeacons, and canons, and all
quiet citizens, were afflicted at this cruel onslaught, and
compassionated with the servants of God who had suffered such unheard-of insults. Thus the blood of her
priests was shed in the very bosom of Holy Mother
Church, and the holy synod was converted into a scene
of riot and mockery.

The archbishop, overwhelmed with consternation, retired to his private apartments, where he concealed himself during the uproar, but shortly afterwards, when the
ecclesiastics had betaken themselves to flight, as we

have already related, his wrath subsided, and going to the church, he put on his stole, and sprinkling holy water, reconciled the church which he had polluted and his sorrowing canons.

From *Ecclesiastical History*, trans. T. Forester (London: Bohn, 1853-56).

The Habits of Priests in Normandy

ODO OF RIGAUD

Thirteenth century

A VISITATION OF RURAL CHURCHES BY
ARCHBISHOP ODO OF RIGAUD

FEBRUARY 1248. We visited the deanery of Brachi near St. Just.

We found that the priest of Ruiville was ill-famed with the wife of a certain stonecarver, and by her is said to have a child; also he is said to have many other children; he does not stay in his church, he plays ball, he does not stay in his church, and he rides around in a short coat [the garb of armed men]; we have letters from him [of confession], and they are written on folio 125.

Also, the priest of Gonnetot is ill-famed with two women, and went to the pope on this account, and after he came back he is said to have relapsed; also with a certain woman of Waletot.

Also, the priest of Wanestanville, with a certain one of his parishioners whose husband on this account went beyond the sea, and he kept her for eight years, and she is pregnant; also he plays at dice and drinks too much;

he frequents taverns, he does not stay in his church, he goes hawking in the country as he wishes; we imposed on him a penance which is found on folio 125.

Also, the priest of Brachi, with a certain woman, and because she left the home of that priest, he goes to eat with her, and has his food and flour brought to her house. The chaplain of Brachi frequents taverns. Simon, the priest of St. Just, is pugnacious and quarrelsome.

Also, the priest of Ribeuf frequents taverns and drinks to excess.

Also, the priest of Lanfreiville drinks too much. The priest of Dufranville does not stay there and goes to England without permission.

Also, the priest of Oville keeps his daughter with him against synodal prohibition.

Also, the priest of Poierville is drunken, quarrelsome, and a fighter.

Also, Henry of Evrard Mesnil is ill-famed of incontinence.

Also, Walter, parson of St. Just, is ill-famed with Matilde de Kaletot.

Also, the priest of Grochet is incontinent, and after he was corrected is said to have relapsed, and he has a child of a certain woman which was sent to Lunerai to be baptized there.

Also, Ralph, priest of Essources, is gravely ill-famed of incontinence.

Also, the parson of Rouville does not stay in his church.

Also, the priest of Gorray is ill-famed with a certain one.

Also, Laurence, the priest of Longeuil, keeps the wife of a certain one who is out of the land, and she is called Beatrice Valeran, and he has a child by her.

THE SINNERS SELF-CONFESSED

To all who shall read this, William, priest of Guile-merville, greetings in the Lord. Know that when I was accused before the reverend father Odo, by God's grace archbishop of Rouen, of this, namely, that I was wont to drink in taverns and to take off my vestments there, and to play at dice, and to pawn the books of my church, the infamy of which I admitted in the presence of the said father; wishing that the said father should not proceed against me as harshly as he is able, I humbly sought from him not justice but pity, and I promised and swore to him, with the holy Gospels before me, and my hand placed on my heart, that if it happens again that I am accused of the aforesaid vices or any others and found guilty concerning this, so that I cannot canonically purge myself, I will surrender my church of Guilemerville to the will of the said father wholly and simply, and without the noise of a trial, and I will consider it as surrendered nor will I claim anything in it from then on for any reason whenever I shall be questioned about this by the said father. In the presence of the venerable men: Peter, archdeacon. . . . In witness of this thing I have handed over to the said father these words sealed with my own seal, given at Mont Alacre, in the year of our Lord 1260, on Friday before the feast of the Holy Cross.

To all those who shall see these presents, master Henry, priest of the church of Gomerville, greetings in the Lord. Know that when the reverend father Odo, by God's grace archbishop of Rouen, visiting the deanery of St. Romain, found me seriously ill-famed with Eustachia, daughter of a former deaçon of Gomerville, I, wishing to reform my ways, spontaneously pledged myself to a penalty of twenty pounds of money of Tours to be paid to him if I should disgrace myself further in this way, unless I can purge myself canonically. In memory and witness of this thing, I gave to the reverend father the present letter confirmed by the mark of my seal. Given on this day . . . 1252.

THE VISITATION OF A COLLEGIATE CHURCH
BY ARCHBISHOP ODO

November 1266. By the grace of God we arrived at the church of Rouen for the sake of exercising the visitation there, and having assembled there in the chapter of the said place, the canons, chaplains, and choir clerks, those specifically beneficed in the said church, according to our mandate by letters which we sent earlier in the week concerning this, we preached the word of God in Latin and after this proceeded to the visitation.

We found that the canons and choir clerks talk and chatter from stall to stall, and across each other, while the divine office is being celebrated. They hasten through the psalms too quickly. We found certain things in the office of the treasurer to be corrected. The chaplains celebrate the mass inadequately; also the chaplains and choir clerks often leave the choir before the office being sung is finished. About the parsons, in truth, we found many ill-famed of incontinence, namely Burnet of Albana scandalously, Visus Lupus with many women, Lords Geoffrey of Sotteville, Peter Pilatus, Peter of Aulagia, Ralph Anglicus, chaplains, and a certain clerk of the choir called Gorgias; also Lord Robert called the Fish, of trading. . . . Also the clerks of Albana do not sleep together in their own house, as they should. Also, we found Lord Gilbert called Barrabas, priest and rector of the parish of St. Stephen, ill-famed many times; for he said that for many years he kept and still keeps his

own niece and had begotten children by her. He did not
have the letters of his ordination; he could not tell by
whom or through whom he had been ordained; he was
also ill-famed of trading; he celebrated [mass] insufficiently, was too solitary, being known to few. We
warned the rectors and canons who were present at the
visitation that they should correct the aforesaid matters
within the octave of the Epiphany; otherwise we should
apply ourselves to them as we were able to do; and then
we asked the chapter for our procuration [expenses] by
reason of the aforesaid visitation.

From *Regestrum visitationum archiepiscopi Rothomagensis*, Th.
Bonnin, éd. (Rouen: A. Le Brument, 1852); trans. J.B.R.

Statutes for a College

ROBERT DE SORBONNE

Thirteenth century

I WISH that the custom which was instituted from the
beginning in this house by the counsel of good men
may be kept, and if anyone ever has transgressed it,
that henceforth he shall not presume to do so.

No one therefore shall eat meat in the house on Advent, nor on Monday or Tuesday of Lent, nor from
Ascension Day to Pentecost.

Also, I will that the community be not charged for
meals taken in rooms. If there cannot be equality, it is
better that the fellow eating in his room be charged
than the entire community.

Also, no one shall eat in his room except for cause. If
anyone has a guest, he shall eat in hall. If, moreover,
it shall not seem expedient to the fellow to bring that

guest to hall, let him eat in his room and he shall have
the usual portion for himself, not for the guest. If, moreover, he wants more for himself or his guest, he should
pay for it himself. . . .

Also, the fellows should be warned by the bearer of
the roll that those eating in private rooms conduct themselves quietly and abstain from too much noise, lest
those passing through the court and street be scandalized
and lest the fellows in rooms adjoining be hindered in
their studies.

Also, those eating in private rooms shall provide themselves with what they need in season as best they can,
so that the service of the community may be disturbed
as little as possible. But if there are any infringers of this
statute who are accustomed to eat in private rooms without cause, they shall be warned by the bearer of the roll
to desist, which if they will not do, he shall report it
to the master. If, moreover, other reasons arise for which
anyone can eat in a private room, it shall be left to the
discretion of the roll-bearer and proctors until otherwise
ordered.

Also, the rule does not apply to the sick. If anyone
eats in a private room because of sickness, he may have
a fellow with him, if he wishes, to entertain and wait
on him, who also shall have his due portion. What shall
be the portion of a fellow shall be left to the discretion
of the dispenser. If a fellow shall come late to lunch, if
he comes from classes or a sermon or business of the
community, he shall have his full portion, but if from his
own affairs, he shall have bread only. . . .

Also, all shall wear closed outer garments, nor shall
they have trimmings of vair or grise or of red or green
silk on the outer garment or hood.

Also, no one shall have loud shoes or clothing by
which scandal might be generated in any way.

Also, no one shall be received in the house unless he shall be willing to leave off such and to observe the aforesaid rules.

Also, no one shall be received in the house unless he pledges faith that, if he happens to receive books from the common store, he will treat them carefully as if his own and on no condition remove or lend them out of the house, and return them in good condition whenever required or whenever he leaves town.

Also, let every fellow have his own mark on his clothes and one only and different from the others. And let all the marks be written on a schedule and over each mark the name of whose it is. And let that schedule be given to the servant so that he may learn to recognize the mark of each one. And the servant shall not receive clothes from any fellow unless he sees the mark. And then the servant can return his clothes to each fellow. . . .

Also, for peace and utility we propound that no secular person living in town—scribe, corrector, or anyone else—unless for great cause eat, sleep in a room, or remain with the fellows when they eat, or have frequent conversation in the gardens or hall or other parts of the house, lest the secrets of the house and the remarks of the fellows be spread abroad.

Also, no outsider shall come to accountings or the special meetings of the fellows, and he whose guest he is shall see to this.

Also, no fellow shall bring in outsiders frequently to drink at commons, and if he does, he shall pay according to the estimate of the dispenser.

Also, no fellow shall have a key to the kitchen.

Also, no fellow shall presume to sleep outside the house in town, and if he did so for reason, he shall take pains to submit his excuse to the bearer of the roll. . . .

Also, no women of any sort shall eat in the private rooms. If anyone violates this rule, he shall pay the assessed penalty, namely, sixpence. . . .

Also, no one shall form the habit of talking too loudly at table. Whoever after he has been warned about this by the prior shall have offended by speaking too loudly, provided this is established afterwards by testimony of several fellows to the prior, shall be held to the usual house penalty, namely two quarts of wine.

The penalty for transgression of statutes which do not fall under an oath is twopence, if the offenders are not reported by someone, or if they were, the penalty becomes sixpence in the case of fines. I understand "not reported" to mean that, if before the matter has come to the attention of the prior, the offender accuses himself to the prior or has told the clerk to write down twopence against him for such an offence, for it is not enough to say to the fellows, "I accuse myself."

From *Chartulary of the University of Paris*, trans. L. Thorndike, *University Records and Life in the Middle Ages* (New York: Columbia University Press, 1944).

How the Student Should Behave

JOHN OF GARLAND

Thirteenth century

LEARN how to entertain at table, to provide food and the sauces that go with the various dishes, and to serve seasonable wine in modest quantity. Once again I touch critically on manners in polite society so that my readers may become more genteel. According to good custom you should place the sauce on the right, the service plate on the left; you should have the servant take the first course to him who sits at the head of the table. Take hold of the base of a goblet so that unsightly finger marks may not show on the side. Polite diners pause over their cup, but gluttons, who live like mules and weevils, empty it with one draught. Pour wine properly with both hands so as not to spill any. Always serve two pieces of bread. Have several well-dressed servants in readiness to bring clean towels and to supply the wants of the guests. Lest I should seem to be in charge of the cooks like Nebuzaradan, I shall not go into the art of preparing fine dishes. Carve the meats which are not to be served in the broth, and skilfully take off the wings of fowl while they are hot. He who takes a walk or a brief nap after dinner preserves his health. If you wish to regain your strength as a convalescent, and keep your health when you are well, drink moderately. All Epicureans live impure lives; they lose their eyesight; they are rude, unclean, and are doomed to die a sudden death. . . .

The sage of Miletus set down these rules of polite behaviour for which we should be grateful. Regulate your household soberly; do your civic duties cheerfully; have a word of greeting for strangers as for friends; do your utmost to avoid altercations with irate associates; with a smile and a witticism cover up the faults of others; be faultless at table, glad even to entertain your enemies; bear your misfortunes with fortitude and do not let your head be turned by good fortune. Make an effort to follow these seven rules of courtliness. May you be decked out with them, you who declare yourself to be a scholar; unless you have such urbanities you are taken for a rustic. . . .

Even though you be a Socrates, if you have rude manners, you are a ditch-digger. Avoid these seven rusticities which are signalled by Thales, the sage. Light-minded talk is unseemly at table; so is presumption and constant contention. It is rude to be ungrateful or cruel towards the poor. It is reprehensible to be haughty towards your dear friends; if you reject good advice, you are a fool; and you lack the light of reason if you fly in the face of God. These good precepts are not hidden away but are written in the public theatre. Avoid these things lest you be consigned behind the gates of hell. . . .

You will be courteous if you perform the following works of mercy: if at night you give beds to the poor, if you heal the sick, if you clothe the freezing, give food to the beggar, console the afflicted, and offer drink to the thirsty. . . .

Regard as models of deportment the graven images of the churches, which you should carry in your mind as living and indelible pictures. Cherish again the violets of civility without blemish so that, when your blindness has vanished, the eyes of your soul may have no wasting disease. Be not a fornicator, O student, a robber, a murderer, a deceitful merchant, a champion at dice. In the choirstalls a cleric should chant without noise and commotion. I advocate that the ordinary layman, who does not sing, be kept out of the choir. A student, who is a churchman, is expected to follow good custom, to be willing to serve, to fee the notary who has drawn up a charter for him, to gladden the giver. Do not constantly urge your horse on with the spur, which should be used only on rare occasions. Give your horse the reins when he mounts an incline; fearing a serious accident, avoid crossing swollen rivers, or the Rhine. If a bridge is not safe, you should dismount and let the horse pick his way over the smooth parts. Mount gently on the left stirrup. Select beautiful equestrian trappings suitable to your clerical station. Ride erect unless you are bent by age. If you are of the elect you should have a rich saddle cloth. The cross should be exalted, the voice be raised in prayer, Christ should be worshipped, the foot should be taken out of the stirrup. The horseman will descend from his horse and say his prayers; no matter how far he then will travel, he will ride in safety. He who wishes to serve should be quick, not go to sleep, and not give way to anger against his lord. Avoid drunkards, those who indulge in secret sin, those who like to beat and strike, those who love lewdness, evil games, and quarrels. Passing a cemetery, if you are well-bred, and if you hope for salvation, you pause to pray that the dead may rest in peace. Have nothing to do with the prostitute, but love your wife; all wives should be honoured but especially those who are distinguished by virtue. A person who is well should not recline at table in the fashion of the ancients. When you walk after dinner keep on frequented streets. Avoid insincere speeches. Unless you wish to be considered a fool learn to keep your mouth shut in season. Stand and sit upright, do not scratch yourself. . . .

I must speak about medical matters and drugs, but Phoebus shows that they are harmful if taken too often. In order that a man be kept entirely healthy this chapter is added so that the mind may be purified and the body strengthened. Nutmeg may be taken as well as cloves, musk may be given, fennel may be eaten by anybody; they expel gas from the stomach and thus, along with the triple compartments of the brain, they comfort the cerebellum. By means of cooked pears you can take away fevers with marvellous results. Pliris is good for weak and melancholy men. The thin flux (usia) is cured by means of diapenidia. Ygia is good for rheumatics, athanasia for flux of the bowels. Give diaciminum and sweet wine to those who have indigestion. Justinum and goat's blood dissolve stone in the bladder. Diaprunis makes you immune to fevers; when given to patients who have fasted, a decoction with prunes from Damascus allays fevers. A sane diet is essential to a life of happiness; thus you will be strong and vigorous when health, the aim of the physician, is yours. . . .

Exhibit a good deportment in deeds, and in words; learn the custom of the country in which you happen to be. Do not be noisy, rash in your actions, odious because of your insulting words, wrathful about little annoyances. You should never despair if you suffer on account of sin; you will bear all the bitterness of poverty, knowing that you are an heir of the eternal Prince. Be peaceful among peaceful citizens, be like a rich patron among the poor. You should disassociate yourself from the rich, for, a celibate on earth, you will dwell with Christ, the celibate, in heaven. Hasten to help a needy friend, give him money if you can. Be a good debtor and hasten to pay your debts lest you be condemned by your burden of sin and by the peasant bewailing his losses. You should take good care of your horse, give him enough water, clean straw when he is worn out, and enough of the kind of food he likes to eat. There are more such precepts for him who wishes to know all the rules of politeness; as such, make it your ambition, by careful study, to learn them.

From *Morale Scholarium*, trans. L. J. Paetow (Berkeley, Calif.: University of California Press, 1927).

THE NOBILITY: THE FIGHTERS

The Function of Knighthood

JOHN OF SALISBURY

Twelfth century

BUT what is the office of the duly ordained soldiery?
To defend the Church, to assail infidelity, to venerate the priesthood, to protect the poor from injuries, to
pacify the province, to pour out their blood for their
brothers (as the formula of their oath instructs them),
and, if need be, to lay down their lives. The high praises
of God are in their throat, and two-edged swords are in
their hands to execute punishment on the nations and
rebuke upon the peoples, and to bind their kings in
chains and their nobles in links of iron. But to what
end? To the end that they may serve madness, vanity,
avarice, or their own private self-will? By no means.
Rather to the end that they may execute the judgment
that is committed to them to execute; wherein each follows not his own will but the deliberate decision of God,
the angels, and men, in accordance with equity and the
public utility. . . . For soldiers that do these things are
"saints," and are the more loyal to their prince in proportion as they more zealously keep the faith of God; and
they advance the more successfully the honour of their
own valour as they seek the more faithfully in all things
the glory of their God.

From *Policraticus*, trans. J. Dickinson.

The Chivalric Ideal

DÍAZ DE GÁMEZ

Fifteenth century

Now is it fitting that I should tell what it is to be a knight: whence comes this name of knight; what manner of a man a knight should be to have a right to be called a knight; and what profit the good knight is to the country wherein he lives. I tell you that men call knight the man who, of custom, rides upon a horse. He who, of custom, rides upon another mount, is no knight; but he who rides upon a horse is not for that reason a knight; he only is rightly called a knight, who makes it his calling. Knights have not been chosen to ride an ass or a mule; they have not been taken from among feeble or timid or cowardly souls, but from among men who are strong and full of energy, bold and without fear; and for this reason there is no other beast that so befits a knight as a good horse. Thus have horses been found that in the thick of battle have shewn themselves as loyal to their masters as if they had been men. There are horses who are so strong, fiery, swift, and faithful, that a brave man, mounted on a good horse, may do more in an hour of fighting than ten or mayhap a hundred could have done afoot. For this reason do men rightly call him knight.

What is required of a good knight? That he should be noble. What means noble and nobility? That the heart should be governed by the virtues. By what virtues? By the four that I have already named. These four virtues are sisters and so bound up one with the other, that he who has one, has all, and he who lacks one, lacks the others also. So the virtuous knight should be wary and prudent, just in the doing of justice, continent and temperate, enduring and courageous; and withal he must have great faith in God, hope at His glory, that he may attain the guerdon of the good that he has done, and finally he must have charity and the love of his neighbour.

Of what profit is a good knight? I tell you that through good knights is the king and the kingdom honoured, protected, feared, and defended. I tell you that the king, when he sends forth a good knight with an army and entrusts him with a great emprise, on sea or on land, has in him a pledge of victory. I tell you that without good knights, the king is like a man who has neither feet nor hands.

From *The Unconquered Knight*, trans. J. Evans (London: Routledge, 1926).

The Murder of a Feudal Lord

GALBERT OF BRUGES

1127

Now the pious count [Charles of Flanders] wishing to bring back good order to his realm, sought to find out who properly pertained to him [i.e., his ministerials, officials, often of high social rank but of servile status], who were serfs, and who free men in the land. While the business of the courts was being carried on, the count was often present, hearing in the discussion of secular liberty and the condition of serfs, that in matters of high justice and general pleas, free men did not deign to make answer to serfs. Those whom the count was able to discover as pertaining to him, he sought to claim for himself.

A certain provost, Bertulf of Bruges, and his brother the castellan in Bruges [Didier Hackett] together with his nephews Borsiard, Robert, Albert, and other well-known members of that kinship, studied with every kind of craft and cleverness how they might remove themselves and escape from the servitude and possession of the count; for those pertaining to the count were of servile condition. At length after taking counsel on the matter, the provost gave his marriageable nieces, whom he had reared in his own home, in marriage to free knights so that by this circumstance of marrying both he and his family might enter upon secular liberty after a certain manner. But it happened that a knight, who had taken to wife one of the nieces of the provost, in the presence of the count challenged to single combat a certain other knight of the count who according to the descent of his family was free; and the one challenged replied vehemently for himself, refusing indignantly, saying that he was not of servile condition but on the contrary born of free rank according to the descent of his family, and for this reason he would not meet the challenger as an equal in single combat. For, according to the law of the count, whoever had taken to wife a servile woman, after he had held her for a year, was no longer free, but became of the same condition as his wife. Then that knight grieved who had lost his liberty on account of his wife through whom he had hoped to be freer when he had accepted her; and then the provost and his family grieved and strove by all means to free themselves from servitude to the count. Therefore when the count had learned from the investigation of the facts, and by the report of the elders of the kingdom, that they pertained to him without doubt, he tried to claim them for himself in servitude. Now all this would have sunk into oblivion, as it were lulled to sleep and neglected after such a long time, because the provost and his kinsmen had not been questioned or challenged about their servile status by the count's predecessors up to this time, if it had not been recalled to mind in the aforesaid summons to battle.

But the provost with all his nephews, who after the count was the most powerful in the land and the most renowned in reputation and religion, affirmed that he himself was free and both his ancestors and his successors, and with a certain excessive pride and arrogance insisted that it was so. He strove therefore by deliberation and by influence to remove himself and his family from the possession and ownership of the count, saying, "That Charles of Denmark would never have attained the countship if I had wished otherwise. Now then, when he has been made count through me, he does not remember that I did well by him but instead tries by all means to cast me with my whole family into servitude, inquiring of the elders whether we are his serfs. But let him seek as much as he wishes, we will always be free and we are free, and there is no man on earth who can make us into serfs." He spoke thus boastfully in vain, however, for the count, on his guard, had perceived the intention of the provost and his family and had heard of their fraud as well as of their treachery. When the provost and his relatives saw that they could not succeed in defending themselves but on the contrary were about to be deprived of their usurped liberty, they preferred to perish rather than to be handed over to the count in servitude. At length in the evil deceit of wicked deliberation they began to discuss among themselves the

death of the most pious count and to consider the place
and the opportunity of killing him.

Now when strife and discord had broken out between
his nephews and Thancmar [of Straeten] whose side the
count justly favoured, the provost rejoiced because he
now had opportunities for betraying the count, for he
had summoned all the knights of our province, some for
a price, others through influence, or claim to the aid of
his nephews against Thancmar. They besieged him on
every side in the place where he had entrenched himself
and finally, in an armed band, they strongly attacked the
besieged and breaking the bolts of the gates, they cut
down the barriers and enclosures of their enemies. The
provost, however, was not present but, acting as if he
had done nothing, he did everything by plan and guile;
he outwardly showed nothing but benevolence and told
his enemies that he regretted that his nephews were responsible for so much strife and murder, whom indeed
he himself had inspired to all kinds of evil.

In the aforesaid conflict many on both sides fell dead
and wounded on that day. For when the provost had
learned that the attack was actually going on, he himself went to the carpenters who were working in the
cloister of the monks, and ordered their tools, that is,
their axes, to be taken there, with which they might
knock down the tower, walls, and houses of their enemies. Then he sent through the several houses in the
suburbium to collect axes which were quickly brought.
And when in the night his nephews had returned with
five hundred armed knights and a great number of foot
soldiers, he took them into the cloister and refectory of
the monks where he refreshed them all with various
kinds of food and drink, and on this occasion he was
elated and boastful. While he was thus assiduously at-

tacking his enemies and making a great outlay for those who were helping his nephews, at first the squires and then the knights began to rob the peasants, even to the extent of seizing and devouring the cattle and herds of the serfs. Whatever the peasants possessed for their own use, the nephews of the provost seized violently and allotted to their expenses. But from the beginning of the realm none of the counts had allowed pillage to be carried on in the land because great slaughter and strife result from it.

Consequently when the peasants heard that the count had come to Ipres, about two hundred of them went to him secretly by night and, bent down at his feet, begged from him his paternal and customary help, that he should order their goods returned to them, namely, their cattle and herds, clothes and silver, as well as all the other equipment of their houses, all of which the nephews of the provost had seized, and those who had fought with them night and day in the execution of that siege. After the count had gravely heard these complaints he called together his councillors and many also who were of the kinship of the provost, inquiring of them by what punishment and severity the law should treat this crime. And they gave counsel that without delay he should destroy the house of Borsiard by fire, because Borsiard had pillaged the peasants of the count; and for this reason they strongly advised that the aforesaid house be destroyed, because as long as it stood, so long would Borsiard carry on strife and plunder and even murder, and so he would continuously lay waste that whole vicinity.

On this advice the count went and burned the house and destroyed the dwelling to the foundations. Then that Borsiard and the provost and their accomplices were troubled beyond measure, both because the count in this deed was seen to have agreed with and lent aid to their enemies, and because the count was daily disturbing them about their servile status and trying in every way to get them handed over to him.

After the house was burned the count came up to Bruges. When he had entered his home and settled down, some of his intimates came to him and put him on his guard, saying that the nephews of the provost would betray him because now they would seize the opportunity given by the burning of the aforesaid house, although even if the count had not done this, nevertheless he would have been betrayed by them. Now after the count had dined, there came into his presence intercessors on behalf of the provost and his nephews who begged the count to turn his indignation away from them and in pity to take them back into his friendship. But the count replied that he would deal justly with them and even mercifully if they would henceforth give up strife and plunder, and he promised to bind himself in addition to restore to Borsiard an even better house. In the place where the house was burned up, however, he swore that, as long as he held the countship, Borsiard would never again obtain any possession, because as long as he had remained there next to Thancmar he had never done anything but engage in strife and discord against his enemies and against the citizens with pillage and slaughter. In truth the intercessors, for the most part conscious of the treachery, did not vex the count very much about the reconciliation, and since the servants were going about offering drinks, they asked the count to order better wine to be brought. When they had drunk this, as drinkers are wont to do, they kept on asking for their healths to be drunk and more abundantly, until, when they had received the count's final dismissal, they should go off to bed. By the order of the count healths were drunk to all who were present until, after final dismissal was received, they withdrew.

Then Isaac, Borsiard, William of Werwicq, Ingran, and their accomplices, with the approval of the provost, hastened what they were about to do by free will indeed, not from the necessity of divine providence. For at once those who were mediators and intercessors between the count and the provost's nephews, having gone to the provost's home, denounced the response of the count, that is, that they had not been able to secure any favour either for the nephews or for their supporters, and that he would act toward them only as the judgment of the primates of the land had determined in the severity of justice. Then the provost and his nephews withdrawing into a [inner] room, having summoned those whom they wished, with the provost himself guarding the door of the room, gave their right hands to each other, pledging that they would betray the count. For this crime they proposed Robert the Young, asking him to give his right hand to them in pledge that he would carry out with them that same thing which they were about to do, for which they had given their right hands to each other. But the noble youth, forewarned by the strength of his soul, and considering that it must be a grievous thing which they were urging on him, resisted, unwilling to be ignorantly led into their compact, unless he should know what things they had agreed to do. When they were constraining him to this, drawing away, he hastened toward the door. But Isaac and William and the others called to the provost who was then watching the door, not to let Robert go out until he had been forced by the provost's order to carry out what they had demanded of him. Immediately, overcome by the blandishments and threats of the provost, the youth came back and gave his hand on their terms, not knowing indeed what act he was about to perform with them, and now in league with the traitors, he asked what he should do. They replied, "That Count Charles is working in every way for our destruction and hastening to claim us as his serfs; his betrayal we have already sworn, and now you must carry through this same treachery with us both in word and deed." Then the youth, terrified and dissolved in tears, said, "Heaven forbid that we should betray our lord and the count of our land. Nay rather, if you do not desist, I shall go and speak openly to the count and to all of your treachery, nor shall I ever, God willing, lend any aid or counsel to this plan." But they forcibly held him as he tried to flee from them, saying, "Listen, friend, we made known the aforesaid treachery to you as if we were about to do it in earnest, in order to try out in this way whether you wish to stay with us in some serious business; there is indeed something else which we have concealed from you so far, by reason of which you are bound to us by faith and compact, which we may tell you about in the future." And turning it off as a joke they concealed the treachery.

Then each one of them, going from the room, went to his own place. When Isaac had finally come home, he went off as if to bed—for he was awaiting the silence of the night—and soon, mounted on his horse, he returned to the castle, stopping at the quarters of Borsiard, and, calling him and others whom he wished, they went separately to the quarters of another, Walter the knight. And when they had entered they straightway extinguished the fire in the house, lest by chance through the lighted fire it should be noted by those awake who were in the house and what business they were carrying on contrary to custom at that time of night. Secure therefore in the darkness they took counsel about the treachery to be done promptly at dawn, choosing from the household of Borsiard the most courageous and bold for this crime, and they promised them great riches. They offered to the knights who should kill the count four marks and to the serving men who should do the same two marks, and they bound themselves together by the most evil compact. And so Isaac returned home about dawn after he had inspired the others by his counsel and made them ready for such a great crime.

Therefore when day had dawned, very dark and foggy so that no one could see anything a spear's length away, Borsiard secretly sent a few servants to the courtyard of the count to watch for his going out into the church. The count indeed had risen early at dawn and had distributed [alms] to the poor, as he was wont to do in his own house, and was about to go to church. (But as his chaplains related, at night when he had composed himself in bed for sleeping, he was troubled by a certain anxiety of wakefulness, his mind confused and disturbed, so that, disquieted by meditation on many things, now turning and tossing, now sitting on his bed, he seemed quite ill.) And when he had proceeded on his way to the church of St. Donatian, the servants who had watched for his exit announced to the traitors that the count had ascended into the *solarium* [gallery] of the church with a few persons. Then that mad Borsiard and his knights and servants, with their bare swords under their cloaks, followed the count into the same *solarium*, dividing into two groups so that none of those whom they wished to betray could escape at either end of the *solarium*, and lo! they saw the count kneeling as was his custom near to the altar on a low stool, where he was devoutly chanting psalms to God and likewise saying prayers and giving pennies to the poor. . . .

In the year 1127, or the sixth day before the nones of March, on the second day, that is, after the beginning

of the same month . . . while the pious count in
Bruges in the church of St. Donatian . . . was bowed
in prayer that he might hear the early morning mass, according to his pious custom he was distributing a profu-
sion of alms to the poor, with his eyes fixed on reading
the psalms and his right hand stretched out to bestow
alms; for his chaplain, who attended to that duty, had
placed near the count many pennies which he was distributing to the poor while in the act of prayer. Now
when the office of the first hour was ended, and the
response of the third hour finished, when "Our Father"
is said, the count according to custom was praying,
reading aloud dutifully; then at length, after so many
plots and oaths and pledges made among themselves,
the wretched traitors, already murderers at heart, left for
dead the count devoutly praying and giving alms, bowed
in supplication to the divine majesty, pierced by the
swords and run through again and again. And so God
gave the palm of the martyrs to the count, washed clean
of his sins by the rivulets of his blood, with the course
of his life terminated in good works. In the last moment of life and at the onset of death, he most fittingly
turned his face and his royal hands to heaven as well as
he could in the midst of so many blows and thrusts of
the swordsmen, and so he gave up his spirit to the Lord
of all, and he offered himself up to God as a morning sacrifice. And now the bloody body of such a great man and
prince lay alone, without the veneration of his people
and the proper reverence of his servants. Whence whoever has heard the circumstance of his death, suffering in
tears that pitiable death, has commended to God such
a great and lamented prince, brought to an end by a
martyr's death.

From *Histoire du meurtre de Charles le Bon*, H. Pirenne, ed.
(Paris: A. Picard, 1891); trans. J.B.R.

The Battle of Poitiers

Geoffrey le Baker

September 19, 1356

THE prince [Edward of Wales, the "Black Prince"]
then entrusted the vanguard of the army to the earls
of Warwick and Oxford, the middle part he himself
commanded, and the rear was led by the earls of Salisbury and Suffolk. In the whole army of the prince there
were not more than four thousand men at arms, one
thousand armed soldiers, and two thousand archers.

The proud nobility of the French approached, very
disdainful of the small numbers of the English, for their
army contained eight thousand fighting soldiers and an
uncounted number of soldiers, under four score and seven
standards. Many of our men murmured on this account,
because recently a large part of our army had been sent
to defend Gascony. . . .

When the armies had been arrayed on both sides,
ready to fight early Sunday morning, which dawned
very fair, the cardinal of Périgord came to the prince.
He besought the prince, for the honour of God who was
crucified and for love of His Virgin Mother, and in
reverence of the ecclesiastical peace and for the sparing
of Christian blood, that it might please him to postpone the war for a time, so that peace might be discussed. This he promised should be carried out honourably, through his own intercession, if he should be
allowed to mediate. The prince, altogether untouched
by tyranny, neither feared war nor refused peace, but
modestly agreed to the request of this holy father. Then

during that whole day, which had been set aside for the making of peace, the army of the French increased by the number of a thousand men of arms, and a great multitude of people. The next morning, on Monday, the cardinal came again from the French king [John], asking for a year's truce, which the prince refused. But at the insistence of the cardinal, he granted a truce lasting until the next Christmas. Then the cardinal, returning to the French king, asked him for pledges of peace, which should be given according to the agreement of the lord prince. But, although the Marshal de Clermont advised the king to agree, this petition was opposed by the Marshal d'Audrehem, Geoffrey de Charny, and Douglas the Scot, by whom the king was greatly influenced. They persuaded him that in the common course of nature the English could not at that time prevail, especially since there were few of them, and in a strange land, miserably fatigued by their laborious travels, against the great numbers of Frenchmen defending their own soil. . . .

When he heard from messengers of the cardinal that the leader of the French wanted no peace at all, except that achieved by force of arms, the prince of Wales called his soldiers together, and made an oration to them . . . and turning to the body of archers, he comforted them by this speech: "Your courage and your loyalty have been sufficiently proved to me. You have shown yourselves, in many and great dangers, not degenerate sons and kinsmen of those who under my father's dukedom and that of my forebears, kings of England, found no labour impossible, no place impassable, nor the steepest hill inaccessible, no tower unscalable, no army impenetrable, nor armed host formidable. Their lively courage tamed the French, the Cyprians, the Syracusans, the Calabrians and Palestinians, and subdued the stiff-necked Scots and Irish, and even the Welsh, most patient in all labours. Occasion, time, and dangers make the timid brave, and the stupid clever; honour also, and love of country, and the rich spoil of the Frenchmen, more than my words, exhort you to follow your fathers' footsteps. Follow your standards, obeying the commands of your leaders fully, both in mind and in body, so that if victory comes with life, we may still continue in firm friendship, always of one mind and will. But if envious fortune, which God forbid, should, in this present struggle, make us run the final race of all flesh, the infamous punishment of hanging will not profane your names, but these noble companions of mine and I will drink the same cup together with you. For us, to vanquish the nobility of France will be glorious, but to be vanquished, which God forbid, not a shameful danger, but a courageous one."

As he was saying these words, the prince saw that there was a hill near by, covered with ditches and hedges on the outside, but of a different sort within. On one side was a pasture, thickly covered with bushes, and on the other side it was planted with vines, and the rest was sown land. On the top of this, he believed, the French army lay. Between our army and the hill there was a large low valley, marshy, and watered by a stream. One company of the prince crossed the stream with baggage-wagons to a narrow path, entered the valley across the hedges and ditches, and took the hill. They hid themselves among the bushes, taking advantage of the place, which lay higher than the enemy. The field, in which the first and second divisions of our army were, was divided from the plain occupied by the French army by a long hedge and ditch, one end of which stretched down into the marsh mentioned above. The slope going down to the marsh was held by the earl of

Warwick, leader and commander of the vanguard. In the upper part of the hedge, at a distance from the slope of the hill, there was an open place or gap, made by the teams in the autumn, and a stone's throw from this stood our rear guard, commanded by the earl of Salisbury.

The enemy, seeing the prince's standard displayed, and moved from place to place, and sometimes quite hidden by the hill, thought that the prince had fled, although Douglas the Scot and Marshal de Clermont said that this was not so. But Marshal d'Audrehem, deceived by his own opinion, thought to pursue the fleeing prince, and with him went Douglas, in order to advance the splendid name of his new warfare. And de Clermont, to clear himself of the suspicion concerning his loyalty, vehemently urged them forward. For to these men the command of the vanguard was entrusted. There advanced before them, as was the custom, certain soldiers to chase and to joust, and against them came our horsemen especially assigned to jousting, from our first division lying under the hill. In order to see the outcome of the jousting, Marshal d'Audrehem held up his attack. Meanwhile, de Clermont, hoping to pass through the gap in the hedge, and to surround our vanguard from behind, encountered the earl of Salisbury who, perceiving the approach of de Clermont, was prudently forewarned of his purpose. And so those who commanded our rear guard, swiftly taking the gap and preventing the passage of the enemy through it, sustained the first charge of the battle.

Then there began a terrible encounter between the armed men, with lances, spears, and battle-axes. Nor did our archers neglect their duties, but rising from their places of safety shot their arrows over the tops of ditches and hedges, to prevail over the armed soldiers, and their arrows flew more swiftly and more profusely than the weapons of those who fought in arms. Then our rear guard, above, meeting the enemy at the gap, and our vanguard, below on the slope of the hill next to the marsh, and commanded by the earl of Warwick, beat down the opposing Frenchmen. Our bowmen of the vanguard stood safely in the marsh, lest the horsemen should attack them, yet even so those did prevail there somewhat. For the horsemen, as has been said, had the special purpose of overrunning the archers, and of protecting their army from the arrows. Standing near their own men they faced the archers with their chests so solidly protected with plated mail and leather shields, that the arrows were either fended off directly or broken in pieces by the hard objects or were diverted upwards, to fall down for the indifferent destruction of friend or enemy.

Perceiving this, the earl of Oxford left the prince, and leading the archers with him to one side, ordered them to shoot at the hind parts of the horses. When this was done, the wounded horses kicked and reared, and threw their riders, and then turning back upon them, wrought great slaughter on their own masters, who had thought to have another end. Since the horsemen were thus beaten back, the archers, retiring to the place from which they had come, pierced the fighting flanks of the French with direct shots. The dreadful fury of battle continued, as the earls of Warwick and Salisbury fought like lions, to see which of them might pour forth more French blood upon the soil of Poitiers, and each gloried in staining his own arms with warm blood. Nor did Thomas Dufford, deservedly duke of Suffolk, neglect his duty, who from youth to advanced age was distinguished by strenuous deeds in every field of military science. Running through every line of battle, comforting the soldiers and inspiring each one to do well, he took care that the furious courage of the young men should not carry them too far or that the bowmen should not direct their arrows uselessly, and, with much-respected words, he fired their ardent spirits. De Clermont, bravely fighting in the battle, not deigning to surrender or flee, was snatched by death, nor was he unavenged. But the prevailing valour of the English forced d'Audrehem to surrender; the wounded Douglas fled, taking with him his brother Archibald and a few Scots of his band. For the fearful fury of war had slain almost all of them, and had compelled the rest of that company to die honourably, to flee, or to be taken prisoner and held for ransom. But our leaders took care that the victors should not pursue those who had fled too far, because, undeceived by that fortunate beginning of the battle, they believed that a more difficult struggle would take place when later armies attacked. Therefore our men put themselves in good array, and the first and second divisions were joined together.

And without delay another army of the French advanced, led by the dauphin of Vienne, the eldest son of the French king. The splendour of this army was more terrible and more fierce than that of the army which had just been beaten back. Yet it could not frighten our men who were avid for honour and most eager to avenge themselves and their comrades who had been wounded in the first struggle. So, boldly, they go at it on both sides, shouting and calling on St. George or St. Denis to favour them in the battle. Soon they are fighting man to man, and each one, ready to die, fights for his life. Nor does the pregnant lioness make the wolf more afraid, nor the tiger seem more terrifying, than did our noblemen, as they threw the enemy into disorder and put them to flight. And although this army withstood ours longer than the first, nevertheless after a great slaughter of

their men, they used a device which the invincible
French are wont to call not flight, but a fair retreat. But
our men, judging that the outcome of the battle was
doubtful, so long as the French king could get there
with his forces which were half-concealed in a neighbouring valley, refused to leave the field to pursue the
fleeing French.

Sir Maurice Berkeley, son of Sir Thomas, and a hero
worthy of illustrious stock, had no regard for this.
Through the whole six-months' expedition of the prince,
he had led his men, and, among the first and most distinguished, he had never willingly left the front line of
battle. In this hour, he was among the first attacking the
enemy, and against them he struck blows worthy of
eternal praise. In the midst of the dauphin's guard, raging among them with armed hand, he did not think of
fleeing from the French so long as he saw them standing
erect, and wholly intent on those in front of him, never
looking behind or upwards, all alone he pursued the
fearless army of the great dauphin, against whom, with
savage strength, he fought with lance and sword and
other weapons. Finally, alone and surrounded by a multitude, frightfully wounded, he was taken alive and held
for ransom.

Meanwhile, our men laid those who were wounded
under bushes and hedges. Others, having lost their own
weapons, took lances and swords from those who were
overcome, and the archers hastened to draw out the
arrows from the poor wretches who were half dead.
There was not one who was not wounded or worn out
in the great struggle, excepting only four hundred, who
kept the chief standard, and were being held in reserve
to meet the French king and his army.

After the dauphin was thus put to flight, a witness of
the battle came to the French king, and said: "My lord,

the field has fallen to the English, and my lord your son has retreated." Answering him, the king swore an inviolable oath that he would not desert the field that day, unless he were captured or slain or taken by force. Then the standard-bearers were ordered to advance, and they were followed by a very numerous armed force from the valley into the spacious field, where they showed themselves to our men. And they inspired such despair of victory that a man of great worth standing near the prince, cried out to him: "Alas, we are overcome!" But the prince, trusting in Christ and the Virgin Mother Mary, upbraided him thus: "You lie, you silly fool, if you blasphemously say that we shall be beaten while I am alive." Not only did the multitude of the enemy strike terror in our men, but also the thought of our notable inferiority in numbers. For many of our wounded had by necessity left the battle, almost all the rest were terribly fatigued, and the archers had used up all their arrows.

Meanwhile, Captain de la Buche, a most worthy man, as soon as he saw the army of the French march forth from their camp, got permission from the prince, and withdrew with sixty knights and a hundred archers, and many of our men thought they had fled. Because our men, except for the leaders, despaired of victory, they commended themselves wholly to God, and as if they valued life as nothing, considered only how they might not die alone and unavenged.

Then the prince ordered his standard-bearer, Sir Walter de Wodelonde, to advance against the enemy, and with a few fresh soldiers he went to meet the great army of the French king. Immediately the trumpets sound, one answering another, and the stone walls of Poitiers sound the echo to the woods, so that you would think that the hills had called out to the valleys, and that it had thundered in the clouds. Such great thunder did not lack terrible lightning, when the light shown on armour shining like gold. . . . Then the menacing company of crossbowmen brought the darkness of night on the field with a dense mass of arrows, which was beaten back by a deadly rain of arrows from the English phalanx, driven to fury by desperation. Out fly darts of ash, which greet the enemy from afar, but the French army, full of troops, their breasts protected by shields, turn away their faces from the missiles. Then the English archers, their quivers emptied in vain, armed only with swords and light shields, try to attack the heavily armed French, fervently desiring to yield themselves to death, which they think will end that day for them. Then the prince of Wales instantly rages, hewing the Frenchmen down with a sharp sword, and he breaks lances, parries blows, annihilates space, lifts up the fallen, and teaches the enemy how furious the desperation of battle can be.

In the meantime, Captain de la Buche marched around on one side, under the slope of the hill which, with the prince, he had left a little while before, and secretly going around the field, he came to the place where the French army lay. Then he ascended to the top of the hill by the path trodden by the French. So, breaking forth suddenly and unexpectedly, he showed by the venerated standards of St. George that he was one of ours. Then the courage of the prince fights to break the ranks of the French, before the captain should have attacked their flanks, which protected the French rear.

So . . . laying about him on every side, the prince, fighting in the midst of the French, breaks the enemy line. . . . The poor wretches, whom those fighting with de la Buche cut to pieces from behind, are attacked on every side, and our archers, placed for that purpose, wound them most cruelly. The whole battle order of the French is then broken. . . . But thrusting swiftly through their broken lines, and pushing aside the few soldiers still engaged in combat with the victors, Prince Edward directs fearful assaults on the king's guard, which still surrounded him, crowded together in a mighty wedge. Then the standards totter, the standard-bearers fall to the ground, some, eviscerated, tread on their own entrails, others vomit forth their teeth, some still standing have their arms cut off. The dying roll about in the blood of strangers, the fallen bodies groan, many are transfixed to the earth, and the proud spirits, abandoning their inert bodies, moan horribly. Servile blood and royal ran together in one stream, and near-by rivers ran red with the delicate nectar, so that the fishes were frightened. So the boar of Cornwall rages who "rejoices to have no other path but through streams of blood" to the French king's guard. Here is met the savage resistance of most courageous men. The English fight and the French strike back at them, and although their leader is of premature age, nevertheless, with the youthful fury of the beginner, he fights admirably, with the strength of two, cleaving the heads of some, and putting others to flight. He cuts off the heads of some, or beats in their faces, some he eviscerates, others he detruncates, showing in everything that he is no degenerate son of the royal line of France. But at length, as Fortune hastens to turn her wheel, the prince of Wales presses forward upon the enemy, and striking down the proud, as if with the savage generosity of a lion, he spares the beaten, and receives the surrender of the French king.

Meanwhile, the French, scattered through the broad fields of Poitiers and seeing their standard, the fleur-de-lys, beaten down, fled with all swiftness to the near-by city. But the English, however badly wounded or worn out from heavy labour, did not think first of the joy of life and victory, but pursued the fleeing French even to

the walls of Poitiers. There, in a very great and dangerous skirmish, they slew many of the beaten French, and
they would have killed many more, if they had not been
more eager to seize the price of their ransom, than to
obtain this chiefest triumph.

At last, when our men had been called back together
by the sound of the trumpet, pavilions and tents were
set up in the fields, and the whole company was quick
to give its attention to the care of the wounded, rest for
the weary, the safekeeping of prisoners, and the refreshment of the famished. Then, seeing that from their company men were absent because of the fighting, many
were chosen to seek out the living, or dutifully to bring
back the dead to the camp. . . .

From *Chronicon Galfridi le Baker*, E. M. Thompson, ed. (Oxford:
Clarendon Press, 1889); trans. M.M.M.

A Knight-Errant
of the Fifteenth Century

Jörg von Ehingen

Fifteenth century

I, Jörg von Ehingen [b. 1428], knight, was sent in
my youth as page to the Court at Innsbruck. At that
time a young prince of Austria, Duke Sigismund, held his
court there. He had married a queen of Scotland, and
I was ordered to serve her. After a time I became carver
and server of the dishes to this queen. But when I grew
older and came to man's estate, and began to be conscious of my strength, I thought myself too lowly employed, and proposed to attach myself to some active

prince, so that I might exercise myself in knightly matters and learn all the practices of knighthood, rather than remain in peace and pleasure at Innsbruck. Now, at that time, Duke Albert of Austria, brother of the Roman Emperor Frederick [III], had returned from the Eastern countries to Swabia and Upper Germany, and my late father assisted me with three horses to enter his service. This same Duke Albert had many worthy people about him, and kept a costly, princelike, and, indeed, a royal court. . . .

In that year it fell out that King Ladislaus, who was a prince of Austria and at the same time king of Hungary and Bohemia, caused himself to be crowned at Prague as king of Bohemia. Then my gracious master, Duke Albert, caused five hundred horses to be equipped, and the Margrave Albert of Brandenburg prepared himself also to accompany my master with three hundred horses. I reported these matters to my late father, and acquainted him with the course I had followed in accordance with his counsel, and of my present position. At this he was much pleased and said: "Dear son, I will fit you out well and honourably for this expedition in such a manner as becomes a knightly man, so that you may exercise yourself in all knightly matters and tournaments, and be prepared to take your place among your equals and superiors who have been dubbed knights, and so you shall return to your place." Accordingly I was provided with armour and cuirass, with stallions, horses, pages, clothes, and other things, and fitted out as a knight, and my gracious master was much pleased with what had been done. His grace was attended by a well-equipped train of many distinguished people. So the two princes rode with each other to Vienna in Austria, where they found King Ladislaus, who received them honourably. From Vienna the princes travelled with the king, who was attended by many powerful men from Hungary, Austria, and other lands thereto belonging, with a train of ten thousand horses, and thus he rode into Prague. But it would take too long to describe all the knightly sports and royal and costly displays which were seen at Vienna and on the road between that place and Prague. But King Ladislaus rode into Prague with many princes and lords, and his ten thousand horses, and was crowned king, and many counts, lords, and nobles were dubbed knights. Five members of my gracious master Duke Albert's train were knighted and accepted into the ranks of chivalry: Lord Jörg, Truchsess of Waldsee, Lord Bernhart of Bach, Lord Conrad of Ramstein, Lord Sigismund of Thun, and I, Jörg von Ehingen, knight. . . .

At this time [1454] my gracious master, Duke Albert, was with his court at Rottenburg-on-the-Neckar. I presented myself to his grace and was very graciously and well received by him, as well as by the courtiers and all the nobles and knights. The duke presented me also with the princely Order of the Salamander, and I remained a whole year with his grace at court, but my desire still was to follow the profession of knighthood. I was preferred by his grace above all other lords and nobles, and became his chief chamberlain. It happened in that year that his grace spoke frequently with me on many matters touching on my sea journeys, and I made his grace aware of my desire, that as soon as I heard of a worthy expedition of knights to attach myself to them, with his gracious consent, and to follow their fortunes, carrying myself therein in such wise as to bring distinction to his grace's name. With this the duke was well content. But at that time there were, so far as I could learn, no warlike disturbances in the country of any king or prince, for peace prevailed in all the kingdoms of the Christian

world. And I began to think that it was useless for me to
waste my time thus sitting still, for my gracious master
also had then no particular business in hand, and spent
the time at his court at Rottenburg or at Freiburg very
pleasantly in racing, tourneys, and dancing, and suchlike
pastimes, wherein I also took part as best I could, and
applied myself very diligently thereto. For my late father said always that slothfulness was a great vice in
young and old. I hoped also by such exercises to obtain
practice and facility which would profit me in my
knightly undertakings and be very serviceable to me, for
I contemplated visiting the most famous kingdoms of
Christendom, intending to wander from one country to
another until I met with serious and important affairs.

From *The Diary of Jörg von Ehingen*, trans. M. Letts (London:
Oxford University Press, H. Milford, 1929).

The Rules of Courtly Love
ANDREAS CAPELLANUS

Twelfth century

LOVE is a certain inborn suffering derived from the
sight of and excessive meditation upon the beauty
of the opposite sex, which causes each one to wish above
all things the embraces of the other and by common desire to carry out all of love's precepts in the other's embrace.

THE RULES

I. Marriage is no real excuse for not loving.
II. He who is not jealous cannot love.

III. No one can be bound by a double love.

IV. It is well known that love is always increasing or decreasing.

V. That which a lover takes against the will of his beloved has no relish.

VI. Boys do not love until they arrive at the age of maturity.

VII. When one lover dies, a widowhood of two years is required of the survivor.

VIII. No one should be deprived of love without the very best of reasons.

IX. No one can love unless he is impelled by the persuasion of love.

X. Love is always a stranger in the home of avarice.

XI. It is not proper to love any woman whom one would be ashamed to seek to marry.

XII. A true lover does not desire to embrace in love anyone except his beloved.

XIII. When made public love rarely endures.

XIV. The easy attainment of love makes it of little value; difficulty of attainment makes it prized

XV. Every lover regularly turns pale in the presence of his beloved.

XVI. When a lover suddenly catches sight of his beloved his heart palpitates.

XVII. A new love puts to flight an old one.

XVIII. Good character alone makes any man worthy of love.

XIX. If love diminishes, it quickly fails and rarely revives.

XX. A man in love is always apprehensive.

XXI. Real jealousy always increases the feeling of love.

XXII. Jealousy, and therefore love, are increased when one suspects his beloved.

XXIII. He whom the thought of love vexes eats and sleeps very little.

XXIV. Every act of a lover ends in the thought of his beloved.

XXV. A true lover considers nothing good except what he thinks will please his beloved.

XXVI. Love can deny nothing to love.

XXVII. A lover can never have enough of the solaces of his beloved.

XXVIII. A slight presumption causes a lover to suspect his beloved.

XXIX. A man who is vexed by too much passion usually does not love.

XXX. A true lover is constantly and without intermission possessed by the thought of his beloved.

XXXI. Nothing forbids one woman being loved by two men or one man by two women.

From *The Art of Courtly Love*, trans. J. J. Parry (New York: Columbia University Press, 1941).

A Noble Household

JEAN FROISSART

Fourteenth century

ON ENTERING his presence the count received me most handsomely, and retained me in his household. Our acquaintance was strengthened by my having brought with me a book which I had made at the desire of Winceslaus of Bohemia, duke of Luxembourg and Brabant; in which book, called *Le Meliador*, are contained all the songs, ballads, roundelays, and virelays, which that gentle duke had composed. Every night after supper I read out to the count parts of it, during which time he and all present preserved the greatest silence; and when any passages were not perfectly clear, the count himself discussed them with me, not in his Gascon language, but in very good French.

I shall now tell you several particulars respecting the count and his household. Count Gascon Phoebus de Foix, at the time of which I am speaking, was about fifty-nine years old; and although I have seen very many knights, squires, kings, princes, and others, I never saw any one so handsome. He was so perfectly formed that no one could praise him too much. He loved earnestly the things he ought to love, and hated those which it became him to hate. He was a prudent knight, full of enterprise and wisdom. He never allowed any men of abandoned character to be about him, reigned prudently, and was constant at his devotions. There were regular nocturnals from the psalter, prayers from the rituals to the Virgin, to the Holy Ghost, and from the burial service. He had, every day, distributed, as alms at his gate, five florins, in small coin, to all comers. He was liberal and courteous in his gifts, and well knew how to take and how to give back. He loved dogs above all other animals; and during summer and winter amused himself much with hunting. He never indulged in any foolish works or ridiculous extravagances, and took account every month of the amount of his expenditure. He chose twelve of the most able of his subjects to receive and administer his finances, two serving two months each, and one of them acting as comptroller. He had certain coffers in his apartment, whence he took money to give to different knights, squires, or gentlemen, when they came to wait on him, for none ever left him without a gift. He was easy of access to all, and entered very freely into discourse, though laconic in his advice and in his answers. He employed four secretaries to write and copy his letters, and these were to be in readiness as soon as he left his room. He called them neither John, Walter, nor William, but his good-for-nothings, to whom he gave his letters, after he had read them, to copy or to do anything else which he might command. In such manner lived the Count de Foix. When he quitted his chamber at midnight for supper, twelve servants bore each a lighted torch before him. The hall was full of knights and squires, and there were plenty of tables laid out for any who chose to sup. No one spoke to him at table unless he first began the conversation. He ate heartily of poultry, but only the wings and thighs. He had great pleasure in hearing minstrels, being himself a proficient in the science. He remained at table about two hours, and was pleased whenever fanciful dishes were served up to him—not that he desired to partake of them, but having seen them, he immediately sent them to the tables of his knights and squires. In short, everything considered, though I had before been in several courts, I never was at one which pleased me more, nor was ever anywhere more delighted with feats of arms. Knights and squires were to be seen in every chamber, hall, and court, conversing on arms and armour. Everything honourable was to be found there. All intelligence from distant countries was there to be learnt; for the gallantry of the count had brought together visitors from all parts of the world.

From *Chronicles*, trans. T. Johnes (Everyman's Library [1906]).

Offices in a Noble Household

JOHN RUSSELL

Fifteenth century

THE duty of a chamberlain is to be diligent in office,
neatly clad, his clothes not torn, hands and face well
washed and head well kempt.

He must be ever careful—not negligent—of fire and
candle. And look you give diligent attendance to your
master, be courteous, glad of cheer, quick of hearing
in every way, and be ever on the lookout for things to
do him pleasure; if you will acquire these qualities, it
may advance you well.

See that your lord has a clean shirt and hose, a short
coat, a doublet, and a long coat, if he wear such, his
hose well brushed, his socks at hand, his shoes or slippers
as brown as a water-leech.

In the morning, against your lord shall rise, take care
that his linen be clean, and warm it at a clear fire, not
smoky, if [the weather] be cold or freezing.

When he rises make ready the foot-sheet, and forget
not to place a chair or some other seat with a cushion
on it before the fire, with another cushion for the feet.
Over the cushion and chair spread this sheet so as to
cover them; and see that you have a kerchief and a comb
to comb your lord's head before he is fully dressed.

Then pray your lord in humble words to come to a
good fire and array him thereby, and there to sit or
stand pleasantly; and wait with due manners to assist
him. First hold out to him his tunic, then his doublet
while he puts in his arms, and have his stomacher well

aired to keep off harm, as also his vamps and socks, and so shall he go warm all day.

Then draw on his socks and his hose by the fire, and lace or buckle his shoes, draw his hosen on well and truss them up to the height that suits him, lace his doublet in every hole, and put round his neck and on his shoulders a kerchief; and then gently comb his head with an ivory comb, and give him water wherewith to wash his hands and face. . . .

If your lord wishes to bathe and wash his body clean, hang sheets round the roof, every one full of flowers and sweet green herbs, and have five or six sponges to sit or lean upon, and see that you have one big sponge to sit upon, and a sheet over so that he may bathe there for a while, and have a sponge also for under his feet, if there be any to spare, and always be careful that the door is shut. Have a basin full of hot fresh herbs and wash his body with a soft sponge, rinse him with fair warm rose-water, and throw it over him; then let him go to bed; but see that the bed be sweet and nice; and first put on his socks and slippers that he may go near the fire and stand on his foot-sheet, wipe him dry with a clean cloth, and take him to bed to cure his troubles. . . .

An usher or marshal, without fail, must know all the estates of the Church, and the excellent estate of a king with his honourable blood. This is a notable nurture, cunning, curious, and commendable.

The estate of the pope has no peer, an emperor is next him everywhere and a king is correspondent, a high cardinal next in dignity, then a king's son (ye call him prince), an archbishop his equal; a duke of the blood royal; a bishop, marquis, and earl coequal; a viscount, legate, baron, suffragan, and mitred abbot; a baron of the exchequer, the three chief justices, and the mayor of

London; a cathedral prior, unmitred abbot, and knight bachelor; a prior, dean, archdeacon, knight, and body esquire; the master of the rolls (as I reckon aright), and puisne judge; clerk of the crown and the exchequer, and you may pleasantly prefer the mayor of Calais.

A provincial, doctor of divinity, and prothonotary may dine together; and you may place the pope's legate or collector with a doctor of both laws. An ex-mayor of London ranks with a serjeant-at-law, next a master of chancery, and then a worshipful preacher of pardons, masters of arts, and religious orders, parsons and vicars, and parish priests with a cure, the bailiffs of a city, a yeoman of the crown, and serjeant-of-arms with his mace, with him a herald, the king's herald in the first place, worshipful merchants and rich artificers, gentlemen well-nurtured and of good manners, together with gentlewomen and lords' foster-mothers—all these may eat with squires.

From "Book of Nurture" in *The Babees' Book*, trans. E. Rickert (London: Chatto and Windus, 1923).

Private Lives of the English Gentry

AN ENGLISH SCHOOLBOY, C. 1380

SIRE and God's servant: Know, if you please, that I have seen your son Edmund and have observed his condition for two nights and a day. His illness grows less from day to day, and he is no longer in bed; but when the fever returns, he lies somewhat ill for about two hours, after which he rises and, according to the demands of the time, goes to school and eats and walks about, well and happy, so that there seems to be nothing dangerous in his condition. And of his own accord he sent his respects to you and to his lady, and his greetings to the others. He is beginning to learn Donatus slowly and modestly, as is proper. He has that copy of Donatus which I feared was lost. Truly I have never seen a boy have such care as he has had during his illness. The master and his wife desire that some of his clothes should be left home, because he has far too many and fewer would suffice, and it is possible that, through no fault of theirs, his clothes might easily become torn and spoiled. I send to you descriptive titles of the books contained in one volume which the owner will not sell for less than twelve shillings; in my opinion and that of others, it is worth that. And if he sells it, he wants to be paid promptly. So, if you please, send me by your boy a reply concerning your wishes about these things. Farewell, in the power of Christ and in the merits of the Virgin and Mother Mary, from your devoted

Brother Edmund

To the honourable Sir Edmund de Stonor.

THE FURNISHINGS OF AN ENGLISH MANOR HOUSE, 1474

Also these are permanent furnishings of Stonor that shall remain in the Manor of Stonor from heir to heir.

First, one standing cup of silver gilded with a covering and two images in the bottom. Likewise, the companion piece of the same cup, gilded without a foot. Likewise a great Bowl of silver with the arms of Stonor and Kyrkeby on the bottom.

Also this is the stuff that is left within the manor of Stonor that shall remain in the said manor from heir to heir. First, in the hall a pair of cobirons left there for permanent furniture. Also, the same hall hung with black say [fine cloth, like serge]. Also, the little chamber annexed to the parlour, the hanging there of striped cloth, purple and green. Also, three chambers hung with striped say, red and green, with a bed of the same. Also, the chamber at the lower end of the hall is hung with green worsted, and the hanging for a bed of white. Also, for the bed in the parlour chamber two pairs of blankets, a pair of sheets, and a red coverlet with green chaplets. Also, a feather bed, which the said Jane Stoner left there in loan to the said chamber. Also, a green coverlet with pots and ostrich feathers, in the same chamber; a pair of sheets, one pair of blankets, and a mattress for the truckle bed in the same chamber. Also, an andiron for the same chamber, and a tin basin. Also, one fire fork for the hall. Also, a chafing-dish of latten [an alloy similar to brass]. Also, two plain chains. Also, one turned chain, two cushions covered with grey skins. Also, two cushions covered with red worsted. Also, two cushions of tapestry work with knots.

Also, in the buttery is left one basin and an ewer of latten. Also, one basin and ewer of tin. Also, a chafing-dish of latten. Also, five canisters of latten. Also, two table cloths of diaper. Also, a long tablecloth and a short. Also, a cupboard cloth with three towels, and one trencher knife, and three leather pots, and two salts of tin. Also, in the kitchen, two large pots, one medium pot, one little pot, two hanging racks for pots, two costrels [a bottle or wooden keg with ears by which it could be hung], two racks to rest them on, two large gridirons, two old pans, two frying pans, and one stone mortar, one broad grate, one large spit, one medium spit, one bird spit, two dressing knives, one meat axe, one wood axe, one meathook, one skimmer of latten, a wooden scale . . . one set of pewter vessels. Also in the backhouse there is left one mashing vat, one eel-tub, seven covers, nine barrels, one large cauldron, one trivet, two bolting-pipes [vessels for sifting meal], one cable, one axe, one wedge of iron.

Likewise, five jacks, three sallets [a light head-piece], two glaives [spears or halberds], and a boar-spear.

A LOVE LETTER, 1476

My own heartily beloved Cousin Katherine, I recommend myself to you with all the inwardness of my heart. And now you shall understand that I lately received a token from you, which was and is right heartily welcome to me, and with glad will I received it. And besides that I had a letter from Howlake, your gentle squire, by which I understand right well that you are in good health of body, and merry at heart. And I pray God heartly to His pleasure to continue the same; for it is to me a very great comfort that you are so, so help me Jesus. And if you would be a good eater of your meat always, so that you might wax and grow fast to be a woman, you should make me the gladdest man in the world, by my troth. For when I remember your favour and your sober loving conduct towards me, truly you make me very glad and joyous in my heart, and on the other hand again when I remember your youth— And therefore I pray you, my own sweet Cousin, even as you love me, to be merry and to eat your meat like a woman. And if you will do so for my love, whatever you desire of me, by my troth, I promise you by the help of our Lord to perform it if I can. I can say no more now, but when I come home, I will tell you much more, between you and me and before God. And when you, full womanly and like a lover, remember me with manifold recommendations in diverse manners, sending the same to my discretion to distribute as I see fit, forsooth, my own sweet Cousin, you know that with good heart and good will I receive and take to myself one half of them, and those I will keep by me, and the other half with hearty love and favour I send to you, my own sweet Cousin, to keep with you; and besides I send you the blessing that our Lady gave her dear Son, to fare well always.

I pray you, greet well my horse, and ask him to give you four of his years to help you, and when I come home I will give him four of my years and four horse loaves to make up for it. Tell him that I asked him this. And, Cousin Katherine, I thank you for him, and my wife shall thank you for him hereafter, for I am told that you take great pains with him. My own sweet cousin, I heard lately that you were in Calais to look for me, but you could not see me or find me; truly you might have come to my counter, and there you would have found me and seen me, and not have failed to find me. But you looked for me in a wrong Calais. . . . I pray you, gentle Cousin, commend me to the Clock, and ask him to amend his unthrifty manners, for he always strikes in undue time, and he will always be ahead, and that is an unsatisfactory condition. Tell him that unless he amends his condition, he will cause strangers to avoid him and come there no more. I trust that he will improve before my coming, which will be shortly, with all hands and all feet, with God's grace. My very faithful Cousin, I trust that though I have not remembered my right worshipful mistress your mother before in this letter, you will of your gentleness recommend me to her as many times as you like. And you may say, if you please, that in Whitsun Week next I plan to go to the market. And I trust you will pray for me, for I shall pray for you, and, it may be, none so well. And Almighty Jesus make you a good woman and send you many good years and long, to live in health and virtue to His pleasure. At great

Calais on this side of the sea, the first day of June, when every man had gone to his dinner, and the Clock struck nine, and all our household called after me and bade me come down: "Come to dinner at once!" and what answer I gave them you know of old.

By your faithful Cousin and lover Thomas Betson. I send you this ring for a token.

To my faithful and heartily Beloved Cousin Katherine Riche at Stonor this letter is delivered in haste.

A WIFE TO HER HUSBAND, 1476

Right entirely and best beloved husband: I recommend myself to you in the most loving way that I can or may. Moreover, may it please you to know that I have received your letter, and a bill enclosed in the same letter which I have read and understood right well; and as for all such stuff as the bill specifies, I have not as yet received it. Nevertheless the barge is coming with the said stuff tonight at seven o'clock, and so, Sir, it will be morning before I can receive it. Furthermore, Sir, may it please you to know that on last Friday I dined with my father and my mother. And there were at dinner with them the friends of the boy who was proposed for one of my daughters when you were last here. And so after dinner they made their communication on the said matter, whereby I understood how they were disposed in this matter. And truly it was not at all as it was spoken of in the beginning; wherefore I answered in this way, that though she were my child, as she is, I could not answer this matter without you, and would do nothing. Nevertheless, I answered in your behalf that I knew right well that you would be a right kind and loving father, if God designs that you and they should deal. And at what you write, that the bargemen are loath to take and receive any stuff of ours, I marvel greatly; for truly I never had anything carried by any of them, but that I paid them truly for it. And Sir, as for the six pair of dried cod which you write for, they shall be bought and sent you right shortly. And as for your gowns of camlet and doublets of silk, I have bought them, and they will please you right well at your coming, I trust to God. And Sir, my son Betson recommends himself to you, and he came home on Monday last, and has brought with him, blessed be God, good tidings, which he and I shall tell you when you come. And as you write that you will send me a wild boar and other venison for Sunday, I thank you as heartily as I can. But truly I would yet pray you to speed hither as soon as you can; for I would trust to God's mercy it should be to your profit and avail in time to come, by the grace of our Lord, who preserve and keep you ever to His pleasure and your heart's comfort. Amen. At London the xi day of December. . . .

And Cousin, when you wrote me I had no leisure; truly I have been sick and busy, or else I would have written to you before this.

By your own Elizabeth Stonor.

To my right well beloved Cousin, Willian Stoner, esquire at Stoner, this be delivered.

From *The Stonor Letters and Papers,* C. L. Kingsford, ed. (London: Camden Society, 3rd series, vols. 29 and 30, nos. 30, 140, 166, 176; 1919); trans. M.M.M.

THE PEASANTS AND BURGHERS:
THE WORKERS

The Feet of the Commonwealth

JOHN OF SALISBURY

Twelfth century

THOSE are called the feet who discharge the humbler offices, and by whose services the members of the whole commonwealth walk upon solid earth. Among these are to be counted the husbandmen, who always cleave to the soil, busied about their plough-lands or vineyards or pastures or flower-gardens. To these must be added the many species of cloth-making, and the mechanic arts, which work in wood, iron, bronze, and the different metals; also the menial occupations, and the manifold forms of getting a livelihood and sustaining life, or increasing household property, all of which, while they do not pertain to the authority of the governing power, are yet in the highest degree useful and profitable to the corporate whole of the commonwealth. All these different occupations are so numerous that the commonwealth in the number of its feet exceeds not only the eight-footed crab but even the centipede, and because of their very multitude they cannot be enumerated; for while they are not infinite by nature, they are yet of so many different varieties that no writer on the subject of offices or duties has ever laid down particular precepts for each special variety. But it applies generally to each and all of them that in their exercise they should not transgress the limits of the law, and should in all things observe constant reference to the public utility. For inferiors owe it to their superiors to provide them with service, just as the superiors in their turn owe it to their inferiors to provide them with all things needful for their protection and succour.

From *Policraticus*, trans. J. Dickinsón.

The Duties of Manorial Officers

Thirteenth century

THE OFFICE OF SENESCHAL

THE seneschal of lands ought to be prudent and faithful and profitable, and he ought to know the law of the realm to protect his lord's business and to instruct and give assurance to the bailiffs who are beneath him in their difficulties. He ought two or three times a year to make his rounds and visit the manors of his stewardship, and then he ought to inquire about the rents, services, and customs, hidden or withdrawn, and about franchises of courts, lands, woods, meadows, pastures, waters, mills, and other things which belong to the manor and are done away with without warrant, by whom, and how: and if he be able let him amend these things in the right way without doing wrong to any, and if he be not, let him show it to his lord, that he may deal with it if he wish to maintain his right.

The seneschal ought, at his first coming to the manors, to cause all the demesne lands of each to be measured by true men, and he ought to know by the perch of the country how many acres there are in each field, and thereby he can know how much wheat, rye, barley, oats, peas, beans, and dredge one ought by right to sow in each acre, and thereby can one see if the provost or the hayward account for more seed than is right, and thereby can he see how many ploughs are required on the manor, for each plough ought by right to plough nine score acres, that is to say: sixty for winter seed, sixty for spring seed, and sixty in fallow. Also he can see how many acres ought to be ploughed yearly by boon or custom, and how many acres remain to be tilled by the ploughs of the manor. And further he can see how many acres ought to be reaped by boon and custom, and how many for money. And if there be any cheating in the sowing, or ploughing, or reaping, he shall easily see it. And he must cause all the meadows and several pastures to be measured by acres, and thereby can one know the cost, and how much hay is necessary every year for the sustenance of the manor, and how much stock can be kept on the several pastures, and how much on the common. . . .

THE OFFICE OF BAILIFF

The bailiff ought to be faithful and profitable, and a good husbandman, and also prudent, that he need not send to his lord or superior seneschal to have advice and instruction about everything connected with his baillie, unless it be an extraordinary matter, or of great danger; for a bailiff is worth little in time of need who knows nothing, and has nothing in himself without the instruction of another. The bailiff ought to rise every morning and survey the woods, corn, meadows, and pastures, and see what damage may have been done. And he ought to see that the ploughs are yoked in the morning, and unyoked at the right time, so that they may do their proper ploughing every day, as much as they can and ought to do by the measured perch. And he must cause the land to be marled, folded, manured, improved, and amended as his knowledge may approve, for the good and bettering of the manor. He ought to see how many measured acres the boon-tenants and customary-tenants ought to plough yearly, and how many the ploughs of the manor ought to till, and so he may lessen the surplus of the cost. And he ought to see and know how many acres of meadow the customary-tenants ought to mow and make, and how many acres of corn the boon-tenants and customary-tenants ought to reap and carry, and thereby he can see how many acres of meadow remain to be mowed, and how many acres of corn remain to be reaped for money, so that nothing shall be wrongfully paid for. And he ought to forbid any provost or bedel or hayward or any other servant of the manor to ride on, or lend, or ill-treat the cart-horses or others. And he ought to see that the horses and oxen and all the stock are well kept, and that no other animals graze in or eat their pasture. . . .

THE OFFICE OF PROVOST

The provost ought to be elected and presented by the common consent of the township, as the best husbandman and the best approver among them. And he must see that all the servants of the court rise in the morning to do their work, and that the ploughs be yoked in time, and the lands well ploughed and cropped, and turned over, and sown with good and clean seed, as much as they can stand. And he ought to see that there be a good fold of wooden hurdles on the demesne, strewed within every night to improve the land. . . .

Let no provost remain over a year as provost, if he

be not proved most profitable and faithful in his doings, and a good husbandman. Each provost ought every year to account with his bailiff, and tally the works and customs commuted in the manor, whereby he can surely answer in money for the surplus in the account, for the money for customs is worth as much as rent. . . .

THE OFFICE OF HAYWARD

The hayward ought to be an active and sharp man, for he must, early and late, look after and go round and keep the woods, corn, and meadows and other things belonging to his office, and he ought to make attachments and approvements faithfully, and make the delivery by pledge before the provost, and deliver them to the bailiff to be heard. And he ought to sow the lands, and be over the ploughers and harrowers at the time of each sowing. And he ought to make all the boon-tenants and customary-tenants who are bound and accustomed to come, do so, to do the work they ought to do. And in haytime he ought to be over the mowers, the making, and the carrying, and in August assemble the reapers and the boon-tenants and the labourers and see that the corn be properly and cleanly gathered; and early and late watch so that nothing be stolen or eaten by beasts or spoilt. . . .

THE OFFICE OF PLOUGHMEN

The ploughmen ought to be men of intelligence, and ought to know how to sow, and how to repair and mend broken ploughs and harrows, and to till the land well, and crop it rightly; and they ought to know also how to yoke and drive the oxen, without beating or hurting them, and they ought to forage them well, and look well after the forage that it be not stolen nor carried off; and they ought to keep them safely in meadows and several pastures, and other beasts which are found therein they ought to impound. . . .

THE OFFICE OF WAGGONERS

The waggoner ought to know his trade, to keep the horses and curry them, and to load and carry without danger to his horses, that they may not be overloaded or overworked, or overdriven, or hurt, and he must know how to mend his harness and the gear of the waggon. And the bailiff and provost ought to see and know how many times the waggoners can go in a day to carry marl or manure, or hay or corn, or timber or firewood, without great stress; and as many times as they can go in a day, the waggoners must answer for each day at the end of the week. . . .

THE OFFICE OF COWHERD

The cowherd ought to be skilful, knowing his business and keeping his cows well, and foster the calves well from time of weaning. And he must see that he has fine bulls and large and of good breed pastured with the cows, to mate when they will. And that no cow be milked or suckle her calf after Michaelmas, to make cheese of rewain; for this milking and this rewain make the cows lose flesh and become weak, and will make them mate later another year, and the milk is better and the cow poorer. . . .

And every night the cowherd shall put the cows and other beasts in the fold during the season, and let the fold be well strewed with litter or fern, as is said above, and he himself shall lie each night with his cows. . . .

THE OFFICE OF SWINEHERD

The swineherd ought to be on those manors where swine can be sustained and kept in the forest, or in woods, or waste, or in marshes, without sustenance from the grange; and if the swine can be kept with little sustenance from the grange during hard frost, then must a pigsty be made in a marsh or wood, where the swine may be night and day. . . .

THE OFFICE OF SHEPHERD

Each shepherd ought to find good pledges to answer for his doings and for good and faithful service, although he be companion to the miller. And he must cover his fold and enclose it with hurdles and mend it within and without, and repair the hurdles and make them. And he ought to sleep in the fold, he and his dog; and he ought to pasture his sheep well, and keep them in forage, and watch them well, so that they be not killed or destroyed by dogs or stolen or lost or changed, nor let them pasture in moors or dry places or bogs, to get sickness and disease for lack of guard. No shepherd ought to leave his sheep to go to fairs, or markets, or wrestling matches, or wakes, or to the tavern, without taking leave or asking it, or without putting a good keeper in his place to keep the sheep, that no harm may arise from his fault. . . .

THE OFFICE OF DAIRYMAID

The dairymaid ought to be faithful and of good repute, and keep herself clean, and ought to know her business and all that belongs to it. She ought not to allow any under-dairymaid or another to take or carry away milk, or butter, or cream, by which the cheese shall be less and the dairy impoverished. And she ought to know well how to make cheese and salt cheese, and she ought to save and keep the vessels of the dairy, that it need not be necessary to buy new ones every year. . . .

The dairymaid ought to help to winnow the corn when she can be present, and she ought to take care of the geese and hens and answer for the returns and keep and cover the fire, that no harm arise from lack of guard.

From *Seneschaucie*, trans. E. Lamond (London, New York: Longmans Green, 1890).

The Peasant's Life
WILLIAM LANGLAND

Fourteenth century

"Can you serve," he said, "or sing in churches,
Or cock hay in my harvest, or handle a hay-fork,
Mow or mound it or makes sheaves or bindings,
Reap, or be an head reaper, and rise early,
Or have an horn and be an hayward, and be out till
    morning,
And keep my corn in my croft from pickers and stealers?
Or make shoes, or sew cloth, or tend sheep or cattle,
Or make hedges, or harrow, or drive geese, or be swine-
    herd?
Or can you work at any craft which the commune calls
    for,
To be means of livelihood to the bed-ridden?"

• • •

"I have no penny," said Piers, "to buy pullets,
Nor geese nor pigs, but two green cheeses,
A few curds of cream, a cake of oatmeal,
Two loaves of beans and bran, baked for my children;
And, by my soul, I swear I have no salt bacon,
Nor cook to make collops, I take Christ to witness!

But I have parsley and pot herbs and a plenty of cab-
    bages,
And a cow and a calf, and a cart mare
To draw my dung afield till the drought is over.
This is the little we must live on till the Lammas season.
And then I hope to have my harvest in the garner.
And then I may spread your supper to my soul's con-
    tent."

So all the poor people fetched peascods,
And brought him beans and baked apples by the lapful,
Ripe cherries, chervils and many small onions,
And offered Piers the present to please Hunger.

· · ·

The needy are our neighbours, if we note rightly;
As prisoners in cells, or poor folk in hovels,
Charged with children and overcharged by landlords.
What they may spare in spinning they spend on rental,
On milk, or on meal to make porridge
To still the sobbing of the children at meal time.
Also they themselves suffer much hunger.
They have woe in winter time, and wake at midnight
To rise and to rock the cradle at the bedside,
To card and to comb, to darn clouts and to wash them,
To rub and to reel and to put rushes on the paving.
The woe of these women who dwell in hovels
Is too sad to speak of or to say in rhyme.
And many other men have much to suffer
From hunger and from thirst; they turn the fair side
    outward,
For they are abashed to beg, lest it should be acknowl-
    edged
At their neighbours what they need at noon and even.

I know all this well; for the world has taught me
What befalls another who has many children,
With no claim but his craft to clothe and feed them,
When the mouths are many and the money scarce.
They have bread and penny ale in place of a pittance,
And cold flesh and cold fish for venison from the
     butcher.
On Fridays and fast days a farthing worth of mussels
Would be a feast for such folk, with a few cockles.
It were an alms to help all with such burdens,
And to comfort such cottagers and crooked men and
     blind folk.

From *The Vision of Piers Plowman*, trans. H. W. Wells (New York: Sheed and Ward, 1935).

The Making of a Merchant: St. Godric of Finchale

REGINALD OF DURHAM

Twelfth century

THIS holy man's father was named Ailward, and his mother Edwenna; both of slender rank and wealth, but abundant in righteousness and virtue. They were born in Norfolk, and had long lived in the township called Walpole. . . . When the boy had passed his childish years quietly at home, then, as he began to grow to manhood, he began to follow more prudent ways of life, and to learn carefully and persistently the teachings of worldly forethought. Wherefore he chose not to follow the life of a husbandman, but rather to study, learn, and exercise the rudiments of more subtle conceptions. For this reason, aspiring to the merchant's trade, he began to follow the chapman's way of life, first learning how to gain in small bargains and things of insignificant price; and thence, while yet a youth, his mind advanced little by little to buy and sell and gain from things of greater expense. For, in his beginnings, he was wont to wander with small wares around the villages and farmsteads of his own neighbourhood; but, in process of time, he gradually associated himself by compact with city merchants. Hence, within a brief space of time, the youth who had trudged for many weary hours from village to village, from farm to farm, did so profit by his increase of age and wisdom as to travel with associates of his own age through towns and boroughs, fortresses and cities, to fairs and to all the various booths of the market-place, in pursuit of his public chaffer. He went along the highway, neither puffed up by the good testimony of his conscience nor downcast in the nobler part of his soul by the reproach of poverty. . . .

Seeing that he then dwelt by the seashore, he went down one day to the strand to seek for some means of livelihood. . . . The place is called Wellstream, hard by the town of Spalding; there, when the tide was out, the country-folk were wont to scour and explore the stretches of sand, discovering and converting to their own use whatever wreckage or drift the sea might have brought to shore; for hence they sometimes get wealth, since they are free to seize there upon whatsoever goods or commodities they may find by the shore. The saint, then, inspired by such hopes, roamed one day over these stretches of foreshore; and, finding nothing at first, he followed on and on to a distance of three miles, where he found three porpoises lying high and dry, either cast upon the sands by the waves or left there by the ebb-tide. Two were still alive and struggling: the third, in the midst, was dead or dying. Moved with pity, he left the living untouched, cut a portion from the dead fish, and began carrying this away upon his back. But the tide soon began to flow; and Godric, halting under his burden, was overtaken by the waves; first they wet his feet, then his legs; then his upper body was compassed about by the deep; at length the waters went even over his head; yet Godric, strong in faith, bare his burden onwards even under the waves, until, by God's help, he struggled out upon the very shore from which he had gone forth. Then, bringing the fish to his parents, he told them the whole tale, and exhorted them to declare the glory of God. . . .

Yet in all things he walked with simplicity; and, in so far as he yet knew how, it was ever his pleasure to follow in the footsteps of the truth. For, having learned the Lord's Prayer and the Creed from his very cradle, he oftentimes turned them over in his mind, even as he went alone on his longer journeys; and, in so far as the truth was revealed to his mind, he clung thereunto most devoutly in all his thoughts concerning God. At first, he lived as a chapman for four years in Lincolnshire, going on foot and carrying the smallest wares; then he travelled abroad, first to St. Andrews in Scotland and then for the first time to Rome. On his return, having formed a familiar friendship with certain other young men who were eager for merchandise, he began to launch upon bolder courses and to coast frequently by sea to the foreign lands that lay around him. Thus, sailing often to and fro between Scotland and Britain, he traded in many divers wares and, amid these occupations, learned much worldly wisdom. . . . He fell into many perils of the sea, yet by God's mercy he was never wrecked; for He who had upheld St. Peter as he walked

upon the waves, by that same strong right arm kept this
His chosen vessel from all misfortune amid these perils.
Thus, having learned by frequent experience his wretchedness amid such dangers, he began to worship certain
of the saints with more ardent zeal, venerating and calling upon their shrines, and giving himself up by whole-
hearted service to those holy names. In such invocations his prayers were oftentimes answered by prompt
consolation; some of which prayers he learned from
his fellows with whom he shared these frequent perils;
others he collected from faithful hearsay; others again
from the custom of the place, for he saw and visited
such holy places with frequent assiduity. Thus aspiring
ever higher and higher, and yearning upward with his
whole heart, at length his great labours and cares bore
much fruit of worldly gain. For he laboured not only as
a merchant but also as a shipman . . . to Denmark and
Flanders and Scotland; in all which lands he found
certain rare, and therefore more precious, wares, which
he carried to other parts wherein he knew them to be
least familiar, and coveted by the inhabitants beyond
the price of gold itself; wherefore he exchanged these
wares for others coveted by men of other lands; and
thus he chaffered most freely and assiduously. Hence
he made great profit in all his bargains, and gathered
much wealth in the sweat of his brow; for he sold dear
in one place the wares which he had bought elsewhere
at a small price.

Then he purchased the half of a merchant-ship with
certain of his partners in the trade; and again by his
prudence he bought the fourth part of another ship. At
length, by his skill in navigation, wherein he excelled
all his fellows, he earned promotion to the post of
steersman. . . .

For he was vigorous and strenuous in mind, whole of

limb and strong in body. He was of middle stature, broad-shouldered and deep-chested, with a long face, grey eyes most clear and piercing, bushy brows, a broad forehead, long and open nostrils, a nose of comely curve, and a pointed chin. His beard was thick, and longer than the ordinary, his mouth well-shaped, with lips of moderate thickness; in youth his hair was black, in age as white as snow; his neck was short and thick, knotted with veins and sinews; his legs were somewhat slender, his instep high, his knees hardened and horny with frequent kneeling; his whole skin rough beyond the ordinary, until all this roughness was softened by old age. . . . In labour he was strenuous, assiduous above all men; and, when by chance his bodily strength proved insufficient, he compassed his ends with great ease by the skill which his daily labours had given, and by a prudence born of long experience. . . . He knew, from the aspect of sea and stars, how to foretell fair or foul weather. In his various voyages he visited many saints' shrines, to whose protection he was wont most devoutly to commend himself; more especially the church of St. Andrew in Scotland, where he most frequently made and paid his vows. On the way thither, he oftentimes touched at the island of Lindisfarne, wherein St. Cuthbert had been bishop, and at the isle of Farne, where that saint had lived as an anchoret, and where St. Godric (as he himself would tell afterwards) would meditate on the saint's life with abundant tears. Thence he began to yearn for solitude, and to hold his merchandise in less esteem than heretofore. . . .

And now he had lived sixteen years as a merchant, and began to think of spending on charity, to God's honour and service, the goods which he had so laboriously acquired. He therefore took the cross as a pilgrim to Jerusalem, and, having visited the Holy Sepulchre, came back to England by way of St. James [of Compostella]. Not long afterwards he became steward to a certain rich man of his own country, with the care of his whole house and household. But certain of the younger household were men of iniquity, who stole their neighbours' cattle and thus held luxurious feasts, whereat Godric, in his ignorance, was sometimes present. Afterwards, discovering the truth, he rebuked and admonished them to cease; but they made no account of his warnings; wherefore he concealed not their iniquity, but disclosed it to the lord of the household, who, however, slighted his advice. Wherefore he begged to be dismissed and went on a pilgrimage, first to St. Gilles and thence to Rome the abode of the Apostles, that thus he might knowingly pay the penalty for those misdeeds wherein he had ignorantly partaken. I have often seen him, even in his old age, weeping for this unknowing transgression. . . .

On his return from Rome, he abode awhile in his father's house; until, inflamed again with holy zeal, he purposed to revisit the abode of the Apostles and made his desire known unto his parents. Not only did they approve his purpose, but his mother besought his leave to bear him company on this pilgrimage; which he gladly granted, and willingly paid her every filial service that was her due. They came therefore to London; and they had scarcely departed from thence when his mother took off her shoes, going thus barefooted to Rome and back to London. Godric, humbly serving his parent, was wont to bear her on his shoulders. . . .

Godric, when he had restored his mother safe to his father's arms, abode but a brief while at home; for he was now already firmly purposed to give himself entirely to God's service. Wherefore, that he might follow Christ the more freely, he sold all his possessions and distributed them among the poor. Then, telling his parents of this purpose and receiving their blessing, he went forth to no certain abode, but whithersoever the Lord should deign to lead him; for above all things he coveted the life of a hermit.

From *Life of St. Godric*, trans. G. G. Coulton, *Social Life in Britain*.

Advice to a Norwegian Merchant

Thirteenth century

Son. I am now in my most vigorous years and have a desire to travel abroad; for I would not venture to seek employment at court before I had observed the customs of other men. Such is my intention at present, unless you should give me other advice.

Father. Although I have been a kingsman rather than a merchant, I have no fault to find with that calling, for often the best of men are chosen for it. But much depends on whether the man is more like those who are true merchants, or those who take the merchant's name but are mere frauds and foisters, buying and selling wrongfully.

Son. It would be more seemly for me to be like the rightful ones; for it would be worse than one might think likely, if your son were to imitate those who are not as they ought. But whatever my fate is to be, I desire to have you inform me as to the practices of such men as seem to be capable in that business.

Father. The man who is to be a trader will have to brave many perils, sometimes at sea and sometimes in heathen lands, but nearly always among alien peoples;

and it must be his constant purpose to act discreetly wherever he happens to be. On the sea he must be alert and fearless.

When you are in the market town, or wherever you are, be polite and agreeable; then you will secure the friendship of all good men. Make it a habit to rise early in the morning, and go first and immediately to church wherever it seems most convenient to hear the canonical hours, and hear all the hours and mass from matins on. Join in the worship, repeating such psalms and prayers as you have learned. When the services are over, go out to look after your business affairs. If you are unacquainted with the traffic of the town, observe carefully how those who are reputed the best and most prominent merchants conduct their business. You must also be careful to examine the wares that you buy before the purchase is finally made to make sure that they are sound and flawless. And whenever you make a purchase, call in a few trusty men to serve as witnesses as to how the bargain was made.

You should keep occupied with your business till breakfast or, if necessity demands it, till midday; after that you should eat your meal. Keep your table well provided and set with a white cloth, clean victuals, and good drinks. Serve enjoyable meals, if you can afford it. After the meal you may either take a nap or stroll about a little while for pastime and to see what other good merchants are employed with, or whether any new wares have come to the borough which you ought to buy. On returning to your lodgings examine your wares, lest they suffer damage after coming into your hands. If they are found to be injured and you are about to dispose of them, do not conceal the flaws from the purchaser: show him what the defects are and make such a bargain as you can; then you cannot be called a deceiver. Also put a good price on your wares, though not too high, and yet very near what you see can be obtained; then you cannot be called a foister.

Finally, remember this, that whenever you have an hour to spare you should give thought to your studies, especially to the law books; for it is clear that those who gain knowledge from books have keener wits than others, since those who are the most learned have the best proofs for their knowledge. Make a study of all the laws, but while you remain a merchant there is no law that you will need to know more thoroughly than the Bjarkey code. If you are acquainted with the law, you will not be annoyed by quibbles when you have suits to bring against men of your own class, but will be able to plead according to law in every case.

But although I have most to say about laws, I regard no man perfect in knowledge unless he has thoroughly learned and mastered the customs of the place where he is sojourning. And if you wish to become perfect in knowledge, you must learn all the languages, first of all Latin and French, for these idioms are most widely used; and yet do not neglect your native tongue or speech. . . .

And further, there are certain things which you must beware of and shun like the devil himself: these are drinking, chess, harlots, quarrelling, and throwing dice for stakes. For upon such foundations the greatest calamities are built; and unless they strive to avoid these things, few only are able to live long without blame or sin.

Observe carefully how the sky is lighted, the course of the heavenly bodies, the grouping of the hours, and the points of the horizon. Learn also how to mark the movements of the ocean and to discern how its turmoil ebbs and swells; for that is knowledge which all must possess who wish to trade abroad. Learn arithmetic thoroughly, for merchants have great need of that.

If you come to a place where the king or some other chief who is in authority has his officials, seek to win their friendship; and if they demand any necessary fees on the ruler's behalf, be prompt to render all such payments, lest by holding too tightly to little things you lose the greater. Also beware lest the king's belongings find their way into your purse; for you cannot know but that he may be covetous who has those things in charge, and it is easier to be cautious beforehand than to crave pardon afterwards. If you can dispose of your wares at suitable prices, do not hold them long; for it is the wont of merchants to buy constantly and to sell rapidly.

If you are preparing to carry on trade beyond the seas and you sail your own ship, have it thoroughly coated with tar in the autumn and, if possible, keep it tarred all winter. But if the ship is placed on timbers too late to be coated in the fall, tar it when spring opens and let it dry thoroughly afterwards. Always buy shares in good vessels or in none at all. Keep your ship attractive, for then capable men will join you and it will be well manned. Be sure to have your ship ready when summer begins and do your travelling while the season is best. Keep reliable tackle on shipboard at all times, and never remain out at sea in late autumn, if you can avoid it. If you attend carefully to all these things, with God's mercy you may hope for success. This, too, you must keep constantly in mind, if you wish to be counted a wise man, that you ought never to let a day pass without learning something that will profit you. . . .

Whenever you travel at sea, keep on board two or three hundred ells of wadmal of a sort suitable for mending sails, if that should be necessary, a large number of needles, and a supply of thread and cord. It may seem trivial to mention these things, but it is often necessary to have them on hand. You will always need to carry a supply of nails, both spikes and rivets, of such sizes as your ship demands: also good boat hooks and broad-axes, gouges and augers, and all such other tools as ship carpenters make use of. All these things that I have now named you must remember to carry with you on ship-board, whenever you sail on a trading voyage and the ship is your own. When you come to a market town where you expect to tarry, seek lodgings from the inn-keeper who is reputed the most discreet and the most popular among both kingsmen and boroughmen. Always buy good clothes and eat good fare if your means permit; and never keep unruly or quarrelsome men as attendants or messmates. . . .

If your wealth takes on rapid growth, divide it and invest it in a partnership trade in fields where you do not yourself travel; but be cautious in selecting partners. Always let Almighty God, the holy Virgin Mary, and the saint whom you have most frequently called upon to intercede for you be counted among your partners. Watch with care over the property which the saints are to share with you and always bring it faithfully to the place to which it was originally promised.

If you have much capital invested in trade, divide it into three parts: put one-third into partnerships with men who are permanently located in market boroughs, are trustworthy, and are experienced in business. Place the other two parts in various business ventures; for if your capital is invested in different places, it is not likely that you will suffer losses in all your wealth at one time; more likely it will be secure in some localities, though frequent losses be suffered. But if you find that the profits of trade bring a decided increase to your funds, draw out the two-thirds and invest them in good farm land, for such property is generally thought the most secure, whether the enjoyment of it falls to one's self or to one's kinsmen. With the remaining third you may do as seems best—continue to keep it in business or place it all in land. However, though you decide to keep your funds invested in trade, discontinue your own journeys at sea or as a trader in foreign fields, as soon as your means have attained sufficient growth and you have studied foreign customs as much as you like. Keep all that you see in careful memory, the evil with the good; remember evil practices as a warning, and the good customs as useful to yourself and to others who may wish to learn from you.

From *The King's Mirror*, trans. L. M. Larson (New York: The American-Scandinavian Foundation, 1917).

The Successful Surgeon

John Arderne

Fourteenth century

FIRST it behooves him that will profit in this craft that he always honour God in all his works, and always call on His help meekly with heart and tongue; and sometimes share his earnings with poor men as he is able, that they by their prayers may get him grace of the Holy Ghost. And let him not be found bold or boastful in his sayings or in his deeds; and let him abstain from much speech, and most among great men; and answer warily to things asked, that he be not tripped up by his own words. Forsooth if his works are often known to be in discord with his words and his behests, he shall be held more unworthy, and he shall blemish his own good fame. . . .

Also a leech should not be given much to laughing or playing. And as much as he can without harm, let him flee the fellowship of knaves and dishonest persons. And let him be always occupied in things that belong to his craft; either reading or studying or writing or praying; for the use of books does honour to a leech, because he shall both be kept busy and become more wise.

And above all this, it profits him to be found always sober; for drunkenness destroys all virtue and brings it to nought. . . . Let him be content in strange places with the meats and drinks found there, using measure in all things. . . .

Let him scorn no man. . . . If any other leech is talked about, let him neither set him at nought nor praise him too much nor commend him but answer thus courteously: "I have no true knowledge of him but I have not learned nor heard of him anything but what is good and honest." And from this shall the honour and thanks of each party increase and multiply to him; after this, honour is in the honourer and not in the honoured.

Let him not observe too openly the lady or the daughters or other fair women in great men's houses nor seek to touch, either privately or openly, their breasts, their hands, or their private parts, that he may not encounter the indignation of the lord or any of his.

Inasmuch as he may, let him do no injury to servants but get their love and their good will.

Let him abstain from harlotry as well in words as in deeds in every place, for if he takes to harlotry in private places, some time in public he may be dishonoured for his evil practices. . . .

When sick men, forsooth, or any others come to the leech to ask help or counsel of him, let him be not too fierce nor too familiar but moderate in bearing according to the requests of the persons, to some reverent, to some familiar. . . . Also it is useful that he have suitable excuses, that he may not incline to their asking without harm or without the indignation of some great man or friend, or out of necessary occupation. Or let him feign to be hurt or sick or some other convenient cause by which he may likely be excused.

Therefore, if he will agree to any man's asking, let him make a covenant for his work and take it beforehand. But let him be careful that he give no certain answer in any case without first seeing the sickness and the manner of it; and when he has seen and assayed it, although it seem to him that the sick may be healed, nevertheless he shall make prognostication to the patient of the perils to come if the cure be differed. And if he sees that the patient eagerly pursues the cure, then according to the status of the patient let him ask boldly more or less; but always let him be wary of asking too little, for asking too little sets at nought both the market and the thing. Therefore, for the cure of *fistula in ano,* when it is curable, let him ask sufficiently of a worthy man and a great one hundred marks, or forty pounds with robes and fees of one hundred shillings for term of life by year. Of lesser men let him ask forty pounds, or forty marks without fees. But let him take not less than one hundred shillings. For never in my life did I take less than one hundred shillings for cure of that sickness. Nevertheless, let another man do as he thinks best and most helpful.

And if the patients or their friends or servants ask in how much time he hopes to heal it, let the leech always say the double that he intends to accomplish in half; that is, if the doctor hopes to heal the patient in twenty weeks—that is the common course of curing—let him

add so many over. For it is better that the term be
lengthened than the cure, for prolongation of the cure
gives cause of despairing to the patients when faith in
the leech is the greatest hope of health.

And if the patient considers or wonders or asks why
the leech set so long a time for curing, seeing that he
healed him in half, let him answer that it was because
the patient was strong-hearted, and suffered well sharp
things, and that he was of good temperament and had
sound flesh to heal; and let him feign other causes pleasing to the patient, for patients are proud and delighted
with such words.

Also let a leech see to it that in clothes and other
apparel he is decent, not likening himself in apparel or
bearing to minstrels but in clothing and bearing let him
show the manner of clerks. Because it is seemly for any
discreet man clad in clerk's clothing to sit at gentlemen's
tables.

Let the leech also have clean hands and well-shapen
nails and cleansed of all blackness and filth. And let him
be courteous at the tables of lords and not displease in
words or deeds the guests sitting by; let him hear many
things but speak few. . . .

And when he shall speak, let the words be short and,
so far as possible, fair and reasonable and without swearing. Beware lest there ever be found a double word in
his mouth for if he be found true in his words few or
none shall doubt his deeds. Let a young leech also learn
good proverbs pertaining to his craft for the comforting
of patients.

Or if patients complain that their medicines are bitter
or sharp or such, then shall the leech say to the patient
thus: "It is read in the last lesson of matins of the Nativity of our Lord that our Lord Jesus Christ came into
this world for the health of mankind in the manner of a

good leech and wise." And when he comes to the sick man, let him show him medicines, some light and some hard, and say to the sick man, "If you will be made whole this and this shall you take." . . .

Besides that, he ought to comfort the patient in admonishing him that in anguish he should be of great heart. For great heart makes a man hardy and strong to suffer sharp things and grievous. And it is a great virtue and a happy, for Boethius says, in *De disciplina scholarium*, "He is not worthy of the height of sweetness that can not endure the grieving of bitterness, because a strong medicine answers to a strong sickness." . . .

It is fitting for a great-hearted man to suffer sharp things; he, forsooth, that is weak of heart is not in the way of being cured. Forsooth in all my life I have seen but few labouring in this vice healed in any sickness; therefore wise men should beware of getting mixed up with such. The wise man says, "All things are hard to a weak-hearted man, for they think always that evils are near them; they are always in dread, they endure nothing, they are always unstable and unwise." . . .

Also it is helpful for a leech to have a stock of good tales and honest that may make the patients laugh, as well from the Bible as from other tragedies; and any other things which are not objectionable as long as they make or induce a light heart in the patient or sick man.

Let the leech never disclose carelessly the counsels of his patients, neither of men nor of women, nor belittle one to another although he have cause, that he be not guilty of breaking confidence. For if a man sees that you hold well another man's counsel, he will trust you better. Many things, forsooth, are to be observed by a leech, besides these that are said before, that may not be noted here for over much occupying. But it is not to be doubted that if the foresaid be well kept that they shall give a gracious going to the user to the height of honour and of success. . . .

From *Treatises of Fistula in Ano*, D'Arcy Power, ed. (London: Early English Texts Society, Orig. Ser., no. 139, 1910); trans. J.B.R.

The Good Wife

Late fourteenth century

Dear Sister,

You being the age of fifteen years and, in the week that you and I were wed, did pray me to be indulgent to your youth and to your small and ignorant service, until you had seen and learned more; to this end you promised me to give all heed and to set all care and diligence to keep my peace and my love, as you spoke full wisely, and, as I well believe, with other wisdom than your own, beseeching me humbly in our bed, as I remember, for the love of God not to correct you harshly before strangers nor before our own folk, but rather each night, or from day to day, in our chamber, to remind you of the unseemly or foolish things done in the day or days past, and chastise you, if it pleased me, and then you would strive to amend yourself according to my teaching and correction, and to serve my will in all things, as you said. And your words were pleasing to me, and won my praise and thanks, and I have often remembered them since. And know, dear sister, that all that I know you have done since we were wed until now, and all that you shall do hereafter with good intent, was and is to my liking, pleaseth me, and has well pleased me, and will please me. For your youth excuses your unwisdom and will still excuse you in all things as long as all you do is with good intent and not displeasing to me. And know that I am pleased rather than displeased that you tend rose-trees, and care for violets, and make chaplets, and dance, and sing: nor would I have you cease to do so among our friends and equals, and it is but good and seemly so to pass the time of your youth, so long as you neither seek nor try to go to the feasts and dances of lords of too high rank, for that does not become you, nor does it sort with your estate, nor mine. And as for the greater service that you say you would willingly do for me, if you were able and I taught it you, know, dear sister, that I am well content that you should do me such service as your good neighbours of like estate do for their husbands, and as your kinswomen do unto their husbands. . . . And lastly, meseems that if your love is as it has appeared in your good words, it can be accomplished in this way, namely in a general instruction that I will write for you and present to you, in three sections containing nineteen principal articles. . . .

CARE OF A HUSBAND

The seventh article of the first section showeth how you should be careful and thoughtful of your husband's person. Wherefore, fair sister, if you have another husband after me, know that you should think much of his person, for after that a woman has lost her first husband and marriage, she commonly findeth it hard to find a second to her liking, according to her estate, and she remaineth long while all lonely and disconsolate and the more so still if she lose the second. Wherefore love your husband's person carefully, and I pray you keep him in clean linen, for that is your business, and because the trouble and care of outside affairs lieth with men, so must husbands take heed, and go and come, and journey hither and thither, in rain and wind, in snow and hail, now drenched, now dry, now sweating, now shivering, ill-fed, ill-lodged, ill-warmed, and ill-bedded. And naught harmeth him, because he is upheld by the hope that he hath of the care which his wife will take of him on his return, and of the ease, the joys, and the pleasures which she will do him, or cause to be done to him in her presence; to be unshod before a good fire, to have his feet washed and fresh shoes and hose, to be given good food and drink, to be well served and well looked after, well bedded in white sheets and nightcaps, well covered with good furs, and assuaged with other joys and desports, privities, loves, and secrets whereof I am silent. And the next day fresh shirts and garments.

Certes, fair sister, such services make a man love and desire to return to his home and to see his goodwife, and to be distant with others. Wherefore I counsel you to make such cheer to your husband at all his comings and stayings, and to persevere therein; and also be peaceable with him, and remember the rustic proverb, which saith that there be three things which drive the goodman from home, to wit, a leaking roof, a smoky chimney, and a scolding woman. And therefore, fair sister, I beseech you that you keep yourself in the love and good favour of your husband, you be unto him gentle, and amiable, and debonair. Do unto him what the good simple women of our country say hath been done to their sons, when these have set their love elsewhere and their mothers cannot wean them therefrom.

Wherefore, dear sister, I beseech you thus to bewitch and bewitch again your husband that shall be, and beware of roofless house and of smoky fire, and scold him not, but be unto him gentle and amiable and peaceable. Have a care that in winter he have a good fire and smokeless and let him rest well and be well covered

between your breasts, and thus bewitch him. And in
summer take heed that there be no fleas in your chamber, nor in your bed, the which you may do in six ways,
as I have heard tell. For I have heard from several that
if the room be strewn with alder leaves, the fleas will be
caught thereon. Item, I have heard tell that if you have
at night one or two trenchers [of bread] slimed with
glue or turpentine and set about the room, with a
lighted candle in the midst of each trencher, they will
come and be stuck thereto. The other way that I have
tried and 'tis true: take a rough cloth and spread it
about your room and over your bed, and all the fleas
that shall hop thereon will be caught, so that you may
carry them away with the cloth wheresoe'er you will.
Item, sheepskins. Item, I have seen blanchets [of white
wool] set on the straw and on the bed, and when the
black fleas hopped thereon, they were the sooner found
upon the white, and killed. But the best way is to guard
oneself against those that be within the coverlets and
the furs, and the stuff of the dresses wherewith one is
covered. For know that I have tried this, and when the
coverlets, furs, or dresses, wherein there be fleas, be
folded and shut tightly up, as in the chest tightly corded
with straps, or in a bag well tied up and pressed, or
otherwise put and pressed so that the aforesaid fleas be
without light and air and kept imprisoned, then will they
perish forthwith and die. Item, I have sometimes seen in
divers chambers, that when one had gone to bed they
were full of mosquitoes, which at the smoke of the
breath came to sit on the faces of those that slept, and
stung them so hard, that they were fain to get up and
light a fire of hay, in order to make a smoke so that they
had to fly away or die, and this may be done by day if
they be suspected, and likewise he that hath a mosquito
net may protect himself therewith.

And if you have a chamber or a passage where there is great resort of flies, take little sprigs of fern and tie them to threads like to tassels, and hang them up and all the flies will settle on them at eventide; then take down the tassels and throw them out. Item, shut up your chamber closely in the evening, but let there be a little opening in the wall towards the east, and as soon as the dawn breaketh, all the flies will go forth through this opening, and then let it be stopped up. . . .

Item, have whisks wherewith to slay them by hand. Item, have little twigs covered with glue on a basin of water. Item, have your windows shut full tight with oiled or other cloth, or with parchment or something else, so tightly that no fly may enter, and let the flies that be within be slain with the whisk or otherwise as above, and no others will come in. Item, have a string hanging soaked in honey, and the flies will come and settle thereon and at eventide let them be taken in a bag. Finally meseemeth that flies will not stop in a room wherein there be no standing tables, forms, dressers or other things whereon they can settle and rest, for if they have naught but straight walls whereon to settle and cling, they will not settle, nor will they in a shady or damp place. Wherefore meseemeth that if the room be well watered and well closed and shut up, and if naught be left lying on the floor, no fly will settle there.

And thus shall you preserve and keep your husband from all discomforts and give him all the comforts whereof you can bethink you, and serve him and have him served in your house, and you shall look to him for outside things, for if he be good he will take even more pains and labour therein than you wish, and by doing what I have said, you will cause him ever to miss you and have his heart with you and your loving service and he will shun all other houses, all other women, all other services and households.

Dinner for a Meat Day Served in Thirty-one Dishes and Six Courses

First course. [Wine of] Grenache and roasts, veal pasties, pimpernel pasties, black-puddings and sausages.

Second course. Hares in civey and cutlets, pea soup [*lit.*, strained peas], salt meat and great joints (*grosse char*), a soringue of eels and other fish.

Third course. Roast: coneys, partridges, capons, etc., luce, bar, carp, and a quartered pottage.

Fourth course. River fish à la dodine, savoury rice, a bourrey with hot sauce and eels reversed.

Fifth course. Lark pasties, rissoles, larded milk, sugared flawns.

Sixth course. Pears and comfits, medlars and peeled nuts. Hippocras and wafers. . . .

A Fish Dinner

First course. Pea soup, herring, salt eels, a black civey of oysters, an almond brewet, a tile, a broth of broach and eels, a cretonnée, a green brewet of eels, silver pasties.

Second course. Salt and freshwater fish, bream and salmon pasties, eels reversed, and a brown herbolace, tench with a larded broth, a blankmanger, crisps, lettuces, losenges, orillettes, and Norwegian pasties, stuffed luce and salmon.

Third course. Porpoise frumenty, glazed pommeaulx, Spanish puffs and chastelettes, roast fish, jelly, lampreys, congers and turbot with green sauce, breams with verjuice, leches fried, darioles and entremet. Then Dessert, Issue, and Sally-Forth. . . .

Rosée of Young Rabbits, Larks and Small Birds or Chickens.

Let the rabbits be skinned, cut up, parboiled, done again in cold water and larded; let the chickens be scalded for plucking, then done again, cut up and larded, and let larks and little birds be plucked only for parboiling in sewe of meat; then have bacon lard cut up into little squares and put them into a frying pan and take away the lumps but leave the fat, and therein fry your meat, or set your meat to boil on the coal, often turning it, in a pot with fat. And while you do this, have peeled almonds and moisten them with beef broth and run it through the strainer, then have ginger, a head of clove, cedar otherwise hight *alexander* [red cedar], make some gravy and strain it and when the meat is cooked set it in a pot with the broth and plenty of sugar; then serve in bowls with glazed spices thereon.

Eel Reversed

Take a large eel and steam it, then slice it along the back the length of the bone on both sides, in such manner that you draw out the bone, tail and head all together, then wash and turn it inside out, to wit the flesh outwards, and let it be tied from place to place; and set it to boil in red wine. Then take it out and cut the thread with a knife or scissors, and set it to cool on a towel. Then take ginger, cinnamon, cloves, flour of cinnamon, grain [of Paradise], nutmegs, and bray them and set them aside. Then take bread toasted and well brayed, and let it not be strained, but moistened with wine wherein the eel hath been cooked and boil all together in an iron pan and put in verjuice, wine, and vinegar and cast them on the eel.

From *The Goodman of Paris*, trans. E. Power (London: Routledge, 1928).

Life in London

THE CASE OF THE MISSING HEAD, 1277

O N MONDAY the morrow of the Close of Easter, in the fifth year of King Edward, the said chamberlain and sheriffs were given to understand that one Symon de Winton, taverner, was lying dead, etc., in the parish of St. Martin, in Ismongerelane in the ward of Chepe, in a house belonging to Robert le Surigien, of Frydaystrete; in which house the said Symon kept a tavern. On hearing which, the said chamberlain and sheriffs went there, and calling together the good men of that ward and of Bassieshawe, and of the ward of Henry de Frowyk, diligent inquisition was made how this had happened.

The jurors say, that on the Eve of St. Nicholas [6 December] in the same year, a dispute arose between the said Symon and a certain man who said that he was called "Roger de Westminster," and who was his servant. And on the morrow also, they were seen by the neighbours in the same house and tavern, abusing each other and quarrelling, by reason of the same dispute; and on the same night they slept there, in the same room together. But as soon as this Roger saw that the said Symon was sound asleep, he seized a knife, and with it cut the throat of Symon quite through, so that the head was entirely severed from the body. After which, he dragged the body out, and put it in a certain secret spot, a dark and narrow place, situate between two walls in the same house, where coals were usually kept; such place being somewhat long, and not quite two feet wide. And on the following day, the same Roger, as was his custom, set out the bench of the tavern, and sold wine there. And as the said Symon had not been seen by the neighbours all that day, they asked Roger what had become of his master; whereupon he made answer that he had gone to Westminster, to recover some debts that were owing to him there; and on the second day and third he gave the same answer. At twilight however on the third day, he departed by the outer door, locking it with the key, and carrying off with him a silver cup, a robe, and some bedclothes, which had belonged to the same Symon. Afterwards he returned, and threw the key into the house of one Hamon Cook, a near neighbour, telling him that he was going to seek the said Symon, his master, and asking him to give him the key, in case he should come back. And from that day the house remained closed and empty until the Eve of our Lord's Circumcision [1 January] following; upon which day John Doget, a taverner, taking with him Gilbert de Colecestre, went to the house aforesaid to recover a debt which the said Symon owed to him for wines. But when he found the door closed and locked, he enquired after the key, of the neighbours who were standing about: upon hearing of which, the said Hamon gave him up the key forthwith. Upon entering the tavern with Gilbert aforesaid, he found there one tun full of wine, and another half full, which he himself had sold to Symon for 50 shillings; and this he at once ordered to be taken out by porters . . . and taken to his own house, for the debt so due to him; together with some small tables, canvas cloths, gallons, and wooden potels, two shillings in value. This being done, the said John Doget shut the door of the house, carrying away with him the key thereof; from which time the house was empty, no one having entered it until the Tuesday before Palm Sunday.

Upon which day, Master Robert aforesaid, to whom the house belonged, came and broke open the door for want of a key, and so entering it, immediately enfeoffed Michael le Oynter thereof; which Michael, on the Saturday in Easter week, went there alone, to examine all the offices belonging thereto, and see which of them required to be cleansed of filth and dust. But when he came to the narrow and dark place aforesaid, he there found the headless body; upon seeing which, he sent word to the said chamberlain and sheriffs.

Being asked if anyone else dwelt in the house, save and except those two persons, or if anyone else had been seen or heard in that house with them on the night the felony was committed, or if any other person had had frequent or especial access to the house by day or night, from which mischief might have arisen, they say, not beyond the usual resort that all persons have to a tavern. Being asked if the said Roger had any well-known or especial [friend] in the City, or without, to whose house he was wont to resort, they say they understand that he had not, seeing that he was a stranger, and had been in the service of this Symon hardly a fortnight. Being asked therefore whither he had taken the goods he had carried off, they say that, seeing that the house was near to the Jewry, they believe that he took them to the Jewry; but to whose house they know not. Being asked what became of the head so cut off, they say they know not, nor can they ascertain anything as to the same. They say also that the said Roger escaped by stealth, and has not since been seen. Chattels he had none.

And the four nearest neighbours were attached, by sureties, and all the persons whose names are above-mentioned.

SPECIFICATIONS FOR BUILDING A HOUSE, 1308

Simon de Canterbury, carpenter, came before the
mayor and aldermen on the Saturday next after the feast
of St. Martin the Bishop [11 November], in the second
year of the reign of King Edward, son of King Edward,
and acknowledged that he would make at his own
proper charges, down to the locks, for William de Hanigtone, pelterer, before the Feast of Easter then next ensu-
ing, a hall and a room with a chimney, and one larder
between the said hall and room; and one sollar over the
room and larder; also, one oriole at the end of the hall,
beyond the high bench, and one step with an oriole,
from the ground to the door of the hall aforesaid, outside of that hall; and two enclosures as cellars, opposite
to each other, beneath the hall; and one enclosure for
a sewer, with two pipes leading to the said sewer; and
one stable . . . in length, between the said hall and
the old kitchen, and twelve feet in width, with a sollar
above such stable, and a garret above the sollar aforesaid; and at one end of such sollar, there is to be a
kitchen with a chimney; and there is to be an oriole
between the said hall and the old chamber, eight feet
in width. And if he shall not do so, then he admits,
etc. . . .

And the said William de Hanigtone acknowledged
that he was bound to pay to Simon before-mentioned,
for the work aforesaid, the sum of 9 £.5s.4d. sterling,
half a hundred of Eastern martenskins, fur for a woman's hood, value five shillings, and fur for a robe of him,
the said Simon. . . .

BAKERS' TRICKS, 1327

A congregation of . . . aldermen, and Roger Chaun-
tecler, one of the sheriffs of London, holden at the Guild-

hall, on Thursday in the week of Pentecost, that is, on the 4th day of June A.D. 1327. . . .

John Brid, baker, was attached to make answer as to certain falsehood, malice, and deceit, by him committed, to the nuisance of the common people; as to which, the mayor, aldermen, and sheriffs of the City were given to understand that the same John, for falsely and maliciously obtaining his own private advantage, did skilfully and artfully cause a certain hole to be made upon a table of his, called a *"moldingborde,"* pertaining to his bakehouse, after the manner of a mouse-trap, in which mice are caught; there being a certain wicket warily provided for closing and opening such hole.

And when his neighbours and others, who were wont to bake their bread at his oven, came with their dough or material for making bread, the said John used to put such dough or other material upon the said table, called a *"moldingborde,"* as aforesaid, and over the hole beforementioned, for the purpose of making loaves therefrom, for baking; and such dough or material being so placed upon the table aforesaid, the same John had one of his household, ready provided for the same, sitting in secret beneath such table; which servant of his, so seated beneath the hole, and carefully opening it, piecemeal and bit by bit craftily withdrew some of the dough aforesaid, frequently collecting great quantities from such dough, falsely, wickedly, and maliciously; to the great loss of all his neighbours and persons living near, and of others, who had come to him with such dough to bake, and to the scandal and disgrace of the whole City, and, in especial, of the mayor and bailiffs for the safe-keeping of the assizes of the City assigned. Which hole, so found in his table aforesaid, was made of aforethought; and in like manner, a great quantity of such dough that had been drawn through the said hole, was found beneath the hole, and was . . . brought here into Court.

And the same John, here present in court, being asked how he will acquit himself of the fraud, malice, and deceit aforesaid, personally in court says that of such fraud, malice, and deceit, he is in no way guilty; and puts himself upon the country thereon, etc. Therefore, let inquisition as to the truth of the matter be made by the country, etc. . . .

And after counsel and treaty had been held among the mayor and aldermen, as to passing judgment upon the falsehood, malice, and deceit aforesaid; seeing that, although there is no one who prosecutes them, or any one of them, the said deed is, as it were, a certain species of theft, and that it is neither consonant with right nor pleasing to God that such falsehood, deceit, and malice shall go unpunished; the more especially as all those who have come to the said bakers, to bake their bread, have been falsely, wickedly, and maliciously deceived, they themselves being wholly ignorant thereof, and have suffered no little loss thereby; it was agreed and ordained, that all those of the bakers aforesaid, beneath whose tables with holes dough had been found, should be put upon the pillory, with a certain quantity of such dough hung from their necks; and that those bakers in whose houses dough was not found beneath the tables aforesaid, should be put upon the pillory, but without dough hung from their necks; and that they should so remain upon the pillory until vespers at St. Paul's in London should be ended.

From *Memorials of London*, H. T. Riley, ed. (London: Longmans Green, 1868).

Fashions in Italy

SACCHETTI

Fourteenth century

Bᴜᴛ was not this fashion of wearing gorgets the most extraordinary of all the fashions in the world? Of all that were ever seen in the world, this was the strangest and the most tiresome. And I, the writer, remember hearing Salvestro Brunelleschi relate that, after having dwelt a long time in Friuli, he returned to Florence just when his kindred were engaged in a very great quarrel with a neighbouring family called Agli. It so happened that one of these Agli, named Guernizo, returned home from Germany at this time; and either on account of the name, or because he was reputed a very fierce man, all the Brunelleschi armed themselves in such a manner that Salvestro was made to wear a gorget. And that morning at dinner a dish of beans was placed before him, and taking a spoonful to put them into his mouth, he dropped them down inside his gorget. The beans were very hot, and scalded his neck and throat so badly that he cried, "I put on the gorget for fear of Guernizo, and it hath caused me to burn my whole throat!" and rising up from table he took off the gorget and cast it on the floor, saying, "I would rather be put to death by mine enemies than kill myself."

How many fashions have been altered in my time by the changeableness of those persons now living, and especially in mine own city! Formerly the women wore their bodices cut so open that they were uncovered to beneath their armpits! Then with one jump, they wore their collars right up to their ears. And these are all outrageous fashions. I, the writer, could recite as many more of the customs and fashions which have been changed in my days as would fill a book as large as this whole volume. But although they were constantly changing in this city of ours, they were not invariable either in most of the other great cities of the world. And although formerly the Genoese never altered the fashion of their dress, and neither the Venetians nor the Catalans altered theirs, nor did their women either, nowadays it seemeth to me that the whole world is united in having but little firmness of mind; for the men and women of Florence, Genoa, Venice, Catalonia, indeed of all the Christian world, go dressed in the same manner, not being able to distinguish one from another. And would to Heaven they all remained fixed upon the same manner, but quite the contrary! For if one jay do but appear with a new fashion, all the world doth copy it. So that the whole world, but most especially Italy, is variable and hastens to adopt the new fashions. The young maidens, who used to dress with so much modesty, have now raised the hanging ends of their hoods and have twisted them into caps, and they go attired like common women, wearing caps, and collars and strings round their necks, with divers kinds of beasts hung upon their breasts. And what more wretched, dangerous, and useless fashion ever existed than that of wearing such sleeves as they do, or great sacks, as they might rather be called? They cannot raise a glass or take a mouthful without soiling both their sleeves and the tablecloth by upsetting the glasses on the table. Likewise do youths wear these immense sleeves, but still worse is it when even sucklings are dressed in them. The women wear hoods and cloaks. The young men for the most part go without cloaks and wear their hair long; they need but divest themselves of their breeches and they will then have left off everything they can, and truly these are so small that they could easily do without them. They put their legs into tight socks and upon their wrists they hang a yard of cloth; they put more cloth into the making of a glove than into a hood. Perchance they will thereby all do penance for their many vanities. For whoever liveth but one day in this world changeth his fashions a thousand times; each one seeketh liberty and yet depriveth himself of it. The Lord created our feet free, yet many persons are unable to walk on account of the long points of their shoes. He created legs with joints, but many have so stiffened them with strings and laces that they can scarcely sit down; their bodies are drawn in tightly, their arms are burdened with a train of cloth, their necks are squeezed into their hoods and their heads into a sort of nightcap, whereby all day they feel as though their heads were being sawn off. Truly there would be no end to describing the women's attire, considering the extravagance of their dress from their feet up to their heads, and how every day they are up on the roofs, some curling their hair, some smoothing it, and some bleaching it, so that often they die of the colds they catch!

Oh, the vanity of human power! Through thee true glory is lost! But I will speak no more of these things, for I should so engross myself in their misdeeds that I should be able to discourse of nothing else.

From *Tales from Sacchetti*, trans. M. G. Steegmann (London: Dent, 1908).

THE JEWS

Papal Protection of the Jews

POPE GREGORY X

1272

GREGORY, bishop, servant of the servants of God, extends greetings and the apostolic benediction to the beloved sons in Christ, the faithful Christians, to those here now and to those in the future. Even as it is not allowed to the Jews in their assemblies presumptuously to undertake for themselves more than that which is permitted them by law, even so they ought not to suffer any disadvantage in those [privileges] which have been granted them. [This sentence, first written by Gregory I in 598, embodies the attitude of the Church to the Jew.] Although they prefer to persist in their stubbornness rather than to recognize the words of their prophets and the mysteries of the Scriptures [which, according to the Church, foretold the coming of Jesus], and thus to arrive at a knowledge of Christian faith and salvation; nevertheless, inasmuch as they have made an appeal for our protection and help, we therefore admit their petition and offer them the shield of our protection through the clemency of Christian piety. In so doing we follow in the footsteps of our predecessors of blessed memory, the popes of Rome—Calixtus, Eugene, Alexander, Clement, Celestine, Innocent, and Honorius.

We decree moreover that no Christian shall compel them or any one of their group to come to baptism unwillingly. But if any one of them shall take refuge of his own accord with Christians, because of conviction, then, after his intention will have been manifest, he shall be made a Christian without any intrigue. For, indeed, that person who is known to have come to Christian baptism not freely, but unwillingly, is not believed to possess the Christian faith. [The Church, in principle, never approved of compulsory baptism of Jews.]

Moreover no Christian shall presume to seize, imprison, wound, torture, mutilate, kill, or inflict violence on them; furthermore no one shall presume, except by judicial action of the authorities of the country, to change the good customs in the land where they live for the purpose of taking their money or goods from them or from others.

In addition, no one shall disturb them in any way during the celebration of their festivals, whether by day or by night, with clubs or stones or anything else. Also no one shall exact any compulsory service of them unless it be that which they have been accustomed to render in previous times. [Up to this point Gregory X has merely repeated the bulls of his predecessors.]

Inasmuch as the Jews are not able to bear witness against the Christians, we decree furthermore that the testimony of Christians against Jews shall not be valid unless there is among these Christians some Jew who is there for the purpose of offering testimony.

[The church council at Carthage, as early as 419, had forbidden Jews to bear witness against Christians; Justinian's law of 531 repeats this prohibition. Gregory X here—in accordance with the medieval legal principle that every man has the right to be judged by his peers—insists that Jews can only be condemned if there are

Jewish as well as Christian witnesses against them. A similar law to protect Jews was issued before 825 by Louis the Pious (814-840) of the Frankish Empire.]

Since it happens occasionally that some Christians lose their Christian children, the Jews are accused by their enemies of secretly carrying off and killing these same Christian children and of making sacrifices of the heart and blood of these very children. It happens, too, that the parents of these children, or some other Christian enemies of these Jews, secretly hide these very children in order that they may be able to injure these Jews, and in order that they may be able to extort from them a certain amount of money by redeeming them from their straits. [Following the lead of Innocent IV, 1247, Gregory attacks the ritual murder charge at length.]

And most falsely do these Christians claim that the Jews have secretly and furtively carried away these children and killed them, and that the Jews offer sacrifice from the heart and the blood of these children, since their law in this matter precisely and expressly forbids Jews to sacrifice, eat, or drink the blood, or to eat the flesh of animals having claws. This has been demonstrated many times at our court by Jews converted to the Christian faith: nevertheless very many Jews are often seized and detained unjustly because of this.

We decree, therefore, that Christians need not be obeyed against Jews in a case or situation of this type, and we order that Jews seized under such a silly pretext be freed from imprisonment, and that they shall not be arrested henceforth on such a miserable pretext, unless —which we do not believe—they be caught in the commission of the crime. We decree that no Christian shall stir up anything new against them, but that they should be maintained in that status and position in which they were in the time of our predecessors, from antiquity till now.

We decree, in order to stop the wickedness and avarice of bad men, that no one shall dare to devastate or to destroy a cemetery of the Jews or to dig up human bodies for the sake of getting money. [The Jews had to pay a ransom before the bodies of their dead were restored to them.] Moreover, if any one, after having known the content of this decree, should—which we hope will not happen—attempt audaciously to act contrary to it, then let him suffer punishment in his rank and position, or let him be punished by the penalty of excommunication, unless he makes amends for his boldness by proper recompense. Moreover, we wish that only those Jews who have not attempted to contrive anything toward the destruction of the Christian faith be fortified by the support of such protection. . . .

Given at Orvieto by the hand of the Magister John Lectator, vice-chancellor of the Holy Roman Church, on the 7th of October, in the first indiction [cycle of fifteen years], in the year 1272 of the divine incarnation, in the first year of the pontificate of our master, the Pope Gregory X.

From *The Jew in the Medieval World*, J. R. Marcus, ed. (Cincinnati: Sinai Press, 1938).

The Cremation of the Strasbourg Jewry

JACOB VON KÖNIGSHOFEN

1349

IN THE year 1349 there occurred the greatest epidemic that ever happened. Death went from one end of the earth to the other, on that side and this side of the sea, and it was greater among the Saracens than among the Christians. In some lands everyone died so that no one was left. Ships were also found on the sea laden with wares; the crew had all died and no one guided the ship. The bishop of Marseilles and priests and monks and more than half of all the people there died with them. In other kingdoms and cities so many people perished that it would be horrible to describe. The pope at Avignon stopped all sessions of court, locked himself in a room, allowed no one to approach him and had a fire burning before him all the time. [This last was probably intended as some sort of disinfectant.] And from what this epidemic came, all wise teachers and physicians could only say that it was God's will. And as the plague was now here, so was it in other places, and lasted more than a whole year. This epidemic also came to Strasbourg in the summer of the above-mentioned year, and it is estimated that about sixteen thousand people died.

In the matter of this plague the Jews throughout the world were reviled and accused in all lands of having caused it through the poison which they are said to have put into the water and the wells—that is what they were accused of—and for this reason the Jews were burnt all the way from the Mediterranean into Germany, but not in Avignon, for the pope protected them there.

Nevertheless they tortured a number of Jews in Berne and Zofingen [Switzerland] who then admitted that they had put poison into many wells, and they also found the poison in the wells. Thereupon they burnt the Jews in many towns and wrote of this affair to Strasbourg, Freiburg, and Basel in order that they too should burn their Jews. But the leaders in these three cities in whose hands the government lay did not believe that anything ought to be done to the Jews. However in Basel the citizens marched to the city hall and compelled the council to take an oath that they would burn the Jews, and that they would allow no Jew to enter the city for the next two hundred years. Thereupon the Jews were arrested in all these places and a conference was arranged to meet at Benfeld [Alsace, February 8, 1349]. The bishop of Strasbourg [Berthold II], all the feudal lords of Alsace, and representatives of the three above-mentioned cities came there. The deputies of the city of Strasbourg were asked what they were going to do with their Jews. They answered and said that they knew no evil of them. Then they asked the Strasbourgers why they had closed the wells and put away the buckets, and there was a great indignation and clamour against the deputies from Strasbourg. So finally the bishop and the lords and the Imperial Cities agreed to do away with the Jews. The result was that they were burnt in many cities, and wherever they were expelled they were caught by the peasants and stabbed to death or drowned. . . .

[The town-council of Strasbourg which wanted to save the Jews was deposed on the 9th/10th of February, and the new council gave in to the mob, who then arrested the Jews on Friday, the 13th.]

On Saturday—that was St. Valentine's Day—they burnt the Jews on a wooden platform in their cemetery. There were about two thousand people of them. Those who wanted to baptize themselves were spared. [Some say that about a thousand accepted baptism.] Many small children were taken out of the fire and baptized against the will of their fathers and mothers. And everything that was owed to the Jews was cancelled, and the Jews had to surrender all pledges and notes that they had taken for debts. The council, however, took the cash that the Jews possessed and divided it among the working-men proportionately. The money was indeed the thing that killed the Jews. If they had been poor and if the feudal lords had not been in debt to them, they would not have been burnt. After this wealth was divided among the artisans some gave their share to the cathedral or to the Church on the advice of their confessors.

Thus were the Jews burnt at Strasbourg, and in the same year in all the cities of the Rhine, whether Free Cities or Imperial Cities or cities belonging to the lords. In some towns they burnt the Jews after a trial, in others, without a trial. In some cities the Jews themselves set fire to their houses and cremated themselves.

It was decided in Strasbourg that no Jew should enter the city for a hundred years, but before twenty years had passed, the council and magistrates agreed that they ought to admit the Jews again into the city for twenty years. And so the Jews came back again to Strasbourg in the year 1368 after the birth of our Lord.

From *Chronicle*, in *The Jew in the Medieval World*, J. R. Marcus, ed.

Conflict, Protest, and Catastrophe

A Revolt of the Commons in London

ROGER OF WENDOVER

1194

A BOUT this time there arose a dispute in the city of
London between the poor and the rich on account
of the talliage, which was exacted by the king's agents
for the benefit of the exchequer: for the principal men
of the city, whom we call mayors and aldermen, having
held a deliberation at their hustings, wished to preserve
themselves free from the burden, and to oppress the
poorer classes. Wherefore William Fitz-Robert, sur-
named "with the beard," because his ancestors in anger
against the Normans never shaved, made opposition to
the same, and called the mayors of the city traitors to
our lord the king for the cause above-named; and the
disturbances were so great in the city that recourse was
had to arms. William stirred up a large number of the
middle and lower classes against the mayors and aldermen, but by their pusillanimity and cowardice the plans
of William's confederates in resisting the injury done
them were dissipated and defeated: the middle and

lower classes were repressed, and the king, his ministers, and the chief men of the city charged the whole crime on William. As the king's party were about to arrest him, he, being a distinguished character in the city, tall of stature and of great personal strength, escaped, notwithstanding their exertions, defending himself with nothing but a knife, and flying into the church of St. Mary of the Arches, demanded the protection of our Lord, St. Mary, and her church, saying that he had resisted an unjust decree for no other purpose than that all might bear an equal share of the public burden, and contribute according to their means. His expostulations, however, were not listened to, the majority prevailed, and the archbishop, to the surprise of many, ordered that he should be dragged from the church to take his trial, because he had created a sedition and made such a disturbance among the people of the city. When this was told to William, he took refuge in the tower of the church, for he knew that the mayors, whom he had contradicted, sought to take away his life. In their obstinacy they applied fire, and sacrilegiously burnt down a great part of the church. Thus William was forced to leave the tower, almost suffocated with the heat and smoke. He was then seized, dragged out of the church, stripped, and, with his hands tied behind his back, conveyed away to the Tower of London. Soon after, at the instigation of the archbishop, the principal citizens, and the king's ministers, he was taken from the Tower, and dragged, tied to a horse's tail, through the middle of London to Ulmet, a pitiable sight to the citizens and to his own respectable relations in the city: after which he was hung in chains on a gallows. Thus William of the Beard was shamefully put to death by his fellow citizens for asserting the truth and defending the cause of the poor: and if the justice of one's cause constitutes a martyr, we may surely set him down as one. With him also were hanged nine of his neighbours or of his family, who espoused his cause.

From *Flowers of History*, Matthew Paris' addition, trans. J. A. Giles (London: Bohn, 1849).

The Peasants' Revolt in England

1381

AND at this moment [c. May 30] a justice was assigned by the king and council to go into Kent with a commission of Trailbaston, as had been done before in Essex, and with him went a sergeant-at-arms of our lord the king, named Master John Legge, bearing with him a great number of indictments against folks of that district, to make the king rich. And they would have held session at Canterbury, but they were turned back by the commons.

And after this the commons of Kent gathered together in great numbers day after day, without a head or a chieftain, and the Friday after Whit-Sunday came to Dartford. . . .

And, on the next Friday after, they came to Rochester and there met a great number of the commons of Essex. . . .

But those who came from Maidstone took their way with the rest of the commons through the countryside. And there they made chief over them Wat Teghler of Maidstone, to maintain them and be their councillor. And on the Monday next after Trinity Sunday they came to Canterbury, before the hour of noon; and four thousand of them entering into the minster at the time of high mass, there made a reverence and cried with one voice to the monks to prepare to choose a monk for archbishop of Canterbury, "for he who is archbishop now is a traitor, and shall be decapitated for his iniquity." And so he was within five days after! And when they had done this, they went into the town to their fellows, and with one assent they summoned the mayor, the bailiffs, and the commons of the said town, and examined them whether they would with good will swear to be faithful and loyal to King Richard and to the true commons of England or no. Then the mayor answered that they would do so willingly, and they made their oath to that effect. Then they (the rebels) asked them if they had any traitors among them, and the townsfolk said that there were three, and named their names. These three the commons dragged out of their houses and cut off their heads. And afterwards they took five hundred men of the town with them to London, but left the rest to guard the town.

At this time the commons had as their councillor a chaplain of evil disposition named Sir John Ball, which Sir John advised them to get rid of all the lords, and of the archbishop and bishops, and abbots, and priors, and most of the monks and canons, saying that there should be no bishop in England save one archbishop only, and that he himself would be that prelate, and they would have no monks or canons in religious houses save two, and that their possessions should be distributed among the laity. For which sayings he was esteemed among the commons as a prophet, and laboured with them day by day to strengthen them in their malice—and a fit reward he got, when he was hung, drawn, and quartered, and beheaded as a traitor. After this the said commons went to many places, and raised all the folk, some willingly and some unwillingly, till they were gathered together full sixty thousand. And in going towards London they met divers men of law, and twelve knights of that country, and made them swear to support them, or otherwise they should have been beheaded. They wrought much damage in Kent, and notably to Thomas Haselden, a servant of the duke of Lancaster, because of the hate that they bore to the said duke. They cast his manors to the ground and all his houses, and sold his beasts— his horses, his good cows, his sheep, and his pigs—and all his store of corn, at a cheap price. And they desired every day to have his head, and the head of Sir Thomas Orgrave, clerk of receipt and subtreasurer of England.

When the king heard of their doings he sent his messengers to them, on Tuesday after Trinity Sunday, asking why they were behaving in this fashion, and for what cause they were making insurrection in his land. And they sent back by his messengers the answer that they had risen to deliver him, and to destroy traitors to him and his kingdom. The king sent again to them bidding them cease their doings, in reverence for him, till he could speak with them, and he would make, according to their will, reasonable amendment of all that was ill-done in the realm. . . .

And on the vigil of Corpus Christi Day the commons of Kent came to Blackheath, three leagues from London, to the number of fifty thousand, to wait for the king, and they displayed two banners of St. George and forty pennons. And the commons of Essex came on the other side of the water to the number of sixty thousand to aid them, and to have their answer from the king. And on the Wednesday, the king being in the Tower of London, thinking to settle the business, had his barge got ready, and took with him in his barge the archbishop, and the treasurer, and certain others of his council, and four other barges for his train, and got him to Greenwich, which is three leagues from London. But there the chancellor and the treasurer said to the king that it would be too great folly to trust himself among the commons, for they were men without reason and had not the sense to behave properly. But the commons of Kent, since the king would not come to them because he was dissuaded by his chancellor and treasurer, sent him a petition, requiring that he should grant them the head of the duke of Lancaster, and the heads of fifteen other lords, of whom fourteen (three?) were bishops, who were present with him in the Tower of London. . . .

This the king would not grant them, wherefore they sent to him again a yeoman, praying that he would come and speak with them: and he said that he would gladly do so, but the said chancellor and treasurer gave him contrary counsel, bidding him tell them that if they would come to Windsor on the next Monday they should there have a suitable answer. . . .

And at this time there came a knight with all the haste that he could, crying to the king to wait; and the king, startled at this, awaited his approach to hear what he would say. And the said knight came to the king telling him that he had heard from his servant, who had been in the hands of the rebels on that day, that if he came to them all the land should be lost, for they would never let him loose, but would take him with them all round England, and that they would make him grant them all their demands, and that their purpose was to slay all the lords and ladies of great renown, and all the archbishops, bishops, abbots and priors, monks and canons, parsons and vicars, by the advice and counsel of the aforesaid Sir John Wraw [Ball].

Therefore the king returned towards London as fast as he could, and came to the Tower at the hour of Tierce. And at this time the yeoman who has been mentioned above hastened to Blackheath, crying to his fellows that the king was departed, and that it would be good for them to go on to London and carry out their purpose that same Wednesday. And before the hour of vespers the commons of Kent came, to the number of sixty thousand to Southwark, where was the Marshalsea. And they broke and threw down all the houses in the Marshalsea, and took out of prison all the prisoners who were imprisoned for debt or for felony. And they levelled to the ground a fine house belonging to John Imworth, then marshal of the Marshalsea of the King's Bench, and warden of the prisoners of the said place, and all the dwellings of the jurors and questmongers belonging to the Marshalsea during that night. But at the same time, the commons of Essex came to Lambeth near London, a manor of the archbishop of Canterbury, and entered into the buildings and destroyed many of the goods of the said archbishop, and burnt all the books of register, and rules of remembrances belonging to the chancellor, which they found there.

And the next day, Thursday, which was the feast of Corpus Christi, the 13th day of June . . . the said commons of Essex went in the morning to Highbury, two leagues north of London, a very fine manor belonging to the master of the Hospitallers. They set it on fire, to the great damage and loss of the Knights Hospitallers of St. John. Then some of them returned to London, but others remained in the open fields all that night. And this same day of Corpus Christi, in the morning, the commons of Kent cast down a certain house of ill-fame near London Bridge, which was in the hands of Flemish women, and they had the said house to rent from the mayor of London. And then they went on to the Bridge to pass into the City, but the mayor was ready before them, and had the chains drawn up, and the drawbridge lifted, to prevent their passage. And the commons of Southwark rose with them and cried to the custodians of the Bridge to lower the drawbridge and let them in, or otherwise they should be undone. And for fear that they had of their lives, the custodians let them enter, much against their will. At this time all the religious and the parsons and vicars of London were going devoutly in procession to pray God for peace. At this same time the commons took their way through the middle of London, and did no harm or damage till they came to Fleet Street. . . . And in Fleet Street the men of Kent broke open the prison of the Fleet, and turned out all the prisoners, and let them go whither they would. Then they stopped, and cast down to the ground and burnt the shop of a certain chandler, and another shop belonging to a blacksmith, in the middle of the said street. And, as is supposed, there shall never be houses there again, defacing the beauty of that street. . . .

And then they went towards the Savoy, and set fire to divers houses of divers unpopular persons on the western side: and at last they came to the Savoy, and broke open the gates, and entered into the place and came to the wardrobe. And they took all the torches they could find, and lighted them, and burnt all the sheets and coverlets and beds and headboards of great worth, for their whole value was estimated at one thousand marks. And all the napery and other things that they could discover they carried to the hall and set on fire with their torches. And they burnt the hall, and the chambers, and all the buildings within the gates of the said palace or manor, which the commons of London had left unburnt. And, as is said, they found three barrels of gunpowder, and thought it was gold or silver, and cast it into the fire, and the powder exploded, and set the hall in a greater blaze than before, to the great loss and damage

of the duke of Lancaster. And the commons of Kent got
the credit of the arson, but some say that the Londoners
were really the guilty parties, for their hatred to the said
duke. . . .

At this time the king was in a turret of the great
Tower of London, and could see the manor of the Savoy
and the Hospital of Clerkenwell, and the house of Simon
Hosteler near Newgate, and John Butterwick's place, all
on fire at once. And he called all his lords about him to
his chamber, and asked counsel what they should do in
such necessity. And none of them could or would give
him any counsel, wherefore the young king said that he
would send to the Mayor of the City, to bid him order
the sheriffs and aldermen to have it cried round their
wards that every man between the age of fifteen and
sixty, on pain of life and members, should go next morning (which was Friday) to Mile End, and meet him
there at seven o'clock. He did this in order that all the
commons who were encamped around the Tower might
be induced to abandon the siege, and come to Mile End
to see him and hear him, so that those who were in the
Tower could get off safely whither they would, and save
themselves. But it came to nought, for some of them
did not get the good fortune to be preserved. And on
that Thursday, the said feast of Corpus Christi, the king,
being in the Tower very sad and sorry, mounted up into
a little turret towards St. Catherine's, where were lying
a great number of the commons, and had proclamation
made to them that they all should go peaceably to their
homes, and he would pardon them all manner of their
trespasses. But all cried with one voice that they would
not go before they had captured the traitors who lay in
the Tower, nor until they had got charters to free them
from all manner of serfdom, and had got certain other
points which they wished to demand. And the king

benevolently granted all, and made a clerk write a bill in their presence . . .

And when the commons had heard the bill, they said that this was nothing but trifles and mockery. Therefore they returned to London and had it cried around the City that all lawyers, and all the clerks of the chancery and the exchequer and every man who could write a brief or a letter should be beheaded, whenever they could be found. At this time they burnt several more houses in the City, and the king himself ascended to a high garret of the Tower and watched the fires. Then he came down again and sent for the lords to have their counsel, but they knew not how they should counsel him, and all were wondrous abashed.

And next day, Friday, the commons of the country-side and the commons of London assembled in fearful strength, to the number of one hundred thousand or more, besides some four score who remained on Tower Hill to watch those who were in the Tower. And some went to Mile End, on the Brentwood Road, to wait for the coming of the king, because of the proclamation that he had made. . . .

And by seven o'clock the king came to Mile End, and with him his mother in a whirlicote, and also the earls of Buckingham, Kent, Warwick, and Oxford, and Sir Thomas Percy, and Sir Robert Knolles, and the mayor of London, and many knights and squires; and Sir Aubrey de Vere carried the sword of state. And when he was come the commons all knelt down to him, saying "Welcome our Lord King Richard, if it pleases you, and we will not have any other king but you." And Wat Tighler, their leader and chief, prayed in the name of the commons that he would suffer them to take and deal with all the traitors against him and the law, and the king granted that they should have at their disposition all who were traitors, and could be proved to be traitors by process of law. The said Walter and the commons were carrying two banners, and many pennons and pennoncels, while they made their petition to the king. And they required that for the future no man should be in serfdom, nor make any manner of homage or suit to any lord, but should give a rent of 4d. an acre for his land. They asked also that no one should serve any man except by his own good will, and on terms of regular covenant.

And at this time the king made the commons draw themselves out in two lines, and proclaimed to them that he would confirm and grant it that they should be free, and generally should have their will, and that they might go through all the realm of England and catch all traitors and bring them to him in safety, and then he would deal with them as the law demanded.

Under colour of this grant Wat Tighler and [some of] the commons took their way to the Tower, to seize the archbishop, while the rest remained at Mile End. . . .

And at the same time the commons made proclamation that whoever could catch any Fleming or other alien of any nation, might cut off his head, and so they did after this. Then they took the heads of the archbishop and of the others and put them on wooden poles, and carried them before them in procession, as far as the shrine of Westminster Abbey, in despite of them and of God and Holy Church; and vengeance descended on them no long time after. Then they returned to London Bridge and set the head of the archbishop above the gate, with eight other heads of those they had murdered, so that all could see them who passed over the Bridge. This done, they went to the church of St. Martin's in the Vintry, and found therein thirty-five Flemings, whom they dragged out and beheaded in the street. On that day there were beheaded in all some one hundred and forty or one hundred and sixty persons. Then they took their way to the houses of Lombards and other aliens, and broke into their dwellings, and robbed them of all their goods that they could lay hands on. This went on for all that day and the night following, with hideous cries and horrid tumult. . . .

Then the king caused a proclamation to be made that all the commons of the country who were still in London should come to Smithfield, to meet him there; and so they did.

And when the king and his train had arrived there they turned into the eastern meadow in front of St. Bartholomew's, which is a house of canons: and the commons arrayed themselves on the west side in great battles. At this moment the mayor of London, William Walworth, came up, and the king bade him go to the commons, and make their chieftain come to him. And when he was summoned by the mayor, by the name of Wat Tighler of Maidstone, he came to the king with great confidence, mounted on a little horse, that the commons might see him. And he dismounted, holding in his hand a dagger which he had taken from another man, and when he had dismounted he half bent his knee, and then took the king by the hand, and shook his arm forcibly and roughly, saying to him, "Brother, be of good comfort and joyful, for you shall have, in the fortnight that is to come, praise from the commons even more than you have yet had, and we shall be good companions." And the king said to Walter, "Why will you not go back to your own country?" But the other answered, with a great oath, that neither he nor his fellows would depart until they had got their charter such as they wished to have it, and had certain points rehearsed, and added to their charter which they wished to demand. And he said in a threatening fashion that the lords of the realm would rue it bitterly if these points were not settled to their pleasure. Then the king asked him what were the points which he wished to have revised, and he should have them freely, without contradiction, written out and sealed. Thereupon the said Walter rehearsed the points which were to be demanded; and he asked that there should be no law within the realm save the law of Winchester, and that from henceforth there should be no outlawry in any process of law, and that no lord should have lordship save civilly, and that there should be equality (?) among all people save only the king, and that the goods of Holy Church should not remain in the hands of the religious, nor of parsons and vicars, and other churchmen; but that clergy already in possession should have a sufficient sustenance from the endowments, and the rest of the goods should be divided among the people of the parish. And he demanded that there should be only one bishop in England and only one prelate, and all the lands and tenements now held by them should be confiscated, and divided among the commons, only reserving for them a reasonable sustenance. And he demanded that there should be no more villeins in England, and no serfdom or villeinage, but that all men should be free and of one condition. To this the king gave an easy answer, and said that he should have all that he could fairly grant, reserving only for himself the regality of his crown. And then he bade him go back to his home without making further delay.

During all this time that the king was speaking, no lord or counsellor dared or wished to give answer to the commons in any place save the king himself. Presently Wat Tighler, in the presence of the king, sent for a flagon of water to rinse his mouth, because of the great heat that he was in, and when it was brought he rinsed his mouth in a very rude and disgusting fashion before the king's face. And then he made them bring him a jug of beer, and drank a great draught, and then, in the presence of the king, climbed on his horse again. At this time a certain valet from Kent, who was among the king's retinue, asked that the said Walter, the chief of the commons, might be pointed out to him. And when he saw him, he said aloud that he knew him for the greatest thief and robber in all Kent. Watt heard these words, and bade him come out to him, wagging his head at him in sign of malice; but the valet refused to approach, for fear that he had of the mob. But at last the lords made him go out to him, to see what he [Watt] would do before the king. And when Watt saw him he ordered one of his followers, who was riding behind him carrying his banner displayed, to dismount and behead the said valet. But the valet answered that he had done nothing worthy of death, for what he had said was true, and he would not deny it, but he could not lawfully make debate in the presence of his liege lord, without leave, except in his own defence: but that he could do without reproof; for if he was struck he would strike back again. And for these words Watt tried to strike him with his dagger, and would have slain him in the king's presence; but because he strove so to do, the mayor of London, William Walworth, reasoned with the said Watt for his violent behaviour and despite, done in the king's presence, and arrested him. And because he arrested him, the said Watt stabbed the mayor with his dagger in the stomach in great wrath. But, as it pleased God, the mayor was wearing armour and took no harm, but like a hardy and vigorous man drew his cutlass, and struck back at the said Watt, and gave him a deep cut on the neck, and then a great cut on the head. And during this scuffle one of the king's household drew his sword, and ran Watt two or three times through the body, mortally wounding him. And he spurred his horse, crying to the commons to avenge him, and the horse carried him some four score paces, and then he fell to the ground half dead. And when the commons saw him fall, and knew not how for certain it was, they began to bend their bows and to shoot, wherefore the king himself spurred his horse, and rode out to them, commanding them that they should all come to him to Clerkenwell Fields.

Meanwhile the mayor of London rode as hastily as he could back to the City, and commanded those who were in charge of the twenty-four wards to make proclamation round their wards, that every man should arm himself as quickly as he could, and come to the king in St. John's Fields, where were the commons, to aid the king, for he was in great trouble and necessity. But at this time most of the knights and squires of the king's household, and many others, for fear that they had to this affray, left their lord and went each one his way. And afterwards, when the king had reached the open fields, he made the commons array themselves on the west side of the fields. And presently the aldermen came to him in a body, bringing with them their wardens, and the wards arrayed in bands, a fine company of well-armed folks in great strength. And they enveloped the commons like sheep within a pen, and after that the mayor had set the wardens of the city on their way to the king, he returned with a company of lances to Smithfield, to make an end of the captain of the commons. And when he came to Smithfield he found not there the said captain Watt Tighler, at which he marvelled much, and asked what was become of the traitor. And it was told him that he had been carried by some of the commons to the hospital for poor folks by St. Bartholomew's, and was put to bed in the chamber of the master of the hospital. And the mayor went thither and found him, and had him carried out to the middle of Smithfield, in presence of his fellows, and there beheaded. And thus ended his wretched life. But the mayor had his head set on a pole and borne before him to the king, who still abode in the Fields. And when the king saw the head he had it brought near him to abash the commons, and thanked the mayor greatly for what he had done. And when the commons saw that their chieftain, Watt Tyler, was dead in such a manner, they fell to the ground there among the wheat, like beaten men, imploring the king for mercy for their misdeeds. And the king benevolently granted them mercy, and most of them took to flight. But the king ordained two knights to conduct the rest of them, namely the Kentishmen, through London, and over London Bridge, without doing them harm, so that each of them could go to his own home. Then the king ordered the mayor to put a helmet on his head because of what was to happen, and the mayor asked for what reason he was to do so, and the king told him that he was much obliged to him, and that for this he was to receive the order of knighthood. And the mayor answered that he was not worthy or able to have or to spend a knight's estate, for he was but a merchant and had to live by traffic; but finally the king made him put on the helmet, and took a sword in both his hands and dubbed him knight with great good will. The same day he made three other knights from among the citizens of London on that same spot . . . and the king gave Sir William Walworth £100 in land, and each of the others £40 in land, for them and their heirs. And after this the king took his way to London to the Wardrobe to ease him of his great toils. . . .

At this same time the commons had risen in Suffolk

in great numbers, and had as their chief Sir John Wraw, who brought with him more than ten thousand men. And they robbed many good folks, and cast their houses to the ground. . . .

At the same time there were great levies in Norfolk, and the rebels did great harm throughout the countryside, for which reason the bishop of Norwich, Sir Henry Despenser, sent letters to the said commons, to bid them cease their malice and go to their homes, without doing any more mischief. But they would not, and went through the land destroying and spoiling many townships, and houses of divers folk. . . .

Afterwards the king sent out his messengers into divers parts, to capture the malefactors and put them to death. And many were taken and hanged at London, and they set up many gallows around the City of London, and in other cities and boroughs of the south country. At last, as it pleased God, the king seeing that too many of his liege subjects would be undone, and too much blood spilt, took pity in his heart, and granted them all pardon, on condition that they should never rise again, under pain of losing life or members, and that each of them should get his charter of pardon, and pay the king as fee for his seal twenty shillings, to make him rich. And so finished this wicked war.

From *Anonimalle Chronicle*, trans. C. Oman, in *The Great Revolt of 1381* (Oxford: Clarendon Press, 1906).

My Brother Man

WALTHER VON DER VOGELWEIDE

Thirteenth century

Who fears not, God, Thy gifts to take,
And then Thy ten commandments break,
Lacks that true love which should be his salvation.
For many call Thee Father, who
Will not own me as brother too:
They speak deep words from shallow meditation.
Mankind arises from one origin;
We are alike both outward and within;
Our mouths are sated with the selfsame fare.
And when their bones into confusion fall,
Say ye, who knew the living man by sight,
Which is the villein now and which the knight,
That worms have gnawed their carcasses so bare?
Christians, Jews, and heathens serve Him all,
And God has all creation in His care.

From *I Saw the World*, trans. I. G. Colvin (London: Arnold,
1938).

Piers Plowman's Protest

WILLIAM LANGLAND

Fourteenth century

Therefore I warn you rich, who are able in this world
On trust of your treasure to have triennials and pardons,
Be never the bolder to break the ten commandments;
And most of all you masters, mayors and judges,
Who have the wealth of this world, and are held wise
     by your neighbours,
You who purchase your pardons and papal charters:
At the dread doom, when the dead shall rise
And all come before Christ, and give full accounting,
When the doom will decide what day by day you
     practised,
How you led your life and were lawful before him,
Though you have pocketfuls of pardons there or pro-
     vincial letters,
Though you be found in the fraternity of all the four
     orders,
Though you have double indulgences—unless Do Well
     help you
I set your patents and your pardons at the worth of a
     peascod!
Therefore I counsel all Christians to cry God mercy,
And Mary His Mother be our mean between Him,
That God may give us grace, ere we go hence,
To work with such a will, while we are here,
That after our death day, and at the Day of Doom,
Do Well may declare that we did as He commanded.

• • •

The poor may plead and pray in the doorway;
They may quake for cold and thirst and hunger;
None receives them rightfully and relieves their suffer-
ing.
They are hooted at like hounds and ordered off.
Little does he love the Lord, who lent him all these
favours,
And who so parts his portion with the poor who are in
trouble.
If there were no more mercy among poor than among
rich men,
Mendicants might go meatless to slumber.
God is often in the gorge of these great masters,
But among lowly men are his mercy and his works;
And so says the psalter, as I have seen it often:
*Ecce audivimus eam in Effrata, invenimus eam in cam-
pis silvae.*
Clerics and other conditions converse of God readily,
And have him much in the mouth, but mean men in
their hearts.

Friars and false men have found such questions
To please proud men since the pestilence season,
And have so preached at Saint Paul's from pure envy of
clerics,
That men are not firm in faith nor free in bounty
Nor sorry for their sins. Pride has so multiplied
In religious orders and in the realm, among rich and
poor folk,
That prayers have no power to prevent the pestilence,
Yet the wretches of this world are not warned by each
other.
The dread of death cannot draw pride from them;

Nor are they plentiful to the poor as plain charity wishes;
But glut themselves with their goods in gaiety and glut-
tony,
And break no bread with the beggar as the Book teaches.

• • •

Lo, lords, lo, and ladies! witness
That the sweet liquor lasts but a little season,
Like peapods, and early pears, plums and cherries.
What lances up lightly lasts but a moment,
And what is readiest to ripen rots soonest.
A fat land full of dung breeds foul weeds rankly,
And so are surely all such bishops,
Earls and archdeacons and other rich clerics
Who traffic with tradesmen and turn on them if they
are beaten,
And have the world at their will to live otherwise.
As weeds run wild on ooze or on the dunghill,
So riches spread upon riches give rise to all vices.
The best wheat is bent before ripening
On land that is overlaid with marle or the dungheap.
And so are surely all such people:
Overplenty feeds the pride which poverty conquers.

The wealth of this world is evil to its keeper,
Howsoever it may be won, unless it be well expended.
If he is far from it, he fears often
That false men or felons will fetch away his treasure.
Moreover wealth makes men on many occasions
To sin, and to seek out subtlety and treason,
Or from coveting of goods to kill the keepers.
Thus many have been murdered for their money or
riches,
And those who did the deed damned forever,

And he himself, perhaps, in hell for his hard holding;
And greed for goods was the encumbrance of all to-
    gether.
Pence have often purchased both palaces and terror;
Riches are the root of robbery and of murder;
He who so gathers his goods prizes God at little.

Ah! well may it be with poverty, for he may pass un-
    troubled,
And in peace among the pillagers if patience follow
    him!
Our Prince Jesus and His Apostles chose poverty to-
    gether,
And the longer they lived the less wealth they mastered.

• • •

"When the kindness of Constantine gave Holy Church
    endowments
In lands and leases, lordships and servants,
The Romans heard an angel cry on high above them:
'This day *dos ecclesiae* has drunk venom
And all who have Peter's power are poisoned forever.'
But a medicine may be given to amend prelates
Who should pray for the peace and whose possessions
    prevent them.
Take your lands, you lords, and let them live by tithing!
If possession is poison and makes imperfect orders,
It were good to dislodge them for the Church's profit,
And purge them of that poison before the peril is greater.

"If priesthood were perfect all the people would be con-
    verted
Who are contrary to Christ's law and who hold Christen-
    dom in dishonour.
All pagans pray and believe rightly

In the great and holy God, and ask His grace to aid
them.
Their mediator is Mohammed to move their petition.
Thus the folk live in a faith but with a false advocate,
Which is rueful for righteous men in the realms of Chris-
tendom,
And a peril to the pope and to the prelates of his crea-
tion
Who bear the names of the bishops of Bethlehem and
Babylon."

• • •

"And would that you, Conscience, were in the court of
the king always,
That Grace, whom you commend so, were the guide of
all clergy,
And that Piers with his plows, the newer and the older,
Were emperor of all the world, and all men Christian!
He is but a poor pope who should be the peoples' helper
And who sends men to slay the souls that they should
rescue.
But well be it with Piers the Plowman who pursues his
duty!
Qui pluit super justos et injustos equally,
Sends forth the sun to shine on the villein's tillage
As brightly as on the best man's and on the best
woman's.
So Piers the Plowman is at pains to harrow
As well for a waster and for wenches in the brothels
As for himself and his servants, though he is served
sooner.
He toils and tills for a traitor as earnestly
As for an honest husbandman, and at all times equally.
May he be worshipped who wrought all, both the good
and the wicked,

And suffers the sinful till the season of their repentance!
God amend the pope, who pillages Holy Church,
Who claims that before the king he is the keeper of
    Christians,
Who accounts it nothing that Christians are killed and
    beaten,
Who leads the people to battle and spills the blood of
    Christians,
Against the Old Law and the New Law, as Luke wit-
    nesses. . . .
Surely it seems that if himself has his wishes
He recks nothing of the right nor of the rest of the peo-
    ple.
But may Christ in His Kindness save the cardinals and
    prelates
And turn their wits into wisdom and to welfare of the
    spirit!"

"Charity is God's champion, like a child that is gentle,
And the merriest of mouth at meat and at table.
For the love that lies in his heart makes him lightsome in
    language,
And he is companionable and cheerful as Christ bids
    him.
Nolite fieri sicut hypocritae tristes, etc.
I have seen him in silk and sometimes in russet,
In grey and in furred gowns and in gilt armour;
And he gave them as gladly to any creature who needed
    them.
Edmund and Edward were each kings
And considered saints when Charity followed them.
I have seen Charity also singing and reading,
Riding, and running in ragged clothing;

But among bidders and beggars I beheld him never.
In rich robes he is most rarely witnessed,
With a cap or a crown glistening and shaven,
Or in cleanly clothes of gauze or Tartary.
In a friar's frock he was found once,
But that was afar back in Saint Francis' lifetime;
In that sect since he has been too seldom witnessed.
He receives the robes of the rich, and praises
All who lead their lives without deception.
Beatus est dives qui, etc.
He comes often in the king's court where the council is
    honest,
But if Covetousness is of the council he will not come
    into it.
He comes but seldom in court with jesters,
Because of brawling and backbiting and bearing false
    witness.
He comes but rarely in the consistory where the com-
    missary is seated,
For their lawsuits are overlong unless they are lifted by
    silver,
And they make and unmake matrimony for money.
Whom Conscience and Christ have combined firmly
They undo unworthily, these Doctors of Justice.
His ways were once among the clergy,
With archbishops and bishops and prelates of Holy
    Church,
To apportion Christ's patrimony to the poor and needy.
But now Avarice keeps the keys and gives to his kins-
    men,
To his executors and his servants and sometimes to his
    children.

"I blame no man living; but Lord amend us

And give us all grace, good God, to follow Charity!
Though he mistrusts such manners in all men who meet
    him,
He neither blames nor bans nor boasts nor praises,
Nor lowers nor lauds nor looks sternly
Nor craves nor covets nor cries after more.
In pace in idipsum dormiam, etc.
The chief livelihood that he lives by is love in God's
    passion.
He neither bids nor begs nor borrows to render.
He misuses no man and his mouth hurts no one."

From *The Vision of Piers Plowman*, trans. H. W. Wells.

The Waldensian Heretics

BERNARD GUI

Early fourteenth century

CONCERNING THE WALDENSIAN SECT AND FIRST OF ALL CONCERNING THEIR ORIGINS AND BEGINNINGS

THE sect and heresy of the Waldensians began in about the year 1170 A.D. Its founder was a certain citizen of Lyons, named Waldes or Waldo, from whom his followers were named. He was a rich man, who, after having given up all his wealth, determined to observe poverty and evangelical perfection, in imitation of the apostles. He caused to be translated into the French tongue, for his use, the Gospels, and some other books of the Bible, and also some authoritative sayings of Saints Augustine, Jerome, Ambrose, and Gregory, arranged under titles, which he and his followers called "sentences." They read these very often, and hardly understood them, since they were quite unlettered, but infatuated with their own interpretation, they usurped the office of the apostles, and presumed to preach the Gospel in the streets and public places. And the said Waldes or Waldo converted many people, both men and women, to a like presumption, and sent them out to preach as his disciples.

Since these people were ignorant and illiterate, they, both men and women, ran about through the towns, and entered the houses. Preaching in public places and also in the churches, they, especially the men, spread many errors around about them.

They were summoned, however, by the archbishop of Lyons, the Lord Jean aux Belles-Mains, and were forbidden such great presumption, but they wished by no means to obey him, and cloaked their madness by saying that it was necessary to obey God rather than man. They said that God had commanded the apostles to preach the Gospel to all men, applying to themselves what was said to the apostles whose imitators and successors they boldly declared themselves to be, by a false profession of poverty and the feigned image of sanctity. They scorned the prelates and the clergy, because they abounded in riches and lived in pleasantness.

So then, by this arrogant usurpation of the office of preaching, they became masters of error. Admonished to cease, they disobeyed and were declared contumacious, and then were excommunicated and expelled from that city and their country. Finally in a certain council which was held at Rome before the Lateran council, since they were obstinate, they were judged schismatic, and then condemned as heretics. Thus, multiplied upon the earth, they dispersed themselves through that province, and through the neighbouring regions, and into Lombardy. Separated and cut off from the Church, mingling with other heretics and imbibing their errors, they mixed the errors and heresies of earlier heretics with their own inventions. . . .

CONCERNING THE ERRORS OF THE WALDENSIANS OF MODERN TIMES (SINCE FORMERLY THEY HAD MANY OTHERS)

The principal heresy, then, of the aforesaid Waldensians was and still remains the contempt for ecclesiastical power. Excommunicated for this reason, and delivered to Satan, they were precipitated into innumerable errors, and mingled the errors of earlier heretics with their own.

The erring followers and sacrilegious masters of this sect hold and teach that they are not subject to the lord pope or Roman pontiff or to any prelates of the Roman Church, declaring that the Roman Church has persecuted and condemned them unjustly and undeservedly. Also they assert that they cannot be excommunicated by the Roman pontiff and the prelates, and that they ought not to obey any of them, when they order or command the followers and teachers of the said sect to abandon or abjure it, although this sect has been condemned as heretical by the Roman Church.

Also, they hold and teach that all oaths, whether in justice or otherwise, without exception and explanation, are forbidden by God, and illicit and sinful, interpreting thus in an excessive and unreasonable sense the words of the holy Gospel and of St. James the Apostle against swearing. Nevertheless, the swearing of oaths is lawful and obligatory for the purpose of declaring the truth in justice, according not only to the same doctrine of the saints and doctors of the Church and the tradition of the same holy Catholic Church, but also to the decree of the Church published against the aforesaid error:

"If any of these should reject the religious obligation of taking an oath by a damnable superstition, and should refuse to swear, from this fact they may be considered heretics."

It should be known, however, that these Waldensians give themselves dispensations in the matter of taking oaths; they have the right to swear an oath to avoid death for themselves or for another, and also in order not to betray their fellows, or reveal the secret of their sect. For they say that it is an inexpiable crime and a sin against the Holy Ghost to betray a "perfect" member of their sect.

Also, from this same fount of error, the said sect and heresy declares that all judgment is forbidden by God, and consequently is sinful, and that any judge violates this prohibition of God, who in whatever case and for whatever cause sentences a man to corporal punishment, or to a penalty of blood, or to death. In this, they apply, without the necessary explanation, the words of the holy Gospel where it is written: "Judge not, that ye be not judged," and "Thou shalt not kill," and other similar texts; they do not understand these or know either their meaning or their interpretation, as the holy Roman Church wisely understands them and transmits them to the faithful according to the doctrines of the fathers and doctors, and the decisions of canon law.

Also, the aforesaid sect, wandering from the straight and narrow path, does not accept or consider valid the canonical sanctions and the decretals and constitutions of the supreme pontiffs, and the regulations concerning fasts and the celebration of feast days, and the decrees of the fathers, but scorns, rejects, and condemns them.

Also, more perniciously in error concerning the sacrament of penance and the power of keys, the aforesaid heretics say, hold, and teach that they have power from

God alone and from no other, just as the apostles had from Christ, of hearing the confessions of the men and women who wish to confess to them and be absolved and have penances imposed on them. And they hear the confessions of such people and absolve them and impose penances, although they are not priests or clerics ordained by any bishop of the Roman Church, but are simply laymen. They do not confess that they hold such power from the Roman Church, but rather deny it, and in fact they hold it neither from God nor from His Church, since they are outside the Church, and are now cut off from that Church outside which there is no true penitence or salvation.

Also, the aforesaid sect and heresy ridicule the indulgences which are made and given by the prelates of the Church and declare that they are worthless.

They are in error indeed concerning the sacrament of the Eucharist, saying, not publicly but secretly, that in the sacrament of the altar the bread and wine do not become the body and blood of Christ if the priest who celebrates or consecrates is a sinner; and they consider any man a sinner who does not belong to their sect. Also, they say that the consecration of the body and blood of Christ may be made by any just person, although he be a layman and not a priest ordained by a Catholic bishop, provided he is a member of their sect. They even believe the same thing concerning women, if they are of their sect, and so they say that every holy person is a priest. . . .

Also, they declare that there are three ranks in their church; deacons, priests, and bishops, and that the power of each of these comes from them only, and not from the Roman Church. They believe that the holy orders of the Roman Church are not from God, but from human tradition and so they falsely deceive when they profess that they believe that there are in the holy church (meaning their own) the holy orders of the episcopate, the priesthood, and the diaconate. . . .

These three doctrines, however, they do not make known indifferently to their "believers," but the "perfect" of this sect hold them among themselves; namely, that the miracles of the saints are not true, that prayers should not be made to them, and that their feasts should not be celebrated, except Sunday, the feasts of the Blessed Virgin Mary, and, some add, the feasts of the apostles and evangelists.

They teach these and other insane and erroneous doctrines, which follow by necessity from those which precede them, secretly to their "believers" in their conventicles. They also preach to them on the Gospels and Epistles and other sacred writings, which these masters of error, who do not know how to be the disciples of truth, distort by their interpretation. For preaching is absolutely forbidden to laymen. It should be known, also, that this sect formerly had and held many other errors, and still in certain regions is said to hold them secretly, such as those concerning the celebration of the mass on Holy Thursday, described above, and the abominable and promiscuous coupling of men and women, under cover of darkness, and concerning the apparition of cats, sprinkling with the tail, and certain others described more fully in the little summaries written on this subject.

CONCERNING THE MANNER OF LIFE OF THE WALDENSIANS

Something should be said concerning the practices and way of life of the Waldensian heretics, in order that they may be known and recognized.

In the first place, then, it should be known that the Waldensians have and establish for themselves one superior whom they call their "majoral" and whom all must obey, just as all Catholics obey the lord pope.

Also, the Waldensians eat and drink at common meals. Also those who can and will, fast on Mondays and Wednesdays; those who fast, however, eat meat. Also, they fast on Fridays, and during Lent, and then they abstain from meat in order not to give scandal to others, since they say that to eat meat on any day whatsoever is not a sin, because Christ did not prohibit the eating of meat, nor order anyone to abstain from it.

Also, after they have been received into this society, which they call a "fraternity," and have promised obedience to their superior, and that they will observe evangelical poverty, from that time they should observe chastity and should not own property, but should sell all that they possess and give the price to the common fund, and live on alms which are given to them by their "believers" and those who sympathize with them. And the superior distributes these among them, and gives to each one according to his needs.

Also, the Waldensians recommend continence to their believers. They concede, however, that burning passion ought to be satisfied, in whatever shameful way, interpreting the words of the Apostle [Paul]: "It is better to marry than to burn," to mean that it is better to appease desire by any shameful act than to be tempted inwardly in the heart. This doctrine they keep very secret, however, in order not to seem vile to their "believers."

Also, they have collections made by their "believers" and friends, and what is given and received they take to their superior.

Also, each year they hold or celebrate one or two general chapters in some important town, as secretly as possible, assembling, as if they were merchants, in a house hired long before by one or more of the "believers." And in those chapters the superior of all orders and disposes matters concerning the priests and deacons and concerning those sent to different parts and regions to their "believers" and friends to hear confessions and to collect alms. He also receives the account of receipts and expenses.

Also, they do not work with their hands after they have been made "perfect," nor do they do any work for profit, except perchance in case it is necessary to dissimulate, so that they may not be recognized and apprehended.

Also, they commonly call themselves brothers, and they say that they are the poor of Christ or the poor of Lyons.

Also, they hypocritically insinuate themselves into the society of the religious and of the clergy, so that they may conceal themselves, and they bestow gifts or presents upon them and pay them reverence and services so that they may obtain a freer opportunity for themselves and theirs to hide, to live, and to injure souls.

Also, they frequent the churches and sermons, and in all externals conduct themselves with religion and compunction, and strive to use unctuous and discreet language.

Also, they say many prayers during the day, and they instruct their "believers" that they should pray as they do, and with them. This is their manner of praying: on bended knees, they bow down on a bench or on something like it, and so, on their knees, bowed down to the ground, they all remain praying in silence for as long as it takes to say the "Our Father" thirty or forty times or more. They do this regularly each day, when they are with their "believers" and sympathizers, with no strangers present, before and after dinner, before and after supper, at night when they go to bed, before they lie down; also in the morning when they arise, and in the course of the day, both in the morning and in the afternoon.

Also, they say and teach and recognize no other prayer besides the "Our Father." They have no regard for the salutation of the Virgin Mary, "Hail, Mary," or for the Apostles' Creed, "I believe in God," for they say that these have been arranged or composed by the Roman Church and not by Christ. They keep, however, seven articles of the faith on divinity, seven on humanity, and the ten commandments of the Decalogue, and the seven works of mercy. They have arranged and compoed these in a sort of résumé and in a certain way, and they say and teach them thus. They glory exceedingly in this and they show themselves immediately ready to answer concerning their faith.

They can thus easily be detected in this way: "Say for me the Apostles' Creed, as the Catholic Church says it, since it contains all the articles" and then they answer: "I do not know it, because no one has taught me thus." . . .

Also, they tell their "believers" that they should in no way betray them to chaplains or clerics or religious or inquisitors, because, if they should be known, they would be seized. They are pursued by the inquisitors and those of the Roman Church unjustly, they say to their "believers," because it is they who serve God and observe the commandments of God and practise poverty and evangelical perfection, just as Christ and the apostles did. They say that they themselves know the truth and the way of God better than the chaplains and clerics and religious of the Roman Church, who persecuted them through ignorance of the truth. . . .

ON THE METHOD OF TEACHING OF THE WALDENSIANS

One can distinguish two categories in this sect; there are the "perfect," and these are properly called Waldensians. These, previously instructed, are received into their order according to a special rite, so that they may know how to teach others. These "perfect" claim that they possess nothing of their own, neither houses nor possessions nor furnishings. Moreover, if they had had wives before, they give them up when they are received. They say that they are the successors of the apostles, and are the masters and confessors of the others. They travel through the country, visiting and confirming their disciples in error. Their disciples and "believers" supply them with necessities. Wherever the "perfect" go, the "believers" spread the news of their arrival, and many come to the house, where they are admitted to see and hear them. All sorts of good things to eat and drink are brought to them, and their preaching is heard in assemblies which gather chiefly at night, when others are sleeping or resting.

The "perfect," moreover, do not immediately in the beginning reveal the secrets of their error. First they say what the disciples of Christ should be like, according to the words of the Gospel and of the apostles. Only those, they say, should be the successors of the apostles who imitate and hold to the example of their life. On this basis, they argue and conclude that the pope, the bishops and prelates, and clergy, who possess the riches of this world and do not imitate the sanctity of the apostles, are not true pastors and guides of the Church of God, but ravening and devouring wolves, to whom Christ did not deign to entrust His spouse the Church, and so they should not be obeyed. They also say that an impure person cannot purify another, nor can one who is bound loose another, nor can an accused person influence a judge, already angered against him, in favour of another accused person. One who is on the road to perdition cannot lead another to heaven. In this way, they slander the clergy and the prelates, in order to render them odious, so that they will not be believed or obeyed.

The Waldensians, then, commonly say and teach to their "believers" certain things which seem good and moral, concerning the virtues which should be practised, the good works which should be done, and the vices to be avoided and fled from. Thus they are more readily listened to in other matters, and they ensnare their hearers. For they say that one should not lie, since everyone who lies slays his soul, according to the Scripture; also that one should not do to another, what he would not want done to him. One should obey the commandments of God. One should not swear in any case because God has forbidden all taking of oaths, saying in the Gospel: "Swear not at all; neither by heaven; for it is God's throne: Nor by the earth for it is the footstool of His feet, nor by any other creature, because a man cannot make one hair white or black, but let your speaking be yea, yea, and nay, nay; for whatever is more than these comes of evil." These words make a great impression on their "believers" and they receive no further interpretation of them. . . .

Also, when they preach on the Gospels and the Epistles, or on the examples or sayings of the saints, they allege: "This is written in the Gospel or in the Epistle of St. Peter or St. Paul or St. James, or the writings of such and such a saint or doctor," so that what they say may be more readily accepted by their hearers.

Moreover, they ordinarily have the Gospels and the Epistles in the vulgar tongue, and also in Latin, since some of them understand it. Some also know how to read, and sometimes they read from a book those things which they say and preach. Sometimes they do not use a book, especially those who do not read, but they have learned these things by heart. . . .

Also, they teach their "believers" that true penitence and the purgatory of sins are only in this life and not in another. And so they instruct their "believers" to confess their sins to them, and they hear confessions, and absolve those who confess to them, and impose penances on them, consisting usually of fasting on Friday and of saying the "Our Father." They say that they have this power from God, just as the apostles had.

Also, according to them, when souls leave their bodies, those which should be saved go immediately to heaven, and those which should be damned immediately to hell. There is no other place for souls, after this life, except paradise or hell.

Also they say that the prayers which are said for the dead are of no avail for them, because those who are in paradise do not need them, and for those who are in hell there is no redemption.

Also, when they hear confessions, they tell those who are confessing that they should not reveal, when they confess to priests, that they have made confessions to those Waldensians.

CONCERNING THE SUBTLETIES AND DECEITS WITH WHICH
THEY CONCEAL THEMSELVES IN ANSWERING

It should be known that it is exceedingly difficult to interrogate and examine the Waldensians, and to get the truth about their errors from them, because of the deception and duplicity with which they answer questions, in order not to be caught. . . .

This is the way they do it. When one of them is arrested and brought for examination, he appears undaunted, and as if he were secure and conscious of no evil in himself. When he is asked if he knows why he has been arrested, he answers very sweetly and with a smile, "My Lord, I should be glad to learn the reason from you." Asked about the faith which he holds and believes, he answers, "I believe everything that a good Christian ought to believe." Questioned as to whom he considers a good Christian, he replies, "He who believes as Holy Church teaches him to believe." When he is asked what he means by "Holy Church," he answers, "My lord, that which you say and believe is the Holy Church." If you say to him, "I believe that the Holy Church is the Roman Church, over which the lord pope rules; and under him, the prelates," he replies, "I believe it," meaning that he believes that you believe it.

Interrogated concerning the articles in which he believes, such as the Incarnation of Christ, His Resurrection and Ascension, he promptly answers, "I firmly believe." Asked if he believes that in the mass the bread and wine are transubstantiated into the body and blood of Christ by the words of the priest and by the divine power, he says, "Should I not, indeed, believe this?" If the inquisitor says, "I do not ask if you should believe, but if you do not believe," he replies, "I believe whatever you and other good doctors command me to believe." . . .

When he is questioned concerning this deception and many others like it, and asked to answer explicitly and directly, he replies, "If you will not interpret what I say simply and sanely, then I do not know how I should answer you. I am a simple and illiterate man. Do not try to ensnare me in my words." If you say to him, "If you are a simple man, answer simply, without dissimulation," he says, "Willingly."

Then if you say, "Will you swear that you have never learned anything contrary to the faith which we say and believe to be true," he answers somewhat timorously, "If I ought to swear, I shall willingly swear." "I am not asking whether you ought to swear, but whether you will swear." Then he replies, "If you command me to swear, I shall swear." I say to him, "I do not compel you to swear, because, since you believe that it is forbidden to take an oath, you will put the blame on me for compelling you; but if you want to swear, I shall listen." Then he answers, "Why should I swear then, if you will not command me?" "To remove the suspicion that you are reputed to be a Waldensian heretic who believes that all swearing of oaths is unlawful and sinful." He then replies, "How ought I to swear?" You say, "Swear as you know." He answers, "My lord, I do not know, unless you teach me." "If I should have to swear, then with hand upraised, and touching the holy Gospels of God, I should say, 'I swear by these holy Gospels that I have never learned or believed anything contrary to the faith which the holy Roman Church believes and holds.'" Then, trembling and as if he did not know how to form the words, he stammers over them, he stops, as if interrupted, and he puts in words, to avoid the direct formula of the oath, but uses certain expressions, which are not swearing, so that he will seem to have sworn. . . .

If, however, one of these heretics consents to swear simply, then you should say to him, "If you now swear in order to be released, you should know that one oath or two or ten or a hundred are not enough for me, but as many as I shall ask. For I know that you are dispensed, and are permitted a certain number of oaths when compelled by necessity, so that you may free yourself or others. But I mean to require of you oaths without number and, moreover, if I have witnesses against you, your oaths will profit you nothing. And then you have stained your conscience by swearing contrary to its dictates and because of this you will not escape."

I have seen some of them who, in such great anxiety, confessed their errors, in order to escape. Others, however, then declared openly that, if it would be of no avail for their escape to swear once or a certain number of times and no more, they refused to swear at all, and said that all swearing is unlawful and sinful. And when one of them was asked why he wished to swear, if he considered it unlawful, he replied: "I wish to deliver myself from death by doing this, and to conserve my life, and I shall do penance afterward for my sin."

From *Manuel de l'inquisiteur*, G. Mollat, ed. (Paris: Champion, 1926); trans. M.M.M.

The Impact of the Black Death

HENRY KNIGHTON

1348-1350

IN THIS year [1348] and in the following one there was a general mortality of men throughout the whole world. It first began in India, then in Tharsis [Taurus?], then it came to the Saracens, and finally to the Christians and Jews, so that in the space of one year, from Easter to Easter, as the rumour spread in the Roman curia, there had died, as if by sudden death, in those remote regions eight thousand legions, besides the Christians. The king of Tharsis, seeing such a sudden and unheard-of slaughter of his people, began a journey to Avignon with a great multitude of his nobles, to propose to the pope that he would become a Christian and be baptized by him, thinking that he might thus mitigate the vengeance of God upon his people because of their wicked unbelief. Then, when he had journeyed for twenty days, he heard that the pestilence had struck among the Christians, just as among other peoples. So, turning in his tracks, he travelled no farther but hastened to return home. The Christians, pursuing these people from behind, slew about seven thousand of them.

There died in Avignon in one day one thousand three hundred and twelve persons, according to a count made for the pope, and, another day, four hundred persons and more. Three hundred and fifty-eight of the Friars Preachers in the region of Provence died during Lent. At Montpellier, there remained out of a hundred and forty friars only seven. There were left at Magdalena only seven friars out of a hundred and sixty, and yet enough. At Marseilles, of a hundred and fifty Friars Minor, there remained only one who could tell the others; that was well, indeed. Of the Carmelites, more than a hundred and sixty-six had died at Avignon before the citizens found out what had happened. For they believed that one had killed another. There was not one of the English Hermits left in Avignon. . . .

At this same time the pestilence became prevalent in England, beginning in the autumn in certain places. It spread throughout the land, ending in the same season of the following year. At the same time many cities in Corinth and Achaia were overturned, and the earth swallowed them. Castles and fortresses were broken, laid low, and swallowed up. Mountains in Cyprus were levelled into one, so that the flow of the rivers was impeded, and many cities were submerged and villages destroyed. Similarly, when a certain friar was preaching at Naples, the whole city was destroyed by an earthquake. Suddenly, the earth was opened up, as if a stone had been thrown into water, and everyone died along with the preaching friar, except for one friar who, fleeing, escaped into a garden outside the city. All of these things were done by an earthquake. . . .

Then that most grievous pestilence penetrated the coastal regions [of England] by way of Southampton, and came to Bristol, and people died as if the whole strength of the city were seized by sudden death. For there were few who lay in their beds more than three days or two and a half days; then that savage death snatched them about the second day. In Leicester, in the little parish of St. Leonard, more than three hundred and eighty died; in the parish of the Holy Cross, more than four hundred, and in the parish of St. Margaret in Leicester, more than seven hundred. And so in each parish, they died in great numbers. Then the bishop of Lincoln sent through the whole diocese, and gave the general power to each and every priest, both regular and secular, to hear confessions and to absolve, by the full and entire power of the bishop, except only in the case of debt. And they might absolve in that case if satisfaction could be made by the person while he lived, or from his property after his death. Likewise, the pope granted full remission of all sins, to be absolved completely, to anyone who was in danger of death, and he granted this power to last until the following Easter. And everyone was allowed to choose his confessor as he pleased.

During this same year, there was a great mortality of sheep everywhere in the kingdom; in one place and in one pasture, more than five thousand sheep died and became so putrefied that neither beast nor bird wanted to touch them. And the price of everything was cheap, because of the fear of death; there were very few who took any care for their wealth, or for anything else. For a man could buy a horse for half a mark, which before was worth forty shillings, a large fat ox for four shillings, a cow for twelve pence, a heifer for sixpence, a large fat sheep for four pence, a sheep for threepence, a lamb for two pence, a fat pig for five pence, a stone of wool for nine pence. And the sheep and cattle wandered about through the fields and among the crops, and there was no one to go after them or to collect them. They perished in countless numbers everywhere, in secluded ditches and hedges, for lack of watching, since there was such a lack of serfs and servants, that no one knew what he should do. For there is no memory of a mortality so severe and so savage from the time of Vortigern, king of the Britons, in whose time, as Bede says, the living did not suffice to bury the dead. In the following autumn, one could not hire a reaper at a lower wage than eight pence with food, or a mower at less than twelve pence with food. Because of this, much grain rotted in the fields for lack of harvesting, but in the year of the plague, as was said above, among other things there was so great an abundance of all kinds of grain that no one seemed to have concerned himself about it.

The Scots, hearing of the cruel pestilence in England, suspected that this had come upon the English by the avenging hand of God, and when they wished to swear an oath, they swore this one, as the vulgar rumour reached the ears of the English, "be the foul deth of Engelond." And so the Scots, believing that the horrible vengeance of God had fallen on the English, came together in the forest of Selkirk to plan an invasion of the whole kingdom of England. But savage mortality supervened, and the sudden and frightful cruelty of death struck the Scots. In a short time, about five thousand died; the rest, indeed, both sick and well, prepared to return home, but the English, pursuing them, caught up with them, and slew a great many of them.

Master Thomas Bradwardine was consecrated archbishop of Canterbury by the pope, and when he returned to England, came to London. In less than two days he was dead. He was famous above all other clerks in Christendom, in theology especially, but also in other liberal studies. At this same time there was so great a lack of priests everywhere that many widowed churches had no divine services, no masses, matins, vespers, sacraments, and sacramentals. One could hardly hire a chaplain to minister to any church for less than ten pounds or ten marks, and whereas, before the pestilence, when there were plenty of priests, one could hire a chaplain for five or four marks or for two marks, with board, there was scarcely anyone at this time who wanted to accept a position for twenty pounds or twenty marks. But within a short time a very great multitude whose wives had died of the plague rushed into holy orders. Of these many were illiterate and, it seemed, simply laymen who knew nothing except how to read to some extent. The hides of cattle went up from a low price to twelve pence, and for shoes the price went to ten, twelve, fourteen pence; for a pair of leggings, to three and four shillings.

Meanwhile, the king ordered that in every county of the kingdom, reapers and other labourers should not receive more than they were accustomed to receive, under the penalty provided in the statute, and he renewed the statute from this time. The labourers, however, were so arrogant and hostile that they did not heed the king's command, but if anyone wished to hire them, he had to pay them what they wanted, and either lose his fruits and crops or satisfy the arrogant and greedy desire of the labourers as they wished. When it was made known to the king that they had not obeyed his mandate, and had

paid higher wages to the labourers, he imposed heavy
fines on the abbots, the priors, the great lords and the
lesser ones, and on others both greater and lesser in the
kingdom. From certain ones he took a hundred shillings,
from some, forty shillings, from others, twenty shillings,
and from each according to what he could pay. And he
took from each ploughland in the whole kingdom twenty
shillings, and not one-fifteenth less than this. Then the
king had many labourers arrested, and put them in
prison. Many such hid themselves and ran away to the
forests and woods for a while, and those who were
captured were heavily fined. And the greater number
swore that they would not take daily wages above those
set by ancient custom, and so they were freed from
prison. It was done in like manner concerning other
artisans in towns and villages. . . .

After the aforesaid pestilence, many buildings, both
large and small, in all cities, towns, and villages had collapsed, and had completely fallen to the ground in the
absence of inhabitants. Likewise, many small villages
and hamlets were completely deserted; there was not
one house left in them, but all those who had lived in
them were dead. It is likely that many such hamlets will
never again be inhabited. In the following summer
[1350], there was so great a lack of servants to do anything that, as one believed, there had hardly been so
great a dearth in past times. For all the beasts and cattle
that a man possessed wandered about without a shepherd, and everything a man had was without a caretaker.
And so all necessities became so dear that anything that
in the past had been worth a penny was now worth four
or five pence. Moreover, both the magnates of the kingdom and the other lesser lords who had tenants, remitted something from the rents, lest the tenants should
leave, because of the lack of servants and the dearth of

things. Some remitted half the rent, some more and others less, some remitted it for two years, some for three, and others for one year, according as they were able to come to an agreement with their tenants. Similarly, those who received day-work from their tenants throughout the year, as is usual from serfs, had to release them and to remit such services. They either had to excuse them entirely or had to fix them in a laxer manner at a small rent, lest very great and irreparable damage be done to the buildings, and the land everywhere remain completely uncultivated. And all foodstuffs and all necessities became exceedingly dear. . . .

From *Chronicon Henrici Knighton*, J. R. Lumby, ed., Rolls Series, vol. 92; trans. M.M.M.

Paris during the Hundred Years' War

THE FALL OF THE GREAT

1413. Also, the first day of July, 1413, the said provost [Pierre des Essarts] was seized in the palace, dragged on a litter to the Heaumerie, and then seated on a plank in the tumbril, holding a wooden cross in his hand, clad in a black greatcoat, fringed and furred with marten, white breeches, with black slippers on his feet; in that condition he was taken to the market-place of Paris and there they cut off his head; and it was put higher than the others by more than three feet. And it is true that, from the time he was put on the litter up to his death, he did nothing but laugh, as he did in his great majesty, from which most people thought him mad; for all those who saw him wept so piteously that you would never hear of greater tears for the death of a man; and he alone laughed. And it was his belief that the common people would prevent his death; but he intended, if he had lived, to betray the city and to deliver it into the hands of the enemy, and himself to make great and cruel slaughter, and to pillage and strip the good citizens of the good city of Paris who had loved him so loyally; for he was wont to order nothing that they did not do as far as possible. It seemed that he had taken such great pride in himself for he had enough offices for six or eight sons of counts or bannerets. First of all, he was provost of Paris, he was grand butler, master of waters and forests, grand general, capitain of Paris, of Cherbourg, of Montgaris, grand falconer, and many other offices; from which he derived such great pride and lost his reason, and thus Fortune led him to this shameful end. And know that when he saw that he was going to die, he knelt before the executioner, and kissed a little image of silver that the executioner wore on his chest; and pardoned him for his death most gently, and begged all the lords that his fate should not be announced before he was decapitated; and they granted him this.

Thus was decapitated Pierre des Essarts, and his body taken to the gibbet, and hung the highest. And about two years before, the duke of Brabant, brother of the duke of Burgundy, who observed his outrageous government, said to him, in the hotel of the king: "Provost of Paris, Jehan de Montaigu took twenty-two years to get his head cut off; but truly you will not take more than three"; and he didn't do it, for he took only about two years and a half from this word; and they said for amusement throughout Paris, that the said duke was a prophet speaking the truth.

INFLATION AND MISERY

1421. Also, at this time, at the feast of the Presentation [February 2], to comfort the poor people, there were again put upon the children of the Enemy of hell, impositions, fourths, and extortionate taxes; and the collectors of them were lazy folk who knew only how to live, who squeezed everything so closely that all merchandise was lacking, both on account of the money as well as the taxes. As a result such high prices followed that at Easter a good ox cost two hundred francs or more, a good calf twelve francs, a flitch of bacon eight or ten francs, a pig sixteen or twenty francs, a small cheese, quite white, sixteen Parisian sous, and all meat a high price; a hundred eggs cost sixteen Parisian sous. And every day and every night there were heard throughout Paris, because of the aforesaid high prices, such long complaints, lamentations, sounds of sorrow, and piteous cries that never, I believe, was Jeremiah the prophet more sorrowful when the city of Jerusalem was entirely destroyed and the children of Israel were led to Babylon in captivity; for night and day cried out men, women, little children, "Alas! I die of cold," or "of hunger."

And in truth it was the longest winter that one had seen for forty years; for at the fairs of Easter it snowed, it froze and brought all the misery of cold that one could imagine. And because of the great poverty that some of the good citizens of the good city of Paris saw being suffered, they went so far as to buy three or four houses which they made into hospitals for the poor children who were dying of hunger within Paris, and they had soup and a good fire and were well bedded down. And in less than three months there were in each hospital forty beds or more well equipped, which the good folk of Paris had given, and there was one in the Heaumerie, another before the Palais, and another in the Place Maubert.

And in truth when good weather came, in April, those who in the winter had made their beverages from apples and sloe plums emptied the residue of their apples and their plums into the street with the intention that the pigs of St. Antoine would eat them. But the pigs did not get to them in time, for as soon as they were thrown out, they were seized by poor folk, women and children, who ate them with great relish, which was a great pity, each for himself; for they ate what the pigs scorned to eat, they ate the cores of cabbages without bread or without cooking, grasses of the fields without bread or salt. In short, it was such a dear time that few households in Paris ate their fill of bread; for flesh they did not eat at all, nor kidney beans, nor peas, only herbs which were marvellously dear. . . .

Also, in this time the wolves were so ravenous, that they unearthed with their claws the bodies of people buried in the villages and fields; for everywhere one went, one found people dead in the fields and towns, from the great poverty, the dear times, and the famine which they suffered, through the cursed war which always grew worse from day to day.

A POPULAR PREACHER

1429. Also, the duke of Burgundy returned to Paris April 4th, the day of St. Ambrose, in a big and fine company of knights and squires; and afterwards, in about eight days there came to Paris a Franciscan named Friar Richard, a man of very great prudence, learned in discourse, a sower of good doctrine to edify his fellow-men. And so much he laboured there that one would scarcely believe it who had not seen it; for as long as he was in

Paris, he missed only one day of preaching; and he began Saturday, April 16, 1429, at St. Geneviève, and Sunday following and the week following, that is, Monday, Tuesday, Wednesday, Thursday, Friday, Saturday, Sunday of the Innocents; and his sermon began about five o'clock in the morning and lasted until between ten and eleven o'clock. And he always had some five or six thousand persons at his sermon; and he was raised, when he preached, on a scaffolding which was almost two meters and a half high. . . .

Also, the aforesaid friar preached the day of St. Mark following at Boulogne-la-Petite; and there were as many people there as mentioned before. And in truth that day, on returning from the said sermon, the people of Paris were so turned to piety and moved, that in less than three or four hours you would have seen more than a hundred fires, in which men burnt gaming tables and boards, cards, billiard balls and cues, and all kinds of things which make one angry and blasphemous at greedy games.

Also, the women that day and the next burned, before all, the adornments of their heads like padding, ornaments, trifles, pieces of leather or of whalebone, which they put in their head-dresses to make them stiff or turned up in front; the young women left their horns and their tails and a great harvest of their luxuries. And truly ten sermons which he preached in Paris, and one in Boulogne, turned more people to devotion than all the preachers who had preached in Paris for a hundred years. . . .

Also, in truth, the friar, who had assembled so many people at his sermon, as told above, went riding off with them [the Armagnacs]; and as soon as those in Paris [partisans of the duke of Burgundy] were certain that he was in truth riding off with them thus, and that by his language he was deflecting cities which had taken oaths to the regent and his agents, they cursed him in the name of God and His saints; and what is worse, the games which he had forbidden began again despite him; and even a medal of pewter on which was carved the name of Jesus, which he had made them wear, they abandoned, and took the cross of St. Andry.

EXTORTIONATE TAXES

1437. In this month of September 1437, they imposed at Paris the strangest tax that had ever been imposed; for no one in all Paris was excepted from it, no matter of what estate he was, neither bishop, abbot, prior, monk, nuns, canon, priest with or without benefice, nor sergeants, musicians, nor parish clerks, nor any person of any estate. And first was imposed a big tax on the clergy, and afterwards on the big merchants, men and women; and the one paid four thousand francs, the other three thousand, or two thousand eight hundred, six hundred, each according to his condition; afterwards from other rich hands, up to one hundred francs or sixty, fifty or forty; everywhere the lesser folk paid twenty francs or above; other smaller folk paid less than twenty francs or more than ten, none exceeded twenty francs, nor paid less than ten; of others even lesser, none exceeded one hundred sous nor less than forty Parisian sous. After this dolorous tax they imposed another very dishonest one; for the rulers took from the churches the vessels of silver, such as censers, patens, chalices, candlesticks, pyxes, in short, all the church vessels which were of silver they took without asking; and afterwards they took the greatest part of all the coined silver which was in the treasury of the brotherhoods. In short they took so much money in Paris that one would scarcely believe it, and all this under the pretence of taking the chateau of Montereau and the city.

THE MENACE OF THE WOLVES

1439. Also, at this time, especially while the king was in Paris, the wolves were so mad to eat the flesh of men, women, or children that, in the last week of September, they strangled and ate fourteen persons, both large and small, between Montmartre and the Porte St. Antoine, both in the vineyards and within the swamps; and if they found a flock of animals, they assailed the shepherd and left the beasts. On the Eve of St. Martin there was chased a wolf so terrible and horrible that they said that he alone had done more of the aforesaid horrors than all the others. On that day he was taken, and he had no tail, and for this he was named Courtaut [short tail]; and they talked as much about him as one does about a bandit or a cruel soldier, and they said to the people who were going out to the fields: "Beware of Courtaut!" On that day he was put in a wheelbarrow, his jaws open, and taken within Paris; and the people left everything they were doing, drinking, eating, or any other necessary thing whatsoever, to go to see Courtaut; and in truth, he was worth to them more than ten francs.

THE INSECURITY OF LIFE

1444. Also, at the beginning of July, there came a great company of thieves and murderers who lodged in the villages around Paris, and it was such that, up to six or about eight leagues from Paris, no man dared go out to the fields or come to Paris, nor dared to pick in the fields anything at all; for no vehicle was taken by them which was not ransomed at eight or ten francs; nor any beast seized, whether ass, cow, or pig, which

was not ransomed at more than it was worth; nor could
a man of any estate, whether monk, priest, or religious
of some order, or nun, or musician, or herald, or woman,
or child of any age go outside Paris that he was not in
great peril of his life. But if they did not take his life,
he was stripped bare, all without exception, regardless of
estate; and when one complained to the rulers of Paris,
they replied, "They must live; the king will put a quick
end to it." And of this company there were chiefly Pierre
Regnault, Floquart, l'Estrac, and several others, all followers of Antichrist, for they were all thieves and murderers, sowers of sedition, violators of women, they and
all their company.

THE SHAME OF AGNES SOREL

1448. Also, the last week of April, there came to
Paris a young woman who was said to be loved publicly
by the king of France, without faith and without law,
and without truth to the good queen whom he had married; and it was apparent that she went in as great state
as a countess or duchess; and she came and went often
with the good queen of France, without having any
shame for her sin. On this account the queen had much
sorrow in her heart, but suffering was then her lot. And
the king, to show and manifest even more his great sin
and his great shame, gave her the castle of Beauty, the
most beautiful and delightful, and the best located in
the Isle de France. And she called herself and had herself called "the beautiful Agnes." And because the people of Paris did not show her such reverence as her great
pride demanded, which she could not conceal, she said
on her departure that they were only villeins, and that if
she had believed that they would not do her greater
honour than they had shown, she would certainly never
have entered nor put her foot within the city; which

would have been a pity, but a small one. Thus went off the beautiful Agnes, the tenth day of May following, to her sin as before. Alas! what a pity when the head of the kingdom gives such a bad example to his people; for if they do as bad or worse, one would not dare speak of it; for it is said in a proverb: "Like master, like valet" . . . for when such a great lord or lady sins so greatly in public, his knights and his people are bolder to sin because of it.

From *Journal d'un bourgeois de Paris sous Charles VI et Charles VII*, A. Mary, ed. (Paris: H. Jonquières, 1929); trans. J.B.R.

II. THE CHRISTIAN COMMONWEALTH

The Spiritual Authority

The Superiority
of the Spiritual Authority

POPE BONIFACE VIII

1302

W E ARE compelled, our faith urging us, to believe and to hold—and we do firmly believe and simply confess—that there is one holy catholic and apostolic Church, outside of which there is neither salvation nor remission of sins; her Spouse proclaiming it in the canticles, "My dove, my undefiled is but one, she is the choice one of her that bare her"; which represents one mystic body, of which body the head is Christ, but of Christ, God. In this Church there is one Lord, one faith, and one baptism. There was one ark of Noah, indeed, at the time of the flood, symbolizing one Church; and this being finished in one cubit had, namely, one Noah as helmsman and commander. And, with the exception of this ark, all things existing upon the earth were, as we read, destroyed. This Church, moreover, we venerate as the only one, the Lord saying through His prophet, "Deliver my soul from the sword, my darling from the power of the dog." He prayed at the same time for His soul—that is, for Himself the head, and for His body—

which body, namely, he called the one and only Church on account of the unity of the faith promised, of the sacraments, and of the love of the Church. She is that seamless garment of the Lord which was not cut but which fell by lot. Therefore of this one and only Church there is one body and one head—not two heads as if it were a monster: Christ, namely, and the vicar of Christ, St. Peter, and the successor of Peter. For the Lord Himself said to Peter, "Feed my sheep." My sheep, He said, using a general term, and not designating these or those particular sheep; from which it is plain that He committed to Him *all* His sheep. If, then, the Greeks or others say that they were not committed to the care of Peter and his successors, they necessarily confess that they are not of the sheep of Christ; for the Lord says, in John, that there is one fold, one shepherd, and one only. We are told by the word of the Gospel that in this His fold there are two swords—a spiritual, namely, and a temporal. For when the apostles said, "Behold here are two swords"—when, namely, the apostles were speaking in the church—the Lord did not reply that this was too much, but enough. Surely he who denies that the temporal sword is in the power of Peter wrongly interprets the word of the Lord when He says, "Put up thy sword in its scabbard." Both swords, the spiritual and the material, therefore, are in the power of the Church; the one, indeed, to be wielded for the Church, the other by the Church; the one by the hand of the priest, the other by the hand of kings and knights, but at the will and sufferance of the priest. One sword, moreover, ought to be under the other, and the temporal authority to be subjected to the spiritual. For when the apostle says "there is no power but of God, and the powers that are of God are ordained," they would not be ordained unless sword were under sword and the lesser one, as it were,

were led by the other to great deeds. For according to St. Dionysius the law of divinity is to lead the lowest through the intermediate to the highest things. Not, therefore, according to the law of the universe, are all things reduced to order equally and immediately; but the lowest through the intermediate, the intermediate through the higher. But that the spiritual exceeds any earthly power in dignity and nobility we ought the more openly to confess the more spiritual things excel temporal ones. This also is made plain to our eyes from the giving of tithes, and the benediction and the sanctification; from the acceptation of this same power, from the control over those same things. For, the truth bearing witness, the spiritual power has to establish the earthly power, and to judge it if it be not good. Thus concerning the Church and the ecclesiastical power is verified the prophecy of Jeremiah: "See, I have this day set thee over the nations and over the kingdoms," and the other things which follow. Therefore if the earthly power err it shall be judged by the spiritual power; but if the lesser spiritual power err, by the greater. But if the greatest, it can be judged by God alone, not by man, the apostle bearing witness. A spiritual man judges all things, but he himself is judged by no one. This authority, moreover, even though it is given to man and exercised through man, is not human but rather divine, being given by divine lips to Peter and founded on a rock for him and his successors through Christ Himself whom he has confessed; the Lord Himself saying to Peter: "Whatsoever thou shalt bind," etc. Whoever, therefore, resists this power thus ordained by God, resists the ordination of God, unless he makes believe, like the Manichean, that there are two beginnings. This we consider false and heretical, since by the testimony of Moses, not "in the beginnings," but "in the beginning" God created the heavens and the earth. Indeed we declare, announce, and define that it is altogether necessary to salvation for every human creature to be subject to the Roman pontiff. The Lateran, November 14, in our eighth year. As a perpetual memorial of this matter.

The Bull, "Unam Sanctam," *Select Historical Documents*, E. Henderson, ed. (London: Bohn, 1892).

The Election and Coronation of a Pope

ADAM OF USK

1404

For the election of a new pontiff of Rome the cardinals entered the conclave [established in 1274], which was entrusted to the safekeeping of the king of Naples and six thousand of his soldiers.

The baleful Roman people rose divided into the two parties of Guelphs and Ghibellines, and for the space of three weeks with slaughter and robbery and murder did they torment each other, either party seeking the creation of a pope on its own side; yet by reason of the said guard could they not come near to the palace of Saint Peter nor to the conclave. And so their partisanship caused the election, as pope, of one who was after the heart of neither side, namely Innocent the Seventh, a native of Solmona. And, when his election was made known, the Romans attacked his palace, and, after their greedy fashion, nay rather from festering corruptness, they sacked it, leaving therein not so much as the bars of the windows.

The conclave is a close-built place, without anything to divide it, and is set apart to the cardinals for the election of the pope; and it must be shut and walled in on all sides, so that, excepting a small wicket for entrance, which is afterwards closed, it shall remain strongly guarded. And therein is a small window for food to be passed in to the cardinals, at their own cost, which is fitted so as to open or shut as required.

And the cardinals have each a small cell on different floors, for sleep and rest; and three rooms alone in common, the privy, the chapel, and the place of election. After the first three days, while they are there, they have but one dish of meat or fish daily, and after five days thence bread and wine only, until they agree. . . .

Such advancement of my lord Innocent I thus saw in a vision, how he went up from the sacristy of St. Peter's to the altar to celebrate mass, robed in the papal vestments of scarlet silk woven with gold.

The dead pope, after the proclamation of the election, was carried to the church of St. Peter for the funeral rites, which lasted for nine days. . . .

On the feast of St. Martin the new pope went down from the palace to the church of St. Peter for the ceremony of his coronation, and at the altar of St. Gregory, the auditors bringing the vestments, he was robed for the mass. And at the moment of his coming forth from the chapel of St. Gregory, the clerk of his chapel, bearing a long rod on the end of which was fixed some tow, cried aloud as he set it aflame: "Holy father, thus passeth the glory of the world"; and again, in the middle of the procession, with a louder voice, thus twice: "Holy father! Most holy father!" and a third time, on arriving at the altar of St. Peter, thrice: "Holy father! Holy father! Holy father!" at his loudest; and forthwith each time is the tow quenched. Just as in the coronation of the emperor, in the very noontide of his glory, stones of every kind and colour, worked with all the cunning of the craft, are wont to be presented to him by the stone-cutters, with these words: "Most excellent prince, of what kind of stone wilt thou that thy tomb be made?" Also, the new pope, the mass being ended, ascends a lofty stage, made for this purpose, and there he is solemnly crowned with the triple golden crown by the cardinal of Ostia as dean of the college. The first crown means power in temporal things; the second, fatherhood in things spiritual; the third, pre-eminence in things of heaven. And afterwards, still robed in the same white vestments, he, as well as all the prelates likewise in albs, rides thence through Rome to the church of St. John Lateran, the cathedral seat of the pope. Then, after turning aside out of abhorrence of Pope Joan, whose image with her son stands in stone in the direct road near St. Clement's, the pope, dismounting from his horse, enters the Lateran for his enthronement. And there he is seated in a chair of porphyry, which is pierced beneath for this purpose, that one of the younger cardinals may make proof of his sex; and then, while a "Te Deum" is chanted, he is borne to the high altar.

On his way to the church, the Jews offered to him their law, that is the Old Testament, seeking his confirmation; and the pope took it gently in his hands, for by it we have come to the knowledge of the Son of God and to our faith, and thus answered: "Your law is good; but ye understand it not, for the old things have passed away, and all things are made new." And, as if for a reproach, since they being hardened in error understand it not, he delivers it back to them over his left shoulder, neither annulling nor confirming it.

There rode with the pope not only those of his court and the clergy, but also the thirteen quaestors of the city with their captains and standards at their heads. During the progress, in order to ease the thronging of the people, small coin was thrice cast among the crowd, and a passage was thus cleared while it was being gathered up.

Now I rejoice that I was present and served in that great solemnity, as also I did in the coronation of King Henry the Fourth of England and in the confirmation of the empire spoken of above.

From *Chronicle*, trans. E. M. Thompson (London: Murray, 1876).

The Creation of Cardinals

POPE PIUS II

1460

PIUS [II], having appointed Saturday [March 8, 1460] for the consistory in the cathedral, commanded that the three new cardinals already at Rome should be summoned and before they arrived he spoke at length about the election and the merits of each, proving that the creation of all had been just and necessary. Then when they entered, he bade them take their places at the chancel and addressed them as follows: "My sons, you have received a most high and exalted dignity. In being called to the Apostolic College you will become our counsellors and co-judges of the world. It will be your duty to decide between cause and cause, blood and blood, leprosy and leprosy. As successors of the apostles you will sit around our throne; you will be senators of the city and the equals of kings, in very truth the hinges of the world, which must turn and regulate the gate of the Church Militant. Consider what men, what minds, what integrity this dignity demands. This office calls for humility, not pride; generosity, not greed;

temperance, not drunkenness; self-control, not lust; knowledge, not ignorance; every virtue, no vice. If heretofore you have been vigilant, you must now practise vigilance against a malignant foe who never sleeps for thinking whom he may devour. If you have been generous, pour out now your wealth in noble causes and especially in succouring the poor. If temperate in food and drink, now especially shun luxury. Refrain from avarice, do away with cruelty, banish arrogance. Have holy books ever in your hands. Day and night be learning something or teaching others. So act that your light shall shine before all men and, finally, be such as you thought cardinals ought to be before you yourselves rose to this eminence."

After these words he summoned them to kiss his foot and then offered them his hand and cheek. The old cardinals also kissed them and made room for them to sit. Then the advocates pleaded a number of cases and when these had been settled, the old cardinals stood in a ring around the pope and the new ones kneeling took their oath according to the ancient formula. Then the pope placed the red hat, the badge of the cardinalate, on the head of each, and a chorus sang a hymn giving thanks to God. The old cardinals, except two who remained with the pope, escorted the new cardinals in procession to the altar of the Blessed Virgin and there the senior cardinal made them an eloquent discourse, invoking many blessings on them and on Holy Church. After this they returned to the pope, who dissolved the consistory and returned to his palace.

A like ceremony was held a few days later on the arrival of the cardinals of Rieti and Siena, one coming to Siena from Bologna and the other from Perugia. The pope praised the cardinal of Rieti as became his merits; the cardinal of Siena, since he was his own nephew and over-young, he said he should never have elevated if he had not been persuaded by the entreaties of the cardinals.

From *The Commentaries of Pius II*, book IV, trans. F. Gragg, L. Gabel, ed., *Smith College Studies in History*, vol. XXX (1947).

The Fourth Lateran Council

ROGER OF WENDOVER

1215

IN THE same year, namely, A.D. 1215, a sacred and general synod was held in the month of November, in the church of the Holy Saviour at Rome, called Constantian, at which our lord Pope Innocent [III], in the eighteenth year of his pontificate, presided, and which was attended by four hundred and twelve bishops. Amongst the principal of these were the two patriarchs of Constantinople and Jerusalem. The patriarch of Antioch could not come, being detained by serious illness, but he sent his vicar, the bishop of Antaradus; the patriarch of Alexandria, being under the dominion of the Saracens, did the best he could, sending a deacon his cousin in his place. There were seventy-seven primates and metropolitans present, more than eight hundred abbats and priors; and of the proxies of archbishops, bishops, abbats, priors, and chapters who were absent the number is not known. There was also present a great multitude of ambassadors from the emperor of Constantinople, the king of Sicily, who was elected emperor of Rome, the kings of France, England, Hungary, Jerusalem, Cyprus, Aragon, and other princes and nobles, and from cities and other places. When all of these were assembled in the place above-mentioned, and, according to the custom of general councils, each was placed according to his rank, the pope himself first delivered an exhortation, and then the sixty articles were recited in full council, which seemed agreeable to some and tedious to others. At length he commenced to preach concerning the business of the cross, and the subjection of the Holy Land, adding as follows: "Moreover, that nothing be omitted in the matter of the cross of Christ, it is our will and command that patriarchs, archbishops, bishops, abbats, priors, and others, who have the charge of spiritual matters, carefully set forth the work of the cross to the people entrusted to their care; and in the name of the Father, the Son, and the Holy Ghost, the one alone and eternal God, supplicate kings, dukes, princes, marquises, earls, barons, and other nobles, and also the communities of cities, towns, and villages, if they cannot go in person to the assistance of the Holy Land, to furnish a suitable number of soldiers, with all supplies necessary for three years, according to their means, in remission of their sins, as in the general letters is expressed; and it is also our will that those who build ships for this purpose be partakers in this remission. But to those who refuse, if any be so ungrateful, let it be on our behalf declared, that they will for a certainty account to us for this at the awful judgment of a rigorous Judge; considering, before they do refuse, with what chance of salvation they will be able to appear before the only God and the only-begotten Son of God, to whose hands the Father has entrusted all things, if they refuse to serve that Crucified One, in this their proper service, by whose gift they hold life, by whose kindness they are supported, and by whose blood they have been redeemed. And we, wishing to set an example to others, give and grant thirty thousand pounds for this business, besides a fleet, which we will supply to those who assume the cross from this city and the neighbouring districts; and we moreover assign for the accomplishment of this three thousand marks of silver, which remain to us out of the alms of some of the true faith. And as we desire to have the other prelates of the churches, and also the clergy in general, as partakers both in the merit and the reward, it is our decree, that all of them, both people and pastors, shall contribute for the assistance of the Holy Land the twentieth portion of their ecclesiastical profits for three years, except those who have assumed the cross or are about to assume it and set out for the Holy Land in person; and we and our brethren the cardinals of the Holy Church of Rome will pay a full tenth part of ours. . . .

And we, trusting to the mercy of the omnipotent God, and to the authority of the blessed apostles Peter and Paul, by virtue of that power which the Lord has granted to us, unworthy though we are, of binding and loosing, grant to all who shall undertake this business in person and at their own expense full pardon for their sins, for which they shall be truly contrite in heart, and of which they shall have made confession; and in the rewarding of the just we promise an increase of eternal salvation; and to those who do not come in person, but at their own expense send suitable persons according to their means, and also to those who come in person though at the expense of others, we likewise grant full pardon for their sins."

From *Flowers of History*, trans. J. A. Giles.

A French Provincial Synod

ODO OF RIGAUD

1259

FEBRUARY, 1259. At dawn, we arrived at the church of St. Aniane, and before we sat down in council, we celebrated mass in pontifical robes, our venerable brothers, our suffragans, being present with us, not rerobed for the celebration of the mass, with the deacon and subdeacon rerobed. . . . After mass was celebrated, we and our suffragans, all clad pontifically, went to our seats on the platform and there the deacon, rerobed, read the Gospel, namely, "Jesus appointed et cetera" [Luke x, 1]. This done, we began in a loud voice, *"Veni Creator spiritus."* This sung, two rerobed in surplices chanted the litany before the altar. Then, after *"Pater noster"* in a low voice, we said the prayer, *"Assumus."* This done, we preached the word of God, God Himself aiding us. Afterward the letter sent to the bishop of Bayeux concerning calling the council was read, and a rescript was read. Third, the procurations of the cathedral chapters were read. Fourth was read the constitution issued in general council [Lyon, 1245], concerning the councils to be held every year by the archbishops and their suffragans, which is contained in the section on purgations and reads, "As it was formerly," and other constitutions of the same general council which seemed to be useful, and those decretals, "From inebriation, and drunkenness, et cetera."

The procurators of the chapter of Rouen were: William, the treasurer, and John of Porta, archdeacon

. . . ; of the chapter of Bayeux . . . ; of the diocese of
Evreux . . . ; of the chapter of Lisieux . . . ; of the
chapter of Coutances . . . ; of the chapter of Avranches . . . ; of the chapter of Séez . . . ; the proc-
urator of the lord of Bayeux was Master Gerard of
Corion, archdeacon of Bayeux.

Afterward, it was asked of the inquisitors, appointed
in the other provincial council, what they wished to report. Some of them had retired, and those who had remained said that they did not wish to make any inquiries
in the absence of their colleagues. Then we installed
others, namely, in the diocese of Rouen . . . deacons;
also in the diocese of Avranches . . . rectors; in the
diocese of Evreux . . . deacons. . . .

And it should be known that in the celebration of the
council, there sat next to us our venerable brothers: on
our right, R. of Evreux, and F., bishop of Lisieux, G.,
bishop of Bayeux, being absent, who if he had been
present would have sat near to us, before the two aforesaid bishops; at our left: R. of Avranches, Th. of Séez,
and J. of Coutances.

Sixth, there were chosen and read aloud certain
statutes in the following form: it is pleasing to the holy
council that those things which follow below should be
strictly observed so that the reverend fathers, Odo, by
God's grace archbishop of Rouen, and his suffragans,
and those subject to them, should in no wise be impeded
in the observation of them, as if they had to be enacted
anew, namely, in respect to those things which are
found stated in law, either in the statutes of Pope
Gregory IX, or in episcopal synods.

We wish that in respect to the expenses of procuration [hospitality], due by reason of visitation, which
should be received by the archbishop and bishops, and
in respect to the damage which should not be inflicted

as a consequence of their accompanying officials, there should be observed what was established in the council of Lyon.

We wish that the statute of the general council against those who form leagues, and against the statutes issued contrary to the liberties of the Church, .should be frequently and solemnly proclaimed in the synods and parish churches, and the transgressors canonically punished.

We decree that secular powers seizing clerics with greater violence than the rebellion of the defendant demands, and detaining them, beyond or against the demand of the ecclesiastical judge, should be denounced as excommunicated by canon law in general, in particular, indeed, after it shall be clearly proved.

We strictly forbid that, in cases pertaining to the Church, a secular judge should be approached by ecclesiastical persons, especially concerning personal actions.

We decree that abbots and priors, and other ecclesiastical persons who receive the greater tithes in parish churches, should be compelled to maintain the building, books and ornaments, in proportion to what they collect in the same.

We wish that the synodal statute be firmly observed, namely that the ecclesiastical persons to whom come mandates of various judges, delegates, conservators, or executors, should carefully see that the names of the judges of the diocese and of the places to which they refer are authentic.

We forbid that any Christian men or women should dare to serve Jews in inns or to live with them, and we order that Jews be forced to wear clear signs by which they can be distinguished from Catholics.

We strongly forbid that any night revels or dances

be carried on in cemeteries and holy places, ordering
that the transgressors be canonically punished.

We solemnly warn clerks in churches, especially the
unmarried ones, to bear a suitable tonsure; and crusaders in truth should be forced to wear the cross openly.

Concerning saddles, bridles, spurs, and gilded breast-
plates or those having other superfluities to whom as
clerics it is forbidden, and concerning the garments,
closed above, to be worn by priests, we wish the statute
of the general council to be observed.

We forbid that any beneficed clergy or any ordained
in holy orders should be intent upon or addicted to hunting or fowling.

We decree that in abbeys and priories in which the
resources are not diminished, the number of religious
persons should be re-established, unless perhaps it is
limited for the time by express licence of the superior
and for a reasonable cause.

This which is established by law, that a monk should
not stay anywhere alone, we wish and order to be observed.

Let the monks staying in priories which are not
conventual be warned, with threat of suspension and
excommunication, and, as it shall seem expedient, be
induced to try to observe the statutes of Pope Gregory,
so far as concerns eating meat, confessions, and fasting.

We decree that regulars should not stay with seculars,
unless by diocesan or special licence.

The statute concerning loans to be drawn by religious,
beyond a certain amount, except by licence of their
abbot, should be strictly observed.

We order that rural deans, exercising jurisdiction,
should not excommunicate or suspend except in writing.

We order that priests should not desist from the

announcement of excommunication, no matter how much the parties make peace among themselves, unless it shall be lawfully established concerning the absolution of the excommunicated.

We wish that absolution should be done with proper solemnity.

We forbid priests that they should presume to excommunicate in general except for theft and injury, and with an adequate forewarning.

Also, we decree that chaplains to whom churches are committed for a time, should be carefully examined on grammar, on their way of life, and on their ordination.

These things so done, and the council celebrated harmoniously, we recessed singing, "*Te Deum laudamus*," and we went before the altar of St. Aniane, and there, when the canticle was finished, we said certain suitable prayers.

From *Regestrum visitationum archiepiscopi Rothomagensis*, trans. J.B.R.

Letter to Henry II

THOMAS BECKET

1166

THESE are the words of the archbishop of Canterbury to the king of the English.

With desire I have desired to see your face and to speak with you; greatly for my own sake but more for yours. For my sake, that when you saw my face you might recall to memory the services which, when I was under your obedience, I rendered faithfully and zealously to the best of my conscience . . . and that so you

might be moved to pity me, who am forced to beg my
bread among strangers; yet, thanks be to God, I have
an abundance. . . . For your sake for three causes:
because you are my lord, because you are my king, and
because you are my spiritual son. In that you are my
lord I owe and offer to you my counsel and service, such
as a bishop owes to his lord according to the honour of
God and the holy Church. And in that you are my king
I am bound to you in reverence and regard. In that you
are my son I am bound by reason of my office to chasten
and correct you. . . . Christ founded the Church and
purchased her liberty with His blood, undergoing the
scourging and spitting, the nails, and the anguish of
death, leaving us an example that we should follow in
His steps. Whence also saith the apostle, "If we suffer
with Him we shall also reign with Him. If we die with
Him, with Him we shall rise again."

The Church of God consists of two orders, clergy and
people. Among the clergy are apostles, apostolic men,
bishops, and other doctors of the Church, to whom is
committed the care and governance of the Church, who
have to perform ecclesiastical business, that the whole
may redound to the saving of souls. Whence also it was
said to Peter, and in Peter to the other rulers of the
Church, not to kings nor to princes, "Thou art Peter,
and upon this rock will I build my Church, and the
gates of hell shall not prevail against it."

Among the people are kings, princes, dukes, earls, and
other powers, who perform secular business, that the
whole may conduce to the peace and unity of the
Church. And since it is certain that kings receive their
power from the Church, not she from them but from
Christ, so, if I may speak with your pardon, you have
not the power to give rules to bishops, nor to absolve
or excommunicate anyone, to draw clerks before secular

tribunals, to judge concerning churches and tithes, to forbid bishops to adjudge causes concerning breach of faith or oath, and many other things of this sort which are written among your customs which you call ancient. Let my lord, therefore, if it pleases him, listen to the counsel of his subject, to the warnings of his bishop, and to the chastisement of his father. And first let him for the future abstain from all communion with schismatics. It is known almost to the whole world with what devotion you formerly received our lord the pope and what attachment you showed to the Church of Rome, and also what respect and deference were shown you in return. Forbear then, my lord, if you value your soul, to deprive that Church of her rights. Remember also the promise which you made, and which you placed in writing on the altar at Westminster when you were consecrated and anointed king by my predecessor, of preserving to the Church her liberty. Restore therefore to the Church of Canterbury, from which you received your promotion and consecration, the rank which it held in the time of your predecessors and mine; together with all its possessions, townships, castles, and farms, and whatsoever else has been taken by violence either from myself or my dependents, laymen as well as clerks. And further, if so please you, permit us to return free and in peace, and with all security to our see, to perform the duties of our office as we ought. And we are ready faithfully and devotedly with all our strength to serve you as our dearest lord and king with all our strength in whatsoever we are able, saving the honour of God and of the Roman Church, and saving our order. Otherwise, know for certain that you shall feel the divine severity and vengeance.

From St. Thomas of Canterbury, W. H. Hutton, ed. (London: D. Nutt, 1889).

The Temporal Authorities

The Nature of a True Prince

JOHN OF SALISBURY

Twelfth century

THE PRINCE AND THE LAW

BETWEEN a tyrant and a prince there is this single or chief difference, that the latter obeys the law and rules the people by its dictates, accounting himself as but their servant. It is by virtue of the law that he makes good his claim to the foremost and chief place in the management of the affairs of the commonwealth and in the bearing of its burdens; and his elevation over others consists in this, that whereas private men are held responsible only for their private affairs, on the prince fall the burdens of the whole community. Wherefore deservedly there is conferred on him, and gathered together in his hands, the power of all his subjects, to the end that he may be sufficient unto himself in seeking and bringing about the advantage of each individually, and of all; and to the end that the state of the human commonwealth may be ordered in the best possible manner, seeing that each and all are members one of another. Wherein we indeed but follow nature, the best guide of life; for nature has gathered together all the

251

senses of her microcosm or little world, which is man, into the head, and has subjected all the members in obedience to it in such wise that they will all function properly so long as they follow the guidance of the head, and the head remains sane. Therefore the prince stands on a pinnacle which is exalted and made splendid with all the great and high privileges which he deems necessary for himself. And rightly so, because nothing is more advantageous to the people than that the needs of the prince should be fully satisfied; since it is impossible that his will should be found opposed to justice. Therefore, according to the usual definition, the prince is the public power, and a kind of likeness on earth of the divine majesty. Beyond doubt a large share of the divine power is shown to be in princes by the fact that at their nod men bow their necks and for the most part offer up their heads to the axe to be struck off, and, as by a divine impulse, the prince is feared by each of those over whom he is set as an object of fear. And this I do not think could be, except as a result of the will of God. For all power is from the Lord God, and has been with Him always, and is from everlasting. The power which the prince has is therefore from God, for the power of God is never lost, nor severed from Him, but He merely exercises it through a subordinate hand, making all things teach His mercy or justice. "Who, therefore, resists the ruling power, resists the ordinance of God," in whose hand is the authority of conferring that power, and when He so desires, of withdrawing it again, or diminishing it. For it is not the ruler's own act when his will is turned to cruelty against his subjects, but it is rather the dispensation of God for His good pleasure to punish or chasten them. . . .

Princes should not deem that it detracts from their princely dignity to believe that the enactments of their own justice are not to be preferred to the justice of God, whose justice is an everlasting justice, and His law is equity. Now equity, as the learned jurists define it, is a certain fitness of things which compares all things rationally, and seeks to apply like rules of right and wrong to like cases, being impartially disposed toward all persons, and allotting to each that which belongs to him. Of this equity the interpreter is the law, to which the will and intention of equity and justice are known. Therefore Crisippus asserted that the power of the law extends over all things, both divine and human, and that it accordingly presides over all goods and ills, and is the ruler and guide of material things as well as of human beings. To which Papinian, a man most learned in the law, and Demosthenes, the great orator, seem to assent, subjecting all men to its obedience because all law is, as it were, a discovery, and a gift from God, a precept of wise men, the corrector of excesses of the will, the bond which knits together the fabric of the state, and the banisher of crime; and it is therefore fitting that all men should live according to it who lead their lives in a corporate political body. All are accordingly bound by the necessity of keeping the law, unless perchance there is any who can be thought to have been given the licence of wrongdoing. However, it is said that the prince is absolved from the obligations of the law; but this is not true in the sense that it is lawful for him to do unjust acts, but only in the sense that his character should be such as to cause him to practise equity not through fear of the penalties of the law but through love of justice; and should also be such as to cause him from the same motive to promote the advantage of the commonwealth, and in all things to prefer the good of others before his private will. Who, indeed, in respect of public matters can properly speak of the will of the prince at all, since therein he may not lawfully have any will of his own apart from that which the law or equity enjoins, or the calculation of the common interest requires? For in these matters his will is to have the force of a judgment; and most properly that which pleases him therein has the force of law, because his decision may not be at variance with the intention of equity. "From thy countenance," says the Lord, "let my judgment go forth, let thine eyes look upon equity"; for the uncorrupted judge is one whose decision, from assiduous contemplation of equity, is the very likeness thereof. The prince accordingly is the minister of the common interest and the bond-servant of equity, and he bears the public person in the sense that he punishes the wrongs and injuries of all, and all crimes, with even-handed equity. His rod and staff, also, administered with wise moderation, restore irregularities and false departures to the straight path of equity, so that deservedly may the Spirit congratulate the power of the prince with the words, "Thy rod and thy staff, they have comforted me." His shield, too, is strong, but it is a shield for the protection of the weak, and one which wards off powerfully the darts of the wicked from the innocent. Those who derive the greatest advantage from his performance of the duties of his office are those who can do least for themselves, and his power is chiefly exercised against those who desire to do harm. Therefore not without reason he bears a sword, wherewith he sheds blood blamelessly, without becoming thereby a man of blood, and frequently puts men to death without incurring the name or guilt of homicide. . . .

This sword, then, the prince receives from the hand of the Church, although she herself has no sword of blood at all. Nevertheless she has this sword, but she uses it by the hand of the prince, upon whom she con-

fers the power of bodily coercion, retaining to herself
authority over spiritual things in the person of the pontiffs. The prince is, then, as it were, a minister of the
priestly power, and one who exercises that side of the
sacred offices which seems unworthy of the hands of
the priesthood. For every office existing under, and concerned with the execution of, the sacred laws is really
a religious office, but that is inferior which consists in
punishing crimes, and which therefore seems to be typi-
fied in the person of the hangman. Wherefore Constantine, most faithful emperor of the Romans, when he had
convoked the council of priests at Nicaea, neither dared
to take the chief place for himself nor even to sit among
the presbyters, but chose the hindmost seat. Moreover,
the decrees which he heard approved by them he rev-
erenced as if he had seen them emanate from the judg-
ment-seat of the divine majesty. Even the rolls of petitions containing accusations against priests which they
brought to him in a steady stream he took and placed in
his bosom without opening them. . . . But if one who
has been appointed prince has performed duly and faithfully the ministry which he has undertaken, as great
honour and reverence are to be shown to him as the
head excels in honour all the members of the body. Now
he performs his ministry faithfully when he is mindful
of his true status, and remembers that he bears the person of the *universitas* of those subject to him; and when
he is fully conscious that he owes his life not to himself
and his own private ends, but to others, and allots it to
them accordingly, with duly ordered charity and affection. Therefore he owes the whole of himself to God,
most of himself to his country, much to his relatives and
friends, very little to foreigners, but still somewhat. He
has duties to the very wise and the very foolish, to little
children and to the aged. Supervision over these classes

of persons is common to all in authority, both those who have care over spiritual things and those who exercise temporal jurisdiction. . . . And so let him be both father and husband to his subjects, or, if he has known some affection more tender still, let him employ that; let him desire to be loved rather than feared, and show himself to them as such a man that they will out of devotion prefer his life to their own, and regard his preservation and safety as a kind of public life; and then all things will prosper well for him, and a small bodyguard will, in case of need, prevail by their loyalty against innumerable adversaries. For love is strong as death; and the wedge which is held together by strands of love is not easily broken. . . .

ON LIBERTY AND TYRANNY

Liberty means judging everything freely in accordance with one's individual judgment, and does not hesitate to reprove what it sees opposed to good morals. Nothing but virtue is more splendid than liberty, if indeed liberty can ever properly be severed from virtue. For to all right-thinking men it is clear that true liberty issues from no other source. Wherefore, since all agree that virtue is the highest good in life, and that it alone can strike off the heavy and hateful yoke of slavery, it has been the opinion of philosophers that men should die, if need arose, for the sake of virtue, which is the only reason for living. But virtue can never be fully attained without liberty, and the absence of liberty proves that virtue in its full perfection is wanting. Therefore a man is free in proportion to the measure of his virtues, and the extent to which he is free determines what his virtues can accomplish; while, on the other hand, it is the vices alone which bring about slavery, and subject a man to persons and things in unmeet obedience; and though slavery of the person may seem at times the more to be pitied, in reality slavery to the vices is ever far the more wretched. And so what is more lovely than liberty? And what more agreeable to a man who has any reverence for virtue? We read that it has been the impelling motive of all good princes; and that none ever trod liberty under foot save the open foes of virtue. The jurists know what good laws were introduced for the sake of liberty, and the testimony of historians has made famous the great deeds done for love of it. . . . If I wished to recall individual instances of this kind, time would run out before the examples were exhausted. The practice of liberty is a notable thing and displeasing only to those who have the character of slaves.

Things which are done or spoken freely avoid the fault of timidity on the one hand and of rashness on the other, and so long as the straight and narrow path is followed, merit praise and win affection. But when under the pretext of liberty rashness unleashes the violence of its spirit, it properly incurs reproach, although, as a thing more pleasing in the ears of the vulgar than convincing to the mind of the wise man, it often finds in the indulgence of others the safety which it does not owe to its own prudence. Nevertheless, it is the part of a good and wise man to give a free rein to the liberty of others and to accept with patience the words of free speaking, whatever they may be. Nor does he oppose himself to its works so long as these do not involve the casting away of virtue. For since each virtue shines by its own proper light, the merit of tolerance is resplendent with a very special glory. . . .

A tyrant, . . . as the philosophers have described him, is one who oppresses the people by rulership based upon force, while he who rules in accordance with the laws is a prince. Law is the gift of God, the model of equity, a standard of justice, a likeness of the divine will, the guardian of well-being, a bond of union and solidarity between peoples, a rule defining duties, a barrier against the vices and the destroyer thereof, a punishment of violence and all wrongdoing. The law is assailed by force or by fraud, and, as it were, either wrecked by the fury of the lion or undermined by the wiles of the serpent. In whatever way this comes to pass, it is plain that it is the grace of God which is being assailed, and that it is God Himself who in a sense is challenged to battle. The prince fights for the laws and the liberty of the people; the tyrant thinks nothing done unless he brings the laws to nought and reduces the people to slavery. Hence the prince is a kind of likeness of divinity; and the tyrant, on the contrary, a likeness of the boldness of the Adversary, even of the wickedness of Lucifer, imitating him that sought to build his throne to the north and make himself like unto the Most High, with the exception of His goodness. For had he desired to be like unto Him in goodness, he would never have striven to tear from Him the glory of His power and wisdom. What he more likely did aspire to was to be equal with him in authority to dispense rewards. The prince, as the likeness of the Deity, is to be loved, worshipped, and cherished; the tyrant, the likeness of wickedness, is generally to be even killed. The origin of tyranny is iniquity, and springing from a poisonous root, it is a tree which grows and sprouts into a baleful pestilent growth, and to which the axe must by all means be laid. For if iniquity and injustice, banishing charity, had not brought about tyranny, firm concord and perpetual peace would have possessed the peoples of the earth forever, and no one would think of enlarging his boundaries. Then kingdoms would be as friendly and peaceful, according to the authority of the great father Augustine, and would enjoy as undisturbed repose, as the separate families in a well-ordered state, or as different persons in the same family; or perhaps, which is even more credible, there would be no kingdoms at all, since it is clear from the ancient historians that in the beginning these were founded by iniquity as presumptuous encroachments against the Lord, or else were extorted from Him.

From *Policraticus*, trans. J. Dickinson.

The Independence
of the Temporal Authority

FREDERICK BARBAROSSA

1157

INASMUCH as the Divine Power, from which is every power in Heaven and on earth, has committed to us, His anointed, the kingdom and the empire to be ruled over, and has ordained that the peace of the Church shall be preserved by the arms of the empire—not without extreme grief of heart are we compelled to complain to you, beloved, that, from the head of the holy Church on which Christ impressed the character of His peace and love, causes of dissension, seeds of evil, the poison of a pestiferous disease seem to emanate. Through these, unless God avert it, we fear that the whole body of the Church will be tainted, the unity riven, a schism be brought about between the kingdom and the priesthood. For recently while we were holding court at Besançon and with due watchfulness were treating of the honour of the empire and of the safety of the Church, there came apostolic legates asserting that they brought such message to our majesty that from it the honour of our empire should receive no little increase. When, on the first day of their coming, we had honourably received them, and, on the second, as is the custom, we sat together with our princes to listen to their report—they, as if inflated with the mammon of unrighteousness, out of the height of their pride, from the summit of their arrogance, in the execrable elation of their swelling hearts, did present to us a message in the form of an apostolic letter, the tenor of which was that we should always keep it before our mind's eye how the lord pope [Adrian IV] had *conferred* upon us the distinction of the imperial crown and that he would not regret it if our highness were to receive from him even greater *benefices*. This was that message of paternal sweetness which was to foster the unity of Church and empire, which strove to bind together both with a bond of peace, which enticed the minds of the hearers to the concord and obedience of both. Of a truth at that word, blasphemous and devoid of all truth, not only did the imperial majesty conceive a righteous indignation, but also all the princes who were present were filled with such fury and wrath that, without doubt, they would have condemned those two unhallowed presbyters to the punishment of death had not our presence prevented them. Whereupon, since many similar letters were found upon them, and sealed forms to be filled out afterwards at their discretion—by means of which, as has hitherto been their custom, they intended to strive throughout all the churches of the kingdom of Germany to scatter the virus conceived by their iniquity, to denude the altars, to carry away the vessels of the house of God, to strip the crosses: lest an opportunity should be given them of proceeding further, we caused them to return to Rome by the way on which they had come. And, inasmuch as the kingdom, together with the empire, is ours by the election of the princes from God alone, who, by the passion of His Son Christ subjected the world to the rule of the two necessary swords; and since the apostle Peter informed the world with this teaching, "Fear God, honour the king": whoever shall say that we received the imperial crown as a benefice from the lord pope, contradicts the divine institutions and the teaching of Peter, and shall be guilty of a lie. Since, moreover, we have hitherto striven to rescue from the hands of the Egyptians the honour and liberty of the Church which has long been oppressed by the yoke of an undue servitude, and are striving to preserve to it all the prerogatives of its dignity: we ask you as one to condole with us over such ignominy inflicted on us and on the empire, trusting that the undivided sincerity of your faith will not permit the honour of the empire, which, from the foundation of Rome and the establishment of the Christian religion up to your own times has remained glorious and undiminished, to be lessened by so unheard-of an innovation. And be it known beyond the shadow of a doubt, that we would rather incur danger of death than in our day to sustain the shame of so great a disaster.

"Manifesto of the Emperor," *Select Historical Documents*, E. F. Henderson, ed. (London: Bohn, 1892).

The Election and Coronation
of an Emperor

OTTO OF FREISING

1152

IN THE year 1800 from the founding of the City
[Rome], in truth from the Incarnation of our Lord
1152, after the most pious King Conrad had died in the
spring . . . in the city of Bamberg . . . there assembled in the city of Frankfort from the vast expanse of
the transalpine kingdom [Germany], marvellous to tell,
the whole strength of the princes, not without certain
of the barons from Italy, in one body, so to speak. Here,
when the primates were taking counsel about the prince
to be elected—for the highest honour of the Roman Empire claims this point of law for itself, as if by special
prerogative, namely, that the kings do not succeed by
heredity but are created by the election of the princes—
finally Frederick, duke of Swabia, son of Duke Frederick, was desired by all, and with the approval of all, was
raised up as king.

The chief reason for such a unanimous agreement of
this deliberation in favour of that person was, as I remember, the following. There were formerly in the Roman world between the confines of Gaul and Germany
two famous families, one of the Henrys of Waiblingen,
the other of the Welfs of Altdorf, the one accustomed to
produce emperors, the other great dukes. These, striving in competition frequently with each other, as is usually the case among great men avid for fame, very often

disturbed the public peace. Now it happened, doubtless by the will of God, providing for the future peace of his people, that, under Henry V, Duke Frederick, the father of this one, who descended from the family of kings, took to wife the daughter [Judith] of Duke Henry of Bavaria from the other family, and from this union was born the present Frederick. The princes, therefore, considering not only the energy and courage of the aforesaid young man, but also this fact, that as a member of both families, he might be able to bridge the gap between these two walls like a cornerstone, judged that he should be made the head of the kingdom. They recognized how great would be the advantage to the state if such a serious and lasting rivalry between the greatest men of the empire for private gain could be finally set at rest by this opportunity. So it was not out of hatred for Conrad but rather out of consideration for the public good, as we have said, that they preferred to elevate this Frederick rather than the son of Conrad, also named Frederick, who was still a boy. With this consideration and arrangement in mind, the election of Frederick was celebrated.

When the king had bound all the princes who had assembled there in fealty and homage, he, together with a few whom he had chosen as suitable, having dismissed the others in peace, took ship with great joy on the fifth day and, going by the Main and Rhine, he landed at the royal palace of Sinzig. There, taking horse, he came to Aachen on the next Saturday; on the following day, Sunday [March 9th] . . . led by the bishops from the palace to the church of the blessed Virgin Mary, and with the applause of all present, crowned by Arnold, archbishop of Cologne, assisted by the other bishops, he was set on the throne of the Franks, which was placed in the same church by Charles the Great. Many were amazed that in such a short space of time not only so many of the princes and nobles of the kingdom had assembled but also that not a few had come even from western Gaul, where, it was thought, the rumour of this event could not yet have penetrated.

I should not omit to tell that, after the sacrament of unction, when the diadem was placed on his head, one of his servants who because of certain serious offences had been cut off from his favour, privately up to this moment, threw himself in the middle of the church at Frederick's feet, hoping, on account of the joy of this day, to be able to soften his heart from the rigour of justice. The emperor, however, persevering in his previous severity and remaining thus fixed, gave not a little evidence to us all of his constancy, saying it was not out of hatred, but from respect for justice that the man had been excluded from his favour. Nor did this happen without the admiration of many that so much glory could not bend such a young man, equipped as it were with the mind of an old man, from the courage of severity to the weakness of forgiveness. What more need I say? Not the intercession of the princes, not the blandishment of smiling fortune, nor the immediate joy of such a great celebration could help that wretched one; he went forth unheard from the inexorable Frederick.

Nor should I pass over in silence that on the same day in the same church the bishop-elect of Münster, also called Frederick, was consecrated as bishop by the same bishops who had consecrated the king; so that in truth the highest king and the priest believed this to be a sort of prognostication in the present joyfulness that, in one church, one day saw the unction of two persons, who alone are anointed sacramentally with the institution of the old and new dispensations and are rightly called the anointed of Christ.

After the completion of all the things which pertained to the coronation, the prince returned to the privacy of the palace, and having called together the wiser and abler ones among the princes, in consideration of the public good, decided that legates should be sent to the Roman pontiff, Eugenius, to the City [Rome] and to all Italy who should tell of his elevation to the kingship.

From *Gesta Friderici I imperatoris*, G. Waitz, ed. (Hanover, 1884); trans. J.B.R.

A German Poet's Attack on the Papacy

WALTHER VON DER VOGELWEIDE

Thirteenth century

KING CONSTANTINE'S FOLLY

King Constantine in folly gave
The Cross, the Crown, the Sacred Stave
That pierced our Lord, all to the Holy See.
The angel mourned his folly so:
"Ah woe, ah woe, ah threefold woe!
For Christendom is now in jeopardy.
I see a subtil poison fall,
Their honey will be turned to gall;
On Man a heavy burden will be laid."
The princes lose all proper awe;
The highest prince is of all power deprived
By this election which the priests contrived.
Let accusation before God be made;
The clerics are perverting civil law.
It was no falsehood that the angel said!

THE ROMAN SHRINE

Ahi, how Christianlike the pope laughs at our wrongs,
When he recites his triumphs to the Romish throngs.
> He boasts of deeds of which he never should have
> thought.
He says: "Two Teutons under one crown I have
> brought,
So that the great rise up with burning and with wast-
> ing.
I herd them with my staff, while ye are casting
> Their goods into my coffers; all that they have is
> mine.
> Their German silver travels to my Roman shrine.
> Eat pullets down, ye priests, and drink your wine,
And leave the foolish German laymen—fasting."

From I Saw the World, trans. I. G. Colvin.

The Seven Electors

ADAM OF USK

Fifteenth century

BUT now as to . . . the election of the emperor, and
how many and what crowns he has, and by whom
he is elected and receives them, and what they mean.
There are seven electors, whence these verses:

> From Mainz and Trier and eke Cologne
> Come chancellors for Caesar's throne.
> A steward, the palgrave serves his lord;
> And Saxony doth bear the sword.
> As chamberlain a marquis bends;

Bohemia's king the wine cup tends.
On whom these princes' choice doth fall,
He reigneth overlord of all.

The first crown, which is of iron, in token of valour,
shall the archbishop of Cologne give to the elect; the
second, of silver, in token of chastity, shall the archbishop of Trier give; the third, of gold, in token of excellence, shall the archbishop of Mainz give, and this
last shall the pope, in the confirmation of the elect, place
upon his head as he kneels at his feet in token of humility and to do honour to the holy Roman Church, whose
vassal he is.

From *Chronicle,* trans. E. M. Thompson.

A Picture of a Good Feudal King:
Louis VI of France

SUGER

Twelfth century

AND so the famous youth Louis, jolly, gracious, and
benevolent, to such an extent that he was considered simple by some, now an adult, illustrious, and zealous defender of the paternal kingdom, looked out for
the needs of the churches, and, what had not been done
for a long time, strove for the security of the clergy, the
workers, and the poor. . . .

The noble church of Reims and the churches pertaining to it were suffering from the devastation of their
goods by the tyranny of the powerful and turbulent
baron Ebles de Roucy and his son Guichard. The more

he concerned himself with warlike activities—of such magnitude that once he set out for Spain with an army of a size which was suitable only for kings—the more mad and rapacious he was in carrying out depredations and persisting in spoliation and all kinds of evil.

Mournful complaints against such a powerful and wicked man had been lodged a hundred times with Lord Philip the King, and now with his son [Louis] twice or thrice. The son, in bitterness, gathered together a modest army of about seven hundred knights chosen from the most noble and valiant barons of France; he hastened to Reims [1102], and in almost two months of severe conflict, he punished the damage done to the churches, depopulated the lands of the aforesaid tyrant and his accomplices, ruined them by fire, and exposed them to plunder. It was an excellent deed, that those who ravaged should be ravaged, and those who tortured should be tortured equally or more. So great was the ardour of the lord and the army that as long as they were there they scarcely ever took any rest, except on Saturday and Sunday, but instead persisted in conflict with lances and swords in hand, or avenged by the ruin of the lands the injuries committed.

They fought there not only against Ebles but against all the barons of those parts whose relationship with the powerful of Lorraine resulted in a strong army of considerable numbers. Meanwhile numerous attempts at peace were made. Since various cares of state and perilous affairs called urgently for the presence of the young lord elsewhere, he, after holding his council, ordered and obtained peace for the churches from the aforesaid tyrant, and having accepted hostages, he made the tyrant confirm it by an oath. Then he dismissed him, thus treated and beaten. . . .

Not less notable was the military aid he bore to the

church of Orleans [1103]. Leo, a noble of the castle of
Meung, vassal of the bishop of Orleans, was in the process of seizing the greater part of this castle and the lordship of another. Louis conquered him by force, and shut
him up in the same castle with many of his men. When
the castle was taken, Leo, in a church near his home,
erected fortifications and undertook to defend himself.
But the strong must yield to the stronger; he was overcome by an intolerable flood of flames and arrows. He
was not alone in paying dearly for the long-continued
anathema since he himself and many others, about sixty,
rolling from the tower as the flames prevailed, were
pierced by the points of the lances raised on high and
the flying arrows; breathing out their last breath in sorrow, they carried their wretched souls to hell. . . .

Meanwhile as the son progressed each day, so his
father, King Philip, each day failed; for after he had
abducted the countess of Anjou he did nothing worthy
of royal majesty but, transported by his passion for the
woman he had carried off, devoted himself to the satisfaction of his desires. Hence he neither took care of the
interests of state nor, in his great slackness, did he look
after the health of his body which was noble and elegant. Only one thing remained which strengthened the
kingdom, that is, the love and fear of his son and successor. When he was almost sixty years old, the king
died, breathing his last in the presence of Lord Louis at
the castle at Melun-sur-Seine [1108].

At his noble obsequies were present venerable men
such as Galo, bishop of Paris, the bishop of Senlis and
Adam of Orleans, of blessed memory, the abbot of St.
Denis, and many other religious personages. These,
bearing the noble corpse of royal majesty to Notre
Dame, passed the whole night in celebrating his obsequies. At dawn following the son had the litter, properly

adorned with rich cloths and all sorts of funeral ornaments, placed on the shoulders of his principal servitors. With filial affection, as was suitable, now on foot, now on horseback with the barons who were there, he strove weeping to help carry the bier. Thus he showed the marvellous generosity of his soul, for in his whole life, neither in the case of the repudiation of his mother nor in that of the Angevin mistress, did he ever offend his father in any way or seek to upset his authority in the kingdom by any fraud, as other young men are wont to do. . . .

Now the aforesaid Louis, since in his youth he had merited by his generous defence the friendship of the Church, had sustained the cause of the poor and orphans and had tamed tyrants by his valiant courage, with the consent of God was called to the summit of the kingdom, according to the wish of good men, as he would have been excluded, if it had been possible, by the avowed machinations of the evil and impious.

It was decided therefore, according to the advice of the most venerable and wise Ivo, bishop of Chartres, in order to counteract the machinations of the impious, to assemble as rapidly as possible in Orleans and to hasten to carry through completely his elevation to the throne. The archbishop of Sens, Daimbert, invited with his suffragans, to wit, Manassus of Meaux, Jean of Orleans, Ivo of Chartres, Hugh of Nevers, and [Humbert] of Auxerre, arrived, and on the day of the discovery of the holy protomartyr Stephen [August 3, 1108], he anointed Louis with the most holy oil of the unction. After celebrating masses of thanksgiving, he removed the secular sword and girded him with the ecclesiastical sword for the punishment of evil-doers, crowned him with the royal diadem and bestowed on him most devoutly the sceptre and the wand, and by this gesture, the defence of the churches and the poor, and other insignia of the kingdom, with the great approval of the clergy and the people. . . .

Now Louis, king of the Franks by the grace of God, did not lose the habit he had grown used to in his youth, that is, of guarding the churches, protecting the poor and needy, and standing for the peace and defence of the kingdom. . . .

Because the hand of kings is most powerful, by the consecrated right of their office the audacity of tyrants is repressed as often as they see them provoke wars, plunder endlessly at their will, confound the poor, and destroy churches. Thus is checked that licence which, if tolerated, inflames them more madly, like those malign spirits who slaughter the more those whom they fear to lose, destroy those whom they wish to save, and put fuel on the flames that they may devour more cruelly.

So it was with Thomas of Marle, a most abandoned man. While the king was attending the aforesaid and many other wars, Thomas, the devil aiding him because the prosperity of fools is wont to ruin them, had ravaged the regions of Laon, Reims, and Amiens, and he had devoured them like a furious wolf. He did not spare the clergy out of any fear of ecclesiastical punishment nor the people out of any sense of humanity, but killed all and ruined all. He went so far as to seize from the convent of nuns of St. Jean of Laon two of their best manors, to fortify as if they were his own the strong castles of Crécy and Nouvion with a marvellous defence and high towers, and, transforming them into a nest of dragons and a cave of thieves, to expose almost the whole land to unmerciful ravaging and fire.

Exhausted by the intolerable damage done by this man, the Church of Gaul assembled in general council at Beauvais that it might begin there to pronounce against the enemy of its true Spouse, Jesus Christ, a first judgment and a sentence of damnation. The venerable legate of the holy Roman Church, Cono, bishop of Palestrina, greatly moved by the innumerable complaints of the churches, and the sufferings of the poor and orphans, striking low his tyranny by the sword of St. Peter, that is, a general anathema, ungirdled from him, although he was absent, the knightly belt, and removed him by the judgment of all from all honour as criminal, infamous and an enemy to the name of Christian.

The king, incited by the lamentation of the council, moves his army quickly against him, and accompanied by the clergy to whom he was humbly attached, turns toward the strongly fortified castle of Crécy. Thanks to a powerful force of armed men, nay, rather to divine aid, he seizes the castle unexpectedly, storms the impregnable tower as if it were a rustic hut, confounds the criminals, piously massacres the impious, and strikes down without pity those whom he attacks because they were pitiless. You could see the castle as if enveloped in infernal flames, so that you would not differ with the prophecy: "The whole universe will fight for him against the mad."

Then, powerful in victory, ready to pursue his success, when he had started toward the other castle by name Nouvion, a man approached him who said, "Your highness should know, my lord king, that in that criminal castle live the most wicked of men who are worthy only of hell. It was they, I say, who, when you ordered the commune to be crushed, set fire not only to the city of Laon but also to the noble church of the Mother of God and many others, martyred almost all the nobles of the city, both as cause and punishment because with true faith they tried to help their lord bishop, and, not afraid to put their hands on the anointed of the Lord, they most cruelly murdered the bishop himself, Gaudry, venerable defender of the Church, exposed him nude to the beasts and birds in the square, cut off his finger with the pontifical ring, and together with their vile counsellor Thomas, concerted to occupy your tower to displace you."

The king, then doubly angered, attacked the wicked castle, broke up these places, full of punishments and sacrilege like hell, dismissing the innocent and gravely punishing the guilty, one alone avenging the injuries of many. Those of the detestable murderers whom he came upon, thirsty for justice, he ordered to be affixed to the gibbet, thus presenting a feeding ground for the rapacity of kites, crows, and vultures, and thus he taught what those deserve who do not fear to put their hands on the anointed of the Lord. . . .

Then he disinherited the detestable Thomas and his heirs in perpetuity of the city [of Amiens].

From *Vie de Louis VI le Gros*, H. Waquet, ed. (Paris: Champion, 1929); trans. J.B.R.

The Coronation of Richard Lion Heart

ROGER OF WENDOVER

1189

DUKE RICHARD, when all the preparations for his coronation were complete, came to London, where were assembled the archbishops of Canterbury, Rouen, and Treves, by whom he had been absolved for having carried arms against his father after he had taken the cross. The archbishop of Dublin was also there, with all the bishops, earls, barons, and nobles of the kingdom.

When all were assembled, he received the crown of the kingdom in the order following: First came the archbishops, bishops, abbats, and clerks, wearing their caps, preceded by the cross, the holy water, and the censers, as far as the door of the inner chamber, where they received the duke, and conducted him to the church of Westminster, as far as the high altar, in a solemn procession. In the midst of the bishops and clerks went four barons carrying candlesticks with wax candles, after whom came two earls, the first of whom carried the royal sceptre, having on its top a golden cross; the other carried the royal sceptre, having a dove on its top. Next to these came two earls with a third between them, carrying three swords with golden sheaths, taken out of the king's treasury. Behind these came six earls and barons carrying a chequer, over which were placed the royal arms and robes, whilst another earl followed them carrying aloft a golden crown. Last of all came Duke Richard, having a bishop on the right hand, and a bishop on the left, and over them was held a silk awning. Proceeding to the altar, as we have said, the holy Gospels were placed before him together with the relics of some of the saints, and he swore, in presence of the clergy and people, that he would observe peace, honour, and reverence, all his life, towards God, the holy Church and its ordinances: he swore also that he would exercise true justice towards the people committed to his charge, and abrogating all bad laws and unjust customs, if any such might be found in his dominions, would steadily observe those which were good. After this they stripped him of all his clothes except his breeches and shirt, which had been ripped apart over his shoulders to receive the unction. He was then shod with sandals interwoven with gold thread, and Baldwin archbishop of Canterbury anointed him king in three places, namely, on his head, his shoulders, and his right arm, using prayers composed for the occasion: then a consecrated linen cloth was placed on his head, over which was put a hat, and when they had again clothed him in his royal robes with the tunic and gown, the archbishop gave into his hand a sword wherewith to crush all the enemies of the Church; this done, two earls placed his shoes upon his feet, and when he had received the mantle, he was adjured by the archbishop, in the name of God, not to presume to accept these honours unless his mind was steadily purposed to observe the oaths which he had made: and he answered that, with God's assistance, he would faithfully observe everything which he had promised. Then the king taking the crown from the altar gave it to the archbishop, who placed it upon the king's head, with the sceptre in his right hand and the royal wand in his left; and so, with his crown on, he was led away by the bishops and barons, preceded by the candles, the cross and the three swords aforesaid. When they came to the offertory of the mass, the two bishops aforesaid led him forwards and again led him back. At length, when the mass was chanted, and everything finished in the proper manner, the two bishops aforesaid led him away with his crown on, and bearing in his right hand the sceptre, in his left the royal wand, and so they returned in procession into the choir, where the king put off his royal robes, and taking others of less weight, and a lighter crown also, he proceeded to the dinner-table, at which the archbishops, bishops, earls, and barons, with the clergy and people, were placed, each according to his rank and dignity, and feasted splendidly, so that the wine flowed along the pavement and walls of the palace.

From *Flowers of History*, trans. J. A. Giles.

The Deposition and Death of Richard II

Adam of Usk

1399-1400

Next, the matter of setting aside King Richard, and of choosing Henry, duke of Lancaster, in his stead, and how it was to be done and for what reasons, was judicially committed to be debated on by certain doctors, bishops, and others, of whom I, who am now noting down these things, was one. And it was found by us that perjuries, sacrileges, unnatural crimes, oppression of his subjects, reduction of his people to slavery, cowardice and weakness of rule—with all of which crimes King Richard was known to be tainted—were cause enough for setting him aside, in accordance with the chapter: "*Ad apostolicae dignitatis,*" under the title: "*De re judicata,*" in the Sextus; and although he was ready himself to yield up the crown, yet was it determined, for the aforesaid reasons, that he should be deposed by the authority of the clergy and people, for which purpose they were summoned.

On St. Matthew's day (21st September), just two years after the beheading of the earl of Arundel, I, the writer of this history, was in the Tower, wherein King Richard was a prisoner, and was present at his dinner, and marked his mood and bearing, having been taken thither for that very purpose by Sir William Beauchamp. And there and then the king discoursed sorrowfully in these words: "My God! a wonderful land is this, and a fickle; which hath exiled, slain, destroyed, or ruined so many kings, rulers, and great men, and is ever filled and toileth with strife and variance and envy"; and then he recounted the histories and names of sufferers from the earliest habitation of the kingdom. Perceiving then the trouble of his mind, and how that none of his own men, nor such as were wont to serve him, but strangers who were but spies upon him, were appointed to his service, and musing on his ancient and wonted glory and on the fickle fortune of the world, I departed thence much moved at heart. . . .

On St. Michael's day there were sent to the king in the Tower, on behalf of the clergy, the archbishop of York and the bishop of Hereford; on behalf of the superior lords temporal, the earls of Northumberland and Westmorland; for the lower prelates, the abbat of Westminster and the prior of Canterbury; for the barons, the lords Berkeley and Burnell; for the lower clergy, Master Thomas Stow and John Borbach; and for the commons of the kingdom, Sir Thomas Grey and Sir Thomas Erpingham, knights, to receive the surrender of the crown from King Richard. And when this was done, on the morrow, the said lords, on behalf of the whole parliament and the clergy and the people of the kingdom, altogether renounced their oath of allegiance, loyalty, submission, service, and what obedience soever, and their fealty to him, setting him aside, and holding him henceforth not for king, but for a private person, Sir Richard of Bordeaux, a simple knight, having taken away his ring in token of deposition and deprival, and bringing the same to the duke of Lancaster, and delivering it to him in full parliament on that day assembled. On the same day the archbishop of York delivered first an address on the text: "I have set my words in thy mouth"; and then, having been made by King Richard his mouthpiece, he, using the first person, as though the king himself were speaking, read in full parliament the surrender of his royal rank and the release of all his lieges and subjects whomsoever from all submission, fealty, and homage openly and publicly drawn up in writings. And this surrender, the consent of all and every in parliament being first called for, was openly and distinctly accepted. Which being done, my lord archbishop of Canterbury made an address on the text: "A man shall reign over my people," wherein he highly lauded the duke of Lancaster and his strength and his understanding and his virtues, rightly exalting him to be their king; and, among other things, he spake of the shortcomings of King Richard, and specially how he had most unjustly stifled in prison his uncle, the duke of Gloucester, treacherously, and without a hearing or leave to answer; and how he strove to overthrow the law of the land to which he had sworn. And so, in short, although he had sufficiently made resignation, the sentence of his deposition, drawn up in writing, by consent and authority of the whole parliament, was there openly, publicly, and solemnly read by Master John Trevour of Powis, bishop of St. Asaph. And so, the throne being vacant, by consent of the whole parliament, the said duke of Lancaster, being raised up to be king, forthwith had enthronement at the hands of the said archbishops, and, thus seated on the king's throne, he there straightway openly and publicly read a certain declaration in writing, wherein was set forth that he, seeing the kingdom of England to be vacant, by lawful right of succession by descent from the body of King Henry the Third, did claim and take upon himself the crown as his by right; and that, in virtue of such succession or conquest, he would in no wise allow the state of the kingdom nor of any man to suffer change in liberties, franchises, inheritances, or in any other right or custom. And he fixed the day of his coronation for St. Edward's day next coming. And for that, through the deposing of King Richard, the parliament which was in his name assembled had become extinct, therefore, by consent of all, he ordained a new parliament in his own name as new king, to begin on the morrow of the coronation. He also thereupon made public proclamation that, if any thought that he had claim to do service or office in the coronation, by right of inheritance or custom, he should send in his petition, setting forth the why and the wherefore, in writing, to the seneschal of England, at Westminster, on the Saturday next following, and that he should have right in all things. . . .

On the morrow of the coronation, which was the first day of the new king's parliament, the commons presented to the king their speaker, Sir John Cheyne, knight. The king received liege homage from all the lords spiritual and temporal. Also, the last parliament of Lord Richard, then king, was declared altogether void. And this took place on the Tuesday. On the Wednesday the king promoted his eldest son Henry, by five symbols, to wit, by delivery of a golden rod, by a kiss, by a belt, by a ring, and by letters of creation, to be prince of Wales. Also the causes of the repeal of that parliament were declared to be because of the fears of, and threats used towards, the peers of the realm if they obeyed not the king's will; secondly, because of the armed violence of the king's supporters, which blazed forth in the parliament; and thirdly, because the counties, cities, and boroughs had not had free election in the choice of the members of the commons. It was also declared that the parliament of the eleventh year of King Richard, which was all the work of the duke of Gloucester and the earl of Arundel, should remain in full force. Also, that anyone who had in any way been deprived of his right by Richard's last parliament should then and there be restored to his own. And the king also granted and gave over to his eldest son the principality of Wales, as well as the duchy of Cornwall, along with the county of Chester. . . .

The lord Richard, late king, after his deposition, was carried away on the Thames, in the silence of dark midnight, weeping and loudly lamenting that he had ever been born. . . .

And now those in whom Richard, late king, did put his trust for help were fallen. And when he heard thereof, he grieved more sorely and mourned even to death, which came to him most miserably on the last day of February [1400], as he lay in chains in the castle of Pontefract, tortured by Sir N. Swinford with scant fare. . . .

Richard, farewell! king indeed (if I may call thee so), most mighty; for after death all might praise thee, hadst thou, with the help of God and thy people, so ordered thy deeds as to deserve such praise. But, though well endowed as Solomon, though fair as Absalom, though glorious as Ahasuerus, though a builder excellent as the great Belus, yet, like Chosroes, king of Persia, who was delivered into the hands of Heraclius, didst thou in the midst of thy glory, as Fortune turned her wheel, fall most miserably into the hands of Duke Henry, amid the curses of thy people.

From *Chronicle*, trans. E. M. Thompson.

An Imperialist View
of the Lombard Communes

OTTO OF FREISING

Twelfth century

NEVERTHELESS the Lombards had laid aside all the bitterness of their barbarous ferocity, in consequence, perhaps, of their marriages with the Italians, so that they had children who inherited something of Roman mildness and intellect from their maternal parentage, or from the influence of the soil and climate, and retain the elegance of the Latin language and a certain courtesy of manners. They also imitate the activity of the ancient Romans in the management of the cities and in the preservation of the state. Finally, they are so attached to their liberty that, to avoid the insolence of rulers, they prefer to be reigned over by consuls than by princes. And since, as it is known, there are three orders among them, of captains, vassals, and the commons, in order to keep down arrogance, these aforesaid consuls are chosen, not from one order, but from each, and, lest they should be seized with a greed for power, they are changed nearly every year. From which it happens that that territory is all divided into cities, which have each reduced those of their own province to live with them, so that there is hardly to be found any noble or great man with so great an influence, as not to owe obedience to the rule of his own city. And they are all accustomed to call these various territories their own *Comitatus*, from this privilege of living together. And in order that the means of restraining their neighbours may not fail, they do not disdain to raise to the badge of knighthood, and to all grades of authority, young men of low condition, and even workmen of contemptible mechanical arts, such as other people drive away like the plague from the more honourable and liberal pursuits. From which it happens that they are pre-eminent among the other countries of the world for riches and power. And to this they are helped also, as has been said, by their own industrious habits, and by the absence of their princes, accustomed to reside north of the Alps. In this, however, they retain a trace of their barbarous dregs, forgetful of ancient nobility, that while they boast of living by law they do not obey the laws. For they seldom or never receive the prince reverently, to whom it would be their duty to show a willing reverence of submission, nor do they obediently accept those things which he, according to the justice of the laws, ordains, unless they are made to feel his authority, constrained by the gathering of many soldiers. On this account it frequently happens that, whereas a citizen has only to be restrained by the law, and an adversary must be coerced with arms according to the law, they find him, from whom as their proper prince they should receive clemency, more often having recourse to hostilities for his own rights. From which results a double evil for the state, both that the prince has his thoughts distracted by the collecting of an army for the subjection of the citizen, while the citizen has to be compelled to obedience to his prince, not without a great expenditure of his own substance. Whence, for the same reason that the people are in such an instance guilty of rashness, the prince is to be excused, by the necessity of the case, before God and man.

Among the other cities of that nation, Milan, situated between the Po and the Alps, now possesses the supremacy. . . . And it is considered more famous than other cities, not only on account of its greater size and its large number of armed men, but also because it has added to its jurisdiction two other cities placed in the same region, namely Como and Lodi. Then, as happens in human affairs, through the blandishments of a smiling fortune, it swelled out into such daring of pride, being elated with success, that it not only did not refrain from attacking all its neighbours, but ventured even without alarm to incur the recently offended majesty of the prince.

From *Gesta Friderici*, trans. U. Balzani, *Early Chroniclers of Italy* (London: Society for Promoting Christian Knowledge, 1883).

City Politics in Siena

POPE PIUS II

Fifteenth century

SIENA is a very famous city of Tuscany and possesses wide lands. Many strange stories are told about its founders, but the stock originated at Rome and took from there the device of the she-wolf with the twins hanging on her teats. Some think they have been mixed with Gallic stock since the time when the Senonese Gauls invaded Rome and were defeated and routed by Camillus. For they say that the remnants of both armies settled where Siena now is and built two towns which afterwards, at the time of Charlemagne, were united in one great city. As evidence for this story they adduce the fact that to this day a third of the state is called Camillia from Camillus and they think that the name of the spring of Fontebranda is derived with a slight change of letters from Brennus, the Gallic chieftain. For our part we neither affirm nor deny these ancient tales, but we can assert that in this city there were many nobles and very powerful men who erected lofty palaces, high towers, and very splendid churches while they administered the state. When however the nobler families began to quarrel about the government and sometimes appealed even to armed force, the nobility decided to resign the management of affairs to the people, reserving for themselves only a few offices; for they thought that the popular party, though they might be administering the government, would do nothing without the permission of the nobles, of whose power they would continue to stand in awe. This turned out to be the case for a time, but when the people became accustomed to rule and had once tasted the sweets of office and the fruits of power, in their increased wealth and splendour they disdained the nobility, banished certain noble families, and sent the rest under the yoke like slaves, although they shared with them a few minor offices. There were five parties in the city (not counting the populace) as follows: the Nine, so named because when they alone were in power, they appointed nine chief magistrates; the Twelve, named on the same principle; the Reformers, so called because it was thought they had made certain reforms in the state; the Nobles who retained the title originally conferred because of their antiquity and influence; the rest were called the Populari. The Twelve had long since been deposed and no longer had any part in the government; the Nobles were entrusted with a fourth part of certain offices, but they were not permitted to command citadels or to live as priors in the palace or to keep the keys of the gates. The entire strength of the government re-

mained in the hands of the Nine, the Reformers, and
the Populari. In the course of time during the pontificate
of Calixtus III bitter feuds grew up among these three
parties and a considerable number of those in power
were accused of having conspired to betray the city to
Piccinino. On this charge some were beheaded, some
driven into exile, some banished and fined; and the
whole city was so torn with civil discord that it was the
universal opinion that she would soon lose her liberty.
But the great God looked with loving eyes on a state
dedicated to His Mother, the Virgin Mary; for when
Pope Pius succeeded to the papacy on the death of
Calixtus, he at once took thought for his dearly loved
country. He disrupted the schemes set on foot against
her and frightened off her enemies by his authority.
Moreover he thought it greatly concerned the city's
welfare that the places of citizens who had been removed from the government should be filled from the
Nobles and that it did not befit her dignity that the
Nobles, to whom he himself belonged by birth, should
be regarded as slaves in his native city. The Sienese,
suspecting this would happen, in order to forestall any
complaint, elected to office Pius's own family, the Pic-
colomini, thinking that he would demand nothing further. But Pius, who was concerned not for his own
house but for the whole state, thought that nothing had
been accomplished unless all the Nobles were returned
to power, and he sent ambassadors to demand that all
the rest of that order should be made equal to the Pic-
colomini. The people were violently excited by this demand; they declared that the pope's request was outrageous and that the state would never consent, even if
they were compelled to stand a siege and starved into
eating their own children. Pius on the other hand in-

sisted and swore that, if they did not obey, he would withdraw his favour from a city which refused to comply with just demands. . . .

The council was recalled repeatedly; a vote was taken again and again, but still it was impossible to get two-thirds of the senators to accept the pope's terms. When however he grew more insistent and demanded a reply before he left, and it appeared that he would be furious if he did not prevail, the senate finally voted to admit the Nobles to all offices and to grant them a fourth of some privileges and an eighth of the others. The announcement of this vote soon filled the whole city with rejoicing. The entire senate and all the magistrates went to acquaint the pope with what had been done. Pius, though he realized that his wishes had not been fully met, still, in order not to cast gloom on the city, appeared pleased and thanked the senate, praising what they had done and saying that he hoped for something more when he returned from Mantua.

From *The Commentaries of Pius II*, book ii, trans. F. Gragg, L. Gabel, ed. *Smith College Studies in History*, vol. xxv, nos. 1-4 (Oct. 1939—July 1940).

A Petty Italian Tyrant

Fourteenth century

THERE was in the Romagna a faithless dog of a Patarine [heretic], a rebel against Holy Church. For thirty years he had been excommunicate and his lands had been under an interdict without the reading of a mass. He held in his power many lands of the Church: the cities of Forlì, Cesena, Forlimpopoli, Castrocaro,

Brettinoro, Imola, and Giazzolo. All these he held and ruled them as a tyrant; not to mention many other castles and communes belonging to local proprietors.

This was Francesco Ordelaffi, a desperate character and a mortal enemy of priests, who never forgot that he had been harshly treated by the former legate, Bertrando del Poggetto, cardinal of Ostia. He refused to live any longer under priestly rule . . . He was a faithless and obstinate tyrant. This Francesco, when he heard the bells ringing for his excommunication, ordered other bells to be rung and excommunicated the pope and the cardinals, and, what was worse, he burned paper images of them filled with straw in the market place. Talking with his good friends, he said, "Well, we are excommunicated, but for all that our bread, our meat, and our wine will taste just as well and do us just as much good."

And this was his way of treating priests and monks: The bishop, after he had pronounced the excommunication and had been outrageously insulted, stayed away, and the captain forced the clergy to celebrate mass, the greater part of them doing as they were ordered in spite of the interdict. Fourteen clerics, seven monks and seven seculars, received the sacred honour of martyrdom. Seven of them were hanged by the neck and seven were flayed. He was absolutely devoted to the people of Forlì and dearly beloved by them. He put on the appearance of pious philanthropy, found husbands for orphan girls, secured places for others, and provided for the poor among his friends.

Trans. E. Emerton, in *Humanism and Tyranny: Studies in the Italian Trecento* (Cambridge, Mass.: Harvard University Press, 1925).

A Picture of a Tyrant

POPE PIUS II

Fifteenth century

SIGISMONDO, of the noble family of the Malatesta but illegitimate, was very vigorous in body and mind, eloquent, and gifted with great military ability. He had a thorough knowledge of history and no slight acquaintance with philosophy. Whatever he attempted he seemed born for, but the evil part of his character had the upper hand. He was such a slave to avarice that he was ready not only to plunder but to steal. His lust was so unbridled that he violated his daughters and his sons-in-law. When he was a lad he often played the bride and after taking the woman's part debauched men. No marriage was sacred to him. He ravished nuns and outraged Jewesses; boys and girls who would not submit to him he had murdered or savagely beaten. He committed adultery with many women to whose children he had been godfather and murdered their husbands. He outdid all barbarians in cruelty. His bloody hand inflicted terrible punishments on innocent and guilty alike. He oppressed the poor, plundered the rich, spared neither widows nor orphans. No one felt safe under his rule. Wealth or a beautiful wife or handsome children were enough to cause a man to be accused of crime. He hated priests and despised religion. He had no belief in another world and thought the soul died with the body. Nevertheless he built at Rimini a splendid church dedicated to St. Francis, though he filled it so full of pagan works of art that it seemed less a Christian sanctuary than a temple of heathen devil-worshippers. In it he erected for his mistress a tomb of magnificent marble and exquisite workmanship with an inscription in the pagan style as follows, "Sacred to the deified Isotta." The two wives he had married before he took Isotta for his mistress he killed one after the other with the sword or poison. The third, whom he married before these, he divorced before he had intercourse with her, but kept her dowry. Meeting not far from Verona a noble lady who was going from Germany to Rome in the jubilee year, he assaulted her (for she was very beautiful) and when she struggled left her wounded and covered with blood. Truth was seldom in his mouth. He was a past master of simulation and dissimulation. He showed himself a perjuror and traitor to Alfonso, king of Sicily, and his son Ferrante. He broke his word to Francesco, duke of Milan, to the Venetians, the Florentines and the Sienese. Repeatedly too he tricked the Church of Rome. Finally when there was no one left in Italy for him to betray, he went on to the French, who allied themselves with him out of hatred for Pope Pius but fared no better than the other princes. When his subjects once begged him to retire at last to a peaceful life and spare his country, which had so often been exposed to pillage on his account, he replied, "Go and be of good courage; never while I live shall you have peace."

Such was Sigismondo, intolerant of peace, a devotee of pleasure, able to endure any hardship, and greedy for war. Of all men who have ever lived or ever will live he was the worst scoundrel, the disgrace of Italy and the infamy of our times.

From *The Commentaries of Pius II*, book II, trans. F. Gragg, L. Gabel, ed.

Renewal and Reform

The Recovery of the Holy Land:
A Plan of Action
and a Scheme for Reform

PIERRE DU BOIS

1305-1307

To THE most illustrious prince, distinguished above all others in the glories of his military art and experience, to the most Christian lord Edward, by divine favour king of England and Scotland, lord of Ireland, duke of Aquitaine, the most lowly advocate of his ecclesiastical cases in this same duchy, in order to serve him, moved long since by the pure ardour of natural affection and royal virtue, seeking nothing and up to now paid no salary, with the greatly desired increase of good fortune, sends greeting in Him through whom all true kings rule and princes govern.

I have recognized in you a true king, magnanimous and splendid, because you have understood not only how to rule, but also at the same time how to fight, and a true legislator, because you have until now devoted the greatest effort to making all your subjects, far and near, good, not only through fear of punishment, but also by the frequent encouragement of great rewards. And now at last, after your wars have been brought to a successful conclusion, your armies aided by the Lord, the King of kings, from whom all good things come, in place of that rest which other princes, after such great labours, and much lesser men are wont to choose, your glorious spirit has been strongly inclined to the recovery of the Holy Land, so that it may be snatched from the hands of the infidel. Thus, at the approach of old age, against the natural and accustomed inclination of men, you would courageously embrace, with fervent desire, the true perfection of fortitude by undertaking fearful struggles, in which the death of the body is threatened, and out of which the life of the soul is born. For this reason, although I am the least in counsel, I . . . propose briefly to discuss, with the help and favour of the highest wisdom of God, those things which seem to me necessary, profitable, and also appropriate to the recovery and preservation of the Holy Land.

But it seems that this cannot be accomplished, unless all impediments have been removed, and all that is profitable and fitting has been ordained, by the most holy father, your friend, by divine providence supreme pontiff of the most holy Roman and universal Church, with the assent of a general council of all Catholic princes and prelates. For that land most excellent beyond all others, according to the testimony of the Saviour, has been extraordinarily populated by the Saracens who occupied it. Because, being devoted to a polygamous way of life and without exception having leisure for it, they were so much more effective in the procreation and education of children, the many regions and kingdoms of the area near the east, west, and south of the same Holy Land were not enough for them. For this reason, they left these lands after the manner of the Tartars. From these surrounding kingdoms those Saracens will quickly and easily have a multitude of people to aid them, if, in great fear of death, they should yield to your kings and princes, to you and others, thinking that they will quickly return to their own lands. Immediately after their retreat, those Saracens will return, more warlike and in greater numbers, so that they may slay those who are there and possess the sweetness of the land. . . .

Therefore, that land [the Holy Land] cannot be taken except by a great multitude, nor, after it has been taken, can it be held.

To the end that such a great multitude may be led there, and may remain there, it will be necessary for Catholic princes to be harmonious, and not to have wars among themselves. For if, while they are there, they should hear that their own lands are overcome and laid waste, they will give up the inheritance of the Lord, and will return to their own to defend it, just as it has happened there many times. For that reason, it is expedient that peace be established among all Catholics, at least among those obedient to the Roman Church, so that there may be one commonwealth, so strongly united that it may not be divided; since "every kingdom divided against itself, will fall," as the Saviour says; and if it should be divided, it is expedient that by this division, the safeguarding of the Holy Land should be strengthened, as will appear below.

For we have seen that although the Germans and the Spaniards are renowned warriors, yet because of the frequent wars of their kingdoms, they have now become idle, and are unable to come to the aid of the Holy Land. The wars of the Catholics among themselves are the very worst, because many die in them in such a state that the everlasting life of such men is truly in doubt.

And as often as they begin wars, so much the more do they desire to wage them, pursuing this course more from habit than for advantage, not seeking or keeping the peace after wars nor through them, and not being afraid to start wars again. They do not pay attention to the words of the philosopher, the teacher of Alexander: "All war is evil and unlawful in itself, so much so that he who seeks war for its own sake has his end in wickedness." But, nevertheless, when it is impossible to have peace by other means than by war, it is permitted to just men to seek and to wage war, so that, when peace has been obtained, after the war, in time of peace men may have leisure for cultivating virtue and knowledge. Otherwise, unless it is for this end, all war is unlawful, also according to the doctors of civil law.

We see that when the fathers and grandfathers have died in unlawful war, the surviving descendants and the wives of the dead, whatever they may promise, prepare themselves again, as quickly as they can, for war and wilful vengeance. These things thus happen, brought about by the maker of dissension through his temptations, persuasions and infinite frauds and deceptions, so that he may cause the number of those damned with him to increase, and may hinder and retard the recovery and preservation of the Holy Land. For this reason he does not wish to allow the strength of the Catholics to be unified, since, as the philosopher says: "All strength united is stronger than it is dispersed and divided. . . ."

To the end, therefore, that the Holy Land can be recovered, and having been recovered, can be held against so many and such great demons, who have followers, protectors, and helpers, the devout prayers of the universal Church seem necessary. And it does not seem possible to have them without a reformation of the condition of the universal Church, which is discussed below. Nor is it possible unless the whole commonwealth of Christians obedient to the Roman Church, bound together by the bond of peace, is united in such a way that Catholics would mutually desist from all warfare among themselves; so that if any should engage in war, out of this warfare and because of it, the recovery and defence of the Holy Land might be strengthened.

This could be accomplished thus. After a general council has been called, because of ardour for the deliverance of the Holy Land, the greatest royal experience will be able to request through the lord pope that the princes and prelates should agree and determine to the end that, when anyone whosoever says that he has suffered injuries according to the laws and customs of the kingdoms and regions, justice will be done, more quickly than is customary, by judges established in those places, and where they have not been established, they should be, in the manner described below. No Catholic should rush to arms against Catholics; no one should shed the blood of a baptized Christian. Whoever wants to fight should strive to fight against the enemies of the Christian faith, of the Holy Land and the holy places of the Lord, not against brothers, seeking an occasion of bodily and spiritual perdition.

Those who should presume, moreover, to carry on warfare against their fellow Catholics, in defiance of this wholesome decision, by that act should incur the loss of all their goods, with everything which aids them in fighting—foodstuffs, arms, and other necessities of life or battle—and in ruling, in any way whatsoever. After the war has ended, those who survive, of whatever estate, condition, and sex, should be exiled forever from their lands and possessions, and, completely deprived, with all of their descendants, they should be sent to people the Holy Land. As much as will be necessary for their expenses and for making the journey should be given to them from the property of which they have been deprived, if they should be obedient and willingly intend to transfer themselves to the Holy Land. . . .

But since these cities [the Italian cities] and many princes do not recognize superiors in their lands, who should administer justice to them according to the laws and customs of these places, will they not begin to cause disputes, and come before those judges and quarrel? It can be answered that the council should establish as judges religious men or others chosen for this purpose, prudent, experienced, and trustworthy men. When these three judges mentioned above and three others on behalf of both sides, men of substance, and such as it is likely cannot be corrupted by love, hatred, fear, greed, or otherwise, have been sworn, they should come together in a place more suitable for this purpose. After these men have taken very binding oaths, and, when the articles of petition and defence of each party have been presented, summarily and easily, they should meet beforehand, and after first rejecting that which is superfluous and inappropriate, they should receive the witnesses and the instruments, and should examine them most diligently. The examination of every witness should be heard by at least two of the sworn, trustworthy, and prudent men. The depositions should be written down, and guarded very carefully by the judges, in order to prevent fraud and deception.

Thus the judges may agree, in order to pay moderate expenses of the parties, that as much will be paid as these expend when they are in their own homes. For the purpose of judging, if it shall seem expedient, the judges may have, according to their consciences, assistants who are very trustworthy and very well trained in divine and canon and civil law.

If either side should not be content with the decision of these judges, the judges may, on behalf of all, send the process of the dispute with the decisions to the apostolic see, to be amended or altered by the supreme pontiff then reigning, in so far as, and if, it seems just; if not, they should be confirmed advantageously for the perpetual memory of the matter, and should be registered in the records of the holy Roman Church.

Since, indeed, the changes in the succession of the empire have been wont to present infinite occasions of war in Germany, obstructing the customary election of the emperor, and because these accustomed discords have hindered the recovery and the preservation of the Holy Land, a firm peace in the Roman Empire would very likely be able to contribute very great aid to that same recovery and preservation. . . . Lest the wellbeing and prestige of the commonwealth, the kingdom and the empire of so noble a people should be extinguished, the kingdom of Germany and the empire should be asked to confirm itself in a modern king, and in his descendants after him. In order to avoid scandal and to quiet the greed of the electors, some compensation with regard to the affairs and liberties of the empire should be made to them. The modern king and future emperor should agree and should promise an annual aid to the Holy Land, as long as it will be in need of it, of a great number of fighting men, whom he will send to the seaports at his own expense, sufficiently armed and prepared. . . .

Just as, moreover, it is necessary and expedient that the harmonious and united temporal resources of the whole commonwealth of Catholics should be brought together for so great a recovery and preservation, so it will be necessary, by the devout prayers of the universal Church, to seek and obtain this great blessing of the recovery and maintenance of so great a peace, from Him from whom all good proceeds, who is God and the Lord of armies, who alone is the cause of peace and victory. For if the leaders of warfare and the fighting men entrusted to them should be confident in their own strength, and should think that this strength suffices to obtain and keep so great a victory, and to resist the evil spirits fighting against them, with their persuasions and temptations . . . it will not be possible in this way to recover and keep the Holy Land. For this reason, it seems expedient that the council should seek to reform and improve the condition of the Church Universal, so that the prelates both greater and lesser may abstain from that which is forbidden by the holy fathers; that they may guard their precepts, commandments, and counsels, as they are understood, according to the saying of the prophet, "Depart from evil, and do good; seek peace and pursue it." And then, when the true peace of the heart has been attained, all Catholic prelates, with all the clergy and people committed to their care, should form one spiritual commonwealth, in order to approach what the apostle says, "And the multitude of them that believed were of one heart and one soul." . . .

If, indeed, it will seem good to strengthen the bonds of universal peace in the manner prescribed, it should be resolved, by agreement of the council of prelates and princes, that all prelates, of whatever rank, and also the secular knights in their own ranks, will firmly swear that they will observe, with all their strength, the covenants of this peace with its penalties, and that they will take care that it is observed, in every way in which they can. Thus anyone who will scorn or neglect to fulfil this oath, because of this, by the apostolic authority and that of the sacred council, will *ipso facto* incur sentence of major excommunication. Thus anyone who assails this covenant of peace in the future will be strongly attacked by all those knights of the spiritual and temporal army, with all their strength, so that he will not be able to resist. . . .

It seems necessary to arrange that four armies should be formed, of which three should go by sea, and the fourth, larger than the others, by dry land, following the example of Charles the Great, of the Emperor Frederick I, and of Godfrey of Bouillon. Then when the enemies of the faith in many places have been besieged and crushed, and thus divided, they may the more easily be driven out. And it is likely that these enemies, knowing that the aforesaid covenant of peace has been confirmed for their ruin, and that so many people are coming and will come against them, will gladly depart from the entire Promised Land without fighting. If they should do this, and if the fortified places and other habitations have not been destroyed, and the relics and sacred vessels of the Church have been left, it seems that they should be spared from violent death, under the threat, that, if they should attack the Christians in any way, they will be destroyed root and branch, and that no place will be left for them in the land. And then it seems best for the princes to leave an army in the Holy Land sufficient to safeguard it, and to return by way of Greece, in order to fight bravely, with the counsel of the Roman Church, on behalf of the Lord Charles [Charles of Valois], against the Paleologus [Andronicus II], the unlawful ruler of the [Byzantine] Empire, unless he should wish to surrender. It should be agreed that, when victory and the possession of the Empire have been obtained, the same Lord Charles should give suitable aid, as much as may be necessary, to the defence of the Holy Land, since he is nearer to it than the others. Thus he will strongly relieve the more distant princes, except the king of Germany, so that in the future all the wars of Christians for the aid of the Holy Land may be effectively organized.

After the aforesaid matters have been arranged by God's grace, the harmonious Catholics will possess the entire shore of the Mediterranean Sea, from the west side to the northeast, and the better part of that touching on the Land of Promise to the south. Thus the Arabs will not be able to live well even physically, unless they have relations with the Catholics for the exchange of their goods, and it will be the same among the eastern peoples, and concerning them.

When this great goal, then, has been perceived by the legislator of Christians, the vicar on earth of the Lord Jesus Christ, the successor of the blessed Peter, prince of the apostles, in order to consummate it successfully, with the help of God, the Lord of armies, it may please the most experienced royal majesty [Philip IV of France], after his own wars have been successfully carried out, to request that these things be done, and with those reinforcements ordained by the Fount of Life from whom all good proceeds, to provide for their accomplishment. In order that these things which have been planned may be begun, it seems expedient to entreat the lord pope to establish a general council, on this side of the Alps, having called the prelates and princes obedient to him to deliberate on these matters, especially the kings and others who do not recognize superiors in their lands. The Paleologus who holds the empire at Constantinople, and he who holds the kingdom of Castile, and his nephews who are striving to obtain it, and the king of Germany with his electors, should by no means be overlooked. And in order that advice, aid, and remedy may be had concerning the recovery, reformation, and preservation of the Holy Land, and also concerning the condition of the whole commonwealth of Christians . . . the present little work should be sent to the lord pope, after it has been corrected by more prudent men with the foresight of the most experienced leader in warfare [Philip IV]. Care should be taken that it should not be shown to the pope except by trusted secretaries who have sworn an oath. For it is certain that such a pious work will have, at the instigation of Satan and his nefarious army, many rivals wickedly opposing it. . . .

After this has been thus accomplished, it may happen that men will be very much dissatisfied, and will murmur together about this plan, saying that it does not seem to them, or is not wont to seem to them, that the legacies bequeathed to the Holy Land and other property, in the names of the Templars and Hospitallers, for the aid of the Holy Land, and other things collected in various ways, have been clearly of advantage in aiding it. For this reason, they will for the most part be in favour of stopping the gifts which have been secured, which is a thing to be condemned. Lest they should stop these, it seems expedient that there should be in the cathedral church of each diocese, that is, in its treasury, a public chest, in which moneys belonging in any way whatsoever to this aid for the Holy Land may be kept. And when it is necessary for the sake of this aid, money should be given, with the counsel of the diocesan of the place and of the masters of the said Provisio [i.e., du Bois' scheme], to the fighting men of the place who are to go to the Holy Land, that is, to the natives of that diocese or to others who are about to cross the sea. This should be done after the elders of the same diocese, province, or kingdom have knowledge of it and have taken counsel with the diocese. On account of these things, if they are done, many more and also far larger donations to the aid of the Holy Land may be made . . . and, because of this, the resources for sending fighters, when it is necessary, will everywhere be acquired far more easily. . . .

It is very likely that after wars have been extinguished in the manner prescribed, and after the lord pope has perpetually entrusted the government, possession, and occupation of his temporalities, in return for a certain annual pension, to the lord king of the French, to be governed, as it will seem expedient, by his brothers and sons, and after the poisonous treacheries of the Romans and Lombards have ceased, the lord pope will live long and healthily in his own native land, the kingdom of France. Thus he will have leisure for the government only of souls, and will avoid the intemperance of the Roman air, which is not native to him. This will be forever advantageous, more than can now be believed, to all friends of the same lord pope, both far and near, and especially for the whole kingdom of the French. For the ultramontanes [Italians] would not use the wealth of the fat benefices of churches on this side of the Alps, as they have been wont to do, in building towers for themselves; and the churches which have been robbed would not be lacking in divine services, and the Italians would not have fat benefices. Also the highest office of the Church would not escape the hands of the French, as has been the case for a long time now, through the craftiness and natural cunning of the Romans, who, striving by their own arrogance to trample underfoot the humility of the French, have presumed to attempt that which otherwise would have been unheard of, to claim temporal lordship over the kingdom of France and its chief prince, by damnably inciting the kingdom from the heights of peace and concord to perpetual sedition.

The presumptuous beginning of their attack has wholesomely been stilled, the King of Peace bestowing the greatest peace among His own vicars.

And since the Roman pope has abused power, and has done this in as much as he is a Roman, it is expedient and just, with regard for what has been established by the holy fathers, and saving and augmenting in all things the dignity of the papacy, that the Romans should for a very long time, although unwillingly, allow this great office to be exercised by those who would not strive to seize the highest office of a most Christian prince; who would not transcend the limits which the holy fathers have set; who would allow each Caesar to reign in his own place, to rule, and to rejoice in his own possessions. This is as our Saviour taught that it ought to be done, as evangelical truth witnesses, since in order to avoid scandal for Himself and Peter, He ordered the tribute that was owed to be paid, saying and leaving this example for Peter and his successors: "Render unto Caesar the things that are Caesar's, and unto God the things that are God's."

From *De recuperatione Terre Sancte*, C. V. Langlois, ed. (Paris: A. Picard, 1891); trans. M.M.M.

On the Supremacy of General Councils in Church and Empire

NICHOLAS OF CUSA

1433

IN SHORT, one conclusion can be drawn from the laws, based in part on the endorsement of the signatories and partly on the reasoning in the councils: that the Roman pontiff does not have, in the making of general statutes, the authority which certain flatterers attribute to him—namely, that he alone has the power to legislate while the others merely serve as counsellors. I do not deny that the pope has always had authority to respond to a consultation, to advise, and to address [the council] in writing; I am talking of statutes that have the force of canons and of decretals that are universally binding in the Church. Whether even today the pope alone may decree, as universally binding, that which has been transmitted by long usage, I am not at present considering. I do say that even though he has such power it does not contradict our thesis, which holds merely that the authority of enacting canons depends, not on the pope alone, but on common agreement.

No rule or custom can prevail against this conclusion any more than against the divine or natural law upon which the conclusion depends. The pre-eminent power of the Roman pontiff in respect to this matter in a general or universal council is no different from that of a metropolitan in a provincial council; or rather the pontiff's power, in respect to authoritative action, is less in a universal council of the whole Catholic Church than in a patriarchal council. In the latter, indeed, the pope is rightly likened to the metropolitan in a provincial council, as we have shown. Accordingly, the Roman pontiff is frequently called "archbishop" by the ancients. Indeed a lesser pre-eminence is attributable to the Roman pontiff in a universal council of the whole Church than to the same pontiff in a patriarchal council or to a metropolitan in a provincial council, as will be shown below.

This will perhaps appear strange to any who have read the writings of Roman pontiffs declaring that plenitude of authority is in the Roman pontiff and that all others may be called by virtue of his favour; as well as to those who have read Gelasius, Sylvester, Nicholas, Symmachus, and other Roman pontiffs, maintaining that the pope passes judgment on other ecclesiastical authorities but that none passes judgment on him: since the authority of the pope is divine, transmitted to him by God with the words "Whatsoever ye shall bind," and accordingly, the pope, as vicar of Christ, presides over the universal Church; and since he himself holds this supreme authority and is known to have condemned and absolved subjects of any bishops whatsoever even when their own bishops were not negligent; and he may be appealed to without any intermediary. The power of making statutes depends on a power of jurisdiction; therefore [according to this argument] it is absurd to say that something more than his will is necessary to the validity of any statute, since what pleases the prince has the force of law. Furthermore: it cannot be doubted that the head of a corporation has authority to exercise jurisdiction, although jurisdiction itself remains ostensibly in the corporation. And no one doubts that the pope is the "rector" of the ship of St. Peter and of the universal Church; wherefore the validity of fundamental laws depends upon him, just as it is impossible to legislate for a corporation without the head. . . .

However, in order to discover the truth of this statement that inferior prelates hold jurisdiction under positive law *papa derivative*—that is derived from the pope himself, it would be necessary, if that were true, that in the beginning Peter should have received something special from Christ and that the pope was his successor in this. Yet we know that Peter received from Christ no more authority than the other apostles; for nothing was said to Peter that was not also said to the others. Is it not true that just as it was said to Peter, "Whatsoever thou shalt bind upon the earth," it was also said to the others, "Whomsoever ye shall bind"? And although it was said to Peter, "Thou art Peter and upon this Rock"; nevertheless by rock we understand Christ, whom Peter confessed. And if by *petra* ("rock"), Peter is to be understood as the foundation stone of the church, then, according to St. Jerome, all the other apostles were similarly foundation stones of the church (concerning which there is a discussion in next to the last chapter of the Apocalypse, wherein by the twelve foundation stones of the city of Jerusalem—that is, the holy Church—no one doubts that the apostles are meant). If it was said to Peter, "Feed the sheep," it is nevertheless clear that this feeding is by word and example. So also, according to St. Augustine in his gloss upon the same passage, the same command was given for all. In the verse—"Go ye into all the world" (Matthew and Mark, at the end), it does not appear that anything was said to Peter that implied any supremacy. Therefore, we rightly say that all the apostles are equal in authority with Peter. It should also be remembered that at the beginning of the Church there was only one general episcopate, diffused throughout the whole world, without division into dioceses. . . .

Therefore, since the power of binding and loosing, on which all ecclesiastical jurisdiction is founded, is immediately from Christ, and since from this power comes the power of divine jurisdiction, it is evident that all bishops, and perhaps even presbyters, are of equal authority in respect to jurisdiction, although not in respect to the execution, which is confined within certain positive limits. . . .

In order that everyone may be better satisfied, I add another consideration, which, if it were practicable, should be set forth at greater length. Seeking to be brief and to please the reader, I shall definitely compress the matter.

Every constitution is founded on natural law (*jure naturali*), and if it contradicts this it cannot be valid. Wherefore, since natural law exists by nature in reason, every law (*lex*) is basically congenital with man. Accordingly, those who are wiser and more excellent than others are chosen as rulers, in order that, endowed with a naturally clear reason and with wisdom and prudence, they may choose just laws and by these govern others and hear cases, so as to preserve the peace; such are the judgments of the wise. Thus those who are strong in reason are by nature masters and rulers of others, yet not by means of coercive laws or of judgments rendered against an unwilling subject.

Since by nature all men are free, all government—whether based on written law or on law embodied in a ruler through whose government the subjects are restrained from evil deeds and their liberty regulated, for a good end, by fear of punishment—arises solely from agreement and consent of the subjects. For if men are by nature powerful and equally free, a valid and ordained authority of any one person, whose power by nature is like that of the rest, cannot be created save by election and consent of the others, just as law is established by consent. . . .

From the foregoing then it is clear that laws and canons constitute the norms for every judge, and that every law or canon is superior to any judge in rendering judgments. Furthermore, if a canon is approved by agreement, usage, and acceptance, then the stability of any constitution rests on acceptance. Accordingly, ecclesiastical canons are rightly decreed by a common council; for the Church is a congregation. A single person cannot rightly issue ecclesiastical canons. Wherefore we see that in councils, canons issue from agreement, acceptance, consent, and approval; and that decretals or judicial decisions of the Roman pontiffs, or of contested incumbents in emergencies, have received the strength of stability and justness, not from a merely powerful will, but from the fact that in accordance with the canons it was right that those decisions should be made. . . .

It is sufficient to know that free election, depending on natural and divine law, does not have its origin in positive law or in any man, in such way that the validity of an election—especially the election of a king or emperor, whose existence and power depend on no one man—should rest in his discretion.

Thus the electors—who were created in the time of Henry the Second by common agreement of all the Germans and other subjects of the empire—have their authority fundamentally from the common consent of all those who could by natural law have created the emperor, not from the Roman pontiff, who has no authority to give to any region in the world a king or emperor without its consent. Gregory V concurred in the arrangement, but in the role of a particular Roman pontiff, who has to participate, according to his rank, in agreeing to the common emperor. So also in general councils, the pontiff's authority rightly concurs by consent, in the first degree, with all others attending the same council. The force of a decree depends, nevertheless, not on the chief pontiff, but on the common consent of himself and the others. The fact that in setting up a king or emperor the consent of priests as well as of laymen must be obtained, is not because the authority of kings is outweighed by the priesthood in matters of government, for we know that the priesthood of the sun and the imperium of the moon are equal, but because the temporal possessions of the Church, without which the priesthood cannot survive in this perishable life, are subject to the imperium and its laws. . . .

In sum and substance then, this ought to be understood: the aim of a ruler should be to establish laws by agreement. It is, therefore, fitting that all general matters affecting the commonwealth should be decided and ordered in a council of the two estates of primates and bishops (*primatum et praesulum*). Indeed the king must be the executor of what is enacted by the council, since this very legislation is the rule according to which the subjects desire the authority of the king to be controlled. No one doubts that a universal council has the power to regulate, by agreement of the head and members, the chief governing (*praesidentialem*) authority, for the good of the commonwealth. . . .

We know that the emperor is head and chief of all; and from him comes the imperial command for the assembling of subordinate kings and princes, while they, as members, have to concur with the head. In this universal council are the heads of the provinces, as representatives of their provinces; also the rectors and teachers of the great universities; and those who are of the senatorial rank, which is called the holy diet, since they are illustrious as closest to the ruler and parts of his body; or they are notable members of the middle group; or those most distinguished in the lowest group—beyond which grades none was found among the well-defined grade (*certum*) of the senators. The first orders are the rulers and electors of the empire and the highest nobles. The second are the dukes, governors, prefects, and others of this sort. The third are the marquises, land-graves, and the like. All those who are superior to the rest and who are nearer to the imperial government, compose that imperial body whose head is the emperor himself; and when they are met in one complete repre-sentative body, the whole imperial authority is brought together. . . .

Let the annual meeting be set for about the feast of Pentecost, in Frankfort, which seems to be the most suit-able place from its situation and from other circum-stances. To this meeting all the judges and electors of the empire should come in person, without pomp or heavy expense. Let his lordship the emperor himself preside, if he can be present in person; otherwise, the chief of the electors in the emperor's name. Let affairs of the empire, and even local affairs that have come be-fore the judges, be dealt with; and let things that need reforming be reformed. If a critical matter of business really demands that a full meeting of all the chief offi-cials take place, there or elsewhere, let whatever is most suitable be done. However, a regular annual council of lords, judges, and electors—in which cases of the princes are to be decided through a common vote—should never be omitted. And since it is useful to introduce any reform on the basis of precedent, I would submit an imperial letter which is credited to Constantine, who ordered a similar meeting of judges to be held at Arles. . . .

Following this form, an annual council should be

established in Frankfort (which, by reason of its situation and the converging of merchandise there, may be correctly likened to Arles), to be held for at least one month, in either May or September; and, with those mentioned above, at least one should come from each city and metropolis and from the large imperial towns. The chief electors should bring with them those whom they wish as counsellors. The nobles and all should be bound by oath to contribute counsels for the public good, according to the right verdict of reason. Let provincial customs be there examined, and harmonized as nearly as possible with the common practices; and especially let captious formalities be completely laid aside; for the simple poor are often most unjustly led outside the case (*extra formam*) by the sophistries of lawyers, and so lose their whole case, since he who loses a syllable loses a case, as I have often seen happen in the diocese of Treves. Moreover, those very bad usages that permit an oath against anyone whomsoever and witnesses of whatever number should be abolished. Throughout Germany there are many such bad practices that are against true justice and are also breeders of crimes which no one could enumerate in detail. Wherefore judges of the provinces ought to come together and put the customs of their provinces into writing and lay them out before the council, so that they may be examined.

From *De concordantia catholica*, trans. F. W. Coker, in *Readings in Political Philosophy* (New York: Macmillan, 1938).

A Plea for the Reform of Germany

c. 1437

ALMIGHTY GOD, Creator of heaven and earth, give strength and grace, give wisdom in the most blessed manner to achieve and to possess an ordinance for the spiritual and temporal estates in which Thy holy name and divinity shall be acknowledged; for Thy wrath is manifest. Thy displeasure has laid hold upon us; we go about like sheep without a shepherd. We go about, O Lord, in Thy pasture without permission. Obedience is dead; justice suffers distress; nothing stands in its proper station.

Therefore God withdraws His grace from us and justly, for we disregard his commandment. What He has commanded is held lightly without all righteousness. But one thing must be known, that matters cannot well go on longer unless there is a proper ordering of the spiritual and temporal estates, for they stand naked and without power. Therefore are admonished first all you high princes, lords, and you worthy members of the knighthood, and you noble imperial cities. For the head is too ill, the spiritual and temporal leaders let drop what has been commanded of them by God, and if one regard it rightly, all now depends upon the imperial cities. If they slept and did not watch, then Christendom would be estranged from God and all His grace, and all righteousness would be worthless before God since the divine order would be extinguished.

The great superiors are not to be admonished, for by force they have taken to themselves injustice. Our lord the emperor or king can no longer maintain his status; that most worthy office is diminished for the empire by the electors and others, so that our empire is ill, infirm, and weak.

Therefore, you noble imperial cities, be admonished through God the Father, through Jesus Christ, through His red blood which He shed on our account, that you recognize how we are liberated by God, how we should conduct ourselves, how all order has no proper structure. Act then, for you are the chief member upon which, indeed, Christendom at this time is built.

Also, it is to be known, that the holy council [Basel] has gathered. There is to take place a reformation, the spiritual and temporal estates shall be well ordered. But the spiritual superiors wish to resist on many points. They do not wish to give up unrighteousness, as you will hear hereafter in the reformation.

But one thing: it should truly be known what an oppression lies upon Christendom and how one may ward it off: the discovery has been made through the grace of God that all defects may be easily remedied [by him] who will be true to God and the Christian faith. All the defects suffer primarily in respect to two things: in the clergy the malady is great simony, that is so much as usury. This same simony has poisoned the whole ecclesiastical estate. In the laity the malady is greed which divides all friendship; enmity, faithlessness, and much wrong arise from it. . . .

CONCERNING TOLLS

It must also be known that all lands are greatly overburdened by tolls. There is a toll at almost every spot, one land wholly refuses to assist another or be of advantage to it, nor will anyone give another his rightful penny's worth. All that happens on account of the tolls.

You shall hear how tolls were first instituted by an emperor. There were wild mountains over which there had to be roads; likewise over the rivers.

So it was held that it should justly be done by a common effort, and a small toll was set in such a measure that no one should be oppressed by it, and help and tax were asked for.

No one pocketed it, except to use it for building [the roads]. For whoever puts tolls somewhere else than where they rightly belong, if he makes use of them he makes use of usury, for he takes it from one who does not owe him anything. He shall do penance for it, as being property acquired by usury. . . .

Therefore let two-thirds of the tolls be abolished and the third part applied [to the roads] and let no one pocket it; thus one will be able to travel more easily.

But whoever will not do this and wishes to collect the common injustice by force, if he is a lord, any one may attack him and be permitted to take from him his property, for he, in turn, unjustly takes the property of everyone. . . .

Item, a priest, a member of a religious order, a knight, and a nobleman shall pay no tolls. . . .

Item, every toll shall always be renewed every ten years [in order to see] if it should be decreased or increased according to the circumstances of the mountains or rivers, so that no one shall be wronged and that no evil fraud should arise.

Item, two men shall be elected in every city who shall personally swear to the council to look after the construction [of roads] whether through the mountains or over rivers, to see to the bridges and ways, so that no one should suffer any loss in his property. . . .

GUILDS

It is also to be known, that in the good cities, namely imperial cities, there are guilds. These have now become very powerful, and [entrance into] the guild must be dearly bought. They make laws among one another as at one time the cities did. In many cities they appoint the council [and determine] how many from each guild shall enter the council. This is called in one city in Latin *una parcialitas* and is not a proper community, as I assure you.

If there is a guild which ought to be punished because of the work which it does, which is not beneficial to a community in a city, such as the butchers who sell meat too dearly, or the bakers who bake too small loaves, or the tailors who take too great fees, as it now is, the [representatives] of the guilds sit in the council and have sworn loyalty and truth to the city and community; still one guild closely assists the other, as if to say: overlook me, I will overlook you. Thus then the community is defrauded and does not get its rightful penny's worth. That now everyone recognizes well is grossly contrary to all justice and God, and the oaths are overlooked, and it is [to be] feared that thus one will clearly and unquestionably go to hell.

This has become so much of a custom that it seems right to them not even to mention in the confessional that they so greatly burden the community and the city. But should one wish to bring it about that cities should become good and every man be faithful to the other, then one would abolish guilds, and everything would be equal and everyone would be helpful to the other and the council would be cleansed. Those then who were members of the council would be moved in their advice neither by fears nor hopes as is now the case, and would give the just penny's worth, and the cities would thrive mightily. Otherwise, everyone speaks thus: I am over-burdened, everything in the city is overburdened, and therefore lords and citizens bear the cities a grudge. If in the cities all things were in common, then lords and everyone else would have a common opportunity. Otherwise if one man in a guild is provoked, the whole guild is provoked. Let it come to a state of community [and] certainly no one will regret it. . . . If there are other associations which wish to come together in which no one excludes another from any trade, then there is neither coldness nor heat and everyone is equal to the other, and the councillors are generally untroubled.

CRAFTS AND TRADES

It is also to be known that it is a bad thing in the cities and in the countryside in many places, that some-one has more trades than are proper for him. One is a vintner and besides sells salt and cloth. One is a tailor and also engages in commerce. Thus whoever is able buys and sells in whatever way it seems to him that he can bring in a penny. But will you hear what imperial law commands—our predecessors were not fools—trades were created to the end that everyone should earn his daily bread by them, and no one should intervene in another's trade. In that way the world will take care of its needs, and everyone will be able to support himself.

Is someone a vintner, let him occupy himself with that, and let him not practise anything else besides. Is he a baker, likewise, no trade excepted. . . .

CONTROL AND JURISDICTION

Now subordination and all jurisdiction should be maintained according to imperial ordinance. It is to be known that the great princes, who have much land, still maintain an almost imperial jurisdiction on their part.

But counts, barons, knights, and nobles, who also have rights of jurisdiction, enserf people and hold them now as serfs and tax them and besides take exceptional daily service from them in addition to making them pay heavily for wood and field.

It is an unheard of thing that, in holy Christendom, one must proclaim the great injustice which exists, that someone is so presumptuous before God that he dares to say to anyone: "You are mine." For let one reflect that our God, by His death and His wounds and torments which, for our sake, He suffered and bore, [did so] to the end that He liberated us and freed us from all bonds, and in this no one is raised one above the other, for we are in the same state of liberation and freedom, whether noble or non-noble, rich or poor, small or great. Whoever is baptized and believes, he is counted among the members of Jesus Christ.

Therefore let everyone know, whoever he is, who calls his fellow Christian his own, that he is not a Christian, and is against Christ and all the ordinances of God are lost on him.

And still more has unfortunately been added, in that cloisters also take people for serfs. Now they wish to belong to God, and ought to support the faith; they all depart from God.

I say it openly: no one may continue to do this any more who wishes to be a Christian.

If he is noble and does not desist, and the act is not done penance for, they [the serfs] shall be taken away and renounced. But if it is a cloister and it does not entirely desist, then it should be completely and utterly destroyed: that is godly work. The cloisters should wait upon the service of God; now they recognize the world and worldly things.

Through their wealth, they cannot live properly according to their rules. They rest well; they are day and night distinguished as great drinkers and eaters, as if, in their evil way of life, they were in the world. They have what they want. They order and do what they want.

They not only say: "This one belongs to us." They create widows, and orphans. When the fathers die, they [the cloisters] inherit and rob the rightful members, and make orphans. They force them, besides, to swear themselves serfs, and thus they rob them of their proper work; they rule like lords.

It should no longer be borne or permitted from anyone, whether temporal or ecclesiastical.

Let us recognize our own advantages and live our great freedom which everything that belongs to God enjoys! But if we permit this and do not prevent what well might be prevented, then there is no expedient, we will go with them to hell, for the sin is greater than other sins: it is called having sinned consciously.

Item, in the countryside there are estates, farm-lands, and meadows as there are farm-houses. They are now heavily loaded with taxes. To the estates, now, belong meadows and grazing lands, woods and fields, which every peasant can cultivate with his animals. Now that is reckoned as interest on the estate, and in addition it is taxed. They [the peasants] are forbidden the woods, they are assessed, day-work is taken, there is no mercy. One takes away lightly but still one lives from their labour, for without them neither can nor may anyone exist. The beast in the forest and the bird in the air live on the peasant.

It should be known that neither forest nor field ought to be placed under any sort of prescription; its cultivators prescribe it to their requirements when they pay taxes for it, as far as their prescription runs.

Excepted are the great forests on the flat or in the mountains, they belong to various jurisdictions and to the highest courts. That is because every lord ought to provide good security and convoy through them so that no harm should come to anyone. Therefore they may enjoy the great forests and exclusive hunting rights. But now they add on a tariff for convoy on the roads, and take what they will. It should be abolished, for it is against God and all justice.

Item, there are placed under prescription all the rivers, which must have their way, which serve all lands and which no one may nor can turn other than as God has ordained. They shall henceforth be free, namely those that are navigable. For in respect to bridges only that shall apply which was previously determined in regard to tolls. But where there is no bridge over the river, there no toll shall either be taken or given.

Where, however, there are little streams they shall also be free to the whole world. It has unhappily come to the point that, wanting to prescribe the whole world and the waters, they were prescribed.

Now we see well how God has ordered; that we reject and do not maintain. The dumb beasts ought verily to cry out and declare about us: "Pious, faithful Christians, according to all of the admonition which has been given you, let your hearts feel all the great unrighteousness, while there is still time, before God avenges it."

From *Die Reformation Kaiser Sigmunds*, trans. H. F. Schwarz, text v, K. Beer, ed. (Stuttgart: F. A. Perthes, 1933).

A Call for Common Action
against the Turks

POPE PIUS II

1459

O N JUNE 1, the day fixed for the opening of the Congress, the pope descended from his palace to the
church accompanied by the cardinals, bishops, and all
the clergy. The monks of every order in the city had also
been bidden to assemble and mass was celebrated with
solemn pomp and with profound reverence on the part
of all present. Then the bishop of Coron, a man distinguished for his learning as well as for his probity, delivered a speech in which he explained the pope's purpose, the reason for the Congress, and the need for
action and exhorted all who had gathered there to
further the pope's desire with ready and willing hearts.
When all were on the point of rising, Pius [II] made a
gesture for silence and from his throne spoke as follows:

"Our brethren and our sons, we hoped on arriving at
this city [Mantua] to find that a throng of royal ambassadors had preceded us. We see that only a few are
here. We have been mistaken. Christians are not so
concerned about religion as we believed. We fixed the
day for the Congress very far ahead. No one can say the
time was too short; no one can plead the difficulties of
travel. We who are old and ill have defied the Apennines
and winter. Not even mother Rome could delay us, although, beset as she is with brigands, she sorely needed
our presence. Not without danger we left the patrimony

of the Church to come to the rescue of the Catholic faith which the Turks are doing their utmost to destroy. We saw their power increasing every day, their armies, which had already occupied Greece and Illyricum, over-running Hungary, and the loyal Hungarians suffering many disasters. We feared (and this will surely happen if we do not take care) that once the Hungarians were conquered, the Germans, Italians, and indeed all Europe would be subdued, a calamity that must bring with it the destruction of our Faith. We took thought to avert this evil; we called a Congress in this place; we summoned princes and peoples that we might together take counsel to defend Christendom. We came full of hope and we grieve to find it vain. We are ashamed that Christians are so indifferent. Some are given over to luxury and pleasure; others are kept away by avarice. The Turks do not hesitate to die for their most vile faith, but we cannot incur the least expense nor endure the smallest hardship for the sake of Christ's gospel. If we continue thus, it will be all over with us. We shall soon perish unless we can summon up a different spirit. There-fore we urge you, who are holy men, to pray God with-out ceasing that He may change the temper of the Christian kings, rouse the spirit of His people, and kindle the hearts of the faithful, so that now at least we may take arms and avenge the wrongs which the Turks day after day are inflicting on our religion. Up, brethren! Up, sons! Turn to God with all your hearts. Watch and pray; atone for your sins by fasting and giving alms; bring forth works meet for repentance; for thus God will be appeased and have mercy on us, and if we show our-selves brave, He will deliver our enemies into our hands. We shall remain here till we have learned the disposition of the princes. If they intend to come, we will together take counsel for our state. If not, we must go home again and endure the lot God has given us. But so long as life and strength last we shall never abandon the purpose of defending our religion nor shall we think it hard, if need be, to risk our life for our sheep."

From *The Commentaries of Pius II*, book III, trans. F. Gragg, L. Gabel, ed. *Smith College Studies in History*, vol. xxv, nos. 1-4 (Oct. 1939—July 1940).

III. THE HOUSE
OF FAME

Bohemond the Crusader

ANNA COMNENA

Early twelfth century

Now the man was such as, to put it briefly, had never before been seen in the land of the Romans, be he either of the barbarians or of the Greeks (for he was a marvel for the eyes to behold, and his reputation was terrifying). Let me describe the barbarian's appearance more particularly—he was so tall in stature that he overtopped the tallest by nearly one cubit, narrow in the waist and loins, with broad shoulders and a deep chest and powerful arms. And in the whole build of the body he was neither too slender nor overweighted with flesh, but perfectly proportioned and, one might say, built in conformity with the canon of Polycleitus. He had powerful hands and stood firmly on his feet, and his neck and back were well compacted. An accurate observer would notice that he stooped slightly, but this was not from any weakness of the vertebrae of his spine but he had probably had this posture slightly from birth. His skin all over his body was very white, and in his face the white was tempered with red. His hair was yellowish, but did not hang down to his waist like that of the other barbarians; for the man was not inordinately vain of his hair, but had it cut short to the ears. Whether his beard was reddish, or any other colour I cannot say, for the razor had passed over it very closely and left a surface smoother than chalk; most likely it too was reddish. His blue eyes indicated both a high spirit and dignity; and his nose and nostrils breathed in the air freely; his chest corresponded to his nostrils and by his nostrils . . . the breadth of his chest. For by his nostrils nature had given free passage for the high spirit which bubbled up from his heart. A certain charm hung about this man but was partly marred by a general air of the horrible. For in the whole of his body the entire man shewed implacable and savage both in his size and glance, methinks, and even his laughter sounded to others like snorting. He was so made in mind and body that both courage and passion reared their crests within him and both inclined to war. His wit was manifold and crafty and able to find a way of escape . . . in every emergency. In conversation he was well informed, and the answers he gave were quite irrefutable. This man who was of such a size and such a character was inferior to the emperor alone in fortune and eloquence and in other gifts of nature.

From *The Alexiad*, trans. E. Dawes (London: Kegan Paul, Trench, Trübner, 1928).

On the Fame of Abelard

HELOISE

Twelfth century

A LETTER of consolation you had written to a friend, my dearest Abelard, was lately as by chance put into my hands. The superscription in a moment told me from whom it came, and the sentiments I felt for the writer compelled me to read it more eagerly. I had lost the reality; I hoped therefore from his words, a faint image of himself, to draw some comfort. But alas! for I well remember it, almost every line was marked with gall and wormwood. It related the lamentable story of our conversion, and the long list of your own unabated sufferings.

Indeed, you amply fulfilled the promises you there made to your friend, that, in comparison of your own, his misfortunes should appear as nothing, or as light as air. Having exposed the persecutions you had suffered from your masters, and the cruel deed of my uncle, you were naturally led to a recital of the hateful and invidious conduct of Albericus of Reims, and Lotulphus of Lombardy. By their suggestions, your admirable work on the Trinity was condemned to the flames, and yourself were thrown into confinement. This you did not omit to mention. The machinations of the abbot of St. Denys and of your false brethren are there brought forward; but chiefly—for from them you had most to suffer—the calumnious aspersions of those false apostles, Norbert and Bernard, whom envy had roused against you.

It was even, you say, imputed as a crime to you to have given the name of Paraclete, contrary to the common practice, to the oratory you had erected. In fine, the incessant persecutions of that cruel tyrant of St. Gildas, and of those execrable monks, whom yet you call your children and to which at this moment you are exposed, close the melancholy tale of a life of sorrow.

Who, think you, could read or hear these things and not be moved to tears? What then must be my situation? The singular precision with which each event is stated could but more strongly renew my sorrows. I was doubly agitated, because I perceived the tide of danger was still rising against you. Are we then to despair of your life? And must our breasts, trembling at every sound, be hourly alarmed by the rumours of that terrible event?

For Christ's sake, my Abelard—and He, I trust, as yet protects you—do inform us, and that repeatedly, of each

circumstance of your present dangers. I and my sisters
are the sole remains of all your friends. Let us, at least,
partake of your joys and sorrows. The condolence of
others is used to bring some relief to the sufferer, and
a load laid on many shoulders is more easily supported.
But should the storm subside a little, then be even more
solicitous to inform us, for your letters will be messengers of joy. In short, whatever be their contents, to
us they must always bring comfort; because this at
least they will tell us, that we are remembered by
you. . . .

My Abelard, you well know how much I lost in
losing you; and that infamous act of treachery which,
by a cruelty before unheard-of, deprived me of you,
even tore me from myself. The loss was great, indeed,
but the manner of it was doubly excruciating. When the
cause of grief is most pungent, then should consolation
apply her strongest medicines. But it is you only can
administer relief: by you I was wounded, and by you I
must be healed. It is in your power alone to give me
pain, to give me joy, and to give me comfort. And it is
you only that are obliged to do it. I have obeyed the
last title of your commands; and so far was I unable to
oppose them, that, to comply with your wishes, I could
bear to sacrifice myself. One thing remains which is
still greater, and will hardly be credited; my love for
you had risen to such a degree of frenzy, that to please
you, it even deprived itself of what alone in the universe
it valued, and that forever. No sooner did I receive your
commands than I quitted at once the habit of the
world, and with it all the reluctance of my nature. I
meant that you should be the sole possessor of whatever
I had once a right to call my own.

Heaven knows! in all my love it was you, and you only
I sought for. I looked for no dowry, no alliances of mar-

riage. I was even insensible to my own pleasures; nor had I a will to gratify. All was absorbed in you. I call Abelard to witness. In the name of wife there may be something more holy, more imposing; but the name of mistress was ever to me a more charming sound. The more I humbled myself before you, the greater right I thought I should have to your favour; and thus also I hoped the less to injure the splendid reputation you had acquired.

This circumstance, on your own account, you did not quite forget to mention in the letter to your friend. You related also some of the arguments I then urged to deter you from that fatal marriage; but you suppressed the greater part, by which I was induced to prefer love to matrimony and liberty to chains. I call Heaven to witness! Should Augustus, master of the world, offer me his hand in marriage, and secure to me the uninterrupted command of the universe, I should deem it at once more eligible and more honourable to be called the mistress of Abelard than the wife of Caesar. The source of merit is not in riches or in power; these are the gifts of fortune; but virtue only gives worth and excellence. . . .

But that happiness which in others is sometimes the effect of fancy, in me was the child of evidence. They might think their husbands perfect, and were happy in the idea, but I knew that you were such, and the universe knew the same. Thus, the more my affection was secured from all possible error, the more steady became its flame. Where was found the king or the philosopher that had emulated your reputation? Was there a village, a city, a kingdom, that did not ardently wish even to see you? When you appeared in public, who did not run to behold you? And when you withdrew, every neck was stretched, every eye sprang forward to pursue you. The married and the unmarried women, when Abelard was away, longed for his company; and when he was present, every bosom was on fire. No lady of distinction, no princess, that did not envy Heloise the possession of her Abelard.

You possessed, indeed, two qualifications—a tone of voice and a grace in singing—which gave you the control over every female heart. These powers were peculiarly yours; for I do not know that they ever fell to the share of any other philosopher. To soften, by playful amusement, the stern labours of philosophy, you composed several sonnets on love and on similar subjects. These you were often heard to sing, when the harmony of your voice gave new charms to the expression. In all circles nothing was talked of but Abelard; even the most ignorant, who could not judge of composition, were enchanted by the melody of your voice. Female hearts were unable to resist the impression. Thus was my name soon carried to distant nations; for the loves of Heloise and Abelard were the constant theme of all your songs. What wonder if I became the subject of general envy?

You possessed, besides, every endowment of mind and body. But, alas! if my happiness then raised the envy of others, will they not now be compelled to pity me? And surely even she who was then my enemy will now drop a tear at my sad reverse of fortune.

You know, Abelard, I was the great cause of your misfortunes; but yet I was not guilty. It is the motive with which we act, and not the event of things, that makes us criminal. Equity weighs the intention, and not the mere actions we may have done. What, at all times, were my dispositions in your regard, you, who knew them, can only judge. To you I refer all my actions, and on your decision I rest my cause. I call no other witness. . . .

By that God, then, to whom your life is consecrated, I conjure you, give me so much of yourself as is at your disposal; that is, send me some lines of consolation. Do it with this design, at least; that, my mind being more at ease, I may serve God with more alacrity. When formerly the love of pleasure was your pursuit, how often did I hear from you? In your songs the name of Heloise was made familiar to every tongue: it was heard in every street; the walls of every house repeated it. With how much greater propriety might you now call me to God, than you did then to pleasure? Weigh your obligations; think on my petition.

I have written you a long letter, but the conclusion shall be short: My only friend, farewell.

From *Abelard and Heloise*, trans. A. S. Richardson (Boston: James R. Osgood & Co., 1884).

Heloise and Abelard: The Later Years

Peter the Venerable

Twelfth century

WHEN I received your affectionate letters, which you sent to me earlier by my son Theobald, I was delighted, and I embraced them as friends for the sake of their sender. I wanted to write immediately what was in my mind, but I could not, because I was hindered by the troublesome demands of my cares, to which very often, indeed, almost always, I am compelled to yield. I have only just snatched what I could seize from a day interrupted by confusions.

It seems that I should have hastened to make at least the recompense of words for your affection towards me, which I have recognized both at that time from your letters and earlier from the gifts you sent me, and that I should have shown how large a place of love for you in the Lord I keep in my heart. For truly I do not now first begin to love a person whom I remember that I have loved for a long time. I had not yet completely passed out of adolescence, I had not yet attained young manhood, when the fame, not yet indeed of your religion, but of your distinguished and praiseworthy studies became known to me.

I heard then that a woman, although she was not yet disentangled from the bonds of the world, devoted the highest zeal to literary studies, which is very unusual, and to the pursuit of wisdom, although it was that of the world. I heard that she could not be hindered by pleasures, frivolities, and delights from this useful purpose of learning the arts. And when almost everyone is kept from these studies by detestable sloth, and when the progress of wisdom can come to a standstill, I do not say among women, by whom it is entirely rejected, but it is scarcely able to find virile minds among men, you, by your praiseworthy zeal, completely excelled all women, and surpassed almost all men.

Soon, indeed, according to the words of the apostle, as it pleased Him who brought you forth from your mother's womb to call you by His grace, you exchanged this devotion to studies for a far better one. Now completely and truly a woman of wisdom, you chose the Gospel instead of logic, the apostle in place of physics, Christ instead of Plato, the cloister instead of the Academy. You snatched the spoils from the defeated enemy, and passing through the desert of this pilgrimage, with the treasures of the Egyptians, you built a precious tabernacle to God in your heart. You sang a song of praise with Miriam, when Pharaoh was drowned; and carrying in your hands the timbrel of holy mortification, as she did formerly, you sent forth with skilled musicianship a new melody to the very ears of God. Now in beginning that which, by divine grace, you will continue well, you have trampled underfoot the ancient serpent always lying in wait for women, and you have so driven it out, that it will never dare to tempt you further. . . .

I say these things, dearest sister in the Lord, not indeed to flatter you, but to encourage you, so that, devoting your attention to that great good in which you have for a long time persevered, you may the more ardently continue to preserve it carefully, and that you may inflame both by words and by example, according to the grace granted to you by God, those holy women who serve the Lord with you, so that they may strive anxiously in this same contest. For you, although you are a woman, are one of those creatures whom the prophet Ezechiel saw, who should not only burn like coals of fire, but should glow and shine like lamps. You are truly a disciple of truth, but you are also by that very obligation, inasmuch as it behooves you for those entrusted to you, a mistress of humility. The complete mastery of humility and of all celestial discipline has been imposed on you by God. Wherefore you ought to take care not only for yourself, but also for the flock entrusted to you, and on behalf of all, you should in all things receive a greater reward. Surely the reward of victory awaits you above all, since, as you know best, as many times as the world and the prince of the world have been overcome by your leadership, so many triumphs, so many glorious trophies, will be prepared for you with the eternal King and Judge.

But it is not altogether unusual among mortals that women should be ruled by women, and not wholly strange also that they should fight in battle, and moreover, accompany men themselves to battle. For if the saying is true that it is lawful also to be taught by the enemy, it is written that, among the Gentiles, Penthesilea, queen of the Amazons, with her Amazons, not men but women, often fought in battle at the time of the Trojan War, and that, among the people of God also, the prophetess Deborah inspired Barach, the judge of Israel, against the heathen. Why then should it not be permitted that women of courage, going forth to battle against a strong army, should be made leaders of the army of the Lord, since that Deborah fought against the enemy with her own hand, which indeed seemed unbecoming? Why should not this Deborah of ours lead, arm, and inspire men themselves to the divine warfare? When King Jabin had been defeated, and the leader Sisera slain, and the godless army destroyed, that other Deborah immediately sang a song, and she sang it devoutly in praise of God. By the grace of God, you shall be doing this, after the victory over enemies stronger by far has been given to you and yours, and you shall never cease to sing, far more gloriously, that song of yours, which thus rejoicing you shall sing, just as you shall never cease rejoicing. Meanwhile you shall be with the handmaidens of God, that is, the celestial army, as that other Deborah was with her own Jewish people, and you shall never rest from so gainful a contest, at any time or in any case, except in victory.

And since the name, Deborah, as your learning knows, means "bee," in the Hebrew tongue, you shall also be in this another Deborah, that is, a bee. For you shall make honey, but not for yourself alone, since whatever good you have gathered, in different ways and from various sources, you shall pour it all forth, by example, by word, and in every possible way, upon the sisters of your house and upon all others. In this short span of mortal life, you shall satisfy yourself with the secret sweetness of sacred learning, and the blessed sisters with public preaching, so that, according to the words of the prophet: "It shall come to pass in that day, that the mountains shall drop down new wine, and the hills shall flow with milk and honey." For although this may be said concerning this time of grace, nothing prevents its being understood concerning the time of glory; in fact, it is even sweeter. It would be sweet to me to continue discussing this longer with you, because I am both delighted by your renowned learning and, far more, attracted by your religion, which is praised by many. Would that our order of Cluny had you! Would that the pleasant prison of Marcigny embraced you, with the other handmaidens of Christ awaiting celestial freedom there! I should prefer the riches of religion and learning to the greatest treasures of any kings whatsoever, and I should rejoice to see that illustrious body of sisters shine more brilliantly with you dwelling there. . . .

But although this may be denied to us concerning you, by the providence of God which disposes all things, it has been granted concerning that one of yours, concerning that Master Peter, I say, often and always to be named with honour, the servant and truly the philosopher of Christ, whom, in the last years of his life, that same divine providence brought to Cluny. And he enriched her in and from that gift more precious than gold and topazes. A brief word cannot tell of his holy, humble, and devout way of life among us, as Cluny bears strong witness. For, unless I am mistaken, I do not recollect that I have seen his like, in the appearance and actions of humility, so much so that, to the very discerning, neither St. Germain would appear more abject, nor St. Martin himself poorer. And when, at my command, he took a superior rank in that great assembly of our brothers, he seemed the least in the plainness of his apparel.

I wondered often, as he preceded me in processions with the others, according to custom, nay, I was almost astounded that a man of so great and so famous a name could thus belittle himself, could thus humble himself. And while there are certain of those who profess religion, who desire that the religious garments which they wear should be exceedingly sumptuous, he was completely sparing in these, and, content with a simple garment of any kind, he asked for nothing more. He observed this practice also in food, and in drink, and in all care of his own body, and he condemned in his words and in his life, I do not say the superfluous only, but everything except what was really necessary, both for himself and for everyone. His reading was continual, his prayer frequent, his silence perpetual, except when familiar intercourse with the brothers or public discussion in their assembly pressed him to speak to them about divine things. He frequented the divine sacraments as much as he was able, offering the sacrifice of the immortal Lamb to God; and indeed, after the apostolic favour had been granted, by letters and through my effort, he frequented them almost constantly.

And what more can I say? His mind, his tongue, his labour, always serving God, always philosophical, ever more learned, he meditated, taught, and spoke. Living thus with us for some time, this simple and upright man, fearing God, and withdrawing from evil, consecrated the last days of his life to God, and to end them (for more than usual, he was troubled by scabies and certain discomforts of body), he was sent by me to [St. Marcel lès] Châlons. For because of the pleasant situation of that place, which surpasses almost all regions of our

Burgundy, I thought to provide a suitable place for him, near the city indeed, but yet near where the Saône flows. There, as much as his illness permitted, he renewed his former studies, and was always bending over his books, and he did not, as Gregory the Great wrote, allow a single moment to be wasted, but always he prayed, or read, or wrote, or dictated. In these holy exercises, the coming of that angelic visitor found him, and discovered him not sleeping, like many, but vigilant. It found him truly watchful, and summoned him, not as the foolish, but as the wise virgin, to the marriage feast of eternity. For he brought with him a lamp full of oil, that is, a conscience filled with the testimony of a holy life. For, in order that the common debt of mortal life should be paid, he was seized by illness, and suffering in it, he was in a short time brought to his end. Then, truly, how holy, how devout, how Catholic, was the confession he made, first, of his faith, and then of his sins. With what longing of his loving heart he received the last repast of the journey, and the pledge of eternal life, the body of the Lord our Redeemer, how faithfully he commended to Him his body and soul here and forever, the brothers are witnesses, and all the members of that monastery where the body of the holy martyr Marcellus lies. Thus Master Peter brought his days to a close, and he who was known throughout almost the whole world for his unique mastery of knowledge, and was everywhere famous, persevering, meek, and humble, in the discipleship of Him who said: "Learn of Me, for I am meek and humble of heart," thus passed over to Him, as it should be believed. Him then, venerable and dearest sister in the Lord, to whom you clung in the bonds of the flesh, and later in the so much stronger and better bond of divine love, with whom and under whom you have long served the Lord; him, I say, in your place, and as another you, Christ cherishes in His own embrace, and He preserves him to be restored to you by His grace, at the coming of the Lord, when He descends from heaven, with the singing of archangels and the sound of the trumpet. Be mindful of him, then, in the Lord; be mindful also of me, if it pleases you, and solicitously commend to those holy sisters who serve the Lord with you, the brothers of our congregation, and the sisters, who everywhere in the world, as much as they can, are serving the same Lord as you do.

"Letter to Heloise," Migne, *Patrologia Latina*, vol. 189; trans. M.M.M.

Arnold of Brescia, a Twelfth-Century Revolutionary

JOHN OF SALISBURY

Twelfth century

BETWEEN the lord pope [Eugenius III] and the Romans peace was being discussed [1148], and frequent embassies ran to and fro from one party to the other. But many things hindered the peacemaking, particularly that the Romans did not wish to cast out Arnold of Brescia, who was said to have pledged himself to the honour of the city and republic of Rome by a sworn oath, and to him the Roman people had in turn promised aid and counsel against all men, and especially against the lord pope; for he had excommunicated Arnold from the Roman Church, and, as it were, warned that he should be shunned as a heretic.

This man was a priest in rank, in condition a canon

regular, and he disciplined the flesh by austerity and
lack of possessions. He was acute in intelligence, stead-
fast in the study of the Scriptures, fluent in speech, and
a vigorous preacher of contempt for the world. But, as
they say, he was seditious and a fomenter of schism,
and wherever he lived he did not allow the laity to have
peace with the clergy. He had been abbot at Brescia,
and when the bishop, who had gone to Rome, delayed
there for a while, Arnold so altered the minds of the
citizens that they scarcely wished to admit the returning
bishop. Deposed because of this by the lord pope Innocent [II], and exiled from Italy, Arnold went to France
and joined Peter Abelard, and zealously favoured his
cause with the Lord Jacintus, who was now cardinal,
against the abbot of Clairvaux.

After Master Peter had gone to Cluny, Arnold, remaining in Paris at Mont Ste. Geneviève, expounded the
Holy Scriptures to the scholars at St. Hilaire, where the
aforesaid Peter had been a guest. But he had no auditors
except poor ones, and those who begged alms publicly
from door to door, while they spent their life with the
master. He said that they agreed very well with the law
of Christ, and that they disagreed as much as possible
with the lives of Christians. He did not spare the
bishops, attacking them because of their avarice and
shameful money-grubbing, and because of their so frequently blemished lives, and because they strove to
build the Church of God by the shedding of blood. That
abbot [St. Bernard], whose name is considered very
famous because of his many merits, he accused of being
a pursuer of vain glory, one who envied all who were
not of his own school. The abbot indeed brought it
about that the most Christian king cast Arnold out of
the kingdom of France. Thence, after the death of the
lord Innocent, he returned to Italy, and when he had

promised satisfaction and obedience to the Roman Church, he was received by the lord Eugenius [III] at Viterbo. Penance was imposed on him, which he agreed that he would do, in fasts, in vigils, and in prayers at the holy places in the city; and indeed he swore a solemn oath to observe obedience.

While living at Rome under the pretext of penitence, he won the city over to himself, and while the lord pope was travelling among the Gauls, Arnold, preaching freely, created a sect of men who are still called Lombard heretics. For he had followers who were continent and who, because of their appearance of honesty and austerity of life, were pleasing to the people, but they found support especially among the religious women. Arnold himself was frequently heard on the Capitol and in public meetings. Now he openly attacked the cardinals, saying that their assembly, because of their pride and avarice, hypocrisy, and manifold wickedness, was not the Church of God, but a house of business and a den of thieves, who acted as scribes and pharisees among the Christian people. He said that the pope himself was not what he professed to be, an apostolic man and a shepherd of souls, but a man of blood, who upheld his authority by fire and slaughter, a tormenter of churches, an oppresser of innocence, who did nothing else in the world but feed on flesh, and fill his own coffers and empty those of others. He said that the pope was so apostolic that he did not follow the doctrine or life of the apostles, and to him obedience and reverence were not due. . . .

From *Historia pontificalis*, R. L. Poole, ed. (Oxford: Clarendon Press, 1927); trans. M.M.M.

Arnold of Brescia

Twelfth century

THIS man was harshly austere throughout his whole life; moderate in his habits, yet in his speech extravagant, he strove for wisdom beyond that which is fitting. He was eloquent and bold and self-assured, a man of much reading. I believe that it is just to describe briefly his teaching and his end, for it will please many to know it.

He attacked and condemned priests as well as lesser people. Believing that he alone lived righteously and that others erred unless they wished to follow his teaching, he also attacked violently the actions of the prelates, and, in short, he spared no one, he mingled the true with the false, and was pleasing to many.

He condemned the laymen for not paying their tithes, and he condemned all taking of usury. Following the Scripture, he taught that shameful greed, war, hatred, lust, perjury, murder, theft, deception, and the evil desires of the flesh are hindrances to eternal life. He spared no vice, and like a foolish doctor, he cut away the healthy along with the diseased. For he censured all priests as wicked and as followers of that Simon who wanted to buy divine things for money, and he made almost no exceptions. . . . He said that the monks were completely irregular, and that truly they could not be called by the name of monks. He declared that the great prelates coveted transitory things, and scorned the things of heaven for those of earth; night and day, they judged legal cases for a price, and considered the office of the episcopate of less account than this. For this, he claimed, they would be condemned to everlasting death, and he asserted that all men of every order were corrupted, loving neither God nor their neighbours.

He cried out that, alas, evils flourished especially in the Roman see, where money was honoured more than justice, and where money was obtained in place of justice. There evil had spread from the head to the body, and all the members sought money and bribes. All things were done with money, the things of the Lord were bought and sold, and anyone who lacked money was completely despised.

This was the teaching of that famous Master Arnold, which pleased many men only because of its novelty. Indeed, Europe was now full of this doctrine. He first gathered bitter fruits in his native city, and you, Brescia, have revelled in the teaching of your citizen. He also stirred up great Milan, and the Roman people, always willing to believe new things. Wherever he was, this man caused sedition, for he deceived people under the image of truth.

The highest apostolic shepherd wished to convert him, yet he could not. And with kind words he frequently admonished him to give up his error and his evil doctrine. But Arnold never ceased to insult the holy father with bitter words, and he did not abandon his wicked teaching. And when, often warned, he became worse, and rejoiced that his fame spread through the world, the pope, grieving because the people were corrupted by false teaching, and wishing to cure the sickness by reason, expelled this schismatic teacher from the bosom of his mother, the Church. Desirous that the rest of the body should retain its health, the wise doctor cut off with a sword the diseased member.

But the tongue of Master Arnold was not so restrained

that he did not spread his customary errors, that he did not snap harder with bared fangs at the Roman Church, that he did not teach the people in opposition to the lord pope. Then he was brought by King Frederick [Barbarossa] to the Roman judge who had been appointed, and was put in chains. And the ruler ordered his case to be judged, and the learned teacher was condemned for his teaching.

But when he saw that his punishment was prepared, and that his neck was to be bound in the halter by hurrying fate, and when he was asked if he would renounce his false doctrine, and confess his sins after the manner of the wise, fearless and self-confident, wonderful to relate, he replied that his own doctrine seemed to him sound, nor would he hesitate to undergo death for his teachings, in which there was nothing absurd or dangerous. And he requested a short delay for time to pray, for he said that he wished to confess his sins to Christ. Then on bended knees, with eyes and hands raised up to heaven, he groaned, sighing from the depths of his breast, and silently communed in spirit with God, commending to Him his soul. And after a short time, prepared to suffer with constancy, he surrendered his body to death. Those who looked on at his punishment shed tears; even the executioners were moved by pity for a little time, while he hung from the noose which held him. And it is said that the king, moved too late by compassion, mourned over this.

Learned Arnold, what did such great learning profit you, and so much fasting, and so many labours? Of what profit was such a hard life, which spurned all slothful leisure and enjoyed no fleshly pleasures? Alas, what made you turn your biting slander upon the Church, so that you should come, O wretched one, to the sad noose! Behold your doctrine, O condemned one, for which you have paid the penalty! Doctrine passes away, and your teaching will not long survive! It has been burned and dissolved with you into a few ashes, lest perchance something might be left to be honoured.

Twelfth-century poem, E. Monachi, ed., *Archivio della Società Romana di Storia Patria* (Rome, 1878); trans. M.M.M.

His Own Deeds

GIRALDUS CAMBRENSIS

Twelfth century

GIRALDUS was born [c. 1145-47] in South Wales, on the coast of Dyfed, not far from the principal town of Pembroke, that is, in the castle of Manorbier, of noble stock. For his mother was Angarath, the daughter of Nesta, the noble daughter of Rhys, prince of South Wales . . . who was married to the distinguished man, William de Barri. Giraldus was the youngest of four blood-brothers. And when the three others in their childish games used to build castles and cities and palaces in the sands or mud, as a prelude to their future life, he, as a like prelude, always devoted himself entirely to building churches and to constructing monasteries. His father, often noting and wondering at his custom, took it as a prophecy of the future, and determined with wise forethought to have him study letters and liberal arts; and, with teasing praise, he used to call him his "little bishop."

It happened one night that the land was harassed by an enemy invasion, and all the able-bodied young men of the castle rushed swiftly to arms. When the boy saw this and when he heard the tumult, he wept aloud and seeking a safe place to hide, asked that he be carried to the church, thus declaring in a marvellous spirit of prophecy that the peace of the church and the immunity of God's house should be most firm and secure. When everyone heard this, the tumult ceased, and pondering these boyish words, and conferring among themselves, they remembered with amazement that his words promised for himself greater safety in this remote church, exposed to the winds and to chance, than in any city filled with men and arms, and well fortified with towers and walls. . . .

In these early days, then, the boy was not a little hindered by the companionship of his brothers, who played with him on holidays and praised as highly as possible the business of their knightly profession, for a boy's manners are formed by those who live with him. Finally, however, he was much moved by the rebuke and immediate correction of that Bishop David of St. David's, of pious memory, who was his own uncle; and also by two clerks of the same bishop, one of whom rebuked him by declining the adjective "*durus, durior, durissimus,*" and the other, "*stultus, stultior, stultissimus.*" This insult stirred him deeply, so that he began to make progress, aided more by shame than by the rod, and by this disgrace rather than by his teacher or by fear. Afterwards, therefore, he was so wrapped in zeal for his studies that within a short time he far surpassed all his schoolfellows of the same age in his native land. In the course of time, he crossed the sea three times to France, for the sake of further study and profit, and studied for three periods of several years in liberal arts at Paris, until at length, rivalling the most excellent teachers, he taught the trivium there with great success, and won distinguished praise in the art of rhetoric. Here he was so wholly given up to study, so completely devoid of frivolity and buffoonery in action and spirit, that, whenever the teachers in arts wanted to provide an example from among their good scholars, they used to name Giraldus first of all. Thus, because of his merits, he was worthy, in youth and adolescence, not to seek but to give an example of excellence and distinction in the duty of a scholar. . . .

After these achievements, Giraldus, who "thought that nothing had been done so long as anything remained to be done," and who never looked backward, but always pressed forward and climbed higher with unfaltering step, determined, for the sake of greater and riper wisdom, and when he had collected his treasure of books, to cross the sea to France, and to apply himself once again with all his heart to the study of liberal arts at Paris. He intended thus to build upon his foundation of arts and literature the walls of civil and canon law, and to complete the building with the sacred roof of theological learning, so that this triple edifice, strengthened by the firmest bonds, should long prevail. After he had applied his studious mind for many years in that city, first to the imperial and then to the pontifical laws, and at last to the sacred Scriptures, at length he attained such popularity by his exposition of canon law, which it was customary to discuss on Sunday, that on the day when it was known in the city that he wished to speak, such a great crowd of almost all the teachers and their students gathered to listen to his pleasant voice, that even the largest hall could scarcely hold his audience. For he expounded the reasoning of canon and civil law in such a lively manner, and supported his exposition with such rhetorical persuasions; he so adorned it with figures and colours of speech as well as with profound wisdom, and by the marvellous art with which he applied them to the proper subjects, he so aptly used the sayings of philosophers and other authors, that the wiser and more learned his hearers were, the more avidly and attentively they applied their ears and minds to listen and to fix it all in their memories. For they were so charmed and entranced by the sweetness of his words that they hung on his lips as he spoke, and listened without weariness or satiety, even if his speech were long and protracted, and such as begets boredom in many people. Therefore, scholars everywhere vied with each other in writing out his lectures word for word, as they came from his own lips, and very eagerly took them to heart. One day, moreover, when a great crowd had gathered from all sides to hear him, after he had finished speaking and while a murmur of praise and applause came from all his hearers, a certain eminent doctor, who had also lectured in arts at Paris, and had long studied law at Bologna, one Master Roger the Norman, afterwards dean of the church of Rouen, burst out with the following words: "Certainly there is no study under the sun which, brought by chance to Paris, does not become incomparably stronger there, and far more excellent than anywhere else." . . .

After a long stay [late 1176-1179] devoted to study, Giraldus thought it time to return to his country. But he had waited long beyond the time set for his messenger to bring money to Paris for him, and his creditors, to whom he was deeply in debt, were impatient and importuned and pressed harder every day for payment. So he went, full of sorrow and anxiety and in almost the last extremity of despair, to the chapel of St. Thomas of Canterbury, which the archbishop of Reims, the brother of King Louis, had built in the church of St. Germain of Auxerre, where Thomas was canonized as a martyr. Giraldus went there with his companions as a last resort, so that he might devoutly implore the help of the martyr to save him from his troubles. For he knew, as the wise Philo said, that when human aid fails, one must turn to the help that comes from God. And after hearing the solemn mass in honour of the martyr and making his offering, he immediately received from heaven the reward of his devotion. For within the hour he received his messengers who brought him both joy and prosperity, thanks to the marvellous dispensation of God. . . .

Proceeding, therefore, on his journey and crossing the Flemish sea, he came to Canterbury, and, at the prior's bidding, dined in the refectory with the monks of that monastery, on the day of the Holy Trinity. Sitting there at the high table with the prior and elder monks, he noticed, as he used to relate, two things, the excessive superfluity of signs, and the multitude of dishes. For the prior gave so many dishes to the monks who served him, and they on their part took these as gifts to the lower tables, and the recipients gave so many thanks, and were so extravagant in their gesticulation of fingers and hands and arms, and in the whisperings by which they avoided open speech, showing in all this a most unedifying levity and licence, that Giraldus felt as if he were sitting at a stage-play, or among actors and buffoons. For it would be more appropriate to order and decency to speak modestly in plain human speech than to use such a mute garrulity of frivolous signs and hissings.

Of the dishes themselves and their number, what can I say but this, that I have often heard Giraldus tell how sixteen or more very sumptuous dishes were laid on the table in order, or shall I say in disorder? At the last, potherbs were brought to all the tables, but they were scarcely touched. For you might see so many kinds of fish, roasted and boiled, stuffed and fried, so many dishes tricked out by the cook's art with eggs and pepper, so many sauces and savouries contrived by that same art to stimulate gluttony and to excite the appetite. In addition to these, there was such an abundance of wine and strong drink, of metheglin and claret, of new wine and mead and mulberry wine, and all intoxicating liquors, that beer, which is brewed excellently in England, and especially in Kent, found no place. But there beer was among other drinks as potherbs are among other dishes. You might see here, I say, so excessive and costly a superfluity in food and drink as might not only disgust the partaker, but also weary the beholder.

What then would Paul the Hermit have said to this, or Anthony, or Benedict, the father and founder of monastic life? Or to seek more recent examples, what would our noble Jerome have said, who in his *Lives of the Fathers* extols with such praise the parsimony, the abstinence, and the moderation of the primitive Church, saying among other things that as the Church grew in wealth, she greatly declined in virtue? Moreover, Giraldus would sometime tell, as is not beside the point to relate here, how the monks of St. Swithin at Winchester, with their prior, grovelled in the mud before King Henry II of England, and complained to him with tears and wailing that their bishop, Richard, who was in place of an abbot to them, had taken away three of their daily dishes. And when the king asked how many dishes remained, they answered ten, since they were wont, by ancient custom, to have thirteen. "And I," said the king, "in my court am content with three. Let your bishop perish, unless he reduces your dishes to the number of mine!" To what purpose is this waste, especially among men vowed to religion and wearing a religious habit? "For these superfluities might have been sold and given to the poor." . . .

Now [c. 1184], as the fame of Giraldus increased and became more widespread from day to day, King Henry II, who was then in the March intent upon the pacification of Wales, summoned him, on the advice of his great men. And although Giraldus was most unwilling (for as he values the life of the scholar above all others, so he detests that of the courtier), yet because of the king's insistence, and also his promises and demands, he finally became a follower of the court, and the king's clerk. After he had rendered loyal service for several years by following the court, and had been of great aid in the pacification of Wales, not least because of his kinship with Rhys ap Gruffydd and other princes of Wales, he received nothing but empty, untruthful promises from the king, who enriched and promoted so many undeserving persons. But secretly the king praised him greatly in front of his counsellors, and spoke highly of his character, his self-restraint, his modesty, and his loyalty. The king said that if Giraldus had not been born in Wales and if he were not so closely related by blood to the magnates of Wales, and especially to Rhys, he would have exalted him by bestowing on him ecclesiastical honours and rich rewards, and would have made him a great man in his kingdom. . . .

At this time [1185] the Patriarch Heraclius of Jerusalem came to England, and offered to the king the keys of that city, humbly requesting him, but accomplishing nothing, that either the king himself would come to the defence of the Holy Land, or would send there one of his sons, three of whom were still living. But the king did neither the one thing nor the other, but despised this great messenger, and was therefore himself despised. Deserting God and deserted by Him, since from this time the king's glory, which had until then grown continually, was turned to shame, he sent his younger son John with a great army to Ireland. And he sent with him Master Giraldus, because he had a great number of kinsmen there, descended from the first conquerors in Ireland, and because he himself was an honest and prudent man. . . .

After Giraldus had thus gained a great name and wide renown in this island [Ireland], between Easter and Pentecost he crossed over into Wales, where he applied his whole mind with all diligence to the completion of his *Topography of Ireland,* which he had already begun. In the course of time, when the work had been completed and corrected, not wishing to put his lighted candle under a bushel but to raise it up on a candlestick, that it might show its full light, he determined to go to Oxford, where the English clergy were most flourishing and most excellent in learning, and there to read his book before this eminent audience. And, since the work was divided into three parts, by reading one daily, he spread it over three days. On the first he received and entertained in his lodging all the poor of the whole city, whom he had called together for the purpose; on the next day he entertained all the doctors of the different faculties, and their pupils of greatest fame and renown; and on the third day the rest of the scholars with the knights, the citizens, and others of the borough. This was indeed a costly and noble undertaking, by which were renewed in some fashion the authentic and ancient times of the poets; nor can either the present age nor any past age in England show such a day.

About that time [1187], after the Holy Land had been conquered by the heathens and Parthians under the leadership of Saladin, King Henry, following the example of his son Richard, count of Poitou, who was the first of all the princes on this side of the Alps to be signed with the cross, took the cross, together with

Philip, king of the French, at Gisors, in the presence of, and persuaded by, the archbishop of Tyre. The king came to England from Normandy, where he had delayed briefly, around the first of February. Immediately, he summoned a council at Geddington in the region of Northampton, and there Baldwin, archbishop of Canterbury, preached and displayed the cross . . . and the great men of England, of both clergy and laity, took the cross upon their shoulders. Moreover, in order to attract and bind good men of Wales as well as of England to the service of the cross, the king sent Archbishop Baldwin into Wales. He came to Hereford with Ranulph de Glanville, who had been sent with him, about the beginning of Lent, and entered Wales at Radnor, where he met Rhys ap Gruffydd and many of the great men of Wales. After the archbishop had delivered a sermon on the service of Christ crucified, Giraldus the archdeacon, giving an example to others, at the earlier request of the king, and the insistence of the archbishop and justiciar in the king's name, and inspired as much by his own devotion as by the exhortation of such great men, first of all took the cross from the hands of the archbishop. . . .

Then the archbishop, going on his way, and taking with him the archdeacon Giraldus as his inseparable companion in the duty of preaching, crossed Wales, and proceeding along the south coast through the diocese of Llandaff towards Mynyw, preached the cross and the service of the Crucified everywhere, in suitable places. When he had entered Dyfed, and approached the region of Mynyw, the archbishop first preached at Haverford in the centre of the province to the clergy and people of those parts whom he had called together there. Then he charged Giraldus to preach the word of God. And in that hour God granted him such grace of speech and of persuasion, that the greatest part of the young men of that whole region, the flower of knighthood, took the cross, and also a countless number of the people. When the archbishop saw that at his own words so few out of so great a multitude had taken the cross, he said, as if in sorrow and wonder, "God, what a hardhearted people this is!" And when he ordered the cross which he held in his hand to be given to the archdeacon, to support him, the archdeacon, who was sitting at the archbishop's side, asked that his bishop, Peter, should be enjoined to speak. But the archbishop answered that in these matters rank should not be regarded, but only him to whom God had given grace. Now the archdeacon had divided his sermon into three parts, saving the greatest force of persuasion for the end of each. . . .

Many were amazed, moreover, that, although the archdeacon spoke only in French and Latin, the common people who knew neither language wept in uncounted numbers, no less than the others, and more than two hundred rushed to receive the sign of the cross. . . .

When this praiseworthy mission had been accomplished, and as the archbishop was passing from the borders of Wales into England, some of his clerks who were travelling with him spoke about this pilgrimage to Jerusalem, and asked him who could worthily handle the glorious tale of the recovery of the land of Palestine by our princes, and of the defeat of Saladin and the Saracens at their hands. The archbishop replied that he had provided for that, and had someone ready who could relate the story very well. When they questioned him further and asked who it was, he turned to Giraldus who was riding by his side, and said, "This is the one who will write it in prose, and my nephew Joseph will tell it in verse . . ." He began, moreover, to commend highly the archdeacon's book, the *Topography of Ire-*

land, which Giraldus had given to the archbishop as they entered Wales and which he had read from beginning to end; he praised it greatly both for its style and for the way in which the subject had been handled. . . .

The archbishop asked Giraldus whether he had taken from any of our hagiographers or expositors some evidence concerning the allegorical interpretations of the natures of birds which he had given in the first book of his *Topography*. When Giraldus answered that he had borrowed nothing, the archbishop replied that these were written in the same spirit in which the fathers wrote. He added this also, that Giraldus should not allow the gift of this excellent style which God had given him to lie idle, but that he should always use it, and write continually, so that his time might not be lost in idleness, but that by constant study and praiseworthy labour, he should extend the memory of his name to future ages. Thus he would earn perpetual grace and favour, not only from future generations, but from all save the envious of the present time. He said and repeated that Giraldus should love God's gift of so gracious a style far more than earthly riches that must soon perish, or worldly dignities that must swiftly pass away. For, he said, Giraldus' works could neither pass away nor perish, but the older they became in process of time, the dearer and more precious they would be to all men for all eternity. . . .

[The purpose of the following journey to Rome, the first of several, was to obtain papal confirmation of his election as bishop of St. David's, and to have this see raised to metropolitan rank. Both aims, which dominated much of Giraldus's career, were opposed by the archbishop of Canterbury.] So, crossing the Alps and passing quickly through Italy and Tuscany, Giraldus arrived in Rome about the feast of St. Andrew [Nov. 30, 1199], and approaching the feet of Pope Innocent III, then in the second year of his reign, he presented to him six books which he had composed with diligent study, saying among other things, "Others give you pounds, I give you books." These books, moreover, the pope, who was very learned and loved literature, kept all together by his bed for almost a month, and displayed their elegant and pithy sayings to the cardinals who visited him. Finally, he gave all except one to various cardinals, at their request. But he would not let himself be parted from the *Gemma Ecclesiastica*, which he loved more than the others. . . .

From *De rebus a se gestis*, J. S. Brewer, ed., Rolls Series, vol. 21; trans. M.M.M.

Moreover, though Master Giraldus had thrice gone to Rome on account of the aforesaid suits, yet after only two years had elapsed, he firmly resolved to seek the thresholds of the apostles for a fourth time [1207], but solely by way of pilgrimage and devotion, in order that by the labours of the journey, by the giving of alms . . . and by true confession and absolution, all the stains contracted in his past life and that also which he had incurred by the security which, with some loss of honour, he had been forced both by Church and state to give, when he was reconciled with the archbishop, might be wiped away past all doubt. . . . Moreover, he resigned into the pope's hands all the churches and ecclesiastical benefices, of which some had been given him in his boyhood while he was unworthy to hold them, and others had been conferred upon him by his parents and kinsmen, who were moved thereto by the bonds of the flesh, and had perhaps been taken from more worthy persons by force, or acquired through the court or in some other unlawful manner; and he committed himself wholly to the pope's wisdom for the guidance of all the days of his life that might be yet to come and for the salvation of his soul at the last. And the pope of pure grace and by his free gift restored all these to him before his departure and gave him salutary instruction for their use and governance and showed him how he should live henceforth and how provide for his final departing. Let the careful reader therefore consider whether the labours of Master Giraldus should be regarded as spent wholly in vain. . . .

And so Giraldus ran the course that was ordained for him, while he could and while the time permitted, nor in his day was he a sluggard or a coward. But now that others run and follow the court and pile up vain vexations, let him take his rest and in his humble habitation indulge his love of books and in the corners of churches weep for his sins and wail for his offences and for the welfare of his soul with penance wash them away and wipe them out.

From *De iure et statu Menuensis ecclesiae*, trans. H. E. Butler, *The Autobiography of Giraldus Cambrensis* (London: Cape, 1937).

Henry II, King of England

Giraldus Cambrensis

Twelfth century

IT WERE not amiss in this place to draw the portrait of the king, so that his person as well as his character may be familiar to posterity; and those who in future ages shall hear and read of his great achievments, may be able to picture him to themselves as he was. For the history on which I am employed must not suffer so noble an ornament of our times to pass away with only a slight notice. But herein we crave pardon for speaking the exact truth, for without it, history not only loses all authority, but does not even merit the name. It is the business of art to copy nature, and the painter is not to be trusted who exaggerates graces and conceals blemishes.

No man indeed is born without faults, but he is best who has the least; and the wise will think that nothing which concerns mankind is devoid of interest. There is no certainty in worldly matters, and no perfect happiness; good is mixed with evil, and virtue with vice. Wherefore, if things spoken in commendation of a man's disposition or conduct are pleasant to the ear, it should not be taken amiss if his faults are told. It was the remark of a philosopher, that princes ought to be treated with deference, and not exasperated by severe things being said of them; and a comic writer tells us that smooth words make friends, but the language of truth makes enemies; so that it is a dangerous matter to say anything against one who has the power of revenging himself; and it is still more perilous, and more arduous than profitable, to describe freely and in many words a prince who, by a single word, can consign you to ruin. It would surely be a pleasing task, but I confess that it is one beyond my powers, to tell the truth respecting a prince in everything without in any way offending him. But to the purpose.

Henry II, king of England, had a reddish complexion, rather dark, and a large round head. His eyes were grey, bloodshot, and flashed in anger. He had a fiery countenance, his voice was tremulous, and his neck a little bent forward; but his chest was broad, and his arms were muscular. His body was fleshy, and he had an enormous paunch, rather by the fault of nature than from gross feeding. For his diet was temperate, and indeed in all things, considering he was a prince, he was moderate, and even parsimonious. In order to reduce and cure, as far as possible, this natural tendency and defect, he waged a continual war, so to speak, with his own belly by taking immoderate exercise. For in time of war, in which he was almost always engaged, he took little rest, even during the intervals of business and action. Times of peace were no seasons of repose and indulgence to him, for he was immoderately fond of the chase, and devoted himself to it with excessive ardour. At the first dawn of day he would mount a fleet horse, and indefatigably spend the day in riding through the woods, penetrating the depths of forests, and crossing the ridges of hills. On his return home in the evening he was seldom seen to sit down, either before he took his supper or after; for notwithstanding his own great fatigue, he would weary all his court by being constantly on his legs. But it is one of the most useful rules in life, not to have too much of any one thing, and even medicine is not in itself perfect and always to be used; even so it befell this king. For he had frequent swellings in his legs and feet, increased much by his violent exercise on horseback, which added to his other complaints, and if they did not bring on serious disorders, at least hastened that which is the source of all, old age. In stature he may be reckoned among men of moderate height, which was not the case with either of his sons; the two eldest being somewhat above the middle height, and the two youngest somewhat below.

When his mind was undisturbed, and he was not in an angry mood, he spoke with great eloquence, and, what was remarkable in those days, he was well learned.

He was also affable, flexible, and facetious, and, however he smothered his inward feelings, second to no one
in courtesy. Withal, he was so clement a prince, that
when he had subdued his enemies, he was overcome
himself by his pity for them. Resolute in war, and provident in peace, he so much feared the doubtful fortune of
the former, that, as the comic poet writes, he tried all
courses before he resorted to arms. Those whom he lost
in battle he lamented with more than a prince's sorrow,
having a more humane feeling for the soldiers who had
fallen than for the survivors; and bewailing the dead
more than he cared for the living. In troublesome times
no man was more courteous, and when all things were
safe, no man more harsh. Severe to the unruly, but clement to the humble; hard towards his own household, but
liberal to strangers; profuse abroad, but sparing at home;
those whom he once hated, he would scarcely ever love,
and from those he loved, he seldom withdrew his regard.
He was inordinately fond of hawking and hunting,
whether his falcons stooped on their prey, or his saga-
cious hounds, quick of scent and swift of foot, pursued
the chase. Would to God he had been as zealous in his
devotions as he was in his sports.

It is said that after the grievous dissensions between
him and his sons, raised by their mother, he had no respect for the obligations of the most solemn treaties.
True it is that from a certain natural inconstancy he
often broke his word, preferring rather, when driven to
straits, to forfeit his promise than depart from his purpose. In all his doings he was provident and circum-
spect, and on this account he was sometimes slack in the
administration of justice, and, to his people's great cost,
his decisions on all proceedings were dilatory. Both God
and right demand that justice should be administered

gratuitously, yet all things were set to sale and brought great wealth both to the clergy and laity; but their end was like Gehazi's gains.

He was a great maker of peace, and kept it himself; a liberal alms-giver, and an especial benefactor to the Holy Land. He loved the humble, curbed the nobility, and trod down the proud; filling the hungry with good things, and sending the rich empty away; exalting the meek, and putting down the mighty from their seat. He ventured on many detestable usurpations in things belonging to God, and through a zeal for justice (but not according to knowledge), he joined the rights of the Church to those of the crown, and therein confused them, in order to centre all in himself. Although he was the son of the Church, and received his crown from her hands, he either dissembled or forgot the sacramental unction. He could scarcely spare an hour to hear mass, and then he was more occupied in counsels and conversation about affairs of state than in his devotions. The revenues of the churches during their avoidance he drew into his own treasury, laying hands on that which belonged to Christ; and as he was always in fresh troubles and engaged in mighty wars, he expended all the money he could get, and lavished upon unrighteous soldiers what was due to the priests. In his great prudence he devised many plans, which, however, did not all turn out according to his expectations; but no great mishap ever occurred, which did not originate in some trifling circumstance.

He was the kindest of fathers to his legitimate children during their childhood and youth, but as they advanced in years looked on them with an evil eye, treating them worse than a stepfather; and although he had such distinguished and illustrious sons, whether it was that he would not have them prosper too fast, or whether they were ill-deserving, he could never bear to think of them as his successors. And as human prosperity can neither be permanent nor perfect, such was the exquisite malice of fortune against this king, that where he should have received comfort he met with opposition; where security, danger; where peace, turmoil; where support, ingratitude; where quiet and tranquillity, disquiet and disturbance. Whether it happened from unhappy marriages, or for the punishment of the father's sins, there was never any good agreement either of the father with his sons, or of the sons with their parent, or between themselves.

At length, all pretenders to the government and disturbers of the peace being put down, and the brothers, his sons, and all others, both at home and abroad, being reconciled, all things succeeded according to his will. Would to God that he had, even late, acknowledged this crowning proof of the divine mercy by works worthy of repentance. I had almost forgotten to mention that his memory was so good, that, notwithstanding the multitudes who continually surrounded him, he never failed of recognizing anyone he had ever seen before, nor did he forget anything important which he had ever heard. He was also master of nearly the whole course of history, and well versed in almost all matters of experience. To conclude in few words; if this king had been finally chosen of God, and had turned himself to obey his commands, such were his natural endowments that he would have been, beyond all comparison, the noblest of all princes of the earth in his times.

From *Conquest of Ireland*, trans. T. Wright (London: Bell, 1881).

The Emperor Frederick II

SALIMBENE

Thirteenth century

FREDERICK II, formerly emperor, although he was great and rich and a mighty emperor, had nevertheless many misfortunes. Concerning these something should be said. The first of all his misfortunes was that his first-born son Henry, who should have ruled after him, went over to the Lombards against his will, and so Frederick captured him, bound him, and put him in prison. Thus the emperor could say with Job, "They whom I loved are turned against me."

His second misfortune was that he wished to subjugate the Church, so that the pope and the cardinals and other prelates should be poor, and should go on foot. And he did not try to do this by divine zeal, but because he was not a good Catholic, and because he was very avaricious and greedy, and wanted to have the riches and treasures of the Church for himself and his sons. He wished to put down the power of the churchmen, so that they could not undertake anything against him. And he told this to certain of his secretaries, from whom, afterwards, it became known. . . .

The third of his misfortunes was that he wanted to conquer the Lombards and could not, because when he had them on one side, he lost them on the other. . . .

His fourth misfortune was that Pope Innocent IV deposed him from the empire in the plenary council of Lyons, and made public there all his wickedness and iniquities. . . .

His fifth misfortune was that while he was still living, his empire was given to another, namely, the landgrave of Thuringia [Henry Raspe]. Although death took him quite soon, yet Frederick was sorrowful when he saw that his empire had been given to another. . . .

His sixth misfortune was when Parma rebelled against him, and went over completely to the Church, which was the cause of all his ruin.

The seventh misfortune was when the men of Parma took his city, Vittoria, which he had built near Parma, and burned, razed, and completely destroyed it, and filled up the holes so that no vestige of it remained, according to the Apocalypse, "A city which was and is no more." Also, they put Frederick and his army shamefully to flight, and killed many of them, and led many captive to their city of Parma. . . . Also they despoiled him and took his whole treasury. . . . The cry of Frederick could be that of Job: "He hath stripped me of my glory, and taken the crown from my head." This can be taken to mean Pope Innocent IV, who deposed him from the empire, or the city of Parma, which literally stripped him and took his crown from his head. A certain man of Parma found this crown in the city of Vittoria when it was destroyed, and carried it publicly in his hand, but the men of Parma took it away from him. . . . I have seen and known this man, and I have also seen the crown, and held it in my hand; it was of great weight and of great value. The men of Parma gave him two hundred pounds imperial for it, and a little house near the church of St. Christine, which formerly was a bathing and drinking place for horses. . . .

Frederick's eighth misfortune was when his princes and barons rebelled against him, like Teobaldo Francesco, who shut himself up in Cappacio, and afterwards died wretchedly; after his eyes had been put out and he had been tortured, he was slain by Frederick. There were also Piero della Vigna and many others, whom it would take too long to name. Concerning these, Frederick could say with Job: "All my inward friends abhorred me, and they whom I loved are turned against me." The one whom he greatly loved was Piero della Vigna, whom he had raised up from nothing, so that he could say, "I have lifted you out of the dust," for Piero had been a poor man, and the emperor had made him his secretary, and had called him "logothete," wishing to honour him greatly. . . .

His ninth misfortune was when his son, King Enzio, was captured by the Bolognese, which was right and just, for he had captured at sea prelates who were going to the council of Pope Gregory IX. . . . Thus it could not be, that the emperor would not be pierced by this sword of sorrow, that is, the capture of his son by his enemies at such a time. For then all hope of his victory perished.

The tenth and last of his misfortunes was when he heard that the Marquis Uberto Pelavicini had greater lordship over the Lombards than he himself could ever have, although Uberto was on his side. He was old and thin and weak and one-eyed, because when he lay as a baby in the cradle, a cock had pecked his eye, that is, it had extracted it from his head with its beak, and eaten it.

To these ten misfortunes of the Emperor Frederick we can add two more, so that we shall have twelve: first, that he was excommunicated by Pope Gregory IX; and second, that the Church tried to take away from him the kingdom of Sicily. And he was not without blame in this, for when the Church sent him across the sea to recover the Holy Land, he made a peace with the Saracens without advantage for the Christians. Moreover, he had the name of Mohammed publicly chanted in the church of God, as we have set down in another chronicle, where we described the twelve crimes of Frederick. . . .

That Frederick who was once emperor died in 1250 A.D., in Apulia, in the little city which is called Fiorentino, which is about ten miles from the Saracen city of Nocera. And because of the very great stench of corruption which came from his body, he could not be carried to Palermo, where the sepulchres of the kings of Sicily are, and where they are buried.

The reasons for the failure to bury this king in the tombs of the kings of Sicily are manifold. The first was the fulfilment of the Scriptures, whence Isaiah: "Thou shalt not be joined with them in burial, because thou hast destroyed thy land and slain thy people." . . . The second was that such a great stench came from his body that it could not be endured. . . . The third reason was that his son Manfred, who was called prince, concealed his death, because he wanted to seize the kingdom of Sicily and Apulia, before his brother Conrad should come from Germany. Hence it was that many believed that he had not died, although he really had; and thus was fulfilled the Sibylline prophecy: "It will be said among the people, 'He lives' and 'He does not live,'" and this happened because his death was hidden. . . .

But know you that Frederick always delighted in having strife with the Church, and that he many times fought her, who had nourished, protected, and exalted him. Of faith in God he had none. He was a crafty man, wily, avaricious, lustful, malicious, and wrathful.

And yet at times he was a worthy man, when he wanted to prove his goodness and his generosity; then he was friendly, merry, full of sweetness and diligence. He could read, write, and sing, and make songs and

music. He was a handsome, well-formed man, but only
of middle height. I have seen him, and once I loved
him, for he wrote on my behalf to Brother Elias, the
minister general of the Franciscan order, to send me
back to my father. He knew how to speak many and
various languages. And, to put it briefly, had he been
a good Catholic, and loved God, the Church, and his
own soul, he would have had as his equals few emperors
in the world. But since, as it is written, a little leaven
leaveneth the lump, so he destroyed all his good qualities through this, that he persecuted the Church of
God, which he would not have done, if he had loved
God and his own soul. . . . So he was deposed from
the imperial office, and died an evil death. . . .

But now I have something to say about the follies of
Frederick. His first folly was that he had the thumb of
a notary cut off, because he spelled his name in a different way from what he wished. Frederick desired that
the first syllable of his name be written "i," like this,
Fridericus, and that notary had written it with an "e,"
Fredericus.

His second folly was that he wanted to find out what
kind of speech and what manner of speech children
would have when they grew up, if they spoke to no one
beforehand. So he bade foster mothers and nurses to
suckle the children, to bathe and wash them, but in no
way to prattle with them or to speak to them, for he
wanted to learn whether they would speak the Hebrew
language, which was the oldest, or Greek, or Latin, or
Arabic, or perhaps the language of their parents, of
whom they had been born. But he laboured in vain,
because the children all died. For they could not live
without the petting and the joyful faces and loving
words of their foster mothers. And so the songs are

called "swaddling songs," which a woman sings while she is rocking the cradle, to put a child to sleep, and without them a child sleeps badly and has no rest.

His third folly was that, when he saw the land across the sea, the Holy Land, which God had so often praised, in that He called it "the land flowing with milk and honey," and the most excellent of all lands, it displeased him, and he said that the God of the Jews had not seen his own lands, namely, the Terra di Lavoro, Calabria, Sicily and Apulia. Otherwise, He would not so often have praised the land that He promised and gave to the Jews. . . .

His fourth folly was that he often sent a certain Nicholas, against his will, to the bottom of the Faro, and many times he returned. But Frederick wanted to discover whether or not he had really gone to the bottom and returned, so he threw his golden cup in the sea, where he thought it was deepest. And Nicholas plunged in, found the cup, and brought it to him, which astonished the emperor. But when Frederick wanted to send him back once again, Nicholas said, "Do not send me there again at any price, for the sea is so troubled in its depths, that if you send me I shall never return." The emperor sent him nevertheless, and he never returned. For at the times of tempests there are great fishes in the depths of the sea and also, as Nicholas himself reported, rocks and many wrecked ships. . . .

Moreover, Frederick had other superstitions and curiosities and curses and incredulities and perversities and abuses, concerning which I have written in another chronicle. . . . For he was an Epicurean, and so whatever could be found in divine Scripture by him and by his wise men, which seemed to show that there is no other life after death, he found it all, for example, the words of the Psalms: "You will destroy them and you will not rebuild them" and the saying, "Their sepulchres will be their homes forever." . . .

The sixth curiosity and folly of Frederick, as I have said in my other chronicle, was that at a certain luncheon he had two men very well beaten, and then sent one of them to sleep and the other to hunt, and on the following evening, he had them defecate in his presence, because he wanted to know which of them had digested the better. And it was decided by the doctors that he who had slept had enjoyed the better digestion.

The seventh and last of his curiosities and follies was that, as I have also written in my other chronicle, when he was in a certain palace on a certain day, he asked Michael Scot, his astrologer, how far he was from the sky, and the astrologer told him how far it seemed to him. Then the emperor took him to other parts of the kingdom, as if for the sake of travel, and he remained for many months. Meanwhile, Frederick had ordered the architects or carpenters to lower the hall of the palace in such a way that no one could detect it. And thus it was done. When after many days, the emperor was staying in the same palace with his astrologer, as if beginning in another way, he asked him whether he was still as far from the sky as he had said the other time. After he had made his computation, the astrologer said that either the sky had been raised or certainly the earth had been lowered. And then the emperor knew that the astrologer spoke truly. I know and I have heard many other follies of Frederick, which for the sake of brevity I do not mention, and because it bores me to relate so many of his follies, and also because I hasten to speak of other things.

From *Chronicle,* F. Bernini, ed.; trans. M.M.M.

A Saintly King

JEAN DE JOINVILLE

Thirteenth century

HIS VIRTUES

IN THE name of God Almighty, I, John, Lord of Joinville, seneschal of Champagne, dictate the life of our holy King Lewis; that which I saw and heard by the space of six years that I was in his company on pilgrimage oversea, and that which I saw and heard after we returned. And before I tell you of his great deeds, and of his prowess, I will tell you what I saw and heard of his good teachings and of his holy words, so that these may be found here set in order for the edifying of those who shall hear thereof.

This holy man loved God with all his heart, and followed Him in His acts; and this appeared in that, as God died for the love He bore His people, so did the king put his body in peril, and that several times, for the love he bore to his people; and such peril he might well have avoided, as you shall be told hereafter.

The great love that he bore to his people appeared in what he said during a very sore sickness that he had at Fontainebleau, unto my lord Lewis, his eldest son. "Fair son," he said, "I pray thee to make thyself beloved of the people of thy kingdom; for truly I would rather that a Scot should come out of Scotland and govern the people of the kingdom well and equitably than that thou shouldest govern it ill in the sight of all men." The holy king so loved truth, that, as you shall hear hereafter, he would never consent to lie to the Saracens as to any covenant that he had made with them.

Of his mouth he was so sober, that on no day of my life did I ever hear him order special meats, as many rich men are wont to do; but he ate patiently whatever his cooks had made ready and was set before him. In his words he was temperate; for on no day of my life did I ever hear him speak evil of any one; nor did I ever hear him name the Devil—which name is very commonly spoken throughout the kingdom, whereby God, as I believe, is not well pleased.

He put water into his wine by measure, according as he saw that the strength of the wine would suffer it. At Cyprus he asked me why I put no water into my wine; and I said this was by order of the physicians, who told me I had a large head and a cold stomach, so that I could not get drunk. And he answered that they deceived me; for if I did not learn to put water into my wine in my youth, and wished to do so in my old age, gout and diseases of the stomach would take hold upon me, and I should never be in health; and if I drank pure wine in my old age, I should get drunk every night, and that it was too foul a thing for a brave man to get drunk.

He asked me if I wished to be honoured in this world, and to go into paradise at my death? And I said, "Yes." And he said, "Keep yourself then from knowingly doing or saying anything which, if the whole world heard thereof, you would be ashamed to acknowledge, saying 'I did this,' or 'I said that.'" He told me to beware not to contradict or impugn anything that was said before me—unless indeed silence would be a sin or to my own hurt—because hard words often move to quarrelling, wherein men by the thousand have found death.

He said that men ought to clothe and arm their bodies in such wise that men of worth and age would never say, this man has done too much, nor young men say, this man has done too little. And I repeated this saying to the father of the king that now is, when speaking of the embroidered coats of arms that are made nowadays; and I told him that never, during our voyage oversea, had I seen embroidered coats, either belonging to the king or to anyone else. And the king that now is told me that he had such suits, with arms embroidered, as had cost him eight hundred pounds *parisis*. And I told him he would have employed the money to better purpose if he had given it to God, and had had his suits made of good taffeta (satin) ornamented with his arms, as his father had done. . . .

He so loved all manner of people who had faith in God and loved Him, that he gave the constableship of France to my lord Giles Le Brun, who was not of the kingdom of France, because men held him in so great repute for his faith and for love to God. And verily I believe that his good repute was well deserved.

He caused Master Robert of Sorbon to eat at his table, because of the great repute in which he was held as a man of uprightness and worth. One day it chanced that Master Robert was eating at my side, and we were talking to one another. The king took us up, and said: "Speak out, for your companions think you are speaking ill of them. If you talk at table of things that can give us pleasure, speak out, and, if not, hold your peace."

When the king would be mirthful he would say to me: "Seneschal, tell me the reasons why a man of uprightness and worth [*prud'homme*] is better than a friar?" Then would begin a discussion between me and Master Robert. When we had disputed for a long while, the king would give sentence and speak thus: "Master Robert, willingly would I bear the title of upright and worthy [*prud'homme*] provided I were such in reality

—and all the rest you might have. For uprightness and worth are such great things and such good things that even to name them fills the mouth pleasantly."

On the contrary, he said it was an evil thing to take other people's goods. "For," said he, "to restore is a thing so grievous, that even in the speaking the word 'restore' scratches the throat by reason of the r's that are in it, and these r's are like so many rakes with which the Devil would draw to himself those who wish to 'restore' what they have taken from others. And very subtly does the Devil do this; for he works on great usurers and great robbers in such sort that they give to God what they ought to 'restore' to men." . . .

The rule of his land was so arranged that every day he heard the hours sung, and a requiem mass without song; and then, if it was convenient, the mass of the day, or of the saint, with song. Every day he rested in his bed after having eaten, and when he had slept and rested, he said, privily in his chamber—he and one of his chaplains together—the office for the dead; and after he heard vespers. At night he heard complines.

A grey friar [Franciscan] came to him at the castle of Hyères, there where we disembarked; and said in his sermon, for the king's instruction, that he had read the Bible, and the books pertaining to heathen princes, and that he had never found, either among believers or mis-believers, that a kingdom had been lost, or had changed lords, save there had first been failure of justice. "Therefore let the king, who is going into France, take good heed," said he, "that he do justice well and speedily among his people, so that our Lord suffer his kingdom to remain in peace all the days of his life." It is said that the right worthy man who thus instructed the king lies buried at Marseilles, where our Lord, for his sake, performs many a fine miracle. He would never consent to remain with the king, however much the king might urge it, for more than a single day.

The king forgat not the teaching of the friar, but ruled his land very loyally and godly, as you shall hear. He had so arranged that my lord of Nesle, and the good count of Soissons, and all of us who were about him, should go, after we had heard our masses, and hear the pleadings at the gate which is now called the Gate of Requests.

And when he came back from church, he would send for us and sit at the foot of his bed, and make us all sit round him, and ask if there were any whose cases could not be settled save by himself in person. And we named the litigants; and he would then send for such and ask, "Why do you not accept what our people offer?" and they would make reply, "Sire, because they offer us very little." Then would he say, "You would do well to accept what is proposed, as our people desire." And the saintly man endeavoured thus, with all his power, to bring them into a straight path and a reasonable.

Ofttimes it happened that he would go, after his mass, and seat himself in the wood of Vincennes, and lean against an oak, and make us sit round him. And all those who had any cause in hand came and spoke to him, without hindrance of usher, or of any other person. Then would he ask, out of his own mouth, "Is there any one who has a cause in hand?" And those who had a cause in hand stood up. Then would he say, "Keep silence all, and you shall be heard in turn, one after the other." Then he would call my lord Peter of Fontaines and my lord Geoffry of Villette, and say to one of them, "Settle me this cause."

And when he saw that there was anything to amend in the words of those who spoke on his behalf, or in the words of those who spoke on behalf of any other person, he would himself, out of his own mouth, amend what they had said. Sometimes have I seen him, in summer, go to do justice among his people in the garden of Paris, clothed in a tunic of camlet, a surcoat of tartan without sleeves, and a mantle of black taffeta about his neck, his hair well combed, no cap, and a hat of white peacock's feathers upon his head. And he would cause a carpet to be laid down, so that we might sit round him, and all the people who had any cause to bring before him stood around. And then would he have their causes settled, as I have told you afore he was wont to do in the wood of Vincennes. . . .

THE DEATH OF HIS MOTHER

To Sayette came news to the king that his mother was dead. He made such lamentation that, for two days, no one could speak to him. After that he sent one of the varlets of his chamber to summon me. When I came before him in his chamber, where he was alone, and he saw me, he stretched out his arms, and said, "Ah, seneschal, I have lost my mother!" "Sire," said I, "I do not marvel at that, since she had to die; but I do marvel that you, who are a wise man, should have made such great mourning; for you know what the sage says: that whatever grief a man may have in his heart, none should appear on his countenance, because he who shows his grief causes his enemies to rejoice and afflicts his friends." He caused many fine services to be held for the queen overseas; and afterwards sent to France a chest full of letters to the churches, asking them to pray for her.

My lady Mary of Vertus, a very good lady and a saintly woman, came to tell me that the queen was making great lamentation, and asked me to go to her and comfort her. And when I came there, I found her weeping; and I told her that he spake sooth who said that none should put faith in woman. "For," said I, "she that is dead is the woman that you most hated, and yet you are showing such sorrow." And she told me it was not for the queen that she was weeping, but because of the king's sorrow in the mourning that he made, and because of her daughter, afterwards the queen of Navarre, who had remained in men's keeping.

The unkindness that the queen Blanche showed to the queen Margaret was such that she would not suffer, in so far as she could help it, that her son should be in his wife's company, except at night when he went to sleep with her. The palace where the king and his queen liked most to dwell was at Pontoise, because there the king's chamber was above and the queen's chamber below; and they had so arranged matters between them that they held their converse in a turning staircase that went from the one chamber to the other; and they had further arranged that when the ushers saw the queen Blanche coming to her son's chamber, they struck the door with their rods, and the king would come running into his chamber so that his mother might find him there; and the ushers of Queen Margaret's chamber did the same when Queen Blanche went thither, so that she might find Queen Margaret there.

Once the king was by his wife's side, and she was in great peril of death, being hurt for a child that she had borne. Queen Blanche came thither, and took her son by the hand, and said, "Come away; you have nothing to do here!" When Queen Margaret saw that the mother was leading her son away, she cried, "Alas! whether dead or alive, you will not suffer me to see my lord!" Then she fainted, and they thought she was dead; and the king, who thought she was dying, turned back; and with great trouble they brought her round. . . .

THE HORROR OF ST. LEWIS FOR ALL BLASPHEMY

The king so loved God and His sweet Mother that he caused all those to be grievously punished who were convinced of speaking of Them evilly or lightly, or with a profane oath. Thus I saw him cause a goldsmith, at Caesarea, to be bound to a ladder, in his drawers and shirt, with a pig's gut and haslet round his neck, and in such quantity that they reached up to his nose. I heard tell that, since I came from overseas, he caused, on this account, a citizen of Paris to be burned in the nose and lip; but this I did not myself witness. And the saintly king was used to say: "I would consent to be branded with a hot iron on condition that all profane oaths were removed out of my realm."

I was full twenty-two years in his company, and never heard him swear by God, nor His Mother, nor His saints. When he wished to affirm anything, he would say: "Truly that was so," or "Truly that is so."

Never did I hear him name the Devil, unless the name came in some book, where it was right that it should come, or in the life of the saints where the book made mention thereof. And great shame it is to the realm of France, and to the king who suffers it, that scarcely can anyone speak without saying, "May the Devil take it!" And it is a great sin of speech to devote to the Devil men or women who were given to God as soon as they were baptized. In the house of Joinville whosoever speaks such a word receives a buffet or pummel, and bad language is nearly outrooted. . . .

THE DEATH OF ST. LEWIS

When the good king had so taught his son, my lord Philip, the infirmity that was upon him began to grow apace; and he asked for the sacraments of Holy

Church, and received them, being clear of thought and of sound understanding, as appeared duly, for when they anointed him with oil and said the seven psalms, he repeated the verses in turn.

And I heard my lord, the count of Alençon, his son, tell that when the king came near to death he called upon the saints to help and succour him, and especially upon my lord St. James, saying St. James's orison, which begins, "*Esto, Domine*," that is to say, "O God, be the sanctifier and guardian of thy people." Then he called to his aid my lord St. Denis of France, saying St. Denis's orison, which is to this effect: "Lord God, grant that we may despise the prosperity of this world, and not stand in fear of any adversity."

And I then heard my lord of Alençon—on whom God have mercy!—relate how his father called on my lady St. Geneviève. After that, the saintly king caused himself to be laid on a bed covered with ashes, and put his hands across his breast, and, looking towards heaven, rendered up his spirit to our Creator; and it was at the same hour that the Son of God died upon the cross for the world's salvation.

A piteous thing, and worthy of tears, is the death of this saintly prince, who kept and guarded his realm so holily, and loyally, and gave alms there so largely, and set therein so many fair foundations. And like as the scribe who, writing his book, illuminates it with gold and azure, so did the said king illuminate his realm with the fair abbeys that he built, and the great number of almshouses, and the houses for Preachers and Franciscans, and other religious orders, as named above.

On the day after the feast of St. Bartholomew the Apostle, did the good King Lewis pass out of this world, and in the year of the incarnation of our Saviour, the year of grace 1270 (the 25th August). And his bones were put in a casket, and borne thence, and buried at St. Denis in France, where he had chosen his place of sepulture; and in the place where they were buried God has sithence performed many fair miracles in his honour, and by his merit.

THE CANONIZATION OF ST. LEWIS

After this, at the instance of the king of France, and by command of the pope, came the archbishop of Rouen, and Brother John of Samois, who has since been made bishop, they came to St. Denis in France, and there remained a long space to make inquisition into the life, the works, and the miracles of the saintly king. And I was summoned to come to them, and they kept me two days. And after they had questioned me and others, what they had ascertained and set down was sent to the court of Rome; and the pope and the cardinals looked diligently into what had been sent to them, and according to what they saw there they did right to the king, and set him among the number of the confessors.

From *Chronicle*, in *Memoirs of the Crusades*, trans. Sir Frank Thomas Marzials (Everyman's Library [1908]).

Pope Boniface VIII

GIOVANNI VILLANI

Early fourteenth century

AFTER the said strife had arisen between Pope Boniface and King Philip [IV] of France, each one sought to abase the other by every method and guise

that was possible: the pope sought to oppress the king
of France with excommunications and by other means
to deprive him of the kingdom; and with this he favoured the Flemings, his rebellious subjects, and entered into negotiations with King Albert of Germany,
encouraging him to come to Rome for the imperial benediction, and to cause the kingdom to be taken from
King Charles, his kinsman, and to stir up war against
the king of France on the borders of his realm on the
side of Germany. The king of France, on the other hand,
was not asleep, but with great caution, and by the counsel of Stefano della Colonna and of other sage Italians,
and men of his own realm, sent one M. William of Nogaret of Provence, a wise and crafty cleric, with M.
Musciatto Franzesi, into Tuscany, furnished with much
ready money, and with drafts on the company of the
Peruzzi (which were then his merchants) for as much
money as might be needed; the Peruzzi not knowing
wherefore. And when they were come to the fortress of
Staggia, which pertained to the said M. Musciatto, they
abode there long time, sending ambassadors and messages and letters; and they caused people to come to
them in secret, giving out openly that they were there
to treat concerning peace between the pope and the
king of France, and that for this cause they had brought
the said money; and under this colour they conducted
secret negotiations to take Pope Boniface prisoner in
Anagna, spending thereupon much money, corrupting
the barons of the country and the citizens of Anagna;
and as it had been purposed, so it came to pass; for
Pope Boniface being with his cardinals, and with all the
court, in the city of Anagna, in Campagna, where he had
been born, and was at home, not thinking or knowing of
this plot, nor being on his guard, or if he heard anything
of it, through his great courage not heeding it, or per-

haps, as it pleased God, by reason of his great sins—in the month of September, 1303, Sciarra della Colonna, with his mounted followers, to the number of three hundred, and many of his friends on foot, paid by money of the French king, with troops of the lords of Ceccano and of Supino, and of other barons of the Campagna, and of the sons of M. Maffio d'Anagna, and, it is said, with the consent of some of the cardinals which were in the plot, one morning early entered into Anagna, with the ensigns and standards of the king of France, crying, "Death to Pope Boniface! Long life to the king of France!" And they rode through the city without any hindrance, or, rather, well-nigh all the ungrateful people of Anagna followed the standards and the rebellion; and when they came to the papal palace, they entered without opposition and took the palace, forasmuch as the present assault was not expected by the pope and his retainers, and they were not upon their guard. Pope Boniface—hearing the uproar, and seeing himself forsaken by all his cardinals, which were fled and in hiding (whether through fear or through set malice), and by the most part of his servants, and seeing that his enemies had taken the city and the palace where he was—gave himself up for lost, but like the high-spirited and valorous man he was, he said, "Since, like Jesus Christ, I am willing to be taken and needs must die by treachery, at the least I desire to die as pope"; and straightway he caused himself to be robed in the mantle of St. Peter, and with the crown of Constantine on his head, and with the keys and the cross in his hand, he seated himself upon the papal chair. And when Sciarra and the others, his enemies, came to him, they mocked at him with vile words, and arrested him and his household which had remained with him; among the others, M. William of Nogaret scorned him, which had conducted the negotiations for the king of France, whereby he had been taken, and threatened him, saying that he would take him bound to Lyons on the Rhone, and there in a general council would cause him to be deposed and condemned. The high-spirited pope answered him, that he was well pleased to be condemned and deposed by Paterines [heretics] such as he, whose father and mother had been burnt as Paterines; whereat M. William was confounded and put to shame. But afterwards, as it pleased God, to preserve the holy dignity of the popes, no man dared to touch him, nor were they pleased to lay hands on him, but they left him robed under gentle ward, and were minded to rob the treasure of the pope and of the Church. In this pain, shame, and torment the great Pope Boniface abode prisoner among his enemies for three days; but, like as Christ rose on the third day, so it pleased Him that Pope Boniface should be set free; for without entreaty or other effort, save the divine aid, the people of Anagna beholding their error, and issuing from their blind ingratitude, suddenly rose in arms, crying, "Long live the pope and his household, and death to the traitors"; and running through the city they drove out Sciarra della Colonna and his followers, with loss to them of prisoners and slain, and freed the pope and his household. Pope Boniface, seeing himself free, and his enemies driven away, did not therefore rejoice in any wise, forasmuch as the pain of his adversity had so entered into his heart and clotted there; wherefore he departed straightway from Anagna with all his court, and came to Rome to St. Peter's to hold a council, purposing to take the heaviest vengeance for his injury and that of Holy Church against the king of France, and whosoever had offended him; but, as it pleased God, the grief which had hardened in the heart of Pope Boniface, by reason of the injury which he had received, produced in him, after he was come to Rome, a strange malady so that he gnawed at himself as if he were mad, and in this state he passed from this life on the twelfth day of October in the year of Christ 1303, and in the church of St. Peter, near the entrance of the doors, in a rich chapel which was built in his lifetime, he was honourably buried.

This Pope Boniface was very wise both in learning and in natural wit, and a man very cautious and experienced, and of great knowledge and memory; very haughty he was, and proud, and cruel towards his enemies and adversaries, and was of a great heart, and much feared by all people; and he exalted and increased greatly the estate and the rights of Holy Church, and he commissioned M. Guglielmo da Bergamo and M. Ricciardi of Siena, who were cardinals, and M. Dino Rosoni of Mugello, all of them supreme masters in laws and in decretals, together with himself, for he too was a great master in divinity and in decretals, to draw up the Sixth Book of the Decretals, which is as it were the light of all the laws and the decretals. A man of large schemes was he, and liberal to folk which pleased him, and which were worthy, very desirous of worldly pomp according to his estate, and very desirous of wealth, not scrupulous, nor having very great or strict conscience about every gain, to enrich the Church and his nephews. He made many of his friends and confidants cardinals in his time, among others two very young nephews, and his uncle, his mother's brother; and twenty of his relations and friends of the little city of Anagna, bishops and archbishops of rich benefices; and to another of his nephews and his sons, which were counts, as we afore made mention, to them he left almost unbounded riches; and after the death of Pope Boniface, their uncle, they were bold and valiant in war, doing vengeance upon all their neighbours and enemies, which had betrayed and injured Pope Boniface, spending largely, and keeping at their own cost three hundred good Catalan horsemen, by force of which they subdued almost all the Campagna and the district of Rome. And if Pope Boniface, while he was alive, had believed that they could be thus bold in arms and valorous in war, certainly he would have made them kings or great lords. And note, that when Pope Boniface was taken prisoner, tidings thereof were sent to the king of France by many couriers in a few days, through great joy; and when the first couriers arrived at Sion, beyond the mountain of Brieg [Sion under Brieg], the bishop of Sion, which then was a man of pure and holy life, when he heard the news was, as it were, amazed, and abode some while in silent contemplation, by reason of the wonderment which took him at the capture of the pope; and coming to himself he said aloud, in the presence of many good folk, "The king of France will rejoice greatly on hearing these tidings, but I have it by divine inspiration, that for this sin he is judged by God, and that great and strange perils and adversities, with shame to him and his lineage, will overtake him very swiftly, and he and his sons will be cast out from the inheritance of the realm." And this we learned a little while after, when we passed by Sion, from persons worthy of belief, which were present to hear. Which sentence was a prophecy in all its parts, as afterwards the truth will show, in due time, when we narrate the doings of the said king of France and of his sons. And the judgment of God is not to be marvelled at; for, albeit Pope Boniface was more worldly than was fitting to his dignity, and had done many things displeasing to God, God caused him to be punished after the fashion that we have said, and afterwards He punished the offender against him, not so much for the injury against the person of Pope Boniface, as for the sin committed against the Divine Majesty, whose countenance he represented on earth.

From *Chronicle*, trans. R. E. Selfe, P. H. Wicksteed, ed. (London: Constable, 1906).

Dante Alighieri

GIOVANNI VILLANI

Fourteenth century

IN THE said year 1321, in the month of July, Dante Alighieri, of Florence, died in the city of Ravenna, in Romagna, having returned from an embassy to Venice in the service of the lords of Polenta, with whom he was living; and in Ravenna, before the door of the chief church, he was buried with great honour, in the garb of a poet and of a great philosopher. He died in exile from the commonwealth of Florence, at the age of about fifty-six years. This Dante was a citizen of an honourable and ancient family in Florence, of the Porta San Piero, and our neighbour; and his exile from Florence was by reason that when M. Charles of Valois, of the house of France, came to Florence in the year 1301 and banished the White party, as has been aforementioned at its due time, the said Dante was among the chief governors of our city, and pertained to that party, albeit he was a Guelph; and, therefore, for no other fault he was driven out and banished from Florence with the White party; and went to the university at Bologna, and afterwards at Paris, and in many parts of the world. This man was a great scholar in almost every branch of learning, albeit he was a layman; he was a great poet and philosopher, and a perfect rhetorician alike in prose and verse, a very noble orator in public speaking, supreme in rhyme, with the most polished and beautiful style which in our language ever was up to his time and beyond it. In his youth he wrote the book of *The New Life*, of love; and afterwards, when he was in exile, he wrote about twenty very excellent odes, treating of moral questions and of love; and he wrote three noble letters among others; one he sent to the government of Florence complaining of his undeserved exile; the second he sent to the Emperor Henry [VII] when he was besieging Brescia, reproving him for his delay, almost in a prophetic strain; the third to the Italian cardinals, at the time of the vacancy after the death of Pope Clement, praying them to unite in the election of an Italian pope; all these in Latin in a lofty style, and with excellent purport and authorities, and much commended by men of wisdom and insight. And he wrote the *Comedy*, wherein, in polished verse, and with great and subtle questions, moral, natural, astrological, philosophical, and theological, with new and beautiful illustrations, comparisons, and poetry, he dealt and treated in one hundred chapters or songs, of the existence and condition of Hell, Purgatory, and Paradise as loftily as it were possible to treat of them, as in his said treatise may be seen and understood by whoso has subtle intellect. It is true that he in this *Comedy* delighted to denounce and to cry out after the manner of poets, perhaps in certain places more than was fitting; but may be his exile was the cause of this. He wrote also the *Monarchy*, in which he treated of the office of pope and of emperor. (And he began a commentary upon fourteen of his aforenamed moral odes in the vulgar tongue which, in consequence of his death, is only completed as to three of them; the which commentary, judging by what can be seen of it, was turning out a lofty, beautiful, subtle, and very great work, adorned by lofty style and fine philosophical and astrological reasonings. Also he wrote a little book entitled *De Vulgari Eloquentia*, of which he promised to write four books, but of these only two exist, perhaps on account of his untimely death; and here, in strong and ornate Latin and with beautiful reasonings, he reproves all the vernaculars of Italy.) This Dante, because of his knowledge, was somewhat haughty and reserved and disdainful, and after the fashion of a philosopher, careless of graces and not easy in his converse with laymen; but because of the lofty virtues and knowledge and worth of so great a citizen, it seems fitting to confer lasting memory upon him in this our chronicle, although, indeed, his noble works left to us in writing are the true testimony to him, and are an honourable report to our city.

From *Chronicle*, trans. R. E. Selfe.

Inscription for a Portrait of Dante

GIOVANNI BOCCACCIO

c. 1373

Dante Alighieri, a dark oracle
　　Of wisdom and of art, I am; whose mind
　　Has to my country such great gifts assign'd
That men account my powers a miracle.
My lofty fancy pass'd as low as Hell,
　　As high as Heaven, secure and unconfined;
　　And in my noble book doth every kind
Of earthly lore and heavenly doctrine dwell.

Renownèd Florence was my mother—nay,
Stepmother unto me her piteous son,
Through sin of cursed slander's tongue and tooth.
Ravenna shelter'd me so cast away;
My body is with her—my soul with One
For whom no envy can make dim the truth.

Trans. D. G. Rossetti, in *The Early Italian Poets* (London: Smith Elder, 1861).

Giotto

LORENZO GHIBERTI

Fourteenth century

THE art of painting began to rise in Tuscany in a village near the city of Florence called Vespignano. There was born a child of marvellous talent who drew a sheep from nature. Cimabue, the painter, passing along the road to Bologna saw the boy sitting on the ground, drawing a sheep on a flat stone. He was seized with great wonder that the child, being of such a tender age, could do so well, seeming to have the gift from nature, and he asked the boy what he was called. He replied and said, "I am called Giotto, and my father is named Bondoni and lives in that house which is close by." Cimabue went with Giotto to the father; he had a very fine appearance, and he asked the father for the boy. And the father was very poor. He gave the boy to Cimabue who took Giotto with him, and Giotto became the pupil of Cimabue.

He [Cimabue] followed the "Greek manner"; in this style he had won very great fame in Tuscany. Giotto made himself great in the art of painting. He brought in

the new art, abandoned the stiffness of the Greeks, rose
to fame most excellently in Tuscany. And he made the
most notable works, especially in the city of Florence,
and in many other places, and about him there were a
number of disciples, all learned like the ancient Greeks.
Giotto saw in art what the others did not add to it; he
brought into being art according to nature and gentleness with it, not exceeding measure. He was most expert
in all aspects of art; he was an inventor and a discoverer
of much knowledge which had been buried about the
year 600. When nature wishes to grant anything, she
grants it in truth without any stint. Giotto was prolific
in everything; he worked in murals, he worked in oil, he
worked on wood. He made in mosaic the Navicella of
St. Piero in Rome and with his own hand painted the
chapel and the altarpiece of St. Piero. He painted most
nobly the hall of King Robert [of Sicily] with pictures
of famous men. In Naples he painted in the Castello
dell' Uovo. He painted, that is, all by his own hand,
in the church of the Arena of Padua, and by his own
hand a Last Judgment. And in the Palazzo della Parte
[Guelph] he did a story of the Christian faith, and many
other things in the said palace. He painted in the church
at Assisi [San Francesco] of the order of Friars Minor
almost all the lower part. He also painted in Santa Maria
degli Angeli in Assisi and in Santa Maria della Minerva
in Rome a crucifix and a panel.

The works painted by him in Florence were the
following. In the Badia of Florence, in an arch above
the portal, our Lady, half-length, with two figures at
the sides, very exquisitely, and also the great chapel
and the panel. In the church of the Friars Minor [Santa
Croce] four chapels and four panels. Very excellently he
painted in Padua in the Friars Minor. Most skilfully in
the church of the Humiliati [Ognissanti] in Florence, a

chapel and a large crucifix, and four panels made very
excellently; in one was shown the death of our Lady
with angels and with the twelve apostles and our Lord
round about, made most perfectly. And there a very
large panel with our Lady sitting on a throne with many
angels round about. And there over the door leading
into the cloister, our Lady, half-length, with the Child
in her arms. And in St. Giorgio a panel and a crucifix.
In the Friars Preachers [Santa Maria Novella] there is
a crucifix and a most perfect panel by his hand; also
many other things there.

He painted for many lords. He painted in the palace
of the podestà in Florence; within he represented the
commune, showing how it was robbed, and the chapel
of Santa Maria Maddalena.

Giotto deserved the highest praise. He was most
worthy in all branches of art, even in the art of sculpture. The first compositions in the edifice which was
built by him, of the bell tower of Santa Reparata [Santa
Maria del Fiore], were sculptured and designed by his
hand. In my time I have seen the models of these reliefs
in his hand, most nobly designed. He was skilled in the
one kind of art and in the other. Since from him came
and developed such great knowledge, he is the one to
whom the highest praise should be given, because nature is seen to produce in him every skill. He led art to
its greatest perfection. He had very many disciples of
the greatest fame. . . .

From *Quellenbuch zur Kunstgeschichte*, J. Schlosser, ed. (Vienna:
C. Graeser, 1896); trans. J.B.R.

Letter to Posterity

FRANCESCO PETRARCA

c. 1370

GREETING. It is possible that some word of me may have come to you, though even this is doubtful, since an insignificant and obscure name will scarcely penetrate far in either time or space. If, however, you should have heard of me, you may desire to know what manner of man I was, or what was the outcome of my labours, especially those of which some description or, at any rate, the bare titles may have reached you.

To begin with myself, then, the utterances of men concerning me will differ widely, since in passing judgment almost everyone is influenced not so much by truth as by preference, and good and evil report alike know no bounds. I was, in truth, a poor mortal like yourself, neither very exalted in my origin, nor, on the other hand, of the most humble birth, but belonging, as Augustus Caesar says of himself, to an ancient family. As to my disposition, I was not naturally perverse or wanting in modesty, however the contagion of evil associations may have corrupted me. My youth was gone before I realized it; I was carried away by the strength of manhood; but a riper age brought me to my senses and taught me by experience the truth I had long before read in books, that youth and pleasure are vanity—nay, that the Author of all ages and times permits us miserable mortals, puffed up with emptiness, thus to wander about, until finally, coming to a tardy consciousness of our sins, we shall learn to know ourselves. In my prime

I was blessed with a quick and active body, although not exceptionally strong; and while I do not lay claim to remarkable personal beauty, I was comely enough in my best days. I was possessed of a clear complexion, between light and dark, lively eyes, and for long years a keen vision, which however deserted me, contrary to my hopes, after I reached my sixtieth birthday, and forced me, to my great annoyance, to resort to glasses. Although I had previously enjoyed perfect health, old age brought with it the usual array of discomforts.

My parents were honourable folk, Florentine in their origin, of medium fortune, or, I may as well admit it, in a condition verging upon poverty. They had been expelled from their native city, and consequently I was born in exile, at Arezzo, in the year 1304 of this latter age which begins with Christ's birth, July the twentieth, on a Monday, at dawn. I have always possessed an extreme contempt for wealth; not that riches are not desirable in themselves, but because I hate the anxiety and care which are invariably associated with them. I certainly do not long to be able to give gorgeous banquets. I have, on the contrary, led a happier existence with plain living and ordinary fare than all the followers of Apicius, with their elaborate dainties. So-called *convivia*, which are but vulgar bouts, sinning against sobriety and good manners, have always been repugnant to me. I have ever felt that it was irksome and profitless to invite others to such affairs, and not less so to be bidden to them myself. On the other hand, the pleasure of dining with one's friends is so great that nothing has ever given me more delight than their unexpected arrival, nor have I ever willingly sat down to table without a companion. Nothing displeases me more than display, for not only is it bad in itself, and opposed to humility, but it is troublesome and distracting.

I struggled in my younger days with a keen but constant and pure attachment, and would have struggled with it longer had not the sinking flame been extinguished by death—premature and bitter, but salutary. I should be glad to be able to say that I had always been entirely free from irregular desires, but I should lie if I did so. I can, however, conscientiously claim that, although I may have been carried away by the fire of youth or by my ardent temperament, I have always abhorred such sins from the depths of my soul. As I approached the age of forty, while my powers were unimpaired and my passions were still strong, I not only abruptly threw off my bad habits, but even the very recollection of them, as if I had never looked upon a woman. This I mention as among the greatest of my blessings, and I render thanks to God, who freed me, while still sound and vigorous, from a disgusting slavery which had always been hateful to me. But let us turn to other matters.

I have taken pride in others, never in myself, and however insignificant I may have been, I have always been still less important in my own judgment. My anger has very often injured myself, but never others. I have always been most desirous of honourable friendships, and have faithfully cherished them. I make this boast without fear, since I am confident that I speak truly. While I am very prone to take offence, I am equally quick to forget injuries, and have a memory tenacious of benefits. In my familiar associations with kings and princes, and in my friendship with noble personages, my good fortune has been such as to excite envy. But it is the cruel fate of those who are growing old that they can commonly only weep for friends who have passed away. The greatest kings of this age have loved and courted me. They may know why; I certainly do not.

With some of them I was on such terms that they seemed in a certain sense my guests rather than I theirs; their lofty position in no way embarrassing me, but, on the contrary, bringing with it many advantages. I fled, however, from many of those to whom I was greatly attached; and such was my innate longing for liberty, that I studiously avoided those whose very name seemed incompatible with the freedom that I loved.

I possessed a well-balanced rather than a keen intellect, one prone to all kinds of good and wholesome study, but especially inclined to moral philosophy and the art of poetry. The latter, indeed, I neglected as time went on, and took delight in sacred literature. Finding in that a hidden sweetness which I had once esteemed but lightly, I came to regard the works of the poets as only amenities. Among the many subjects which interested me, I dwelt especially upon antiquity, for our own age has always repelled me, so that, had it not been for the love of those dear to me, I should have preferred to have been born in any other period than our own. In order to forget my own time, I have constantly striven to place myself in spirit in other ages, and consequently I delighted in history; not that the conflicting statements did not offend me, but when in doubt I accepted what appeared to me most probable, or yielded to the authority of the writer.

My style, as many claimed, was clear and forcible; but to me it seemed weak and obscure. In ordinary conversation with friends, or with those about me, I never gave any thought to my language, and I have always wondered that Augustus Caesar should have taken such pains in this respect. When, however, the subject itself, or the place or listener, seemed to demand it, I gave some attention to style, with what success I cannot pretend to say; let them judge in whose presence I

spoke. If only I have lived well, it matters little to me
how I talked. Mere elegance of language can produce
at best but an empty renown.

My life up to the present has, either through fate or
my own choice, fallen into the following divisions. A part
only of my first year was spent at Arezzo, where I first
saw the light. The six following years were, owing to
the recall of my mother from exile, spent upon my father's estate in Ancisa, about fourteen miles above Florence. I passed my eighth year at Pisa, the ninth and following years in Farther Gaul, at Avignon, on the left
bank of the Rhone, where the Roman pontiff holds
and has long held the Church of Christ in shameful
exile. . . .

On the windy banks of the river Rhone I spent my
boyhood, guided by my parents, and then, guided by my
own fancies, the whole of my youth. Yet there were long
intervals spent elsewhere, for I first passed four years
at the little town of Carpentras, somewhat to the east
of Avignon: in these two places I learned as much of
grammar, logic, and rhetoric as my age permitted, or
rather, as much as it is customary to teach in school: how
little that is, dear reader, thou knowest. I then set out
for Montpellier to study law, and spent four years there,
then three at Bologna. I heard the whole body of the
civil law, and would, as many thought, have distinguished myself later, had I but continued my studies. I
gave up the subject altogether, however, so soon as it
was no longer necessary to consult the wishes of my
parents. My reason was that, although the dignity of
the law, which is doubtless very great, and especially
the numerous references it contains to Roman antiquity,
did not fail to delight me, I felt it to be habitually de-
graded by those who practise it. It went against me
painfully to acquire an art which I would not practise

dishonestly, and could hardly hope to exercise otherwise. Had I made the latter attempt, my scrupulousness would doubtless have been ascribed to simplicity.

So at the age of two and twenty I returned home. I call my place of exile home, Avignon, where I had been since childhood; for habit has almost the potency of nature itself. I had already begun to be known there, and my friendship was sought by prominent men; wherefore I cannot say. I confess this is now a source of surprise to me, although it seemed natural enough at an age when we are used to regard ourselves as worthy of the highest respect. I was courted first and foremost by that very distinguished and noble family, the Colonnesi, who, at that period, adorned the Roman Curia with their presence. However it might be now, I was at that time certainly quite unworthy of the esteem in which I was held by them. . . .

About this time, a youthful desire impelled me to visit France and Germany. While I invented certain reasons to satisfy my elders of the propriety of the journey, the real explanation was a great inclination and longing to see new sights. I first visited Paris, as I was anxious to discover what was true and what fabulous in the accounts I had heard of that city. On my return from this journey I went to Rome, which I had since my infancy ardently desired to visit. There I soon came to venerate Stephano, the noble head of the family of the Colonnesi, like some ancient hero, and was in turn treated by him in every respect like a son. . . .

On my return, since I experienced a deep-seated and innate repugnance to town life, especially in that disgusting city of Avignon which I heartily abhorred, I sought some means of escape. I fortunately discovered, about fifteen miles from Avignon, a delightful valley, narrow and secluded, called Vaucluse, where the Sorgue, the prince of streams, takes its rise. Captivated by the charms of the place, I transferred thither myself and my books. Were I to describe what I did there during many years, it would prove a long story. Indeed, almost every bit of writing which I have put forth was either accomplished or begun, or at least conceived, there, and my undertakings have been so numerous that they still continue to vex and weary me. My mind, like my body, is characterized by a certain versatility and readiness, rather than by strength, so that many tasks that were easy of conception have been given up by reason of the difficulty of their execution. . . .

While I was wandering in those mountains upon a Friday in Holy Week, the strong desire seized me to write an epic in an heroic strain, taking as my theme Scipio Africanus the Great, who had, strange to say, been dear to me from my childhood. But although I began the execution of this project with enthusiasm, I straightway abandoned it, owing to a variety of distractions. The poem was, however, christened *Africa*, from the name of its hero, and, whether from his fortunes or mine, it did not fail to arouse the interest of many before they had seen it.

While leading a leisurely existence in this region, I received, remarkable as it may seem, upon one and the same day, letters both from the Senate at Rome and the chancellor of the University of Paris, pressing me to appear in Rome and Paris, respectively, to receive the poet's crown of laurel. In my youthful elation I convinced myself that I was quite worthy of this honour; the recognition came from eminent judges, and I accepted their verdict rather than that of my own better judgment. I hesitated for a time which I should give ear to, and sent a letter to Cardinal Giovanni Colonna, of whom I have already spoken, asking his opinion. He was so near that, although I wrote late in the day, I received his reply before the third hour on the morrow. I followed his advice, and recognized the claims of Rome as superior to all others. . . .

So I decided, first to visit Naples, and that celebrated king and philosopher, Robert, who was not more distinguished as a ruler than as a man of culture. He was, indeed, the only monarch of our age who was the friend at once of learning and of virtue, and I trusted that he might correct such things as he found to criticize in my work. The way in which he received and welcomed me is a source of astonishment to me now, and, I doubt not, to the reader also, if he happens to know anything of the matter. Having learned the reason of my coming, the king seemed mightily pleased. He was gratified, doubtless, by my youthful faith in him, and felt, perhaps, that he shared in a way the glory of my coronation, since I had chosen him from all others as the only suitable critic. After talking over a great many things, I showed him my *Africa*, which so delighted him that he asked that it might be dedicated to him in consideration of a handsome reward. This was a request that I could not well refuse, nor, indeed, would I have wished to refuse it, had it been in my power. He then fixed a day upon which we could consider the object of my visit. This occupied us from noon until evening, and the time proving too short, on account of the many matters which arose for discussion, we passed the two following days in the same manner. Having thus tested my poor attainments for three days, the king at last pronounced me worthy of the laurel. He offered to bestow that honour upon me at Naples, and urged me to consent to receive it there, but my veneration for Rome prevailed over the insistence of even so great a monarch as Robert. At length, seeing that I was inflexible in my purpose, he sent me on my way accompanied by royal messengers and letters to the Roman Senate, in which he gave enthusiastic expression to his flattering opinion of me. This royal estimate was, indeed, quite in accord with that of many others, and especially with my own, but today I cannot approve either his or my own verdict. In his case, affection and the natural partiality to youth were stronger than his devotion to truth.

On arriving at Rome, I continued, in spite of my unworthiness, to rely upon the judgment of so eminent a critic, and, to the great delight of the Romans who were present, I who had been hitherto a simple student received the laurel crown. . . .

On leaving Rome, I went to Parma, and spent some time with the members of the house of Correggio, who, while they were most kind and generous towards me, agreed but ill among themselves. They governed Parma, however, in a way unknown to that city within the memory of man, and the like of which it will hardly again enjoy in this present age. . . .

I had already passed my thirty-fourth year when I returned thence to the Fountain of the Sorgue, and to my transalpine solitude. I had made a long stay both in Parma and Verona, and everywhere I had, I am thankful to say, been treated with much greater esteem than I merited.

Some time after this, my growing reputation procured for me the goodwill of a most excellent man, Giacomo the Younger, of Carrara, whose equal I do not know among the rulers of his time. For years he wearied me with messengers and letters when I was beyond the Alps, and with his petitions whenever I happened to be in Italy, urging me to accept his friendship. . . . I appeared, though tardily, at Padua, where I was received by him of illustrious memory, not as a mortal, but as the blessed are greeted in heaven—with such delight and such unspeakable affection and esteem, that I cannot adequately describe my welcome in words, and must, therefore, be silent. Among other things, learning that I had led a clerical life from boyhood, he had me made a canon of Padua, in order to bind me the closer to himself and his city. In fine, had his life been spared, I should have found there an end to all my wanderings. But alas! nothing mortal is enduring, and there is nothing sweet which does not presently end in bitterness. Scarcely two years was he spared to me, to his country, and to the world. . . .

I returned to Gaul, not so much from a desire to see again what I had already beheld a thousand times, as from the hope, common to the afflicted, of coming to terms with my misfortunes by a change of scene.

From *Petrarch, the First Modern Scholar and Man of Letters,* trans. J. R. Robinson and H. W. Rolfe (New York and London: Putnam, 1898).

Charles the Bold
and the Fall of the House of Burgundy

PHILIPPE DE COMMINES

Fifteenth century

I SAW a seal ring of his [Duke Charles the Bold], after his death, at Milan, with his arms cut curiously upon a sardonyx that I have often seen him wear in a riband at his breast, which was sold at Milan for two ducats, and had been stolen from him by a varlet that waited on him in his chamber. I have often seen the duke dressed

and undressed in great state and formality, and by very
great persons; but, at his last hour, all this pomp and
magnificence ceased, and both he and his family perished (as you have heard already) on the very spot
where he had delivered up the constable not long before, out of a base and avaricious motive; but may God
forgive him! I have known him a powerful and honourable prince, in as great esteem and as much courted by
his neighbours (when his affairs were in a prosperous
condition), as any prince in Europe, and perhaps more
so; and I cannot conceive what should have provoked
God Almighty's displeasure so highly against him, unless
it was his self-love and arrogance, in attributing all the
success of his enterprises, and all the renown he ever
acquired, to his own wisdom and conduct, without
ascribing anything to God: yet, to speak truth, he was
endowed with many good qualities. No prince ever had
a greater desire to entertain young noblemen than he;
or was more careful of their education. His presents and
bounty were never profuse and extravagant, because he
gave to many, and wished everybody should taste of
his generosity. No prince was ever more easy of access
to his servants and subjects. Whilst I was in his service
he was never cruel, but a little before his death he became so, which was an infallible sign of the shortness of
his life. He was very splendid and pompous in his dress,
and in everything else, and, indeed, a little too much. He
paid great honours to all ambassadors and foreigners,
and entertained them nobly. His ambitious desire of
glory was insatiable, and it was that which more than
any other motive induced him to engage eternally in
wars. He earnestly desired to imitate the old kings and
heroes of antiquity, who are still so much talked of in
the world, and his courage was equal to that of any
prince of his time.

But all his designs and imaginations were vain, and turned afterwards to his own dishonour and confusion, for it is the conquerors and not the conquered that win renown. I cannot easily determine towards whom God Almighty showed his anger most, whether towards him who died suddenly without pain or sickness in the field of battle, or towards his subjects, who never enjoyed peace after his death, but were continually involved in wars against which they were not able to maintain themselves, upon account of the civil dissensions and cruel animosities that arose among them; and that which was the most insupportable was, that the very people to whom they were now indebted for their defence and preservation, were the Germans, who were strangers, and not long since had been their enemies. In short, after the duke's death, there was not a man who wished them to prosper, whoever defended them. And by the management of their affairs, their understanding seemed to be as much infatuated as their master's was just before his death; for they rejected all good counsel, and pursued such methods as directly tended to their destruction; and they are still in great danger of a relapse into calamity, and it will be well if it turn not in the end to their utter ruin.

I am partly of the opinion of those who maintain that God gives princes, as He in His wisdom thinks fit, to punish or chastise their subjects: and He disposes the affections of subjects to their princes, as He has determined to exalt or depress them. Just so it has pleased Him to deal with the house of Burgundy; for after a long series of riches and prosperity, and sixscore years' peace under three illustrious princes, predecessors to Duke Charles (all of them of great prudence and discretion), it pleased God to send this Duke Charles, who continually involved them in bloody wars, as well winter as summer, to their great affliction and expense, in which most of their richest and stoutest men were either killed or taken prisoners. Their misfortunes began at the siege of Nuz, and continued for three or four battles successively, to the very hour of his death; so much so, that at the last, the whole strength of the country was destroyed, and all were killed or taken prisoners who had any zeal or affection for the house of Burgundy, or power to defend the state and dignity of that family; so that in a manner their losses equalled, if they did not overbalance, their former prosperity; for as I had seen these princes puissant, rich, and honourable, so it fared with their subjects: for I think I have seen and known the greatest part of Europe, yet I never knew any province or country, though of a larger extent, so abounding in money, so extravagantly fine in their furniture, so sumptuous in their buildings, so profuse in their expenses, so luxurious in their feasts and entertainments, and so prodigal in all respects, as the subjects of these princes in my time; and if any think I have exaggerated, others who lived in my time will be of opinion that I have rather said too little.

But it pleased God, at one blow, to subvert this great and sumptuous edifice, and ruin this powerful and illustrious family, which had maintained and bred up so many brave men, and had acquired such mighty honour and renown far and near, by so many victo ies and successful enterprises, as none of all its neighbouring states could pretend to boast of. A hundred and twenty years it continued in this flourishing condition, by the grace of God; all its neighbours having, in the meantime, been involved in troubles and commotions, and all of them applying to it for succour or protection: to wit, France, England, and Spain, as you have seen by experience of our master the king of France, who in his minority, and during the reign of Charles VII, his father, retired to this court, where he lived six years, and was nobly entertained all that time by Duke Philip the Good. Out of England I saw there also two of King Edward's brothers, the dukes of Clarence and Gloucester (the last of whom was afterwards called King Richard the Third); and of the house of Lancaster, the whole family or very near, with all their party. In short, I have seen this family in all respects the most flourishing and celebrated of any in Christendom: and then, in a short space of time, it was quite ruined and turned upside down, and left the most desolate and miserable of any house in Europe, as regards both prince and subjects. Such changes and revolutions of states and kingdoms, God in His providence has wrought before we were born, and will do again when we are dead; for this is a certain maxim, that the prosperity or adversity of princes depends wholly on His divine disposal.

From *Memoirs of Philippe de Commines*, A. R. Scoble, ed. (London: Bell, 1896).

IV. THE
WORLD PICTURE

The Frontiers of Europe: Conquest and Assimilation of Peoples

Anglo-Saxons and Normans

WILLIAM OF MALMESBURY

Twelfth century

THIS was a fatal day to England, a melancholy havoc of our dear country, through its change of masters [1066]. For it had long since adopted the manners of the Angles, which had been very various according to the times: for in the first years of their arrival, they were barbarians in their look and manners, warlike in their usages, heathens in their rites; but, after embracing the faith of Christ, by degrees, and in process of time, from the peace they enjoyed, regarding arms only in a secondary light, they gave their whole attention to religion. . . . Many during their whole lives in outward appearance only embraced the present world, in order that they might exhaust their treasures on the poor, or divide them amongst monasteries. What shall I say of the multitudes of bishops, hermits, and abbats? Does not the whole island blaze with such numerous relics of

its natives, that you can scarcely pass a village of any
consequence but you hear the name of some new saint,
besides the numbers of whom all notices have perished
through the want of records? Nevertheless, in process of
time, the desire after literature and religion had decayed,
for several years before the arrival of the Normans. The
clergy, contented with a very slight degree of learning,
could scarcely stammer out the words of the sacraments:
and a person who understood grammar was an object
of wonder and astonishment. The monks mocked the
rule of their order by fine vestments, and the use of
every kind of food. The nobility, given up to luxury and
wantonness, went not to church in the morning after
the manner of Christians, but merely, in a careless manner, heard matins and masses from a hurrying priest in
their chambers, amid the blandishments of their wives.
. . . Drinking in parties was a universal practice, in
which occupation they passed entire nights as well as
days. They consumed their whole substance in mean
and despicable houses; unlike the Normans and French,
who, in noble and splendid mansions, lived with frugality. The vices attendant on drunkenness, which enervate
the human mind, followed; hence it arose that engaging
William, more with rashness, and precipitate fury, than
military skill, they doomed themselves and their country
to slavery, by one, and that an easy, victory. "For nothing is less effective than rashness; and what begins with
violence, quickly ceases, or is repelled." In fine, the English, at that time, wore short garments reaching to the
midknee; they had their hair cropped; their beards
shaven; their arms laden with golden bracelets; their
skin adorned with punctured designs. They were accustomed to eat till they became surfeited, and to drink
till they were sick. These latter qualities they imparted
to their conquerors; as to the rest, they adopted their

manners. I would not, however, have these bad propensities universally ascribed to the English. I know that many of the clergy, at that day, trod the path of sanctity, by a blameless life; I know that many of the laity, of all ranks and conditions, in this nation, were well-pleasing to God. . . .

Moreover, the Normans, that I may speak of them also, were at that time, and are even now, proudly apparelled, delicate in their food, but not excessive. They are a race inured to war, and can hardly live without it; fierce in rushing against the enemy; and where strength fails of success, ready to use stratagem, or to corrupt by bribery. As I have related, they live in large edifices with economy; envy their equals; wish to excel their superiors; and plunder their subjects, though they defend them from others; they are faithful to their lords, though a slight offence renders them perfidious. They weigh treachery by its chance of success, and change their sentiments with money. They are, however, the kindest of nations, and they esteem strangers worthy of equal honour with themselves. They also intermarry with their vassals. They revived, by their arrival, the observances of religion, which were everywhere grown lifeless in England. You might see churches rise in every village, and monasteries in the towns and cities built after a style unknown before; you might behold the country flourishing with renovated rites; so that each wealthy man accounted that day lost to him, which he had neglected to signalize by some magnificent action.

From *Chronicle*, trans. J. A. Giles.

The Character and Customs of the Irish

GIRALDUS CAMBRENSIS

Twelfth century

I HAVE considered it not superfluous to give a short account of the condition of this nation, both bodily and mentally; I mean their state of cultivation, both interior and exterior. This people are not tenderly nursed from their birth, as others are; for besides the rude fare they receive from their parents, which is only just sufficient for their sustenance, as to the rest, almost all is left to nature. They are not placed in cradles, or swathed, nor are their tender limbs either fomented by constant bathings, or adjusted with art. For the midwives make no use of warm water, nor raise their noses, nor depress the face, nor stretch the legs; but nature alone, with very slight aids from art, disposes and adjusts the limbs to which she has given birth, just as she pleases. As if to prove that what she is able to form she does not cease to shape also, she gives growth and proportions to these people, until they arrive at perfect vigour, tall and handsome in person, and with agreeable and ruddy countenances. But although they are richly endowed with the gifts of nature, their want of civilization, shown both in their dress and mental culture, makes them a barbarous people. For they wear but little woollen, and nearly all they use is black, that being the colour of the sheep in this country. Their clothes are also made after a barbarous fashion.

Their custom is to wear small, close-fitting hoods, hanging below the shoulders a cubit's length, and generally made of parti-coloured strips sewn together. Under these, they use woollen rugs instead of cloaks, with breeches and hose of one piece, or hose and breeches joined together, which are usually dyed of some colour. Likewise, in riding, they neither use saddles, nor boots, nor spurs, but only carry a rod in their hand, having a crook at the upper end, with which they both urge forward and guide their horses. They use reins which serve the purpose both of a bridle and a bit, and do not prevent the horses from feeding, as they always live on grass. Moreover, they go to battle without armour, considering it a burthen and esteeming it brave and honourable to fight without it. . . .

The Irish are a rude people, subsisting on the produce of their cattle only, and living themselves like beasts—a people that has not yet departed from the primitive habits of pastoral life. In the common course of things, mankind progresses from the forest to the field, from the field to the town, and to the social condition of citizens; but this nation, holding agricultural labour in contempt, and little coveting the wealth of towns, as well as being exceedingly averse to civil institutions, lead the same life their fathers did in the woods and open pastures, neither willing to abandon their old habits nor learn anything new. They, therefore, only make patches of tillage; their pastures are short of herbage; cultivation is very rare, and there is scarcely any land sown. This want of tilled fields arises from the neglect of those who should cultivate them; for there are large tracts which are naturally fertile and productive. The whole habits of the people are contrary to agricultural pursuits, so that the rich glebe is barren for want of husbandmen, the fields demanding labour which is not forthcoming.

Very few sorts of fruit trees are found in this country, a defect arising not from the nature of the soil, but from want of industry in planting them; for the lazy husband-man does not take the trouble to plant the foreign sorts which would grow very well here. . . .

There are also veins of various kinds of metals rami-fying in the bowels of the earth, which, from the same idle habits, are not worked and turned to account. Even gold, which the people require in large quantities, and still covet in a way that speaks their Spanish origin, is brought here by the merchants who traverse the ocean for the purposes of commerce. They neither employ themselves in the manufacture of flax or wool, nor in any kind of trade or mechanical art; but abandoning them-selves to idleness, and immersed in sloth, their greatest delight is to be exempt from toil, their richest possession the enjoyment of liberty.

This people, then, is truly barbarous, being not only barbarous in their dress, but suffering their hair and beards (*barbis*) to grow enormously in an uncouth man-ner, just like the modern fashion recently introduced; indeed, all their habits are barbarisms. But habits are formed by mutual intercourse; and as this people in-habit a country so remote from the rest of the world, and lying at its farthest extremity, forming, as it were, another world, and are thus secluded from civilized na-tions, they learn nothing, and practise nothing but the barbarism in which they are born and bred, and which sticks to them like a second nature. Whatever natural gifts they possess are excellent, in whatever requires industry they are worthless. . . .

The faith having been planted in the island from the time of St. Patrick, so many ages ago, and propagated almost ever since, it is wonderful that this nation should remain to this day so very ignorant of the rudiments of

Christianity. It is indeed a most filthy race, a race sunk in vice, a race more ignorant than all other nations of the first principles of the faith. Hitherto they neither pay tithes nor first fruits; they do not contract marriages, nor shun incestuous connections; they frequent not the church of God with proper reverence. Nay, what is most detestable, and not only contrary to the gospel, but to everything that is right, in many parts of Ireland brothers (I will not say marry) seduce and debauch the wives of their brothers deceased, and have incestuous intercourse with them; adhering in this to the letter, and not to the spirit, of the Old Testament; and following the example of men of old in their vices more willingly than in their virtues.

They are given to treachery more than any other nation, and never keep the faith they have pledged, neither shame nor fear withholding them from constantly violating the most solemn obligations, which, when entered into with themselves, they are above all things anxious to have observed. So that, when you have used the utmost precaution, when you have been most vigilant, for your own security and safety, by requiring oaths and hostages, by treaties of alliance firmly made, and by benefits of all kinds conferred, then begins your time to fear; for then especially their treachery is awake, when they suppose that, relying on the fulness of your security, you are off your guard. That is the moment for them to fly to their citadel of wickedness, turn against you their weapons of deceit, and endeavour to do you injury, by taking the opportunity of catching you unawares. . . .

It must be observed also, that the men who enjoy ecclesiastical immunity, and are called ecclesiastical men, although they be laics, and have wives, and wear long hair hanging down below their shoulders, but only do

not bear arms, wear for their protection, by authority of
the pope, fillets on the crown of their heads, as a mark
of distinction. Moreover, these people, who have customs so very different from others, and so opposite to
them, on making signs either with the hands or the head,
beckon when they mean that you should go away, and
nod backward as often as they wish to be rid of you.
Likewise, in this nation, the men pass their water sitting,
the women standing. They are also prone to the failing
of jealousy beyond any other nation. The women, also,
as well as the men, ride astride, with their legs stuck
out on each side of the horse.

We come now to the clerical order. The clergy, then,
of this country are commendable enough for their piety;
and among many other virtues in which they excel, are
especially eminent for that of continence. They also perform with great regularity the services of the psalms,
hours, lessons, and prayers, and, confining themselves to
the precincts of the churches, employ their whole time in
the offices to which they are appointed. They also pay
due attention to the rules of abstinence and a spare diet,
the greatest part of them fasting almost every day till
dusk, when by singing complines they have finished the
offices of the several hours for the day. Would that after
these long fasts, they were as sober as they are serious, as
true as they are severe, as pure as they are enduring,
such in reality as they are in appearance. But among so
many thousands you will scarcely find one who, after his
devotion to long fastings and prayers, does not make up
by night for his privations during the day by the enormous quantities of wine and other liquors in which he
indulges more than is becoming.

Dividing the day of twenty-four hours into two equal
parts, they devote the hours of light to spiritual offices,
and those of night to the flesh; so that in the light they

apply themselves to the works of the light, and in the dark they turn to the works of darkness. Hence it may be considered almost a miracle, that where wine has the dominion lust does not reign also. This appears to have been thought difficult by St. Jerome; still more so by the apostle; one of whom forbids men to be drunken with wine, wherein there is excess: the other teaches that the belly, when it is inflamed by drink, easily vents itself in lust.

There are, however, some among the clergy who are most excellent men, and have no leaven of impurity. Indeed this people are intemperate in all their actions, and most vehement in all their feelings. Thus the bad are bad indeed—there are nowhere worse; and than the good you cannot find better. But there is not much wheat among the oats and the tares. Many, you find, are called, but few chosen: there is very little grain, but much chaff.

From *Topography of Ireland*, trans. T. Wright (London: Bell, 1881).

The Conversion and Subjugation of the Slavs

HELMOLD

Twelfth century

SINCE he was confident that he was called by Heaven to the work of the Gospel, Vicelin went [c. 1126] to the venerable Adalbero, archbishop of Hamburg, who happened to be staying in Bremen, to reveal to him the purpose of his heart. Not a little delighted, Adalbero approved of his purpose and commissioned him [to preach] the word of God among the Slavic folk and in his name to extirpate idolatry. Vicelin immediately began the journey into the land of the Slavs, accompanied by the worthy priests, Rotholph of Hildesheim and Ludolph, a canon of Verden, who had devoted themselves to the work of this ministry. And they went together to seek Prince Henry in the city of Lübeck and asked that permission be given them to preach the name of the Lord. In the presence of his people without hesitation he raised these most worthy men to great honours and gave them the church at Lübeck that they might live in a secure abode with him and carry on the work of God. . . .

Since the illustrious Caesar Lothar and his very worthy consort Richenza were most devoutly solicitous for the divine service, the priest of Christ, Vicelin, went to him while he was tarrying at Bardowiek [1131] and suggested to him that he should provide for the Slavic race some means of salvation in keeping with the power that had been bestowed on him by Heaven. Vicelin, moreover, made known to him that there is in the province of Wagria a mountain adapted for the erection of a royal castle for the protection of the land. . . . The emperor attended to the prudent counsel of the priest and sent competent men to determine the fitness of the mountain. On being assured by the reports of the messengers, he crossed the river [Elbe] and went into the land of the Slavs to the place appointed. He ordered all the Nordalbingian people to come together for the building of the castle [Segeberg]. In obedience to the emperor, the princes of the Slavs also were present, taking part in the business, but with great sadness, for they discerned that the structure was being erected for their oppression. . . .

Matters having been arranged in this manner, Adolph

[II, Count of Holstein] began to rebuild [1143] the fortress at Segeberg and girded it with a wall. As the land was without inhabitants, he sent messengers into all parts, namely, to Flanders and Holland, to Utrecht, Westphalia, and Frisia, proclaiming that whosoever were in straits for lack of fields should come with their families and receive a very good land—spacious land, rich in crops, abounding in fish and flesh and exceeding good pasturage. To the Holzatians and Sturmarians he said: "Have you not subjugated the land of the Slavs and bought it with the blood of your brothers and fathers? Why, then, are you the last to enter into possession of it? Be the first to go over into a delectable land and inhabit it and partake of its delights, for the best of it is due you who have wrested it from the hands of the enemy."

An innumerable multitude of different peoples rose up at this call and they came with their families and their goods into the land of Wagria to Count Adolph that they might possess the country which he had promised them. . . .

The bishop [Gerold of Bremen] returned to Wagria [1155], taking with him his brother, the abbot of Riddagshausen, and went to Oldenburg to solemnize the feast of the Epiphany in the cathedral city. The city was entirely deserted, having neither walls nor an inhabitant, only a little chapel which Vicelin of saintly memory had erected there. In the bitterest cold, amid piles of snow, we went through the mass there. Besides Pribislav and a few others, not a Slav attended. After the sacred mysteries were finished, Pribislav asked us to come to his house which was in a remoter town. He received us with much gladness and prepared a sumptuous repast for us. Twenty dishes of food loaded the table set before us. There I learned from experience what before

I knew by report, that no people is more distinguished in its regard for hospitality than the Slavs. . . .

After staying that night and the following day and night with the ruler, we crossed [1156] into farther Slavia to be the guests of an influential man, Thessemar, who had invited us. It happened that on our journey we came into a forest, which is the only one in that country, for it all stretches out in a plain. Among very old trees we saw there the sacred oaks which had been consecrated to the god of that land, Prove. There was a courtyard about them and a fence very carefully constructed of wood and having two gates. For, besides the household gods and the idols with which each village abounded, that place was the sanctuary of the whole land for which a flamen and feast days and a variety of sacrificial rites had been appointed. On the second weekday the people of the land were wont to assemble there for holding court with the ruler and with the flamen. Entrance to this courtyard was forbidden to all, except only to the priest and to those wishing to make sacrifices, or to those in danger of death, because they were never to be denied asylum. For the Slavs show such reverence for their holy things that they do not allow the neighbourhood of a fane to be defiled by blood even in time of war. They admit oaths with the greatest reluctance; for among the Slavs to swear is, as it were, to forswear oneself, because of the avenging wrath of the gods. The Slavs have many forms of idol worship, for they are not all agreed upon the same superstitious customs. Some display in the temples fantastically formed images, as, for example, the idol at Plön, the name of which is Pogada; other deities live in the woods and groves, like Prove, the god of Oldenburg; of these no effigies are fashioned. They also carve out many deities with two, three, or more heads. But they do not deny that there is among the multiform godheads to whom they attribute plains and woods, sorrows and joys, one god in the heavens ruling over the others. They hold that he, the all-powerful one, looks only after heavenly matters; that the others, discharging the duties assigned to them in obedience to him, proceeded from his blood; and that one excels another in the measure that he is nearer to this god of gods.

When we came to that wood and place of profanation, the bishop exhorted us to proceed energetically to the destruction of the grove. Leaping from his horse, he himself with his staff broke in pieces the decorated fronts of the gates and, entering the courtyard, we heaped up all the hedging of the enclosure about those sacred trees and made a pyre of the heap of wood by setting fire to it, not, however, without fear that perchance we might be overwhelmed in a tumult of the inhabitants. But we were protected by heaven. After this we betook ourselves to the lodge where Thessemar received us with great pomp. Still the cups of the Slavs were neither sweet nor pleasing to us because we saw the shackles and the diverse kinds of instruments of torture which they were wont to use on the Christians brought here from Denmark. We saw there priests of the Lord, emaciated by their long detention in captivity, whom the bishop could not help either by force or by prayer.

The following Lord's day all the people of the land convened in the market place at Lübeck and the lord bishop came and exhorted the assemblage to give up their idols and worship the one God who is in heaven, to receive the grace of baptism and renounce their evil works; namely, the plundering and killing of Christians. And when he had finished speaking to the congregation, Pribislav, with the consent of the others, said: "Your words, O venerable prelate, are the words of God and are meet for our salvation. But how shall we, ensnared by so many evils, enter upon this way? In order that you may understand our affliction, hear patiently my words, because the people whom you see are your people, and it is proper for us to make known to you our need. Then it will be reasonable for you to pity us. Your princes rage against us with such severity that, because of the taxes and most burdensome services, death is better for us than life. Behold, this year we, the inhabitants of this tiny place, have paid the duke in all a thousand marks, so many hundred besides to the count, and yet we are not through but every day we are outdone and oppressed even to the point of exhaustion. How, therefore, shall we, for whom flight is a matter of daily consideration, be free to build churches for this new religion and to receive baptism? Were there but a place to which we could flee! On crossing the Trave, behold, like ruin is there; on coming to the Peene River, it is not less there. What remains, therefore, but to leave the land and take to the sea and live with the waves? Or what fault is it of ours, if, driven from our fatherland, we have troubled the sea and got our livelihood by plunder of the Danes or the merchants who fare the sea? Will not this be the fault of the princes who are hounding us?"

To these words the lord bishop replied: "That our princes have hitherto used your people ill is not to be wondered at, for they do not think that they do much wrong to those who are worshippers of idols and to those who are without God. Nay, rather return to the Christian worship and subject yourselves to your Creator before whom they stoop who bear up the world. Do not the Saxons and the other peoples who bear the Christian name live in tranquillity, content with what is legitimately theirs? Indeed, as you alone differ from the religion of all, so you are subject to the plundering of all."

And Pribislav said: "If it pleases the lord duke and you that we have the same mode of worship as the count, let the rights of the Saxons in respect of property and taxes be extended to us and we shall willingly be Christians, build churches, and pay our tithes." . . .

The work of God thus increased in the land of Wagria and the count and the bishop co-operated one with the other. About this time the count rebuilt the stronghold at Plön and made there a city and market place. The Slavs who lived in the villages round about withdrew and Saxons came and dwelt there; and the Slavs little by little failed in the land.

From *Chronicle of the Slavs*, trans. F. J. Tschan (New York: Columbia University Press, 1935).

The German Push to the East

Thirteenth century

CONCERNING BROTHER HERMANN VON SALZA, FOURTH MASTER OF THE GERMAN HOUSE

THIS powerful hero received God's blessing in many manifestations of grace. In all his actions he was eloquent, wise, far-seeing, just, honourable, and kind. When he saw the order, as master of which the brothers had elected him, in such a miserable condition, he said with a sigh: "Oh, Heavenly God, I would gladly lose an eye if only the order, in my time, would increase enough so that it could equip ten knightly Brothers." Thus he prayed fervently. And You, most gentle Christ, who are always willing to fulfil the wishes of the just who beseech You, what did You do? Did You let his prayer go unheard? No, Your sweet kindness gave him all he prayed for: while he was master, the order increased in wealth and power so greatly that after his death it numbered two thousand Brothers of German origin and of excellent manly strength . . .

Master Hermann also acquired for his order the most useful and best papal and imperial privileges. Also the order was given many a territory in Apulia, Greece, Cilicia, and Germany, Transylvania, Livonia, and Prussia . . .

God loved Master Hermann because he obeyed His orders, and He therefore helped him to rise high. All people loved him; pope and emperor, kings, dukes, famous princes, and other courageous lords were drawn to Master Hermann to such an extent that all his wishes were fulfilled to the benefit, honour, and advantage of the order.

HOW THE PRUSSIANS DEVASTATED THE LANDS OF DUKE CONRAD OF MASOVIA AND KUJAVIA

The Prussians often did much harm to these lands. They burned, destroyed, murdered men and drove women and children into eternal slavery. And if a pregnant woman could not keep up with their army, they killed her, together with the unborn child. They tore children from their mothers' arms and impaled them on fence poles where the little ones died in great misery, kicking and screaming. They devastated the duke's lands to such an extent that, of all the weaker and stronger fortresses of his territory, only Plock on the Vistula was left to him.

The heathen also destroyed about two hundred and fifty parish houses and many beautiful monasteries in which monks, nuns, and the secular clergy had served

God. The heathen stormed about everywhere like mad-men. They killed the priests before their altars while the body and blood of our Lord Jesus Christ were devoutly being consecrated. The heathen threw God upon the ground to the outrage and infamy of the sacred object, and stamped upon the sacred body of Christ and His blood in their fury. One could further see the unclean heathen stealing in their hate chalices, lamps, and all sorts of sacred vessels. It was pitiful to see how they treated not only the worldly virgins but also those de-voted to God. The devilish crowd dragged them out of the cloisters by force and, to their great distress of heart, used them for their disgusting lust.

THE BROTHERS OF THE SWORD

When Duke Conrad saw his land so miserably de-stroyed, and he was not able to protect it, he conferred with Bishop Christian of Prussia and the great nobles of his court about what would help him and them most. He thus created for the protection of his country the Brotherhood of the Knights of Christ. They wore white tunics with red swords and stars on them. (The duke gave the order the castle of Dobrin on the Vistula.)

HOW THE LANDS OF PRUSSIA AND KULM WERE GIVEN TO THE BROTHERS OF THE ORDER OF THE GERMAN HOUSE

The fame of the heroic deeds of the Teutonic order spread so far that Conrad of Masovia heard of it. Then the idea came to him—and the spirit of God moved him so that he did not relinquish it again—to invite these Brothers for the protection of his country; to ask them whether they could not, with their force, free the Chris-tians from their heathen oppressors since the Brothers of the Sword were unable to do so.

IMPERIAL CONFIRMATION OF THE GIFT OF LAND OF
KULM TO THE TEUTONIC ORDER (1226)

In the name of the holy and undivided Trinity, Amen.
Frederick II, by the grace of God, emperor of the Romans, Augustus, king of Jerusalem and Sicily. God has
raised our emperorship over all kings of the earth, and
expanded the sphere of our power over different zones
that His name may be magnified in this world and the
faith be spread among the heathen peoples. Just as He
created the Holy Roman Empire for the preaching of
the gospel, so likewise we must turn our care and attention to the conquest and conversion of the heathen. . . .

For this reason we make known to and inform with
this proclamation all living and future members of our
empire: Brother Hermann, the worthy master of the
Holy German Hospital of St. Mary at Jerusalem and our
trustworthy servant, has informed us in all submissive-
ness that our dear Conrad, duke of Masovia and Kujavia,
intends to make provision for him and his Brothers
in the land of Kulm and the land between his march
and the territories of the Prussians. Therefore the Brothers shall take upon themselves the trouble and, on a
suitable occasion, to the honour and glory of the true
God, enter into the Prussian land and occupy it. Hermann postponed the acceptance of this offer and approached our majesty first with his submissive application; if we should deign to agree, he would begin the
great task, trusting in our authorization. Our majesty
should then confirm to him and his house all the land
which the duke gave him, as well as all the land they
would gain in Prussia through their efforts; also we
should grant his house through a charter all rights and
liberties for this area. Then he would accept the gift of
said duke and use the goods and men of his house for the

invasion and conquest of the county in tireless, unremitting effort.

Considering the attitude of active Christianity of this
Master, and how he eagerly desires to acquire these
lands for his house in the name of God, and since this
land belongs to our empire; trusting also in the wisdom
of this master, a man mighty in word and deed, who
will take up the matter forcefully with his Brothers
and carry through the conquest manfully, not abandoning it as many did before him, who wasted so much
energy in this undertaking for nothing, we give this
master the authority to invade the land of Prussia with
the forces of his house, and with all means at his disposal.

We also permit and confirm to this master, his successors, and his house for all time that they shall hold
the said land which they will get from Duke Conrad
according to his promise, any other lands which he may
give them in the future, finally, all they conquer in
Prussia with the grace of God, with rights to the
mountains, the flat country, rivers, forests, and lakes as
if it were an ancient imperial right, freely and unen-
cumbered by any services or taxes, without any ordinary
burdens, and no one shall have to give account for this,
their land. They also shall be allowed in the land they
conquer now or in the future, for the benefit of their
house to erect road and other toll stations, hold fairs and
markets, coin money, collect taxes and other tributes,
set up traffic laws for their rivers and the sea, as it
seems good to them; they also shall always have the
right of mining gold, silver, and other metals, and salt,
if such are at present found in their territories, or should
be found there in the future. We also give them the
right to set up judges and administrators, thus to govern
and lead justly the people subject to them, both those

who have been converted to the true faith as well as those who live in their delusion; to punish crimes of evil-doers wisely, to examine civil and criminal matters and to make decisions according to the dictates of reason. To this we add, out of our especial grace, that this master and his successors shall have and exercise sovereign rights in all their lands in the same manner as they are enjoyed by princes of the empire exercising the fullest rights in their lands, so that they may introduce good customs and promulgate regulations through which the faith of the Christians may be strengthened and their subjects enjoy peace and quiet.

Through this charter we prohibit any prince, duke, margrave, count, court official, magistrate, bailiff, every person of high or low estate, whether temporal or spiritual, to enfringe on these privileges and authorizations. Should anyone dare to do so, let him know that he will have to pay a fine of one thousand pounds of gold, one half to our treasury, the other to the ones that were injured.

THE BUILDING OF THE CASTLE OF THORN

In the year of our Lord, 1231, Hermann Balk [the first "landmeister" of Prussia] crossed the Vistula in the name of God to the Kulm side with his men and built the castle of Thorn on the bank. This was done as follows: on a hill stood a big oak; into its branches they built strong fortifications and defendable battlements, and around the fortress they built dense barricades so that one could get into it only by one path. Only seven Brothers were there; they had to have their boats always ready to escape to Nessau if necessary in case of an assault by the Prussians. Some time later the Brothers founded a town outside the castle of Thorn. Later on it was necessary to move the town to its present location, since the Vistula often completely flooded it.

OF THE IMAGES, DISBELIEFS, AND CUSTOMS OF THE PRUSSIANS

(The Prussians knew neither writing nor books,) and they were very much surprised at first when they saw the letters of the knights. And thus God was unknown to them; and thence came their error that they, in their foolishness, worshipped any creature as a god: thunder, sun, moon, stars, birds, animals, and even toads. They also had fields, woods, and waters which were holy to them, so that they neither plowed nor fished nor cut wood in them. . . .

The Prussians also believed in a resurrection, but not correctly. They believed that as he is on earth, noble or common, poor or rich, powerful or not, just so would he be after the resurrection. Therefore it was customary after the death of a noble to burn with him his weapons and horse, servants and maids, beautiful clothes, hunting dogs, falcons, and whatever else belongs to the equipment of a noble. Also with the common people everything they owned was burned, because they believed it all would rise with them and continue to serve them.

Also there was a devilish fraud connected with such a death, for the relative of the dead came to the priest and asked if he had seen somebody go or drive by his house at such and such a time of the day or night. The priest then generally described to them exactly the figure of the dead man, his gestures, his weapons and dress, servants and horses. And to make them believe him more readily, he often showed them some mark which the dead man cut or scratched into his door while driving by.

After a victory, the heathen, for their salvation, usually sacrificed to their idols one-third of their booty which they gave to the priest, who burned it for the gods. (They also sacrifice horses and cast the lot.). . .

Wealth and good-looking clothes they value very slightly; as they take off their furs today, they put them on tomorrow. They are ignorant of soft beds and fine food. They drink, since ancient times, only three things: water, mead, and mares' milk. . . .

(Their greatest virtue is hospitality.) They freely and willingly share food and drink. They think they have not treated their guests politely and well if they are not so full of drink that they vomit. Usually they urge each other mutually to take an innumerable number of drinks of equal measure. When they sit down to drink, every member of the household brings a measure to his host, drinks to him out of it, and the host then gladly finishes the drink. Thus they drink to each other, and let the cup go round without rest, and it runs to and fro, now full, now empty. They do this until man and woman, host and friends, big and small, all are drunk; that is pastime to them and a great honour—to me that does not seem honourable at all.

According to an old custom, they buy their women with money. The husband keeps his wife like a maid; she is not allowed to eat at his table, and daily has to wash the feet of the members of the household and the guests.

Nobody has to beg, because the poor man can go from house to house and eat wherever he likes.

If there is a murder, there is no reconciliation until the friends of the dead have killed the guilty person or one of his close relatives.

If a Prussian is met suddenly by a great calamity, he usually kills himself in his distress.

(To count the days, they make knots in a cord or notches on a piece of wood.)

Some Prussians, in honour of their gods, bathe daily; others never. Man and woman spin thread; some wool, the others linen, whichever they think the gods like most. Some never mount a black horse; some never a white one, or one of some other colour.

Trans. H. F. Schwarz, from *Ordensritter und Kirchenfürsten*, J. Bühler, ed. (Leipzig: Insel-Verlag, 1927).

The Near East:
Pilgrimage and Crusade

The Great German Pilgrimage

LAMBERT OF HERSFELD

1064-1065

IN THE autumn, Archbishop Siegfried of Mainz and Bishop Gunther of Bamberg, Otto of Regensberg and William of Utrecht, and many others with them, the pillars and heads of Germany, set out for Jerusalem. . . .

Meanwhile, since the bishops who were travelling to Jerusalem indiscreetly displayed their great wealth to the peoples through whose territories they journeyed, they would have brought upon themselves the most extreme danger, had not divine mercy restored that which was lost through human rashness. For the barbarians, who flocked in crowds from the towns and fields to behold such distinguished men, were seized at first by a vast wonder at their strange dress and magnificent equipment, and then, as is often the case, not less by the hope and desire of plunder. Therefore, when, after crossing Licia, they entered the territory of the Saracens and were now one day's journey or a little more from the city called Ramleh, they suffered an attack from the Arabs on Good Friday about the third hour of the day.

The Arabs, upon learning of the approach of such distinguished men, had flocked together from every side, in great numbers and armed to seize spoils. Most of the Christians thought it was impious to supply themselves with military aid, and to safeguard with material arms the lives which, upon setting forth into foreign lands, they had consecrated to God; they were immediately laid low, weakened by many wounds, and despoiled of all they possessed, "from a thread even to a shoelatchet." Among these Bishop William of Utrecht, with his arm almost crippled by blows, was left behind, naked and half-dead. By throwing stones, a kind of weapon which by chance the place itself provided abundantly, the other Christians were not so much warding off danger as trying to postpone the death which was upon them.

Withdrawing little by little, they turned aside to a village, which was at a moderate distance from their route itself. They conjectured from the similarity of the name that this was Capharnaum. When they had entered, all the bishops occupied a certain atrium, which was enclosed by a low wall, so fragile that even if no force had been applied, it could easily have fallen down from sheer age. In the middle of this there was a house which had an upper story sufficiently lofty and prepared, as if purposely, to resist siege. The bishops of Mainz and Bamberg, with their clergy, claimed for themselves the upper story; the other bishops the lower story. All the laymen rushed about energetically, trying to hinder the attack of the enemy and defend the wall, and indeed they withstood the first of the attack by throwing stones, as was mentioned before. Then, when the barbarians cast a thick mass of spears into the fortification and most of the Christians, having rushed at them, wrested their

shields and swords from their hands by force, not only
were the Christians able now to defend the wall, but
they even ventured now and then to make a sortie from
the gates and engage in hand-to-hand combat.

Since the Arabs were now unable to sustain the attack in any place or in any line, they finally changed
their plan from a disorderly attack to a siege and undertook to subdue by hunger and fatigue those whom they
were unable to overcome by the sword. Therefore they
divided their multitude, of which they had more than
enough, having massed together about twelve thousand,
in such a way that, with one part regularly succeeding
another in carrying on the siege, they should give little
or no opportunity for respite to the Christians, surmising
that, because of the lack of everything which could sustain human life, they would not be able to endure the
labour of fighting for long.

So the Christians were besieged without intermission
all of Good Friday, all of Holy Saturday, up to almost
the third hour of Easter Sunday, and the wickedness of
the enemy did not grant them even a brief respite in
which at least they might refresh their bodies with
sleep. For, having death before their eyes, they desired
neither food nor drink, and if they had greatly desired
anything, they could not have taken it, since they were
without everything. And when, on the third day, worn
out with exertion and with hunger, they had reached
the end, and since their strength, broken by fasting,
betrayed the many brave attempts they made, a certain
priest cried out that they were not acting righteously,
since they put their hope and strength in their arms
rather than in God and tried to ward off, by their own
power, this misfortune into which He had permitted
them to fall. On this account he thought they should
surrender, especially since this three-day fast now ren-

dered them utterly useless for fighting. When they had surrendered and had been sent under the yoke by the enemy, it would not be difficult for the God who had so often, even in the last necessity, saved them miraculously when they were hard pressed, now to grant them His mercy. And he also impressed this upon them: the barbarians were not at all raging in so great an effort for the sake of killing them, but rather because they wished to take away their money; if the barbarians got possession of this, the Christians would in time be allowed to depart free and henceforth unharmed, without attack or molestation.

This plan was pleasing to everyone and, turning immediately from arms to prayers, they begged through an interpreter that they be received in surrender. When he learned this, the Arab leader hastened at a gallop into the first ranks, and, indeed, withdrew the others to some distance away because he feared that if the multitude were to be rashly admitted, the booty would be divided in a disorderly manner. He himself, taking with him seventeen of the most honoured men of his tribe, entered the open camp, having left his son to guard the gates, lest perchance someone avid for plunder, who had not been asked to follow him, should break in. And after he and a few others had ascended on ladders which had been moved to the upper story where the bishops of Mainz and Bamberg were concealed, the bishop of Bamberg, to whom before all others, in spite of his youth, but because of the superiority of his courage and the admirable dignity of his whole appearance, the honour had been given, began to ask him that, when they had taken away everything they had, "even to the uttermost farthing," he should permit them to go away stripped.

The Arab leader, both elated by the victory and ex-

cessively furious beyond the inborn barbarity of his
manners because of the defeats received in so many
battles, said that he had waged war against them for
three days now, with great injury to his own army, to
the end that he might make his own terms with the
conquered, rather than accept those which they themselves established. Lest, therefore, they should be deceived by a false hope, he said that the Arabs, when
they had taken away everything the Christians had,
would eat their flesh and drink their blood. Without
delay, loosening the turban with which, according to
the custom of his people, he covered his head, and
making of it a lasso, he threw it over the neck of the
bishop. Since the bishop was a man with a noble's sense
of honour and of almost exaggerated dignity, he did not
suffer this ignominy, but struck him such a violent blow
of the fist in the face, that with one punch he knocked
the startled Arab headlong to the pavement, and shouted
that he would first punish him for his impiety, since he,
a profane man and an idolater, had presumed to lay
impure hands upon a priest of Christ.

Immediately the other clerics and laymen rushed forward and with fetters bound the hands of both the
leaders and the others, who had ascended into the upper
story, so tightly behind their backs, that the skin was
broken in many places and the blood flowed over their
fingernails. When the news of this bold deed was
brought to those who were standing in the lower part
of the house, they did likewise to those Arab nobles who
were with them. Then, raising on high a mighty shout
and calling to their aid God, the maker of all things, all
the laymen took up arms again, occupied the wall, and,
with an organized band, routed and put to flight the
guard which had been placed at the gates. They fought
everywhere so eagerly and with their strength so re-

newed by the unexpected success that you would have thought they suffered no fatigue and no discomfort from the fasting and exertion of three days.

Wondering greatly at the amazing eagerness arising from alarming circumstances and, in fact, from the utmost desperation, and suspecting no other cause for this strange occurrence than that punishment had been inflicted upon their leaders, the Arabs, in a most hostile spirit, rushed into the fight and, crowding together, prepared to break into the camp by force of arms and men. And they would have done so, had not the Christians, acting upon a quickly worked out plan, placed the captive leaders in the place where the most fearful force of the enemy and the thickest rain of spears were falling, and set a scout above their heads, who, with drawn sword in his hands, shouted through an interpreter that, unless they stopped attacking, the Christians would fight against them not with arms, but with the heads of their leaders.

Then the leaders themselves, who, besides the painfulness of their bonds, were also tormented exceedingly by the swords threatening their necks, with great lamentation implored their people to act more moderately and not, by obstinately continuing to fight, to incite the Christians, now that the hope of pardon had been cut off, to torture and murder them. Terrified by the danger to his father, the son of the Arab leader, whom I mentioned above as having been left by his father to guard the gate of the atrium, with swift steps pushed through the crowded ranks of his own men and, chiding them by word and gesture, held back the attack of the raging array and forbade them to cast their spears at the enemy, since not the enemy, as they thought, but rather their own nobles would receive those weapons in their breasts.

Because of this, when the Christians had been little by little freed from arms and attack, a messenger came to them in the fortification, who had been sent by those who, on Good Friday, after losing everything, naked and wounded had pushed on to Ramleh. He brought great refreshment to spirits that had been worn out by bitterness and fear, revealing that the prince of the city mentioned above, although a pagan [Moslem], had, nevertheless, been inspired by what might be thought to be a divine feeling and was coming with huge forces to free them. Nor could the news of the approaching enemy be concealed from the Arabs. Immediately, they all turned their thoughts from attacking the Christians to saving themselves, and everyone disappeared, fleeing blindly whither any hope of escape called. In this confusion, while some ran about caring for other matters, one of the captives escaped, aided by a certain Saracen whom the Christians had used as a guide for the journey, and such was the grief, such the sorrow, of everyone that they could scarcely keep their hands off him through whose negligence the captive had escaped.

Not long afterwards, the leader himself, as had been announced, came with his army and was received peacefully in the atrium by the Christians, who were all, nevertheless, suspended between hope and fear, lest by chance the calamity had not been averted, but only the enemy changed, and because of the strangeness of the thing it was hard to believe that "Satan should cast out Satan," that is, that a pagan should wish to restrain a pagan from attacking Christians. First he ordered all the captives to be brought to him. When he had seen them and had heard in order what had been done, he thanked the Christians very heartily for the magnificent things they had done, and for defeating these most violent enemies of the state, who had now for many years harassed the kingdom of Babylon [Caliphate of Cairo] with thoroughgoing devastations, and who had often destroyed the great lines arrayed against them in battle. He ordered them to be turned over to guards and to be preserved alive for the king of Babylon. When he had received from the Christians as much money as had been stipulated, he himself took them with him to Ramleh. Then, supplying them with a guard of light-armed youth, so that they would not be in further danger of any attack from brigands, he commanded that they be escorted as far as Jerusalem. They suffered no further difficulty on the journey there, and none in returning, and they reached Licia, giving thanks to God for their having survived so many calamities and for His having preserved them alive and unharmed.

From *Annales*, O. Holder-Egger, ed. (Hanover: 1894); trans. M.M.M.

The First Contact of Crusaders and Turks

1097-1099

IMPRESSIONS OF THE PEOPLE AND THE COUNTRY IN ANATOLIA

THE first day of our departure from the city [Constantinople], we reached a bridge and we stayed there two days. The third day our men rose before dawn and, since it was still night, they did not see well enough to hold to the same route, and they divided into two corps which were separated by two days' march. In the first group were Bohemond, Robert of Normandy, the prudent Tancred and many others; in the second were the count of St. Giles, Duke Godfrey, the bishop of Puy, Hugh the Great, the count of Flanders and many others.

The third day [July 1, 1097], the [Seljuk] Turks violently burst upon Bohemond and his companions. At once the Turks began to shriek, scream, and cry out in high voices, repeating some diabolical sound in their own language. The wise Bohemond, seeing the innumerable Turks at a distance, shrieking and crying out in demoniac voices, at once ordered all the knights to dismount and the tents to be pitched quickly. Before the tents were pitched, he said to all the soldiers: "Lords, and valiant soldiers of Christ, here we are confronted on all sides by a difficult battle. Let all the knights advance bravely and let the foot soldiers quickly and carefully pitch the tents."

When all this was done, the Turks had already surrounded us on all sides, fighting, throwing javelins and shooting arrows marvellously far and wide. And we, although we did not know how to resist them nor to endure the weight of so great an enemy, nevertheless we met that encounter with united spirit. And our women on that day were a great help to us, in bearing drinking water to our fighters and perhaps also in always comforting those fighting and defending. The wise Bohemond sent word forthwith to the others, that is, to the count of St. Giles, to Duke Godfrey, Hugh the Great, the bishop of Puy and all the other knights of Christ, to hasten and come quickly to the battle, saying, "If today they wish to fight, let them come bravely." . . .

Our men wondered greatly whence could have sprung such a great multitude of Turks, Arabs, Saracens, and others too numerous to count, for almost all the mountains and hills and valleys and all the plains, both within and without, were covered entirely by that excommunicated race. There was among us a quiet exchange of words, praising God and taking counsel and saying: "Be unanimous in every way in the faith of Christ and the victory of the holy cross, for today, if it pleases God, you will all become rich." . . .

On the approach of our knights, the Turks, Arabs, Saracens, Angulans [unidentifiable], and all the barbarous peoples fled quickly through the passes of the mountains and the plains. The number of the Turks, Persians, Paulicians, Saracens, Angulans, and other pagans was three hundred and sixty thousand, without counting the Arabs, whose number no one knows except God alone. They fled extremely quickly to their tents but were not allowed to remain there long. Again they resumed their flight and we pursued them, killing them during one whole day; and we took much booty, gold, silver, horses, asses, camels, sheep, cows, and many other things which we do not know. If the Lord had not been with us in this battle, if He had not quickly sent us the other division, none of ours would have escaped, because from the third hour up to the ninth hour the battle continued. But God all-powerful, pious and merciful, who did not permit His knights to perish nor to fall into the hands of the enemy, sent aid to us rapidly. But two of our knights died there honourably . . . and other knights and foot soldiers whose names I do not know, found death there.

Who will ever be wise or learned enough to describe the prudence, the military skill, and the fortitude of the Turks? They thought to terrorize the race of the Franks by the threats of their arrows, as they have terrorized the Arabs, Saracens and Armenians, Syrians and Greeks. But, if it pleases God, they will never prevail over such a great people as ours. In truth they say they are of the race of the Franks and that no man, except the Franks and themselves, ought rightly to be called a knight. Let me speak the truth which no one will dare to contest; certainly, if they had always been firm in the faith of Christ and holy Christianity, if they had been willing to confess one Lord in three persons, and the Son of God born of a virgin, who suffered, rose from the dead, ascended into heaven in the sight of His disciples and sent the consolation of the Holy Spirit, and if they had believed in right mind and faith that He reigns in heaven and on earth, no one could have been found more powerful or courageous or gifted in war; and nevertheless, by the grace of God, they were conquered by our men. This battle took place on the first of July. . . .

And we kept going on [July—August, 1097], pursuing the most iniquitous Turks who fled each day before us. . . . And we pursued them through deserts and a land without water or inhabitants from which we scarcely escaped and got out alive. Hunger and thirst pressed us on all sides, and there was almost nothing for us to eat, except the thorns which we pulled and rubbed between our hands; on such food we lived miserably. In that place there died most of our horses, so that many of our knights became foot soldiers; and from lack of horses, cattle took the place of war steeds and in this extreme necessity goats, sheep, and dogs were used by us for carrying.

Then we began to enter an excellent region, full of nourishment for the body, of delights and all kinds of good things, and soon we approached Iconium. The inhabitants of this country [probably Armenians] persuaded and warned us to carry with us skins full of water, because for the journey one day thence there is a great dearth of water. We did so until we came to a certain river and there we camped for two days. . . .

We . . . penetrated into a diabolic mountain [in the Antitaurus], so high and so narrow that no one dared to go before another on the path which lay open on the mountain; there the horses plunged down and one pack-horse dragged over another. On all sides the knights were in despair; they beat their breasts in sorrow and sadness, wondering what to do with themselves and their arms. They sold their shields and their best coats of mail with helmets for only three or five pennies or for anything at all; those who failed to sell them, threw them away for nothing and proceeded. . . .

Finally [October, 1097] our knights reached the valley in which is situated the royal city of Antioch, which is the capital of all Syria and which the Lord Jesus Christ gave to St. Peter, prince of the apostles, in order that he might recall it to the cult of the holy faith, he who lives and reigns with God the Father in the unity of the Holy Spirit, God through all the ages. Amen. . . .

AT THE SIEGE OF ANTIOCH

The next day [March 7, 1098], at dawn, some Turks went forth from the city and collected all the fetid corpses of the Turkish dead which they could find on the bank of the river and buried them at the mosque beyond the bridge, before the gate of the city. With the bodies they buried cloaks, bezants [gold coins], pieces of gold, bows, arrows, and many other objects which we cannot name. Our men, hearing that the Turks had buried their dead, all prepared themselves and hastened to the diabolic edifice. They ordered the tombs to be dug up and broken, and dragged from the burial places. They threw all the corpses into a certain ditch and carried the severed heads to our tents so that the num-

ber of them should be known exactly. . . . At this sight
the Turks mourned exceedingly and were sad unto
death for on that day they did nothing in their sorrow
except weep and utter cries. . . .

THE TAKING OF MARRA

The Saracens, seeing that our men had sapped the
wall, were struck with terror and fled within the city.
All this took place on Saturday at the hour of vespers, at
sunset, December 11th [1098]. Bohemond sent word
by an interpreter to the Saracen chiefs that they with
their wives and children and other belongings should
take refuge in a palace which is above the gate and he
himself would protect them from sentence of death.

Then all our men entered the city and whatever of
value they found in the houses or hiding places each
one took for his own. When day came, wherever they
found anyone of the enemy, either man or woman, they
killed him. No corner of the city was empty of Saracen
corpses, and no one could go through the streets of the
city without stepping on these corpses. At length Bohemond seized those whom he had ordered to go to the
palace and took from them everything they had, gold,
silver, and other ornaments; some he had killed, others
he ordered to be led to Antioch to be sold.

Now the stay of the Franks in this city was one month
and four days, during which the bishop of Orange died.
There were some of our men who did not find there
what they needed, both because of the long stay and
the pressure of hunger, for outside the city they could
find nothing to take. They sawed open the bodies of the
dead because in their bellies they found bezants hidden;
others cut the flesh in strips and cooked them for eating. . . .

THE SACK OF JERUSALEM

Entering the city [July 15, 1099], our pilgrims pursued and killed Saracens up to the Temple of Solomon, in which they had assembled and where they gave battle to us furiously for the whole day so that their blood flowed throughout the whole temple. Finally, having overcome the pagans, our knights seized a great number of men and women, and they killed whom they wished and whom they wished they let live. . . . Soon the crusaders ran throughout the city, seizing gold, silver, horses, mules, and houses full of all kinds of goods.

Then rejoicing and weeping from extreme joy our men went to worship at the sepulchre of our Saviour Jesus and thus fulfilled their pledge to Him. . . .

Then, our knights decided in council that each one should give alms with prayers so that God should elect whom He wished to reign over the others and rule the city. They also ordered that all the Saracen dead should be thrown out of the city because of the extreme stench, for the city was almost full of their cadavers. The live Saracens dragged the dead out before the gates and made piles of them, like houses. No one has ever heard of or seen such a slaughter of pagan peoples since pyres were made of them like boundary marks, and no one except God knows their number.

From *Histoire anonyme de la première croisade,* L. Bréhier, ed. (Paris: Champion, 1924); trans. J.B.R.

A Greek View of the Crusaders

ANNA COMNENA

Early twelfth century

BEFORE he had enjoyed even a short rest, he [Emperor Alexis] heard a report of the approach of innumerable Frankish armies. Now he dreaded their arrival for he knew their irresistible manner of attack, their unstable and mobile character, and all the peculiar natural and concomitant characteristics which the Frank retains throughout; and he also knew that they were always agape for money, and seemed to disregard their truces readily for any reason that cropped up. For he had always heard this reported of them, and found it very true. However, he did not lose heart, but prepared himself in every way so that, when the occasion called, he would be ready for battle. And indeed the actual facts were far greater and more terrible than rumour made them. For the whole of the West and all the barbarian tribes which dwell between the farther side of the Adriatic and the pillars of Heracles, had all migrated in a body and were marching into Asia through the intervening Europe, and were making the journey with all their household. . . .

The incidents of the barbarians' approach followed in the order I have described, and persons of intelligence could feel that they were witnessing a strange occurrence. The arrival of these multitudes did not take place at the same time nor by the same road (for how indeed could such masses starting from different places have crossed the straits of Lombardy all together?). Some first, some next, others after them, and thus successively all accomplished the transit, and then marched through the continent. Each army was preceded, as we said, by an unspeakable number of locusts; and all who saw this more than once recognized them as forerunners of the Frankish armies. When the first of them began crossing the straits of Lombardy sporadically the emperor summoned certain leaders of the Roman forces, and sent them to the parts of Dyrrhachium and Valona with instructions to offer a courteous welcome to the Franks who had crossed, and to collect abundant supplies from all the countries along their route; then to follow and watch them covertly all the time, and if they saw them making any foraging excursions, they were to come out from under cover and check them by light skirmishing. These captains were accompanied by some men who knew the Latin tongue, so that they might settle any disputes that arose between them. . . .

Now the Frankish counts are naturally shameless and violent, naturally greedy of money too, and immoderate in everything they wish, and possess a flow of language greater than any other human race; and they did not make their visits to the emperor in any order, but each count as he came brought in as many men as he liked with him; and one came after another, and another in turn after him. And when they came in, they did not regulate their conversation by a waterglass, as the rule was for orators formerly, but for as long as each wished to talk to the emperor, be he even a mere nobody, for so long he was allowed to talk. Now, as this was their character, and their speech very long-winded, and as they had no reverence for the emperor, nor took heed of the lapse of time nor suspected the indignation of the onlookers, not one of them gave place to those who came after them, but kept on unceasingly with their talk and requests. Their talkativeness and hunting instinct and their finicking speech are known to all who are interested in studying the manners of mankind, but we who were then present learnt them more thoroughly from experience. For even when evening came, the emperor who had remained without food all through the day, rose from his throne to retire to his private bedroom; but not even then was he freed from the Franks' importunity. For one came after the other and not only those who had not been heard during the day, but the same came over again, always preferring one excuse after another for further talk, whilst he stood unmoved in the midst of the Franks, quietly bearing their endless chatter. And you could see him all alone and with unchanging countenance ever giving a ready answer to all their questions. And there was no end to their unseasonable loquacity. If any one of the ministers tried to cut them short, the emperor prevented him. For knowing the Franks' natural irritability he was afraid lest from some trifling pretext a great fire of scandal should be lighted and great harm ensue to the Roman rule. And really it was a most wonderful sight. For like a hammer-wrought statue, made perhaps of bronze or cold iron, he would sit the whole night through, from the evening until midnight perhaps, and often even till the third cockcrow, and very occasionally almost till the sun's rays were bright.

From *The Alexiad*, trans. E. Dawes.

An Arab Opinion of the Crusaders

USÁMAH

Twelfth century

THEIR LACK OF SENSE

MYSTERIOUS are the works of the Creator, the author of all things! When one comes to recount cases regarding the Franks, he cannot but glorify Allah (exalted is he!) and sanctify him, for he sees them as animals possessing the virtues of courage and fighting, but nothing else; just as animals have only the virtues of strength and carrying loads. I shall now give some instances of their doings and their curious mentality.

In the army of King Fulk, son of Fulk, was a Frankish reverend knight who had just arrived from their land in order to make the holy pilgrimage and then return home. He was of my intimate fellowship and kept such constant company with me that he began to call me "my brother." Between us were mutual bonds of amity and friendship. When he resolved to return by sea to his homeland, he said to me:

"My brother, I am leaving for my country and I want thee to send with me thy son"—my son, who was then fourteen years old, was at that time in my company—"to our country, where he can see the knights and learn wisdom and chivalry. When he returns, he will be like a wise man."

Thus there fell upon my ears words which would never come out of the head of a sensible man; for even if my son were to be taken captive, his captivity could

not bring him a worse misfortune than carrying him into
the lands of the Franks. However, I said to the man:

"By thy life, this has exactly been my idea. But the
only thing that prevented me from carrying it out was
the fact that his grandmother, my mother, is so fond of
him and did not this time let him come out with me
until she exacted an oath from me to the effect that I
would return him to her."

Thereupon he asked, "Is thy mother still alive?"

"Yes," I replied.

"Well," said he, "disobey her not."

THEIR CURIOUS MEDICATION

A case illustrating their curious medicine is the following:

The lord of al-Munaytirah wrote to my uncle asking
him to dispatch a physician to treat certain sick persons
among his people. My uncle sent him a Christian physician named Thabit. Thabit was absent but ten days
when he returned. So we said to him, "How quickly
hast thou healed thy patients!" He said:

"They brought before me a knight in whose leg an
abscess had grown; and a woman afflicted with imbecility. To the knight I applied a small poultice until the
abscess opened and became well; and the woman I put
on diet and made her humour wet. Then a Frankish
physician came to them and said, 'This man knows nothing about treating them.' He then said to the knight,
'Which wouldst thou prefer, living with one leg or dying
with two?' The latter replied, 'Living with one leg.' The
physician said, 'Bring me a strong knight and a sharp
axe.' A knight came with the axe. And I was standing
by. Then the physician laid the leg of the patient on a
block of wood and bade the knight strike his leg with

the axe and chop it off at one blow. Accordingly he struck it—while I was looking on—one blow, but the leg was not severed. He dealt another blow, upon which the marrow of the leg flowed out and the patient died on the spot. He then examined the woman and said, 'This is a woman in whose head there is a devil which has possessed her. Shave off her hair.' Accordingly they shaved it off and the woman began once more to eat their ordinary diet—garlic and mustard. Her imbecility took a turn for the worse. The physician then said, 'The devil has penetrated through her head.' He therefore took a razor, made a deep cruciform incision on it, peeled off the skin at the middle of the incision until the bone of the skull was exposed and rubbed it with salt. The woman also expired instantly. Thereupon I asked them whether my services were needed any longer, and when they replied in the negative I returned home, having learned of their medicine what I knew not before."

I have, however, witnessed a case of their medicine which was quite different from that.

The king of the Franks had for treasurer a knight named Bernard . . . who (may Allah's curse be upon him!) was one of the most accursed and wicked among the Franks. A horse kicked him in the leg, which was subsequently infected and which opened in fourteen different places. Every time one of these cuts would close in one place, another would open in another place. All this happened while I was praying for his perdition. Then came to him a Frankish physician and removed from the leg all the ointments which were on it and began to wash it with very strong vinegar. By this treatment all the cuts were healed and the man became well again. He was up again like a devil. . . .

NEWLY ARRIVED FRANKS ARE ESPECIALLY ROUGH: ONE INSISTS THAT USĀMAH SHOULD PRAY EASTWARD

Everyone who is a fresh emigrant from the Frankish lands is ruder in character than those who have become acclimatized and have held long association with the Moslems. Here is an illustration of their rude character.

Whenever I visited Jerusalem I always entered the Aqsa Mosque, beside which stood a small mosque which the Franks had converted into a church. When I used to enter the Aqsa Mosque, which was occupied by the Templars . . . who were my friends, the Templars would evacuate the little adjoining mosque so that I might pray in it. One day, I entered this mosque, repeated the first formula, "Allah is great," and stood up in the act of praying, upon which one of the Franks rushed on me, got hold of me and turned my face eastward saying, "This is the way thou shouldst pray!" A group of Templars hastened to him, seized him, and repelled him from me. I resumed my prayer. The same man, while the others were otherwise busy, rushed once more on me and turned my face eastward, saying, "This is the way thou shouldst pray!" The Templars again came in to him and expelled him. They apologized to me, saying, "This is a stranger who has only recently arrived from the land of the Franks and he has never before seen anyone praying except eastward." Thereupon I said to myself, "I have had enough prayer." So I went out and have ever been surprised at the conduct of this devil of a man, at the change in the colour of his face, his trembling and his sentiment at the sight of one praying towards the *qiblah*.

ANOTHER WANTS TO SHOW TO A MOSLEM GOD AS A CHILD

I saw one of the Franks come to al-Amir Mu'in-al-Din (may Allah's mercy rest upon his soul!) when he was in the Dome of the Rock, and say to him, "Dost thou want to see God as a child?" Mu'in-al-Din said, "Yes." The Frank walked ahead of us until he showed us the picture of Mary with Christ (may peace be upon him!) as an infant in her lap. He then said, "This is God as a child." But Allah is exalted far above what the infidels say about him!

FRANKS LACK JEALOUSY IN SEX AFFAIRS

The Franks are void of all zeal and jealousy. One of them may be walking along with his wife. He meets another man who takes the wife by the hand and steps aside to converse with her while the husband is standing on one side waiting for his wife to conclude the conversation. If she lingers too long for him, he leaves her alone with the conversant and goes away.

Here is an illustration which I myself witnessed:

When I used to visit Nablus, I always took lodging with a man named Mu'izz, whose home was a lodging-house for the Moslems. The house had windows which opened to the road, and there stood opposite to it on the other side of the road a house belonging to a Frank who sold wine for the merchants. He would take some wine in a bottle and go around announcing it by shouting, "So and so, the merchant, has just opened a cask full of this wine. He who wants to buy some of it will find it in such and such a place." The Frank's pay for the announcement made would be the wine in that bottle. One day this Frank went home and found a man with his wife in the same bed. He asked him, "What could have made thee enter into my wife's room?" The man replied, "I was tired, so I went in to rest." "But how," asked he, "didst thou get into my bed?" The other replied, "Well, I found a bed that was spread, so I slept in it." "But," said he, "my wife was sleeping together with thee!" The other replied, "Well, the bed is hers. How could I therefore have prevented her from using her own bed?" "By the truth of my religion," said the husband, "if thou shouldst do it again, thou and I would have a quarrel." Such was for the Frank the entire expression of his disapproval and the limit of his jealousy. . . .

From *Memoirs of Usamah*, trans. P. K. Hitti (New York: Columbia University Press, 1929).

A Crusader's Criticism of the Greeks

ODO OF DEUIL

c. 1148

AND then the Greeks degenerated entirely into women; putting aside all manly vigour, both of words and of spirit, they lightly swore whatever they thought would please us, but they neither kept faith with us nor maintained respect for themselves. In general they really have the opinion that anything which is done for the holy empire cannot be considered perjury. Let no one think that I am taking vengeance on a race of men hateful to me and that because of my hatred I am inventing a Greek whom I have not seen. Whoever has known the Greeks will, if asked, say that when they are afraid they become despicable in their excessive debasement and when they have the upper hand they are arrogant in their severe violence to those subjected to them. . . .

The city [Constantinople] itself is squalid and fetid and in many places harmed by permanent darkness, for the wealthy overshadow the streets with buildings and leave these dirty, dark places to the poor and to travellers; there murders and robberies and other crimes which love the darkness are committed. Moreover, since people live lawlessly in this city, which has as many lords as rich men and almost as many thieves as poor men, a criminal knows neither fear nor shame, because crime is not punished by law and never entirely comes to light. In every respect she exceeds moderation; for, just as she surpasses other cities in wealth, so, too, does she surpass them in vice. Also, she possesses many churches unequal to Santa Sophia in size but equal to it in beauty, which are to be marvelled at for their beauty and their many saintly relics. Those who had the opportunity entered these places, some to see the sights and others to worship faithfully.

Conducted by the emperor [Manuel Comnenus], the king [Louis VII of France] also visited the shrines and, after returning, when won over by the urgency of his host's requests, dined with him. That banquet afforded pleasure to ear, mouth, and eye with pomp as marvellous, viands as delicate, and pastimes as pleasant as the guests were illustrious. There many of the king's men feared for him; but he, who had entrusted the care of himself to God, feared nothing at all, since he had faith and courage; for one who is not inclined to do harm does not easily believe that anyone will harm him.

Although the Greeks furnished us no proof that they were treacherous, I believe that they would not have exhibited such unremitting servitude if they had had good intentions. . . .

Distrusting their pledge, scorning their favours, and

foretelling the injuries which we afterwards endured, the bishop of Langres, however, urged us to take the city. He proved that the walls, a great part of which collapsed before our eyes, were weak, that the people were inert, that by cutting the conduits the fresh water supply could be withdrawn without delay or effort. He, a man of wise intellect and saintly piety, said that if that city were taken it would not be necessary to conquer the others, since they would yield obedience voluntarily to him who possessed their capital. He added further that Constantinople is Christian only in name, not in fact, and, whereas for her part she should not prevent others from bringing aid to Christians, her emperor had ventured a few years previously to attack the prince of Antioch. He said: "First he took Tarsus and Mamistra and numerous strongholds and a broad expanse of land, and, after expelling the Catholic bishops in the cities and replacing them with heretics, he besieged Antioch. And although it was his duty to ward off the near-by infidels by uniting the Christian forces, with the aid of the infidels he strove to destroy the Christians." . . .

To us who suffered the Greeks' evil deeds, however, divine justice, and the fact that our people are not accustomed to endure shameful injuries for long, give hope of vengeance. Thus we comfort our sad hearts, and we shall follow the course of our misfortunes so that posterity may know about the Greeks' treacherous actions.

From *De profectione Ludovici VII in orientem*, trans. V. G. Berry (New York: Columbia University Press, 1948).

Why the Crusaders Failed

WILLIAM OF TYRE

Late twelfth century

A T THIS point I must digress somewhat from the course of my story, not to wander about aimlessly, but to bring out something of value. The question is often asked, and quite justly, why it was that our fathers, though less in number, so often bravely withstood in battle the far larger forces of the enemy and that often by divine grace a small force destroyed the multitudes of the enemy, with the result that the very name of Christian became a terror to nations ignorant of God, and thus the Lord was glorified in the works of our fathers. In contrast to this, the men of our times too often have been conquered by inferior forces; in fact, when with superior numbers they have attempted some exploit against adversaries less strong, their efforts have been fruitless and they have usually been forced to succumb.

The first reason that presents itself, as we carefully and thoughtfully study this condition of our times, looking for aid to God, the Author of all things, is that our forefathers were religious men and feared God. Now in their places a wicked generation has grown up, sinful sons, falsifiers of the Christian faith, who run the course of all unlawful things without discrimination. . . .

A second reason occurs to us in passing. In earlier times, those first revered men who came to the lands of the East led by divine zeal and aflame with spiritual enthusiasm for the faith were accustomed to military discipline; they were trained in battle and familiar with the use of weapons. The people of the East, on the contrary, through long-continued peace, had become enervated; they were unused to the art of war, unfamiliar with the rules of battle, and gloried in their state of inactivity. Therefore it is not strange that men of war, even though few in number, easily held their own even against larger numbers and could boast of their superiority in carrying off the palm of victory. For in such matters (as those who have had more experience in war know better than I), facility in arms due to long and continual practice, when opposed to untrained strength and lack of persistence, generally wins.

A third reason, no less important and effective, forces itself upon my attention. In former times almost every city had its own ruler. To speak after the manner of Aristotle, they were not dependent on one another; they were rarely actuated by the same motives, but, in fact, very often by those directly opposite. To contend in battle against adversaries of widely differing and frequently conflicting ideas, adversaries who distrusted each other, involved less peril. Those who feared their own allies not less than the Christians could not or would not readily unite to repulse the common danger or arm themselves for our destruction. But now, since God has so willed it, all the kingdoms adjacent to us have been brought under the power of one man. Within quite recent times, Zangi, a monster who abhorred the name of Christian as he would a pestilence, the father of this Nureddin who has lately died, first conquered many other kingdoms by force and then laid violent hands on Rages, also called Edessa, which even within our memory was the splendid and notable metropolis of the Medes. He took this city with all its territories and put to death all faithful believers found within its borders.

Then his son, Nureddin, drove the king of Damascus from his own land, more through the treachery of the latter's subjects than by any real valour, seized that realm for himself, and added it to his paternal heritage. Still more recently, the same Nureddin, with the assiduous aid of Shirkuh, seized the ancient and wealthy kingdom of Egypt as his own, in the manner already related more fully when the reign of King Amaury was under discussion.

Thus, as has been said, all the kingdoms round about us obey one ruler, they do the will of one man, and at his command alone, however reluctantly, they are ready, as a unit, to take up arms for our injury. Not one among them is free to indulge any inclination of his own or may with impunity disregard the commands of his overlord. This Saladin, whom we have had occasion to mention so frequently, a man of humble antecedents and lowly station, now holds under his control all these kingdoms, for fortune has smiled too graciously upon him. From Egypt and the countries adjacent to it, he draws an inestimable supply of the purest gold of the first quality known as *obryzum*. Other provinces furnish him numberless companies of horsemen and fighters, men thirsty for gold, since it is an easy matter for those possessing a plenteous supply of this commodity to draw men to them. . . .

From A *History of Deeds Done beyond the Seas*, trans. E. A. Babcock and A. C. Krey (New York: Columbia University Press, 1943).

The Expedition of the Grand Company to Constantinople

RAMÓN MUNTANER

1302

"THEN, Lord," said Frey Roger, "by your leave, I shall send two knights with an armed galley to the emperor of Constantinople [Andronicus II Palaeologus], and shall let him know that I am ready to go to him with as great a company of horse and foot, all Catalans and Aragonese, as he wishes, and that he should give us pay and all necessaries; that I know he greatly needs these succours, for the Turks have taken from him land of the extent of thirty journeys; and he could not do as much with any people as with Catalans and Aragonese, and especially with those who have carried on this war against King Charles." And the lord king [Fadrique I of Sicily] answered, "Frey Roger, you know more in these matters than we do; nevertheless, it seems to us that your idea is good, and so ordain what you please, we shall be well satisfied with what you ordain." And upon this Frey Roger kissed the king's hand and departed from him and went to his lodging where he remained all that day arranging matters. And the lord king and the others attended the feast and the diversions and disportings.

And when the next day came, he had a galley equipped and called two knights whom he trusted, and told them all he had planned; and also told them that, above all, they should make a treaty by which he would obtain, as wife, the niece [daughter] of the emperor of Lantzaura [Bulgaria] and also that he be made grand duke of the empire; and again, that the emperor give pay for four months to all those he would bring, at the rate of four onzas a month to each armed horseman and one onza a month to each man afoot. And that he keep them at this pay all the time they wished to remain, and that they find the pay at Monemvasia. And Frey Roger gave them the articles of all this, as well of these matters as of all they were to do. And I know this, as I, myself, was present at the dictating and ordering of these articles. And he gave them power, by an adequate permit, to sign everything for him, as well about the marriage as about other matters. And, assuredly, the knights were worthy and wise, and when they had heard the plan, a few articles would have sufficed them; nevertheless all was done in regular order.

With that, when they were ready, they took leave of Frey Roger who held the matter for concluded, because his renown was great in the house of the emperor, from the time he was commanding the ship of the Templars, called the *Falcon*, when he had done many favours to ships of the emperor which he met beyond the seas, and he knew Greek very well. And so, likewise, he was very renowned in Romania and throughout all the world for the help he had given so freely to the lord king of Sicily, and so he was able to provide himself very fully with followers. Thus En Berenguer de Entenza, with whom he had sworn brotherhood, promised to follow him . . . and many other Catalan and Aragonese knights; and of the almugavars [special infantry] full four thousand, all expert, who, from the time of the lord king En Pedro until that day, had carried on the war in Sicily. He was very cheerful, and helped all meanwhile as much as he could; he did not leave them in want of anything.

And the galley went so fast that, in a short time, it was at Constantinople where it found the emperor, Skyr Andronicus and his eldest son, Skyr Miqueli. And when the emperor had heard the message, he was very joyous and content and received the messengers well and, in the end, the matter came to pass as Frey Roger had dictated; the emperor wished Frey Roger to have to wife his niece, daughter of the emperor of Lantzaura. She was at once affianced to one of the knights for Frey Roger. Then Skyr Andronicus agreed that all the company Frey Roger would bring should be in the pay of the emperor; four onzas pay for each armed horse and one onza for each man afoot, and four onzas for each boatswain and one onza for each steersman, and twenty silver reales for each crossbowman and twenty-five silver reales for each seaman of the prow; and they should be paid every four months. And if, at any time, there was anyone who wished to go west, that the reckoning be made according to the agreement and that he be paid and allowed to return, and receive pay for two months whilst returning; and that Frey Roger be made grand duke of all the empire. And grand duke is a title which means the same as prince and lord over all the soldiers of the empire, with authority over the admiral; and all the islands of Romania are subject to him and also the places on the seacoasts.

And the emperor sent the charter of his title of grand duke to Frey Roger in a handsome gold casket, signed by him and his sons, and he sent him the baton of the office and the banner and hat (all the officials of Romania have a special hat the like of which no other man may wear). And so likewise he granted that they should find provision of pay at Monemvasia and of all they would need on arrival.

And so, joyous and content, the messengers returned

to Sicily with everything signed, and found Frey Roger at Alicata and told him all they had done and gave him the grants of everything, and the baton and the hat and the banner and the seal of the office of grand duke. And henceforth he will be called the grand duke.

And when the grand duke had received everything, he went to the lord king whom he found at Palermo with my lady the queen, and then he told him all about the matter. And the lord king was very joyous thereat and, incontinent, had ten galleys of the dockyard and two lenys given him, and had them repaired and fitted out for him. And the grand duke already had eight of his own, and so he had eighteen and two lenys; and then he freighted three large ships and many terides and more lenys, and sent word to all parts that everyone who was to go with him should come to Messina. And the lord king assisted everyone as much as he could with money and gave each person, man, woman and child, who was going with the grand duke, whether Catalan or Aragonese, one quintal of biscuits and five cheeses, and between every four persons one baco of salted meat and also garlic and onions.

So all embarked with their wives and children, very joyous and satisfied with the lord king; there never was a lord who behaved more liberally to people who had served him than he did, as much as he could and even above his power. Everyone may know that the lord king had no treasure; he had come out of such great wars that he had nothing left. And so, likewise, the rich homens and knights embarked, and the knights and horsemen had double rations of everything. . . . And so, when they had embarked, there were, between galleys and lenys and ships and terides, thirty-six sails; and there were one thousand five hundred horsemen, according as it was written down, fitted out with everything except horses. And there were full four thousand almugavars and full a thousand men afoot; without the galley-slaves and seamen who belonged to the shipping. And all these were Catalans and Aragonese and the greater part brought their wives or their mistresses and their children. And so they took leave of the lord king and departed from Messina at a suitable hour with great cheer and content.

Then God gave them fine weather and in a few days they landed at Monemvasia and there they found those who showed them great honour, and they were given great refreshment of all things. And they found there an order of the emperor to go straight to Constantinople, and so they did. They left Monemvasia and went to Constantinople. And when they were at Constantinople, the emperors, the father and the son, and all the people of the empire, received them with great joy and great pleasure. But if these were pleased at their arrival, the Genoese were sorry. They saw well that if these people remained there, they themselves would lose the honour and power they had in the empire; that the emperor had dared do nothing but what they wished, but that, henceforth, he would despise them. What shall I tell you? The wedding was celebrated, the grand duke took to wife the niece of the emperor, who was one of the beautiful and learned damsels of the world and was about sixteen; and the wedding was celebrated with great joy and content and every man received pay for four months.

But whilst this feast was great, some Genoese, by their arrogance, caused a fight with the Catalans; it was a great fight. And a wicked man, called Roso de Finar, carried the banner of the Genoese and came before the palace of Blanquerna; and our almugavars and the seamen came out against them, and even the grand duke and the rich homens and the knights could not hold them back; and they came out with a royal pennon carried before them and only about thirty squires and light horse went with them. And when they came near each other, the thirty squires proceeded to attack; and they attacked where the banner was and felled Roso de Finar to the ground and the almugavars hit out amongst them. What shall I tell you? This Roso and over three thousand Genoese were killed there; and the emperor saw all this from his palace and had great joy and content thereat. He said before all: "Now the Genoese, who have behaved with such arrogance, have found their match; and the Catalans were quite in the right, it was the fault of the Genoese."

And when the banner of the Genoese was on the ground and Roso and other important people had been killed, the almugavars, engaged in killing their enemies, wanted to go and pillage Pera, which is a select city of the Genoese, in which are all their treasure and merchandise. But upon this, when the emperor saw they were going to plunder Pera, he called the grand duke and said to him: "My son, go to your people and make them turn back; if they sack Pera the empire is destroyed, for the Genoese have much of our property and of that of the barons and the other people of our empire."

And, at once, the grand duke mounted a horse and, mace in hand, with all the rich homens and knights who had come with him, he went towards the almugavars, who already were preparing to demolish Pera, and he made them turn back. And so the emperor was very content and joyous.

And next day he had more pay given to all and ordered all to prepare to proceed to Boca Daner and attack the Turks, who, at that place, had taken from the emperor land to the extent of more than thirty days' journeys, covered with good cities and towns and castles which they had subdued and which paid tribute to them. And also, which is a greater disgrace, if a Turk wished to marry the daughter of the most important man in one of these cities or towns or castles which they had conquered, her parents or friends had to give her to him to wife. And when children were born, if they were males, they made them Turks and had them circumcised as if they were Saracens; but if they were females, they could follow which law they pleased. You see in what grief and subjection they were, to the great disgrace of all Christendom. Wherefore you may well see how necessary it was that that company should go there. And what is more, the Turks had, in truth, made such conquests, that an army of them came opposite Constantinople; there was not more than an arm of the sea, less than two miles broad, between them and the city, and they drew their swords and threatened the emperor, and the emperor could see it all. Imagine with what grief he beheld it. If they had had wherewith to cross this arm of the sea, they could have taken Constantinople.

From *The Chronicle of Muntaner*, trans. Lady Goodenough (London: Hakluyt Society, 2nd ser., vol. 50, 1921).

The Far East:
Missionaries and Merchants

The Tartar Menace to Europe

MATTHEW PARIS

1238

About this time, special ambassadors were sent by the Saracens, chiefly on behalf of the old man of the mountain, to the French king, telling him that a monstrous and inhuman race of men had burst forth from the northern mountains, and had taken possession of the extensive, rich lands of the East; that they had depopulated Hungary Major, and had sent threatening letters, with dreadful embassies; the chief of whom declared, that he was the messenger of God on high, sent to subdue the nations who rebelled against him. . . .

The inhabitants of Gothland and Friesland, dreading their attacks, did not, as was their custom, come to Yarmouth, in England, at the time of the herring-fisheries, at which place their ships usually loaded; and, owing to this, herrings in that year were considered of no value, on account of their abundance, and about forty or fifty, although very good, were sold for one piece of silver, even in places at a great distance from the sea. This

465

powerful and noble Saracen messenger, who had come to the French king, was sent on behalf of the whole of the people of the East to tell these things; and he asked assistance from the Western nations, the better to be able to repress the fury of the Tartars; he also sent a Saracen messenger from his own company to the king of England, who had arrived in England, to tell these events, and to say, that if they themselves could not withstand the attacks of such people, nothing remained to prevent their devastating the countries of the West. . . .

He therefore asked assistance in this urgent and general emergency, that the Saracens, with the assistance of the Christians, might resist the attacks of these people. The bishop of Winchester, who happened to be then present, and wearing the sign of the cross, interrupted his speech, and replied jocosely, "Let us leave these dogs to devour one another, that they may all be consumed, and perish; and we, when we proceed against the enemies of Christ who remain, will slay them, and cleanse the face of the earth, so that all the world will be subject to the one Catholic Church, and there will be one shepherd and one fold."

From *English History*, trans. J. A. Giles (London: Bohn, 1852).

A Mission to the Great Khan

WILLIAM OF RUBRUCK

1253-54

TO THE most excellent lord and most Christian Louis, by the grace of God illustrious king of the French [Louis IX], from Friar William of Rubruck, the meanest in the order of Minor Friars, greetings, and may he always triumph in Christ. It is written in Ecclesiasticus of the wise man: "He shall go through the land of foreign peoples, and shall try the good and evil in all things." This, my lord King, have I done, and may it have been as a wise man and not as a fool; for many do what the wise man doth, though not wisely, but most foolishly; of this number I fear I may be. Nevertheless in whatever way I may have done, since you commanded me when I took my leave of you that I should write you whatever I should see among the Tartars, and you did also admonish me not to fear writing a long letter, so I do what you enjoined on me, with fear, however, and diffidence, for the proper words that I should write to so great a monarch do not suggest themselves to me.

Be it known then to your Sacred Majesty that in the year of our Lord one thousand CCLIII, on the nones of May (7th May), I entered the Sea of Pontus, which is commonly called Mare Majus, or the Greater Sea. . . .

On the Octave of the Innocents (3rd January, 1254) we were taken to court; and there came certain Nestorian priests, whom I did not know to be Christians, and they asked me in what direction I prayed. I said, "To the east." And they asked that because we had shaved our beards, at the suggestion of our guide, so as to appear before the chan according to the fashion of our country. 'Twas for this that they took us for Tuins, that is idolaters. They also made us explain the Bible. Then they asked us what kind of reverence we wanted to make the chan, according to our fashion, or according to theirs. I replied to them, "We are priests given to the service of God. Noblemen in our country do not, for the glory of God, allow priests to bend the knee before them. Nevertheless, we want to humble ourselves to every man for the love of God. We come from afar: so in the first place then, if it please you, we will sing praises to God who has brought us here in safety from so far, and after that we will do as it shall please your lord, this only excepted, that nothing be required of us contrary to the worship and glory of God." Then they went into the house, and repeated what I had said. It pleased the lord, and so they placed us before the door of the dwelling, holding up the felt which hung before it; and, as it was the Nativity, we began to sing:

> "A solis ortus cardine
> Et usque terre limitem
> Christum canamus principem
> Natum Maria virgine."

When we had sung this hymn, they searched our legs and breasts and arms to see if we had knives upon us. They had the interpreter examined, and made him leave his belt and knife in the custody of a door-keeper. Then we entered, and there was a bench in the entry with cosmos, and near by it they made the interpreter stand. They made us, however, sit down on a bench near the ladies. The house was all covered inside with cloth of gold, and there was a fire of briars and wormwood roots —which grow here to great size—and of cattle dung, in a grate in the centre of the dwelling. He (Mangu) was seated on a couch, and was dressed in a skin spotted and glossy, like a seal's skin. He is a little man, of medium height, aged forty-five years, and a young wife sat beside him; and a very ugly, full-grown girl called Cirina, with other children sat on a couch after them. This dwelling had belonged to a certain Christian lady, whom he had much loved, and of whom he had had this girl. Afterwards he had taken this young wife, but the

girl was the mistress of all this *ordu,* which had been
her mother's.

He had us asked what we wanted to drink, wine or
terracina, which is rice wine (*cervisia*), or *caracosmos,*
which is clarified mare's milk, or *bal,* which is honey
mead. For in winter they make use of these four kinds
of drinks. I replied: "My lord, we are not men who seek
to satisfy our fancies about drinks; whatever pleases you
will suit us." So he had us given of the rice drink, which
was clear and flavoured like white wine, and of which
I tasted a little out of respect for him, but for our misfortune our interpreter was standing by the butlers, who
gave him so much to drink, that he was drunk in a short
time. After this the chan had brought some falcons and
other birds, which he took on his hand and looked at,
and after a long while he bade us speak. Then we had
to bend our knees. He had his interpreter, a certain Nestorian, who I did not know was a Christian, and we had
our interpreter, such as he was, and already drunk. Then
I said: "In the first place we render thanks and praise
to God, who has brought us from so far to see Mangu
Chan, to whom God has given so much power on earth.
And we pray Christ, by whose will we all live and die,
to grant him a happy and long life." For it is their desire, that one shall pray for their lives. Then I told him:
"My lord, we have heard of Sartach that he was a Christian, and the Christians who heard it rejoiced greatly,
and principally my lord the king of the French. So we
came to him, and my lord the king sent him letters by
us in which were words of peace, and among other
things he bore witness to him as to the kind of men we
were, and he begged him to allow us to remain in his
country, for it is our office to teach men to live according to the law of God. He sent us, however, to his father Baatu, and Baatu sent us to you. You it is to whom

God has given great power in the world. We pray then your mightiness to give us permission to remain in your dominion, to perform the service of God for you, for your wives and your children. We have neither gold, nor silver, nor precious stones to present to you, but only ourselves to offer to you to serve God, and to pray to God for you. At all events give us leave to remain here till this cold has passed away, for my companion is so feeble that he cannot with safety to his life stand any more the fatigue of travelling on horseback."

My companion had told me of his infirm condition, and had adjured me to ask for permission to stay, for we supposed that we would have to go back to Baatu, unless by special grace he gave us permission to stay. Then he began his reply: "As the sun sends its rays everywhere, likewise my sway and that of Baatu reach everywhere, so we do not want your gold or silver." So far I understood my interpreter, but after that I could not understand the whole of any one sentence: 'twas by this that I found out he was drunk, and Mangu himself appeared to me tipsy. His speech, it seemed to me, however, showed that he was not pleased that we had come to Sartach in the first place rather than to him. Then I, seeing that I was without interpreter, said nothing, save to beg him not to be displeased with what I had said of gold and silver, for I had not said that he needed or wanted such things, but only that we would gladly honour him with things temporal as well as spiritual. Then he made us arise and sit down again, and after awhile we saluted him and went out, and with us his secretaries and his interpreter, who was bringing up one of his daughters. And they began to question us greatly about the kingdom of France, whether there were many sheep and cattle and horses there, and whether they had not better go there at once and take it all. And I had to use all my strength to conceal my indignation and anger; but I answered, "There are many good things there, which you would see if it befell you to go there."

Then they appointed someone to take care of us, and we went to the monk. And as we were coming out of there to go to our lodgings, the interpreter I have mentioned came to me and said: "Mangu Chan takes compassion on you and allows you to stay here for the space of two months: then the great cold will be over. And he informs you that ten days hence there is a goodly city called Caracarum. If you wish to go there, he will have you given all you may require; if, however, you wish to remain here, you may do so, and you shall have what you need. It will, however, be fatiguing for you to ride with the court." I answered: "May the Lord keep Mangu Chan and give him a happy and long life! We have found this monk here, whom we believe to be a holy man and come here by the will of God. So we would willingly remain here with him, for we are monks, and we would say our prayers with him for the life of the chan." Then he left us without a word. And we went to a big house, which we found cold and without a supply of fuel, and we were still without food, and it was night. Then he to whom we had been entrusted gave us fuel and a little food. . . .

A certain woman from Metz in Lorraine, Paquette by name, and who had been made a prisoner in Hungary, found us out, and she gave us the best food she could. She belonged to the *ordu* of the Christian lady of whom I have spoken, and she told me of the unheard-of misery she had endured before coming to the *ordu*. But now she was fairly well off. She had a young Ruthenian husband, of whom she had had three right fine-looking boys, and he knew how to make houses, a very good trade among them. Furthermore, she told us that there was in Caracarum a certain master goldsmith, William by name, a native of Paris: and his family name was Buchier, and the name of his father was Laurent Buchier.

She believed that he had still a brother living on the Grand Pont, called Roger Buchier. She also told me that he supported a young man whom he considered as his son, and who was a most excellent interpreter. But as Mangu Chan had given this said master three hundred iascot, that is three thousand marks, and L workmen to do a certain work, she feared he would not be able to send his son to me. She had heard people in the *ordu* saying, "The men who have come from your country are good men, and Mangu Chan would be pleased to speak with them, but their interpreter is worth nothing." 'Twas for this that she was solicitous about an interpreter. So I wrote to this master of my coming, asking him if he could send me his son; and he replied that in that month he could not, but the following he would have finished his task and then he would send him to me. . . .

Toward the middle of Lent, the son of Master William arrived bringing a beautiful crucifix, made in French style, with a silver image of the Christ fixed on it. Seeing it, the monks and priests stole it, though he was to have presented it from his master to Bulgai, the grand secretary of the court; when I heard of this I was greatly scandalized.

This young man also informed Mangu Chan that the work he had ordered to be done was finished; and this work I shall here describe to you. Mangu had at Caracarum a great palace, situated next to the city walls, enclosed within a high wall like those which enclose monks' priories among us. Here is a great palace, where he has his drinkings twice a year: once about Easter, when he passes there, and once in summer, when he goes back (westward). And the latter is the greater (feast), for then come to his court all the nobles, even though distant two months' journey; and then he makes them largess of robes and presents, and shows his great glory. There are there many buildings as long as barns, in which are stored his provisions and his treasures. In the entry of this great palace, it being unseemly to bring in there skins of milk and other drinks, Master William the Parisian had made for him a great silver tree, and at its roots are four lions of silver, each with a conduit through it, and all belching forth white milk of mares. And four conduits are led inside the tree to its tops, which are bent downward, and on each of these is also a gilded serpent, whose tail twines round the tree. And from one of these pipes flows wine, from another *caracosmos,* or clarified mare's milk, from another *bal,* a drink made with honey, and from another rice mead, which is called *terracina;* and for each liquor there is a special silver bowl at the foot of the tree to receive it. Between these four conduits in the top, he made an angel holding a trumpet, and underneath the tree he made a vault in which a man can be hid. And pipes go up through the heart of the tree to the angel. In the first place he made bellows, but they did not give enough wind. Outside the palace is a cellar in which the liquors are stored, and there are servants all ready to pour them out when they hear the angel trumpeting. And there are branches of silver on the tree, and leaves and fruit. When then drink is wanted, the head butler cries to the angel to blow his trumpet. Then he who is concealed in the vault, hearing this, blows with all his might in the pipe leading to the angel, and the angel places the trumpet to his mouth, and blows the trumpet right loudly. Then the servants who are in the cellar, hearing this, pour the different liquors into the proper conduits, and the conduits lead them down into the bowls prepared for that, and then the butlers draw it and carry it to the palace to the men and women. . . .

Finally, the letters he [Mangu Chan] sends you being finished, they called me and interpreted them to me. I wrote down their tenor, as well as I could understand through an interpreter, and it is as follows:

"The commandment of the eternal God is, in Heaven there is only one eternal God, and on Earth there is only one lord, Chingis Chan, the Son of God, Demugin, (or) Chingis, 'sound of iron.' " (For they call him Chingis, "sound of iron," because he was a blacksmith; and puffed up in their pride they even say that he is the son of God.) "This is what is told you. Wherever there be a Moal [Mongol], or a Naiman, or a Merkit or a Musteleman, wherever ears can hear, wherever horses can travel, there let it be heard and known; those who shall have heard my commandments and understood them, and who shall not believe and shall make war against us, shall hear and see that they have eyes and see not; and when they shall want to hold anything they shall be without hands, and when they shall want to walk they shall be without feet: this is the eternal command of God. . . .

"This, through the virtue of the eternal God, through the great world of the Moal, is the word of Mangu Chan to the lord of the French, King Louis, and to all the other lords and priests and to all the great realm of the French, that they may understand our words. For the word of the eternal God to Chingis Chan has not reached unto you, either through Chingis Chan or others who have come after him." . . .

Master William, once your subject, sends you a girdle ornamented with a precious stone, such as they wear against lightning and thunder; and he sends you endless

salutations, praying always for you; and I cannot sufficiently express to God or to you the thanks I owe him.
In all I baptized vi persons there.

So we separated with tears, my companion remaining
with Master William, and I alone with my interpreter
going back with my guide and one servant, who had an
order by which we were to receive every four days one
sheep for the iiii of us.

In two months and ten days we came to Baatu, and
(on the way there) we never saw a town, nor the trace
of any building save tombs, with the exception of one
little village, in which we did not eat bread; neither did
we ever take a rest in those two months and x days,
except for one day only, when we could not get horses.
We came back for the most part of the way through the
same peoples, though generally through different districts; for we went in winter and came back in summer
by parts farther to the north, fifteen days excepted, when
both in going and in coming back we had to keep along
a river between mountains, where there is no grass except close to the river. We had to go for two days—
sometimes for three days—without taking any other
nourishment than *cosmos*. Sometimes we were in great
danger, not being able to find any people, at moments
when we were short of food, and with worn-out horses.

It seems to me inexpedient to send another friar to
the Tartars, as I went, or as the preaching friars go; but
if the lord pope, who is the head of all Christians, wishes
to send with proper state a bishop, and reply to the
foolishness they have already written three times to the
Franks (once to Pope Innocent the Fourth of blessed
memory, and twice to you: once by David, who deceived you, and now by me), he would be able to tell
them whatever he pleased, and also make them reply
in writing. They listen to whatever an ambassador has

to say, and always ask if he has more to say; but he must have a good interpreter—nay, several interpreters—abundant travelling funds, etc.

From *Journey of William of Rubruck*, William Woodville Rockhill, ed. (London: Hakluyt Society, 2nd ser., vol. 4, 1900).

The Labours of a Friar in Cathay

JOHN OF MONTE CORVINO

1305

I FRIAR JOHN of Monte Corvino, of the order of Minor Friars, departed from Tauris, a city of the Persians, in the year of the Lord 1291, and proceeded to India. And I remained in the country of India, wherein stands the church of St. Thomas the Apostle, for thirteen months, and in that region baptized in different places about one hundred persons. The companion of my journey was Friar Nicholas of Pistoia, of the order of Preachers, who died there, and was buried in the church aforesaid.

I proceeded on my farther journey and made my way to Cathay, the realm of the emperor of the Tartars who is called the grand cham. To him I presented the letter of our lord the pope, and invited him to adopt the Catholic faith of our Lord Jesus Christ, but he had grown too old in idolatry. However he bestows many kindnesses upon the Christians, and these two years past I am abiding with him.

The Nestorians, a certain body who profess to bear the Christian name, but who deviate sadly from the Christian religion, have grown so powerful in those parts that they will not allow a Christian of another ritual to have ever so small a chapel, or to publish any doctrine different from their own.

To these regions there never came anyone of the apostles, nor yet of the disciples. And so the Nestorians aforesaid, either directly or through others whom they bribed, have brought on me persecutions of the sharpest. For they got up stories that I was not sent by our lord the pope, but was a great spy and impostor; and after a while they produced false witnesses who declared that there was indeed an envoy sent with presents of immense value for the emperor, but that I had murdered him in India, and stolen what he had in charge. And these intrigues and calumnies went on for some five years. And thus it came to pass that many a time I was dragged before the judgment seat with ignominy and threats of death. At last, by God's providence, the emperor, through the confessions of a certain individual, came to know my innocence and the malice of my adversaries; and he banished them with their wives and children.

In this mission I abode alone and without any associate for eleven years; but it is now going on for two years since I was joined by Friar Arnold, a German of the province of Cologne.

I have built a church in the city of Cambaliech, in which the king has his chief residence. This I completed six years ago; and I have built a bell-tower to it, and put three bells in it. I have baptized there, as well as I can estimate, up to this time some six thousand persons; and if those charges against me of which I have spoken had not been made, I should have baptized more than thirty thousand. And I am often still engaged in baptizing.

Also I have gradually bought one hundred and fifty boys, the children of pagan parents, and of ages varying from seven to eleven, who had never learned any religion. These boys I have baptized, and I have taught them Greek and Latin after our manner. Also I have written out psalters for them, with thirty hymnaries and two breviaries. By help of these, eleven of the boys already know our service, and form a choir and take their weekly turn of duty as they do in convents, whether I am there or not. Many of the boys are also employed in writing out psalters and other things suitable. His majesty the emperor moreover delights much to hear them chaunting. I have the bells rung at all the canonical hours, and with my congregation of babes and sucklings I perform divine service, and the chaunting we do by ear because I have no service book with the notes.

A certain king of this part of the world, by name George, belonging to the sect of Nestorian Christians, and of the illustrious family of that great king who was called Prester John of India, in the first year of my arrival here attached himself to me, and being converted by me to the truth of the Catholic faith, took the lesser orders, and when I celebrated mass he used to attend me wearing his royal robes. Certain others of the Nestorians on this account accused him of apostasy, but he brought over a great part of his people with him to the true Catholic faith, and built a church on a scale of royal magnificence in honour of our God, of the Holy Trinity, and of our lord the pope, giving it the name of the "Roman church."

This King George six years ago departed to the Lord a true Christian, leaving as his heir a son scarcely out of the cradle, and who is now nine years old. And after King George's death his brothers, perfidious followers of the errors of Nestorius, perverted again all those whom he had brought over to the church, and carried them back to their original schismatical creed. And being all alone, and not able to leave his majesty the cham, I could not go to visit the church above-mentioned, which is twenty days' journey distant.

Yet, if I could but get some good fellow-workers to help me, I trust in God that all this might be retrieved, for I still possess the grant which was made in our favour by the late King George before mentioned. So I say again that if it had not been for the slanderous charges which I have spoken of, the harvest reaped by this time would have been great!

Indeed if I had had but two or three comrades to aid me 'tis possible that the emperor cham would have been baptized by this time! I ask then for such brethren to come, if any are willing to come, such I mean as will make it their great business to lead exemplary lives, and not to make broad their own phylacteries.

As for the road hither I may tell you that the way through the land of the Goths, subject to the emperor of the Northern Tartars, is the shortest and safest; and by it the friars might come, along with the letter-carriers, in five or six months. The other route again is very long and very dangerous, involving two sea-voyages; the first of which is about as long as that from Acre to the province of Provence, whilst the second is as long as from Acre to England. And it is possible that it might take more than two years to accomplish the journey that way. But, on the other hand, the first-mentioned route has not been open for a considerable time, on account of wars that have been going on.

It is twelve years since I have had any news of the papal court, or of our order, or of the state of affairs generally in the West. Two years ago indeed there came hither a certain Lombard leech and chirurgeon, who spread abroad in these parts the most incredible blasphemies about the court of Rome and our order and the state of things in the West, and on this account I exceedingly desire to obtain true intelligence. I pray the brethren whom this letter may reach to do their possible to bring its contents to the knowledge of our lord the pope, and the cardinals, and the agents of the order at the court of Rome.

I beg the minister general of our order to supply me with an antiphonarium, with the legends of the saints, a gradual, and a psalter with the musical notes, as a copy; for I have nothing but a pocket breviary with the short lessons, and a little missal: if I had one for a copy, the boys of whom I have spoken could transcribe others from it. Just now I am engaged in building a second church, with the view of distributing the boys in more places than one.

I have myself grown old and grey, more with toil and trouble than with years; for I am not more than fifty-eight. I have got a competent knowledge of the language and character which is most generally used by the Tartars. And I have already translated into that language and character the New Testament and the psalter, and have caused them to be written out in the fairest penmanship they have; and so by writing, reading, and preaching, I bear open and public testimony to the law of Christ. And I had been in treaty with the late King George, if he had lived, to translate the whole Latin ritual, that it might be sung throughout the whole extent of his territory; and whilst he was alive I used to celebrate mass in his church, according to the Latin ritual, reading in the before-mentioned language and character the words of both the preface and the canon.

And the son of the king before-mentioned is called after my name, John; and I hope in God that he will walk in his father's steps.

As far as I ever saw or heard tell, I do not believe that

any king or prince in the world can be compared to his majesty the cham in respect of the extent of his dominions, the vastness of their population, or the amount of his wealth. Here I stop.

Dated at the city of Cambalec in the kingdom of Cathay, in the year of the Lord 1305, and on the 8th day of January.

From *Cathay and the Way Thither*, H. Yule, ed., 2nd ed., rev. H. Cordier (London: Hakluyt Society, 2nd Ser., vol. 37, 1914).

A Last Mission to Cathay

JOHN OF MARIGNOLLI

1338-1353

I, FRIAR JOHN [of Marignolli] of Florence, of the order of Minors, and now unworthy bishop of Bisignano, was sent with certain others, in the year of our Lord one thousand three hundred and thirty [eight], by the holy pope Benedict the Eleventh, to carry letters and presents from the apostolic see to the kaan or chief emperor of all the Tartars, a sovereign who holds the sway of nearly half the eastern world, and whose power and wealth, with the multitude of cities and provinces and languages under him, and the countless number, as I may say, of the nations over which he rules, pass all telling.

We set out from Avignon in the month of December, came to Naples in the beginning of Lent, and stopped there till Easter (which fell at the end of March), waiting for a ship of Genoa, which was coming with the Tartar envoys whom the kaan had sent from his great city of Cambalec to the pope, to request the latter to despatch an embassy to his court, whereby communication might be established, and a treaty of alliance struck between him and the Christians; for he greatly loves and honours our faith. Moreover the chief princes of his whole empire, more than thirty thousand in number, who are called alans, and govern the whole Orient, are Christians either in fact or in name, calling themselves "the Pope's slaves," and ready to die for the "Franks." For so they term us, not indeed from France, but from Frank-land. Their first apostle was Friar John, called de Monte Corvino, who seventy-two years previously, after having been soldier, judge, and doctor in the service of the Emperor Frederic, had become a Minor Friar, and a most wise and learned one.

Howbeit on the first of May we arrived by sea at Constantinople, and stopped at Pera till the feast of St. John Baptist. We had no idle time of it however, for we were engaged in a most weighty controversy with the patriarch of the Greeks and their whole council in the palace of St. Sophia. And there God wrought in us a new miracle, giving us a mouth and wisdom which they were not able to resist; for they were constrained to confess that they must needs be schismatics, and had no plea to urge against their own condemnation except the intolerable arrogance of the Roman prelates.

Thence we sailed across the Black Sea, and in eight days arrived at Caffa, where there are Christians of many sects. From that place we went on to the first emperor of the Tartars, Usbec, and laid before him the letters which we bore, with certain pieces of cloth, a great warhorse, some strong liquor, and the pope's presents. And after the winter was over, having been well fed, well clothed, loaded with handsome presents, and supplied by the king with horses and travelling expenses, we proceeded to ARMALEC [the capital] of the Middle

Empire. There we built a church, bought a piece of ground, dug wells, sung masses, and baptized several; preaching freely and openly, notwithstanding the fact that only the year before the bishop and six other Minor Friars had there undergone for Christ's sake a glorious martyrdom, illustrated by brilliant miracles. The names of these martyrs were Friar Richard the Bishop, a Burgundian by nation, Friar Francis of Alessandria, Friar Paschal of Spain (this one was a prophet and saw the heavens open, and foretold the martyrdom which should befall him and his brethren, and the overthrow of the Tartars of Saray by a flood, and the destruction of Armalec in vengeance for their martyrdom, and that the emperor would be slain on the third day after their martyrdom, and many other glorious things); Friar Laurence of Ancona, Friar Peter, an Indian friar who acted as their interpreter, and Gillott [Gilottus], a merchant.

Towards the end of the third year after our departure from the papal court, quitting Armalec we came to the CYOLLOS KAGON, i.e., to the Sand Hills thrown up by the wind. Before the days of the Tartars nobody believed that the earth was habitable beyond these, nor indeed was it believed that there was any country at all beyond. But the Tartars by God's permission, and with wonderful exertion, did cross them, and found themselves in what the philosophers call the torrid and impassable zone. Pass it however the Tartars did; and so did I, and that twice. 'Tis of this that David speaketh in the Psalms, *"Posuit desertum,"* &c. After having passed it we came to CAMBALEC, the chief seat of the empire of the East. Of its incredible magnitude, population, and military array, we will say nothing. But the grand kaam, when he beheld the great horses, and the pope's presents, with his letter, and King Robert's too, with their golden seals, and when he saw us also, rejoiced greatly, being delighted, yea exceedingly delighted with everything, and treated us with the greatest honour. And when I entered the kaam's presence it was in full festival vestments, with a very fine cross carried before me, and candles and incense, whilst *Credo in Unum Deum* was chaunted, in that glorious palace where he dwells. And when the chaunt was ended I bestowed a full benediction, which he received with all humility.

And so we were dismissed to one of the imperial apartments which had been most elegantly fitted up for us; and two princes were appointed to attend to all our wants. And this they did in the most liberal manner, not merely as regards meat and drink, but even down to such things as paper for lanterns, whilst all necessary servants also were detached from the court to wait upon us. And so they tended us for nearly four years, never failing to treat us with unbounded respect. And I should add that they kept us and all our establishment clothed in costly raiment. And considering that we were thirty-two persons, what the kaam expended for everything on our account must have amounted, as well as I can calculate, to more than four thousand marks. And we had many and glorious disputations with the Jews and other sectaries; and we made also a great harvest of souls in that empire.

The Minor Friars in Cambalec have a cathedral church immediately adjoining the palace, with a proper residence for the archbishop, and other churches in the city besides, and they have bells too, and all the clergy have their subsistence from the emperor's table in the most honourable manner.

And when the emperor saw that nothing would induce me to abide there, he gave me leave to return to the pope, carrying presents from him, with an allowance for three years' expenses, and with a request that either I or some one else should be sent speedily back with the rank of cardinal, and with full powers, to be bishop there; for the office of bishop is highly venerated by all the Orientals, whether they be Christians or no. He should also be of the Minorite Order, because these are the only priests that they are acquainted with; and they think that the pope is always of that order because Pope Girolamo was so who sent them that legate whom the Tartars and Alans venerate as a saint, viz., Friar John of Monte Corvino of the order of Minorites, of whom we have already spoken.

We abode in Cambalec about three years, and then we took our way through MANZI [South China], with a magnificent provision for our expenses from the emperor, besides about two hundred horses; and on our way we beheld the glory of this world in such a multitude of cities, towns, and villages, and in other ways displayed, that no tongue can give it fit expression.

And sailing on the feast of St. Stephen, we navigated the Indian Sea until Palm Sunday, and then arrived at a very noble city of India called COLUMBUM, where the whole world's pepper is produced. Now this pepper grows on a kind of vines, which are planted just like in our vineyards. These vines produce clusters which are at first like those of the wild vine, of a green colour, and afterwards are almost like bunches of our grapes, and they have a red wine in them which I have squeezed out on my plate as a condiment. When they have ripened, they are left to dry upon the tree, and when shrivelled by the excessive heat the dry clusters are knocked off with a stick and caught upon linen cloths, and so the harvest is gathered.

These are things that I have seen with mine eyes and handled with my hands during the fourteen months that I stayed there. And there is no roasting of the pepper, as authors have falsely asserted, nor does it grow in forests, but in regular gardens; nor are the Saracens the proprietors but the Christians of St. Thomas. And these latter are the masters of the public steelyard, from which I derived, as a perquisite of my office as pope's legate, every month a hundred gold *fan*, and a thousand when I left.

There is a church of St. George there, of the Latin communion, at which I dwelt. And I adorned it with fine paintings, and taught there the holy law. And after I had been there some time I went beyond the glory of Alexander the Great, when he set up his column (in India). For I erected a stone as my landmark and memorial, in the corner of the world over against Paradise, and anointed it with oil! In sooth it was a marble pillar with a stone cross upon it, intended to last till the world's end. And it had the pope's arms and my own engraved upon it, with inscriptions both in Indian and Latin characters. I consecrated and blessed it in the presence of an infinite multitude of people, and I was carried on the shoulders of the chiefs in a litter or palankin like Solomon's.

So after a year and four months I took leave of the brethren, and after accomplishing many glorious works I went to see the famous queen of SABA. By her I was honourably treated, and after some harvest of souls (for there are a few Christians there) I proceeded by sea to SEYLLAN, a glorious mountain opposite to Paradise. And from Seyllan to Paradise, according to what the natives say after the tradition of their fathers, is a distance of forty Italian miles; so that, 'tis said, the sound of the waters falling from the fountain of Paradise is heard there.

From *Cathay and the Way Thither,* H. Yule, ed., 2nd ed. rev. H. Cordier.

Advice to Merchants Bound for Cathay

FRANCESCO PEGOLOTTI

C. 1340

In the name of the Lord, Amen!

This book is called the Book of Descriptions of Countries and of measures employed in business, and of other things needful to be known by merchants of different parts of the world, and by all who have to do with merchandise and exchanges; showing also what relation the merchandise of one country or of one city bears to that of others; and how one kind of goods is better than another kind; and where the various wares come from, and how they may be kept as long as possible.

The book was compiled by Francis Balducci Pegolotti of Florence, who was with the Company of the Bardi of Florence, and during the time that he was in the service of the said Company, for the good and honour and prosperity of the said Company, and for his own, and for that of whosoever shall read or transcribe the said book. And this copy has been made from the book of Agnolo di Lotti of Antella, and the said book was transcribed from the original book of the said Francesco Balducci.

In the first place, you must let your beard grow long

and not shave. And at Tana you should furnish yourself with a dragoman. And you must not try to save money in the matter of dragomen by taking a bad one instead of a good one. For the additional wages of the good one will not cost you so much as you will save by having him. And besides the dragoman it will be well to take at least two good menservants, who are acquainted with the Cumanian tongue. And if the merchant likes to take a woman with him from Tana, he can do so; if he does not like to take one there is no obligation, only if he does take one he will be kept much more comfortably than if he does not take one. Howbeit, if he do take one, it will be well that she be acquainted with the Cumanian tongue as well as the men.

And from Tana travelling to Gittarchan [Astrakhan] you should take with you twenty-five days' provisions, that is to say, flour and salt fish, for as to meat you will find enough of it at all the places along the road. And so also at all the chief stations noted in going from one country to another in the route, according to the number of days set down above, you should furnish yourself with flour and salt fish; other things you will find in sufficiency, and especially meat.

The road you travel from Tana to Cathay is perfectly safe, whether by day or by night, according to what the merchants say who have used it. Only if the merchant, in going or coming, should die upon the road, everything belonging to him will become the perquisite of the lord of the country in which he dies, and the officers of the lord will take possession of all. And in like manner if he die in Cathay. But if his brother be with him, or an intimate friend and comrade calling himself his brother, then to such an one they will surrender the property of the deceased, and so it will be rescued.

And there is another danger: this is when the lord of

the country dies, and before the new lord who is to have the lordship is proclaimed; during such intervals there have sometimes been irregularities practised on the Franks, and other foreigners. (They call "Franks" all the Christians of these parts from Romania westward.) And neither will the roads be safe to travel until the other lord be proclaimed who is to reign in room of him who is deceased.

Cathay is a province which contains a multitude of cities and towns. Among others there is one in particular, that is to say the capital city, to which is great resort of merchants, and in which there is a vast amount of trade; and this city is called Cambalec. And the said city hath a circuit of one hundred miles, and is all full of people and houses and of dwellers in the said city.

You may calculate that a merchant with a dragoman, and with two menservants, and with goods to the value of twenty-five thousand golden florins, should spend on his way to Cathay from sixty to eighty sommi of silver, and not more if he manage well; and for all the road back again from Cathay to Tana, including the expenses of living and the pay of servants, and all other charges, the cost will be about five sommi per head of pack animals, or something less. And you may reckon the sommo to be worth five golden florins. You may reckon also that each ox-waggon will require one ox, and will carry ten cantars Genoese weight; and the camel-waggon will require three camels, and will carry thirty cantars Genoese weight; and the horse-waggon will require one horse, and will commonly carry six and a half cantars of silk, at two hundred and fifty Genoese pounds to the cantar. And a bale of silk may be reckoned at between one hundred and ten and one hundred and fifteen Genoese pounds.

You may reckon also that from Tana to Sara the road

is less safe than on any other part of the journey; and yet even when this part of the road is at its worst, if you are some sixty men in the company you will go as safely as if you were in your own house.

Anyone from Genoa or from Venice, wishing to go to the places above-named, and to make the journey to Cathay, should carry linens with him, and if he visit Organci he will dispose of these well. In Organci he should purchase sommi of silver, and with these he should proceed without making any further investment, unless it be some bales of the very finest stuffs which go in small bulk, and cost no more for carriage than coarser stuffs would do.

Merchants who travel this road can ride on horseback or on asses, or mounted in any way that they list to be mounted.

Whatever silver the merchants may carry with them as far as Cathay the lord of Cathay will take from them and put into his treasury. And to merchants who thus bring silver they give that paper money of theirs in exchange. This is of yellow paper, stamped with the seal of the lord aforesaid. And this money is called balishi; and with this money you can readily buy silk and all other merchandise that you have a desire to buy. And all the people of the country are bound to receive it. And yet you shall not pay a higher price for your goods because your money is of paper. And of the said paper money there are three kinds, one being worth more than another, according to the value which has been established for each by that lord.

And you may reckon that you can buy for one sommo of silver nineteen or twenty pounds of Cathay silk, when reduced to Genoese weight, and that the sommo should weigh eight and a half ounces of Genoa, and should be of the alloy of eleven ounces and seventeen deniers to the pound.

You may reckon also that in Cathay you should get three or three and a half pieces of damasked silk for a sommo; and from three and a half to five pieces of nacchetti of silk and gold, likewise for a sommo of silver.

From *Cathay and the Way Thither*, H. Yule, ed., 2nd ed., rev. H. Cordier.

Henry the Navigator's Search for New Lands

GOMES DE AZURARA

1434

AND you should note well that the noble spirit of this prince, by a sort of natural constraint, was ever urging him both to begin and to carry out very great deeds. For which reason, after the taking of Ceuta he always kept ships well armed against the Infidel, both for war, and because he had also a wish to know the land that lay beyond the isles of Canary and that cape called Bojador, for that up to his time, neither by writings, nor by the memory of man, was known with any certainty the nature of the land beyond that cape. Some said indeed that Saint Brandan had passed that way; and there was another tale of two galleys rounding the cape, which never returned. But this doth not appear at all likely to be true, for it is not to be presumed that if the said galleys went there, some other ships would not have endeavoured to learn what voyage they had made. And be-

cause the said Lord Infant wished to know the truth of
this—since it seemed to him that if he or some other
lord did not endeavour to gain that knowledge, no
mariners or merchants would ever dare to attempt it
(for it is clear that none of them ever trouble themselves
to sail to a place where there is not a sure and certain
hope of profit)—and seeing also that no other prince
took any pains in this matter, he sent out his own ships
against those parts, to have manifest certainty of them
all. And to this he was stirred up by his zeal for the service of God and of the king Edward his lord and brother,
who then reigned. And this was the first reason of his
action.

The second reason was that if there chanced to be in
those lands some population of Christians, or some ha-
vens, into which it would be possible to sail without
peril, many kinds of merchandise might be brought to
this realm, which would find a ready market, and reasonably so, because no other people of these parts traded
with them, nor yet people of any other that were known;
and also the products of this realm might be taken there,
which traffic would bring great profit to our countrymen.

The third reason was that, as it was said that the
power of the Moors in that land of Africa was very much
greater than was commonly supposed, and that there
were no Christians among them, nor any other race of
men; and because every wise man is obliged by natural
prudence to wish for a knowledge of the power of his
enemy; therefore the said Lord Infant exerted himself to
cause this to be fully discovered, and to make it known
determinately how far the power of those infidels extended.

The fourth reason was because during the one and
thirty years that he had warred against the Moors, he
had never found a Christian king, nor a lord outside this

land, who for the love of our Lord Jesus Christ would aid him in the said war. Therefore he sought to know if there were in those parts any Christian princes, in whom the charity and the love of Christ was so ingrained that they would aid him against those enemies of the faith.

The fifth reason was his great desire to make increase in the faith of our Lord Jesus Christ and to bring to him all the souls that should be saved—understanding that all the mystery of the Incarnation, Death, and Passion of our Lord Jesus Christ was for this sole end—namely the salvation of lost souls—whom the said Lord Infant by his travail and spending would fain bring into the true path. . . .

Now the Infant always received home again with great patience those whom he had sent out, as captains of his ships, in search of that land, never upbraiding them with their failure, but with gracious countenance listening to the story of the events of their voyage, giving them such rewards as he was wont to give to those who served him well, and then either sending them back to search again or despatching other picked men of his household, with their ships well furnished, making more urgent his charge to them, with promise of greater guerdons, if they added anything to the voyage that those before them had made, all to the intent that he might arrive at some comprehension of that difficulty. And at last, after twelve years, the Infant armed a "barcha" and gave it to Gil Eannes, one of his squires, whom he afterwards knighted and cared for right nobly. And he followed the course that others had taken; but touched by the selfsame terror, he only went as far as the Canary Islands, where he took some captives and returned to the kingdom. Now this was in the year of Jesus Christ 1433, and in the next year the Infant made ready the same vessel, and calling Gil Eannes apart, charged him earnestly to strain every nerve to pass that cape, and even if he could do nothing else on that voyage, yet he should consider that to be enough. "You cannot find," said the Infant, "a peril so great that the hope of reward will not be greater, and in truth I wonder much at the notion you have all taken on so uncertain a matter—for even if these things that are reported had any authority, however small, I would not blame you, but you tell me only the opinions of four mariners, who come but from the Flanders trade or from some other ports that are very commonly sailed to, and know nothing of the needle or sailing-chart. Go forth, then, and heed none of their words, but make your voyage straightway, inasmuch as with the grace of God you cannot but gain from this journey honour and profit." The Infant was a man of very great authority, so that his admonitions, mild though they were, had much effect on the serious-minded. And so it appeared by the deed of this man, for he, after these words, resolved not to return to the presence of his lord without assured tidings of that for which he was sent. And as he purposed, so he performed—for in that voyage he doubled the cape, despising all danger, and found the lands beyond quite contrary to what he, like others, had expected.

From *Chronicle of the Discovery and Conquest of Guinea*, trans. C. R. Beazley and E. Prestage (London: Hakluyt Society, vol. 95, 1896).

V. THE
NOBLE CASTLE

The Makers

POETS AND STORY-TELLERS

The Vision of Viands

ANIAR MacCONGLINNE

Irish; twelfth century

In a slumber visional,
Wonders apparitional
  Sudden shone on me:
Was it not a miracle?
Built of lard, a coracle
  Swam a sweet milk sea.

With high hearts heroical,
We stepped in it, stoical,
  Braving billow-bounds;
Then we rode so dashingly,
Smote the sea so splashingly,
That the surge sent, washingly,
  Honey up for grounds.

497

Ramparts rose of custard all
Where a castle muster'd all
   Forces o'er the lake;
Butter was the bridge of it,
Wheaten meal the ridge of it,
   Bacon every stake.

Strong it stood, and pleasantly
There I entered presently
   Hying to the hosts;
Dry beef was the door of it,
Bare bread was the floor of it,
   Whey-curds were the posts.

Old cheese-columns happily,
Pork that pillared sappily,
   Raised their heads aloof;
While curd-rafters mellowly
Crossing cream-beams yellowly,
   Held aloft the roof.

Wine in well rose sparklingly,
Beer was rolling darklingly,
   Bragget brimmed the pond.
Lard was oozing heavily,
Merry malt moved wavily,
   Through the floor beyond.

Lake of broth lay spicily,
Fat froze o'er it icily,
   'Tween the wall and shore;
Butter rose in hedges high,
Cloaking all its edges high
   White lard blossomed o'er.

Apple alleys bowering,
Pink-topped orchards flowering,
Fenced off hill and wind;
Leek-tree forests loftily,
Carrots branching tuftily,
Guarded it behind.

Ruddy warders rosily
Welcomed us right cosily
To the fire and rest;
Seven coils of sausages,
Twined in twisted passages,
Round each brawny breast.

Their chief I discover him,
Suet mantle over him,
By his lady bland;
Where the cauldron boiled away,
The Dispenser toiled away,
With his fork in hand.

Good King Cathal, royally,
Surely will enjoy a lay,
Fair and fine as silk;
From his heart his woe I call,
When I sing, heroical,
How we rode, so stoical,
O'er the Sea of Milk.

Trans. G. Sigerson, in *Bards of the Gael and Gall* (London: Unwin, 1897).

Hymn for Good Friday

PETER ABELARD

Latin; twelfth century

Alone to sacrifice Thou goest, Lord,
Giving Thyself to death whom Thou hast slain.
For us Thy wretched folk is any word,
Who know that for our sins this is Thy pain?

For they are ours, O Lord, our deeds, our deeds,
Why must Thou suffer torture for our sin?
Let our hearts suffer for Thy passion, Lord,
That sheer compassion may Thy mercy win.

This is that night of tears, the three days' space,
Sorrow abiding of the eventide,
Until the day break with the risen Christ,
And hearts that sorrowed shall be satisfied.

So may our hearts have pity on Thee, Lord,
That they may sharers of Thy glory be:
Heavy with weeping may the three days pass,
To win the laughter of Thine Easter Day.

Trans. Helen Waddell, in *Mediaeval Latin Lyrics* (New York: Holt, 1938).

David's Lament for Jonathan

Peter Abelard

Latin; twelfth century

Low in thy grave with thee
    Happy to lie,
Since there's no greater thing left Love to do;
    And to live after thee
    Is but to die,
For with but half a soul what can Life do?

So share thy victory,
    Or else thy grave,
Either to rescue thee, or with thee lie:
    Ending that life for thee,
    That thou didst save,
So Death that sundereth might bring more nigh.

Peace, O my stricken lute!
    Thy strings are sleeping.
Would that my heart could still
    Its bitter weeping!

Trans. Helen Waddell, in *Mediaeval Latin Lyrics*.

Let's Away with Study

Latin; twelfth century

Let's away with study,
   Folly's sweet.
Treasure all the pleasure
   Of our youth:
Time enough for age
   To think on Truth.
So short a day,
And life so quickly hasting,
And in study wasting
   Youth that would be gay!

'Tis our spring that's slipping,
   Winter draweth near,
Life itself we're losing,
   And this sorry cheer
Dries the blood and chills the heart,
   Shrivels all delight.
Age and all its crowd of ills
   Terrifies our sight.
So short a day,
And life so quickly hasting,
And in study wasting
   Youth that would be gay!

Let us as the gods do,
   'Tis the wiser part:
Leisure and love's pleasure
   Seek the young in heart

Follow the old fashion,
    Down into the street!
Down among the maidens,
    And the dancing feet!
So short a day,
And life so quickly hasting,
And in study wasting
    Youth that would be gay!

There for the seeing
    Is all loveliness,
White limbs moving
    Light in wantonness.
Gay go the dancers,
    I stand and see,
Gaze, till their glances
    Steal myself from me.
So short a day,
And life so quickly hasting,
And in study wasting
    Youth that would be gay!

Trans. Helen Waddell, in *Mediaeval Latin Lyrics.*

When Diana Lighteth

Latin; twelfth century

When Diana lighteth
Late her crystal lamp,
Her pale glory kindleth
From her brother's fire,
Little straying west winds
Wander over heaven,

Moonlight falleth,
And recalleth
With a sound of lute-strings shaken,
Hearts that have denied his reign
To love again.
Hesperus, the evening star,
To all things that mortal are
Grants the dew of sleep.

Thrice happy Sleep!
The antidote to care,
Thou dost allay the storm
Of grief and sore despair;
Through the fast-closed gates
Thou stealest light;
Thy coming gracious is
As Love's delight.

Sleep through the wearied brain
Breathes a soft wind
From fields of ripening grain,
The sound
Of running water over clearest sand,
A millwheel turning, turning slowly round,
These steal the light
From eyes weary of sight.

Love's sweet exchange and barter, then the brain
Sinks to repose;
Swimming in strangeness of a new delight
The eyelids close;
Oh sweet the passing o'er from love to sleep.
But sweeter the awakening to love.

Under the kind branching trees
Where Philomel complains and sings
Most sweet to lie at ease,
Sweeter to take delight
Of beauty and the night
On the fresh springing grass,
With smell of mint and thyme,
And for Love's bed, the rose.
Sleep's dew doth ever bless,
But most distilled on lovers' weariness.

Trans. Helen Waddell, in *Mediaeval Latin Lyrics*.

To Bel Vezer
on Her Dismissal of the Poet

BERNART DE VENTADORN

Provençal; twelfth century

In vain at Ventadorn full many a friend
　Will seek me, for my lady doth refuse me,
And thither small my wish my way to wend,
　If ever thus despitefully she use me.
On me she frowningly her brow doth bend,
For why? My love to her hath ne'er an end,
　But of no other crime can she accuse me.

The fish full heedless falleth on the prey,
　And by the hook is caught; e'en so I found me
Falling full heedless upon love one day,
　Nor knew my plight till flames raged high around me,
That fiercer burn than furnace by my fay;

Yet ne'er an inch from them can I away,
  So fast the fetters of her love have bound me.

I marvel not her love should fetter me,
  Unto such beauty none hath e'er attained;
So courteous, gay, and fair, and good, is she,
  That for her worth all other worth hath waned;
I cannot blame her, she of blame is free,
Yet I would gladly speak if blame there be,
  But finding none, from speaking have refrained.

I send unto Provence great love and joy,
  And greater joy than ever tongue expresseth,
Great wonders work thereby, strange arts employ,
  Since that I give my heart no whit possesseth.

Trans. Ida Farnell, in *The Lives of the Troubadours* (London: Nutt, 1896).

Dawn Song

French; twelfth century

In orchard where the leaves of hawthorn hide,
The lady holds a lover to her side,
Until the watcher in the dawning cried.
Ah God, ah God, the dawn! it comes how soon.

Ah, would to God that never night must end,
Nor this my lover far from me should wend,
Nor watcher day nor dawning ever send!
Ah God, ah God, the dawn! it comes how soon.

Come let us kiss, dear lover, you and I,
Within the meads where pretty song-birds fly;
We will do all despite the jealous eye:
Ah God, ah God, the dawn! it comes how soon.

Sweet lover come, renew our lovemaking
Within the garden where the light birds sing,
Until the watcher sound the severing.
Ah God, ah God, the dawn! it comes how soon.

Through the soft breezes that are blown from there,
From my own lover, courteous, noble and fair,
From his breath have I drunk a draught most rare.
Ah God, ah God, the dawn! it comes how soon.

Gracious the lady is, and debonaire,
For her beauty a many look at her,
And in her heart is loyal love astir.
Ah God, ah God, the dawn! it comes how soon.

Trans. C. C. Abbott, in *Early Medieval French Lyrics* (London: Oxford University Press, 1932).

The Pretty Fruits of Love

French; twelfth century

I rose up early yestermorn
Before the sun was shining bright,
And stepped within a garden fair
Letting my sleeves trail in the light,
And heard a pretty maid dark-eyed
Singing in a meadow near

And delight it was to hear
Her sweet confiding:
　　"The pretty fruits of love
　　There's no more hiding."

And her lament of full intent
I heard as she spoke sighing there:
"God, I have lost my lover, he
Who loved me so, handsome and fair.
That I should ever be his dear
'Twas such an oath I had from him:
And I have done a foolish thing
None should be chiding.
　　The pretty fruits of love
　　There's no more hiding.

"And where is now the young squire gone
Who begged me ever, night and day,
Lady, take me, body and heart,
And keep me for your love, I pray,
I am your loyal knight alway.
And now I'm all alone; what's done
No longer lets my girdle run
With clasp confining.
　　The pretty fruits of love
　　There's no more hiding.

"Now it behooves me loosen out
My girdle span a little mite;
Already is my belly big,
A bigger still I must requite.
Then while I carry this in sight—
No more a maiden stand confessed—
I'll sing this song, within my breast
For ever hiding:

'The pretty fruits of love
There's no more hiding.'"

And I who heard with full intent
Adventured then a shade more near;
No sooner had she looked on me
Than she began to blush with fear
And I to her said, laughing clear,
"To many a maid it happens so."
For shame her blushes paler grown
No more confiding.
    "The pretty fruits of love
    There's no more hiding."

Trans. C. C. Abbott in *Early Medieval French Lyrics.*

This Song Wants Drink

French; twelfth century

Who has good wine should flagon it out
And thrust the bad where the fungus sprout;
Then must merry companions shout:
    This song wants drink!

When I see wine into the clear glass slip
How I long to be matched with it;
My heart sings gay at the thought of it:
    This song wants drink!

I thirst for a sup; come circle the cup:
    This song wants drink!

Trans. C. C. Abbott, in *Early Medieval French Lyrics.*

The Love of Tristan and Iseult

GOTTFRIED VON STRASSBURG

German; thirteenth century

Now, when the man and the maid, Tristan and Iseult, had drunk of the potion, Love, who never resteth but besetteth all hearts, crept softly into the hearts of the twain, and ere they were ware of it had she planted her banner of conquest therein, and brought them under her rule. They were one and undivided who but now were twain and at enmity. Gone was Iseult's hatred, no longer might there be strife between them, for Love, the great reconciler, had purified their hearts from all ill will, and so united them that each was clear as a mirror to the other. But one heart had they—her grief was his sadness, his sadness her grief. Both were one in love and sorrow, and yet both would hide it in shame and doubt. She felt shame of her love, and the like did he. She doubted of his love, and he of hers. For though both their hearts were blindly bent to one will, yet was the chance and the beginning heavy to them, and both alike would hide their desire.

When Tristan felt the pangs of love, then he bethought him straightway of his faith and honour, and would fain have set himself free. "Nay," he said to himself, "let such things be, Tristan; guard thee well, lest others perceive thy thoughts." So would he turn his heart, fighting against his own will, and desiring against his own desire. He would and would not, and, a prisoner, struggled in his fetters. There was a strife within him, for ever as he looked on Iseult, and love stirred his heart and soul, then did honour draw him back. Yet he must needs follow Love, for his liege lady was she, and in sooth she wounded him more sorely than did his honour and faith to his uncle, though they strove hard for the mastery. For Love looked smiling upon his heart, and led heart and eyes captive; and yet if he saw her not, then was he even more sorrowful. Much he vexed himself, marvelling how he might escape, and saying to his heart: "Turn thee here or there, let thy desire be other, love and long elsewhere." Yet ever the more he looked into his heart the more he found that therein was nought but Love—and Iseult.

Even so was it with the maiden: she was as a bird that is snared with lime. When she knew the snare of love and saw that her heart was indeed taken therein, she strove with all her power to free herself, yet the more she struggled the faster was the hold Love laid upon her, and, unwilling, she must follow whither Love led. As with hands and feet she strove to free herself, so were hands and feet even more bound and fettered by the blinding sweetness of the man and his love, and never half a foot's length might she stir save that Love were with her. Never a thought might Iseult think save of Love and Tristan, yet she fain would hide it. Heart and eyes strove with each other; Love drew her heart towards him, and shame drove her eyes away. Thus Love and maiden shame strove together till Iseult wearied of the fruitless strife, and did as many have done before her—vanquished, she yielded herself body and soul to the man, and to Love.

Shyly she looked on him, and he on her, till heart and eyes had done their work. And Tristan, too, was vanquished, since Love would have it none otherwise. Knight and maiden sought each other as often as they might do so, and each found the other fairer day by day.

For such is the way of Love, as it was of old, and is to-day, and shall be while the world endures, that lovers please each other more as love within them waxeth stronger, even as flowers and fruit are fairer in their fulness than in their beginning; and Love that beareth fruit waxeth fairer day by day till the fulness of time be come.

> Love doth the loved one fairer make,
> So love a stronger life doth take.
> Love's eyes wax keener day by day,
> Else would love fade and pass away.

So the ship sailed gaily onwards, even though Love had thus turned two hearts aside, for she who turneth honey to gall, sweet to sour, and dew to flame, had laid her burden on Tristan and Iseult, and as they looked on each other their colour changed from white to red and from red to white, even as it pleased Love to paint them. Each knew the mind of the other, yet was their speech of other things.

From *The Story of Tristan and Iseult*, trans. J. L. Weston (London: Nutt, 1899).

Of the Churl Who Won Paradise

French; twelfth–thirteenth century

WE FIND in writing a wondrous adventure that of old befell a churl. He died of a Friday morning, and it so chanced, neither angel nor devil came thither, and at the hour of his death when the soul departed out of his body, he found none to ask aught of him or to lay any command upon him. Know ye that full glad was that soul for he was sore afraid. And now as he looked to the right towards Heaven, he saw Saint Michael the Archangel who was bearing a soul in great joy; forthright he set out after the angel, and followed him so long, meseemeth, that he came into Paradise.

Saint Peter who kept the gate, received the soul borne by the angel, and after he had so done, turned back towards the entrance. There he found the soul all alone, and asked him who had brought him thither: "For herein none hath lodging and if he have it not by judgment. Moreover, by Saint Alain, we have l'ttle love for churls, for into this place the vile may not enter." "Yet greater churl than you yourself is there none, fair Sir Peter," saith the soul, "for you were ever harder than a stone; and by the holy Paternoster, God did folly when he made you His apostle, little honour shall be His thereby, in that three times you denied your Lord. Full little was your faith when thrice you denied Him, and though you be of His fellowship, Paradise is not for you. Go forth, and that straightway, ye disloyal soul, but I am true and of good faith, and bliss is rightfully mine."

Strangely shamed was Saint Peter; quickly he turned away, and as he went, he met Saint Thomas, to whom he told all his misadventure word for word, and all his wrath and bitterness. Then saith Saint Thomas; "I myself will go to this churl; here he shall not abide, and it please God." So he goeth into the square to the countryman. "Churl," quoth the apostle, "this dwelling belongeth of right to us and to the martyrs and confessors; wherein have you done such righteousness that you think to abide in it? Here you cannot stay, for this is the hostel of the true-hearted." "Thomas, Thomas, like unto a man of law ye are overquick to make answer; yet are not you he who, as is well known, spake with the apostles when they had seen the Lord after His resurrection? Then you made oath that never would you believe it and if you felt not His wounds with your hands; false and unbelieving were ye." Then Saint Thomas hung his head, and yielded him in the dispute; and thereafter he went to Saint Paul and told him of his discomfiture. "By my head," quoth Saint Paul, "I will go thither, and try if he will argue."

Meantime, the soul who feareth not destruction taketh his delight down in Paradise. "Soul," quoth Saint Paul, "who brought thee hither, and wherein have you done such righteousness that the gate should be opened to you? Get you gone out of Paradise, you false churl." "How is this, Don Paul of the bald pate, are you now so wrathful who erst was so fell a tyrant? Never will there be another so cruel; Saint Stephen paid dear for it when you had him stoned to death. Well know I the story of your life; through you many a brave man died, but in the end God gave you a good big blow. Have we not had to pay for the bargain and the buffet? Ha, what a divine and what a saint! Do ye think that I know you not?" Then had Saint Paul great sorrow.

Swiftly he went thence, and met Saint Thomas who was taking counsel with Saint Peter, and privately he told him of the churl who had so vanquished him: "Rightfully hath he won Paradise of me, and I grant it to him." Then all three went to bring complaint to God. Fairly Saint Peter told Him of the churl who had spoken shame of them: "By his tongue hath he silenced us, and I myself was so abashed that never again will I speak thereof." Then spoke our Lord: "I will go thither, for I myself would hear this new thing."

He cometh to the soul and bespeaketh him, and asked how it chanced that he had come there without leave: "For herein without consent hath no soul, whether of man or woman, ever entered. My apostles you have slandered and scorned and outraged, yet none the less you think to abide here!" "Lord," saith the churl, "if judgment be accorded me, my right to dwell here is as good as theirs: for never did I deny You, or doubt You, nor did any man ever come to his death through me, but all these things have they done, and yet are now in Paradise. While I lived on earth my life was just and upright; I gave of my bread to the poor, I harboured them morning and evening, I warmed them at my fire, and saw that they lacked not for shirt or hose; I kept them even till death, and bore them to holy church: and now I know not if I did wisely. Furthermore, I made true confession, and received Your body with due rites; and we are told that to the man who so dies God forgiveth his sins. Well know You if I speak the truth. I entered in and was not denied, and now I am here, why go hence? Were it so, You would gainsay Your word, for surely You have declared that whoso entereth here goeth not out again; and You would never lie because of me." "Churl," saith the Lord, "I grant it. You have made good your case against Paradise, and have won it by debate. You were brought up in a good school; ready of tongue are you, and know right well how to turn a tale."

The countryman saith in proverb that many a man who hath sought wrong hath won it by argument; wit hath falsified justice, and falsity hath conquered nature; wrong goeth before and right falleth behind. Wit is mightier than force.

From *Tales from the Old French*, trans. I. Butler (Boston: Houghton Mifflin, 1910).

Gather Ye Rosebuds

French; thirteenth century

Woman should gather roses ere
Time's ceaseless foot o'ertaketh her,
For if too long she make delay,
Her chance of love may pass away,
And well it is she seek it while
Health, strength, and youth around her smile.
To pluck the fruits of love in youth
Is each wise woman's rule forsooth,
For when age creepeth o'er us, hence
Go also the sweet joys of sense,
And ill doth she her days employ
Who lets life pass without love's joy.
And if my counsel she despise,
Not knowing how 'tis just and wise,
Too late, alas! will she repent
When age is come, and beauty spent.
But witful women will believe
My words, and thankfully receive
My counsels and my rules will foster
With care, and many a paternoster
Say for my soul's health when I die
For teaching them so worthily.
Well know I that these golden rules
Shall long be taught in noblest schools.

From *Romance of the Rose*, trans. F. S. Ellis (London: Dent, 1900).

The Canticle of the Sun

SAINT FRANCIS OF ASSISI

Italian; thirteenth century

Here begin the praises of the creatures which the Blessed Francis made to the praise and honour of God while he was ill at St. Damian's:

Most high, omnipotent, good Lord,
Praise, glory, and honour and benediction all, are Thine.
To Thee alone do they belong, most High,
And there is no man fit to mention Thee.

Praise be to Thee, my Lord, with all Thy creatures,
Especially to my worshipful brother sun,
The which lights up the day, and through him dost Thou
    brightness give;
And beautiful is he and radiant with splendour great;
Of Thee, most High, signification gives.

Praised be my Lord, for sister moon and for the stars,
In heaven Thou hast formed them clear and precious
    and fair.

Praised be my Lord for brother wind
And for the air and clouds and fair and every kind of
    weather,
By the which Thou givest to Thy creatures nourishment.

Praised be my Lord for sister water,
The which is greatly helpful and humble and precious
    and pure.

Praised be my Lord for brother fire,
By the which Thou lightest up the dark.
And fair is he and gay and mighty and strong.

Praised be my Lord for our sister, mother earth,
The which sustains and keeps us
And brings forth diverse fruits with grass and flowers
    bright.

Praised be my Lord for those who for Thy love forgive
And weakness bear and tribulation.
Blessed those who shall in peace endure,
And by Thee, most High, shall they be crowned.

Praised be my Lord for our sister, the bodily death,
From the which no living man can flee.
Woe to them who die in mortal sin;
Blessed those who shall find themselves in Thy most
    holy will,
For the second death shall do them no ill.

Praise ye and bless ye my Lord, and give Him thanks,
And be subject unto Him with great humility.

From *The Writings of Saint Francis of Assisi*, trans. Father P.
Robinson (Philadelphia: Dolphin Press, 1906).

Of the Gentle Heart

Guido Guinicelli

Italian; thirteenth century

Within the gentle heart Love shelters him,
    As birds within the green shade of the grove.
Before the gentle heart, in Nature's scheme,
    Love was not, nor the gentle heart ere Love.
        For with the sun, at once,
So sprang the light immediately; nor was
        Its birth before the sun's.
And Love hath his effect in gentleness
        Of very self; even as
Within the middle fire the heat's excess.

The fire of Love comes to the gentle heart
    Like as its virtue to a precious stone;
To which no star its influence can impart
    Till it is made a pure thing by the sun:
        For when the sun hath smit
From out its essence that which there was vile,
        The star endoweth it.
And so the heart created by God's breath
        Pure, true, and clean from guile,
A woman, like a star, enamoureth.

In gentle heart Love for like reason is
    For which the lamp's high flame is fann'd and bow'd:
Clear, piercing bright, it shines for its own bliss;
    Nor would it burn there else, it is so proud.

For evil natures meet
With Love as it were water met with fire,
   As cold abhorring heat.
Through gentle heart Love doth a track divine,—
   Like knowing like; the same
As diamond runs through iron in the mine.

The sun strikes full upon the mud all day;
   It remains vile, nor the sun's worth is less.
"By race I am gentle," the proud man doth say:
   He is the mud, the sun is gentleness.
     Let no man predicate
That aught the name of gentleness should have,
   Even in a king's estate,
Except the heart there be a gentle man's.
     The star-beam lights the wave—
Heaven holds the star and the star's radiance.

God, in the understanding of high Heaven,
   Burns more than in our sight the living sun;
There to behold His face unveil'd is given;
   And Heaven, whose will is homage paid to One,
     Fulfils the things which live
In God, from the beginning excellent.
     So should my lady give
That truth which in her eyes is glorified,
   On which her heart is bent,
To me whose service waiteth at her side.

My lady, God shall ask, "What dared'st thou?"
   (When my soul stands with all her acts review'd;)
"Thou passed'st Heaven, into My sight, as now,
   To make Me of vain love similitude.
     To Me doth praise belong,

And to the Queen of all the realm of grace
    Who endeth fraud and wrong."
Then may I plead: "As though from Thee he came,
    Love wore an angel's face:
Lord, if I loved her, count it not my shame."

Trans. D. G. Rossetti, in *The Early Italian Poets* (London: Smith, Elder, 1861).

My Lady Looks So Gentle

DANTE ALIGHIERI

Italian; thirteenth century

My lady looks so gentle and so pure
    When yielding salutation by the way,
    That the tongue trembles and has nought to say,
And the eyes, which fain would see, may not endure.
And still, amid the praise she hears secure,
    She walks with humbleness for her array;
    Seeming a creature sent from Heaven to stay
On earth, and show a miracle made sure.
She is so pleasant in the eyes of men
That through the sight the inmost heart doth gain
    A sweetness which needs proof to know it by:
And from between her lips there seems to move
A soothing spirit that is full of love,
    Saying for ever to the soul, "O sigh!"

Trans. D. G. Rossetti in *The Early Italian Poets*.

Beauty in Women

GUIDO CAVALCANTI

Italian; thirteenth century

Beauty in woman; the high will's decree;
　　Fair knighthood arm'd for manly exercise;
　　The pleasant song of birds; love's soft replies;
The strength of rapid ships upon the sea;
The serene air when light begins to be;
　　The white snow, without wind that falls and lies;
　　Fields of all flower; the place where waters rise;
Silver and gold; azure in jewellery:
Weigh'd against these, the sweet and quiet worth
　　Which my dear lady cherishes at heart
　　　　Might seem a little matter to be shown;
　　Being truly, over these, as much apart
As the whole heaven is greater than this earth.
　　All good to kindred natures cleaveth soon.

Trans. D. G. Rossetti, in *The Early Italian Poets.*

Of the Blessed Virgin Mary, and of the Sinner

JACOPONE DA TODI

Italian; thirteenth century

O Queen of all courtesy,
 To thee I come and I kneel,
 My wounded heart to heal,
  To thee for succour I pray—

To thee I come and I kneel,
 For lo! I am in despair;
None other help can heal,
 Thou only wilt hear my prayer:
 And if I should lose thy care,
  My spirit must waste away.

My heart is wounded more,
 Madonna, than tongue can tell;
Pierced to the very core;
 Rottenness there doth dwell.
 Hasten to make me well!
  How canst thou say me nay?

Madonna, so fierce the strain
 Of this my perilous hour,
Nature is turned to pain,
 So strong is evil's power;
 Be gracious, O Ivory Tower!
  My anguish touch and allay.

All that I had is spent:
　　In nothingness am I drest;
Make me thine instrument,
　　Thy servant ransomed and blest:
　　—He who drank from thy breast,
　　Madonna, the price will pay.

Thy Son, who loved me first,—
　　By His dear love I entreat,
Madonna, pity my thirst,
　　Grant me thy counsel meet!
　　Succor me, Lily most sweet!
　　Haste, and do not delay!

From *Lauda I*, trans. Mrs. T. Beck in E. Underhill, *Jacopone da Todi* (London: Dent, 1919).

Merciless Beauty: A Triple Roundel

GEOFFREY CHAUCER

English; fourteenth century

I

Your two bright eyes will slay me suddenly,
The beauty of them I cannot sustain,
So keenly strikes it through my heart and brain.

Unless your word will heal right speedily
Mine head's confusion and mine heart's sore pain,
　　Your two bright eyes will slay me suddenly,
　　The beauty of them I cannot sustain.

Upon my troth I tell you faithfully,
You of my life and death are sovereign,

And by my death the world shall see it plain—
    Your two bright eyes will slay me suddenly,
    The beauty of them I cannot sustain,
    So keenly strikes it through my heart and brain.

II

    So has your Beauty from your bosom chaséd
    Pity, that it avails not to complain;
    For Pride fetters your Mercy in his chain.

To death all guiltless thus am I abaséd—
I say the sooth, I have no need to feign;
    So has your Beauty from your bosom chaséd
    Pity, that it avails not to complain.

Alas, that Nature in your visage placéd
Beauty so great that no man shall attain
To Mercy, though he perish for the pain!
    So has your Beauty from your bosom chaséd
    Pity, that it avails not to complain;
    For Pride fetters your Mercy in his chain.

III

    Since I from Love escapéd am so fat,
    I think no more to be in prison lean;
    Since I am free, I count him not a bean.

He may reply, and say or this or that;
I reck not on't, I speak right as I mean—
    Since I from Love escapéd am so fat,
    I think no more to be in prison lean.

For evermore Love has abjured me flat,
And he for evermore is stricken clean
Out of my books, as he had never been.

Since I from Love escapéd am so fat,
I think no more to be in prison lean;
Since I am free, I count him not a bean.

Explicit.

Trans. J. S. P. Tatlock and P. MacKaye, *The Modern Reader's Chaucer* (New York: Macmillan, 1912).

Roundel

CHRISTINE DE PISAN

French; fifteenth century

Laughing grey eyes, whose light in me I bear.
Deep in my heart's remembrance and delight,
Remembrance is so infinite delight
Of your brightness, O soft eyes that I fear.

Of love-sickness my life had perished here,
But you raise up my strength in death's respite,
Laughing grey eyes, whose light in me I bear.

Certes, by you my heart, I see full clear,
Shall of desire attain at last the height,
Even that my lady, through your sovereign might,
May we continue in her service dear,
Laughing grey eyes, whose light in me I bear.

From *The Book of the Duke of True Lovers*, trans. Alice Kemp-Welch (London: Chatto and Windus, 1908).

Miracles of the Virgin

JOHANNES HEROLT

Latin; fifteenth century

I

A CERTAIN woman of simple and upright life used to worship the Holy Mary, Mother of God, often strewing flowers and herbs before her image.

Now it chanced that the woman's only son was taken prisoner. And the mother weeping for him would not be comforted, and prayed with all her heart to the Blessed Virgin Mary for her son's deliverance. But seeing it was all in vain, she entered the church and thus addressed the image of the Blessed Virgin, "O Blessed Virgin Mary, often have I asked thee for the deliverance of my son and thou hast not heard me. Therefore, as my son was taken from me, so will I take away thine and will put him in durance as hostage for mine."

And taking the image of the Child from the bosom of Mary, she went home, wrapped him up in a clean cloth, and shut him up carefully in a chest. And, behold, the following night the Blessed Mary appeared to the captive youth bidding him to go forth and said to him: "Tell your mother to give me my Son." And he coming to his mother, described how he had been set free. But she with great rejoicing carried back the image of Jesus to Mary and gave her thanks.

II

In a certain convent of nuns many years ago there lived a virgin named Beatrice under vow of chastity. Devout in soul and a zealous servant of the Mother of God, she counted it her greatest joy to offer up her prayers to her in secret and, when she was made custodian, her devotion increased with her greater freedom. A certain cleric, seeing and desiring her, began to use enticements. When she scorned his wanton talk, he became so much the more eager, and the old serpent hotly tempted her, so that her heart could no longer endure the fires of passion, but going to the altar of the Blessed Virgin Mary, who was the patron saint there, she said: "Lady, I have served thee as faithfully as I could; behold I resign to thee thy keys. I can no longer withstand the temptations of the flesh." Placing the keys on the altar she went in secret after the cleric, and he, after dishonouring her, within a few days deserted her. And she having no means of living and being ashamed to return to the cloister, became a harlot.

Having lived publicly for many years in this wickedness, one day she came in her secular dress to the gate of the convent, and said to the gatekeeper: "Do you know one Beatrice, formerly the custodian of this convent?" And he replied: "Yes, she is a very worthy lady, holy and without reproach from her childhood, who has lived in this convent to this day."

She, hearing these words, but not weighing their meaning, was about to go away, when the Mother of Mercy appeared to her in the form of a woman and said: "For fifteen years I have filled your office in your absence. Return now to your home and do penance, for no one knows of your departure." The Mother of God had actually in her shape and dress taken her place as guardian. At once she returned, and as long as she lived gave thanks to the Virgin Mary, and in confession made known to her confessor all that had happened to her.

III

A certain man lived carnally with another woman, his wife being aware of it. She finding it hard to endure this, made complaint in the church of St. Mary, praying to be avenged on her who had taken away her husband. St. Mary, appearing to her, said, "How can I bring harm upon her, for each day she bends her knee a hundred times to me?" But the woman in much vexation said: "Why will you not avenge me? I will make my complaint to your Son."

She went out of the church muttering those words. But the adulteress met her, and when she inquired what she was saying, the other replied: "I was complaining about you to the Virgin Mary, and she replied that she would do you no harm because every day you made a hundred genuflexions to her, and it is for that I am murmuring. But I hope that her Son will avenge me." Hearing that, the adulteress at once threw herself at her feet begging her pardon and faithfully promising never again to commit sin with her husband.

From *Miracles of the Blessed Virgin Mary*, trans. C. C. S. Bland (London: Routledge, 1928).

PAINTERS AND BUILDERS

Of Pictures and Images

WILLIAM DURANDUS

Thirteenth century

PICTURES and ornaments in churches are the lessons and the scriptures of the laity. Whence Gregory: It is one thing to adore a picture, and another by means of a picture historically to learn what should be adored. For what writing supplieth to him which can read, that doth a picture supply to him which is unlearned, and can only look. Because they who are uninstructed, thus see what they ought to follow: and *things* are read, though letters be unknown. True is it that the Chaldeans, which worship fire, compel others to do the same, and burn other idols. . . . But we worship not images, nor account them to be gods, nor put any hope of salvation in them: for that were idolatry. Yet we adore them for the memory and remembrance of things done long agone. . . .

But Gregory saith, that pictures are not to be put away because they are not to be worshipped: for paintings appear to move the mind more than descriptions: for deeds are placed before the eyes in paintings, and so appear to be actually carrying on. But in description, the deed is done as it were by hearsay: which affecteth the mind less when recalled to memory. Hence, also, is it that in churches we pay less reverence to books than to images and pictures.

Of pictures and images some are above the church, as the cock and the eagle: some without the church, namely, in the air in front of the church, as the ox and the cow: others within, as images, and statues, and various kinds of painting and sculpture: and these be represented either in garments, or on walls, or in stained glass. . . .

The Image of the Saviour is more commonly represented in churches three ways: as sitting on His throne, or hanging on His cross, or laying on the bosom of His mother. And because John Baptist pointed to Him, saying "BEHOLD THE LAMB OF GOD," therefore some represented Christ under the form of a Lamb. But because the light passeth away, and because Christ is very man, therefore, saith Adrian, Pope, He must be represented in the form of a man. A Holy Lamb must not be depicted on the cross, as a principal object: but there is no let when Christ hath been represented as a man, to paint a Lamb in a lower or less prominent part of the picture: since He is the True Lamb *which taketh away the sins of the world.* In these and divers other manners is the Image of the Saviour painted, on account of diversity of significations.

Represented in the Cradle, the artist commemorateth His Nativity: on the bosom of His Mother, His Childhood: the painting or carving His Cross signifieth His Passion (and sometimes the sun and moon are represented on the Cross itself, as suffering an eclipse): when depicted on a flight of steps, His Ascension is signified: when on a state or lofty throne, we be taught His present power: as if He said, "All things are given to me in heaven and in earth": according to that saying, "I saw the Lord sitting upon His throne": that is, reigning over the angels: as the text, "Which sitteth upon the cherubim." Sometimes He is represented as He was seen of Moses and Aaron, Nadab and Abihu, on the mountain: when "under His feet was as it were a paved work of sapphire stones, and as the body of heaven in His clearness": and as "they shall see," as saith St. Luke, "The Son of Man coming in the clouds with power and great glory." Wherefore sometimes He is represented surrounded by the Seven Angels that serve Him, and stand by His Throne, each being pourtrayed with six wings, according to the vision of Isaiah, "And by it stood the Seraphim: each one had six wings: with twain he covered his face, and with twain he covered his feet, and with twain he did fly."

The Angels are also represented as in the flower of youthful age; for they never grow old. Sometimes St. Michael is represented trampling the dragon, according to that of John, "There was war in Heaven: Michael fought with the dragon." Which was to represent the dissentions of the angels: the confirmation of them that were good, and the ruin of them that were bad: or the persecution of the faithful in the Church Militant. Sometimes the twenty-four Elders are painted around the Saviour, according to the Vision of the said John, with *white garments, and they have on their heads crowns of gold.* By which are signified the Doctors of the Old and New Testament; which are twelve, on account of Faith in the Holy Trinity preached through the *four* quarters of the world: or twenty-four, on account of good works, and the keeping of the Gospels. If the seven lamps be added, the Gifts of the Holy Spirit are represented: if the Sea of Glass, Baptism.

Sometimes also representation is made of the four living creatures spoken of in the visions of Ezekiel and the aforesaid John: the face of a man and the face of a lion on the right, the face of an ox on the left, and the face of an eagle above the four. These be the Four Evangelists. Whence they be painted with books by their feet, because by their words and writings they have instructed the minds of the Faithful, and accomplished their own works. Matthew hath the figure of a man, Mark of a lion. These be painted on the right hand: because of the Nativity and the Resurrection of Christ were the general joy of all: whence in the Psalms: "And Gladness at the Morning." But Luke is the ox: because he beginneth from Zachary the Priest, and treateth more specially of the Passion and Sacrifice of Christ: now the ox is an animal fitted for sacrifice. He is also compared to the ox, because of the two horns, as containing the two testaments; and the four hoofs, as having the sentences of the four Evangelists. By this also Christ is figured, who was the Sacrifice for us: and therefore the ox is painted on the left side, because the Death of Christ was the trouble of the Apostles. Concerning this, and how Blessed Mark is depicted, in the seventh part. But John hath the figure of the Eagle: because, soaring to the utmost height, he saith, "In the beginning was the Word." This also representeth *Christ, whose youth is renewed like the eagle's:* because, rising from the dead, He ascendeth into Heaven. Here, however, it is not pourtrayed as by the side, but as above, since it denoteth the Ascension, and the word pronounced of God.

From *Rationale divinorum officiorum,* trans. J. M. Neale and B. Webb (Leeds: Green, 1843).

How to Represent the Arts and Sciences

Early fifteenth century

SEVEN noble pictures of the seven liberal and mechanical arts, theology, and medicine with the most excellent sentences of the philosophers.

A bearded man in a cap: Tully [Cicero]. "It is for philosophy to investigate the causes of all human and divine things." This in the book on utility.

Rhetoric. The image of a woman, having in her hands sprays of flowers.

Logic. The image of a woman standing, having a lectern before her and an open book in which she writes.

Fourth, Grammar. The image of a beautiful woman, having a branch in one hand and a wand in the other, and she is standing.

Fifth, Philosophy, mistress of the sciences. The image of a woman dressed in enough garments, sitting, having a sceptre in her left hand and before her a lectern with an open book, on which is placed her right hand.

Seneca. The image of an antique man. "Philosophy forms and moulds the soul, orders life, rules the emotions, shows what things are to be done and what omitted." . . .

In accordance with the threefold philosophy, namely, rational, natural, and moral, the threefold science of speaking arose, namely, of the suitable, the true, and the ornamental. Of appropriate speaking is Grammar, of true speaking is Logic, of ornamental speaking is Rhetoric.

The first of these says: "I write perfectly; what I have written I convey rightly."

The second says in truth: "I teach how to distinguish clearly the true from the false."

The third boasts thus: "I offer the means of teaching with the flower of eloquence."

Now this is the trivium.

The quadrivium is made up of mathematical subjects, that is Arithmetic, Music, Geometry and Astronomy. Arithmetic is the science of numbers. It is named from "Ares," which is courage and "rismus," number. Music is the division of sounds and the variety of voices, which derives its name from water. Geometry is the fount of speaking and the origin of expressions and explains the measure of the earth. Astronomy is the discipline investigating space, motion, and the return of the celestial bodies at certain times. On this, Hugh [of St. Victor]. . . .

These are the things which are pictured and written on one part of the wall. . . .

On the other wall, on one side one old man. The first one has this verse: "It seems to me the first effort must be given to the arts, where lie the foundations of all, and pure and simple truth is revealed." This, Hugh in the *Didascalicon*. The second old man from the other side speaks thus: "The glory of any kingdom whatsoever grows to immense splendour where the studies of the liberal arts flourish." This, Alexander [of Neckam] in *De naturis rerum*.

The image of a woman, having a book in her right hand and with her left she points with her forefinger to the stars of heaven. And it has written above: Astronomy.

The second image is similarly a woman in the garb of

a virgin having a circle in her right hand and a triangle in her left, and it has written above: Geometry.

The third, Music. A woman adorned sufficiently, singing to a zither.

The fourth, Arithmetic. A woman, having in her hand a tablet with numbers.

Below these images is found this saying: "Among all the men of ancient authority," etc. . . . These are said in the arithmetic of the venerable Boethius, first chapter.

On the other part of the wall is depicted a storeroom with boxes, in which an apothecary pounds material in a mortar. Also an old doctor of grave countenance with all propriety is taking the pulse of a pretty woman. Also a sick man lying in bed, in front of whom stands a beautiful girl having a fan in one hand, in the other holding out a vessel to the sick man so that he may drink. Near her stands a respectable matron who is weeping. Also a young doctor examining urine.

St. Cosmas on the right side with a box in one hand and with a crown on his head. St. Damian similarly on the left side. In the middle is an image of a pretty woman, sitting on a high seat, a lectern with an open book, holding her right hand on the book, in her left a box, a crown on her head, a verse above her: Medicine. At the sides on the right near St. Cosmas, Avicenna, holding in his hand the definition of medicine, in the first canon, on the other side near and behind St. Damian, Johannicius, saying in verse: "Medicine is divided into two parts, as in Johannicius, etc."

THE ART OF WRITING

The image of a little old man, sitting, having in his right hand a strainer and in the other an open written book.

Two are disputing at the same time, between whom stands written: Sophists.

The image of a school teacher, having a rod in one hand and a branch in the other; before him sit his pupils.

Also a scribe writing.

Also a smith, having a book in one hand, in the other a pair of tongs and a hammer.

SACRED THEOLOGY

The image of a very beautiful woman, sitting on a throne, a royal crown on her head, under which is the fillet of a bishop, having a sceptre in the right hand, an apple in the left, with flowing hair, a book before her lying open on a lectern.

St. Gregory sits on a throne, a book lying open on the lectern, a long staff with a cross in the other hand.

St. Jerome, shown as a cardinal, sitting on a bishop's chair, writing on a book lying on a lectern. In the other hand he holds an open book on his lap.

St. Ambrose and St. Augustine, in the guise of bishops.

These four doctors are located in the four corners, a woman in the middle; behind the doctors stand, in one part a cardinal with certain monks, in the other a bishop in a chasuble, likewise accompanied by certain monks and students, having books in their hands.

Below, under the queen is depicted a fountain in a greensward, surrounded by a wall, from which come rivulets watering the greensward, above which is the verse: "Theology is the source and origin of all virtues."

Two very beautiful images in the guise of women are depicted, who sit together in a high and elevated place, grasping each other's hands. The one on the left, in truth, holds a sceptre. On their heads they wear golden crowns. The one on the right has the moon under her feet and there stands written: Civil Law. The one on the left has the sun under her feet and there is written: Canon Law. Standing around are teachers in doctoral and black gowns, old and young, birettas on their heads, suitably clad in long robes. In the first place are two figures, placed before the others, on each side of those; each has an apple in his right hand and a closed book in the left.

From *Quellenbuch zur Kunstgeschichte*, J. Schlosser, ed.; trans. J.B.R.

The Identity of Individual Artists

HOW A CARPENTER GAVE THANKS FOR HIS CURE
(LATE ELEVENTH CENTURY)

[A certain one of the parishioners of the village of Isigny, in the district of Bayeux] confessing and weeping for the guilt of his sins, was borne to Coutances on a litter, a priest accompanying him, and was carried, misshapen, before the altar; and although weakened by suffering and crying aloud, nevertheless, the mercy of God intervening, he was made whole again in his entire body, on that same night which dawned on Sunday. On the following day, which is the second day of the week, he besought the chamberlain, Lord Peter, the deacon and bursar of the church, that he should order an axe to be given him so that he could labour with the other carpenters on the work of the church. When this was done, he worked with the others both that whole and the following week, cleverly and tastefully on the [wooden] window frames of the panes which are called *capsilia* and which were made in those days. After this was completed, when the aforesaid chamberlain had offered him freely a suitable and generous payment of money for his labour, he refused it completely, surrendering himself to the Virgin Mary and [saying] that he would be one of the bond serfs of that church, and that he would pay annually, as long as he lived, to the same church the tax on his own head. After this for a long time he devoutly took part in the special feast days of that same glorious mother of God, Mary.

HOW A SERF ACQUIRED FREEDOM BY HIS ART, C. 1100

A certain man, by name Fulco, endowed with the art of the painter, came to the chapter of St. Aubin [of Angers] and there made the following agreement before the Abbot Girard and the whole convent: he would paint the whole monastery of theirs and whatever they should order him to do, and he would make glass windows. And thereupon he became their brother and in addition he was made a free man of the abbot; and the abbot and monks gave him one acre and a half of vineyard in fee and a house, on these terms, that he should hold them in his lifetime, and after his death they should go back to the saint, unless he should have a son who would know the art of his father and hence could serve St. Aubin. At this act there were present these laymen: Reginald Grandis and Warin the cellarer. . . .

From *Recueil de textes relatifs à l'histoire de l'architecture en France, XI* et *XII* siècles*, V. Mortet, ed. (Paris: A. Picard, 1911); trans. J.B.R.

Abbots as Builders

St. Albans, thirteenth century

RELYING, then, on the advice of these two brothers, and sustained by their support, his conscience pricking him (for he had received from his predecessor, Abbot Warin, as told above, one hundred marks, put aside and designated for the work of the church), Abbot John [1195-1214] demolished completely the wall of the front of our church, made up of old tiles and indissoluble mortar.

Little expecting, however, that mockery of which mention is made in the gospel, namely, that he who is about to build should compute the expenses which are necessary to finish it, lest, after he has laid the foundation, being unable to finish it, all begin to mock him, saying, "This man began to build, and he was not able to finish," the abbot began both to haul wood and to pile up a lot of stones, together with columns and boards. When he had assembled the chosen masons, many in number, over whom stood Master Hugh Goldcliff (a deceitful and lying man, indeed, but an excellent workman), and the trench had been dug and extended, in a short time he spent the hundred marks mentioned, as well as many more, without counting the daily allowances, not a small amount, and the wall did not yet reach the level of its foundation. It happened that by the perfidious advice of the aforesaid Hugh, after carvings had been added that were inappropriate and trifling and much too expensive, before half the work rose to the height of a house-story, the abbot was tired and began to grow weary of it and fearful, and the work languished. And since the walls lay uncovered in the winter weather, the stones, being fragile, broke into bits, and the wall, looking like a tumbled-down ruin, collapsed to such an extent under its own weight, together with its columns, bases, and capitals, that the fragments of images and flowers drew laughter and jeers from the observers. Then the workmen in despair departed, and their wages were not paid to them.

The abbot, nevertheless, not despairing on this account, appointed as custodian of the work Brother Gilbert of Eversolt; and he contributed to the work one sheaf from every acre of sown land. And this lasted from the time it was first given (that is, in the third year of his prelacy) throughout his whole life, namely, seventeen years, and into the life of the following abbot about ten years. That unfortunate work, however, never showed any visible growth, and not being completed as he desired in the time of Abbot John, his heart could not rejoice, so that he grieved inconsolably. He added, therefore, many gifts of gold and silver, if perchance he could thus advance the work. He had it [the work] preached throughout all the lands of St. Alban, and through many episcopal dioceses, and relics carried around, and by a certain clerk, by name Amphibalus (whom the Lord had raised from the dead after four days by the merits of Saints Alban and Amphibalus, so that to the miracles of these saints he might furnish testimony with the faith of an eye-witness), he collected quite a lot of money. But that unfortunate work absorbed it all, as the sea absorbs the rivers, and it still had not made any progress.

After the years had passed by vainly, so far as that work was concerned, and Brother Gilbert Eversolt had died, the custody of that work, dying and languishing, fell into the hands of Brother Gilbert of Sisseverne who held it for about thirty years. Having spent the aforesaid contributions on it, in his whole time he added scarcely two feet to the whole.

With eyes averted, though with heavy heart, the aforesaid Abbot John turned his attention to other works by happier advice, leaving untouched the contributions assigned to the first work, as we have said. And, when the old refectory had been demolished, which was ruinous and dark, he began a most elegant new one which he deserved [to see] completed happily in his lifetime and to dine within joyfully with the brothers.

Raised to better hopes, he had the old dormitory, ruinous and collapsing from age, completely torn down, together with its outbuildings, namely, the latrine, and a most handsome new one built in its place, and finished absolutely to perfection. For the construction of these two noble buildings the convent gave up its wine for the continuous course of fifteen years; but because he [the abbot] abandoned the work of the church, he never deserved to see the completion of it in his lifetime. . . .

Also to the honour of the same Abbot John should belong what is known to have been laudably done by his monks. For in the time of Abbot John, by the industry and the lawful efforts of Prior Raymond, the brother of Roger of Park, the cellarer, there was made a great frontal partly of metal and partly of wood, executed with the greatest artistry, which is before the high altar in our church. Also two tablets of silver gilt, on one of which a cross with a crucifix, and Mary and John, are represented; on the other God in majesty with the four evangelists is cut in the most elegant engraving by the skilful work and diligence of Brother Walter of Colchester who, through the persuasion and prompting of

Brother Ralph Gubiun, took the habit of religion in our church, by a fortunate omen.

Now by the hand of his [Walter's] brother, William, a painted panel before the altar of the Blessed Virgin with a superaltar carved and a cross placed upon it, and a painting above and on the side, was very skilfully made (the same Ralph supplying the things necessary for this); also all the frontals before the altars of our church, namely, of St. John, St. Stephen, St. Amphibalus, and St. Benedict. Also by the hand of his brother and disciple, Master Simon, the painter, the frontals of St. Peter and St. Michael. By the hand also of Brother Richard, nephew of the aforesaid Master William, and son of Master Simon, the frontal of St. Thomas, in two sections above and below, partly by his and partly by his father's hand, was executed. The frontal also of St. Benedict, with many other carvings and paintings, by the labour of the aforesaid (although it was not in the time of Abbot John but later), were made for the honour and the decoration of the house of God.

We have considered, therefore, that these things should be commended to immortal writing and memory so that there may flourish with blessings among us, not ungrateful, the recollection of those who by their zealous labour left after them the works of our church so adorned. . . .

At first he [Abbot William, 1214-35] finished the dormitory most suitably (as well as the private place belonging to it, as said above) with beds of oaken material, and in it he assembled the convent. Moreover, in his time, the two wings of the church were strengthened in the roof with oak, well bound together and joined by small beams; these consumed by rot and worms had previously admitted an abundance of rain.

The spire of the tower, which rises like a great scaffolding, was constructed out of the best material well joined together and raised much higher than the old one which was threatening ruin. And all these, not without great expense, were covered with lead. They were carried out in fact by the diligence and industry of Richard of Thidenhanger, a lay monk of ours, and chamberlain, without neglecting or detracting from his office; they should be ascribed, however, to the abbot, out of reverence. For he is the doer, by whose authority anything is known to be done.

The abbot himself, however, after the death of that Richard of blessed memory, had the same tower uncovered because it had been improperly covered, and adding not a small quantity of lead, had it reroofed properly and durably. Decorations were added on the sides, namely, eight rectilinear pilasters, extending from the top to the wall so that the tower would seem more clearly octagonal; all this was done at his own expense, by the persuasion and instigation of Lord Matthew, then bailiff and keeper of the seal, called "of Cambridge." This was known because he was appointed overseer and adviser and diligent custodian of that work. . . . And these lines which are popularly called *aristae* wonderfully strengthened the tower and adorned what was strengthened and, besides, more surely kept out the rain; this tower previously, with the eight sides undistinguishable, displayed a form which was rounded, plain and meagre, harmonizing poorly and unsuitably with the wall.

And the front work of the same church, after very destructive ruin, the Abbot William, moved to pity and compassion, because it had dragged out in such a wearisome delay, took upon his shoulders to be carried out.

This, in a short time, with a roof of selected material, with timbers and beams, with rafters, and with glass windows executed perfectly, he joined to the old work, suitably covered over with lead.

He also repaired the stone work with glass panes of those windows which are in the great wall above the place where the great missal lies and where the lesser clerics usually sing matins and the hours; moreover, he completed the stone work with glass panes of many other windows in the wings of the church, north and south, with the aid of the custodian of the altar of St. Amphibalus. And so the church, illuminated by the benefit of the new light, seemed as if made new.

Also, in his time, when Master Walter of Colchester, then sacristan (an incomparable painter and sculptor) had completed a rood loft in the middle of the church, with its great cross, and Mary and John, and with other carvings and suitable decorations, at the expense of the sacristy but by the diligence of his own labour, that Abbot William solemnly removed the shrine with the relics of St. Amphibalus and his companions, from the place where it had formerly been located (namely, beside the high altar next to the shrine of St. Alban), towards the north, to the place which is enclosed in the middle of the church by an iron lattice-work grill where a very handsome altar had been constructed with a richly painted frontal and super-altar. . . .

Moreover, to the increase of the fame of that same Abbot William it should, I think, be remembered that he constructed some very noble structures about the high altar, with a certain beam representing the story of St. Alban, which surmounts all that work of artistry. This most splendid work was executed, not without great and laborious zeal and zealous labour, by Master

Walter of Colchester whom we have often mentioned in praise; the abbot, however, freely gave ample funds for this purpose.

From *Gesta abbatum sancti Albani*, H. T. Riley, ed., Rolls Series, vol. 28; trans. J.B.R.

A Painter on His Craft

CENNINO CENNINI

1370

SO THEN, either as a labour of love for all those who feel within them a desire to understand; or as a means of embellishing these fundamental theories with some jewel, that they may be set forth royally, without reserve; offering to these theories whatever little understanding God has granted me, as an unimportant practising member of the profession of painting: I, Cennino, the son of Andrea Cennini of Colle di Val d'Elsa (I was trained in this profession for twelve years by my master, Agnolo di Taddeo of Florence; he learned this profession from Taddeo, his father; and his father was christened under Giotto, and was his follower for four-and-twenty years; and that Giotto changed the profession of painting from Greek back into Latin, and brought it up to date; and he had more finished craftsmanship than anyone has had since), to minister to all those who wish to enter the profession, I will make note of what was taught me by the aforesaid Agnolo, my master, and of what I have tried out with my own hand; first invoking [the aid of] High Almighty God, the Father, Son, and Holy Ghost; then [of] that most beloved advocate of all sinners, Virgin Mary; and of Saint Luke, the evangelist, the first Christian painter; and of my advocate, Saint Eustace; and, in general, of all the Saints of Paradise, AMEN. . . .

It is not without the impulse of a lofty spirit that some are moved to enter this profession, attractive to them through natural enthusiasm. Their intellect will take delight in drawing, provided their nature attracts them to it of themselves, without any master's guidance, out of loftiness of spirit. And then, through this delight, they come to want to find a master; and they bind themselves to him with respect for authority, undergoing an apprenticeship in order to achieve perfection in all this. There are those who pursue it, because of poverty and domestic need, for profit and enthusiasm for the profession too; but above all these are to be extolled the ones who enter the profession through a sense of enthusiasm and exaltation. . . .

The basis of the profession, the very beginning of all these manual operations, is drawing and painting. These two sections call for a knowledge of the following: how to work up or grind, how to apply size, to put on cloth, to gesso, to scrape the gessos and smooth them down, to model with gesso, to lay bole, to gild, to burnish; to temper, to lay in; to pounce, to scrape through, to stamp or punch; to mark out, to paint, to embellish, and to varnish, on panel or ancona. To work on a wall you have to wet down, to plaster, to true up, to smooth off, to draw, to paint in fresco. To carry to completion in secco: to temper, to embellish, to finish on the wall. And let this be the schedule of the aforesaid stages which I, with what little knowledge I have acquired, will expound, section by section. . . .

Now you must forge ahead again, so that you may pursue the course of this theory. You have made your tinted papers; the next thing is to draw. You should adopt this method. Having first practised drawing for a while as I have taught you above, that is, on a little panel, take pains and pleasure in constantly copying the best things which you can find done by the hand of great masters. And if you are in a place where many good masters have been, so much the better for you. But I give you this advice: take care to select the best one every time, and the one who has the greatest reputation. And, as you go on from day to day, it will be against nature if you do not get some grasp of his style and of his spirit. For if you undertake to copy after one master today and after another one tomorrow, you will not acquire the style of either one or the other, and you will inevitably, through enthusiasm, become capricious, because each style will be distracting your mind. You will try to work in this man's way today, and in the other's tomorrow, and so you will not get either of them right. If you follow the course of one man through constant practice, your intelligence would have to be crude indeed for you not to get some nourishment from it. Then you will find, if nature has granted you any imagination at all, that you will eventually acquire a style individual to yourself, and it cannot help being good; because your hand and your mind, being always accustomed to gather flowers, would ill know how to pluck thorns.

Mind you, the most perfect steersman that you can have, and the best helm lie in the triumphal gateway of copying from nature. And this outdoes all other models; and always rely on this with a stout heart, especially as you begin to gain some judgment in draughtsmanship. Do not fail, as you go on, to draw something every day, for no matter how little it is it will be well worth while, and will do you a world of good.

Your life should always be arranged just as if you were

studying theology, or philosophy, or other theories, that is to say, eating and drinking moderately, at least twice a day, electing digestible and wholesome dishes, and light wines; saving and sparing your hand, preserving it from such strains as heaving stones, crowbars, and many other things which are bad for your hand, from giving them a chance to weary it. There is another cause which, if you indulge it, can make your hand so unsteady that it will waver more, and flutter far more, than leaves do in the wind, and this is indulging too much in the company of women. Let us get back to our subject. Have a sort of pouch made of pasteboard, or just thin wood, made large enough in every dimension for you to put in a royal folio, that is, a half; and this is good for you to keep your drawings in, and likewise to hold the paper on for drawing. Then always go out alone, or in such company as will be inclined to do as you do, and not apt to disturb you. And the more understanding this company displays, the better it is for you. When you are in churches or chapels, and beginning to draw, consider, in the first place, from what section you think you wish to copy a scene or figure; and notice where its darks and half tones and high lights come; and this means that you have to apply your shadow with washes of ink; to leave the natural ground in the half tones; and to apply the high lights with white lead. . . .

If you want to get the effect of a velvet, do the drapery with any colour you wish, tempered with yolk of egg. Then make the cut threads, as the velvet requires, with a miniver brush, in a colour tempered with oil; and make the cut threads rather coarse. And you may make black velvets in this way, and red ones, and any coloured ones, tempering in this way. . . .

If you happen to have to work on woollen cloth, on

account of tourneys or jousts, for gentlemen or great lords sometimes teem with desire for distinctive things, and want their arms in gold or silver on this sort of cloth: first, according to the colour of the stuff or cloth, select the crayon which it requires for drawing; and fix it with a pen, just as you did on the velvet. Then take white of egg, well beaten as I taught you before, and an equal amount of size, in the usual way; and put it on the nap of this cloth, on the part where you have to do gilding. Then when it is dry take a crook, and burnish over this cloth; then apply two more coats of this tempera. When it is quite dry, apply your mordant so as not to go outside the tempered part, and lay whatever gold or silver you think fit.

From *The Craftsman's Handbook*, trans. D. V. Thompson (New Haven: Yale University Press, 1933).

Nature as the Supreme Authority

LEONARDO DA VINCI

Fifteenth century

How from age to age the art of painting continually declines and deteriorates when painters have no other standard than work already done:

The painter will produce pictures of little merit if he takes the works of others as his standard; but if he will apply himself to learn from the objects of nature he will produce good results. This we see was the case with the painters who came after the time of the Romans, for they continually imitated each other, and from age to age their art steadily declined.

After these came Giotto the Florentine, and he—

reared in mountain solitudes, inhabited only by goats and suchlike beasts—turning straight from nature to his art, began to draw on the rocks the movements of the goats which he was tending, and so began to draw the figures of all the animals which were to be found in the country, in such a way that after much study he not only surpassed the masters of his own time but all those of many preceding centuries. After him art again declined, because all were imitating paintings already done; and so for centuries it continued to decline until such time as Tommaso the Florentine, nicknamed Masaccio, showed by the perfection of his work how those who took as their standard anything other than nature, the supreme guide of all the masters, were wearying themselves in vain. Similarly I would say about these mathematical subjects, that those who study only the authorities and not the works of nature are in art the grandsons and not the sons of nature, which is the supreme guide of the good authorities.

Mark the supreme folly of those who censure such as learn from nature, leaving uncensured the authorities who were themselves the disciples of this same nature!

From *The Notebooks of Leonardo da Vinci*, trans. E. MacCurdy (New York: Reynal & Hitchcock; London: Cape, 1938).

MUSICIANS

Celtic Music and Music in General

GIRALDUS CAMBRENSIS

Twelfth century

WELSH MUSIC AND SONG

THEIR musical instruments charm and delight the
ear with their sweetness, are borne along by such
celerity and delicacy of modulation, producing such a
consonance from the rapidity of seemingly discordant
touches, that I shall briefly repeat what is set forth in
our Irish *Topography* on the subject of the musical
instruments of the three nations. It is astonishing that in
so complex and rapid a movement of the fingers, the musical proportions can be preserved, and that throughout
the difficult modulations on their various instruments,
the harmony is completed with such a sweet velocity, so
unequal an equality, so discordant a concord, as if the
chords sounded together fourths or fifths. They always
begin from B flat, and return to the same, that the whole
may be completed under the sweetness of a pleasing
sound. They enter into a movement, and conclude it in
so delicate a manner, and play the little notes so spor-
tively under the blunter sounds of the base strings, en-
livening with wanton levity, or communicating a deeper
internal sensation of pleasure, so that the perfection of
their art appears in the concealment of it. . . . From

this cause, those very strains which afford deep and unspeakable mental delight to those who have skilfully penetrated into the mysteries of the art, fatigue rather than gratify the ears of others, who seeing, do not perceive, and hearing, do not understand; and by whom the finest music is esteemed no better than a confused and disorderly noise, and will be heard with unwillingness and disgust.

They make use of three instruments, the harp, the pipes, and the crwth or crowd (*chorus*).

They omit no part of natural rhetoric in the management of civil actions, in quickness of invention, disposition, refutation, and confirmation. In their rhymed songs and set speeches they are so subtile and ingenious, that they produce, in their native tongue, ornaments of wonderful and exquisite invention both in the words and sentences. Hence arise those poets whom they call Bards, of whom you will find many in this nation, endowed with the above faculty. . . .

In their musical concerts they do not sing in unison like the inhabitants of other countries, but in many different parts; so that in a company of singers, which one very frequently meets with in Wales, you will hear as many different parts and voices as there are performers, who all at length unite, with organic melody, in one consonance and the soft sweetness of B flat. In the northern district of Britain, beyond the Humber, and on the borders of Yorkshire, the inhabitants make use of the same kind of symphonious harmony, but with less variety; singing only in two parts, one murmuring in the base, the other warbling in the acute or treble. Neither of the two nations has acquired this peculiarity by art, but by long habit, which has rendered it natural and familiar; and the practice is now so firmly rooted in them, that it is unusual to hear a simple and single melody well sung; and, what is still more wonderful, the children, even from their infancy, sing in the same manner. As the English in general do not adopt this mode of singing, but only those of the northern countries, I believe that it was from the Danes and Norwegians, by whom these parts of the island were more frequently invaded, and held longer under their dominion, that the natives contracted their mode of singing as well as speaking.

From *Itinerary through Wales*, trans. Sir. R. C. Hoare.

IRISH MUSIC AND MUSIC IN GENERAL

The only thing to which I find that this people apply a commendable industry is playing upon musical instruments; in which they are incomparably more skilful than any other nation I have ever seen. For their modulation on these instruments, unlike that of the Britons to which I am accustomed, is not slow and harsh, but lively and rapid, while the harmony is both sweet and gay. . . .

It must be remarked, however, that both Scotland and Wales strive to rival Ireland in the art of music; the former from its community of race, the latter from its contiguity and facility of communication. Ireland only uses and delights in two instruments, the harp and the tabor. Scotland has three, the harp, the tabor, and the crowth or crowd; and Wales, the harp, the pipes, and the crowd. The Irish also use strings of brass instead of leather. Scotland at the present day, in the opinion of many persons, is not only equal to Ireland, her teacher, in musical skill, but excels her; so that they now look to that country as the fountain head of this science.

The sweet harmony of music not only affords us pleasures, but renders us important services. It greatly cheers the drooping spirit, clears the face from clouds, smooths the wrinkled brow, checks moroseness, promotes hilarity; of all the most pleasant things in the world, nothing more delights and enlivens the human heart. There are two things which, more than any other, refresh and delight the mind, namely, sweet odours and music. Man, as it were, feeds upon sweet odours and music. In whatever pursuit the mind is engaged, it draws forth the genius, and by means of insensible things quickens the senses with sensible effect. Hence in bold men it excites courage, and in the religious it nourishes and promotes good feeling.

Moreover, music soothes disease and pain; the sounds which strike the ear operating within, and either healing our maladies, or enabling us to bear them with greater patience. It is a comfort to all, and an effectual remedy to many; for there are no sufferings which it will not mitigate, and there are some which it cures. . . .

It appears, then, that music acts in contrary ways; when employed to give intensity to the feelings, it inflames, when to abate them, it lulls. Hence the Irish and Spaniards, and some other nations, mix plaintive music with their funeral wailings, giving poignancy to their present grief, as well as, perhaps, tranquillizing the mind when the worst is past. Music also alleviates toil, and in labour of various kinds the fatigue is cheered by sounds uttered in measured time. Hence, artificers of all sorts relieve the weariness of their tasks by songs. The very beasts, not to speak of serpents, and birds, and porpoises, are attracted by musical harmony to listen to its melody; and what is still more remarkable, swarms of bees are recalled to their hives, and induced to settle, by musical sounds. I have sometimes observed, when on a voyage, shoals of porpoises long following in the wake of the ship when she was pursuing her course, and how they leaped above the surface, and erected their ears to listen to the tones of the harp or the trumpet.

Moreover, as Isidore remarks, "No teaching can be perfect without harmony. Indeed, there is nothing in which it is not found. The world itself is said to be harmoniously formed, and the very heavens revolve amidst the harmony of the spheres. Sounds, the materials of which melodies are composed, are threefold: first they are harmonic, being produced by the voices of singers; secondly, they are organic, being produced by wind; thirdly, they are rhythmical, produced by the touch of the fingers. For sounds are either produced by the voice, through the throat; or by wind, as a trumpet or pipe; or by the touch, as by the harp, or any other instrument the melody of which is produced by the finger."

From *Topography of Ireland*, trans. T. Wright.

Two Musical Friars

SALIMBENE

Thirteenth century

BROTHER HENRY of Pisa was a handsome man, of medium height, generous, amiable, charitable, and merry. He knew how to get along well with everyone, condescending and adapting himself to the personality of each one, and he won the love of his own brethren as well as that of the laymen, which is given to few. Moreover, he was a celebrated preacher, beloved by both the clergy and the laity. He knew how to write beautifully, and to paint, which some call illuminate, to write music, and to compose the sweetest and loveliest songs, both in harmony and in plain song. He himself was an excellent singer, and had a strong and sonorous voice, so that it filled the whole choir. And his treble sounded light, very high and clear, but sweet, lovely, and pleasing beyond measure. He was my *custos* in the convent at Siena, and my master of song in the time of Pope Gregory IX. . . .

That Brother Henry of Pisa was a man of admirable manners, devoted to God and to the Holy Virgin, and to the Blessed Magdalen. No wonder, for the church of his quarter of Pisa bore the name of this saint; the cathedral of the city, in which he had been ordained by the archbishop of Pisa, bore the name of the Blessed Virgin. Brother Henry composed many *cantilena* and many sequences, for example, the words and melody of the following song:

> O Christ, my God,
> O Christ, my Refuge
> O Christ, King and Lord,

after the song of a maid who was going through the cathedral church of Pisa, singing in the popular tongue:

> If thou carest not for me,
> I'll no longer care for thee.

He made, moreover, the three-part song: "Wretched man, think thou on thy Creator's works!" Also, he composed for the text of Master Philip, the chancellor of Paris:

> O Man, how anxious
> Is my care for thee!

And then once, when he was *custos* of the custody of Siena, and lay sick in bed in the infirmary, and could not write, he called me to him, and I was the first to note down one of his songs, while he sang it. Then for another text of that same chancellor, he wrote the melody: "O Cross, for thee shall I mourn." . . .

He composed a noble melody to the sequence: "He has watered the tree of Jesse," which until then had had a crude one, discordant for singing. Richard of St. Victor wrote the words of this sequence, as well as those of many others. For one of the hymns to the Blessed Magdalen, which Chancellor Philip of Paris had written, "Mourn, tongue of Magdalen" . . . Brother Henry composed a lovely melody. He wrote a sequence, words and melody, on the Resurrection of the Lord, namely: "The Lord, who suffered, is risen today." The second air which belongs to this, the antiphonal chant, was composed by the Franciscan friar, Vita of Lucca, in his time the best singer in the world, in both kinds of song, harmony and plain-chant.

He [Vita] had a lovely, delicate voice, delightful to hear. There was no one so stern that he did not hear him gladly. He sang before bishops, archbishops, cardinals, even before the pope himself, and gladly did they listen to him. If anyone spoke while Brother Vita sang, he immediately had thrown up to him the words of Ecclesiasticus, "Hinder not the music." And when a nightingale sang in hedge or thicket, it would stop when he began to sing, and listen most earnestly to him, as if rooted to the spot, and then take up its song again, and so the voices of bird and friar sounded charming and sweet, singing alternately. So generously did he squander his song that he never made excuses when he was asked to sing, pleading that he had strained his voice, or was hoarse from a cold, or any other reason. Therefore, no one could apply to him the often quoted verses [of Horace]: "All singers have this fault, that they never can be found ready to sing, when they are asked to perform among friends."

His mother and sister were also gifted with excellent, sweet voices. Brother Vita composed the sequence, "Hail Mary, hope of the world," both verse and melody. He composed many hymns in harmony, in which the secular clergy especially delight. He was my master of song in his native city of Lucca in that year [1239] when the sun was so terribly eclipsed. Now when the Lord Thomas of Capua, cardinal of the Roman curia . . . had written the sequence: "Let the Virgin Mother rejoice," and had begged Brother Henry of Pisa to compose an air to it, he made one beautiful and delightful and sweet to hear, and to this Brother Vita composed the secondary melody, that is, the harmony. For always, when he found any plain-song of Brother Henry's, he composed a harmony to it.

The Lord Philip, archbishop of Ravenna, took this Brother Vita into his retinue when he went as legate to the patriarchates of Aquileia and Grado, to the cities of Ragusa, Ravenna, Milan, Genoa, and their dioceses and provinces, and in general, to Lombardy, the Romagna, and the mark of Treviso. He took him, moreover, because he was from his own country, and because he was a Friar Minor, and finally because he knew how to sing and to compose so admirably. He died in Milan, and was buried in the convent of the Friars Minor. He was a slender and elegant man, taller than Brother Henry. His voice was more suitable for the chamber than for the choir. He often left the order, and often returned; in between times he joined the Benedictine order. And when he wanted to return, Pope Gregory IX always dealt gently with him, for love of the holy Francis and for the sweetness of his song. Once, for example, he sang so enchantingly that a nun who heard him threw herself from her window, in order to follow him. But she could not do this, for she broke her leg in the fall.

. . . This was no such listening as is written in the last chapter of the Song of Songs, "Thou that dwellest in the gardens, the friends hearken: make me hear thy voice."

From Chronicle, F. Bernini, ed.; trans. M.M.M.

An Orchestra of the Fourteenth Century

Guillaume de Machaut

Fourteenth century

AFTERWARDS all came into the hall which was not ugly or dull, where each was, in my opinion, honoured and served both with wine and meat as his body and appetite demanded. And there I took my sustenance by looking at the countenance, the condition, the carriage, and the bearing of her in whom is all my joy. But here come the musicians after eating, without mishap, combed and dressed up! There they made many different harmonies. For I saw there all in one circle viol, rebec, gittern, lute, micanon, citole, and the psaltery, harp, tabor, trumpets, nakers, organs, horns, more than ten pairs, bagpipes [cornemuses], flutes [flajos], bagpipes [chevrettes], krumhorns, cymbals, bells, timbrel, the Bohemian flute [la flaüste brehaingne], and the big German cornet, flutes [flajos de saus], flute [fistule], pipe, bagpipe [muse d'Aussay], little trumpet, buzines, panpipes, monochord where there is only one string, and bagpipe [muse de blef] all together. And certainly, it seems to me that such a melody was never seen or heard, for each of them, according to the tune of his instrument, without discord, viol, gittern, citole, harp, trumpet, horn,

flute, pipe, bellows [*?souffle*], bagpipe, nakers, tabor,
and whatever one can do with finger, feather, and bow,
I have seen and heard on this floor.

From "Remède de Fortune," in *Œuvres*, E. Hoepffner, ed. (Paris:
Firmin Didot, 1911); trans. J.B.R.

The Mirror of History

A Philosophy of History

OTTO OF FREISING

Twelfth century

IN PONDERING long and often in my heart upon the
changes and vicissitudes of temporal affairs and their
varied and irregular issues, even as I hold that a wise
man ought by no means to cleave to the things of time,
so I find that it is by the faculty of reason alone that one
must escape and find release from them. For it is the
part of a wise man not to be whirled about after the
manner of a revolving wheel, but through the stability
of his powers to be firmly fashioned as a thing four-
square. Accordingly, since things are changeable and
can never be at rest, what man in his right mind will
deny that the wise man ought, as I have said, to depart
from them to that city which stays at rest and abides
to all eternity? This is the City of God, the heavenly
Jerusalem, for which the children of God sigh while
they are set in this land of sojourn, oppressed by the
turmoil of the things of time as if they were oppressed
by the Babylonian captivity. For, inasmuch as there are
two cities—the one of time, the other of eternity; the
one of the earth, earthy, the other of heaven, heavenly;

562

the one of the devil, the other of Christ—ecclesiastical writers have declared that the former is Babylon, the latter Jerusalem.

But, whereas many of the Gentiles have written much regarding one of these cities, to hand down to posterity the great exploits of men of old (the many evidences of their merits, as they fancied), they have yet left to us the task of setting forth what, in the judgment of our writers, is rather the tale of human miseries. . . .

In those writings the discerning reader will be able to find not so much histories as pitiful tragedies made up of mortal woes. We believe that this has come to pass by what is surely a wise and proper dispensation of the Creator, in order that, whereas men in their folly desire to cleave to earthly and transitory things, they may be frightened away from them by their own vicissitudes, if by nothing else, so as to be directed by the wretchedness of this fleeting life from the creature to a knowledge of the Creator. But we, set down as it were at the end of time, do not so much read of the miseries of mortals in the books of the writers named above as find them for ourselves in consequence of the experiences of our own time. For, to pass over other things, the empire of the Romans, which in Daniel is compared to iron on account of its sole lordship—monarchy, the Greeks call it —over the whole world, a world subdued by war, has in consequence of so many fluctuations and changes, particularly in our day, become, instead of the noblest and the foremost, almost the last. . . .

For being transferred from the City [Rome] to the Greeks, from the Greeks to the Franks, from the Franks to the Lombards, from the Lombards again to the German Franks, that empire not only became decrepit and senile through lapse of time, but also, like a once smooth pebble that has been rolled this way and that by the waters, contracted many a stain and developed many a defect. The world's misery is exhibited, therefore, even in the case of the chief power in the world, and Rome's fall foreshadows the dissolution of the whole structure.

But what wonder if human power is changeable, seeing that even mortal wisdom is prone to slip? We read that in Egypt there was so great wisdom that, as Plato states, the Egyptians called the philosophers of the Greeks childish and immature. . . . And yet Babylon the great, not only renowned for wisdom, but also "the glory of kingdoms, the beauty of the Chaldeans' pride," has become, in the words of the prophecy of Isaiah, without hope of restoration, a shrine of owls, a house of serpents and of ostriches, the lurking-place of creeping things. Egypt too is said to be in large measure uninhabitable and impassable. The careful student of history will find that learning was transferred from Egypt to the Greeks, then to the Romans, and finally to the Gauls and the Spaniards. And so it is to be observed that all human power or learning had its origin in the East, but is coming to an end in the West, that thereby the transitoriness and decay of all things human may be displayed. This, by God's grace, we shall show more fully in what follows.

Since, then, the changeable nature of the world is proved by this and like evidence, I thought it necessary, my dear brother Isingrim, in response to your request, to compose a history whereby through God's favour I might display the miseries of the citizens of Babylon and also the glory of the kingdom of Christ to which the citizens of Jerusalem are to look forward with hope, and of which they are to have a foretaste even in this life. I have undertaken therefore to bring down as far as our own time, according to the ability that God has given me, the record of the conflicts and miseries of the one city, Babylon; and furthermore, not to be silent concerning our hopes regarding that other city, so far as I can gather hints from the Scriptures, but to make mention also of its citizens who are now sojourning in the worldly city. In this work I follow most of all those illustrious lights of the Church, Augustine and Orosius, and have planned to draw from their fountains what is pertinent to my theme and my purpose. The one of these has discoursed most keenly and eloquently on the origin and the progress of the glorious City of God and its ordained limits, setting forth how it has ever spread among the citizens of the world, and showing which of its citizens or princes stood forth pre-eminent in the various epochs of the princes or citizens of the world. The other, in answer to those who, uttering vain babblings, preferred the former times to Christian times, has composed a very valuable history of the fluctuations and wretched issues of human greatness, the wars and the hazards of wars, and the shifting of thrones, from the foundation of the world down to his own time. Following in their steps I have undertaken to speak of the two cities in such a way that we shall not lose the thread of history, that the devout reader may observe what is to be avoided in mundane affairs by reason of the countless miseries wrought by their unstable character, and that the studious and painstaking investigator may find a record of past happenings free from all obscurity. . . .

For it is not because of indiscretion or frivolity, but out of devotion, which always knows how to excuse ignorance, that I, though I am without proper training, have ventured to undertake so arduous a task. Nor can anyone rightfully accuse me of falsehood in matters which—compared with the customs of the present time —will appear incredible, since down to the days still fresh in our memory I have recorded nothing save what

I found in the writings of trustworthy men, and then only a few instances out of many. For I should never hold the view that these men are to be held in contempt if certain of them have preserved in their writings the apostolic simplicity, for, as overshrewd subtlety sometimes kindles error, so a devout rusticity is ever the friend of truth.

As we are about to speak, then, concerning the sorrow-burdened insecurity of the one city and the blessed permanence of the other, let us call upon God, who endures with patience the turbulence and confusion of this world, and by the vision of Himself augments and glorifies the joyous peace of that other city, to the end that by His aid we may be able to say the things which are pleasing to Him. . . .

But when the Lord wished His city to spread abroad and to be extended from that people [the Jews] to all nations, He permitted the realm to be weakened under pressure of the people's sins, and the people itself to be led into captivity. But among the nations which He was to summon to faith in Himself, He established the sovereignty of the Romans to rule over the rest. When this had reached its fullest development and the pinnacle of power, He willed that His Son Christ should appear in the flesh. . . . So then the Lord, transferring His city from that people to the Gentiles, willed that they should first be humbled, despised, and afflicted by many misfortunes—even as it is written, "He scourgeth every son whom He receiveth." But because scourgings, when they exceed due measure, break the spirit rather than heal it (as medicines taken to excess), at the proper time, as I have said before, He exalted His forsaken and humbled Church. That it might therefore become more tranquil with respect to the promised heavenly kingdom, He bestowed upon it the greatest temporal power possessed by any realm. And thus as I have said the City of God, increasing gradually, reached its pinnacle and undivided authority. And observe that before His incarnation His city was not honoured to the full, but that afterwards, when He had risen to the skies with the body He had assumed and had, so to say, accepted His throne, [then] according to the parable He exalted His kingdom, which is the Church, to the highest dignity—than which there is nothing loftier on earth—that hereby He might reveal Himself to the citizens of the world as not only the God of heaven but also as Lord of the earth, and that through the prosperity of this land of our sojourn He might teach His citizens that the delights of their own country were eagerly to be sought. . . .

Furthermore, enough has been said above, I think, regarding the two cities: how one made progress, first by remaining hidden in the other until the coming of Christ, after that by advancing gradually to the time of Constantine. But after Constantine, when troubles from without had finally ceased, it began to be grievously troubled at the instigation of the devil by internal strife even to the time of the Elder Theodosius; Arius was the author of this and the lords of the world, the Augusti, were his coadjutors. But from that time on, since not only all the people but also the emperors (except a few) were orthodox Catholics, I seem to myself to have composed a history not of two cities but virtually of one only, which I call the Church. For although the elect and the reprobate are in one household, yet I cannot call these cities two as I did above; I must call them properly but one—composite, however, as the grain is mixed with the chaff. Wherefore in the books that follow let us pursue the course of history which we have begun. Since not only emperors of the Romans but also other kings (kings of renowned realms) became Christians, inasmuch as the sound of the word of God went out into all the earth and unto the ends of the world, the City of Earth was laid to rest and destined to be utterly exterminated in the end; hence our history is a history of the City of Christ, but that city, so long as it is in the land of sojourn, is "like unto a net, that was cast into the sea," containing the good and the bad. However, the faithless city of unbelieving Jews and Gentiles still remains, but, since nobler kingdoms have been won by our people, while these unbelieving Jews and Gentiles are insignificant not only in the sight of God but even in that of the world, hardly anything done by these unbelievers is found to be worthy of record or to be handed on to posterity.

From *The Two Cities*, trans. C. C. Mierow (New York: Columbia University Press, 1928).

The Problems and Motives of the Historian

WILLIAM OF TYRE

Twelfth century

THAT it is an arduous task, fraught with many risks and perils, to write of the deeds of kings no wise man can doubt. To say nothing of the toil, the never-ending application, and the constant vigilance which works of this nature always demand, a double abyss inevitably yawns before the writer of history. It is only with the greatest difficulty that he avoids one or the other, for, while he is trying to escape Charybdis, he usually falls into the clutches of Scylla, who, surrounded by her dogs, understands equally well how to bring about disaster. For either he will kindle the anger of many persons against him while he is in pursuit of the actual facts of achievements; or, in the hope of rousing less resentment, he will be silent about the course of events, wherein, obviously, he is not without fault. For to pass over the actual truth of events and conceal the facts intentionally is well recognized as contrary to the duty of a historian. But to fail in one's duty is unquestionably a fault, if indeed duty is truly defined as "the fitting conduct of each individual, in accordance with the customs and institutions of his country." On the other hand, to trace out a succession of events without changing them or deviating from the rule of truth is a course which always excites wrath; for, as says the old proverb, "Compliance wins friends; truth, hatred." As a result, historians either fall short of the duty of their profession by showing undue deference, or, while eagerly seeking the truth of a matter, they must needs endure hatred, of which truth herself is the mother. Thus all too commonly, these two courses are wont to be opposed to one another and to become equally troublesome by the insistent demands which they make. . . .

As for those who, in the desire to flatter, deliberately weave untruths into their record of history, the conduct of such writers is looked upon as so detestable that they ought not to be regarded as belonging to the rank of historians. For, if to conceal the true facts about achievements is wrong and falls far short of a writer's duty, it will certainly be regarded as a much more serious sin to mingle untruth with truth and to hand to a trusting posterity as verity that which is essentially untrue.

In addition to these risks, the writer of history usually meets with an equal or even more formidable difficulty, which he should endeavour to avoid in so far as in him lies. It is, namely, that the lofty dignity of historical events may suffer loss through feeble presentation and lack of eloquence. For the style of his discourse ought to be on the same high plane as are the deeds which he is relating. Nor should the language and spirit of the writer fall below the nobility of his subject.

It is greatly to be feared, therefore, that the grandeur of the theme may be impaired by faulty handling and that deeds which are of intrinsic value and importance in themselves may appear insignificant and trivial through fault in the narration. For, as the distinguished orator remarks in the first *Tusculan Disputation*, "To commit one's thoughts to writing without being able to arrange them well, present them clearly, or attract the reader by any charm is the act of a man who foolishly abuses literature and his own leisure." . . .

In view of the many dangerous complications and pitfalls attending this task, it would have been far safer if I had remained silent. I ought to have held my peace and forced my pen to rest. But an insistent love of my country [the kingdom of Jerusalem] urges me on, and for her, if the needs of the time demand, a man of loyal instincts is bound to lay down his life. She spurs me on, I repeat, and with that authority which belongs to her imperiously commands that those things which have been accomplished by her during the course of almost a century be not buried in silence and allowed to fall into undeserved oblivion. On the contrary, she bids me preserve them for the benefit of posterity by the diligent use of my pen.

Accordingly we have obeyed her behest and have put our hand to a task which we cannot with honour refuse. We care but little what the criticism of posterity concerning us may be, or what verdict may be given as to our feeble style of writing while dealing with a subject so noble. . . .

Wearied by the sad disasters which are occurring in the kingdom so frequently—indeed, almost continually—we had resolved to abandon the pen and commit to the silence of the tomb the chronicle of events which we had undertaken to write for posterity. For there is no one who is not reluctant to recount the failings of his country and to bring forth into the light the faults of his own people. It has come to be almost habitual among men, and indeed is regarded as natural, that each one should strive with all his might to extol his own land and not disparage the good fame of his fellow-countrymen.

But now every source of glorious renown is taken from us, and the only subjects that present themselves are the disasters of a sorrowing country and its manifold misfortune, themes which can serve only to draw forth lamentations and tears. . . .

It is therefore time to hold our peace; for it seems more fitting to draw the shades of night over our failures than to turn the light of the sun upon our disgrace. There are some, however, who desire us to continue the task once undertaken, who earnestly entreat that every phase of the kingdom of Jerusalem, adverse as well as prosperous, be recorded in this work for posterity. For our encouragement, they cite the example of most distinguished historians, namely Titus Livius, who recorded in his history not only the successes of the Romans, but also their reverses, and Josephus, who made known in his comprehensive works not only the brilliant deeds of the Jews, but also those shameful things which were done to them.

In their efforts to persuade us to continue this work, they offer many other examples also. We are the more readily influenced to acquiesce in this request, since it is indeed evident that chroniclers of past events have recorded without partiality adverse as well as auspicious happenings. For, by narrating successful achievements, they hope to inspire posterity with courage, while by furnishing examples of misfortunes patiently endured they may render later generations more cautious under similar conditions.

From *A History of Deeds Done beyond the Seas*, trans. E. A. Babcock and A. C. Krey.

The Seven Liberal Arts

On Study and Teaching

HUGH OF ST. VICTOR

Twelfth century

THERE are many whom nature itself has left so deficient in intelligence that they are scarcely able to grasp intellectually even those things which are easy, and of these, it seems, there are two sorts. For there are some who, although they are not ignorant of their dullness, nevertheless strive eagerly for knowledge, with all the effort of which they are capable. And they incessantly sweat in study, so that what they might have less as a result of labour, they seem to achieve by an act of will. But there are others who, since they feel themselves unable by any means to comprehend the most difficult things, neglect the least; and as if resting secure in their own torpor, the more they avoid learning those lesser things which they can understand, the more they lose the light of truth in the greatest things. As the Psalmist says, "They do not wish to know so that they may do well." For not to know something is far different from not wanting to know something, since not to know is a weakness, but to detest knowledge is a perversion of the will.

573

There is another kind of men whom nature has to a great degree enriched intellectually and to whom nature has given an easy access to truth. Although intellectual power may be equal in all, yet the same virtue or will has not been given to all of them to cultivate the natural intellect through exercises and learning. For there are many who, engrossed in the business and cares of the world beyond what is necessary, or abandoned to the vices and pleasures of the body, bury the talent of God in the earth, and seek from it neither the fruit of wisdom nor the profit of good work, and these indeed are most detestable men. Again, for others the lack of resources and little means lessen the possibility of learning. But we believe that it is not possible to pardon them fully for this reason, since we may see many labouring in hunger, thirst, and nakedness to attain the fruit of knowledge. It is one thing when you cannot learn, or to speak more truly, cannot *easily* learn, and another when you are able, and do not wish to know. For just as it is more glorious, with no facilities at hand, to attain wisdom by excellence alone, so it is more shameful to be vigorous in mind, to abound in riches, and to grow torpid in laziness. . . .

Philosophy is divided into the theoretical, the practical, the mechanical, and the logical. Theory is divided into theology, physics, and mathematics. Mathematics includes arithmetic, music, and geometry. Practical philosophy is divided into the solitary, the private, and the public [i.e., ethics, economics, and politics]. The mechanical arts include spinning, arms-making, navigation, agriculture, hunting, medicine, and the theatrical art. Logic includes grammar and expression; there are two kinds of expression, probable and sophistical demonstration. Probable demonstration is divided into dialectic and rhetoric. In this division, only the chief parts of philosophy are contained; there are still other subdivisions of these parts, but the parts can suffice for now. As to these, if you have regard only for number, there are twenty-one; if you wish to compute stages, you will find thirty-eight. Different authors are read in these fields of knowledge; some show how to begin the arts, others, how to advance in them, and others, how to perfect them. . . .

Among all the sciences enumerated above, however, the ancients settled on seven especially in their own studies, for the work of teaching. In these seven, they perceived that there was greater utility than in the others, so that anyone who would firmly comprehend the discipline of these would afterwards, by investigating and practising diligently more than by listening, attain a knowledge of the others. For they are, as it were, the best instruments and the best beginnings, by which the way is prepared in the mind for the full knowledge of philosophical truth. Hence they are called the *trivium* and *quadrivium,* since by these roads, so to speak, the lively mind may enter the secret places of wisdom.

In those former times, no one seemed worthy of the name of master who could not profess the knowledge of these seven. Pythagoras [of Samos, 6th century B.C.] is said to have observed this custom in his schools, that for seven years, according to the number of the seven liberal arts, none of his pupils should dare to ask the reason for anything which was said by him. But the pupil should put his trust in the master's words until he had heard everything, and thus he could then discover the reason for things by himself. Certain ones are said to have learned these seven arts with such great zeal, and kept them all so firmly in memory, that, whatever writings they then took in hand, whatever questions they proposed for solution or proof, they did not seek the pages of books, but had instantly ready by heart, one by one, rules and reasons from the liberal arts, to define whatever was in dispute. Hence it happened at that time that there were so many wise men that they wrote more books than we are able to read.

But our scholars either do not wish or are not able to observe a suitable method of learning, and for that reason we find many students, but few learned men. It seems to me, indeed, that not less care should be taken lest the student expend his labour on unprofitable studies, than lest he should remain lukewarm in a good and useful plan. It is bad to carry out a good plan negligently, it is worse to expend much labour in vain. But since not all can have enough discretion to know what is good for them, I shall briefly show the student which writings seem to me more useful, and then I shall add something also on the method of learning.

There are two kinds of writings. The first kind consists of those which are properly called arts. The second comprises those which are appendages of the arts. The arts are those which are placed under philosophy, that is, which contain definite and established material of philosophy, such as grammar, dialectic, and others of that sort. Appendages of the arts are those which only look at philosophy, that is, they are concerned with material which is outside philosophy; yet sometimes they touch, in a spotty and confused manner, on certain fragments of the arts, or, to put it simply, they prepare the way to philosophy. Of this kind are all the songs of the poets, like tragedies, comedies, satires, heroic, lyric, iambic poetry, and certain didactic works, also stories and histories, and the writings of those whom we are accustomed to call philosophers, who are wont to stretch out a little matter with long circumlocutions, and to obscure plain sense with confused phrases. They also bring together diverse things, as if to make a single picture out of many colours and shapes. Note the distinction I have made for you. The arts and the appendages of the arts are two things. It seems to me that there is as great a distance between these two as that described in the lines: "The sluggish willow yields to the pale olive, as the humble wild nard to a garden of red roses" [Virgil, *Eclog*. v]. Thus if anyone who wishes to attain to knowledge abandons the truth and wants to entangle himself in the remnants of the arts, he will bear not only great but infinite labour, and scanty fruit.

Finally, the arts without their appendages are able to make a perfect scholar, but the appendages without the arts can confer no perfection, especially, moreover, since they possess nothing desirable in themselves which may attract the reader, unless it has been taken over and adapted from the arts, and no one will seek in them anything except what belongs to the arts. For this reason it seems to me that effort should first of all be devoted to those arts which are the foundations of all, and where pure and simple truth is revealed, especially to those seven which I have mentioned, which are the instruments of all of philosophy. Then, if there is time, the others may be read, since sometimes the playful mingled with the serious is wont to delight more, and rarity makes a good thing precious. Thus we sometimes more eagerly retain a maxim which is found in the middle of a tale. Nevertheless, the foundation of all learning is in the seven liberal arts, which beyond all others should be kept at hand, since without them philosophic discipline does not or cannot explain or define anything.

These arts indeed are so closely connected, and are each in turn so dependent on the principles of the others, that if one is lacking, the others are not able to mould the philosopher. Therefore, it seems to me that those err who, not paying attention to such coherence in the arts, select for themselves certain of these arts, and leaving the others untouched, think that they can perfect themselves in those which they have chosen.

There is again another error not much less serious than this, which is very much to be avoided. For there are some who, although they pass over nothing in their reading, yet do not know how to attribute to any art what is proper to it, but read all into each of them. In grammar they dispute concerning the meaning of syllogisms, in dialectic they investigate "case" endings, and what is more worthy of ridicule, they read almost a whole book in its title, and by the third lecture, they have scarcely got beyond the "incipit." They do not thus teach others, but they display their own learning. But would that they appeared to others as they seem to me! Look how perverse this custom would be, if indeed the more you collected superfluities, the less you would be able to hold or to retain those things which are useful.

In each art, therefore, two things especially should be discerned and distinguished by us. First, how one should practise the art itself, and second, how one should apply the principles of that art to any other matters. These are two different things: to practise an art, and to do something else by means of an art. For the sake of an example of practising an art, take grammar. He practises the art of grammar, who treats of the rules concerning the use of words, and the precepts relating to this. Everyone who speaks or writes in accordance with rules acts grammatically. It is therefore suitable only for certain writers, like Priscian, Donatus, Servius, and the like, to practise the art of grammar. But it befits everyone to speak or write grammatically.

When therefore we are occupied with any art, especially in teaching it, when everything should be restricted and confined to what is brief and easy to understand, it should suffice to explain that which we are dealing with as briefly and aptly as possible, lest, if we should multiply irrelevant ideas to excess, we should confuse rather than edify the student. Not everything should be said which we are able to say, lest those things which we should say are said less profitably. In every art, then, you should seek that which has been established as pertaining especially to that art. Then when you are lecturing on the arts and recognize something in any one of them which is appropriate for disputation and discussion, it will be permissible to apply reciprocally the principles of each, and by considering each in turn to investigate those which you have formerly understood less well. Do not multiply the byways until you have learned the highways. You will travel safely when you are not afraid of making mistakes.

Three things are necessary for study: nature, exercise, discipline. By nature is meant that what is heard is easily understood, and that which has been understood is firmly retained. By exercise is meant that the natural capacity for understanding is cultivated by labour and application. By discipline is meant that the student who lives in praiseworthy manner joins morals to knowledge. Let us touch briefly by way of introduction on each of these three. . . .

Those who are devoted to learning should be strong in both intelligence and memory; these two are so closely joined together in every study and discipline, that if one of them is lacking, the other can lead no one to perfection, just as no riches can be of use, where safekeeping is lacking. And he keeps hiding places in vain who has nothing to hide. Natural intelligence discovers, and memory safeguards wisdom. Intelligence is a certain natural power innate in the mind, and is powerful in itself. It springs from nature, is aided by use, is blunted by immoderate labour, and is sharpened by temperate exercise. . . . There are two things which exercise natural capacity, reading and meditation. Reading is when we are informed by the rules and precepts in the writings which we read. There are three kinds of reading, for teaching, for learning, and reading for its own sake. For we say, "I read a book to that person," and "I read a book by that person," and, simply, "I read a book." In reading, order and method are especially to be considered.

Order means one thing in disciplines, as when I speak of grammar as more ancient than dialectic, or arithmetic as prior to music, and another in books, as when I say the Catalinarian before the Jugurthine [orations of Sallust], and another in narration which is in a continuous series, and still another in exposition. Order in disciplines is according to nature; in books, according to the character of the author, or the subject matter. In narration it is according to orderly arrangement, which is twofold: natural, that is, when a thing is related in the order in which it was done, and artificial, when that which happened later is told first, and that which happened first is told later. In exposition we consider order according to inquiry. Exposition consists in three things: the letter, the sense, and the conception. By the letter is meant the suitable arrangement of words, which we also call construction. The sense is a certain easy and evident meaning, which is manifested by the letter at first glance. The conception is a deeper meaning, which is found neither in exposition nor interpretation. In these things order consists in seeking first the letter, then the sense, and finally the conception. When this is done, the exposition is perfect.

Method in reading consists in dividing. All division

begins with the finite and progresses to the infinite. Everything finite, moreover, is better known, and is comprehensible to knowledge. Learning then begins from these things which are better known, and through a knowledge of them attains a knowledge of those which are hidden. Further, we investigate by means of reason, and it properly pertains to reason to divide, when, by dividing, and by investigating the natures of individual things, we descend from universals to particulars. For every universal is better determined by its own particulars. Therefore when we learn, we ought to begin from those things which are better known and determined and comprehended, and thus, by descending little by little and distinguishing individual things by means of division, investigate the nature of those things which are related.

Meditation is frequent and planned cogitation, which prudently investigates the cause and origin, the method and usefulness, of anything. Meditation has its beginning in reading, yet it is not constrained by any rules and precepts of reading. For it is delightful to have recourse to a certain suitable distance, where a free vision is possible for the contemplation of truth, and sometimes to touch lightly now these and then those causes of things, and sometimes to penetrate into them more deeply, and to leave nothing uncertain, and nothing obscure. The beginning of learning, therefore, is in reading, its consummation is in meditation. If anyone learns to love it intimately, and wants to have time for it more often, it bestows an exceedingly pleasant life, and offers the greatest consolation in time of trouble. For that is best which removes the spirit from the clash of earthly tumults, and also makes it possible in a certain sense to taste in this life the sweetness of everlasting peace. And then through those things which have been created, one will learn to seek and to know Him who created all things; then, equally, knowledge will instruct and joy will fill the mind. And thus it is that the greatest solace is in meditation. . . .

As to memory, I think it should not at present be forgotten that just as intelligence investigates and discovers by means of division, so memory safeguards the results by bringing them together. It is necessary, then, that what we have separated in learning, we should bring together to be committed to memory. To bring together means to make a short and concise summary of those things which in writing and discussion are more prolix; this the ancients called an "epilogue," that is, a brief recapitulation of what has been said before. For every treatment of a subject has some beginning on which the whole truth of the matter and the power of judgment depends, and to this everything else is referred. To seek out and to consider this is to bring things together. There is one fount, and many rivulets; why do you follow the windings of the streams? Reach the fount, and you have it all. I say this because man's memory is sluggish, and rejoices in brevity, and if it is dispersed among many things, it does less well in particulars. We ought, then, in all learning to collect something brief and certain, which may be hidden in the secret places of the memory, whence afterward, when it is necessary, the rest may be derived. It is necessary to repeat this often, and to recall the taste from the belly of the memory to the palate, lest, by long interruption, it should fall into disuse. Therefore I beg you, reader, not to rejoice too greatly if you have read much, but if you have understood much, nor that you have understood much, but that you have been able to retain it. Otherwise it is of little profit either to read or to understand. For this reason I repeat what I have said above, that those who give labour to learning need natural capacity and memory.

When a certain wise man [Bernard of Chartres] was asked what is the method and form of learning, he replied, "A humble mind, zeal for inquiry, a quiet life, silent investigation, poverty, and a foreign land: these are wont to reveal to many what is obscure in their reading." I think that he had heard the saying, "Manners adorn knowledge," and so he joined together precepts for study and precepts for living, so that the reader may perceive both the manner of his own life and the meaning of study. Knowledge is unworthy of praise when it is stained by a shameless life. Therefore, he who seeks knowledge should take the greatest care not to neglect discipline.

Humility is the beginning of discipline, and although there are many examples of this, these three especially are important to the reader: first, that he should hold no knowledge and no writing cheap; second, that he should not be ashamed to learn from anyone; third, that when he himself will have attained knowledge, he should not scorn others. This has deceived many, who wished to seem wise prematurely. Hence they swell up with self-importance, so that now they begin to pretend to be what they are not, and to be ashamed of what they are, and thus they withdraw further from wisdom, because they wish, not to be wise, but to be considered wise. I have known many of this sort, who, while they are still lacking in the first elements, deign to interest themselves only in the most advanced, and on this account they think that they themselves have become great, if only they have read the writings, or heard the words of the great and wise. "We," they say, "have seen them; we have read their works; they often speak to us; those distinguished, those famous men know us."

But would that no one recognized me, if I might know everything! You glory in having seen Plato, not in having understood him; I think then that it is not worthy of you to listen to me. I am not Plato, nor do I deserve to see Plato. It is enough for you that you have drunk at the fount of philosophy, but would that you were still thirsty! A king drinks from an earthen pot after he has drunk from a cup of gold. What are you ashamed of? You have heard Plato, you will also hear Chrysippus. As the proverb says: "What you do not know, perhaps Ofellus knows." It is given to no one to know everything, and yet there is no one who has not received from nature something peculiar to himself. The prudent scholar, therefore, hears everyone freely, reads everything, and rejects no book, no person, no doctrine. He seeks from all indifferently what he sees is lacking in himself; he considers not how much he may know, but how much he may not know. Hence the Platonic saying: "I prefer to learn modestly from another, rather than shamelessly to thrust forward my own knowledge." Why are you ashamed to learn and not ashamed to be ignorant? This is more shameful than that. Or why do you strive for the heights, when you are lying in the depths? Consider rather what your powers are strong enough to bear. He advances most suitably who proceeds in an orderly way. When some desire to make a great leap, they fall into the abyss. Do not, therefore, hasten too fast, and thus you will more quickly achieve wisdom. Learn gladly from everyone what you do not know, since humility can make that yours which nature made the possession of someone else. You will be wiser than everyone, if you will learn from everyone. Those who receive from everyone are richer than anyone. Finally, hold no knowledge cheap, since all knowledge is good. If there is time, scorn no writing, or at least read it, since if you gain nothing, you will lose nothing, especially as in my estimation there is no book which does not set forth something to be desired. If it is treated in an appropriate place and order, there is none which does not have something special, which the diligent reader has found nowhere else. The rarer it is, the more gratefully it should be enjoyed. Yet there is nothing good which is not made better.

If you cannot read everything, read that which is more useful. Even if you can read everything, the same amount of labor should not be expended on all. But some things are to be read so that they may not be unknown, and some so that they may not be unheard of, since sometimes we believe that of which we have not heard to be of greater importance, and a thing is more easily judged when its results are known. You can see now how necessary for you this humility is, that you may hold no knowledge cheap, and may learn freely from all. Likewise it behooves you not to despise others when you begin to know something. This vice of arrogance takes possession of some so that they contemplate their own knowledge too lovingly, and since they seem to themselves to be something, they think that others whom they do not know can neither be nor become such as they. Hence also these peddlers of trifles, boasting I do not know of what, accuse their ancestors of simplicity, and believe that wisdom was born with them, and will die with them. They say that in sermons the manner of speaking is so simple that it is not necessary to listen to teachers in these matters, that each of them can penetrate the secrets of truth well enough by his own intelligence. They turn up their noses and make wry mouths at the lecturers in divinity, and they do not understand that they do God an injury, whose words are simple indeed in the beauty of their expression, but they proclaim stupidities with deformed sense. I do not advise imitating such as these. For the good student should be humble and gentle, a stranger to senseless cares and the enticements of pleasure; he should be diligent and zealous, so that he may learn freely from all. He is never presumptuous about his own knowledge, he shuns the authors of perverse teaching like poison, he learns to consider a matter for a long time before he makes a judgment, he knows or seeks not how to seem learned, but to be truly learned, he loves the words of the wise when they have been understood, and he strives to keep them always before his eyes, as a mirror in front of his face. And if perchance his understanding does not have access to the more obscure things, he does not immediately burst out into vituperation, believing that nothing is good unless he himself can understand it. This is the humility of the students' discipline.

Zeal for inquiry pertains to exercise, in which the student needs encouragement more than instruction. For he who will diligently examine what the ancients achieved because of their love of wisdom, and what monuments of their power they left to be remembered by posterity, will see how inferior is his own diligence. Some spurned honours, others threw away riches, some rejoiced when they received injuries, others scorned punishments, others, abandoning the society of men and penetrating the inmost recesses and secret places of the desert, dedicated themselves solely to philosophy, in order that they might have leisure for contemplating it more freely, because they did not subject their minds to any of those desires which are wont to obstruct the path of virtue. The philosopher Parmenides is said to have sat for fifteen years on a rock in Egypt, and Prometheus is remembered because of his excessive attention to meditation while he was exposed to the vultures on Mount Caucasus. For they knew that the true good is

not concealed in the opinion of men, but in a pure conscience, and that those are not really men who, clinging
to transitory things, do not recognize their own good.
The ancients knew also how much they differed from
the others in mind and in intelligence; the very remote-
ness of their dwellings shows that one habitation may
not hold those who are not associated in the same purpose. A certain man once said to a philosopher, "Don't
you see how men mock you?" And the philosopher answered, "They mock me and the asses deride them."
Think, if you can, how much he valued being praised
by those whose scorn he did not fear. Again, we read of
another that, after the study of all disciplines and after
reaching the heights of the arts, he descended to the
potter's trade. And of still another that his disciples
loaded their master with praises, and did not fail to
boast of his skill as a shoemaker. I would desire such
diligence, then, to be in our students, that in them wisdom should never grow old.

Abishag the Shunammite alone kept the old David
warm, since the love of wisdom does not desert its lover
even when the body grows feeble. Almost all virtues of
the body change in the old, and while wisdom alone increases, the others decline. For in the old age of those
who furnish their youth with honourable arts, they
become more learned, more practised, wiser in the
course of time, and reap the sweetest fruits of earlier
studies. Whence also it is said that after that wise man
of Greece, Themistocles, had lived one hundred and
seven years, he saw that he was about to die, and said
that he grieved because he had to abandon life just when
he had begun to be wise. Plato died after eighty-one
years, and Socrates filled ninety-nine years with teaching and writing and painful labour. I say nothing of the
other philosophers, Pythagoras, Democritus, Xenocrates,

Zeno, and Eleatus, who flourished for a long time in the studies of wisdom.

I come now to the poets, Homer, Hesiod, Simonides, Tersilochus, who, when they were very old, sang their swan songs, I know not what, but sweeter than ever at the approach of death. When Sophocles, at a very great age and because of his neglect of family affairs was accused by his own family of madness, he recited to the judge that tale of Oedipus which he had written earlier, and gave so great an example of wisdom in his broken old age, that he converted the severity of his judges into acclamation of his performance. Nor is it to be wondered at that when Cato the Censor, the most eloquent of the Romans, took up the study of Greek as an old man, he was not ashamed, nor did he despair. Certainly Homer tells us that sweeter discourse flowed from the tongue of Nestor when he was an old and decrepit man. Behold, then, how much those men loved wisdom whom not even infirm old age could keep from its pursuit. . . .

The four remaining precepts which follow are so arranged, that, in alternation, one has regard to discipline and the other to practice.

Quietness of life is either interior, that the mind is not distracted by unlawful desires, or exterior, that leisure and opportunity suffice for honourable and useful studies. Both of these pertain to discipline.

But investigation, that is, meditation, pertains to practice. It seems, however, that investigation is included under the zeal for inquiry. If this is true, it is superfluous to repeat what has been said above. But it should be known that there is this difference between the two, that the zeal for inquiry means urgency of effort, but investigation, diligence in meditation. Labour and love complete a work, but care and vigilance bring forth counsel. You act in labour, you perfect in love, you prepare with care, and you are attentive in vigilance. These are the four footmen who bear the litter of Philology, since they exercise the mind in which wisdom rules. The chair of philology is the seat of wisdom, which is said to be carried by these bearers, since it advances by exercising itself in them. Therefore, the handsome youths, Philos and Kophos, that is, Labour and Love, because of their strength are said [Martianus Capella, *De nuptiis philologiae*, bk. II] to bear the litter in front, since they complete a work externally; and behind, the two maidens, Philemia and Agrimina, that is, Care and Vigilance, since they bring forth counsel within and in secret. There are some who think that by the chair of philology is meant the human body, which is governed by the rational mind, that four servants carry the body, that is, that it is composed of four elements. Of these, two are superior, that is, fire and air, masculine in name and in fact, but two are inferior and feminine, earth and water.

Frugality also should be recommended to students, that is, not to strive after superfluities; this is especially related to discipline. For, as it is said, a fat belly does not beget a keen mind. But what can the scholars of our time reply to this, who not only scorn frugality, but also strive to seem richer than they are? Now no one boasts of what he has learned, but of what he has spent. But perhaps they do not want to imitate their own masters, concerning whom I have not discovered what I can say worthy of them.

Finally, a foreign land has been mentioned, which in itself exercises a man. The whole world is a place of exile to those who pursue philosophy. But yet, as someone says [Ovid, *Epistulae ex Pont.*, I, iii, 35], "I do not know what sweetness of the native land alone draws us all, and does not let us be unmindful of it." It is a great beginning of virtue that the trained mind should little by little first learn to change these visible and transitory things, so that afterwards it will be able to give them up entirely. He is still weak for whom his native land is sweet, but he is strong for whom every country is a fatherland, and he is perfect for whom the whole world is a place of exile. The first confirms his love for the world, the second disperses it, and the last extinguishes it. From boyhood, I have lived in exile, and I know with what grief the spirit sometimes deserts the narrow limits of the poor man's hut, and with what a sense of freedom it afterwards despises marble halls and panelled ceilings.

From *Didascalicon*, C. H. Buttimer, ed. (Washington: Catholic University Press, 1939); trans. M.M.M.

The Battle of the Arts

HENRI D'ANDELI

Thirteenth century

Civil Law rode gorgeously
And Canon Law rode haughtily
Ahead of all the other arts.
There was many a Lombard knight,
Marshalled by Rhetoric.
Darts they have of feathered tongues
To pierce the hearts of foolish people
Who come to attack their strongholds;
For they snatch up many a heritage
With the lances of their eloquence.
Augustine, Ambrose, Gregory,
Jerome, Bede, and Isidore,
They quoted to Divinity as authorities

That she might avoid their vanity.
Madam Exalted Science,
Who did not care a fig about their dispute,
Left the arts to fight it out together.
Methinks she went to Paris
To drink the wines of her cellar.

*   *

Villainous Chirurgy
Was seated near a bloody cemetery;
She loved discord much better
Than bringing about nice concord.
She carried boxes and ointments
And a great plenty of instruments
To draw arrows from paunches.
It did not take her long to patch up
The bellies she saw pierced:
However, she is a science.
But she has such bold hands
That she spares no one
From whom she may be able to get money.
I would have had much respect for them
If they had cured my eyes;
But they dupe many people,
While with the copper and silver
Which they receive for their poisons
They build them fine houses in Paris.

*   *   *

Madam Music, she of the little bells,
And her clerks full of songs,
Carried fiddles and viols,
Psalteries and small flutes;
From the sound of the first *fa*
They ascended to *cc sol fa*.

The sweet tones diatessaron
Diapente, diapason,
Are struck in various combinations.
In groups of four and three,
Through the army they went singing,
They go enchanting them with their song.
These do not engage in battle.

* * *

One of the pupils of Dame Logic
Was sent to Grammar;
He bore letters to make peace.
Now I simply cannot refrain from telling this,
That when he arrived at his destination
He did not know the sense
Of the presents nor the preterits;
And that there where he had been brought up,
He had dwelt on them but little.
He had not learned thoroughly
Irregular conjugations,
Which are most difficult to inflect,
Adverbs and parts of speech,
Articles and declensions,
Genders and nominatives,
Supines and imperatives,
Cases, figures, formations,
Singulars, plurals, a thousand terms;
For in the court of Grammar are more corners
Than in all of Logic's prattlings.
The boy did not know how to come to the point;
And came back in shame.
But Logic comforted him,
Carried him to her high tower,
And tried to make him fly
Before he was able to walk.

* * *

Grammar withdrew
Into Egypt, where she was born.
But Logic is now in vogue,
Every boy runs her course
Ere he has passed his fifteenth year;
Logic is now for children!
Logic is in a very bad situation
In the tower on Montlhéry;
There she practises her art;
But Grammar opposes her
With her authors and authorlings
Sententious and frivolous.
Echo answered in the tower
To the great blows given all around,
For there they all hurl their rhymes.

* * *

Sirs, the times are given to emptiness;
Soon they will go entirely to naught,
For thirty years this will continue,
Until a new generation will arise,
Who will go back to Grammar,
Just as it was the fashion
When Henri d'Andeli was born,
Who gives it us as his opinion
That one should destroy the glib student
Who cannot construe his lesson;
For in every science that master is an apprentice
Who has not mastered his parts of speech.
Here ends The Battle of the Seven Arts.

From *The Battle of the Seven Arts*, trans. L. J. Paetow (Berkeley, Calif.: University of California Press, 1914).

Rules of the University of Paris

1215

ROBERT, servant of the cross of Christ by divine pity, cardinal priest of the title, St. Stephen in Mons Caelius, legate of the apostolic see, to all the masters and scholars of Paris, eternal greeting in the Lord. Let all know that, since we have had a special mandate from the pope to take effective measures to reform the state of the Parisian scholars for the better, wishing with the counsel of good men to provide for the tranquillity of the scholars in the future, we have decreed and ordained in this wise:

No one shall lecture in the arts at Paris before he is twenty-one years of age, and he shall have heard lectures for at least six years before he begins to lecture, and he shall promise to lecture for at least two years, unless a reasonable cause prevents, which he ought to prove publicly or before examiners. He shall not be stained by any infamy, and when he is ready to lecture, he shall be examined according to the form which is contained in the writing of the lord bishop of Paris . . . And they shall lecture on the books of Aristotle on dialectic old and new in the schools ordinarily and not *ad cursum*. They shall also lecture on both Priscians ordinarily, or at least on one. They shall not lecture on feast days except on philosophers and rhetoric and the quadrivium and *Barbarismus* and ethics, if it please them, and the fourth book of the *Topics*. They shall not lecture on the books of Aristotle on metaphysics and natural philosophy or on summaries of them or concerning the doctrine of

Master David of Dinant or the heretic Amaury or Mauritius of Spain.

In the *principia* and meetings of the masters and in the responsions or oppositions of the boys and youths there shall be no drinking. They may summon some friends or associates, but only a few. Donations of clothing or other things as has been customary, or more, we urge should be made, especially to the poor. None of the masters lecturing in arts shall have a cope except one round, black, and reaching to the ankles, at least while it is new. Use of the pallium is permitted. No one shall wear with the round cope shoes that are ornamented or with elongated pointed toes. If any scholar in arts or theology dies, half of the masters of arts shall attend the funeral at one time, the other half the next time, and no one shall leave until the sepulture is finished, unless he has reasonable cause. . . .

Each master shall have jurisdiction over his scholar. No one shall occupy a classroom or house without asking the consent of the tenant, provided one has a chance to ask it. No one shall receive the licentiate from the chancellor or another for money given or promise made or other condition agreed upon. Also, the masters and scholars can make both between themselves and with other persons obligations and constitutions supported by faith or penalty or oath in these cases: namely, the murder or mutilation of a scholar or atrocious injury done a scholar, if justice should not be forthcoming, arranging the prices of lodgings, costume, burial, lectures and disputations, so, however, that the university be not thereby dissolved or destroyed.

As to the status of the theologians, we decree that no one shall lecture at Paris before his thirty-fifth year and unless he has studied for eight years at least, and has heard the books faithfully and in classrooms, and has attended lectures in theology for five years before he gives lectures himself publicly. And none of these shall lecture before the third hour on days when masters lecture. No one shall be admitted at Paris to formal lectures or to preachings unless he shall be of approved life and science. No one shall be a scholar at Paris who has no definite master.

Moreover, that these decrees may be observed inviolate, we by virtue of our legatine authority have bound by the knot of excommunication all who shall contumaciously presume to go against these our statutes, unless within fifteen days after the offence they have taken care to emend their presumption before the university of masters and scholars or other persons constituted by the university. Done in the year of Grace 1215, the month of August.

From *Chartulary of the University of Paris*, trans. L. Thorndike, *University Records and Life in the Middle Ages*.

Fernando of Cordova, the Boy Wonder

LAUNOY

1445

IN THE year 1445 there came to the Collège de Navarre a certain youth of twenty summers who was past master of all good arts, as the most skilled masters of the university testified with one accord. He sang beautifully to the flute: he surpassed all in numbers, voice, modes, and symphony. He was a painter and laid colours on images best of all. In military matters he was most expert: he swung a sword with both hands so well and mightily that none dared fight with him. No sooner did he espy his foe than he would leap at him with one spring from a distance of twenty or twenty-four feet. He was a master in arts, in medicine, in both laws, in theology. With us in the school of Navarre he engaged in disputation, although we numbered more than fifty of the most perfect masters. I omit three thousand others and more who attended the bout. So shrewdly and cumulatively did he reply to all the questions which were proposed that he surpassed the belief, if not of those present, certainly of those absent. Latin, Greek, Hebrew, Arabic, and many more tongues he spoke in a most polished manner. He was a very skilful horseman. Nay more, if any man should live to be a hundred and pass days and sleepless nights without food and drink, he would never acquire the knowledge which that lad's mind embraced. And indeed he filled us with deep awe, for he knew more than human nature can bear. He argued four doctors of the church out of countenance, no one seemed comparable to him in wisdom, he was taken for Antichrist. Such are the quotations of Stephen Paschal, book v of *Disquisitions*, chapter 23, from a history in manuscript made by an eyewitness.

Trans. L. Thorndike, in *University Records and Life in the Middle Ages.*

The Problems of a Christian Humanist

John of Salisbury

Twelfth century

CONSIDER the leading teachers of philosophy of our own day, those who are most loudly acclaimed, surrounded by a noisy throng of disciples. Mark them carefully; you will find them dwelling on one rule, or on two or three words, or else they have selected (as though it were an important matter) a small number of questions suitable for dispute, on which to exercise their talent and waste their life. They do not however succeed in solving them but hand down to posterity for solution by their disciples their problems, with all the ambiguity with which they have invested them.

In their lecture room they invite you to battle with them, become pressing, and demand the clash of wit. If you hesitate to engage, if you delay but for a moment, they are upon you. If you advance and, though unwillingly, engage them and press them hard, they take refuge in subterfuge; they change front; they torture words; with tricks of magic they transform themselves until you marvel at the reappearance of the slippery, changing Proteus. But he can be trapped more easily if you insist on understanding his meaning and intention despite his voluble and erratic language. He will finally be vanquished by his own meaning and be caught by the words of his mouth, if you can grasp their significance and hold it firmly.

The points of dispute of our modern Proteus however are as useless as they are trivial. If in disgust over time wasted on such trifles you press your attack he again has recourse to evasion. As if taking refuge in the bosom of Mother Earth like Antaeus, he strives to recover his strength in the element in which he was born and brought up. Such a roundabout way; so many detours! As though it were necessary to traverse a labyrinth to reach the common place! . . .

If therefore you hoist them with their own petard you may well pity them their poverty in almost every capacity. Some seem to excel in details; others offer for sale all branches of philosophy, and yet in the details they are without the proper philosophic background. There are some who hope to attain perfection as the result of excellence in one branch; there are others who devote their energy to the whole field though they lack the knowledge of its parts. I find it hard to say which are in greater error, since perfection is not derived from one and no one has the power to devote himself faithfully to all. However he who seeks perfection in all from one is the more absurd, while he who claims proficiency in all is the more arrogant. It is the mark of the indolent to occupy himself with one thing to the exclusion of all else; of the dilettante to embrace them all.

At any rate he who makes a wide survey in order to select his specialty displays discretion and is the more devoted to his choice after having weighed the value of others. Perhaps that is the intention of the moralist who enjoins the reading of books. . . .

All reading should be done in such a way that some of it when finished should be disregarded, some condemned, and some viewed *en passant*, that the subject matter be not entirely unknown; but above all careful attention should be given to those matters which lay the foundation of the life of the state, be it by the law of the state or else by ethical principles, or which have in view the health of body and soul. Since then the chief branch [grammar] among the liberal arts, without which no one can teach or be taught properly, is to be merely greeted *en passant* and as it were from the door, who can imagine that time should be devoted to other branches which being difficult to understand or impractical and harmful do not conduce to the betterment of man? For even those things that are required for man's use prove very harmful if they occupy his attention to the exclusion of all others.

Does anyone doubt the desirability of reading the historians, the orators, and the authorities on approved mathematics, since without a knowledge of them men cannot be, or at least usually are not, liberally educated? Indeed those who are ignorant of those writers are termed illiterate even if they can read and write. But when such writers lay claim to the mind as though it belonged exclusively to them, although they praise learning they do not teach; rather they hinder the cultivation of virtue. This is the reason that Cicero when dealing with the poets, to make his remarks more effective, burst out, "The shout of approbation of the populace, as though it were some great and wise teacher qualified to recommend, puts the stamp of genius upon whom it wishes. But they who are so lauded, what darkness do they spread, what fears engender, and what passions inflame!" . . . Elsewhere however Cicero highly commends writers. He says, "He alone who fears no contempt himself casts contempt upon poets and writers in other branches of artistic literature, as well as upon the historians. They know what virtue is and offer the material for philosophic study, for they brand vices; they do not teach them. Their works are attractive too on account of the help and pleasure they give to the reader. They make their way amid dangers which threaten character, with the intention of securing a foothold for virtue." . . . I myself am of the opinion of those who believe that a man cannot be literate without a knowledge of the authors. Copious reading, however, by no means makes the philosopher, since it is grace alone that leads to wisdom. . . . It may be assumed that all writings except those that have been disapproved should be read, since it is believed that all that has been written and all that has been done have been ordained for man's utility although at times he makes bad use of them. For the angels too were, so to speak, ordained on account of the soul, but the corporeal world, according to the statement of the fathers, for the use of the body. . . . Just so in books there is something profitable for everybody provided, be it understood, the reading is done with discrimination and that only is selected which is edifying to faith and morals. There is matter which is of profit to stronger minds but is to be kept from the artless; there is that which an innately sound mind rejects; there is that which it digests for character-building or perfecting eloquence; there is that which hardens the soul and causes spiritual indigestion in matters of faith and good works. There is scarcely a piece of writing in which something is not found either in meaning or expression that the discriminating reader will not reject. The safe and cautious thing to do is to read only Catholic books. It is somewhat dangerous to expose the unsophisticated to pagan literature; but a training in both is very useful to those safe in the faith, for accurate reading on a wide range of subjects makes the scholar; careful selection of the better makes the saint. . . .

Therefore let the pagan writers be read in a way that their authority be not prejudicial to reason; for the burning weed, as the rose is plucked, sometimes burns the hand of him who touches it.

Wisdom is as it were a spring from which rivers go out watering all the land, and its divine pages not only fill with delight the place of its birth but also make their way among the nations to such an extent that they are not entirely unknown even to the Ethiopians. It is from this source that the flowering, perfumed, fruitful works of the pagan world spring, and should perchance any artless reader enter their field let him keep in mind this quotation:

> Flee hence, O ye who gather flowers
> Or berries growing on the ground; the clammy
> Snake is hiding in the grass.
> > [Virgil, *Eclogues*, III, 92-93]

It is no sluggard who carries off the apples of the Hesperides guarded by the ever-sleepless dragon, nor one who reads as though not awake but drowsing and dreaming as if eager to reach the end of his task. It is certain that the pious and wise reader who spends time lovingly over his books always rejects errors and comes close to life in all things.

From *Policraticus*, book VII, trans. J. B. Pike, *Frivolities of Courtiers and Footprints of Philosophers* (Minneapolis, Minn.: University of Minnesota Press, 1938).

The Ancients and the Moderns

WALTER MAP

Twelfth century

THE diligent achievement of the ancients is still in our possession; they make their own past present to our times, and we ourselves wax dumb: whence the memory of them liveth in us and we are unmindful of ours. Notable miracle! The dead live, the living are buried in their stead. Our times offer perchance something not unworthy of "the buskin of Sophocles." But the illustrious deeds of modern men of might are little valued, and the castaway odds and ends of antiquity are exalted. This is surely because we know how to blame and because we know not how to write; we seek to tear to pieces and we deserve to be torn. Thus the forked tongues of detractors are responsible for the rarity of poets. Thus minds grow slack, wits are undone; thus the native strength of this time is unduly extinguished, and the lamp is quenched, not indeed by lack of fuel, but craftsmen wax inert and the record of the present is lightly reckoned. So Caesar liveth in the praises of Lucan, Aeneas in those of Virgil, not the more by their great merits than by the watchfulness of poets. Only the (trifling) of mimes in vulgar rhymes celebrateth among us the godlike nobility of the Charleses and the Pepins—no one speaketh of living Caesars; but their characters, full of bravery and self-control, and inviting everybody's wonder, are ready to the pen. Alexander of Macedon, blaming the narrowness of the world open to his conquest, said with a sigh, when he looked upon the tomb of Achilles, "O thou happy youth, who enjoyest so great a publisher of thy merits!" meaning Homer. This mighty Alexander is my witness that many who have deserved to live among men after death, live (only) by the interpretation of poets. But to what purport the sighs of Alexander—certainly this, that he was bemourning the lack of a great poet to chant his merits, lest on his last day he should wholly die. But who would dare to put upon a page what is passing today, or to pen even these names of ours? . . . But if thou lookest upon "Hannibal" or "Menestratus," or any name of a sweetness hallowed by time, thou givest all thine attention; and, eager to plunge into the fabled cycles of the golden age, thou exultest in their deeds. Thou embracest with all reverence the tyranny of Nero and the avarice of Juba, and whatever else antiquity doth offer; thou rejectest the gentleness of Louis and the generosity of Henry.

From *Courtiers' Trifles*, trans. F. Tupper and M. B. Ogle (London: Chatto and Windus, New York: Macmillan, 1924).

A Plea for the Study of Languages

Roger Bacon

Thirteenth century

For it is impossible for the Latins to reach what is necessary in matters divine and human except through the knowledge of other languages, nor will wisdom be perfected for them absolutely, nor relatively to the Church of God and to the remaining three matters noted above. This I now wish to state, and first with respect to absolute knowledge. For the whole sacred text has been drawn from the Greek and Hebrew, and philosophy has been derived from these sources and from Arabic: but it is impossible that the peculiar quality of one language should be preserved in another. For even dialects of the same tongue vary among different sections, as is clear from the Gallic language, which is divided into many dialects among the Gauls, Picards, Normans, Burgundians, and others. . . . Therefore an excellent piece of work in one language cannot be transferred into another as regards the peculiar quality that it possessed in the former. . . .

For let any one with an excellent knowledge of some

science like logic or any other subject at all strive to turn this into his mother tongue, he will see that he is lacking not only in thoughts, but words, so that no one will be able to understand the science so translated as regards its potency. Therefore no Latin will be able to understand as he should the wisdom of the sacred Scripture and of philosophy, unless he understands the languages from which they were translated.

Secondly, we must consider the fact that translators did not have the words in Latin for translating scientific works, because they were not first composed in the Latin tongue. For this reason they employed very many words from other languages. Just as these words are not understood by those ignorant of those languages, so are they neither pronounced correctly nor are they written as they should be. . . .

Thirdly, although the translator ought to be perfectly acquainted with the subject which he wishes to translate and the two languages from which and into which he is translating, Boëthius alone, the first translator, had full mastery of the languages; and Master Robert, called Grosse-Teste, lately bishop of Lincoln, alone knew the sciences. . . .

The fourth reason for this condition is the fact that the Latins up to the present time lack very many philosophical and theological works. For I have seen two books of the Maccabees in Greek, namely the third and the fourth, and Scripture makes mention of the books of Samuel and Nathan and Gad the seer, and of others which we do not have. And since the whole confirmation of sacred history is given by Josephus in his books on Antiquities, and all the sacred writers take the fundamentals of their expositions from those books, it is necessary for the Latins to have that work in an uncorrupted form. But it has been proved that the Latin codices are wholly corrupt in all places on which the import of history rests, so that the text is self-contradictory everywhere. This is not the fault of so great an author, but arises from a bad translation and from the corruption by the Latins, nor can it be remedied except by a new translation or by adequate correction in all fundamental points. Likewise the books of the great doctors like the blessed Dionysius, Basil, John Chrysostom, John of Damascus, and of many others are lacking; some of which, however, Master Robert, the aforesaid bishop, has turned into Latin, and others before him translated certain other works. His work is very pleasing to theologians. If the books of these authors had been translated, not only would the learning of the Latins be augmented in a glorious way, but the Church would have stronger supports against the heresies and schisms of the Greeks, since they would be convinced by their own sacred writers whom they cannot contradict.

Likewise almost all the secrets of philosophy up to the present time lie hidden in foreign languages. For as in many instances only what is common and worthless has been translated; and much even of this character is lacking. . . .

The seventh reason why it is necessary that the Latins should know languages is particularly false interpretation, although the text be absolutely correct. For in both theology and philosophy interpretations are necessary, especially so in the sacred text and in the text of medicine and in that of the secret sciences, which are too obscure owing to the ignorance of interpretations. . . .

Since I have now shown how a knowledge of languages is necessary to the Latins owing to the pure zeal for knowledge, I now wish to state why this should be secured because of the wisdom established for the Church of God, and the commonwealth of the faithful, and the conversion of unbelievers, and the repression of those who cannot be converted. . . .

In the second place, a knowledge of languages is very necessary for directing the commonwealth of the Latins for three reasons. One is the sharing in utilities necessary in commerce and in business, without which the Latins cannot exist, because medicines and all precious things are received from other nations, and hence arises great loss to the Latins, and fraud without limit is practised on them, because they are ignorant of foreign tongues, however much they may talk through interpreters; for rarely do interpreters suffice for full understanding, and more rarely are they found faithful. A second reason is the securing of justice. For countless injuries are done the Latins by the people of other nations, the sufferers being the clergy as well as the laity, members of religious orders, and friars of the Dominicans and Franciscans who travel owing to the varied interests of the Latins. But owing to their ignorance of languages they cannot plead their cases before judges nor do they secure justice. The third reason is the securing of peace among the princes of other nations and among the Latins that wars may cease. For when formal messages along with letters and documents are drawn up in the respective languages of both sides, very often matters which have been set on foot with great labour and expense come to naught owing to ignorance of a foreign tongue. And not only is it harmful, but very embarrassing, when among all the learned men of the Latins prelates and princes do not find a single one who knows how to interpret a letter of Arabic or Greek nor to reply to a message, as is sometimes the case. For example, I learned that Soldanus of Babylonia wrote to my lord, the present king of France, and there was not found in the whole learned body in Paris nor in the whole kingdom of France a man who knew how satisfactorily to explain a letter nor to make the necessary reply to the message. And the lord king marvelled greatly at such dense ignorance, and he was very much displeased with the clergy because he found them so ignorant. . . .

In the third place, the knowledge of languages is necessary to the Latins for the conversion of unbelievers. For in the hands of the Latins rests the power to convert. And for this reason Jews without number perish among us because no one knows how to preach to them nor to interpret the Scriptures in their tongue, nor to confer with them nor to dispute as to the literal sense. . . . Then the Greeks and the Rutheni and many other schismatics likewise grow hardened in error because the truth is not preached to them in their tongue; and the Saracens likewise and the Pagans and the Tartars, and the other unbelievers throughout the whole world. . . . Oh, how we should consider this matter and fear lest God may hold the Latins responsible because they are neglecting the languages so that in this way they neglect the preaching of the faith. For Christians are few, and the whole broad world is occupied by unbelievers; and there is no one to show them the truth.

From *Opus majus* of Roger Bacon, trans. R. B. Burke (Philadelphia: University of Pennsylvania Press, 1928).

Statute of the Council of Vienne on Languages

1312

CLEMENT, bishop, servant of the servants of God. In perpetual memory of the matter . . . imitating the example of Him whose place on earth we unworthily fill who wished the apostles to go throughout the world preaching the Gospel trained in every language, we desire Holy Church to abound in Catholics acquainted with the languages which the infidels chiefly use, who may come to know the infidels themselves, and be able to instruct them in sacred institutions, and add them to the company of worshippers of Christ by knowledge of the Christian faith and reception of baptism. Therefore, that linguistic ability of this sort may be obtained by efficacy of instruction, with the approval of this holy council we have provided for establishing courses in the languages to be mentioned, wherever the Roman curia happens to reside, also in the universities of Paris, Oxford, Bologna, and Salamanca, decreeing that in each of these places Catholics having sufficient knowledge of the Hebrew, Greek, Arabic, and Aramaic languages, namely, two trained in each tongue, shall offer courses there and, translating books faithfully from those languages into Latin, teach others those languages carefully and transfer their ability to these by painstaking instruction, so that, sufficiently instructed and trained in these languages, they may produce the hoped-for fruit with God's aid and spread the faith salubriously to infidel nations.

For whom we wish provision made: for those lecturing at the Roman curia by the apostolic see; in the university of Paris by the king of France; at Oxford by that of England, Scotland, Ireland, and Wales; in Bologna by Italy's and in Salamanca by Spain's prelates, monasteries, chapters, convents, colleges, exempt or not, and rectors of churches in competent stipends and expenses, imposing the burden of contribution according to the ability of each to pay regardless of any privileges and exemptions to the contrary, by which however we do not wish prejudice to be generated so far as other matters are concerned.

From *Chartulary of the University of Paris*, trans. L. Thorndike, *University Records and Life in the Middle Ages*.

An English Humanist

Richard de Bury

Fourteenth century

ALTHOUGH the novelties of the moderns were never disagreeable to our desires, who have always cherished with grateful affection those who devote themselves to study and who add anything either ingenious or useful to the opinions of our forefathers, yet we have always desired with more undoubting avidity to investigate the well-tested labours of the ancients. For whether they had by nature a greater vigour of mental sagacity, or whether they perhaps indulged in closer application to study, or whether they were assisted in their progress by both these things, one thing we are perfectly clear about, that their successors are barely capable of discussing the discoveries of their forerunners, and of acquiring those things as pupils which the ancients dug out by difficult efforts of discovery. For as we read that the men of old were of a more excellent degree of bodily development than modern times are found to produce, it is by no means absurd to suppose that most of the ancients were distinguished by brighter faculties, seeing that in the labours they accomplished of both kinds they are inimitable by posterity. . . . But in truth, if we speak of fervour of learning and diligence in study, they gave up all their lives to philosophy; while nowadays our contemporaries carelessly spend a few years of hot youth, alternating with the excesses of vice, and when the passions have been calmed, and they have attained the capacity of discerning truth so difficult to discover, they soon become involved in worldly affairs and retire, bidding farewell to the schools of philosophy. They offer the fuming must of their youthful intellect to the difficulties of philosophy, and bestow the clearer wine upon the money-making business of life. . . .

Admirable Minerva seems to bend her course to all the nations of the earth, and reacheth from end to end mightily, that she may reveal herself to all mankind. We see that she has already visited the Indians, the Babylonians, the Egyptians and Greeks, the Arabs and the Romans. Now she has passed by Paris, and now has happily come to Britain, the most noble of islands, nay, rather a microcosm in itself, that she may show herself a debtor both to the Greeks and to the Barbarians. At which wondrous sight it is conceived by most men, that as philosophy is now lukewarm in France, so her soldiery are unmanned and languishing. . . .

While assiduously seeking out the wisdom of the men of old, according to the counsel of the wise man (Eccles. xxxix): the wise man, he says, will seek out the wisdom of all the ancients, we have not thought fit

to be misled into the opinion that the first founders of
the arts have purged away all crudeness, knowing that
the discoveries of each of the faithful, when weighed in
a faithful balance, makes a tiny portion of science, but
that by the anxious investigations of a multitude of
scholars, each as it were contributing his share, the
mighty bodies of the sciences have grown by successive
augmentations to the immense bulk that we now behold. . . .

For as in the writers of annals it is not difficult to see
that the later writer always presupposes the earlier,
without whom he could by no means relate the former
times, so too we are to think of the authors of the sciences. For no man by himself has brought forth any
science, since between the earliest students and those
of the latter time we find intermediaries, ancient, if they
be compared with our own age, but modern if we think
of the foundations of learning, and these men we consider the most learned. What would Virgil, the chief
poet among the Latins, have achieved, if he had not
despoiled Theocritus, Lucretius, and Homer, and had
not ploughed with their heifer? What, unless again and
again he had read somewhat of Parthenius and Pindar,
whose eloquence he could by no means imitate? What
could Sallust, Tully, Boëthius, Macrobius, Lactantius,
Martianus, and in short the whole troop of Latin writers
have done, if they had not seen the productions of
Athens or the volumes of the Greeks? Certes, little
would Jerome, master of three languages, Ambrosius,
Augustine, though he confesses that he hated Greek, or
even Gregory, who is said to have been wholly ignorant
of it, have contributed to the doctrine of the Church if
more learned Greece had not furnished them from its
stores. As Rome, watered by the streams of Greece, had
earlier brought forth philosophers in the image of the

Greeks, in like fashion afterwards it produced doctors of the orthodox faith. The creeds we chant are the sweat of Grecian brows, promulgated by their councils, and established by the martyrdom of many. . . .

One thing, however, we conclude from the premises, that the ignorance of the Greek tongue is now a great hindrance to the study of the Latin writers, since without it the doctrines of the ancient authors, whether Christian or Gentile, cannot be understood. And we must come to a like judgment as to Arabic in numerous astronomical treatises, and as to Hebrew as regards the text of the Holy Bible, which deficiencies, indeed, Clement V provides for, if only the bishops would faithfully observe what they so lightly decree. Wherefore we have taken care to provide a Greek as well as a Hebrew grammar for our scholars, with certain other aids, by the help of which studious readers may greatly inform themselves in the writing, reading, and understanding of the said tongues, although only the hearing of them can teach correctness of idiom.

From *Philobiblon*, trans. E. C. Thomas (London: Chatto and Windus, 1913).

In Defence of Liberal Studies

Coluccio Salutati

1378

AND now, my dear colleague, I will come to a matter in which you have stirred me up in no slight degree. I wrote to you asking you to buy for me a copy of Virgil, and you reply reproving me for not occupying myself with quite different matters and calling Virgil—

to quote your own words—a "lying soothsayer." You say that, since it is forbidden in the canon law to concern oneself with books of that sort, I ought not to burden you with such an errand, and you generously offer me a number of volumes of pious literature. I beg you, my dearest Giuliano, to pardon me if, in order that due supremacy of honour be maintained for the prince of Roman eloquence, the divinest of all poets, our own countryman, Virgil, and also that I may set you free from the error in which you seem to be involved, I address you in language rather more severe than is my wont.

I seem to feel a deep obligation to defend Virgil, of whom Horace says that earth never bore a purer spirit, lest he be shut out from the sanctuaries of Christians. I am bound also to clear up that error of yours which gives you such a horror of Virgil that you fear to be polluted by the mere purchase of the book.

How do you happen, my dear colleague, to have this dread of Virgil? You say that he records the monstrous doings of the gods and the vicious practices of men, and that, because he did not, as you say, walk in the way of the Lord, he leads his readers away from the straight path of the faith. But, if you think Virgil ought not to be touched because he was a heathen, why do you read Donatus, or Priscian, who was something far worse, an apostate? Or Job, to whom you yourself call attention, was he a Christian or was he of the circumcision? Or shall we give up Seneca and his writings because he was not renewed with the water of regeneration? If we throw aside the heritage of the Gentiles, whence shall we draw the rules of literary composition? Cicero is the fountain of eloquence, and everyone who since his day has handed on the art of rhetoric has drawn from that source. Read Augustine on Christian doctrine where he seems to touch [the heights of] eloquence, and certainly you will find the Ciceronian tradition renewed in the style of that great man. Not to read the inventions of the heathen out of devotion to the faith is a very weak foundation, especially when with their assistance you can the more easily combat the futilities of the Gentiles. Don't imagine that I have ever so read Virgil as to be led to accept his fables about the heathen gods! What I enjoy is his style, hitherto unequalled in verse, and I do not believe it is possible that human talent can ever attain to its loftiness and its charm.

I admire the majesty of his language, the appropriateness of his words, the harmony of his verses, the smoothness of his speech, the elegance of his composition, and the sweetly flowing structure of his sentences. I admire the profundity of his thought and his ideas drawn from the depths of ancient learning and from the loftiest heights of philosophy.

In these days there is no mixture of heathenism among Christians throughout the civilized world; . . . [those gods] whom that accursed blind superstition worshipped have vanished from their altars and their shrines and have abandoned their glory to the true God, to Christ our Lord. It may have been worth while to warn Christians against the study of the poets at a time when heathens still lingered among them, but since that pest has been exterminated, what harm can it be for consecrated men to have read the poets who, even if they are of [no] profit for the moral conduct of life, nevertheless cannot spread such poison for the destruction of our faith that we shall cease humbly to adore our Creator. . . .

But you will say, that when we are reading these vain things we are wandering away from the study of sacred literature, since—to continue the Psalm which I began elsewhere—that man is blessed, "whose delight is in the law of the Lord and in his law doth he meditate day and night." I grant you, it is a more holy thing to apply oneself without ceasing to the reading of the sacred page; but these devices of the heathen, even the songs of the poets of which you have such a horror, if one reads them in a lofty spirit are of no little profit and incline us toward those writings which pertain to the faith and the reading of which you urge in your letters. . . .

I have dwelt upon this at such length that you may not suppose the reading of Virgil to be a mere idle occupation if one is willing to take the right view of it and to separate the wheat from the tares. Not, indeed, that I believe one should look there for the teachings of our faith or for the Truth; but, as Seneca says of himself, I go over into the enemy's camp, not as a guest or as a deserter, but as a spy. I, as a Christian, do not read my Virgil as if I were to rest in it forever or for any considerable time; but as I read I examine diligently to see if I can find anything that tends toward virtuous and honourable conduct, and as I run through the foreshadowings of his poetry, often with the aid of allegory and not without enjoyment, if I find something not compatible with the truth, or obscurely stated, I try to make it clear by the use of reason. But, when it is my good fortune to find something in harmony with our faith, even though it be wrapped up in fiction, I admire it and rejoice in it, and, since our poet himself thought it well to learn even from an enemy, I joyfully accept it and make a note of it. . . .

As to Jerome, on whose authority the sacred canons forbid the reading of Virgil and other poets, I would maintain without hesitation that if he had been ignorant of the poetry and rhetoric against which he inveighs so beautifully he would never have handed down to us the

volumes of Holy Writ translated in his sweetly flowing
style from both Greek and Hebrew into the Latin
tongue. Never could he have spoken against his critics
with such brilliancy of ideas and such charm of language. Nor, in his criticism of rhetoric—which I should
regard as a fault in another man—would he have made
use of the forces of rhetoric.

Furthermore, Aurelius Augustine, exponent and
champion of the Christian faith, displayed such knowledge of the poets in all his writings that there is scarcely
a single letter or treatise of his which is not crowded
with poetic ornament. Not to speak of others, his *City
of God* could never have been so strongly and so elabo-
rately fortified against the vanity of the heathen if he
had not been familiar with the poets and especially with
Virgil. . . .

Now, if you, through the power of your intellect,
without a knowledge of the poets can understand grammar or most of the writings of the holy fathers, filled as
they are with poetical allusions, do not forbid the reading of Virgil to me and to others, who delight in such
studies, but who have not attained to the lofty heights
of your genius. If you enjoy reading your books as by
a most brilliant illumination, allow me, whose eyes do
not admit so much light, in the midst of my darkness to
gaze upon the stars of poetry, whereby the darkness of
my night is brightened, and to search out a something
for the upbuilding of truth and of our faith from amidst
those fables whose bitter rind conceals a savour of exceeding sweetness. If you neither can nor will do this,
then, with all good will on my part, leave the poets
alone! . . .

So, good-bye! And, according to that verse of Cato—
for that apocryphal book has by usage come to be thus
known—go right on reading your Virgil, secure, since

you are not a priest, against any prohibition by your law. You will find in him delight for your eyes, food for your mind, refreshment for your thought, and you will gain from him no little instruction in the art of eloquence.

Fare you well again and again, my dearest friend and colleague! Don't forget me and do give me not only your approval, but your love!

From "Letters," trans. Ephraim Emerton, in *Humanism and Tyranny: Studies in the Italian Trecento.*

In Praise of Greek

LEONARDO BRUNI

Fifteenth century

THEN first came the knowledge of Greek letters, which for seven hundred years had been lost among us. It was the Byzantine, Chrysoloras, a nobleman in his own country and most skilled in literature, who brought Greek learning back to us. Because his country was invaded by the Turks, he came by sea to Venice; but as soon as his fame went abroad, he was cordially invited and eagerly besought to come to Florence on a public salary to spread his abundant riches before the youth of the city. At that time [1396] I was studying civil law. But my nature was afire with the love of learning and I had already given no little time to dialectic and rhetoric. Therefore at the coming of Chrysoloras I was divided in my mind, feeling that it was a shame to desert the law and no less wrong to let slip such an occasion for learning Greek. And often with youthful impulsiveness I addressed myself thus: "When you are privileged to gaze upon and have converse with Homer, Plato, and Demosthenes as well as the other poets, philosophers, and orators of whom such wonderful things are reported, and when you might saturate yourself with their admirable teachings, will you turn your back and flee? Will you permit this opportunity, divinely offered you, to slip by? For seven hundred years now no one in Italy has been in possession of Greek and yet we agree that all knowledge comes from that source. What great advancement of knowledge, enlargement of fame, and increase of pleasure will come to you from an acquaintance with this tongue! There are everywhere quantities of doctors of the civil law and the opportunity of completing your study in this field will not fail you. However, should the one and only doctor of Greek letters disappear, there will be no one from whom to acquire them."

Overcome at last by these arguments, I gave myself to Chrysoloras and developed such ardour that whatever I learned by day, I revolved with myself in the night while asleep. I had many fellow-students, two of the number who were particularly proficient belonging to the Florentine nobility.

Trans. F. Schevill, in *The First Century of Italian Humanism* (New York: Crofts, 1928).

The Mirror of Nature

Questions on Nature

ADELARD OF BATH

Early twelfth century

WHEN I returned to England not long ago, while Henry [I, 1100-1135], the son of William, was ruling, the reunion with my friends was both delightful and satisfactory to me, for I had long been absent from my homeland for the sake of study. When, therefore, in our first meeting, as is often the case, many questions were asked concerning our own welfare and that of our friends, I consequently became aware that I should know about the morals of our people. When, on investigation, I found princes violent, prelates drunken, judges mercenary, patrons inconstant, the common people flatterers, promisers untruthful, friends envious, almost everyone ambitious, nothing, I said, is more impossible to me than to give myself up to this wretchedness. Then they said, "But what do you think can be done, since you neither wish to engage in this moral evil nor are able to prevent it?" I said, "Deliver it to oblivion, for forgetfulness is the one remedy of unanswerable evils. For he who thinks again of what he hates, in a certain measure suffers that which he does not love."

Then, after these things had been said on one side and the other, since a considerable part of the day was left, there was time to talk of other things. A certain nephew of mine who had come along with the others, being more involved in the causes of things than able to explain them, asked me to relate something new from my Arab studies. When the others agreed I had the following discussion with him, which I know was profitable to its hearers, but I do not know if it was pleasant. For this generation has a gigantic vice, that it considers nothing discovered by moderns worthy of being accepted. Thus it is usual that if I should wish to make public my own discovery, I should attribute it to another, saying, "This person says it, not I." Therefore, lest I should be altogether unheard, I say that a certain lord discovered all my ideas, not I. But enough of this. Now, since it is fitting that I should say something at the request of my friends, I wish to be more certain that it is rightly said by having you [Bishop Richard of Bayeux, to whom this work is dedicated] consider it. For nothing in the liberal arts is so well discussed that it can not shine more splendidly through you. Be present, then, in spirit! For in order to present things succinctly, I set down the chapter headings first. Then I shall reply to my nephew on the causes of things.

1. Why plants are produced without the sowing of seed.
2. How some plants are called hot, since all are more of the earth than of fire.
3. How different plants grow in the same region.
4. Why they are not produced from water, or air, or even from fire, as they are from the earth.
6. Why, when a plant is grafted, the fruit is that of the grafted part, not the trunk.

7. Why certain beasts chew the cud, and certain others not at all.

8. Why those which ruminate lie down first on their hind legs and last on their forelegs.

10. Why all animals which drink do not make water.

11. Why certain animals have a stomach, and others do not.

12. Why certain of them see more sharply by night than by day.

13. Whether beasts have souls.

15. Why men are not born with horns or other weapons.

17. Why those who have good intelligence are lacking in memory and vice versa.

18. Why the seats of imagination, reason, and memory are found in the brain.

19. Why the nose is located above the mouth.

20. Why men get bald in front.

21. Why we hear echoes.

22. How, as the voice comes to the ear, it may penetrate any obstacle.

23. What opinions should be held concerning vision.

24. Whether the visible spirit is substance or accident.

30. Why, as one can see from the darkness into the light, one cannot similarly see from the light into the darkness.

31. Why we smell, taste, and touch.

32. Why joy is the cause of weeping.

33. Why we breathe out of the same mouth now hot and now cold air.

34. Why the motion of fanning produces heat.

36. Why the fingers were made unequal.

37. Why the palm is concave.

38. Why men cannot walk when they are born, as animals do.

39. Why men are nourished more by milk.

42. Why women, if they are more frigid than men, are more wanton in desire.

43. Why men universally die.

46. Why the living are afraid of dead bodies.
48. How or why the globe of the earth is held up in the middle of the air.
49. If the sphere of the earth were perforated, where a stone thrown into it would fall.
50. How the earth moves.
51. Why the waters of the sea are salty.
52. Whence the ebb and flow of the tides come.
53. How the ocean does not increase from the influx of rivers.
54. Why certain rivers are not salty.
55. How the course of rivers can be perpetual.
56. How springs burst forth on a mountain top.
57. Whether there may be other true springs.
58. Why water does not go out of a full vessel open in the lower part, unless an opening is made above.
59. Whence the winds arise.
60. Whence the first movement of air proceeds.
61. Whether, if one atom is set in motion, all are set in motion, since whatever is moved moves something.
62. Why the wind does not move around the earth to the upper regions.
63. Where or whence such great impetus comes to it.
64. Where thunder comes from.
65. Where lightning comes from.
66. Why lightning does not come forth from all thunder.
67. By what power lightning penetrates stones and masses of metal.
68. Why, when we see the fire, we do not hear the crash, either at once or ever.
71. Why the planets and especially the sun do not keep their courses through the middle of the *aplanon* [outermost and immovable sphere of heaven] without revolution.
73. Whether the stars fall, as they seem to fall.
74. Whether the stars are animated.
75. What food the stars eat, if they are animals.
76. Whether the *aplanon* should be called an animate body or God. . . .

Nephew. You have said more than is necessary concerning these childish things. Therefore, let us advance to the nature of animals in itself. For there I have a presentiment that I may cause you uneasiness.

Adelard. It is difficult for me to discuss animals with you, for I have learned from the Arab masters by the guidance of reason, while you, deceived by the picture of authority, follow a halter. For what else should authority be called but a halter? Indeed, just as brute beasts are led by any kind of a halter, and know neither where nor how they are led, and only follow the rope by which they are held, so the authority of your writers leads into danger not a few who have been seized and bound by animal credulity. Whence, usurping for themselves the name of authority, some employ very great licence in writing, so that they have not hesitated to make known to bestial men the false instead of the true. For why do you not fill up sheets of parchment, and why do you not write on the backs, since you usually have hearers in this age who demand no reasonable judgment, but have faith simply in the mention of an old title? For they do not know that reason has been given to each person, so that with it as the first judge he may distinguish between the true and the false. For unless reason should be the universal judge, it is given in vain to individuals. It would suffice that it be given to a writer of precepts, to one, I say, or to many; the rest of them may be content with customs and authorities. Further, those who are called authorities would not have obtained the confidence of lesser men in the first place, unless they had followed reason. Whoever does not know or neglects reason, should deservedly be considered blind. I do not take it too literally that authority ought to be rejected by my judgment. I do, however, claim that reason should first investigate, and what reason has discovered, authority, if it applies, should then support. Authority alone cannot induce belief in the philosopher, nor should it be used for this purpose. Whence the logicians agree that a point is probable, not inevitable, on the basis of authority. Therefore, if you want to hear more from me, give and take reason. For I am not one who can be fed by the picture of a beefsteak. All that is written, to be sure, is like a harlot, showing affection now to this one, now to that one.

Nephew. It may be sensible to do as you ask, since it may be easy for me to oppose you rationally, and so it may not be safe to follow the authority of your Arabs. Let it stand then; let reason be the sole judge between you and me. And since we are to discuss animals, I ask why some of them ruminate and others do not.

Adelard. The natures of animals, like those of men, are different. Some, indeed, are naturally hot, others cold, some humid, others dry. Those which are hot digest better the food they have taken, and more easily convert it into blood, but those which are cold do this more poorly. For everything that is changed is more easily changed by heat than by cold. For fire has as a sort of property that it melts that which is joined together. Those animals, therefore, which have a warm stomach digest their food easily. But those whose natures are cold, since they are unable to digest their food from lack of heat, bring it back again to their mouths, so that there they may be able to soften it more easily by a second chewing. Such are cows, deer, goats and the like kind, which doctors call by the Greek term melancholic. That all of these, moreover, are of a cold nature, although it may be clear to doctors, can thus be shown to you. For, on this account, they have harder and more solid fat, which the ordinary person calls tallow. But others, since they are hotter, have softer fat, since it is better digested, which by common usage is called lard.

From *Quaestiones naturales*, M. Müller, ed. (Münster, 1924); trans. M.M.M.

Experimental Science

ROGER BACON

Thirteenth century

I NOW wish to unfold the principles of experimental science, since without experience nothing can be sufficiently known. For there are two modes of acquiring knowledge, namely, by reasoning and experience. Reasoning draws a conclusion and makes us grant the conclusion, but does not make the conclusion certain, nor does it remove doubt so that the mind may rest on the intuition of truth, unless the mind discovers it by the path of experience; since many have the arguments relating to what can be known, but because they lack experience they neglect the arguments, and neither avoid what is harmful nor follow what is good. For if a man who has never seen fire should prove by adequate reasoning that fire burns and injures things and destroys them, his mind would not be satisfied thereby, nor would he avoid fire, until he placed his hand or some combustible substance in the fire, so that he might prove by experience that which reasoning taught. But when he has had actual experience of combustion his mind is made certain and rests in the full light of truth. Therefore reasoning does not suffice, but experience does.

This is also evident in mathematics, where proof is

most convincing. But the mind of one who has the most convincing proof in regard to the equilateral triangle will never cleave to the conclusion without experience, nor will he heed it, but will disregard it until experience is offered him by the intersection of two circles, from either intersection of which two lines may be drawn to the extremities of the given line; but then the man accepts the conclusion without any question. Aristotle's statement, then, that proof is reasoning that causes us to know is to be understood with the proviso that the proof is accompanied by its appropriate experience, and is not to be understood of the bare proof. . . .

He therefore who wishes to rejoice without doubt in regard to the truths underlying phenomena must know how to devote himself to experiment. For authors write many statements, and people believe them through reasoning which they formulate without experience. Their reasoning is wholly false. For it is generally believed that the diamond cannot be broken except by goat's blood, and philosophers and theologians misuse this idea. But fracture by means of blood of this kind has never been verified, although the effort has been made; and without that blood it can be broken easily. For I have seen this with my own eyes, and this is necessary, because gems cannot be carved except by fragments of this stone. Similarly it is generally believed that the castors employed by physicians are the testicles of the male animal. But this is not true, because the beaver has these under its breast, and both the male and female produce testicles of this kind. Besides these castors the male beaver has its testicles in their natural place; and therefore what is subjoined is a dreadful lie, namely, that when the hunters pursue the beaver, he himself knowing what they are seeking cuts out with his teeth these glands. Moreover, it is generally believed that hot water freezes more quickly than cold water in vessels, and the argument in support of this is advanced that contrary is excited by contrary, just like enemies meeting each other. But it is certain that cold water freezes more quickly for any one who makes the experiment. People attribute this to Aristotle in the second book of the *Meteorologics;* but he certainly does not make this statement, but he does make one like it, by which they have been deceived, namely, that if cold water and hot water are poured on a cold place, as upon ice, the hot water freezes more quickly, and this is true. But if hot water and cold are placed in two vessels, the cold will freeze more quickly. Therefore all things must be verified by experience.

But experience is of two kinds; one is gained through our external senses, and in this way we gain our experience of those things that are in the heavens by instruments made for this purpose, and of those things here below by means attested by our vision. Things that do not belong in our part of the world we know through other scientists who have had experience of them. As, for example, Aristotle on the authority of Alexander sent two thousand men through different parts of the world to gain experimental knowledge of all things that are on the surface of the earth, as Pliny bears witness in his *Natural History*. This experience is both human and philosophical, as far as man can act in accordance with the grace given him; but this experience does not suffice him, because it does not give full attestation in regard to things corporeal owing to its difficulty, and does not touch at all on things spiritual. It is necessary, therefore, that the intellect of man should be otherwise aided, and for this reason the holy patriarchs and prophets, who first gave sciences to the world, received illumination within and were not dependent on sense alone. The same is true of many believers since the time of Christ.

For the grace of faith illuminates greatly, as also do divine inspirations, not only in things spiritual, but in things corporeal and in the sciences of philosophy; as Ptolemy states in the *Centilogium*, namely, that there are two roads by which we arrive at the knowledge of facts, one through the experience of philosophy, the other through divine inspiration, which is far the better way, as he says. . . .

Since this experimental science is wholly unknown to the rank and file of students, I am therefore unable to convince people of its utility unless at the same time I disclose its excellence and its proper signification. This science alone, therefore, knows how to test perfectly what can be done by nature, what by the effort of art, what by trickery, what the incantations, conjurations, invocations, deprecations, sacrifices, that belong to magic, mean and dream of, and what is in them, so that all falsity may be removed and the truth alone of art and nature may be retained. This science alone teaches us how to view the mad acts of magicians, that they may not be ratified but shunned, just as logic considers sophistical reasoning.

This science has three leading characteristics with respect to other sciences. The first is that it investigates by experiment the notable conclusions of all those sciences. For the other sciences know how to discover their principles by experiments, but their conclusions are reached by reasoning drawn from the principles discovered. But if they should have a particular and complete experience of their own conclusions, they must have it with the aid of this noble science. For it is true that mathematics has general experiments as regards its conclusions in its figures and calculations, which also are applied to all sciences and to this kind of experiment, because no science can be known without mathematics. But if we give our attention to particular and complete experiments and such as are attested wholly by the proper method, we must employ the principles of this science which is called experimental. I give as an example the rainbow and phenomena connected with it, of which nature are the circle around the sun and the stars, the streak [*virga*] also lying at the side of the sun or of a star, which is apparent to the eye in a straight line, and is called by Aristotle in the third book of the *Meteorologics* a perpendicular, but by Seneca a streak, and the circle is called a corona, phenomena which frequently have the colours of the rainbow. The natural philosopher discusses these phenomena, and the writer on perspective has much to add pertaining to the mode of vision that is necessary in this case. But neither Aristotle nor Avicenna in their natural histories has given us a knowledge of phenomena of this kind, nor has Seneca, who composed a special book on them. But experimental science attests them.

Let the experimenter first, then, examine visible objects, in order that he may find colours arranged as in the phenomena mentioned above and also the same figure. For let him take hexagonal stones from Ireland or from India, which are called rainbows in Solinus on the *Wonders of the World,* and let him hold these in a solar ray falling through the window, so that he may find all the colours of the rainbow, arranged as in it, in the shadow near the ray. And further let the same experimenter turn to a somewhat dark place and apply the stone to one of his eyes which is almost closed, and he will see the colours of the rainbow clearly arranged just as in the bow. And since many employing these stones think that the phenomenon is due to the special virtue of those stones and to their hexagonal shape, therefore let the experimenter proceed further, and he will find this same peculiarity in crystalline stones correctly shaped, and in other transparent stones. Moreover, he will find this not only in white stones like the Irish crystals, but also in black ones, as is evident in the dark crystal and in all stones of similar transparency. He will find it besides in crystals of a shape differing from the hexagonal, provided they have a roughened surface, like the Irish crystals, neither altogether smooth, nor rougher than they are. Nature produces some that have surfaces like the Irish crystals. For a difference in the corrugations causes a difference in the colours. And further let him observe rowers, and in the drops falling from the raised oars he finds the same colours when the solar rays penetrate drops of this kind. The same phenomenon is seen in water falling from the wheels of a mill; and likewise when one sees on a summer's morning the drops of dew on the grass in meadow or field, he will observe the colours. Likewise when it is raining, if he stands in a dark place and the rays beyond it pass through the falling rain, the colours will appear in the shadow near by; and frequently at night colours appear around a candle. Moreover, if a man in summer, when he rises from sleep and has his eyes only partly open, suddenly looks at a hole through which a ray of the sun enters, he will see colours. Moreover, if seated beyond the sun he draws his cap beyond his eyes, he will see colours; and similarly if he closes an eye the same thing happens under the shade of the eyebrows; and again the same phenomenon appears through a glass vessel filled with water and placed in the sun's rays. Or similarly if one having water in his mouth sprinkles it vigorously into the rays and stands at the side of the rays. So, too, if rays in the required position pass through an oil lamp hanging in the air so that the light falls on the surface of the oil, colours will be produced. Thus in an infinite number of ways colours of this kind appear, which the diligent experimenter knows how to discover. . . .

Another example can be given in the field of medicine in regard to the prolongation of human life, for which the medical art has nothing to offer except the regimen of health. But a far longer extension of life is possible. . . .

Not only are remedies possible against the conditions of old age coming at the time of one's prime and before the time of old age, but also if the regimen of old age should be completed, the conditions of old age and senility can still be retarded, so that they do not arrive at their ordinary time, and when they do come they can be mitigated and moderated, so that both by retarding and mitigating them life may be prolonged beyond the limit, which according to the full regimen of health depends on the six articles mentioned. And there is another farther limit, which has been set by God and nature, in accordance with the property of the remedies retarding the accidents of old age and senility and mitigating their evil. The first limit can be passed but the second cannot be. . . .

Therefore the excellent experimenter in the book on the *Regimen of the Aged* says that if what is tempered in the fourth degree, and what swims in the sea, and what grows in the air, and what is cast up by the sea, and a plant of India, and what is found in the vitals of a long-lived animal, and the two snakes which are the food of Tyrians and Aethiopians, be prepared and used in the proper way, and the *minera* [blood?] of the noble animal be present, the life of man could be greatly prolonged and the conditions of old age and senility could be retarded and mitigated. But that which is tempered in the fourth degree is gold, as is stated in the book on *Spirits and Bodies*, which among all things is most friendly to nature. And if by a certain experiment gold should be made the best possible, or at any rate far better than nature and the art of alchemy can make it, as was the vessel found by the rustic, and it should be dissolved in such water as the ploughman drank, it would then produce a wonderful action on the body of man. And if there is added that which swims in the sea, namely, the pearl, which is a thing most efficacious for preserving life, and there is added also the thing that grows in the air. This last is an *anthos* [flower] and is the flower of seadew, which possesses an ineffable virtue against the condition of old age. But the *dianthos* that is put in an electuary is not a flower, but is a mixture of leaves and fragments of wood and a small portion of flower. For the pure flower should be gathered in its proper season, and in many ways it is used in foods and drinks and electuaries. To these must be added what is cast up by the sea. This last is ambergris, which is spermaceti, a thing of wondrous virtue in this matter. The plant of India is similar to these, and is the excellent wood of the aloe, fresh and not seasoned. To these ingredients there is added that which is in the heart of a long-lived animal, namely, the stag. This is a bone growing in the stag's heart, which possesses great power against premature old age. The snake which is the food of the Tyrians is the Tyrian snake from which Tyriaca is made, and whose flesh is properly prepared and eaten with spices. This is an excellent remedy for the condition of old age and for all the corruptions of the constitution, if it is taken with things suitable to one's constitution and condition, as we are taught in the book on the *Regimen of the Aged*. Aristotle, moreover, in the book of *Secrets* recommends strongly the flesh of the Tyrian snake for our ills. The snake that is the food of the Aethiopians is the dragon, as David says in the Psalm, "Thou hast given it as food to the tribes of the Aethiopians." For it is certain that wise men of Aethiopia have come to Italy, Spain, France, England, and those lands of the Christians in which there are good flying dragons, and by the secret art they possess lure the dragons from their caverns. They have saddles and bridles in readiness, and they ride on these dragons and drive them in the air at high speed, so that the rigidity of their flesh may be overcome and its hardness tempered, just as in the case of boars and bears and bulls that are driven about by dogs and beaten in various ways before they are killed for food. After they have domesticated them in this way they have the art of preparing their flesh, similar to the art of preparing the flesh of the Tyrian snake, and they use the flesh against the accidents of old age, and they prolong life and sharpen their intellect beyond all conception. For no instruction that can be given by man can produce such wisdom as the eating of this flesh, as we have learned through men of proved reliability on whose word no doubt can be cast.

If the elements should be prepared and purified in some mixture, so that there would be no action of one element on another, but so that they would be reduced to pure simplicity, the wisest have judged that they would have the most perfect medicine. . . .

But owing to the difficulty of this very great experiment, and because few take an interest in experiments, since the labour involved is complicated and the expense very great, and because men pay no heed to the secrets of nature and the possibilities of art, it happens that very few have laboured on this very great secret of science, and still fewer have reached a laudable end. . . .

The formation of judgments, as I have said, is a function of this science, in regard to what can happen by nature or be effected in art, and what not. This science, moreover, knows how to separate the illusions of magic and to detect all their errors in incantations, invocations, conjurations, sacrifices, and cults. But unbelievers busy themselves in these mad acts and trust in them, and have believed that the Christians used such means in working their miracles. Wherefore this science is of the greatest advantage in persuading men to accept the faith, since this branch alone of philosophy happens to proceed in this way, because this is the only branch that considers matters of this kind, and is able to overcome all falsehood and superstition and error of unbelievers in regard to magic, such as incantations and the like already mentioned. How far, moreover, it may serve to reprobate obstinate unbelievers is already shown by the violent means that have just been touched upon, and therefore I pass on.

From Opus majus of Roger Bacon, trans. R. B. Burke.

The Case of a Woman Doctor in Paris

1322

WITNESSES were brought before us . . . in the inquisition made at the instance of the masters in medicine at Paris against Jacoba Felicie and others practising the art of medicine and surgery in Paris and the suburbs without the knowledge and authority of the said masters, to the end that they be punished, and that this practice be forbidden them. . . .

The dean and the regent masters of the faculty of medicine at Paris intend to prove against the accused, Mistress Jacoba Felicie, (1) that the said Jacoba visited, in Paris and in the suburbs, many sick persons afflicted with grave illness, inspecting their urine both in common and individually, and touching, feeling, and holding their pulses, body, and limbs. Also (2) that after this inspection of urine and this touching, she said and has said to those sick persons: "I shall make you well, God willing, if you will have faith in me," making an agreement concerning the cure with them, and receiving money for it. Also (3) that after an agreement had been made between the said defendant and the sick persons or their friends, concerning curing them of their internal illness, or from a wound or ulcer appearing on the outside of the bodies of the said sick persons, the said defendant visited and visits the sick persons very often, inspecting their urine carefully and continually, after the manner of physicians and doctors, and feeling their pulse, and their body, and touching and holding their limbs. Also (4) that after these actions, she gave and gives to the sick persons syrups to drink, comforting, laxative, digestive, both liquid and nonliquid, and aromatic, and other drinks, which they take and drink and have drunk very often in the presence of the said defendant, she prescribing and giving them. Also (5) that she has exercised and exercises, in the aforesaid matters, this function of practising medicine in Paris and in the suburbs, that she has practised and practises from day to day although she has not been approved in any official *studium* at Paris or elsewhere. . . .

Jean Faber, living near the Tower in Paris . . . when he was asked if he knew the parties, said that he knew some of the masters by sight, others not, but that he knew the said Jacoba, because she has done well by him, as he said. Asked what he knows of those matters contained in the articles, he replied that he was suffering from a certain sickness in his head and ears at a time of great heat, that is, before the feast of the nativity of St. John [June 24], and that the said Jacoba had visited him, and had shown such great care for him that he was cured from his illness by the potations which she gave him, and by the aid of God. When he was asked what potions she had given to him, he answered that Jacoba had administered potions to him, of which the first was green, and the second and third more colourless, but how they were made he did not know. Asked if the said Jacoba has been wont to visit the sick, he said that she has, as he has heard many say. When he was asked if he had made a contract with her about curing him, he said that he had not. After he had been made well he paid her as he wished. . . .

The lord Odo de Cormessiaco, a brother of the hospital of Paris, a witness, when he was asked what he knew of the matters contained in the articles, etc., answered this by law on his oath, that is, that when, around the feast of the nativity of St. John, he had been seized by a severe illness, to such an extent that his own limbs could not support him, Master Jean de Turre had visited him, and many other masters in medicine, Masters Martin and Herman and many others. And he had had himself taken to the house of the said Jacoba, and was there for a while, and then afterwards this Jacoba visited him both at the baths and in the aforesaid hospital. And Master Jean, who lives with this Jacoba, gave him a purgative, and they prepared many baths and bandages for him, and anointed him very often. The said Jacoba and Jean worked over him with such great care that he was completely restored to health. They also gave him herbs, that is, camomile leaves, melilot, and very many others, which he did not recall. Also, on the advice of the said Jacoba, the said Jean made a certain charcoal fire of the length and breadth of the witness, and upon this fire he placed many herbs, and afterwards he had him lie down on these herbs, and lie there until this made him sweat exceedingly. Afterwards they wrapped him in linen cloth and put him in his own bed, and cared for him with such diligence that by means of God's help and the said care, he was cured. When he was asked if Jacoba had made a contract with him concerning visiting and healing him, he said she had not. He paid as he wished when he got well, and he believed better than otherwise. . . .

Jeanne, wife of Denis called Bilbaut, living in the Rue de la Ferronnerie in Paris . . . answered on oath that around the feast of St. Christopher [July 25], just passed, she had been seized with a fever, and very many physicians had visited her in the said illness, that is, a certain brother de Cordelis, Master Herman, Manfred, and very many others. And she was so weighed down by the said illness that on a certain Tuesday around the said feast, she was not able to speak, and the said physicians gave her up for dead. And so it would have been, if the said Jacoba had not come to her at her request. When she had come, she inspected her urine and felt her pulse, and afterwards gave her a certain clear liquid to drink, and gave her also a syrup, so that she would go to the toilet. And Jacoba so laboured over her that by the grace of God she was cured of the said illness. . . .

These are the arguments which Jacoba said and set forth in her trial. . . .

The said Jacoba said that if the statute, decree, admonition, prohibition, and excommunication which the said dean and masters are trying to use against her, Jacoba, had ever been made, this had been only once, on account of and against ignorant women and inexperienced fools, who, untrained in the medical art and totally ignorant of its precepts, usurped the office of practising it.

From their number the said Jacoba is excepted, being expert in the art of medicine and instructed in the precepts of said art. For these reasons, the statute, decree, admonition, prohibition, and excommunication aforesaid are not binding and cannot be binding on her, since when the cause ceases, the effect ceases. . . .

Also the said statute and decree, etc., had been made on account of and against ignorant women and foolish usurpers who were then exercising the office of practice in Paris, and who are either dead or so ancient and decrepit that they are not able to exercise the said office, as it appears from the tenor of the said statute and decree, etc., which were made a hundred and two years ago, at which time the said Jacoba was not, nor was she for sixty years afterwards, in the nature of things; indeed, she is young, thirty or thereabouts, as it appears from her aspect. . . .

Also it is better and more becoming that a woman clever and expert in the art should visit a sick woman, and should see and look into the secrets of nature and her private parts, than a man, to whom it is not permitted to see and investigate the aforesaid, nor to feel the hands, breasts, belly and feet, etc., of women. Indeed a man ought to avoid and to shun the secrets of women and their intimate associations as much as he can. And a woman would allow herself to die before she would reveal the secrets of her illness to a man, because of the virtue of the female sex and because of the shame which she would endure by revealing them. And from these causes many women and also men have perished in their illnesses, not wishing to have doctors, lest they see their secret parts. . . .

Also, supposing without prejudice that it is bad that a woman should visit, care for, and investigate, as has been said, it is, however, less bad that a woman wise, discreet, and expert in the aforesaid matters has done and does these things, since the sick persons of both sexes, who have not dared to reveal the aforesaid secrets to a man, would not have wished to die. Thus it is that the laws say that lesser evils should be permitted, so that greater ones may be avoided. For this reason, since the said Jacoba is expert in the art of medicine, it is, therefore, better that she be permitted to make visits, in order to exercise the office of practice, than that the sick should die, especially since she has cured and healed all those. . . .

Also, it has been ascertained and thus proved, that some sick persons of both sexes, seized by many severe illnesses and enduring the care of very many expert masters in the art of medicine, have not been able to recover at all from their illnesses, although the masters applied as much care and diligence to these as they were able. And the said Jacoba, called afterwards, has cured these sick persons in a short time, by an art which is suitable for accomplishing this.

From *Chartulary of the University of Paris*, H. Denifle and E. Chatelain, eds. (Paris: Delalain, 1891); trans. M.M.M.

The History of Surgery

GUI DE CHAULIAC

1363

THE workers in this art, from whom I have had knowledge and theory, and from whom you will find observations and maxims in this work, in order that you may know which has spoken better than the other, should be arranged in a certain order.

The first of all was Hippocrates [5th century B.C.] who (as one reads in the *Introduction to Medicine*) surpassed all the others, and first among the Greeks led medicine to perfect enlightenment. For according to Macrobius and Isidore, in the fourth book of the *Etymologies* . . . medicine had been silent for the space of five hundred years before Hippocrates, since the time of Apollo and Aesculapius, who were its first discoverers. He lived ninety-five years, and wrote many books on surgery, as it appears from the fourth of the *Therapeutics* and many other passages of Galen. But I believe that on account of the good arrangement of the books of Galen the books of Hippocrates and of many others have been neglected.

Galen [2nd century A.D.] followed him, and what Hippocrates sowed, as a good labourer he cultivated and increased. He wrote many books, indeed, in which he included much about surgery, and especially the *Book on Tumors Contrary to Nature,* written in summary; and the six first *Books on Therapeutics,* containing wounds and ulcers, and the last two concerning boils and many other maladies which require manual operation. In addition, seven books which he arranged, *Catagent* (that is, about the composition of medicaments according to kinds), of which we have only a summary. Now he was a master in demonstrative science in the time of the Emperor Antoninus [Marcus Aurelius], after Jesus Christ about one hundred and fifty years. He lived eighty years, as is told in *The Book of the Life and Customs of the Philosophers.* Between Hippocrates and Galen there was a very long time, as Avicenna says in the fourth of the *Fractures,* three hundred and twenty-five years, as they gloss it there, but in truth there were five hundred and eighty-six years.

After Galen we find Paul [of Aegina, 7th century]

who . . . did many things in surgery; however, I have found only the sixth book of his *Surgery*.

Going on we find Rhazes [d c. 923], Albucasis [d. c. 1013], and Alcaran [?], who (whether they were all one and the same, or several) did very well, especially in the *Books for Almansor* [by Rhazes] and in the *Divisions*, and in the *Surgery* called Albucasis. In these as Haly Abbas [late 10th century] says, he put all his particulars, and in all the *Continens* (which is called *Helham* in Arabic) he repeated the same things, and he collected all the sayings of the ancients, his predecessors; but because he did not select and is long and without conclusion, he has been less prized.

Haly Abbas was a great master, and besides what he sowed in the books on *The Royal Disposition*, he arranged on surgery the ninth part of his *Second Sermon*.

Avicenna [980-1037], illustrious prince, followed him, and in very good order (as in other things) treated surgery in his fourth book.

And we find that up to him all were both physicians and surgeons, but since then, either through refinement or because of too great occupation with cures, surgery was separated and left in the hands of *mechanics*. Of these the first were Roger [of Salerno, fl. c.1170], Roland [of Parma, fl. c.1200], and the Four Masters [anonymous], who wrote separate books on surgery, and put in them much that was empirical. Then we find Jamerius [fl. c.1230-1252] who did some rude surgery in which he included a lot of nonsense; however, in many things he followed Roger. Later, we find Bruno [of Longoburgo, fl. c.1252], who, prudently enough, made a summary of the findings of Galen and Avicenna, and of the operations of Albucasis; however, he did not have all the translation of the books of Galen and entirely omitted anatomy. Immediately after him came Theodoric [Borgognoni, 1205-1298], who gathering up all that Bruno said, with some fables of Hugh of Lucca [d. c.1252-1258], his master, made a book out of them.

William of Saliceto [c.1210-c.1280] was a man of worth who composed two compendia, one on medicine and the other on surgery; and in my opinion, what he treated he did very well. Lanfranc [d. before 1306] also wrote a book in which he put scarcely anything but what he took from William; however, he changed the arrangement.

At that time Master Arnald of Villanova [d. 1311] was flourishing in both skills, and wrote many fine works. Henry of Mondeville [d. c. 1325] began in Paris a very notable treatise in which he tried to make a marriage between Theodoric and Lanfranc, but being prevented by death he did not finish the treatise.

In this present time, in Calabria, Master Nicholas of Reggio [d. 1350], very expert in Greek and Latin, has translated at the order of King Robert many books of Galen and has sent them to us at court; they seem to be of finer and more perfect style than those which have been translated from the Arabic. Finally there appeared a faded English rose [*Rosa Anglica* of John of Gaddesden, d. 1361] which was sent to me, and I have seen it. I had thought to find in it sweetness of odour, but I have found only the fables of the Spaniard, of Gilbert, and of Theodoric.

In my time there have been operating surgeons, at Toulouse, Master Nicholas Catalan; at Montpellier, Master Bonet, son of Lanfranc; at Bologna, Masters Peregrin and Mercadant; at Paris, Master Peter of Argentière; at Lyons (where I have practised for a long time), Peter of Bonant; at Avignon, Master Peter of Arles and my companion, Jean of Parma.

And I, Guy of Chauliac, surgeon and master in medicine, from the borders of Auvergne, diocese of Mende, doctor and personal chaplain to our lord the pope, I have seen many operations and many of the writings of the masters mentioned, principally of Galen; for as many books of his as are found in the two translations, I have seen and studied with as much diligence as possible, and for a long time I have operated in many places. And at present I am in Avignon, in the year of our Lord 1363, the first year of the pontificate of Urban V. In which year, from the teachings of the above named, and from my experiences, with the aid of my companions, I have compiled this work, as God has willed.

The sects which were current in my time among the workers in this art, besides the two general ones, which are still in vigour, namely, that of the Logicians or rationalists, and that of the Empiricists (condemned by Galen in the *Book of Sects* and throughout the *Therapeutics*), were five.

The first was of Roger, Roland, and the Four Masters who, indiscriminately for all wounds and boils, produced healing or suppuration with their poultices and cataplasms; relying for this on the fifth of the *Aphorisms,* "The loose are good, the hard are bad."

The second was of Bruno and Theodoric who indiscriminately dried up all wounds with wine alone, relying for this on the fourth of the *Therapeutics,* "The dry comes closer to the healthy, and the wet to the unhealthy."

The third sect was of Wiliam of Saliceto and of Lanfranc, who wishing to hold the middle ground between the above, cared for or dressed all wounds with unguents and sweet salves, relying for this on the fourth of the *Therapeutics,* that there is only one way to healing, namely, that it be done safely and painlessly.

The fourth sect is composed of all the men at arms or

Teutonic Knights and others following war; who treat all wounds with conjurations and liquors, oil, wool, and cabbage leaves, relying on this, that God has put his efficacy in words, in herbs, and in stones.

The fifth sect is composed of women and many ignorant ones who entrust those sick with all maladies only to the saints, relying on this: the Lord has given it to me as it has pleased Him; the Lord will take it from me when it shall please Him; blessed be the name of the Lord, Amen.

And because such sects will be refuted in the course of this book, let them be put aside for the present. But I am amazed at one thing, that they follow each other like cranes. For one says only what the other has said. I do not know whether it is from fear or love that they scorn to hear anything except what is traditional or proved by authority. They have read Aristotle badly in the second of the *Metaphysics* where he shows that these two things most of all prevent the sight and knowledge of the truth. Let us abandon such friendships and fears, for Socrates or Plato is our friend, but truth is still more a friend. It is a holy and worthy thing to honour truth in the first place. Let them follow the dogmatic doctrine of Galen approved in the *Book of Sects* and throughout the *Therapeutics,* which is entirely composed of experience and reason, in which one seeks things and scorns words. And he himself has taught the means of seeking truth, in the book on *The Constitution of the Dogmatic Art,* chapter seven, which under a certain epilogue he put in the third book of the *Natural Faculties,* chapter ten, in this way: he who would know something better than the others must suddenly be very different from the others (that is, at the beginning and by nature, and by first knowledge). And when he is a boy, or at the age of puberty, he must be seized with a certain amorous rage for the truth; he must not cease to study day and night, to learn all that has been said by the most famous of the ancients. And when he shall reach the flower of his age and learning, then he must judge what he has learned by examining it very well for a long time and perceive all that agrees with the things which are clearly apparent, and all that disagrees with them, and thus choose the one, and reject the other. To such a one, I hope my observations will be very useful; but to the others, these writings will be as superfluous as a fable told to an ass.

I do not say, however, that it is not a very good thing to cite witnesses in one's discourse, for Galen in many places, besides reason and experience, which are for all men the two instruments of judging (as he says in the first of the *Therapeutics*, chapter three), brings in the third, by witnesses. Of which in the first of the *Miamin* or *Compositions according to Plans*, he says that the belief in things which one writes increases with the agreement of those who repeat them; and therefore he says that he will write down all the medicaments which have been made up by expert doctors. And thus I shall do (as I have said) in my procedure, with the aid of the glorious God.

Let us return to our theme, and put down the conditions which are requisite to every surgeon, who wishes by art to exercise on the human body the aforesaid manner and form of operating, which conditions Hippocrates, who guides us well in everything, concludes with a certain subtle implication, in the first of the *Aphorisms:* life is short, and art prolix, time and chance sharp or sudden, experience fallacious and dangerous, judgment difficult. But not only the doctor must busy himself in doing his duty but also the sick person and the attendants, and he must also put in order external things.

There are then four conditions which are valued here, according to Arnald, a very eloquent Latinist. Some are required of the surgeon, others of the sick, others of those present, others in those things which come in from outside.

The conditions required of a surgeon are four: the first is that he be educated; the second, that he be skilled; the third, that he be ingenious; the fourth, that he be well behaved. It is then required in the first place that the surgeon be educated, not only in the principles of surgery, but also of medicine, both in theory and practice.

In theory he must know things natural, non-natural and unnatural. And first, he must understand natural things, principally anatomy, for without it nothing can be done in surgery, as will appear below. He must also understand temperament, for according to the diversity of the nature of bodies it is necessary to diversify the medicament (Galen against Thessales, in all the *Therapeutics*). This is shown by the virtue and strength of the patient. He must also know the things which are not natural, such as air, meat, drink, etc., for these are the causes of all sickness and health. He must also know the things which are contrary to nature, that is sickness, for from this rightly comes the curative purpose. Let him not be ignorant in any way of the cause; for if he cures without the knowledge of that, the cure will not be by his abilities but by chance. Let him not forget or scorn accidents; for sometimes they override their cause, and deceive or divert, and pervert the whole cure, as is said in the first to Glauconius.

In practice, he must know how to put in order the way of living and the medicaments; for without this surgery, which is the third instrument of medicine, is not perfect. Of which Galen speaks in the *Introduction:* as pharmacy has need of regimen and of surgery, so surgery has need of regimen and pharmacy.

Thus it appears that the surgeon working in his art should know the principles of medicine. And with this, it is very fitting that he know something of the other arts. That is what Galen says in the first of his *Therapeutics* against Thessales, that if the doctors have nothing to do with geometry, or astronomy, or dialectics, or any other good discipline, soon the leather workers, carpenters, smiths, and others, leaving their own occupations, will run to medicine and make themselves into doctors.

In the second place, I have said he must be skilled and have seen others operate; I add the maxim of the sage Avenzoar [12th century], that every doctor must have knowledge first of all, and after that he must have practice and experience. To the same testify Rhazes, in the fourth *Book for Almansor,* and Haly Abbas on the testimony of Hippocrates, in the first of his *Theory.*

Thirdly, he must be ingenious, and of good judgment and good memory. That is what Haly Rodan [11th century] says in the third of his *Techni;* the doctor must have good memory, good judgment, good motives, good presence, and sound understanding, and that he be well formed, for example, that he have slender fingers, hands steady and not trembling, clear eyes, etc.

Fourth, I have said, he should be well mannered. Let him be bold in safe things, fearful in dangers, let him flee false cures or practices. Let him be gracious to the sick, benevolent to his companions, wise in his predictions. Let him be chaste, sober, compassionate, and merciful; not covetous, or extortionate, so that he may reasonably receive a salary in proportion to his work, the ability of his patient to pay, the nature of the outcome, and his own dignity.

The conditions required of the sick man are three: that he be obedient to the doctor, as the servant is to the master, in the first of the *Therapeutics;* that he have faith in the doctor, in the first of the *Prognostics;* that he be patient, for patience conquers malice, as it is said in other writing.

The conditions for the attendants are four, that they be peaceable, polite or agreeable, faithful, and discreet.

The conditions for things coming from outside are many, all of which ought to be arranged for the advantage of the sick, as Galen says, at the end of the commentary of the *Aphorisms* mentioned above.

From *La grande chirurgie de Guy de Chauliac,* E. Nicaise, ed. (Paris: F. Alcan, 1890); trans. J.B.R.

The Mirror of Wisdom

The Place of Logic in Philosophy

PETER ABELARD

Twelfth century

WE MAY open our introduction to logic by examining something of the characteristic property of logic in its genus which is philosophy. Boëthius says that not any knowledge whatever is philosophy, but only that which consists in the greatest things; for we do not call all wise men philosophers, but only those whose intelligence penetrates subtle matters. Moreover, Boëthius distinguishes three species of philosophy, speculative, which is concerned with speculation on the nature of things, moral, for the consideration of the honourableness of life, rational, for compounding the relation of arguments, which the Greeks call logic. However, some writers separated logic from philosophy and did not call it, according to Boëthius, a part of philosophy, but an instrument, because obviously the other parts work in logic in a manner, when they use its arguments to prove their own questions. As, if a question should arise in natural or moral speculation, arguments are derived from logic. Boëthius himself holds, against them, that there is nothing to prevent the same thing from being both an instrument and a part of a single thing, as the hand is both a part and an instrument of the human body. Logic moreover seems itself often its own instrument when it demonstrates a question pertaining to itself by its own arguments, as for example: man is the species of animal. It is none the less logic, however, because it is the instrument of logic. So too it is none the less philosophy because it is the instrument of philosophy. Moreover, Boëthius distinguishes it from the other two species of philosophy by its proper end, which consists in compounding arguments. For although the physicist compounds arguments, it is not physics but only logic which instructs him in that.

He noted too in regard to logic that it was composed of and reduced to certain rules of argumentation for this reason, namely, lest it lead inconstant minds into error by false inferences, since it seems to construct by its reasons what is not found in the nature of things, and since it seems often to infer things contrary in their conditions, in the following manner: *Socrates is body, but body is white, therefore Socrates is white.* On the other hand: *Socrates is body, but body is black, therefore Socrates is black.*

Moreover in writing logic the following order is extremely necessary, that since arguments are constructed from propositions, and propositions from words, he who will write logic perfectly, must first write of simple words, then of propositions, and finally devote the end of logic to argumentations, just as our prince Aristotle did, who wrote the *Categories* on the science of words, the *On Interpretation* on the science of propositions, the *Topics* and the *Analytics* on the science of argumentations.

Porphyry himself moreover, as the very statement of the title shows, prepares this introduction for the *Cate-*

gories of Aristotle, but later he himself shows that it is necessary to the whole art. The *intention* of it, the *matter*, the *manner of treatment*, the *utility* or *the part of dialectic to which the present science is to be subordinated*, will now be distinguished briefly and precisely.

The intention is particularly to instruct the reader in the *Categories* of Aristotle, that he may be able to understand more easily the things that are there treated. This makes necessary the treatment of the five subjects which are its materials, namely genus, species, difference, property, and accident. He judged the knowledge of these to be particularly useful to the *Categories* because the investigation is concerning them in almost the whole course of the *Categories*. That which we spoke of as five, however, can be referred to the words, genus, species, and the others, and also in a certain sense to the things signified by them. For he appropriately makes clear the significance of these five words which Aristotle uses, lest one be ignorant, when one has come to the *Categories*, of what is to be understood by these words; and he is able, moreover, to treat of all the things signified by these words, as if of five things, since, although they are infinite taken singly, inasmuch as genera are infinite and likewise species and the others, nevertheless as has been said, all are considered as five, because all are treated according to five characteristics, all genera according to what constitutes genera, and the others in the same way, for in this same way the eight parts of speech are considered according to their eight characteristics, although taken singly they are infinite.

The manner of treatment here is the following: having first distinguished the natures of each singly in separate treatments of them, he proceeds then for further knowledge of them to their common properties and characteristics.

Its utility, as Boëthius himself teaches, is principally as it is directed to the *Categories*. But it is spread in four directions which we shall disclose more carefully later when he himself takes it up.

If the parts of logic have first been distinguished carefully, it is seen at once what is the part through which the science of the present work leads to logic. On the authority of Cicero and Boëthius, there are two parts of which logic is composed, namely, the science of discovering arguments and of judging them, that is, of confirming and proving the arguments discovered. For two things are necessary to one who argues, first to find the arguments by which to argue, then if any should criticize the arguments as defective or as insufficiently firm to be able to confirm them. Wherefore Cicero says that discovery is by nature prior. The present science, however, is concerned with both parts of logic, but most of all with discovery. And it is a part of the science of discovering. For how can an argument be deduced from genus or species or the others, if the things which are here treated are not known? Wherefore Aristotle himself introduces the definition of the predicables into the *Topics*, when he treats of their places, as Cicero likewise does in his *Topics*. But since an argument is confirmed from the same considerations from which it is discovered, this science is not unrelated to judgment. For as an argument is derived from the nature of genus and species, so, once derived, it is confirmed from the nature of genus and species. For considering the nature of species in man, so far as it is related to animal, I find at once from the nature of the species the argument for proving animal. But if any one should criticize the argument, I show that it is suitable immediately by indicating the nature of the species and the genus in both, so that from the same conditions of the terms the argument

may be found and when it has been found it may be
confirmed.

From *Glosses on Porphyry*, trans. R. McKeon, *Selections from
Medieval Philosophers* (New York: Scribner, 1929).

The End of Man

SAINT THOMAS AQUINAS

Thirteenth century

WE HAVE shown in the preceding books that there
is one First Being, possessing the full perfection
of all being, whom we call God, and who of the abundance of His perfection, bestows being on all that exists,
so that He is proved to be not only the firs: of beings,
but also the beginning of all. Moreover He bestows being on others, not through natural necessity, but according to the decree of His will, as we have shown above.
Hence it follows that He is the Lord of the things made
by Him: since we dominate over those things that are
subject to our will. And this is a perfect dominion that
He exercises over things made by Him, forasmuch as in
their making He needs neither the help of an extrinsic
agent, nor matter as the foundation of His work: since
He is the universal efficient cause of all being.

Now everything that is produced through the will of
an agent is directed to an end by that agent: because the
good and the end are the proper object of the will,
wherefore whatever proceeds from a will must needs be
directed to an end. And each thing attains its end by its
own action, which action needs to be directed by him who
endowed things with the principles whereby they act.

Consequently God, who in Himself is perfect in every way, and by His power endows all things with being, must needs be the Ruler of all, Himself ruled by none: nor is anything to be excepted from His ruling, as neither is there anything that does not owe its being to Him. Therefore as He is perfect in being and causing, so is He perfect in ruling.

The effect of this ruling is seen to differ in different things, according to the difference of natures. For some things are so produced by God that, being intelligent, they bear a resemblance to Him and reflect His image: wherefore not only are they directed, but they direct themselves to their appointed end by their own actions. And if in thus directing themselves they be subject to the divine ruling, they are admitted by that divine ruling to the attainment of their last end; but are excluded therefrom if they direct themselves otherwise.

Others there are, bereft of intelligence, which do not direct themselves to their end, but are directed by another. Of these some being incorruptible, even as they are not patient of defects in their natural being, so neither do they wander, in their own action, from the direction to their appointed end, but are subject, without fail, to the ruling of the Supreme Ruler; such are the heavenly bodies, whose movements are invariable. Others, however, being corruptible, are patient of defects in their natural being; yet this defect is supplied to the advantage of another: since when one thing is corrupted, another is generated. Likewise, they fail from their natural direction in their own actions, yet this failing is compensated by some resultant good. Whence it is clear that not even those things which are seen to wander from the direction of the supreme ruling, escape from the power of the Supreme Ruler: because also these corruptible bodies, even as they are created by God, so too are they perfectly subject to Him. . . .

Since then in the First Book we have treated of the perfection of the divine nature, and, in the Second, of the perfection of the divine power, inasmuch as He is the Creator and Lord of all: it remains for us in this Third Book to treat of His perfect authority or dignity, inasmuch as He is the end and Governor of all. We must therefore proceed in this wise, so as first to treat of Him as the end of all things; secondly of His universal government, inasmuch as He governs every creature: thirdly, of that special government, whereby He governs creatures endowed with intelligence.

Accordingly we must first show that every agent, by its action, intends an end.

For in those things which clearly act for an end, we declare the end to be that towards which the movement of the agent tends: for when this is reached, the end is said to be reached, and to fail in this is to fail in the end intended; as may be seen in the physician who aims at health, and in a man who runs towards an appointed goal. Nor does it matter, as to this, whether that which tends to an end be cognitive or not: for just as the target is the end of the archer, so is it the end of the arrow's flight. Now the movement of every agent tends to something determinate: since it is not from any force that any action proceeds, but heating proceeds from heat, and cooling from cold; wherefore actions are differentiated by their active principles. Action sometimes terminates in something made, for instance, building terminates in a house, healing ends in health: while sometimes it does not so terminate, for instance, understanding and sensation. And if action terminate in something made, the movement of the agent tends by that action towards that thing made: while if it does not terminate in something made, the movement of the agent tends to the action itself. It follows therefore that every agent intends an end while acting, which end is sometimes the action itself, sometimes a thing made by the action.

Again. In all things that act for an end, that is said to be the last end, beyond which the agent seeks nothing further: thus the physician's action goes as far as health, and this being attained, his efforts cease. But in the action of every agent, a point can be reached beyond which the agent does not desire to go; else actions would tend to infinity, which is impossible, for since *it is not possible to pass through an infinite medium,* the agent would never begin to act, because nothing moves towards what it cannot reach. Therefore every agent acts for an end. . . .

Again. Every agent acts either by nature or by intelligence. Now there can be no doubt that those which act by intelligence act for an end; since they act with an intellectual preconception of what they attain by their action, and act through such preconception, for this is to act by intelligence. Now just as in the preconceiving intellect there exists the entire likeness of the effect that is attained by the action of the intellectual being, so in the natural agent there pre-exists the similitude of the natural effect, by virtue of which similitude its action is determined to the appointed effect: for fire begets fire, and an olive produces an olive. Wherefore even as that which acts by intelligence tends by its action to a definite end, so also does that which acts by nature. Therefore every agent acts for an end.

Moreover. Fault is not found save in those things which are for an end: for we do not find fault with one who fails in that to which he is not appointed; thus we find fault with a physician if he fails to heal, but not with a builder or a grammarian. But we find fault in things done according to art, as when a grammarian fails to speak correctly; and in things that are ruled by nature, as in the case of monstrosities. Therefore every agent, whether according to nature, or according to art, or acting of set purpose, acts for an end. . . .

There are, however, certain actions which would seem not to be for an end, such as playful and contemplative actions, and those which are done without attention, such as scratching one's beard, and the like: whence some might be led to think that there is an agent that acts not for an end. But we must observe that contemplative actions are not for another end, but are themselves an end. Playful actions are sometimes an end, when one plays for the mere pleasure of play; and sometimes they are for an end, as when we play that afterwards we may study better. Actions done without attention do not proceed from the intellect, but from some sudden act of the imagination, or some natural principle: thus a disordered humour produces an itching sensation and is the cause of a man scratching his beard, which he does without his mind attending to it. Such actions do tend to an end, although outside the order of the intellect. Hereby is excluded the error of certain natural philosophers of old, who maintained that all things happen by natural necessity, thus utterly banishing the final cause from things.

Hence we must go on to prove that every agent acts for a good.

For that every agent acts for an end clearly follows from the fact that every agent tends to something definite. Now that to which an agent tends definitely must needs be befitting to that agent: since the latter would not tend to it save on account of some fittingness thereto.

But that which is befitting to a thing is good for it. Therefore every agent acts for a good.

Further. The end is that wherein the appetite of the agent or mover is at rest, as also the appetite of that which is moved. Now it is the very notion of good to be the term of appetite, since *good is the object of every appetite.* Therefore all action and movement is for a good.

Again. All action and movement would seem to be directed in some way to being: either for the preservation of being in the species or in the individual; or for the acquisition of being. Now this itself, being, to wit, is a good: and for this reason all things desire being. Therefore all action and movement is for a good.

Furthermore. All action and movement is for some perfection. For if the action itself be the end, it is clearly a second perfection of the agent. And if the action consist in the transformation of external matter, clearly the mover intends to induce some perfection into the thing moved: towards which perfection the movable tends, if the movement be natural. Now when we say a thing is perfect, we mean that it is good. Therefore every action and movement is for a good. . . .

Moreover. The intellectual agent acts for an end, as determining on its end: whereas the natural agent, though it acts for an end, as proved above, does not determine on its end, since it knows not the ratio of end, but is moved to the end determined for it by another. Now an intellectual agent does not determine the end for itself except under the aspect of good; for the intelligible object does not move except it be considered as a good, which is the object of the will. Therefore also the natural agent is not moved, nor does it act for an end, except in so far as this end is a good: since the end is determined for the natural agent by an appetite. Therefore every agent acts for a good. . . .

Moreover. Whatever is moved is brought to the term of movement by the mover and agent. Therefore mover and moved tend to the same term. Now that which is moved, since it is in potentiality, tends to an act, and consequently to perfection and goodness: for by its movement it passes from potentiality to act. Therefore mover and agent by moving and acting always intend a good.

Hence the philosophers in defining the good said: "The good is the object of every appetite," and Dionysius (De Div. Nom., IV) says that "all things desire the good and the best." . . .

From the foregoing it is clear that all things are directed to one good as their last end.

For if nothing tends to something as its end, except in so far as this is good, it follows that good, as such, is an end. Consequently that which is the supreme good is supremely the end of all. Now there is but one supreme good, namely God, as we have shown in the First Book. Therefore all things are directed to the supreme good, namely God, as their end. . . .

Further. In every series of causes, the first cause is more a cause than the second cause: since the second cause is not a cause save through the first. Therefore that which is the first cause in the series of final causes, must needs be more the final cause of each thing, than the proximate final cause. Now God is the first cause in the series of final causes: for He is supreme in the order of good things. Therefore He is the end of each thing more even than any proximate end. . . .

Furthermore. The particular good is directed to the common good as its end: for the being of the part is on account of the whole: wherefore *the good of the nation is more godlike than the good of one man.* Now the supreme good, namely God, is the common good, since the good of all things depends on Him: and the good whereby each thing is good, is the particular good of that thing, and of those that depend thereon. Therefore all things are directed to one good, God, to wit, as their end. . . .

Furthermore. In all mutually subordinate agents and movers, the end of the first agent must be the end of all; even as the end of the commander-in-chief is the end of all who are soldiering under him. Now of all the parts of man, the intellect is the highest mover: for it moves the appetite, by proposing its object to it; and the intellective appetite, or will, moves the sensitive appetites, namely the irascible and concupiscible, so that we do not obey the concupiscence, unless the will command; and the sensitive appetite, the will consenting, moves the body. Therefore the end of the intellect is the end of all human actions. *Now the intellect's end and good are the true;* and its last end is the first truth. Therefore the last end of all man and of all his deeds and desires, is to know the first truth, namely God.

Moreover. Man has a natural desire to know the causes of whatever he sees: wherefore through wondering at what they saw, and ignoring its cause, men first began to philosophize, and when they had discovered the cause they were at rest. Nor do they cease inquiring until they come to the first cause; and *then do we deem ourselves to know perfectly when we know the first cause.* Therefore man naturally desires, as his last end, to know the first cause. But God is the first cause of all. Therefore man's last end is to know God. . . .

Now the last end of man and of any intelligent substance is called happiness or beatitude; for it is this that every intelligent substance desires as its last end, and for its own sake alone. Therefore the last beatitude or happiness of any intelligent substance is to know God.

Hence it is said (Matthew v, 8): "Blessed are the clean of heart, for they shall see God": and (John xvii, 3): "This is eternal life: that they may know Thee, the only true God." Aristotle agrees with this statement (10 *Ethic*, vii) when he says that man's ultimate happiness is "contemplative, in regard to his contemplating the highest object of contemplation." . . .

It remains for us to inquire in what kind of knowledge of God the ultimate happiness of the intellectual substance consists. For there is a certain general and confused knowledge of God, which is in almost all men, whether from the fact that, as some think, the existence of God, like other principles of demonstration, is self-evident, as we have stated in the First Book: or, as seems nearer to the truth, because by his natural reason, man is able at once to arrive at some knowledge of God. For seeing that natural things are arranged in a certain order—since there cannot be order without a cause of order—men, for the most part, perceive that there is one who arranges in order the things that we see. But who or of what kind this cause of order may be, or whether there be but one, cannot be gathered from this general consideration: even, so, when we see a man in motion, and performing other works, we perceive that in him there is a cause of these operations, which is not in other things, and we give this cause the name of "soul," but without knowing yet what the soul is, whether it be a body, or how it brings about operations in question.

Now, this knowledge of God cannot possibly suffice for happiness. . . .

There is yet another knowledge of God, in one respect superior to the knowledge we have been discussing, namely that whereby God is known to men through faith. In this respect it surpasses the knowledge of God through demonstration, because by faith we know certain things about God, which are so sublime that reason cannot reach them by means of demonstration, as we have stated at the beginning of this work. But not even in this knowledge of God can man's ultimate happiness consist.

For happiness is the intellect's perfect operation, as already declared. But in knowledge by faith the operation of the intellect is found to be most imperfect as regards that which is on the part of the intellect: although it is the most perfect on the part of the object: for the intellect in believing does not grasp the object of its assent. Therefore neither does man's happiness consist in this knowledge of God.

Again. It has been shown that ultimate happiness does not consist chiefly in an act of will. Now in knowledge by faith the will has the leading place: for the intellect assents by faith to things proposed to it, because it wills, and not through being constrained by the evidence of their truth. Therefore man's final happiness does not consist in this knowledge. . . .

Seeing that man's ultimate happiness does not consist in that knowledge of God whereby He is known by all or many in a vague kind of opinion, nor again in that knowledge of God whereby He is known in science through demonstration; nor in that knowledge whereby He is known through faith, as we have proved above: and seeing that it is not possible in this life to arrive at a higher knowledge of God in His essence, or at least so that we understand other separate substances, and thus know God through that which is nearest to Him, so to say, as we have proved; and since we must place our ultimate happiness in some kind of knowledge of

God, as we have shown; it is impossible for man's happiness to be in this life.

Again. Man's last end is the term of his natural appetite, so that when he has obtained it, he desires nothing more: because if he still has a movement towards something, he has not yet reached an end wherein to be at rest. Now, this cannot happen in this life: since the more man understands, the more is the desire to understand increased in him—this being natural to man—unless perhaps someone there be who understands all things: and in this life this never did nor can happen to anyone that was a mere man; seeing that in this life we are unable to know separate substances which in themselves are most intelligible, as we have proved. Therefore man's ultimate happiness cannot possibly be in this life.

Besides. Whatever is in motion towards an end has a natural desire to be established and at rest therein: hence a body does not move away from the place towards which it has a natural movement, except by a violent movement which is contrary to that appetite. Now happiness is the last end which man desires naturally. Therefore it is his natural desire to be established in happiness. Consequently unless together with happiness he acquires a state of immobility, he is not yet happy, since his natural desire is not yet at rest. When therefore a man acquires happiness, he also acquires stability and rest; so that all agree in conceiving stability as a necessary condition of happiness: hence the philosopher says (1 *Ethic*, x): "We do not look upon the happy man as a kind of chameleon." Now, in this life there is no sure stability; since, however happy a man may be, sickness and misfortune may come upon him, so that he is hindered in the operation, whatever it be, in which his happiness consists. Therefore man's ultimate happiness cannot be in this life. . . .

Further. All admit that happiness is a perfect good: else it would not bring rest to the appetite. Now perfect good is that which is wholly free from any admixture of evil: just as that which is perfectly white is that which is entirely free from any admixture of black. But man cannot be wholly free from evils in this state of life; not only from evils of the body, such as hunger, thirst, heat, cold, and the like, but also from evils of the soul. For no one is there who at times is not disturbed by inordinate passion; who sometimes does not go beyond the mean, wherein virtue consists, either in excess or in deficiency; who is not deceived in some thing or another; or at least ignores what he would wish to know, or feels doubtful about an opinion of which he would like to be certain. Therefore no man is happy in this life.

Again. Man naturally shuns death, and is sad about it: not only shunning it now when he feels its presence, but also when he thinks about it. But man, in this life, cannot obtain not to die. Therefore it is not possible for man to be happy in this life. . . .

Again. The natural desire cannot be void; since *nature does nothing in vain*. But nature's desire would be void if it could never be fulfilled. Therefore man's natural desire can be fulfilled. But not in this life, as we have shown. Therefore it must be fulfilled after this life. Therefore man's ultimate happiness is after this life.

Besides. As long as a thing is in motion towards perfection it has not reached its last end. Now in the knowledge of truth all men are ever in motion and tending towards perfection: because those who follow, make discoveries in addition to those made by their predecessors, as stated in 2 *Metaph*. Therefore in the knowledge of truth man is not situated as though he had arrived at his last end. Since then as Aristotle himself shows (10 *Ethic,* vii) man's ultimate happiness in this life consists apparently in speculation, whereby he seeks the knowledge of truth, we cannot possibly allow that man obtains his last end in this life. . . .

For these and like reasons Alexander and Averroes held that man's ultimate happiness does not consist in human knowledge obtained through speculative sciences, but in that which results from conjunction with a separate substance, which conjunction they deemed possible to man in this life. But as Aristotle realized that man has no knowledge in this life other than that which he obtains through speculative sciences, he maintained that man attains to happiness, not perfect, but proportionate to his capacity.

Hence it becomes sufficiently clear how these great minds suffered from being so straitened on every side. We, however, will avoid these straits if we suppose, in accordance with the foregoing arguments, that man is able to reach perfect happiness after this life, since man has an immortal soul; and that in that state his soul will understand in the same way as separate substances understand, as we proved in the Second Book.

Therefore man's ultimate happiness will consist in that knowledge of God which he possesses after this life; a knowledge similar to that by which separate substances know him. Hence our Lord promises us a "reward . . . in heaven" (Matthew v, 12) and (Matthew xxii, 30) states that the saints "shall be as the angels": who always see God in heaven (Matthew xviii, 10).

From *Summa contra gentiles,* book iii, trans. English Dominican Fathers (London: Burns, Oates, and Washbourne, 1928).

On Learned Ignorance

NICHOLAS OF CUSA

Fifteenth century

HOW "TO KNOW" IS "NOT TO KNOW"

WE SEE that, by divine grace, there is within all things a certain natural desire to be better, in the manner which the natural condition of each one permits, and that those beings in whom judgment is innate act toward this end and have the necessary instruments; this is in accord with the goal of knowledge so that the longing for it may not be vain, and that it may be able to reach repose in the desired equilibrium of its own nature. If, by chance, it happens otherwise, that comes necessarily from an accident, as when sickness warps the taste or simple opinion warps reasoning. For this reason we say that the sound and free intellect which insatiably, from an innate quest, longs to attain the true by examining all, knows the true when it apprehends it in an amorous embrace, for we do not doubt the perfect truth of that which all sound minds are unable to reject.

Now all those who investigate judge of the uncertain by comparing it to a reliable presupposition by a system of proportion. All inquiry, therefore, is comparative, using the means of proportion so that as long as the objects of inquiry can be compared to the presupposition by a close proportional reduction, the judgment of apprehension is easy; but if we have need of many intermediaries, then difficulty and trouble arise. This is well known in mathematics where the first propositions are easily referred to the first principles which are very well known, but the later ones, since they need the intermediary of the first, present much more difficulty. All inquiry, therefore, consists in comparative proportion, easy or difficult, and that is why the infinite which as infinite escapes all proportion, is unknown.

Now proportion, since in any thing it expresses agreement together with difference, cannot be understood without number. Number, consequently, includes all that is susceptible to proportion. Number, therefore, does not create proportion in quantity only but in all those things which in any way, by substance or accident, can agree or differ. Hence Pythagoras judged with vigour that everything was constituted and understood through the force of numbers. But the precision of combinations in material things and the exact adaptation of the known to the unknown so far surpass human reason that it seemed to Socrates that he knew nothing except his ignorance, and the very wise Solomon affirmed that all things are difficult and inexplicable in language. And another man of divine spirit says that wisdom is hidden, and also the seat of intelligence, from the eyes of the living. If, therefore, it is true, as likewise the very profound Aristotle affirms in his *First Philosophy*, that such a difficulty befalls us in the things most manifest in nature, like owls trying to see the sun, since the divine in us is certainly not vain, we need to know that we are ignorant. If we can attain this end completely, we shall attain "learned ignorance." For nothing becomes a man, even the most zealous, more perfectly in learning than to be found very learned in ignorance itself, which is his characteristic, and anyone will be the more learned the more he knows his own ignorance. On this goal of learned ignorance I have assumed the labour of writing a few words.

Before treating the greatest doctrine, that of ignorance, I consider it necessary to take up the nature of "the quality of being maximum" [*maximitas*]. Now I call "maximum" a thing than which nothing can be greater. Plenitude, in truth, is appropriate to one; that is why unity coincides with "the quality of being maximum," and it is also entity. Now if such unity is absolute universally, beyond all relation and all concreteness, it is clear, since it is the absolute "quality of being maximum," that nothing is opposed to it. And so the absolute maximum is one, which is all, in which all is, because it is the maximum. And since nothing is opposed to it, with it at the same time coincides the minimum; wherefore it is thus in everything. And because it is absolute, then it is actually all possible being, undergoing no restrictions from things and imposing them on all.

This maximum which by the indubitable faith of all nations is accepted also as God, I shall, in my first book on human reason, labour to seek, though incomprehensibly, led by that One who, alone, lives in inaccessible light.

In the second place, as the absolute quality of being maximum is absolute entity, by which all things are what they are, so universal unity of being comes from that which is called absolute maximum, and therefore exists concretely as universe whose unity, indeed, is restricted in plurality without which it cannot be. This maximum, indeed, although in its universal unity it embraces everything, so that all which comes from the absolute is in it and it is in all, does not, however, have subsistence outside of plurality, in which it is, because it does not exist without concreteness from which it cannot be freed. Concerning this maximum, which appears as the universe, I shall add some remarks in my second book.

In the third place, the maximum will show the necessity of a third order of consideration. For, as the universe subsists concretely only in plurality, we shall seek in the multiple things themselves, the maximum one, in whom the universe subsists most greatly and most perfectly both in its realization and in its end. And since this universe unites itself with the absolute, which is the universal goal, because it is the end which is most perfect and beyond all our capacities, I shall add below on this maximum, at the same time concrete and absolute, which we call by the name forever blessed of Jesus, some words as Jesus Himself shall inspire. He who wishes to attain the meaning of what I am going to say, must raise the intelligence above the force of the words themselves, rather than insist on the properties of words, which cannot be adapted properly to such great intellectual mysteries. It is necessary to use in a transcendental fashion the examples which my hand will trace, so that the reader, leaving aside sensible things, should rise easily to simple intellectuality. I have applied myself to seeking this way with ordinary talents, as clearly as I could, avoiding any roughness of style, to lay bare the root of learned ignorance, making it manifest at once although not with the comprehensible precision of truth.

THAT PRECISE TRUTH IS INCOMPREHENSIBLE

Because it is clear in itself that there is no proportion of the infinite to the finite, from this it is most clear that where one finds something which exceeds and something which is exceeded, one does not arrive at the simple maximum, since what exceeds and what is exceeded are finite objects while the simple maximum is necessarily infinite. No matter what has been given, if it is not the simple maximum itself, it is clear that a greater one can be given.

And because we find that equality permits degrees, so that a certain thing is more equal to one than to another, according to the points of agreement and difference, in genus, in species, of place, of influence, and of time, with similar things, it is clear that one cannot find two or more objects similar and equal to such a point that objects more similar still can not exist in infinite number. Let the measures and the objects measured be as equal as can be, there will always be differences. Therefore, our finite intellect cannot, by means of similitude, understand with precision the truth of things. For truth, existing in a certain indivisible nature, is not either more or less, and all that is not true itself is not able to measure it with precision; thus what is not circle cannot measure the circle whose being consists in something indivisible. Therefore the understanding, which is not truth, never attains truth with such precision that it cannot be attained more precisely by the infinite; for it is to truth as the polygon is to the circle; the greater the number of angles inscribed in the polygon, the more it will be like the circle, but nevertheless it is never made equal to the circle, even if one multiplies the angles infinitely, unless it breaks down into identity with the circle. It is clear, therefore, that we know nothing concerning the true except that we know it to be incomprehensible precisely as it is; for truth being absolute necessity, which cannot be more or less than it is, presents itself to our understanding as possibility. Therefore, the quiddity of things, which is the truth of beings, is unattainable in its purity; all philosophers have sought it, none has found it, such as it is; and the more we shall be profoundly learned in this ignorance, the more we shall approach truth itself.

THE MYSTERIES OF FAITH

Our ancestors assert with one voice that faith is the beginning of understanding. For in every discipline certain things are presupposed as first principles which are apprehended by faith alone and from which springs the comprehension of the matters treated. Every man who wishes to raise himself to knowledge must necessarily believe in the things without which he cannot raise himself. As Isaiah says: "Unless you believe, you will not understand." Faith, therefore, comprises in herself all that is intelligible. Understanding is the explication of faith. Understanding is, therefore, directed by faith, and faith is developed by understanding. Where there is no sound faith, there is no true understanding. It is clear to what conclusion error in principle and fragility in foundations lead. There is no faith more perfect than the truth itself, which is Jesus. Who does not understand that the most excellent gift of God is perfect faith? The apostle John says that faith in the incarnation of the Word of God leads us to truth, in order that we may become sons of God; that is what he shows simply in his exordium, and then he recounts numerous works of Christ consonant with this belief that understanding is illuminated by faith. Therefore he comes finally to this conclusion saying: "These things were written so that you might believe that Jesus is the Son of God."

Now that sweetest faith in Christ, firmly sustained in simplicity, may by stages of ascent be extended and developed according to the aforesaid doctrine, that of ignorance. For the greatest and most profound mysteries of God, hidden from those who go about in the world, however wise they may be, have been revealed to the small and humble in the faith of Jesus, because Jesus is the one in whom all the treasures of wisdom and science are enclosed, and without whom no one can do anything. For He is the Word and the power by whom God created the very ages, alone, the highest, having power over all things in heaven and on earth. This one, since He is not knowable in this world, where reason, opinion, and knowledge lead us by symbols through the better known to the unknown, can be grasped only there where proofs cease and faith begins, by which we are ravished in simplicity so that beyond all reason and intelligence, in the third heaven of the most simple intellectuality, we may contemplate Him in His body incorporeally, because in spirit, and in the world but not of the world, but celestially and incomprehensibly in order that it may be understood that He is incomprehensible by reason of His infinite excellence.

And this is that learned ignorance by which the most blessed Paul himself, arising, saw that Christ whom he formerly only had knowledge of, he did not know when he was raised higher up to Him. We are led, therefore, we faithful in Christ, in learned ignorance to that mountain which is Christ, which the nature of our animality prevents us from attaining, and when we try to perceive it with the intellectual eye, we fall down in the fog, knowing only that this fog hides us from the mountain, on which only those may live who flourish in understanding. If we approach this with a greater firmness in our faith we are snatched away from the eyes of those who wander in the world of the senses, so that with internal hearing we perceive the voices, the thunder, and the terrible signs of the majesty of God, easily perceiving the Lord Himself, whom all things obey, advancing by stages in the imperishable traces of His steps, like I do not know what divine creatures; and hearing the voice, not of mortal creatures but of God Himself in the holy organs and in the signs of His prophets and saints, we contemplate Him more clearly, as if through the cloud of reason. Then the believers, with more burning desire, rising continually, are carried up to intellectuality in its simplicity, passing beyond all sensible things, as if from sleep to waking, from hearing to sight, where those things are seen which cannot be revealed, because they are beyond all hearing and the teaching of the voice. For if what is revealed there had to be expressed, then the inexpressible would be expressed and the inaudible would be heard, just as the invisible is seen there. For Jesus, blessed throughout the ages, end of all intellection, since He is truth; end of all sensibility since He is life; end ultimately of all being, because He is entity; perfection of every created being as God and man, is incomprehensibly heard there as the limit of every word. For from Him proceeds, to Him returns every word; all that is true in the word comes from Him. Every word has as its goal edification, therefore Him, who is wisdom itself. All that has been written has been for our edification. The words are represented in the Scriptures, the heavens are sustained by the Word of God. Therefore, all created things are signs of the Word of God. Every corporeal word is the sign of the spiritual Word. The cause of every spiritual corruptible word is the incorruptible Word, which is reason. Christ is the incarnate reason of all reasons, because the Word was made flesh. Jesus therefore is the end of everything.

Such are the verities which reveal themselves by degrees to him who raises himself to Christ by faith. The divine efficacy of this faith is inexplicable for, if it is great, it unites the believer to Jesus so that he is above all that is not in unity with Jesus Himself.

From *De docta ignorantia*, P. Rotta, ed. (Bari, Italy: G. Laterza, 1913); trans. J.B.R.

The Vision of God

The Soul Complains to God

JACOPONE DA TODI

Thirteenth century

Love, that art Charity,
Why has thou hurt me so?
My heart is smote in two,
And burns with ardent love.

Glowing and flaming, refuge finding none,
　My heart is fettered fast, it cannot flee;
It is consumed, like wax set in the sun;
　Living, yet dying, swooning passionately,
It prays for strength a little way to run,
　Yet in this furnace must it bide and be:
Where am I led, ah me!
　　To depths so high?
　　Living I die,
So fierce the fire of Love.

Before I knew its power, I asked in prayer
　For love of Christ, believing it was sweet;
I thought to breathe a calm and tranquil air,
　On peaceful heights, where tempests never beat.

Torment I find, instead of sweetness there!
 My heart is riven by the dreadful heat:
 Of these strange things to treat
  All words are vain;
  By bliss I am slain,
And yet I live and move.

For I have lost my heart, my will, my wit,
 My hopes, desires, my pleasures and my taste;
Beauty seems vile, corruption crawls on it,
 Riches, delights, and honours all are waste:
—A Tree of Love, with fruits both fair and fit
 To feed me, in my heart is rooted fast,
 It flings away in haste
  All it can find,
  Will, strength, and mind:
With Love in vain I strove.

   • • •

More would I love, if more were possible;
 Yet can I give no more than all my heart;
I give my all—my life, my soul, my will,
 Nor needs it proof that all is more than part.
I give Thee all, O Lover Terrible—
 Take all, fresh life for ever to impart;
 So old, so new, Thou art;
  Yea, I have found Thee,
  Soft light around Thee,
And whiter than the Dove.

Gazing on Thee, Thou Bright and Morning Star,
 I am. led far, I know not where I be;
My heart is melted like a waxen bar,
 That moulded in Christ's likeness it may be;
O Christ, Thy barters keen and wondrous are!

I am stript naked, to be drest in Thee:
My heart transformed in me,
　　My mind lies dumb,
　　To see Thee come,
In sweetness and in Love.

So linkèd with that sweetness is my mind,
　It leans and strains, its Lover to embrace:
And all in Him, and naught in self to find,
　It learns, by gazing ever on His face.
Riches, and powers, and memories strong to bind,
　It casts away, as burdens in the race;
　　It hath no resting-place,
　　　No will, no care;
　　　It mounts the stair,
　　Towards which its being strove.

In Christ transformed, almost my soul is Christ;
　Conjoined with God, all, all is now divine,
So great, so high, its marvellous acquist—
　—Possessing, Jesu, all that once was Thine:
Nor need I now, set free from mortal mist,
　Ask medicine for the guilt that once was mine;
　　No more in grief I pine,
　　　My sinful soul
　　　Is purged and whole,
　　Yea, it is cleansed and shrove.

Now, a new creature, I in Christ am born,
　The old man stripped away;—I am new-made;
And mounting in me, like the sun at morn,
　Love breaks my heart, even as a broken blade:
Christ, First and Only Fair, from me hath shorn
　My will, my wits, and all that in me stayed,
　　I in His arms am laid,

I cry and call—
"O Thou my All,
O let me die of Love!"

For Thee, O Love, my heart consumes away,
    I cry, I call, I yearn for Thy caress;
Living, I perish when Thou dost not stay,
    Sighing and mourning for my Blessedness:
Dost Thou return, I strain and strive and pray,
    To lose amidst Thine All my Nothingness:
      Then tarry not to bless,
        Love, think on me;
      Bind me to Thee,
Consume my heart with Love!

• • •

From *Lauda XC*, trans. Mrs. T. Beck, in E. Underhill, *Jacopone da Todi.*

A Crying Mystic

MARGERY KEMPE

Fourteenth century

S° THEY went forth into the Holy Land till they could
see Jerusalem. And when this creature saw Jerusalem, riding on an ass, she thanked God with all her
heart, praying Him for His mercy that, as He had
brought her to see His earthly city of Jerusalem, He
would grant her grace to see the blissful city of Jerusalem above, the city of Heaven. Our Lord Jesus Christ,
answering her thought, granted her to have her desire.
Then for the joy she had, and the sweetness she felt

in the dalliance with our Lord, she was on the point of falling off her ass, for she could not bear the sweetness and grace that God wrought in her soul. Then two pilgrims, Duchemen, went to her, and kept her from falling; one of whom was a priest, and he put spices in her mouth to comfort her, thinking she had been sick. And so they helped her on to Jerusalem, and when she came there, she said:

"Sirs, I pray you be not displeased though I weep sore in this holy place where our Lord Jesus Christ was quick and dead."

Then went they to the temple in Jerusalem and they were let in on the same day at evensong time, and abode there till the next day at evensong time. Then the friars lifted up a cross and led the pilgrims about from one place to another where our Lord suffered . . . His passion, every man and woman bearing a wax candle in one hand. And the friars always, as they went about, told them what our Lord suffered in every place. The aforesaid creature wept and sobbed as plenteously as though she had seen our Lord with her bodily eye, suffering His passion at that time. Before her in her soul she saw Him verily by contemplation, and that caused her to have compassion. And when they came up on to the Mount of Calvary, she fell down because she could not stand or kneel, and rolled and wrested with her body, spreading her arms abroad, and cried with a loud voice as though her heart would have burst asunder; for, in the city of her soul, she saw verily and clearly how our Lord was crucified. Before her face, she heard and saw, in her ghostly sight, the mourning of our Lady, of Saint John, and Mary Magdalene and of many others that loved our Lord.

And she had such great compassion and such great pain, at seeing our Lord's pain, that she could not keep herself from crying and roaring though she should have died for it. And this was the first cry that ever she cried in any contemplation. And this manner of crying endured many years after this time, for aught any man might do, and therefore, suffered she much despite and much reproof. The crying was so loud and so wonderful that it made the people astounded unless they had heard it before, or unless they knew the cause of the crying. And she had them so often that they made her right weak in her bodily might, and especially if she heard of our Lord's passion.

And sometimes, when she saw the crucifix, or if she saw a man with a wound, or a beast, whichever it were, or if a man beat a child before her, or smote a horse or other beast with a whip, if she saw it or heard it, she thought she saw our Lord being beaten or wounded, just as she saw it in the man or the beast either in the field or the town, and by herself alone as well as amongst the people.

First when she had her cryings in Jerusalem, she had them often, and in Rome also. And when she came home to England, first at her coming home, it came but seldom, as it were once a month, then once a week, afterwards daily, and once she had fourteen in one day, and another day she had seven, and so on, as God would visit her, sometimes in church, sometimes in the street, sometimes in her chamber, sometimes in the fields, whenever God would send them, for she never knew the time nor the hour when they would come. And they never came without passing great sweetness of devotion and high contemplation. And as soon as she perceived that she would cry, she would keep it in as much as she might that the people should not hear it, to their annoyance. For some said that a wicked spirit vexed her; some said it was a sickness; some said she had drunk too much wine; some banned her; some wished she was in the harbour; some wished she was on the sea in a bottomless boat; and thus each man as he thought. Other ghostly men loved her and favoured her the more. Some great clerks said our Lady cried never so, nor any saint in Heaven, but they knew full little what she felt, nor would they believe that she could not stop crying if she wished.

And therefore when she knew that she would cry, she kept it in as long as she might, and did all she could to withstand it or put it away, till she waxed as livid as any lead, and ever it would labour in her mind more and more till the time it broke out. And when the body might no longer endure the ghostly labour, but was overcome with the unspeakable love that wrought so fervently in her soul, then she fell down and cried wondrous loud, and the more she laboured to keep it in or put it away, so much the more would she cry, and the louder. Thus she did on the Mount of Calvary, as is written before.

From *The Book of Margery Kempe*, W. Butler-Bowdon, ed. (London: Cape, 1936; New York: Devin-Adair, 1944).

The Vision of God

NICHOLAS OF CUSA

Fifteenth century

I WILL now show you, dearest brethren, as I promised you, an easy path unto mystical theology. For, knowing you to be led by zeal for God, I think you worthy of the opening up of this treasure, as assuredly very precious and most fruitful. And first I pray the Almighty to give me utterance, and the heavenly Word who alone can express Himself, that I may be able, as ye can receive it, to relate the marvels of revelation, which are beyond all sight of our eyes, our reason, and our understanding. I will endeavour by a very simple and commonplace method to lead you by experience into the divine darkness; wherein while ye abide ye shall perceive present with you the light inaccessible, and shall each endeavour, in the measure that God shall grant him, to draw ever nearer thereunto, and to partake here, by a sweetest foretaste, of that feast of everlasting bliss, whereunto we are called in the word of life, through the gospel of Christ, who is blessed for ever.

If I strive in human fashion to transport you to things divine, I must needs use a comparison of some kind. Now among men's works I have found no image better suited to our purpose than that of an image which is omnivoyant—its face, by the painter's cunning art, being made to appear as though looking on all around it. There are many excellent pictures of such faces—for example, that of the archeress in the market-place of Nuremberg; that by the eminent painter, Roger, in his priceless picture in the governor's house at Brussels; the Veronica in my chapel at Coblenz, and, in the castle of Brixen, the angel holding the arms of the Church, and many others elsewhere. Yet, lest ye should fail in the exercise, which requireth a figure of this description to be looked upon, I send for your indulgence such a picture as I have been able to procure, setting forth the figure of an omnivoyant, and this I call the icon of God.

This picture, brethren, ye shall set up in some place, let us say, on a north wall, and shall stand round it, a little way off, and look upon it. And each of you shall find that, from whatsoever quarter he regardeth it, it looketh upon him as if it looked on none other. And it shall seem to a brother standing to eastward as if that face looketh toward the east, while one to southward shall think it looketh toward the south, and one to westward, toward the west. First, then, ye will marvel how it can be that the face should look on all and each at the same time. For the imagination of him standing to eastward cannot conceive the gaze of the icon to be turned unto any other quarter, such as west or south. Then let the brother who stood to eastward place himself to westward and he will find its gaze fastened on him in the west just as it was afore in the east. And, as he knoweth the icon to be fixed and unmoved, he will marvel at the motion of its immovable gaze. . . .

And while he observeth how that gaze never quitteth any, he seeth that it taketh such diligent care of each one who findeth himself observed as though it cared only for him, and for no other, and this to such a degree that one on whom it resteth cannot even conceive that it should take care of any other. He will also see that it taketh the same most diligent care of the least of creatures as of the greatest, and of the whole universe.

'Tis by means of this perceptible image that I purpose to uplift you, my most loving brethren, by a certain devotional exercise, unto mystical Theology, premising three things that be serviceable thereunto.

In the first place, I think, it should be presupposed that there is nothing which seemeth proper to the gaze of the icon of God which doth not more really exist in the veritable gaze of God Himself. For God, who is the very summit of all perfection, and greater than can be conceived, is called *Theos* from this very fact that He beholdeth all things. Wherefore, if the countenance portrayed in a picture can seem to look upon each and all at one and the same time, this faculty (since it is the perfection of seeing) must no less really pertain unto the reality than it doth apparently unto the icon or appearance. For if the sight of one man is keener than that of another among us, if one will with difficulty distinguish objects near him, while another can make out those at a distance, if one perceive an object slowly, the other more quickly—there is no doubt but that Absolute Sight, whence all sight springeth, surpasseth in keenness, in speed, and in strength the sight of all who actually see and who can become capable of sight. . . .

Approach thee now, brother contemplative, unto the icon of God, and place thyself first to the east thereof, then to the south, and finally to the west. Then, because its glance regardeth thee alike in each position, and leaveth thee not whithersoever thou goest, a questioning will arise in thee and thou wilt stir it up, saying: Lord, in this image of Thee I now behold Thy providence by a certain experience of sense. For if Thou leavest not me, who am the vilest of men, never and to none wilt Thou be lacking. For Thou art present to all and to each, even as to those same, all and each, is present the Being without whom they cannot exist. For Thou, the Absolute Being of all, art as entirely present to all as though Thou hadst no care for any other. And this befalleth because there is none that doth not prefer its own being to all others, and its own mode of being to that of all others, and so defendeth its own being as that it would rather allow the being of all others to go to perdition than its own. Even so, Thou, Lord, dost regard every living thing in such wise that none of them can conceive that Thou hast any other care but that it alone should exist, in the best mode possible to it, and that each thinketh all other existing things exist for the sole purpose of serving this end, namely, the best state of him whom Thou beholdest.

Thou dost not, Lord, permit me to conceive by any

imagining whatsoever that Thou, Lord, lovest aught else more than me; since Thy regard leaveth not me, me only. And, since where the eye is, there is love, I prove by experience that Thou lovest me because Thine eyes are so attentively upon me, Thy poor little servant. Lord, Thy glance is love. And just as Thy gaze beholdeth me so attentively that it never turneth aside from me, even so is it with Thy love. And since 'tis deathless, it abideth ever with me, and Thy love, Lord, is naught else but Thy very Self, who lovest me. Hence Thou art ever with me, Lord; Thou desertest me not, Lord; on all sides Thou guardest me, for that Thou takest most diligent care for me. Thy Being, Lord, letteth not go of my being. I exist in that measure in which Thou art with me, and, since Thy look is Thy being, I am because Thou dost look at me, and if Thou didst turn Thy glance from me I should cease to be.

But I know that Thy glance is that supreme Goodness which cannot fail to communicate itself to all able to receive it. Thou, therefore, canst never let me go so long as I am able to receive Thee. Wherefore it behooveth me to make myself, in so far as I can, ever more able to receive Thee. But I know that the capacity which maketh union possible is naught else save likeness. And incapacity springeth from lack of likeness. If, therefore, I have rendered myself by all possible means like unto Thy goodness, then, according to the degree of that likeness, I shall be capable of the truth.

Lord, Thou hast given me my being, of such a nature that it can make itself continuously more able to receive Thy grace and goodness. And this power, which I have of Thee, wherein I possess a living image of Thine almighty power, is free will. By this I can either enlarge or restrict my capacity for Thy grace. The enlarging is by conformity with Thee, when I strive to be good because Thou art good, to be just because Thou art just, to be merciful because Thou art merciful; when all my endeavour is turned toward Thee because all Thy endeavour is turned toward me; when I look unto Thee alone with all my attention, nor ever turn aside the eyes of my mind, because Thou dost enfold me with Thy constant regard; when I direct my love toward Thee alone because Thou, who art Love's self, hast turned Thee toward me alone. And what, Lord, is my life, save that embrace wherein Thy delightsome sweetness doth so lovingly enfold me? I love my life supremely because Thou art my life's sweetness.

Now I behold as in a mirror, in an icon, in a riddle, life eternal, for that is naught other than that blessed regard wherewith Thou never ceasest most lovingly to behold me, yea, even the secret places of my soul. With Thee, to behold is to give life; 'tis unceasingly to impart sweetest love of Thee; 'tis to inflame me to love of Thee by love's imparting, and to feed me by inflaming, and by feeding to kindle my yearnings, and by kindling to make me drink of the dew of gladness, and by drinking to infuse in me a fountain of life, and by infusing to make it increase and endure. 'Tis to cause me to share Thine immortality, to endow me with the glory imperishable of Thy heavenly and most high and most mighty kingdom; 'tis to make me partaker of that inheritance which is only of Thy Son, to stablish me in possession of eternal bliss. There is the source of all delights that can be desired; not only can naught better be thought out by men and angels, but naught better can exist in any mode of being! For it is the absolute maximum of every rational desire, than which a greater cannot be.

From *The Vision of God*, trans. E. Gurney-Salter (London: Dent, 1928).

ACKNOWLEDGMENTS

The editors wish to thank the following publishers and agents for their kind permission to reprint in this volume excerpts from the books listed below:

The American-Scandinavian Foundation, New York, *The King's Mirror*, translated by L. M. Larson.

Appleton-Century-Crofts, Inc., New York, *The First Century of Italian Humanism* by Ferdinand Schevill, copyright 1928 by Appleton-Century-Crofts, Inc.; and *The Statesman's Book of John of Salisbury* translated by John Dickinson, coyright 1927 by Appleton-Century-Crofts, Inc.

Edward Arnold & Co., London, *I Saw the World* by Walther von der Vogelweide, translated by Ian G. Colvin.

Ernest Benn, Limited, London, the poem by Aniar MacConglinne from *Bards of the Gael and Gall*, by G. Sigerson.

Curtis Brown, Ltd., New York, and Helen Waddell, *Mediaeval Latin Lyrics*, translated by Helen Waddell.

Burns, Oates & Washbourne, Ltd., London, *Summa contra Gentiles* by Saint Thomas Aquinas, translated by the English Dominican Fathers.

Cambridge University Press, Cambridge, *Social Life in Britain*, edited by G. G. Coulton.

Jonathan Cape, Limited, London, *The Book of Margery Kempe*, translated by W. Butler-Bowdon; *The Notebooks of Leonardo da Vinci*, translated by Edward Mac-Curdy; and *The Autobiography of Giraldus Cambrensis*, translated by H. E. Butler.

Chatto & Windus, London, *The Babees' Book*, edited by E. Rickert; *The Book of the Duke of True Lovers* by Christine de Pisan, translated by Alice Kemp-Welch; *Philobiblon* by Richard de Bury, translated by E. C. Thomas; and *Couriers' Trifles* by Walter Map, translated by F. Tupper and M. B. Ogle.

The Clarendon Press, Oxford, *The Great Revolt of 1381* by C. Oman; and *The Battle of Poitiers* by Geoffrey le Baker, edited by Sir E. M. Thompson.

Columbia University Press, New York, *Chronicle of the Slavs* by Helmold, priest of Bosau, translated by Francis Joseph Tschan, copyright 1935 by Columbia University Press; *An Arab-Syrian Gentleman and Warrior in the Period of the Crusades, Memoirs of Usāmah ibn-Murshid*, translated by Philip K. Hitti, copyright 1929 by Columbia University Press; *De profectione Ludovici VII in orientem* by Odo of Deuil, translated by Virginia Gingerick Berry, copyright 1948 by Columbia University Press; *A History of Deeds Done Beyond the Seas* by William, Archbishop of Tyre, translated by Emily Atwater Babcock and A. C. Krey, copyright 1943 by Columbia University Press; *The Two Cities* by Otto, Bishop of Freising, translated by Charles Christopher Mierow, copyright 1928 by Columbia University Press; *The Art of Courtly Love* by Andreas Capellanus, translated by John Jay Parry, copyright 1941 by Columbia University Press; and *University Records and Life in the Middle Ages*, edited by Lynn Thorndike, copyright 1944 by Columbia University Press.

Constable and Company, Ltd., London, *Mediaeval Latin Lyrics*, translated by Helen Waddell; and *The Chronicles of Giovanni Villani*, translated by Rose E. Selfe and edited by P. H. Wicksteed.

J. M. Dent & Sons, Ltd., London, *Tales from Sacchetti*, translated by M. G. Steegman; *The Vision of God* by Nicholas of Cusa, translated by E. Gurney-Salter; the poems by Jacopone da Todi, translated by Mrs. T. Beck, from *Jacopone da Todi* by E. Underhill; *Romance of the Rose,* translated by F. S. Ellis; and *Memoirs of the Crusades,* translated by Sir Frank Thomas Marzials.

The Devin-Adair Company, New York, *The Book of Margery Kempe,* translated by W. Butler-Bowdon.

Hakluyt Society, London, *Chronicle of Muntaner,* translated by Lady Goodenough; *Journey of William of Rubruck,* edited by William Woodville Rockhill; *Cathay and the Way Thither,* edited by H. Yule, revised by H. Cordier; and *Chronicle of the Discovery and Conquest of Guinea* by Gomes de Azurara, translated by C. R. Beazley and E. Prestage.

Harvard University Press, Cambridge, *Humanism and Tyranny: Studies in the Italian Trecento* by Ephraim Emerton, copyright 1925 by Harvard University Press.

Malcolm Letts, London, *The Diary of Jörg von Ehingen,* translated by Malcolm Letts.

The Macmillan Company, New York, *The Modern Reader's Chaucer,* edited by John S. P. Tatlock and Percy MacKaye, copyright 1912 by The Macmillan Company; *Readings in Political Philosophy,* revised edition, edited by F. W. Coker, copyright 1938 by The Macmillan Company; and *Courtiers' Trifles* by Walter Map, translated by F. Tupper and M. B. Ogle.

Oxford University Press, London, *Chronicle* by Adam of Usk, translated by Sir E. M. Thompson; and *Early Medieval French Lyrics,* translated by Claude Colleer Abbott.

G. P. Putnam's Sons, New York, *Petrarch, The First Modern Scholar and Man of Letters,*

translated by J. H. Robinson and H. W. Rolfe.

Reynal & Hitchcock, New York, *The Notebooks of Leonardo da Vinci,* translated by Edward MacCurdy.

Routledge and Kegan Paul, Ltd., London, *The Alexiad of Princess Anna Comnena,* translated by E. Dawes; *The Unconquered Knight* by Díaz de Gámez, translated by J. Evans; *The Goodman of Paris,* translated by E. Power; and *Miracles of the Blessed Virgin Mary* by Johannes Herolt, translated by C. C. S. Bland.

Charles Scribner's Sons, New York, *Selections from Medieval Philosophers,* edited and translated by Richard McKeon.

Sheed and Ward, Inc., and H. W. Wells, New York, *The Vision of Piers Plowman,* translated by H. W. Wells.

Smith College, Northampton, Mass., "The Commentaries of Pius II," translated by Florence Gragg, with notes by Leona Gabel, published in *Smith College Studies in History.*

Union of American Hebrew Congregations, Cincinnati, *The Jew in the Medieval World* by Dr. Jacob R. Marcus.

University of California Press, Berkeley, *The Battle of the Seven Arts* by Henri d'Andeli, and *Morale Scholarium* by John of Garland, both translated by L. J. Paetow, in the Memoirs of the University of California series.

University of Minnesota Press, Minneapolis, *John of Salisbury's Frivolities of Courtiers,* translated by J. B. Pike, copyright 1938 by the University of Minnesota.

University of Pennsylvania Press, Philadelphia, *Opus Majus of Roger Bacon,* translated by R. B. Burke, copyright 1928 by University of Pennsylvania Press.

Yale University Press, New Haven, *The Craftsman's Handbook* by Cennino Cennini, translated by D. V. Thompson.